THE HAB THEORY

BOOKS BY ALLAN W. ECKERT
[in order of publication]

The Great Auk
A Time of Terror: The Great Dayton Flood
The Silent Sky: The Incredible Extinction of the Passenger Pigeon
Wild Season
The Frontiersmen
Bayou Backwaters
The Writer's Digest Course in Article Writing ·
The Writer's Digest Course in Short Story Writing
The Dreaming Tree
Wilderness Empire
Blue Jacket: War Chief of the Shawnees
The Crossbreed
The King Snake
In Search of a Whale
The Legend of Koo-Tan [screenplay]
The Conquerors
Incident at Hawk's Hill
The Court-Martial of Daniel Boone
The Owls of North America
Tecumseh! [drama]
The HAB Theory
The Wilderness War
The Wading Birds of North America
Savage Journey
Song of the Wild
Whattizzit?
Gateway to Empire
Johnny Logan: Shawnee Spy
The Dark Green Tunnel
The Wand
The Scarlet Mansion
Earth Treasures: The Northeastern Quadrant
Earth Treasures: The Southeastern Quadrant
Earth Treasures: The Northwestern Quadrant
Earth Treasures: The Southeastern Quadrant
Twilight of Empire
A Sorrow in Our Heart: The Life of Tecumseh
That Dark and Bloody River: Chronicles of the Ohio River Valley
The World of Opals
Return to Hawk's Hill

THE HAB THEORY

Allan W. Eckert

AN AUTHORS GUILD BACKINPRINT.COM EDITION

THE HAB THEORY

All Rights Reserved © 1976, 2001 by Allan W. Eckert

AN AUTHORS GUILD BACKINPRINT.COM EDITION

Published by iUniverse.com, Inc.

For information address:
iUniverse.com, Inc.
5220 S 16th, Ste. 200
Lincoln, NE 68512
www.iuniverse.com

Originally published by Little, Brown & Co.

ISBN: 0-595-00820-8

Printed in the United States of America

DEDICATION

With the greatest of affection and esteem,
this book is dedicated to
LORIE MEIER
who was responsible for its inception,
and whose interest and encouragement
helped to keep the project alive...
...and to her husband,
DON T. MEIER
producer of television's *Wild Kingdom,*
who is beyond doubt one of the
most remarkable and admirable
human beings the author
has ever had the privilege
and good fortune
of knowing.

ACKNOWLEDGMENT

For her extensive assistance in many aspects concerning the preparation of this work—research, filing, indexing, editing, proofreading, and related efforts—and for her valuable suggestions and encouragement during the long period that this novel was in preparation, the author extends his special appreciation to

LINDA A. CAHILL

AUTHOR'S NOTE

Many of the scientists mentioned in this novel were actual people who lived in the past and who performed the work they are described as having accomplished. However, those characters who are portrayed in these pages in the story-line sense are entirely fictional and any resemblance they may bear to people living or dead is purely coincidental.

ALLAN W. ECKERT

Nashville, Tennessee
March 1975

1

We have found a strange footprint on the shores of the unknown. We have devised profound theories, one after another, to account for its origin. At last we have succeeded in reconstructing the creature that made the footprint. And lo! it is our own.

—Sir Arthur Stanley Eddington

I've never encountered anything like it before. I don't think the world ever has! I truly believe, Mr. President, that we are at this moment crossing a threshold into a great renaissance of science.

—Dr. Irma Dowde

I

Even though he had worked with it, studied it, several times dismantled and reassembled it, Herbert Allen Boardman could not seem to grow accustomed to the feel of the revolver he held. For one thing, it was heavy—considerably heavier for its size than he had anticipated it would be. Also, though he was sure it was merely a product of his own state of mind at present, there was a paradoxically repulsive and compelling aura which emanated from the weapon. He could feel it in his palm where it gripped the checkering of the grip plates, and in his fingers and thumb as they curled firmly around it. A detached part of his mind was stimulated by the sensation, curious about it, tending to stand to one side and analyze. In essence, it was merely steel and wood which he held, yet he knew there would be no such sensation, no such aura, were this simply a box or a tool or a nonlethal implement of some sort.

Boardman reflected that this was perhaps what was felt by the criminal—the armed robber or assassin—as he geared himself for what lay ahead. It was almost a fusing of inanimate object with flesh and blood, the object taking on a sense of the warmth and vital flow running down the arm into hand and fingers, while at the same time issuing to the flesh its own aura of extended power and dominance.

"The great equalizer," he murmured, hefting the weapon. For the first time the full significance of that time-worn phrase struck home with him. Perhaps he would not have experienced it at all had he been more familiar with guns, but Herbert Allen Boardman was distinctly unfamiliar with firearms of any kind. Two or three times previously in his life he had fired shoulder weapons—shotguns or rifles—but so far as he could recall, Boardman had never before today fired a handgun. Not once in his entire life, and that was a considerable span, since Boardman was now well into his ninety-fifth year.

The faint sound of a door closing upstairs sent his gaze to the closed door of his study. Then, without haste, he opened the top right drawer of his desk and carefully placed the revolver inside. A moment later the six stubby bullets that had been resting on the desk blotter were dropped into an envelope and put into the drawer beside the gun. He quietly slid the drawer closed just as the expected gentle tapping came on the study door and it opened.

The woman who entered, smiling, was well dressed and nearly as thin as he. At fifty-six, Elizabeth Boardman was still an attractive woman, easily belying her age by a dozen years or more. Her skin was firm and smooth and of good complexion and she seemed to exude an inner vitality. Her dark hair was fairly short but very nicely coiffed, and though her mouth was wide, a certain pleasing squareness of jaw made it just right. There was just the faintest suggestion of crow's-feet wrinkles at the outer corners of her warm gray eyes whenever she laughed or even smiled, as now. She moved with an easy grace and poise, coming to a stop a few feet in front of the desk and tilting her head at him in a rather charming way as she spoke.

"Sure you don't mind my going out, Dad? It's really nothing important and if you'd rather I stayed, I wouldn't mind. Really."

Boardman was shaking his head even as she spoke. "I wouldn't think of it, honey," he said, then added casually, "especially since you're going with Paul. Is he going to pop the question tonight?"

Elizabeth colored faintly and then smiled wryly at the old man. "You're something else," she said. "No one but you has been able to make me blush for thirty years or more, but somehow you manage it every time." She paused for a moment and then went on. "Yes, Paul Neely and I are going out, but what he will or won't ask, I haven't the foggiest notion. What I'd like to know is how is it that you can make a once-divorced high school librarian in middle age, on the verge of going out with a twice-divorced high school principal, feel as flustered as one of the giggly girls she sees every day?"

"I?" Boardman replied with an air of injured innocence. "How could I make you feel that way?"

"I'm not quite sure I know," she answered, "and I suppose I never will. Somehow, though, you make me feel not much different than when I was first dating Sam and you asked the same kind of question."

Herbert Boardman grimaced. He had never really liked Sam Kaiser, not from the very first time he'd met him, when Liz was attending Northwestern and only twenty, and Sam a year older. What irked him was that he had never been quite able to put his finger on what it was about Kaiser that he didn't like. Later on, of course, there were many things that he learned to dislike about him, but they came only after a long time and didn't explain the immediate instinctive antagonism he experienced. When Liz, at age twenty-two, finally had called from Washington, D.C., and excitedly announced to her parents that she and Sam were going to get married, he was neither surprised nor happy. With reservations that he had never been able to express to Liz, he had given his approval and the wedding had taken place. Secretly, he never expected it to last more than a couple of years at best, but he had underestimated Liz. At first, she and Sam had stayed in Washington, where Liz was working. Sam was turning out to be a loser insofar as holding jobs was concerned and more often than not they lived off the salary Liz earned at the Library of Congress. That was where, after getting her degree in library science from Northwestern, she had gotten a job. She'd shown remarkable aptitude and quickly became expert in all phases of library work, especially in the job of cross-reference and Dewey Decimal System filing. She soon had become section chief and then full department head. This irked Sam greatly because he not only couldn't do well in any kind of work he tried, he didn't seem to be able to do well in anything except drinking and carousing.

In those first eight years of their marriage there'd been more than enough grounds for divorce and Liz was seriously considering it when she'd unexpectedly become pregnant. She determined then to make a go of things, come what may. And she had. She'd taken an indefinite leave of absence from her job shortly before David was born, and they'd made out on Sam's odd-jobs income for a couple of years, but then it had become too much. When she received notification from the Library of Congress that they'd like her to come back, she accepted, and things were better then, at least for her and David. Sam was gone most of the time. Not until David had finished high school and gone into the army had she quit her job and returned here to Oak Park to look after her father. It was then that she'd at last filed for divorce, but it took nearly a year for the decree to become final. Since then she'd been librarian at Oakmont High School.

Five years ago that had been, and Boardman realized with a pang how much he had come to love having her here; how much he depended upon her; how strongly in his mind he associated her with her mother until of late when he thought of Norma, it was a picture of Elizabeth that filled his mind. Odd, he thought, perhaps even prophetic at the time, that of his three daughters, although she was the second one, it was she whom he and Norma had given the middle name of Mellon, Norma's maiden name.

Liz was looking at him curiously, the trace of a smile still curving her lips. How often Norma had looked at him in just that way. The pang he was experiencing became stronger and he closed his eyes momentarily.

"You're just like her," he said softly, looking at her again.

"I'm just like who, Dad?"

"Your mother. Just like her. You're almost the same age now that she was when..." He let the sentence trail away and there was a heavy stillness in the room. Liz moved closer, reached across the desk and put her hand atop his, her features softening.

"That was thirty years ago, Pop."

"More like yesterday, honey," he said. He added in a brisker tone of voice, "Well, go on now, and have a good time with Paul. Give him my best."

"You'll be all right?"

He nodded. "I'll be all right."

She looked at him for a long moment, marveling at what an incredible individual he continued to be. Tall and lean and craggy, just as he'd always been for as long as she could remember, and not in the least stooped with age or too often faltering in his movements. True, he was a little unsteady at times, and occasionally the words he spoke came with a bit of hesitation, but he was still sharp, alert. She had the fleeting thought that she hoped she would be that alert when she was seventy-four, much less ninety-four. His skin was still firm and his features, if not handsome, were certainly distinguished.

She squeezed his hand, nodded back at him, and moved toward the door. With the knob in her hand, she looked back. He was watching her, a vague tender sadness in his expression. She felt a sudden little twinge of guilt at leaving him.

"I may be late getting in, Dad, but don't worry. I'll be at Paul's if you want to reach me. We're going back to his place after dinner."

"Why don't you stay all night?" There was no malice in the remark and he was smiling fondly at her. Once again she colored faintly.

"It's not beyond the realm of possibility, Dad," she responded lightly.

"I didn't think it was."

Elizabeth Boardman shook her head and laughed aloud. "You're something else," she said. "Good night, Dad."

"Good night, honey," he responded and then, as she turned to leave the room, he spoke her name, stopping her. She looked back over her shoulder and he shook his head. "Nothing," he said. "Just wanted to say I love you very much."

"That's nothing?" She tossed her head. "That's something very important, Dad. I love you, too."

The door clicked shut quietly behind her, but Boardman remained unmoving. After a few seconds he heard the muted closing of the front door. The mantel clock chimed four notes for the quarter-hour in a softly melodious strain. He glanced at the dial and saw that it was 5:15 and immediately reopened the desk drawer and brought out the revolver and shells. He held the weapon in both hands and studied it closely. It was a wickedly lethal-looking gun, a marvel of compact engineering. Stamped in the blued metal were the words: *Smith & Wesson Centennial*, and, adjacent to that, *Model 42 Airweight, .38 Special*. The snub-nosed barrel was only two inches in length; the entire gun six and a half inches. The cylinder was chambered for five bullets. Smooth walnut stocks were etched with checkering for better grip, and the empty weapon weighed only thirteen ounces. After a few minutes he lay the little revolver on the desk blotter and picked up one of the six shells. Small bright scratches marred the brass casing and instead of a lead slug there was an accurately bullet-shaped plug of paraffin wax. He looked at the base of the cartridge but could detect nothing unusual, although the normal primer was supposed to have been replaced by a primer from a magnum rifle bullet. Holding the cartridge close to his ear, he shook it, but could hear nothing. He looked at the shell and muttered, "For discouraging a big dog," and then smiled faintly.

That was the story he had given the slovenly gunsmith and reloading hobbyist who had made up the shells for him. He had told the man that the pawnshop owner who had sold him the gun had recommended him for the job and explained that he and his daughter lately had been terrorized by a big dog belonging to a neighbor. Complaints to the neighbor, he added, had had little effect. He didn't want to kill the dog, but he did want to hurt it enough that it would think twice before charging at them out of the night again, as it had taken to doing lately when they came home after dark. Wasn't there some way he could take some of the gunpowder out of the shell so that when it was fired the bullet would hit and hurt, but not break the skin or kill? The gunsmith, a beer-bellied, unshaven individual named Roy Bujalski, had shaken his head as he wiped greasy hands on his T-shirt.

"No way," he'd declared. "If you got enough powder in the shell to shove the slug outta the barrel, then you're gonna kill 'im. Nope, only one way I know of that might work."

Bujalski then had gone on to explain that the .38 caliber shell would have to be dismantled, all the powder removed from inside the shell, and the primer replaced with a magnum rifle primer. When this was done, a paraffin bullet molded to the size and shape of the normal lead slug could be fitted into the casing. Bujalski had warmed to his favorite subject and talked as if he were lecturing a child.

"Y'see," he'd said, "the primer in a casing's got a little charge of nitro in it. When you squeeze the trigger, the firing pin hits the primer. When that happens, it jars the nitro enough to make it explode and the flash of this explosion inside the shell sets off the gunpowder, and that's what shoots the slug out. It all happens in about a hundredth of a second. So, okay. Now, like I said, with a slug, if you got enough powder behind it to get the bullet outta the gun barrel, then that slug's gonna damn well have enough power to kill. No two ways about it, at least at close range like you expect to be shootin' at that dog. So, okay, we get rid of the gunpowder and leave only the primer charge. But that ain't enough to shove a regular lead slug outta the gun. So we replace the normal .38 primer with a magnum rifle primer and then we replace the lead slug with a wax one, and I think we got the answer. Might kill the damn dog if you hit 'im in the eye, but as long as you hit the bony part of his head, it oughta not do no more'n knock 'im silly for a while. So, okay. You want I should make up some for you?"

Boardman had agreed, saying six bullets rigged like that would be ample, then wincing when Bujalski quoted a price for the job that was almost half as much as Boardman had paid for the secondhand revolver. But he had paid the gunsmith half in advance and the remainder earlier today when he picked up the doctored ammunition.

Now Herbert Boardman took the paraffin-slugged shell he was holding and, opening the cylinder of the revolver, slid it into one of the chambers. He turned the cylinder and then carefully closed it so the loaded chamber was in line with the barrel and firing pin. A thick, yellow-paged RedBook—the Chicago classified telephone directory—was on one side of the desk and Boardman propped it up against the slender metal stem of the desk light. Standing, he held the gun so the muzzle was no more than four feet from the directory and pulled the trigger.

The hammer merely clicked and, puzzled, Boardman inspected the gun. The bullet he had inserted in the cylinder was now one chamber clockwise away from the barrel. He realized then what had happened and he shook his head at his own ignorance of guns. Opening the cylinder again, he took the bullet out and put it into the chamber which was first to the left of the barrel. Again he pointed the weapon at the telephone book and slowly squeezed the trigger. He watched the cylinder as he did so and saw it advance clockwise one chamber as the hammer went back. This time, when the hammer leaped forward, it drove the firing pin into the primer of the shell.

The gun bucked in his hand less than expected, but with a much louder explosion than he had anticipated with only the primer firing. The directory jumped and fell to one side and then to the floor. Replacing the gun on his desk, Boardman picked up the telephone book and studied it carefully. The slick, heavy paper cover of the volume had a pronounced dent in the center, barely broken here and there with small radial cracks, and the pages of the directory for about a quarter of an inch inward showed the effects of the impact. Fragments of wax had melded with the cover at various places and smaller chunks sprinkled the top of the desk. Trying to estimate what the effect would be on skin with hard bone behind it, Boardman slowly nodded. It looked about right.

Reopening the cylinder, he extracted the spent cartridge and carefully reloaded all five chambers. He took off his suit coat, opened the bottom drawer of his desk, and extracted a contrivance of leather and elastic which, after some difficulty, he managed to place and secure properly over his left shoulder. The flat pouch which now hugged his side just under the armpit seemed ridiculously small to him, but the .38 revolver slipped into it neatly and firmly. He brought up his right hand and smoothly withdrew the weapon, reholstered it, and then did the same thing again. At last he put his coat back on, buttoned the front and then twice more drew the gun and returned it to the holster. Now he walked across the room and for a long moment looked at himself in one of the full-length mirrors which flanked the fireplace. He nodded approvingly.

The image he saw reflected was that of a somewhat towering, rather thin and angular individual with very bushy gray eyebrows and a neatly combed shock of nearly pure white hair. He stood five inches over six feet in height, his gauntness along with the deeply-etched lines of his face and the white hair attesting fully to his advanced age, but the blue-gray eyes were very clear and alert. His penetrating gaze locked on the image of his own left side. There was no telltale swell or lump in the frontal reflection, and none that he could detect from either side as he turned. With a small grunt of satisfaction, he returned to the desk and began to write a letter.

Several times he paused to rub his eyes wearily or just sit and think. At last he finished, folded the sheets neatly in half and then looked around the room slowly. Twice he shook his head and then, as he glanced down at the folded letter on the desktop blotter in front of him, he smiled faintly and reached into the top drawer. A minute or so later, the blotter now clear of everything, he stood up and switched off the desk light and walked to the door.

He paused there, his hand on the wall switch, as he took a final lingering look at the room, fully aware there was every likelihood that this was the last time he would see it. Then he turned off the overhead light and walked crisply from the study and the house, his step firm and his back straight.

Herbert Allen Boardman, ninety-four, was on his way to make an assassination attempt against the President of the United States.

I I

Undoubtedly, it was a great tribute to Marie Grant's self-control and inner strength that she looked as good as she did right now, considering what she had gone through today. Hearing John entering the front door, she touched her freshly combed hair here and there a final time in a thoroughly feminine gesture before switching off the bathroom light and starting toward the stairs to go down and greet him.

Decidedly attractive, Marie looked far more to be a woman in her early to mid-thirties than one rapidly approaching forty-five. Though not overly vain, she nevertheless always had prided herself on her appearance, and it had paid dividends. Five and a half feet tall, she moved with unconscious grace. Her hair was fairly long, rolling gently on her shoulders and naturally honey-blond with the lovely, almost shimmering quality seen on models who posed for the better shampoo ads. Only the first, vague, barely discernible lines at the outer corners of her eyes and on her classic neck just below the angle of her jaw, along with a few small brown spots on the backs of her hands, belied the more youthful impression she imparted. Her figure had never lost the quality that turned men's heads.

As she passed through the bedroom now, she glanced at the second drawer of the huge satiny-smooth solid mahogany dresser and shook her head slightly, only too aware of the neatly folded papers she had hidden there a short time before. It was not until this moment that she made her decision not to tell him. At least not yet. Maybe never, depending on what the next day or two held in store.

That something was going was going sour between her and John over these many months had been quite evident, but though she had begun some time ago to watch more closely for clues, she had found nothing of a concrete nature until now.

In a married woman there is a psychological trauma at the sudden realization that she is forty-five. Even if she has retained her physical grace and well-being, as Marie certainly had, there is the inescapable knowledge that a threshold has been crossed. Estrogenic resources run down and the confidence she has enjoyed for a quarter-century abruptly diminishes. She begins to experience the fear that a major factor in what first attracted her husband to her and then kept him there for so many years—that elemental asset of pure animalistic appeal for the opposite sex—is leaving forever. It's a traumatic time; one of deep self-doubts and sometimes suspicions, justified or not, of her mate. This described Marie Grant well, but in her case there now seemed to be that justification.

The change in John had been gradual but steady. A moodiness, a disinclination to talk with her and a desire more often to be by himself, a marked increase in his desire to plunge himself more deeply into his work and yet, at the same time, a seeming inability on his part to accomplish what he wanted to do. At times a black depression came over him and he would become so morose that she literally yearned to take his head in her lap and stroke his hair and, as if he were a little child, console him and tell him that everything would be all right. But somehow, conditions never lent themselves to that. Marie always had held a dislike for entering areas where she was not wanted; and it was clear that whatever was bothering John was just such an area. Thus, she guessed about it and watched for clues, but she really didn't know.

The possibility of there being another woman—that monstrous fear which, even though it may be deep in the subconscious, sometimes plagues even the happiest of wives—occurred to her more frequently these days, but she always managed to throw it off. In seventeen years of marriage, John had never slipped. Yet, she watched him, while pretending not to watch him, and John knew this and it irked him considerably.

But if not another woman, then what could be upsetting him so badly? They'd skirted the edge of the subject in conversations lately and John had hinted that the cause was his work. As a writer it was imperative to him never to be at a loss for words, to never be thwarted in letting his creative thoughts flow regularly onto paper, but that was what seemed to have happened to him in the past couple of years. He had been working long and hard at writing assignments since then which were simply mundane jobs to him, requiring considerable manual effort, but no real measure of creativity. Recently, whenever he faced the blank page poised for creative thoughts, that page had remained blank and his depression deepened.

Today he'd gone to check out an assignment that a national magazine wanted him to do—an in-depth personality profile on a popular evangelist—but she was almost certain little would come of it. The blank page would remain blank in the typewriter before him.

With a fervency that surprised her, Marie hoped John wasn't planning to spend much time in his den this evening trying to write. The intensity of that hope was deeply rooted in what she had discovered in that room today. The den originally had been an oversized bedroom when they'd bought this five-bedroom house four years ago, but it had served John's needs ideally as a combination office and library, always simply called the den. Skilled carpenters had been hired to construct sturdy floor-to-ceiling bookshelves on three walls to hold John's voluminous research library and bound manuscripts, as well as his numerous diaries.

John Grant had kept diaries ever since he was a boy of twelve. Sometimes, especially during those younger years, though he made regular entries for long periods, there were gaps of weeks or months when he hadn't written. But the habit of writing each day's events had become ingrained as the years passed and the gaps became fewer. There was only one major lapse in the entire chronology and it had occurred in his adult years—the two years which were the first half of his tour of duty in the United States Air Force. But he had come back to it eventually and now, on that special shelf, there were thirty of the fiber-bound diaries, each labeled with the year it covered.

Not uncommonly in the past—though at the moment she could not recall when the last time had been— John had read excerpts to her from them and they had laughed together at the things he had written as a boy—his activities, his yearnings, his dreams, his problems; so intense and important and insoluble then, so poignantly simple and fresh and touching now. Once, when he had been reading from a diary kept long before she and John had met, she'd noticed over his shoulder that at the bottom of a day's entry there were several lines written in an unintelligible string of letters. She had asked him about it and he'd grinned a bit sheepishly and explained it was a simple little code he'd devised at age twelve in which to write some of his innermost thoughts, which he preferred having no one else be able to read. At the time, he had explained, it was mainly because of his mother, who had a proclivity for surreptitiously reading his diary, but even after he left home he had continued the habit on occasion. He had flipped through the pages and pointed out other coded entries here and there, laughingly saying that maybe one day he would decode them and then read them aloud to her and thereby let her enter that highly secret world of a young man growing up.

It was among these neatly handbound volumes, as Marie had been cleaning this morning in the den, that she had become sidetracked. While dusting the shelves she had paused and considered the books, vaguely wishing that she had been possessed of the discipline to keep a diary. She would then have had a clear record of her life— not of her birth and very young years as Marie Fischer in North Carolina, of course, but probably beginning about the time the Fischer family had moved to Reading, Pennsylvania, and, after that, during her sophomore year of high school, to Tampa, Florida. There would have been a record then, too, of her thoughts and dreams as she finished high school there, attended the University of South Florida for two years and then got the civil service job as a secretary at McDill Air Force Base. And it was there at McDill that she had met and begun to date a handsome young air force captain by the name of John Charles Grant.

On sudden impulse, and feeling deliciously guilty about it, Marie had extracted the volume for the year she and John met in the spring and were married in the autumn, and she leafed through it, becoming absorbed in the scattered entries she read. They were a beautiful record of romance and marriage intermingled with the daily struggles of life itself. More than once her eyes flooded with tears as the words brought back into sharp focus events she had all but forgotten. She truly had intended to do no more than glance at that one volume, but that one led to the next, and so on, until by the end of an hour she had rapidly flicked through years of entries of their lives together, with passages here and there underlining the highlights of John Grant's life. They were beautiful words and she wondered why John had not shown them to her before. While feeling guilty at reading them, she nevertheless reveled in what they said.

Shortly after their wedding and John's subsequent honorable discharge, they'd moved to his home city of Chicago where, after working on several different newspapers, he began hitting his writing stride by preparing free-lance articles for major magazines. The conciseness of his writing and his knack for homing in unwaveringly on issues of tremendous interest had put his talents in great demand and earned him respect from many—as well as enmity from a few—and, ultimately, a Pulitzer Prize eight years ago.

Here in these volumes was recorded the excitement and profound joy, too, of the birth of their first child, Carol Ann, almost fifteen years ago, and their son, William Arthur, better known as Billy, thirty months later. At length, after skimming a few more of the earlier volumes, Marie's glance shifted to the far right on the shelf and she took out the final volume, considerably more slender than the others since it was for the current year and far from finished. She had flipped it open at random to an entry of several months ago and then became stunned to see that the ordinary writing of the day's events was followed by an even longer entry in code. As if she had touched a hot coal, she slammed the book shut and slid it back into its place on the shelf.

For several minutes thereafter she had dusted furiously across the room, but her mind was elsewhere. Why would John be writing coded entries now? No one ever touched his diaries here, so why would he feel it necessary to write in code? Certainly he was entitled to his own private thoughts, but why as private as that? All at once the coded entry was the enemy, an insidious threat, something between John and John, with Marie excluded.

In another moment the volume was back in her hands and she was riffling the pages rapidly from back to front. There were other coded entries. They were not daily, but where they occurred they usually were more extensive than the regular entry they followed. She replaced the book and took out the one next to it—last year's. Again she riffled from back to front and again there were codes, but growing less frequent toward the beginning. As if possessed, she had continued looking. The diary for two years ago held far fewer and much shorter coded entries, and the one before that held only seven or eight, with all of those occurring during the last four months of the year.

On the verge of returning this volume to the shelf, she hesitated a moment, considering, and then abruptly took it to the desk and sat there looking at it, closely examining the first coded entry it contained. Initially it was nothing more than a confused hodgepodge of unrelated letters, but then she leaned back and closed her eyes, trying to remember exactly what John had said so casually in passing about the code several years ago…that he'd devised it when he was twelve…that it was simple…that it wasn't meant not to be broken, but only to prevent just anyone from picking it up and reading it. If it was *that* simple, then she ought to be able to decipher it.

There was a legal pad on the right of the desk and she snatched it to her and copied the relatively short entry, leaving plenty of space between letters, words and lines. She was certainly no cryptographer, and though the code was, as John had said, ridiculously simple, it still took her the better part of an hour to crack it. Once she had the key, however, it was child's play to decipher and she was able to do it nearly as fast as ordinary writing. Little wonder that John wrote so extensively in it, since it was every bit as simple to code as to decode.

She had the strange sensation, as she decoded that first relatively brief entry of nearly two and a half years ago, of being two people simultaneously—the person who methodically, almost mechanically, changed the letters to their proper form, and the person who read them with mounting fear mingled with a strange admixture of understanding and incomprehension. After completing it, she went back and read it through twice more.

This next portion encoded, not because I am ashamed of it, but because, should Marie read it, she would find it hard to understand and her feelings would be hurt, and I wouldn't want that. There has been growing within me a hunger for another woman. Not anyone specific; simply someone different. I think perhaps all men, or at least most, have such feelings. I've certainly experienced this inexplicable hunger off and on over the years, but tonight it is especially keen and wrenching. Lately I've been experiencing a peculiar restlessness and I'm not exactly sure why. I'm hesitant about even expressing this next thought but I have to be honest with myself; I'm beginning to find Marie pretty dull. I suppose that's fairly normal after so many years of marriage, but why with such keenness all of a sudden? I love Marie so much; she has always been such a fine and good woman, and yet…oh, for a brief, exciting variation! Why should I feel this way? Perhaps this indicates a deep moral weakness but, if so, then why no sense of guilt or shame inside? I don't know, but damn it, I'm edgy and, I guess when you get right down to it, unhappy.

Marie closed her eyes. She was trembling and her breath was short. An unnerving fear flooded her and she felt as if she had been punched in the stomach. Sitting perfectly still, she forced herself to breathe deeply in an effort to calm herself. It helped only a little. The fact that John could have been harboring such an inner restlessness and craving without her even sensing a suggestion of it both stunned and angered her. After a few moments she opened her eyes and stared at the damnable book before her, then abruptly clenched her hand into a fist and slammed it savagely onto the open entry. Her impulse as she had begun decoding was to close the book, replace it on the shelf and pry no further, but now that was out of the question. How could she stop? She *had* to know more and there was an almost hypnotic effect in the very process of decoding. Despising her own lack of strength to resist, she began turning the pages. The next coded entry followed a regular entry about two weeks later and, because it was much shorter, she swiftly decoded it even while a portion of her mind continued to argue against carrying this any further.

The feeling persists. Oddly, even though I'd like to be with another woman, I don't mean that strictly on the basis of sex. It's more than that. I long for someone stimulating, someone to converse with, to enjoy things with, to experience new things with.

Marie dropped the pencil onto the desktop, leaned back in the chair and again closed her eyes, but this time only briefly. If this was the way John was feeling over two and a half years ago, then what had happened since then, and what was the significance of the increasing number and length of coded entries up to the present? She wanted to know and yet she didn't; she wanted to stop, but couldn't.

Abruptly she glanced at her watch and saw that John almost certainly would not get home from his downtown business meeting before another hour and a half had passed, but realizing that she herself might well lose track of time, she went to the bedroom and returned with the alarm clock, setting it to ring in exactly an hour. Again, thrusting back the guilt she felt inside over what she was doing, she began paging through the diary, decoding rapidly as she came to the entries she sought. She finished that volume and returned it to the shelf, bringing back the diary for the next year—the one for two years previously—becoming immersed in it at once. So absorbed in her efforts did she become that when the alarm went off she practically jumped in her seat. In something of a daze then, she replaced the diary which she had all but finished. With her own papers in hand, she returned the clock to the bedroom and then sat on the edge of the bed reading and digesting better what she had deciphered.

Much of it was similar to what she had read in the first couple of entries, phrased perhaps differently and certainly expressed with an ever-increasing intensity. The progression of his outlook bothered her enormously, yet at some of his remarks she felt a soaring of her spirits and a huge welling of love for her man, along with a deep sympathy for the mental upset he was so obviously enduring as he wrote the words. At other times she felt virtually shattered by the weight of her own increasing fear, and with it an anger at him not only for feeling as he did but for having the temerity to put such matters in writing, an anger bred of a growing sense of inadequacy within herself. Often, quite often, she experienced a surge of embarrassment, not only by what she read but by what she herself had done this day. She had become a Pandora and the box of evils she had so casually opened could not now be closed.

During this past hour she had frequently encountered gaps of many days, even weeks, occasionally months, when there had been no coded entries, but whatever relief she may have gleaned from this was invariably lost as the next one was found. Again, as she reread the words now in her own handwriting, there were words, phrases, sentences, even lengthy passages which struck her with numbing impact.

…As I've mentioned previously, I have felt this great unease sporadically over the years. As for what I plan to do about the problem, I don't in all honesty have any idea. I will just take things as they come and if an opportunity for…whatever…should come along, chances are I won't hesitate much. I'm very tired of holding myself in check against this gnawing frustration…

His unrest was clearly becoming stronger and often he mentioned his desire for a new relationship. As Marie suspected, he definitely wanted sex with another woman. That bothered her enormously, but it wasn't what bothered her most. What he seemed to crave much more than a mere sexual encounter was someone different from Marie herself in all respects, and the niggling anxiety and vague feeling of inadequacy within her grew intense and terrifying. Am I so horrible, she wondered, so dull and lacking? God, what more can I do? She had no answer but she knew he was on the verge of breaking loose and she was deeply frightened.

…For days I've been putting myself through a very special mental wringer, trying to analyze how I feel, what I want, and why; and the one great truth I seem to come up with is that I'm being pretty damned selfish. There appears to be a need for me to think considerably less of self and considerably more of others. I don't believe any person can keep from thinking mean thoughts—thoughts detrimental, or at least debasing, to the character of the thinker. In this respect, we must all be somewhat weak. If the easy thing is to think of no one but self and to submit to every desire which rises, then is not the strength of a man's character predicated upon his ability to live with such desire, fight it successfully, and give the outward appearance of calm. If this premise is true, then do I have enough resolve and strength of character to continue

*holding myself in check? I sincerely hope so. One does not throw down his morals lightly, but as for **thinking** of throwing down one's morals—ah, that's another matter entirely...*

Very slowly Marie Grant stood up, automatically smoothed the bedspread, and then folded the sheets of paper in her hand in half. She moved to her dresser and, in the second drawer, slid the papers between two neatly folded nylon tricot slips. Then she went into the bathroom, sat on the toilet seat, and cried. Afterwards, she looked at herself in the mirror and was appalled at her own reflection. She set about repairing her appearance and was still working at it when John Grant entered the house ten minutes later.

III

"I'm sorry," Elizabeth Boardman said. "I guess my mind was elsewhere. What did you say?"

They were seated in a small Oak Park restaurant and Paul Neely was looking at her curiously. He smiled across the table and touched the back of her hand gently, tracing a little circle with his index finger.

"Exactly the point, Liz," he said. "I asked where you were."

"Drifting," she replied, "and I really shouldn't have been. It's certainly not the company." She smiled at him and squeezed his hand briefly and then picked up her glass. "To us?" she asked.

"To us," he responded, picking up his own, and they touched rims and sipped lightly. He was still looking at her speculatively and she sighed.

"To tell the truth," she said, setting her drink down, "I'm a little worried about Father."

Paul frowned. "What's the matter? Is he ill?"

"No, not really. Just not acting quite the same lately. As if he has something on his mind. Not really as if he's concerned about something, but just preoccupied."

"I don't think I've ever seen him when he wasn't," Paul reminded.

"Oh, I don't mean with his theory and studies," Liz said quickly. "As you say, he's always occupied that way. I mean there's something else, and I can't quite place my finger on it. For one thing, he mentioned my mother again this evening.

"Is that so unusual?"

"Well, yes, it is, Paul. Mother died thirty years ago. Occasionally he'd mention her, but lately he's been talking about her a lot, almost as if she were still around...or..."

"Or what?" he prompted.

"Well," she answered reluctantly, "sometimes I get the feeling he's talking as if he's soon going to be joining her."

They were silent for a long moment and then Paul sipped his drink again and, still holding it in both hands with his elbows on the checkered tablecloth, said gently, "He may be, Liz. He's a very old man. When you get to be ninety-four like he is, it's not so unexpected that he considers what lies ahead."

She made a soft sound. "I suppose so, but I still can't help worrying. He hasn't done any work on his project for weeks, and that's not like him either. He's devoted his whole life to that theory."

"Hasn't it been more a hobby than anything else, though?"

"I've considered it to be that," she admitted, "but I don't think he ever has. It's always consumed his interest above everything else. And now suddenly he's not doing anything on it, and I'm worried."

They were silent again and then Paul spoke abruptly. "Why don't you give him a call and see if everything's okay?"

She shook her head. "No. I thought of that, but I don't think I will. He may have gone to bed early and I wouldn't want to disturb him. He's all right, I'm sure of it—and once again I apologize for being inattentive." She paused and then added lightly, "What we really should be concentrating on now is what we're going to order. I don't know about you, but I'm famished."

"Me, too," he grinned.

They studied the menu as they finished their cocktails and it was the last mention of her father for some time.

I V

John Charles Grant put the papers he would need into his briefcase from where he had stacked them atop the dresser, his brow furrowed slightly in concentration as he considered what else he might need to take.

Marie sat on the edge of the bed watching him closely, thinking of the many years she had loved this man and how her own life had become melded to his. Just looking at him sometimes had the power to cause an intense welling of love to rise in her. It might be caused by a glimpse of the light brown hair neatly combed except for that one persistent cowlick which defied control. Perhaps it would be the wide, boyish grin below dancing blue eyes. Or maybe it simply would be the six-foot-tall, slightly rugged, total physical aspect of the man she had married.

Now, in a manner which she had only begun to perceive, this love, this secure and wonderful life, was in jeopardy, and perhaps even far more than she realized. Right at this moment he seemed no different than his usual, normal self. Marie knew better now. A veil of complacency had been ripped away from her today and odd little pieces of a puzzle she really hadn't perceived before had begun to fit together: his preoccupation of late, his too-frequent moods of gloominess which he attributed with self-deprecating smile to "just one of those nasty depressions you sometimes fall into when you're working too hard," his growing tendency to remain aloof from her, apart, moving in a world that was peripheral to the one they had shared for so many years.

"How long will you be out of town?" she asked suddenly. When he didn't reply at once, she added, "You *will* be back for Carol's birthday, won't you?"

John Grant looked at her and smiled in a way that might have been considered condescending and nodded. "You've got to be kidding, Marie. She's going to be fifteen and at that age she'd never forgive me if I weren't. Of course I'll be back for her birthday, but that's not for a week yet. I'd hope I wouldn't be gone more than two days—three at most." He slid the final papers and a cassette tape recorder into the briefcase and snapped the lid.

"God knows," he continued, "I'd rather not go at all. I'm not looking forward to it. You know how I feel about pompous people, and if you'll forgive my alliteration, Peter Proctor's a pinnacle of pomposity."

Marie winced in an exaggerated way and then shook her head. "My word artist. You do have a way of turning a phrase. If the esteemed Peter Proctor heard you say that, he'd command fire and brimstone to rain about your head."

"Probably," he said dryly, "and I'm sure you can see how dreadfully concerned about it I am."

"What did they tell you at his office today?"

"Oh, they were properly cordial; and properly descending, I might add. In a rare moment of frankness, his chief aide—"

"Farmington?"

"Right, Lamar Farmington, admitted that he had in fact heard of me and that while Proctor considered anything but the most inferential of publicity as being, in his words, 'earthy and detrimental' to his image, he might possibly consider an in-depth interview for *The Covenant* as being important to the people of the world. He also suggested that Peter—and I'll swear he almost said *Saint* Peter—might consider that I was an instrument of the Lord, being sent to help bring His word to the world. How's that for deductive justification?"

"You're kidding?"

"I'm not. Farmington's a disciple in every sense of the word and he really believes what he says. More to the point, I suppose, he seems to believe implicitly whatever Proctor says."

"So then he did express an interest in your doing the profile on Proctor?"

"Guardedly, yes, and with certain reservations."

"What kind of reservations?"

"Well, clearly he doesn't want flagrant publicity for Proctor, any more than he'd want to see a sharply critical piece. I got the very strong impression that he's really looking to see me write a piece that's more a profile on God than on Proctor, but giving Proctor the credit that's due him as God's own special messenger."

"Wow," Marie murmured, "*that* fanatical?"

John nodded. "He very nearly turned me off entirely. But *The Covenant* very much wants the piece and I promised George Benedict I'd look into it. I can't honestly wash my hands of it until I've at least talked with Proctor himself and decide then either that I'll do it or else that it's not my meat. But I have to admit, I'm not expecting a lot. You know how I feel about religion."

Marie nodded, her expression tightening. She was suddenly angry and unable to check the remark which sprang from her tongue. "Catholicism, anyway," she said.

"No, Marie," he retorted, spinning around from the dresser and facing her, "not just Catholicism. Organized religion, period. I find that any one religion is just as repugnant in many respects to me as any other. I don't buy the idea of men in gowns or robes—or business suits, for that matter—setting themselves up as conscience, judge, jury, and sometimes executioner, of anyone. And in man's recorded history, you damned well know that more rotten wrongs have been committed in the name of God than for practically any other reason."

"Oh, for God's sake, John!" Marie rose to her feet quickly, her small fists clenched at her sides. "And I mean that literally: for *God's* sake, don't start orating again on your narrow-minded views of religion. It works for untold millions of people. Just because it doesn't work for you, don't consider that this makes your own personal viewpoint a yardstick for everyone else!"

"A wave of anger washed through Grant and he was momentarily on the point of responding heatedly. What she said was patently unfair to him and she knew it. If there was anything he always consciously did his damnedest *not* to be, it was narrow-minded—whether in the religious connotation or any other. He couldn't afford to be. He knew, and openly admitted, that he was not an expert on religion, but neither did he have only a cursory knowledge of religious doctrines. On his own he had made a point of rather intensively studying various religions over a period of five years. In the process he had become more than merely casually familiar with them and, in addition to learning their virtues, which he readily acknowledged, he also had learned many of their faults. In all these religions, at least the major faiths, he found a basic similarity, a fundamental root from which belief sprang and then expanded. There was God and there was God's messenger. The latter might be called Jesus Christ or Mohammed or Buddha, Joseph Smith or even Peter Proctor. And around God and His messenger, whoever this messenger was, the interpretations grew more entrenched and revered with each passing interpreter. And each new disciple or priest or pastor, or whatever, reinforced the idea that the religion *he* taught was the True Word, the Only Belief, the Only Real Religion. And, equally, each had new ideas about the benevolence of God and His messenger—new ideas which, while stressing the merciful character and forgiveness of God, constantly heaped new and more stringent restrictions upon man until man himself became such a ball of guilt and frustration that the mere act of living became a burden too great to be borne. Grant shook his head faintly and looked at Marie for a long quiet moment, the flash of anger disappearing almost as quickly as it had come. Long ago he had learned the utter pointlessness of trying to discuss religion with her reasonably and logically.

"Sorry," he murmured. "Guess maybe I was warming up for the confrontation with Saint Peter Proctor." He glanced at his watch. "Better get a move on," he said, "or I'll miss both the plane and the interview with His Eminence."

Marie was still stiff. "I don't see why," she said, an edge of petulance in her voice, "it's necessary for you to fly off to St. Louis this evening to talk with him there first thing in the morning, when his office is right here in Chicago."

"Simply because he's just begun his latest tour to evangelize the wayward of America and he'll be gone for three weeks. St. Louis, then New Orleans, followed by Dallas, Los Angeles, and elsewhere. The point is, I told Benedict at *The Covenant* I'd give him an answer within three days. Ergo, I don't have time to wait for Proctor to get back."

"I don't get it," Marie said, more heatedly than called for. "Feeling the way you do about religion of *any* kind, which I assume Mister Editor Benedict knows, then why would he ask you to consider doing the Proctor profile in the first place? And, secondly, also feeling the way you do, how could you even *hope* to write a piece that wasn't prejudicial?"

Grant puffed out his cheeks in a characteristic mannerism of impatience he reserved for presaging an explanation of what he felt to be self-evident. "George Benedict, he explained, "wants me to do it precisely *because* of the way I feel; because he knows that only someone who is not religiously committed can possibly hope to write a piece about the man that is *not* prejudicial—either for or against him. If the piece makes Proctor look good, assuming

I do write it, it'll have to be because Proctor *is* good; and if it makes him look bad, it'll be because that's how, after a close look at all the factors, he appeared.

She shook her head, not pretending to understand and suddenly weary of the conversation. "You have your bag ready?" she asked listlessly.

"It's by the front door. Kids aren't home yet?"

"No. Carol's practicing for the play at school and then going to that slumber party at Peggy's. She'll stay there all night. I called Peggy's mother and it's all right. Six of the girls are going to be there and Mae said she'll keep a close eye on them. I don't envy her. As for Billy, he's out romping around the neighborhood somewhere with his friends. He might be at Jack's house. You want me to call?"

He shook his head. "Haven't time. Tell them I said good-bye and I'll see them when I get home. Take care of yourself, honey. I'll be back soon."

He took a step toward her and the stiffness evaporated and she came easily into his arms, pressing her face against his shoulder and holding him tightly to her. Still in the embrace, she leaned her head back and looked up at him, loving the feel of his arms around her, loving the depth and gentleness of his eyes, loving him still so much after all these years that sometimes it was a huge ache inside her breast. They kissed and it was a good kiss, warm and tender, unlike so many of late that had seemed to her to be perfunctory. Together, then, arms about each other's waist, they walked to the front door, he carrying the briefcase in his free hand. When they stopped, they kissed again, but briefly. She touched his forearm as he picked up the two-suiter and opened the door.

"You're driving?"

"Yes, since it's only for a couple or three days. I'll park in the garage at O'Hare. It'll be a little more convenient than trying to get cabs going and coming."

"Well," she said, looking out at the abnormally hazy early evening sky, "be careful. The weatherman said this morning that there could be some very heavy fog beginning this evening."

"No problem," he said lightly. "It'd take more than a little fog to close down O'Hare. But don't worry, I'll be careful."

He raised the arm holding the briefcase enough so he could bend his head and press his lips to the back of her hand, then stepped outside. Marie placed her other hand over the spot where he had kissed her, pushed the door shut with her shoulder, and then leaned with her back against it, closed her eyes, and fought to put down the enormous welling of apprehension. Was there someone else? Was he going to her now? If there were someone else, who was it? More importantly, if there were someone else, then the question became *Why?* She wanted to know— desperately wanted to know—and yet, just as desperately, she was afraid. What she had already learned lay like a great weight inside her chest.

Now, with a renewed sense of guilt and shame but doggedly determined all the same, she headed for John's den to study the remaining pages of neat handwriting in the diaries.

V

Having caught the elevated train two blocks from his home in Oak Park, Herbert Allen Boardman sat quietly by a window seat in the second car, staring unseeingly at the buildings passing by. He had always been a man of even keel, rarely giving way to temper or worry, blessed with that rare attribute of being at peace within himself and able to meet fortune or misfortune with the same degree of aplomb. This evening, however, was an exception, since Boardman could not seem to shake the sense of foreboding that had settled over him since leaving the house. The full impact of what he was embarked upon was assailing him and the realization was there that his likelihood of success tonight was indeed remote.

Two major points of worry were plaguing him. The first was that he would be unable to get close enough to the President. His knowledge of what sort of security measures customarily were taken to protect the President was sketchy at best, though he was sure such security must be very good. It could well turn out that he might not be able to get within half a block of the Chief Executive, much less within the few feet required for effective aiming of the weapon he carried. His planning at this point was nebulous. If he could get close enough to see the President, then perhaps he could somehow, unsuspected, work his way close enough for the attempt. If nothing else, a sudden rush on his part might, because of its unexpectedness, afford him the opportunity he sought. This, however, he doubted very much. Chances were if he attempted that, he would be stopped before he was anywhere near close enough, and all his plans depended upon his getting off at least one shot at the President from close range before being subdued.

The second point of concern was that, whether successful or not in his attempt to shoot the President, he himself might be killed. Not that, at this stage of his life, Herbert Boardman was worried about death; he never really had been and he wasn't now, except insofar as his being killed would make this effort thoroughly pointless. The whole aim in his scheme was not the assassination attempt upon the President, but what would follow. *That* was what was important, and if he were slain it would largely defeat his whole object in doing this.

The fact that it was not his intent to kill President Sanders, but merely to make it *appear* that such was his intent, was not a matter of great consideration. When he had first read in the newspaper of the possible visit of Sanders to Chicago and then had decided to shoot him, his initial plan was simply to get the gun and use ordinary bullets. His hope then was only to wound the President, but he was not overly concerned if the man were killed. He harbored no feelings of dislike or antipathy in any form for President Sanders, but if his plan had required actual killing, Boardman knew that he could have done so. However, the death of Robert Sanders was not requisite and, in fact, the incredulity of a would-be assassin using a weapon with bullets specifically designed *not* to kill would be far more important.

In respect to the first point of concern, Boardman quickly decided that he simply would look for his opportunity and, if it came, take it. If not, he would quietly withdraw and bide his time until another opportunity could be found. That might require a trip to the nation's capital or elsewhere, along with a delay he did not especially like, but that couldn't be helped.

On the second concern, Boardman decided that his own greatest likelihood of not being killed lay in remaining as close as possible to bystanders, thus increasing the odds in favor of his being manually subdued rather than shot.

A barely audible chuckle left his thin lips at the irony of this situation. It had been an assassination of an American President that initially had deprived him of what he wanted most out of life; so now there was something of poetic justice in the knowledge that if all went well, it would be the attempted assassination of an American President that would achieve this end for him.

It was when the El stopped at the State and Lake station that Herbert Boardman left the train and slowly walked down the iron steps to the southeast corner. State Street was alive with lights and activity, with the huge marquees of the Chicago Theater, State & Lake, and other gaudy movie houses dispelling the gloom of the evening with their brittle, artificial cheer. Continuing east on Lake Street, Boardman walked the two blocks to Michigan Avenue and turned left. He briefly considered taking a taxi the remaining fifteen blocks, but then decided against it. As always, the Wrigley Building gleamed in startling whiteness, bathed by the incredible bank of floodlights on the far side of the river, their combined wattage more than enough to light an entire small city. The huge clock in its tower showed the time to be 8:15, so there was no need to hurry. It was unlikely that the President would arrive at the Continental Plaza more than just a few minutes ahead of his scheduled meeting time of ten o'clock.

He crossed to the east side of Michigan Avenue in front of the Tribune Tower and then continued walking north. A noisy, evening-dress-clad group of conventioneers practically blocked the sidewalk in front of the Sheraton Chicago and he picked his way through them, smiling pleasantly and wholly unnoticed by anyone. Half a dozen times or more he paused to look in the windows of the Michigan Avenue shops, grunting with mild disapproval at the ridiculous fashions and shoes being displayed which were the current mode. A nicely cut woman's knit suit of beige in the window of Saks Fifth Avenue caught his eye and he paused to inspect it more closely, thinking that it would look very handsome on Liz. The small, thick windows of Tiffany's contained a scattering of relatively inexpensive jewelry, and he remembered how they always had displayed beautiful precious gemstones and gold and platinum until robberies had forced a change. Numerous times those thick panes had been smashed by thieves and now Tiffany's no longer provided the temptation.

The Walgreens Drug Store on the southeast corner at Chicago Avenue, diagonally across the intersection from the old, yellow-stoned Water Tower landmark, was still open and so Boardman entered and took a seat at a small table by the windows fronting onto Chicago Avenue. He ordered a cup of coffee and, while sipping it, watched with interest the group of placard carriers, mostly women, milling about in the small park area at the base of the Water Tower. Numerous policemen were on hand, watchful but not interfering. At least a dozen police cars passed, all of them heading north, during the short time it took Boardman to finish drinking his coffee.

Resuming his walk, Boardman noted the rapidly increasing amount of pedestrian traffic as he neared Chestnut. Another block ahead, a veritable battery of police vehicles was stopped along the curbs of both Michigan Avenue and Delaware Place, their blue revolving lights flashing monotonously. Officers on foot were keeping both vehicular and pedestrian traffic moving. Despite this, a considerable knot of onlookers had gathered in front of the towering John Hancock Building across Delaware Place from the main entrance of the Continental Plaza Hotel. Quite a few had welcoming signs and the majority ostensibly seemed to be supporters of the

President. Yet, the nonsupporters were making their presence strongly felt. A somewhat close-knit group carrying poorly lettered placards walked in an endless oval procession on the Michigan Avenue side of the big hotel. They were under the watchful eyes of six or seven uniformed officers and a number of plainclothesmen standing at the corner of the building. The marchers were not being permitted to come closer than about ten yards from the corner, so they had no view at all of the hotel's modernistically arched glass and steel main entry.

Boardman crossed Delaware Place, scarcely glancing at the Continental's entrance to his right, and continued north on Michigan, past the circling marchers but giving them no more than a curious look, as any passerby might.

At the next corner, Walton Street, he turned right and walked past the entrance to the Playboy Building on his side of the street, and the main entrance of the Drake Hotel directly across Walton from him. The next corner was Seneca Street and here he turned right again. In a few minutes he was back to Delaware, one block east of Michigan. The activity near the entrance to the Continental Plaza had changed a little. The crowd had increased in numbers in just this short time, and now two or three local network affiliate television news teams were getting their cameras ready; one of which was being set up atop a panel truck.

It was clear that no one was being allowed to loiter anywhere near the hotel entrance on the north side of Delaware, but a sizable crowd lined the sidewalk across the street at the base of the Hancock Building. Boardman crossed to the south side of Delaware and turned right. A few minutes later he had become just another of the milling spectators hoping for a glimpse of the President of the United States.

V I

John Grant was whistling a faint, tuneless strain as he backed the car out of his driveway and onto Bobolink Terrace. He drove west a quarter of a block and turned right on Kostner, then right again on Lee, those two streets running adjacent to the Evanston Golf Club in Skokie. This was a quiet residential area, its streets lined with huge old elms that the Skokie City Council had been spending tens of thousands of dollars to save from the ravages of Dutch elm disease, but thus far with little success. At the next intersection, Keeler, he turned left and, now following the eastern boundary of the country club, drove the four blocks north to Dempster. But instead of turning left again on Dempster toward the cloverleaf for the Edens Expressway, which subsequently would take him most directly to O'Hare International Airport, he turned right. In less than twenty blocks he had entered Evanston. When he reached the Ridge Boulevard intersection, he pulled up at a service station's pumps and told the attendant to fill the tank. Then he sauntered to the isolated telephone booth and placed a call. An answer came in the midst of the second ring; a woman's voice, brisk and clear.

"Hello?"

"Ma'am," Grant said in drawling tones, "I'm workin' my way through college sellin' magazine subscriptions an' I wondered if—"

"John!" she breathed, cutting him off. "Oh, I was hoping you'd call. God, but I've missed you today."

"Ditto, the other way around," he replied, delighting as always in the change that came into Anne Carpenter's voice when she spoke to him, the warmth and depth of love that became so clear. He added, "But, then, I always do."

Her voice was low, touched with a trace of wistfulness. "I feel the same, but today more than usual."

"How come?"

"Because I saw you today and wanted to be near you and with you, but couldn't, and I didn't like it and it made me sad."

"Where?"

"Downtown. You were going into the Ogilvie Building with one very effete-looking individual. Tell me, is there something about you I don't know and should?"

He grinned. "You've heard me mention him. That, my dear girl, was none other than Lamar Farmington."

"Really? A swisher like that?"

"Where were you," Grant asked, ignoring the pejorative question, "that you saw me and I didn't see you?"

"About fifty feet behind. I'd probably have overtaken you in another few seconds—with a flying tackle, if necessary—but I hardly realized it was you before you entered the Ogilvie Building."

"Mind telling me," he inquired dryly, "how you came to the conclusion in a few seconds and from fifty feet behind at that, that the individual with me might be gay?"

"Apart from the mincing walk that would've been tipoff enough, the looks he was giving you were positively adorable. He's so precious I felt like planting my foot in the middle of his cute little bottom. I'm the only one who's supposed to be giving you looks like that. Five'll get you ten he has a simply darling lisp."

"You lose."

She sighed extravagantly. "Win some, lose some. But you can't convince me he's not gay. I was downright jealous, especially when you still hadn't come out after about twenty minutes."

"You waited that long?"

"Uh-huh. Had an appointment, but with a little time to spare, so I crossed over to the coffee shop and sat in the window nursing a cup of tea and watching. I knew you had to be on business and didn't want to interfere. No," she amended at once, "that's not right. I *did* want to interfere, but didn't think it would be too wise. So I waited. In vain, I might add."

"Wish I'd known," Grant said, genuinely regretful. I could have joined you and finished the business meeting later on."

"Ummm, I like that. You have a way of saying nice things. But it's just as well you didn't, I guess. It gave me a chance to write to you."

"Really? What did you write?"

"You'll find out soon enough. Anyway, I didn't finish it. When am I going to see you?"

"Is half an hour too long to wait?"

"Oh, John, *really*? You're coming by this evening? How long can you stay?"

"I have to be at a meeting in St. Louis at nine-thirty tomorrow morning. There's a plane leaving O'Hare for St. Louis in just over an hour from now. There's also one that leaves O'Hare at seven-twenty-five tomorrow morning which lands at St. Louis at eight-twenty. Guess which one I'll be on?"

"Wonderful! Wonderful! Is the trip something to do with Proctor or his gaymate?"

"Tell you all about it when I get there," he said. "Right now there's a service station attendant glaring at me and wondering why I don't hang up, pay my bill and pull the car away from his pumps."

"Okay. I'll be waiting. Hurry, John. I love you. I want you here."

"Which is where I'll be damned soon. I love you, too. 'Bye for now."

In another few moments Grant was pulling out of the station and heading for Sheridan Road and then Lake Shore Drive, which would take him toward downtown, where Anne Carpenter lived in the east tower of Marina City.

V I I

As always when his schedule was disrupted, the President of the United States showed no outward sign of annoyance, but inwardly he was concerned. His strong features were calm and pleasant, the salt-and-pepper hair neatly combed and the dark eyes never straying from his guest.

President Robert Morton Sanders was a tall man—an inch over six feet and always conscious of physical appearance. Often he was referred to as being very handsome, though, since he was sixty-three, more in a paternal than a romantic sense. He also had remarkable self-control and few people had ever heard him even raise his voice, much less become obviously angry. Irritation over inconvenience, such as the delay in plans he was now experiencing, rarely, if ever, manifested itself in any visible way.

This meeting with Daniel Ngoromu, which began on time, obviously was now going to run considerably longer than anticipated, and there simply was no way in which to cut it short discreetly. Part of the problem, of course, and one which should have been taken into consideration earlier, was Ngoromu's manner of speech.

President of Kenya, East Africa, Ngoromu was a cultured, highly intelligent individual. His command of the English language was superb, his well-modulated bass voice articulating with utmost precision the words he chose to speak. What was bothersome was the length of time it took for him to reply to President Sanders's comments and questions. After each remark by the President, a silence would fill the Oval Office while Ngoromu considered his reply, silences which might last for as long as thirty seconds before the African leader made his response. It was an aggravating mannerism and Robert Sanders was not entirely sure it had not been cultivated for this express purpose. Yet, he allowed no inkling of irritation to show. It could have been presumed that nothing was of more importance to him now than this discussion and that nothing on his agenda following the meeting was of any urgency. That was not quite the case. Highly important though the present meeting with Ngoromu was, there was equally considerable urgency that it be concluded. President Sanders was to have been on his way to Andrews Air Force Base by 7:30 P.M. Obviously that could not be, since 7:30 already had come and gone.

At 7:20 P.M. the tiny red light in the knee alcove of his desk had come alive and had begun pulsating at two-second intervals. Sanders knew it was his personal secretary, Hazel Tierney, reminding him of the 7:30 appointment. Ngoromu, in his chair across from the desk, had no idea that the little light had come on, nor was he aware of the discreet movement of Robert Sanders's knee as it depressed a button close to the light and extinguished it as well as the similarly winking light at Mrs. Tierney's desk. The President's attention remained on Daniel Ngoromu, and not with forced interest; the importance of their discussion could not be underestimated.

Deteriorating relations between the United States and the Arab nations because of continued Arab-Israeli friction and America's posture of close ties and support for Israel long ago made it clear that in the not-too-distant future, Arabian oil exports to the United States inevitably would be either sharply curtailed or cut off completely. Most likely the latter. Russia and China were all too willing to shoulder the economic burden of purchasing most of what the United States now purchased, and what they did not want or could not afford, France, East Germany, Canada, Great Britain, Argentina and Japan were eager to take. Such an event, if it occurred—and it was almost certain to—must have a severely crippling effect on the United States unless another extensive oil source was found. The well-remembered oil crisis suffered by the United States during the Nixon administration early in 1974 was still something of a threat overhanging America; yet that crisis was only a mere taste of what might occur should Mideast oil supplies be completely cut off, with no likelihood of relief. And that, quite simply, underlined the critical nature of the meeting this evening between Presidents Robert Morton Sanders and Daniel Ngoromu.

The recent discovery of two massive oil fields, perhaps rivaling those of the Arab nations, in East Africa was a matter of utmost importance. Until then, East Africa in general and Kenya in particular were primarily tourist havens where camera-laden travelers from all over the world could go to the national parks and ogle the remaining herds of zebra, elephant, giraffe, and other impressive animals of the veldt. But until then, East Africa, including Kenya, had precious little in an export sense to make them important on a global scale. Exports had been almost entirely agricultural, with coffee and pineapples among the most important. Now all that was changing. Sophisticated new oil-locating devices and techniques had revealed the presence of heretofore unsuspected and almost unbelievably rich oil deposits in Kenya and Somali. The Somali field was relatively small—at best contained within an area of two hundred square miles. That in Kenya was another matter entirely. It was an enormous crescent-shaped oil field which began in the tri-country border area of Uganda, the Sudan, and Kenya, then swept eastward in a great expanding arc from this point through Lake Rudolph and southward through the entire Northern Frontier District of Kenya, barely touching the southern border of Ethiopia and sweeping across the southwestern portion of Somali to the Indian Ocean in the vicinity of Bur Gavo. The offshore oil resources were no less impressive, stretching four hundred fifty miles southwestward from Bur Gavo in the continuing crescentic arc, with the tip of the southern cusp coming to its termination almost at the Tanzania capital, Dar es Salaam. The southern portion of the crescent took in all of Kenya's Indian ocean coastline, including the islands of Zanzibar, and with the already well-developed deepwater port of Mombasa at the heart of it all. Kenya was on the threshold of an economic revolution unparalleled in its history and likely to surpass even that of Saudi Arabia. Thus, the talk President Sanders was at this time having with President Ngoromu could well be a keystone to America's continued role as a foremost world power.

Robert Morton Sanders was pertinently aware that even though Ngoromu was married to a white woman from America and held a strong affection for the United States—having himself been educated here—he was neither a stupid man nor one who could be taken advantage of in international trade negotiations. Circumstance had provided the United States with a fortuitous and enviable bargaining position, but it would be the utmost folly to underestimate Ngoromu's intelligence or negotiating ability. The most reliable sources in the State Department had assured President Sanders that Daniel Ngoromu knew precisely what cards he held and exactly how best to play them for the benefit of his own country.

The two leaders continued their discussion in a warmly cordial manner for fifty-five minutes past the time when President Sanders had planned on leaving the White House. With a firm handshake between them and a promise on the part of Robert Sanders that he would seriously consider President Ngoromu's invitation to visit Kenya to further discuss oil field development and trade alliances in the near future, Daniel Ngoromu left the Oval Office at exactly 8:25 P.M. Within fifteen minutes after that, flanked by his Secret Service chief of security, Alexander Gordon, and two of Gordon's top men, President Sanders, walking with his characteristic faint limp, boarded the helicopter on the south lawn of the White House and quickly was borne aloft, heading for Andrews Air Force Base, ten miles southeast.

Air Force One was ready and waiting when they arrived. The transfer to the powerful jet aircraft was made without fanfare but with no little concern on the part of Gordon. A ruggedly handsome black who often smiled, and formerly SAC of the Los Angeles FBI office, Alexander Gordon was a UCLA graduate in law and had played for two years as a linebacker for the Los Angeles Rams before joining the FBI and, after that, the Secret Service. Since leaving the White House, Gordon had been alternately talking into and listening to a small but powerful hand communication device almost constantly. Now, inside Air Force One, he faced his chief, who was just buckling his seat belt.

"Mr. President, I'd like to prevail on you if I may, sir, to cancel this Chicago meeting."

Robert Sanders shook his head. "Impossible, Alex. I'd cancel if I could, but it's just too important. Why?" His dark eyes narrowed. "What's the matter?"

"The weather for one thing, sir," Gordon said. "Control here reports that there's some fog moving in around Chicago. Dense in places. Midway's already been shut down for half an hour because of it."

"Midway Airport, as I recall," the President remarked, "tends to shut down for anything worse than a light drizzle. O'Hare's not affected, is it?"

"Well, not insofar as being shut down is concerned, but air traffic is already slowing. Holding patterns began some time ago and they're only bringing one in about every three or four minutes."

"I'm sure that won't affect us in particular, Alex. I know we've landed there in worse weather."

"Yes, sir, that's true, but you're quite late already and if it's not really necessary to take the risk, then—"

"It's necessary, I'm afraid," the President interjected. "They are prepared for us on the ground, aren't they?"

"Yes, sir. No adverse reports in that respect at all. Except that..." he hesitated.

The President had turned his attention to some papers he was removing from a manila envelope he had taken from his briefcase, but now he paused and looked up at Gordon. "Except what?"

"Evidently someone leaked the prospect of your meeting there."

"Over a week ago the *Chicago Tribune* speculated on it," President Sanders remarked. "The papers are bound to get rumors like that. They don't know anything definite, though."

"Sir," Gordon said, obviously discomfited now, "I'm afraid they do. I talked with Ed Grinelski. He said the *Daily News* carried a banner late this afternoon telling of your planned ten o'clock meeting at the Continental Plaza tonight. I guess there's a small demonstration going on at O'Hare right now, along with a few placard carriers beginning to assemble at the old Water Tower Park on Michigan Avenue already. Plus the usual crowd forming and moving in as close as they can get to the hotel."

Robert Sanders became irked at this. "I wanted no fanfare on this one," he said. "Who the hell leaked it?"

Gordon shrugged. "We can only guess. Probably someone from among the invited group."

The Chief Executive shook his head. "Well, I suppose it was too much to expect that we'd get in and out without coverage." He paused a moment, then asked, "Placards about what, this time?"

"Cost of living. Rising inflation, especially for groceries—milk at a dollar and a half a gallon, bread at a dollar a loaf, hamburger approaching two-fifty a pound. That sort of thing's not making anyone happy. There are placards demanding price controls, price rollbacks, the whole bit. Poorly organized, according to Grinelski. Seems to be mostly housewives."

The President rolled his eyes. "Lord save us from the irate American housewife," he murmured, "but I'll have to admit, I sympathize with them." He fell silent, lost in a thought, then added, "All right, Alex, I guess there's nothing to do but face it." He chuckled dryly. "At least we're making these demonstrators wait longer than they expected. I suppose it's too much to hope for that the delay will make them give up and go home. Let's get moving."

Gordon, obviously not happy at his failure to dissuade the Chief Executive, touched a button a few feet away on the bulkhead. Almost immediately the timbre of the jet engines changed, climbing to a more powerfully high-pitched whine, and the aircraft began moving along the apron toward the runway. Gordon stepped toward the rear but remained in the President's compartment, seating himself by the aft bulkhead door, which was closed.

President Sanders glanced at the papers he was holding: a listing of the points he planned to cover at the forthcoming meeting. Only eight months remained now of his first term as President, and this Chicago meeting was the foundation block being laid for his reelection. He had no definite plans to campaign actively during this election year. As incumbent, and without much threat from the Republicans this time, any extensive campaigning would be unnecessary, but it certainly wasn't too soon to begin laying the groundwork to insure reelection. A score of the most important and influential financiers and industrialists in the Midwest would be at the meeting; each, the President was sure, with his own particular demand. There would be no way to satisfy them all, but the fundamental goals of all were identical and tonight, with his personal assurance of his cognizance of those goals and his willingness to achieve them, it should result in general support among them for his reelection. They were sharp businessmen and his own task would not be easy. Nevertheless, he felt reasonably sure that he would be able to convince them to pledge their support while at the same time not commit himself to any promises he couldn't expect to fulfill.

It was exactly one minute of nine in Washington, D.C., when Air Force One thrust itself into the air at a steep upward angle and with a powerful roaring of the engines. The President of the United States leaned back and closed his eyes, regretful after all that he had not brought Grace with him. The smile which came at the thought of his wife smoothed the lines of concern that etched his face. Abruptly he looked like a very ordinary and very gentle man.

VIII

Marie Grant's ability to fall asleep with phenomenal speed had become something of a standing joke between her and John over the years. Quite early in their marriage, John Grant had teasingly compared her to one of those dolls which has wide-open eyes when standing erect but closes them in a facsimile of sleep when laid upon its back. They had laughed about it together, but the analogy was not far from wrong. The times were rare indeed when sleep did not come for Marie within mere minutes of the time her head hit the pillow. There even had been an occasion when she had fallen asleep in the midst of a conversation. John had never quite gotten over his amusement at that. Sometimes, with close friends, when the subject of sleep was being discussed, John would grin, wink at Marie and say, "Don't ever try to converse with Marie when she's horizontal."

This was not to imply that Marie was not a good bedmate. However deeply asleep she might be, it had become practically automatic with her to awaken as he got into bed and snuggle close to him, molding her body against his and murmuring soft, warm sounds. If he, or she, were inclined toward making love, the sleepiness would vanish and they would fulfill one another in an aura of mutual pleasure and satisfaction. But, almost as if a switch were thrown, when the lovemaking was over Marie would again be asleep.

Tonight had been one of those exceptional nights for her when sleep positively refused to come. The evening had been interminable. Half an hour after John's departure, Billy had called, apologizing in his breathless, twelve-year-old way because he was not yet home and had she started to fix dinner yet and if she hadn't could he stay overnight at Jack's house, because Jack's mother had invited him to dinner and Jack wanted him to stay all night and Jack's mother had said it was all right if it was all right his mother and so was it? Marie hesitated, then asked Billy to let her speak with Jean Coblaum. A brief conversation with her indicated that she was willing to put up with those two wild Indians for the night and so Marie gave her consent. With Carol Ann at Peggy's slumber party and John away, this was going to be one of those extremely unusual occasions when she would be wholly alone in the big house all night.

Having been interrupted by the call while at John's desk in the upstairs den, she had left her papers where they were and went to the kitchen, unwilling to prepare a full meal for herself alone, but knowing she ought to eat at least a sandwich or something. Nothing in the refrigerator looked appealing and the same was true of the cupboards she opened. She decided against eating after all and went into the front room, switched on the television and watched it for fifteen minutes before realizing she hadn't the foggiest notion of what was happening on the tube. She switched it off and picked up a copy of John's *U.S. News and World Report*, stared unseeingly for a minute or so at the cover, which depicted Kenya's President Ngoromu, and then threw it down.

Abruptly, with considerable determination, she marched upstairs to the den and swiftly, methodically, put everything back in its former position and then left the room, mentally berating herself for invading her husband's privacy and vowing not to do so again.

She felt intolerably weary, and even though it was only now beginning to get dark outside, she showered and got into bed, feeling it would be the best thing possible for her to get a good solid night's sleep. Twenty minutes later, her eyes still wide open in the early darkness of the bedroom, she sat up, switched on the light, punched her pillow angrily into a ball against the headboard, and picked up a magazine from the nightstand on John's side of the bed. In less than a minute she threw it aside, got out of bed, and snatched up her robe. She put it on as she went down to the kitchen and brewed herself a cup of tea. Two swallows of it was all she could get down. She sat at the kitchen table, divorced from everything except the struggle being waged in her mind, and then finally slammed her small fist to the tabletop and said aloud, "Damn it all, you know what you're going to do, so *do* it!"

Although she could utter profanity well when occasion demanded, Marie Grant only rarely used it, but as she left the kitchen and stalked purposefully back up to John's den, she spoke the same word aloud, fervently, at least a dozen times. "Damn!…Damn!…Damn!…

As she came to a stop in front of the bookshelf, she caught her breath with a real stab of apprehension as she noted something that had not dawned on her earlier. The final, slender volume —the diary for the current year— was gone. It took her a moment or so to deduce the cause, but then she relaxed. It was not so startling at that. Usually the last thing John did each night before going to bed was to write in his diary. When he was home, it was convenient to keep that in-progress volume on the shelf with the others. However, he also always took it with him whenever he went on trips so he could continue to record his thoughts and impressions of the time for future reference. Marie found herself unexpectedly relieved that it was gone.

That left her with the remainder of entries in the diary for two years ago, plus all of last year's. She took the former volume to the desk, sat there a while staring at the cover, and then heaved a sigh and began deciphering again. Only one coded entry remained in that book, and it was brief…no more than the others had been; a commentary on restlessness and dissatisfaction. The hint was there that he wanted sex with another woman but refused to buy such gratification and was leery of simply going out to seek it. Much more, though, he yearned for what he termed a satisfactory relationship, whatever that meant. At the moment, Marie was in no mood to figure it out. She merely deciphered automatically.

As soon as she was finished, expressionlessly she returned the volume to the shelf. That left only last year's diary, which she took from the shelf and carried to the desk. She set it down, letting her hands fall to each side on the desktop, then noted, as if they belonged to someone else, that they were trembling. She put them together atop the closed diary and tightly interlaced the fingers. She was strongly tempted to leap ahead, to go to the final entries and read them, but somehow it had become important to her to follow the chronological progression of her husband's upset and maybe, in that manner, learn not only what was wrong with him, but what was wrong with herself.

As before, she hesitated. In one way, she was reluctant to go on. She knew very well she could stop right here and now without much damage having been done. Certainly John had expressed feelings and thoughts she had not known were troubling him, but it was obvious that he loved her deeply and that, despite his inner torment, his powerful yearnings, he had remained faithful. That was the important thing. If she stopped deciphering now, that simple fact could remain her ray of hope, the sturdy rock to which she could cling. She was deeply afraid that by the end of the book before her now, that ray of hope would be extinguished and she would be swimming helplessly in a sea of damning facts which had engulfed her rock.

She shuddered uncontrollably for a moment and then unclenched her hands and opened the book. Page after page went by without a coded entry. Then, fully five weeks after the final such entry in the previous volume, she encountered one.

…I'm continually more perplexed with my own feelings. Consider last night: Marie and I made love; joyfully, beautifully, satiating us both to the point of utter exhaustion physically. Yet, I remained awake after she had fallen asleep. I lay there with Marie still in my arms, but longing to be with someone else. Good Christ, how do I reconcile **that**? *And why do I feel such a sense of stagnation where my writing is concerned? How long has it been since I've written anything really good? How long since I've become truly inflamed over any writing project? Years.* **Years!** *Is it a sexual frustration that's eroding the excitement and enthusiasm that I've always found in writing? If so, then my very* **reason** *for existence is gone. If I should find outside gratification, would it stop the erosion? I really doubt it. Even if it did, at what cost? Marital tragedy? God knows I want no sort of emotional attachment with another woman. Ever more frequently I tend to fantasize, and rarely do I see any attractive woman—stranger, acquaintance, friend—that I do not mentally undress her and have sex with her. Yet, even though I fantasize about sex, what I* **really** *long for even more is a* **different** *sort of association, more on a level of mental companionship rather than physical. I seem to vacillate dizzyingly between fidelity and desire.…*

Early in the deciphering of this entry, Marie's eyes had filled and she had difficulty seeing, blinking frequently and as often wiping away the tears on her cheeks with a hanky from her robe pocket that had now become a soggy ball in her left hand. Perhaps it was the whole tenor of the entry that had engendered the tears, but more likely it was his reference to his writing, over which she knew he had been greatly concerned for many months, which very suddenly made her sense that she had lost in that mental battle of which he wrote in the last line. Entry after entry followed in which these subjects were discussed again, sometimes briefly, occasionally at considerable length, once in a while with self-demeaning humor, more often with pained and bewildered seriousness. Her rock of fidelity was sinking and, in flailing about for something else—*anything!*—to which she might cling, she found a sturdier purchase than the one she had abandoned. Only one thing was certain—he loved her. It was there in every entry, whether written on the lines or between them, it was there. He might stray; husbands were known to do that. But he was hers. John loves Marie. *That* was the rock.

In the remainder of the entries for the year, a new factor was becoming manifest through the remarks John wrote, in the regular entries as well as those written in code. This was a constantly growing dejection on his part which was soon worrying Marie as much or even more than what the ultimate result might be of his long-suppressed restlessness. Two of the remaining entries were especially fearful to her; one written on the third day of December, another written on New Year's Eve. The December third entry was like a knife thrust into her heart.

I've had depression in the past, but certainly none quite like the one I've been experiencing lately, almost to the point of physical sickness. If this is what those poor souls experience who wind up blowing their heads off or diving off high buildings or whatever, I'm better able to understand what motivates their suicides. I'm not contemplating that, but the bleakness of my mood is demoralizing. I suppose if I were a heavy drinker I could find some handy bar and conveniently get stoned, thereby blocking out the brooding over whatever it is that is causing this bleakness in the first place, but I am not an escapist.

The final entry in the volume vigorously and viciously twisted the blade driven into Marie's heart by the previous one.

Ever since the onslaught of this damnable depression, I've been trying to determine the causes and see what I might be able to do to alleviate them. I can't go on like this because it's tearing me apart. Perhaps if I put into writing what I've been thinking, I can reach some conclusions. Although the matter of love is, and always has been, far more important to me than sex, still I recognize a keen sense of desire within me for sexual contact with a woman other than marie. I've fought this off successfully for a very long time, but at what cost? Is it not just possible that the internal frustration in this respect is the very cause of the depression? Is it not possible that if I deliberately set about to relieve the frustration, I will at the same time relieve the depression? Is it really so strange that I feel the need of another woman? Of course not. I'm hardly unique in experiencing such feelings; most men have them, I guess, but they seem to cope well with the problem. They cope because they do something about it. My trouble has been, and continues to be, a strong, ingrained reticence to put the wheels into motion which would allow me to achieve such a union. Perhaps I need, more than anything else, to overcome that reticence. Perhaps a strong resolve is in order for the New Year—a resolution to take very positive steps in that direction. So be it.

For long minutes Marie sat still after finishing this last entry. Outwardly she was entirely motionless, but her mind was racing. She felt so all alone right now, so unwanted, unneeded. John was drifting away from her and she tried fiercely to figure out how to bring him back, to renew his interest in her. Would a new hairdo help? Maybe new lingerie? What about fancier meals for him? Was she gaining weight and should she go on a diet? She groaned mentally. These were all superficialities. What was the real *root* of the problem? She couldn't find it. She knew only that she always had been true to John, always had done all she could for him. God, she *lived* just for him. Couldn't he see that? What more could she do? She just didn't know and abruptly she was trembling uncontrollably.

I X

As much as President Robert Sanders required and appreciated the speed with which Air Force One carried him to his various destinations, he nevertheless disliked flying. It afflicted him with a sensation of nervousness he had never experienced when he was himself a jet pilot during the Vietnam War. Perhaps it was the fact that it was not he who was at the controls. More likely, he admitted to himself, it was related to the crash of his plane near Hanoi and his memory of the terrible moments of going down, as well as the pain of the injury and the years of imprisonment which followed.

Although he'd wanted to, he'd never again flown a plane after escaping from the North Vietnamese POW camp in 1969. Nowadays when he flew, it was with someone else at the controls and the nervousness was constantly there. During such times he tried to keep himself busy with paperwork, as much to take his mind off the fact that he was hurtling along in a jet some five or six miles high as to try to catch up on backlogged paperwork details.

Taking off and landing made him especially nervous; and air turbulence, which really had never bothered him much before, now had the effect of causing him to become positively clammy with perspiration. The problem became aggravated when cloud cover blanketed the ground and he could not estimate to his own satisfaction the height at which he was flying. Even worse was when the plane itself became so enveloped by clouds that outside the windows there was only a gray wall of nothingness. When that sort of situation became compounded by accompanying air turbulence and the necessity of making an instrument landing because of poor visibility, his nerves seemed to stretch nearly to the breaking point and he would find himself gripping the armrests fiercely and staring outward and downward through the window at the gray pall. The discomfort might have been eased were he able to experience the thread of security which came through radio contact with the ground. Without that, there was a sense of being lost in a great void.

Only four people besides himself were fully aware of how severely the President was affected—his wife, Grace; his personal physician, Victor Aiken; his chief of security who almost invariably flew with him, Alexander Gordon; his good friend since boyhood, Mark Shepard, whom he hadn't seen too often in recent years, but who still wrote to him regularly. When Grace flew with him, her very presence and the pressure of her hand atop his tended to have a settling effect upon him. When she did not, Sanders often swallowed one of the little yellow pills given to him by Dr. Aiken. It was a mild tranquilizer which in no way hampered the President's faculties and yet almost always provided a calming effect. Tonight, unfortunately, was not one of those times.

The President sat with eyes closed, feeling distinctly uncomfortable until the big aircraft finished its initial steep climb. Then he opened his briefcase again and began going through the stack of material Hazel Tierney had gathered, as usual, for him to study while on the flight—budget reports, House and Senate bill introduction summarizations and vote tallies, brief notes from his press secretary and principal advisers, plus a half-dozen or so letters which, because of their nature or importance, finally had reached him after going through the echelon of White House mail personnel who carefully screened everything.

As the Chief Executive was going through this material for a first quick look at each, Alex Gordon walked past him and disappeared through the forward door on his way to the pilot's cabin. Sanders paid no attention to him. He paged through the material swiftly, occasionally making notes to himself in a small leather-covered pad, writing in the peculiar backhanded manner of left-handed people.

A sudden jarring turbulence rocked Air Force One just as the President was replacing his mail and notes in his briefcase. He glanced outside and saw that now the moon and stars were gone and all was gray darkness as clouds engulfed the huge jet, increasing so rapidly that within mere seconds even the wingtip outside his window was no longer visible.

He glanced at his watch and saw they'd been airborne for just five minutes short of two hours. After several more minutes, during which time the turbulence ended but his nervousness increased by giant strides, Sanders heard a click as the loudspeaker in his compartment came to life.

"Mr. President." It was the voice of the pilot, Colonel William Byrd, known to his subordinates at Andrews as "the Byrd colonel." Now Byrd cleared his throat and spoke carefully. "There's a bit of a traffic problem below. Ground Control has some forty planes in the holding pattern at present and all landing is GCA. Visibility's less than three hundred feet. We'll be given landing priority as soon as possible, but some of the holding aircraft are pretty low on fuel and have to be brought in first. Milwaukee's socked in as badly as O'Hare and Detroit's starting to get it now, too. GC's been redirecting quite a few incoming flights to St. Louis and Indianapolis, but traffic's still very heavy here."

The President leaned forward and depressed the white button beside the communicator built into the wall just forward of his window. "How much of a wait, Bill?" he asked.

"Well, right now, sir, the estimate is about ten minutes. Some of the commercial airliners have been holding for nearly an hour already." Byrd paused, but when there was no further communication from the President, he spoke again. "Sir, we've plenty of fuel and if it's not really a matter of urgency, I'd recommend we cancel out and return to Andrews.

No," Sanders replied, a glaze of perspiration beading his forehead, "we'll land as planned. We're pretty late, so just take her in as soon as you possibly can, please."

"Yes, sir. Mr. Gordon's been on the radio ever since he came up here and he's on his way back to you right now." The faint hum of the intercom was silenced.

In just a moment the forward bulkhead door opened and Alexander Gordon reentered the President's compartment. At the Chief Executive's nod he settled into an adjacent seat with a deep sigh and buckled himself in. The sigh was his only indication that matters might not be ideal. His features were calm.

"All right," Sanders said, "let's have it. What's the situation down there, Alex?"

"Not terribly promising, Mr. President," the chief of security answered. "The fog's very bad. We'll be able to land all right, but there's no possibility of using the helicopter from here to Meigs Field on the lakeshore. We'll have to use ground transportation to the downtown area."

"You've set it up?"

"Yes, sir. They've been alerted and have the cars and escort ready and waiting. My men will be in cars ahead and behind. As usual, I'll be riding with you. Police escorts will be flanking us all the way in. It shouldn't take us more than thirty or forty minutes to reach the hotel. Grinelski reports that he's thrown up a cordon around the entrance."

"What about the meeting? What's the mood of those who are waiting?"

"Sir, Grinelski also said that he's personally spoken to the group, explained the delay and apologized for it. They seem to be taking it in good grace and are waiting patiently. In fact, Ed says there seems to be a feeling of admiration and appreciation prevailing because of your determination not to cancel out and return to Washington."

"Praise God for small favors," President Sanders murmured. "What about the demonstrators?"

"They're there. Not too many, though. The ones down below at the terminal we needn't worry about. We won't be going anywhere near them. Those near the hotel the police are keeping on the move in two lines—one circling on the Michigan Avenue side of the Continental Plaza out of sight of the entrance, the other on the Michigan Avenue sidewalk of the John Hancock Building. They're orderly but determined. Other than that, maybe three or four hundred bystanders waiting around, mostly on the north side of the Hancock, opposite the Continental.

No real problem that Ed can see."

"All right, Alex, thanks. Let's plan to move out immediately after we leave the plane. No interviews, introductions, anything."

"No, sir, none planned or anticipated."

The President lapsed into silence and stared into the darkness outside the window. The perspiration on his brow increased. He glanced at his watch and saw that it was now 10:19 Chicago time—nineteen minutes beyond the time his meeting was scheduled to begin, and he was not yet even on the ground. In sudden exasperation he leaned forward and punched the button beside the communicator.

"Yes, sir?" It was Bill Byrd's voice.

"Colonel, exactly *when* are we going to land?"

The edge in the President's voice and the fact that he had addressed the pilot by his rank rather than by his first name, as he customarily did, were indications of his agitation. Byrd's reply came swiftly, respectfully.

"Sir, we've just now been given clearance and are turning onto final approach. We should be on the ground in three or four minutes maximum."

The time ticked by slowly and then the landing lights came on, but they only illuminated the gray-white blanket of fog enshrouding them. The pitch of engine noise indicated they must be nearly down, but still there was no sign of the ground. Another fifteen seconds passed and then, at exactly 10:23 P.M., the jet sharply leveled off, the engines cut back, and almost at the same instant there was a solid thump as the wheels hit the landing strip. The plane bounced, stabilized, and then, after a moment, the engines roared out their braking thrust. Blue landing lights along the edge of the runway were finally visible to the President, flashing past with diminishing speed.

Within two minutes more, Air Force One had taxied to a stop on the broad holding pad before the operations center of the Sixth Troop Carrier Squadron on the northeast quadrant of the field, nearly a mile and a half from the O'Hare control tower and terminal buildings. Over a hundred yards away a phalanx of Air National Guardsmen stood in stiff formation.

Even before the engines had been shut down, six cars—a large black Cadillac limousine, three official O'Hare security cars, and two black Cadillac sedans—had nosed their way past the rigid troops and pulled to a stop beside the jet. The drivers remained inside each vehicle but from the two sedans, one of which parked in front of the limousine and the other behind, a total of twelve Secret Service men in business suits emerged and took up a loose formation, creating a sort of broad aisle through which the President could walk from ramp to vehicle.

With Gordon beside him, President Sanders moved briskly down the stairs and across the concrete pad to the limousine, tossing a brief casual salute toward the Guardsmen in passage. Gordon opened the rear door for the President to enter, then shut it behind himself as he too climbed into the back seat. Gordon nodded to the agent seated in the right front seat and leaned forward to murmur a few words of instruction to the driver.

In a moment the six vehicles were moving out in a procession which carried them to the Squadron Gate. At this point the O'Hare security cars fell away and immediately their places were taken by three City of Chicago police cars which pulled in front of the remaining three cars and began leading the way; then four others fell in behind, all with their blue roof flashers revolving steadily. They continued out the squadron road to the Mannheim Road entry and here four motorcycle officers, two on each side, moved in and took positions flanking the limousine. Behind them Gordon could see that the southbound Mannheim Road traffic had been stopped about five hundred yards away to permit the procession access to the highway. Within a minute they swung around a cloverleaf onto the regular O'Hare Airport entry road and about a mile from there merged with the John F. Kennedy Expressway heading for downtown Chicago.

Robert Sanders was much more relaxed, now that they were on the ground. He rested comfortably in the seat, his eyes lidded, not really paying any attention to the passing scene outside. As soon as they had entered the broad, four-lane strip of expressway, the three leading police cars had fanned out to drive abreast, maintaining a steady speed of about 45 miles per hour. The four police cars following also spread out, side by side, each in a separate lane. They held their places about fifty yards behind, preventing any other traffic from overtaking and passing. Those private vehicles which did catch up had no choice but to follow the pace set by the procession.

Hectic schedules were a way of life in politics and Sanders had pretty well become accustomed to taking them in stride, even though sometimes, such as tonight, they placed considerable stress on the mind and physical system. And now, as he frequently did during brief intervals at such times, he composed himself by thinking of the ranch near Lander and the peacefulness of the Wyoming rolling plains, with the jutting peaks of the snow-topped Wind River Range serrating the horizon to the west. There were times, more frequent of late, when he found himself wishing he were there again, permanently. Life there had a crispness, an openness about it which, once experienced, never let a man forget it, never stopped subtly pulling him back. They were carefree times: fly-fishing for cutthroat trout in the icy streams, elk hunting in the mountains near Dubois, antelope hunting in the sage-speckled hills east of Riverton...

Sanders idly wondered why he had left it all for a life in the political jungle. But he knew why; because politics was in his blood just as thoroughly as the ranch life was in his heart, which was why, when he finished high school and went directly to Harvard to major in political science, he wound up graduating near the top of his class. And deep inside, he had to admit that no trout striking a dry fly, no form of hunting—not even the exhilaration of riding horseback across the Continental Divide in search of bighorn sheep—had ever quite equaled the feeling that had come the night he won the election and became the junior United States Senator from Wyoming.

True, if old Clepperson hadn't decided to retire, if he hadn't strongly endorsed Sanders for his own seat in the

Senate, it all might never have happened, or at least not as quickly as it had. Robert Sanders had always been popular in his own district and became even more so when he'd returned from Vietnam, having escaped his long internment as a POW, limping badly then because of the loss of his left foot when he'd been shot down and still not accustomed to walking on the prosthetic foot the air force doctors had fitted on him. But popularity in a home district is not popularity on a statewide basis and without the endorsement by the old family friend

Charles Clepperson, it simply wouldn't have happened. The state Democratic party hadn't liked it at all, especially since at that time, despite his degree in political science, he had held no elective office whatever and had adamantly refused until then to join a political party. He liked the independence of being an Independent and supporting the candidates he thought were best qualified, irrespective of party affiliation. No, the state party hadn't liked it but, well familiar with Clepperson's obstinacy, they hadn't dared to try to balk him, especially when the craggy old man had threatened to encourage Sanders to run on the Independent ticket if the party didn't back him, and then still publicly give Sanders his own personal endorsement.

They had backed him, all right, and the bittersweet memory of election night and the day that followed had never dimmed for Robert Sanders. The old senator had spent much of election night with Robert and Grace in their suite at the Frontier Hotel in Cheyenne. The couple had left eight-year-old Robbie at home with Grace's mother and, at the hotel with Clepperson, they watched the returns on television. Clepperson chortled with glee as Sanders took an early lead which gradually increased until, even with less than half the precincts reporting, it was obvious he was going to be a shoo-in. With his hearty congratulations and best wishes, the old senator had decided to leave then, complaining that he didn't feel quite right and wouldn't it be tragic if, at this stage of life, he was to discover that alcohol made him sick?

"By God," he'd rumbled, turning to shake hands with Sanders at the doorway, "that would be one damned terrible development! I'd just naturally spend the rest of my life vomiting my fool head off. 'Stead of calling me Chuck, like they do now, they'd soon be calling me Upchuck!"

He'd winked broadly at Grace's faint embarrassment and squeezed Sanders's shoulder warmly. He turned to leave, then suddenly turned back and his expression had become serious.

"Bob," he'd added, "you're on the brink. No more being a political maverick. You're strong in the state party now and it's only the start for you, I can feel it.

I've known you since you were a runny-nosed kid no older'n your own boy right now, trying like hell to do everything your paw and I did, so let me be a Dutch uncle for a moment and give you a thought to carry to Washington and maybe remember now and then. Two thoughts, really.

"Don't ever," he said firmly, "make the mistake of trying to please everyone. You can't. You never will. If you try, you'll wind up ineffective on all issues and in everyone's eyes including your own. This is good advice, believe me. Take it without reservation, but let it be the last advice you ever accept without reservation. Here's the second thought: *listen* to advice after this and cogitate on it but, by damn, let the decisions be yours, not *anyone* else's, because no one else is ever going to have to live as close to them as you, or be haunted as much by them if they're wrong. So, if mistakes are going to be made—and by God you'll make 'em, believe me, because we all do—then let them be your own. It's never pleasant being taken to task for your own mistakes, but it's a hell of a lot harder to bear taking the blame for someone else's. The less you try to please everyone and the less advice you accept whole cloth, the better off you'll be and the easier it'll be to live with yourself. Good night, son...and, goddammit, congratulations, Senator!"

With that, Clepperson had stridden down the long hallway toward the alcoved bank of elevators. When he moved from sight, Sanders had closed the door and rejoined Grace to await the televised concession of his opponent. It wasn't until forenoon of the next day that they learned what had happened. Clepperson had been found on the floor of the elevator when it reached the lobby. He was still conscious then, still able to mutter a demand that no one tell Robert Sanders about this tonight, because this was his night and no doddering old man was going to ruin it. It had been a heart attack, the first that Charles Clepperson had ever suffered. He had been rushed to Cheyenne's Memorial Hospital, not far from the Democratic party headquarters, and was responding reasonably well to treatment when the second attack hit and killed him.

But, as Clepperson had predicted, Robert Sanders won the U.S. senatorial race handily, and then three terms of reelection which followed. Over those twenty-four years as the senator from Wyoming, he had come to be recognized as one of the strongest, steadiest and most reliable men in the United States Senate. He also had become a significantly powerful figure in that legislative body, chairing a number of the most important Senate committees and becoming one of the most influential figures in the Democratic party nationally.

Then, in the prelude to the last national elections, the then vice-president, James Warfield, failed to receive the endorsement of the outgoing President or the necessary support of the Democratic National Committee in his bid to become the party's candidate for that office. It was no great surprise. Just prior to the Democratic Convention, Warfield had been rocked by scandal. A beautiful, high-strung movie actress had committed suicide and left behind a damning note concerning her torrid affair with him. Warfield already was married and the father of four, so when the suicide note somehow fell into the hands of an opposition newspaper, it marked the end of Warfield's political career. The Democratic National Convention suddenly found itself in dire need of a strong nominee. For nine ballots the nominations remained deadlocked, and then the name of Robert Morton Sanders was entered as a dark horse. On the tenth ballot he showed surprising strength; on the eleventh, even more; on the twelfth he had sewn up the party's nomination.

The Presidential campaign which followed was a lively one and, because of his middle name, he often was referred to as "The Salt of the Senate." Among his supporters he was affectionately dubbed "The Colonel," not because of his air force rank, which had been only major at the time of his discharge, but because of the familiar "finger-lickin' Kentucky colonel with the same last name, but who was no relation whatever.

Had the Republicans been able to come up with a candidate with any real degree of strength, it could have been a very close election, but they didn't and, as a result, Sanders—riding on his highly respectable Senate record and projecting a much greater television image of charisma, charm, ability and potential than his opponent—had gone on to win the November election with a nice majority of electoral votes and a popular vote of just under fifty-eight percent. The fact that he was quite a handsome man as well, who wore a ready smile and had a decided degree of *savoir faire* and dignity, made him a favorite among many women voters who really didn't care much about issues.

Sanders's first inauguration had occurred just over three years ago and during this first term he had made two mistakes which might yet become his undoing. He failed early in his administration, for the first time in his political career, to follow the sage advice given to him so long ago by Charles Clepperson. He tried to please everyone without actually realizing that he was doing so, acting in what he felt to be a refreshingly nonpartisan manner on almost every early issue. In the process, he wound up pleasing practically no one and appearing wishy-washy and ineffective, neither of which, in actuality, he was. Secondly, he also surrounded himself with economic advisers who were not really as erudite as he had initially believed, and then he compounded his error by accepting their advice without question for much too long. The result was that the present economic picture in the United States was far from healthy. The rapidly upward-spiraling inflation refused to be stopped, despite his efforts to curb it; and wages, while increasing also, simply could not keep pace. The dollar now could buy only sixty-seven cent of what it could buy when he took office a little over three years earlier, and it had been in fairly bad shape then.

As an added burr to his problems, he had made a third mistake. It was of much lesser importance than the initial two, but it certainly created difficulties that need not have occurred. Because of his vacillation on many of the early issues, his nonpartisan consideration which he himself thought to be so refreshing in a Chief Executive, he had come under criticism of the press. Even the most sanguine of supportive newspapers had raised editorial eyebrows at his peculiar lack of partisanship on so many issues, and the opposition press had openly and harshly depicted him as a weak leader. These latter newspapers not infrequently referred to him as "Chicken" Sanders— an appellation he loathed. Instead of ignoring it, he became highly caustic in his remarks about the press and thus earned its enmity, which was all too often reflected in the news stories, columns, editorials and broadcasts about him which followed. He knew he should try to mend these fences and, in fact, was actively taking steps in that direction, but the wounds on both sides were slow in healing.

More important, and aggravated by the bad press he had been receiving because of the continually escalating inflation, his popularity had lately suffered considerably. The damnable thing of it was that everyone wanted to make a lot more and spend a lot less, but there was just no way for this to happen. Rising prices kept pace with or exceeded the cost-of-living increases and, of course, the President had to shoulder the blame for most of it. The latest Roper poll had shown him with barely a majority of public support, and Gallup had published a poll showing the support ratio to be 49 to 51, and *not* in his favor. With an election year coming up, something had to be done about it if he were to be assured of reelection. It would be less than prudent to neglect doing anything possible to improve both his image and his economic policies, and the sooner the better.

That, in essence, was the basis of the urgency he felt to attend this meeting tonight in Chicago. It would be a give-and-take session with the twenty financiers and industrialists and he hoped he would be able to dangle enough carrots to win their support while at the same time not make any promises he would be unable to keep. It would not be an easy meeting for him, he knew, because the primary object of those attending would be approximately the same as his own—to take more than to give—but their support was crucial.

Now, as the procession, of which his limousine was the center, passed the area where the Edens Expressway merged into the one they were on, the President grunted faintly. Only a few minutes more and they'd be downtown and the final important function of a very long day could take place.

X

The thirty-ton Davis-Strick, Incorporated, high-octane tanker that had been coming south on the Edens Expressway en route to its depot in Gary, Indiana, merged smoothly with the traffic on the Kennedy Expressway for the final sweep into the downtown Chicago area at about half past ten.

The driver, Harry Stockbridge, straightened his shoulders and groaned faintly with fatigue. The haul from Minneapolis today had been grueling. First there had been the blown tire, which had caused a forty-minute delay at the Eau Claire Interchange. Then had come another delay with the lecture he'd received from the Wisconsin state trooper who'd stopped him when he'd been goosing the giant rig to make up lost time. A stern warning, but no ticket. But, worst of all, ever since crossing the state line into Illinois near Zion, he'd been enveloped in the heavy fog, creeping along at 20 miles an hour, when he normally drove this final stretch of interstate into Chicago at 60 miles an hour or better.

The fog had begun lifting a little only a few miles back, as he'd passed the Dempster cloverleaf in Skokie. Visibility improved until it was possible to see half a mile ahead most of the time, and Stockbridge gradually increased his speed until his big tanker was rolling along at about 45 miles an hour.

As he straightened out from the merging, he saw in his rearview mirror the flashing of a series of blue lights maybe a third of a mile behind him. He paid little attention except to note that they were moving in the same direction he was going, so evidently it wasn't an accident. He kept his truck in the right lane, expecting that the emergency vehicles would soon pass him on one of the lanes to his left. They didn't, but remained in view far behind, indicating they were traveling at about the same speed he was driving.

In another eight or nine minutes he passed the Damen Avenue Exit and for the first time in hours he relaxed a little. The next exit, about a mile ahead, would be Ashland-Armitage. Just a block this side of it, to the right, would be Marshfield Street, where his own house would be visible from the expressway.

As he approached that area, he reduced his speed slightly and was moving at about 40 miles an hour when he passed the street which dead-ended at the expressway. He craned his head to the right, trying to pick out 1892, the big old frame house on the east side of Marshfield that he and Millie had bought a few years ago, just before Debra Lynn's first birthday. He saw it, and saw too that the windows were aglow with warm yellow light. Considerably cheered, he expelled a breath of relief and, as his house was lost from sight, looked ahead again.

His attention had not been off the road more than six or seven seconds, but it was a fateful distraction. The two unlighted cars stopped in his lane weren't more than thirty feet ahead when he saw them. In the split second before he reacted, his mind assessed what had happened. For some reason the first car had stopped in the traffic lane. The second car had left brief, black skid marks as it attempted to stop in time, but it had smacked into the back of the first car with enough force to cripple both vehicles. Apparently it had happened only moments before, because the driver of the second car was just then opening his door to get out.

There was no time to brake, no time even to glance in the rearview mirror. With an action bordering on the instinctive, Harry Stockbridge jerked the steering wheel savagely in a desperate effort to whip his rig out of that lane and into the lane to his left. A pickup truck, which suddenly had accelerated and was then in the process of passing him on the left, slammed into the tractor just behind the cab. The smaller truck was traveling close to 60 miles an hour and the impact on the joint where tractor and tank connected, combined with the imbalance already occurring because of the attempt to change lanes so rapidly, instantly caused the mammoth rig to jackknife. The front of the pickup truck was pinned and crushed between tractor and tank. The forward momentum carried the rear quarter of the tank into the disabled car ahead. There was a fearful grinding thud as the collision occurred. The left wheels of the rig left the road and the tanker flipped over, landing on the roof of the car and squashing that vehicle as if it were cardboard. The giant tank itself split at mid-point on the collision side with the wrenching force of the impact and a great gout of high-octane gasoline spewed out as if from a geyser. A sickening, deep-throated *whoomp* muffled the continuing screeching of torn metal against pavement as the escaped fuel ignited. Instantly a fantastic ball of fire engulfed the overturned tanker, the pickup truck, and the two disabled cars.

The collision occurred just at the forward edge of the Ashland-Armitage overpass and the ball of flame that rose belched over the road in a spectacular, searing conflagration. Flaming liquid spewed down onto the streets below and three cars traveling south on Ashland were momentarily engulfed in the flame, lost control, and crashed, two into the concrete wall, the third into one of those two.

At the same time, on the expressway above, more tragedy was occurring. Two cars, a taxicab, and a Volkswagen minibus decorated with huge hand-painted flowers, were all too close behind to stop in time and plunged into the roaring conflagration which had burst across all the lanes. One car and the taxi struck the overturned tanker which now lay across most of the outer three lanes. In a moment they were burning as fiercely as the tanker itself. The other car was veering violently left as it hit the flames. It crashed through two steel railings, crossing the two center express lanes and rolling over and over directly into the path of rather heavy, high-speed traffic heading away from the downtown area. In a series of screeching crashes and thuds accompanied by the brittle sound of breaking glass, a chain-reaction accident occurred there involving eleven vehicles in a matter of five seconds. At the same time, the VW minibus had veered just as violently to the right, left the road, and slammed against the low guardrail of the overpass, spun around until it was moving backward, and plunged completely through the wall of flame on the extreme right, narrowly missing the wreckage and finally stopping of its own volition some sixty yards beyond the conflagration. Some patches of flaming gasoline clung to the sides of the Volkswagen and its tires were burning. The doors burst open and half a dozen young men and women tumbled out into the road, stumbling, falling, recovering their feet as they scrambled away from their own vehicle and the scorching heat of the enormous fire behind them.

Two other cars collided in a less serious way. A short distance behind the Volkswagen when it first lost control, the two cars were almost side by side in their lanes. Both were still far enough back to react in an effort to shoot down the exit ramp. One alone probably could have made it, but the exit was not wide enough for the yawing attempt by two vehicles simultaneously. They sideswiped, locked together, and, spinning out of control, struck the railing. The impact broke them apart and both came to a stop partway down the ramp, immobilized and effectively blocking traffic. Their drivers and passengers spilled out and made a frenzied scramble over the railing away from the intense heat.

It was one of the worst wrecks in the history of the Chicago expressway system and certainly by far the most spectacular, with the whole thing occurring in less than half a minute. Traffic already was stopped and backing up great distances in both directions, not only on the expressway, but equally on Ashland and Armitage avenues below. At least eight people had died already and twenty-three vehicles had been involved in the tragedy.

As for Harry Stockbridge, he was still alive. The cab of his D-S tractor lay on its right side, broken away from the tanker and separated from it by over a hundred feet. In the moment of jackknifing, when the back of the tractor had been struck by the pickup truck, Stockbridge's left arm had been pinned between the left door and the steering wheel. Now, suspended from the mangled limb, he hung grotesquely inside the cab, his feet not quite touching the right door beneath him.

The heat was excruciating but as yet the cab was not burning. Miraculously, the large fuel tank that was part of the tractor and directly behind the cab wall had neither ruptured nor punctured. That tank was only about half full at this time, but the searing flames licking at the outside had heated the diesel fuel to a perilous degree.

Harry Stockbridge, still conscious, was screaming in pain and fear, over and over shrieking out his wife's name. Then, with a tremendous blast, the diesel fuel tank exploded.

XI

In the sleek black limousine, President Robert Sanders was concentrating on what he would say very shortly in the meeting at the Continental Plaza Hotel. There was no longer any indication of the nervousness that had afflicted him aboard the aircraft. Only a moment ago they had passed the Damen Avenue Exit, and all seemed well when, from the roadway a couple thousand yards ahead of them, an enormous fireball blossomed, appearing even larger than it actually was because of its reflection on the overhanging blanket of fog.

Even from this distance and inside the closed, moving limousine, they still clearly heard the heavy *whoomp*. Immediately the procession slowed and stopped. A score or more cars and trucks were stopped ahead of the three leading police cars, and some of them already were in the process of backing up for greater safety away from the conflagration.

"Oh, Christ!" Gordon murmured as the limousine stopped. He touched the shoulder of the agent on the seat ahead of him. "Larry, you and Mel stay in here. I'll be back. Mr. President," he added, turning toward Sanders, "please remain still and do not become silhouetted in the windows."

Without waiting for a reply he left the car, slamming the door after him and sprinting down the roadway toward the fire. Already agents from the other two cars had moved to encircle the limousine. All were keenly alert and sharply suspicious, their eyes probing the road edges, the houses and other buildings adjacent to the expressway, the traffic that only briefly continued to pass in the other direction on the expressway. Additional heavy traffic coming up from behind already had backed up for more than a mile, but the four stopped police cars at the rear of the presidential procession prevented their coming any nearer, and the two officers of each car were in the road, keeping the situation back there under control.

Five or six minutes after they stopped, a second explosion came from ahead, louder but with a smaller fireball. Within a few minutes more screaming sirens were approaching. Here at the scene of the accident, stopped motorists were endeavoring to help anyone who could be reached who was involved in the wreck. As emergency equipment arrived, the vehicles were badly hampered by the traffic blockages on both sides of the Kennedy Expressway as well as on Ashland and Armitage avenues below. Some fire trucks, ambulances and rescue vehicles managed to move in close to the fences on side streets, and others, with much jockeying, inched their way through the jammed traffic. But it was fully half an hour before any effective controlling action was begun at the disaster scene, and fifteen minutes after that before Alexander Gordon returned to the limousine.

He was breathing heavily and his black face was glistening as he settled in the back seat beside the President and explained the situation to him. A number of people had been killed, he said, and there was no way to skirt the scene of the wreckage. At this point there was nothing left to do but wait. He had hoped he could call the chopper in from Meigs Field to land on the expressway and pick up the President, but the fog was still too heavy to permit it. Consideration had been given to moving the Chief Executive on foot to the nearest point off the expressway where he could be picked up and taken downtown, but this idea was flatly rejected by Gordon on the grounds that it would expose the President to grave risk. It finally had been decided simply to wait until the fire had been brought under control and the charred vehicles could be shoved aside to allow passage of the presidential procession.

Robert Sanders heard out his chief security officer in silence and then finally shook his head wearily and sighed. Gordon experienced a pang of sympathy for him; it seemed as if the cards were stacked against the President's reaching that meeting tonight which he felt to be so urgent. But Gordon had misinterpreted the Chief Executive's thoughts.

"Alex," President Sanders said softly, "I want you to talk with the police official in charge here. Tell him that I wish to have a list of the names and addresses of those who were killed in this accident, and their next of kin. I intend to send personal condolences."

Alexander Gordon had always held the President in the highest esteem, but in his eyes at this moment there was an expression which bordered on adoration.

X I I

John Grant squinted his eyes in the dim light and turned his wrist back and forth slowly in an effort to read the nonluminous hands of his watch. The counter light aglow in the kitchen was a room and an alcove away from the open bedroom door, but little of its light illuminated the room where he lay. Not enough, at any rate, to make the face of the timepiece any more than a faintly lighter circle on the darkness of his arm.

Behind him on the nightstand, humming at just the lower limit of audibility, was the electric alarm clock with a green-lighted dial easily readable from anywhere in the room. He had only to change his position—roll from his side to his back and turn his head—to see it, but he didn't want to do that. The movement would awaken Anne, and he was reluctant to have that happen.

He was wide awake now, but he knew he couldn't have been asleep for more than an hour. A deep sense of well-being filled him and he smiled broadly in the dimness, then was momentarily amused at himself for having done so. How was it, he wondered, that whenever he was with Anne Carpenter he somehow always felt more vibrantly alive? It was as if senses which at other times lay dormant or at least dulled suddenly became keenly alert, sharpened.

In the front room the stereo was still playing LP records, with the beautiful, poignant notes of Beethoven's Moonlight Sonata drifting pleasantly to him. He listened, enjoying it and not thinking of anything in particular until it concluded and another piece, "Strangers in the Night," began just as softly. He reached behind him without turning, felt the nightstand under his hand, and moved carefully, touching the ashtray briefly and then the pack of cigarettes lying beside it. He shook one partially free and put it between his lips.

The slim gold butane lighter was on the nightstand, too, and, as always, it seemed warm in his hand as he picked it up. This was the first gift Anne had given him and he treasured it. Oddly, though, somehow he never could seem to make it light on the first try. Always it took at least a double clicking to make the smooth, slender flame spring to life. Even more oddly, each time Anne tried it the lighter worked perfectly on the first click. It had become something of a joke between them, as if the lighter had a personality of its own. Now, holding it carefully and depressing the thumb button smoothly, his first attempt still resulted in no more than a single loud click in the stillness. He grinned and tried again, successfully this time, and the sudden yellow pencil of flame was very bright to his expanded pupils. He squinted his eyes nearly closed as he lighted the cigarette. In a moment he had replaced the lighter on the table and eased his head back on the pillow.

God, but he felt good! Such an indefinable sense of peace and satisfaction and quiet happiness. A very rare and elusive feeling for him over these past years; something to hold and treasure for as long as it lasted, and then to remember and cherish when it was no longer there.

"Strangers in the Night" was just concluding and its final notes made him more strongly aware of the woman beside him. Less than five full months ago—so short a time!—he and Anne were just such strangers in the night, meeting, talking, measuring one another at that New Year's Eve party and then finding themselves oblivious to anything but each other, though the room was filled with party-goers milling noisily about them. She had at first been pleasant enough but reserved, standing quietly by the big sliding glass doors leading out onto a narrow, ice-encrusted balcony. Even with her back turned she was exceptional enough to have attracted Grant's admiration from across the room. He had found himself very curious to discover whether or not the front view lived up to the breathtaking promise of the back and so he sauntered toward her.

Grant stopped behind her, letting his gaze follow hers. She was looking at the streets of the city, thirty floors below, and at the seemingly endless stream of traffic filtering out of the downtown area and onto the Outer Drive, heading north toward them along the Gold Coast. She hadn't moved, hadn't looked at him, yet he knew she was aware of his presence. The brilliant beacon atop the Playboy Tower flashed as its steadily revolving beam momentarily swept across them and then was gone.

"Count thirty and it'll be back," he said.

She hadn't replied but he smiled as he saw her lips begin barely moving in a silent count and be paced the same count in his own mind. At "twenty-two" he began to hear her), and as she reached "thirty" the beacon once more passed them. Her lips spread and then, without turning, she murmured, "Observant. You must live here."

"No."

She turned and looked at him appraisingly and he was more than merely impressed with her appearance. She was not just pretty or attractive. Rather, she was strikingly beautiful. Her hair was black and long, framing a face with nicely sculpted features—high cheekbones, wide jaw, full and decidedly sensuous lips, a nose neither dainty nor large but just proportionately right for her face, and large eyes beneath unplucked and naturally well-formed eyebrows.

"I didn't mean in this apartment," she said. "I was talking about the building."

"It's still no," he said. "I live in Skokie." He looked through the glass doors again. "When I was a little boy I used to lie in bed at night and watch it pass. It would make a glow in the room for just an instant. Every thirty seconds."

She turned and looked outward again without answering comment. He thought she would turn back to him in a moment, but she didn't. She seemed to have lost interest in conversing and, taking that as an indication that she wished to be alone, he began to move away. Immediately she faced him, her smile stopping him. He saw that her teeth were white and even and perfect.

"I'm Anne Carpenter," she said.

"John Grant."

There was a definite quickening of interest in her green eyes. "Ah. Frank was supposed to introduce us. Our host has been remiss. You're responsible for my being here. You weren't here when I arrived."

"I was late." He dipped his head at the drink he was holding. "This is still my first. Frank was already feeling no pain when I got here. By now he's probably having difficulty remembering his own name, much less being able to make introductions." He paused, then added, "You said I'm responsible for your being here. Frank promised he wasn't going to broadcast my being invited."

She shrugged. "He mentioned you as a last resort. He dropped by the bureau before Christmas to invite me to the party. He seemed anxious to have me come." She laughed lightly, remembering. "Very anxious."

"That's Frank Ventry."

"You've known him and Barbara for a long time?"

We attended Northwestern together, Frank and I. He was an aspiring lecher then."

"I didn't know that was one of Northwestern's courses," she said, "but evidently he graduated at least cum laude."

Grant grinned. "Magna cum laude. It keeps Barbara on her toes."

"I've noticed. Anyway, when he invited me I wasn't inclined to come. I don't very often go to parties and I've grown to loathe New Year's Eve gatherings in particular. When he saw I wasn't interested, he began rattling off names of who was going to be here. I still wasn't impressed. Yours was the last he mentioned. Hesitantly, I might add. As I said, apparently it was a last resort."

"And that turned the trick?"

She looked at him directly and he was struck with the beauty of her eyes; he'd never seen such clear green eyes before. They were, he realized, almost on a level with his own, which made her quite tall, since his own height was six feet.

"I came," she said simply.

Grant was pleased that she was not the gushing type. It always bothered him to be nailed by wide-eyed admirers who lavished him with some form of adulation and then usually wound up discussing the great idea they had for a book, if they could ever get around to writing it. Or, even worse, it was such a tremendous idea that they just knew he'd jump at the chance to write up their story for them. Anne Carpenter thus far had only obliquely made any reference to his notability and he was glad of it. He steered the conversation in another direction.

"You said Frank came by the bureau to invite you. What kind of bureau? Governmental?"

"No," she replied, "so don't get alarmed." She laughed with genuine delight at his expression and went on. "I'm not one of Big Brother's people trying once again to nail you. I own a travel bureau—A-C Tours—in the 333 Michigan Avenue Building. A gigantic operation on the fifth floor, four miles from the elevator and adjacent to the executive broom closet, only not as large."

He chuckled. "Tours only?"

"Mainly. Usually package deals, but I also set up itineraries for individuals at times."

He nodded and said seriously, "I may take advantage of that sometime. I do a good bit of traveling, here and abroad."

"Be my guest. I'd be honored. I've set up a number of trips for Frank Ventry in the past, so that's how he came to stop by and make the invitation for tonight." She paused, looking at him, then touched his arm. "I think I'd like a drink," she said, "and you look about ready for another. Then, if we can find a quiet corner away from the general roar in here, I'd like to talk about your writing. Provided, of course, that Mrs. Grant won't mind my continuing to monopolize you for a while longer."

"She didn't come," Grant told her. "She'd planned on it, because Barbara's a fairly close friend, but she picked up some kind of bug the day before yesterday and she's been snorting and sneezing and just plain miserable ever since. She insisted I come alone tonight, but I very nearly didn't. I expected to be bored silly. It hasn't turned out that way. So, to answer your question, feel free to monopolize me for as long as you like."

The evening had passed swiftly after that. Anne already was quite familiar with his work; she had, in fact, several of his books and had read many of his magazine articles and approved of them. She also was aware of his having received a Pulitzer eight years previously for his penetrating series on high-echelon governmental corruption entitled *The Interior Motive*. It had not been quite the same sort of scandal as Teapot Dome in the early twenties, or Watergate in the seventies, but it was nonetheless extremely important and involved figures as high as Cabinet level, especially in the Department of the Interior, as alluded to in the series title. Despite being subtly harassed by the government and thoroughly investigated by both the FBI and CIA, turning his back equally on attempts to buy him off or threaten him into silence, Grant, on a special reportorial assignment, had painstakingly developed material subsequently published in the *Washington Post*, material that had been directly responsible for the resignation of the Secretary of the Interior, its undersecretary, and the undersecretary of Commerce, as well as a whole string of underlings, many of whom, following lengthy Congressional investigations inspired by John Grant's work, subsequently were indicted, tried, and shuffled off to prison still crying aloud that they merely had been following orders from higher up.

At that time Grant's free-lance writing had been primarily of magazine articles, and the incisive, well-researched pieces—especially his exposés—were very much in demand. They still were now, but he did few of them any longer, preferring to write books on topics that especially appealed to him. In books he found greater latitude for development of his subject and more opportunity for the expression of his own ideas and philosophies. He now had six volumes to his credit and all of them had been well received. Two of them, including a political novel a couple of years ago about the vice-presidency, entitled *Monument to Destiny*, had spent many weeks on the national best-seller lists.

Grant was pleased with Anne Carpenter's familiarity with his work and impressed with the sharpness of her observations, her comments and questions. Reasonably alone together in as remote a corner as they could find, at the stroke of midnight their only contribution to the boisterous, howling festivities swirling in the apartment around them was to lean toward one another and kiss. They had left the party together when they suddenly realized that they were among only a small handful of never-say-die guests and Barbara Ventry, still smiling and gracious, was beginning to show the strain. They had crunched through old snow together past the towering apartment buildings fronting on the Gold Coast district of Lake Shore Drive. At an all-night coffee shop on Rush Street they talked for another hour or two over steaming coffee and a couple of doughnuts each.

During the cab ride from there to where Anne lived in one of the twin apartment buildings called Marina City—or "the Corn Cobs" by those who disparaged their unusual modern design—Anne told Grant that she had three of his six books and suggested that one day, perhaps, he might sign them for her. That day had come quickly. At her insistence that he merely drop her off at the main entrance to Marina City—it was by then nearly 4:00 A.M. on New Year's Day—Grant had impulsively suggested they have lunch together the next day, at which time he could sign the books if she liked. She had agreed, and at noon on January second, he'd picked her up at the same entrance. They had lunched in the 71 Club atop the Executive House Hotel, from which she had pointed out the 42nd floor of Marina City's east tower across the river from them. That was where her apartment was located, on the opposite side of the building. Somehow—and he was never quite sure exactly how it happened—they wound up there. It wasn't to sign books, because she'd brought them along and he'd signed them while they'd sipped cocktails before lunch. However it came about, they were there and he was kissing her and, still not fully realizing it, stepping into a whole new plateau of his life.

They hadn't made love then, but they both knew they would before long. Two lunches, three dinners, and eighteen days later—on January 28—they had. It was the beginning of something very special and strong for both of them, and now, just over four months after their meeting, John Grant was as familiar with the little pie-shaped apartment as he was with his own home. He was also deeply, incredibly deeply, in love with Anne Carpenter.

Still without turning around or moving much, Grant reached behind him and, by feel, carefully put out his cigarette in the ashtray. He kept his eyes on the sleeping form of Anne and felt the warmth of that love filling him, driving all other thoughts away. Her head nestled comfortably on his upper right arm and she lay, as did he, mostly on her right side. Her knees were drawn up and together, as if in a sitting posture. His position behind her was nearly identical and she had wriggled her way against him, molding their bodies so firmly together before falling asleep that there was hardly any place for the entire lengths of their bodies that they did not touch. Even in sleep her left hand remained atop his right hand, pressing it against her breast as she had once, twenty years ago, held her beloved stuffed rabbit, Bun, to her not-yet-budded eight-year-old chest. But Anne Carpenter, child, had never gained so great a sense of comfort from the proximity of the battered, noseless Bun as Anne Carpenter, woman, now found in the touch of John Grant.

As he often did when they lay together like this, Grant marveled at his incredibly good fortune in having her. The fresh, clean smell of her hair was a scent that had the power to make his nostrils tingle in a delightful and wholly indescribable manner. The skin of her shoulders and upper back was smooth, warm, unblemished, filling him anew with that overabundant awareness of her. Briefly, lightly, like the caress of a gentle breeze, he touched his lips to her shoulder near the sweeping upward curve of her neckline and then, cobweb soft, let them move to the point of her shoulder.

"John."

Just that whisper, so soft as almost to have been imagined. Not a question; not anything, really, except a sound of love, of knowing a nearness and being infinitely comforted with it. She might yet have been asleep and the whisper of his name a fragment of her dreaming, but he knew that she was awake again and he buried his face in her hair. Six inches away his words would have been inaudible, but her ear was much closer.

"At the risk of becoming redundant, and on the off-chance that I haven't mentioned it lately, I love you."

He felt her cheek swell faintly and knew she had smiled. Because it had pleased her, he was pleased with himself. He heard her breath draw more sharply, breaking the rhythm that sleep had brought, and her reply came like a sleek, well-muscled cat suddenly rising from sleep and stretching luxuriously.

"You are. You have. But if there's anything better to hear, I don't know what it might be. Been asleep?"

"Only a short while. Mostly thinking."

"Of?"

"Three people."

She was silent for several breaths and then she stirred faintly and said, "Three?"

He grinned. "Uh-huh. You, thee, and thou."

"Something of a triumvirate—like me, myself, and I?"

"Something like that. There's just too much love in me to squander it only on one. You'll just have to learn to share it."

She moved, stretching, forcing his legs straight with the pressure of hers. Then she turned onto her left side and moved into his embrace. Her face was nearly hidden in shadow but it raised toward him and their lips met in a gentle touch—not really a kiss, but the mere touch of lips touching lips. He felt hers move against his, and a distant part of his mind catalogued it as a new form of lip-reading.

"I feel," her lips formed the words, "like a harem."

"You are. Mine."

She was silent again, and then said, "What time is it, Mister?"

He smiled, enjoying her use of the word "Mister" for him, which she frequently used, just as he often called her "Lady." He touched his lips to hers again and replied, "Can't see the clock. Too dim to see my watch."

She raised her head briefly to look over his shoulder, then settled back. "Two-ten."

"Then it's time I made a confession," he said, his tone of voice suddenly more serious.

"Confession?" Her eyes were wide open now, less than an inch from his own. "Confession of what?"

"Before I bare my soul," he said, "do you realize that at this range you have just one huge eye?"

"So call me a Cyclops," she said, continuing to stare at him, "but don't change the subject. What confession?"

"I confess," he was grave again, "that for at least the past hour and a half, my right arm has been without blood circulation and undoubtedly by now has become gangrenous."

"Oh, John, I'm sorry!" She sat up quickly and began kneading and rubbing his upper arm where her head had been.

He sat up also and put a fingertip to her lips. "Hush," he said. "Don't you remember that a guy named Segal once wrote that love means never having to say you're sorry?"

"I don't know who he is, but the hell with him. What did he know about making love in Peoria?"

Grant grinned at the old punch line. "This is Chicago, not Peoria."

"Close enough. Hungry?"

He looked at her, at the swell of her breasts forming highlighted crescents in the faint glow of light, with deep shadows between them. He brought up his hand, cupping her left breast, raising it, bending his head to touch his lips to the nipple. Immediately it began to grow more firm, more erect, and he closed his lips over it, touching the tip of his tongue to it. She trembled slightly and put her hand behind his head, pressing him to her, but only for a moment. The pressure became a grip as she clenched the hair at his nape and gently but firmly pulled his head back. She looked into his eyes deeply, smiling.

"The word, darling, was hungry, not horny." Her voice was husky as she rubbed her palm gently across the cowlick at the back of his head, trying and yet not really trying to smooth down the rebellious little clump of hair. "My man," she murmured, and then, with an effort, brought her voice back to normal. "I repeat, are you hungry?"

"Aren't I always, afterward?"

She grimaced. "Always. Keep on eating after each time we make love, Mister, and you'll be a blimp in six months."

"If I keep on eating after each time we make love, Lady," he amended, "I'll be a blimp in six days."

"Braggart!"

"No, just humble, lovable, little old me."

"Humble, possibly. Lovable, definitely. Old, never, not to me."

"Bear in mind, child," and now there was a vague sadness in what he said, "that three days after you were born, I graduated from high school."

"John," she pressed her hand to his mouth, "don't. You promised."

He raised his hand and pulled hers a little distance away from his mouth. Then he leaned forward and kissed the center of her palm and touched it with his tongue. Her lips parted and her teeth gleamed in the dimness. She disengaged her hand and stood up beside the bed, facing him, then took his head between her hands as he leaned forward again and gently kissed the marvelously soft skin just below her navel. She caressed his hair for a long moment and then, more firmly this time, pushed him away.

"Sustenance you wanted," she said lightly, turning toward the glow of light from the other room, "and sustenance you shall have. Bacon, eggs, and coffee in a jiffy."

He watched her go, seeing her momentarily silhouetted in the doorway, the long dark hair cascading in lovely disarray over her shoulders and to the middle of her back, her nakedness and lithe grace bringing a strong new tingle of warmth to his loins.

"Oh, Christ," he muttered, throwing himself onto his back and then rolling over to reach for his cigarettes, "you are so goddamned beautiful!"

Leaning on one elbow, he extracted a cigarette from the pack and clenched the white filter between strong, straight teeth. His craggy features were set in harsh lines in the steady yellow flame of the lighter, and John Grant suddenly felt every day of his forty-six years pressing down on him. He dropped the lighter back onto the nightstand and idly noted that the time on the green-faced alarm clock was exactly 2:22 A.M.

XIII

Herbert Allen Boardman was cold and tired, his eyes grainy from lack of sleep. Over the past decade or more he had become accustomed to retiring immediately following the ten o'clock newscast on television, and sometimes even before that. He could not remember the last time he had stayed up as late as midnight. For his age he was still remarkably vigorous, both physically and mentally. But Boardman, better than anyone else, knew that the old body was wearing out. Even ordinary things constantly grew harder to do, and any kind of unusual exertion quickly left him spent. This night he had undergone more unusual exertion than he had for a very long time.

The very fact of what he was doing and what he was planning to do had helped buoy him during those initial hours after leaving Oak Park. He had been alert and sprightly at the time he had merged with the crowd at the base of the John Hancock Building across from the Continental Plaza's entrance. That buoyancy had lasted until close to midnight in anticipation of the momentary arrival of the President, but now a great weariness was weighing upon him.

When one o'clock had come and then gone without Robert Sanders arriving as expected, a hum of speculation had risen from the waiting crowd. Before long word had filtered through them that the President was delayed because of fog, but that he was still planning to be here, so Boardman had waited.

It was a pleasantly warm late May night. Nevertheless, no longer accustomed to night air, Boardman had begun getting very chilled around eleven o'clock. It was at about that time when new word swept through the people massed on the sidewalk—word which evidently originated from the waiting television crews or news reporters—that there had been a terrible accident on the Kennedy Expressway and that, while not involved in the wreck, the President's car was tied up in the resultant traffic jam. But there was still that tantalizing bit of information that he would be coming yet, just as soon as the way was cleared for traffic. By this time the enthusiasm of many of the onlookers and even some of the demonstrators had waned considerably and during the next quarter-hour or so, quite a few people drifted away. The three or four hundred individuals crowding the sidewalk opposite the hotel dwindled to about half that number, and the two placard-carrying groups lost enough marchers that they broke up and then consolidated into one listlessly circling group on the Michigan Avenue frontage of the Hancock.

The fatigue and cold that gripped Boardman were obvious—so apparent that at one point a security man in plainclothes walking past in the street stopped and looked up at Boardman briefly, suggesting in a kindly way that the night air might be detrimental to his health and he really ought to go home now. Boardman, who correctly took the man to be a Secret Service agent, felt his insides suddenly churning at the confrontation, but he showed no outward indication of it. He merely smiled tiredly, shook his head and replied, "No. Thanks for your concern, but I want very much to see the President."

The man had grunted in a sympathetic way and then moved off. About five minutes later the cold weariness abruptly evaporated when ululating sirens on Michigan Avenue announced the approach of the President's procession. It was just then 11:50 P.M., and immediately there was a general jockeying for position against the ropes the police had stretched from sawhorse to sawhorse along the south curb of Delaware Place. Traffic, both vehicular and pedestrian, was stopped in all directions as the bevy of blue-blinking police cars and motorcycles moved into view, leading, flanking, and trailing the three black cars.

Boardman had been ready and was in place against the ropes directly opposite the Continental Plaza's doors within seconds of the time the first notes of the sirens were heard. As the crowd jostled him on both sides and behind, he held his place firmly and smiled expectantly, amused at the strong impulse he felt to reach a hand up and touch the small, unfamiliar bulk of the weapon under his left arm. He resisted the urge and merely craned and stared along with the rest of the spectators.

Police cars turned off Michigan onto Delaware, slowing as they came but not stopping until they had passed the hotel entrance by three or four car lengths. The four motorcycles came to a stop in midstreet, mere feet away from Boardman. The officers dismounted and stood near their machines, their attention focused on the three big sedans which similarly had turned the corner and were rolling smoothly to a stop along the north curb.

Instantly all doors of the first and third sedans opened and disgorged six business-suited men from each car. The twelve Secret Service men moved quickly, spreading themselves in a loose semicircle on the street side of the limousine in the middle and forming a group of five on the sidewalk to escort the President inside. Unlike the local police, who watched the car and the President, the Secret Service men looked searchingly in all directions except at the President, their gazes flashing from face to face in the crowd, watching closely for that elusive factor which might forecast a possible threat to the Chief Executive. Their eyes frequently went to the windows of the towering Hancock Building, and equally they studied the banks of windows of the hotel the President would be entering.

There were shouts of welcome and simple yells for recognition from the crowd, along with less audible but stridently angry cries from the placard-carriers who were being restrained farther away. A handful of dignitaries from within the hotel emerged, accompanied by chief Secret Service advance agent Ed Grinelski. They immediately fell under the suspicious scrutiny of the outside agents but, at Grinelski's sign of reassurance, they were not interfered with as they moved toward the President's car.

It was Grinelski who opened the back door of the limousine and it was Security Chief Alexander Gordon who was first to alight and look swiftly all around. After a murmured word or two with Grinelski he nodded and leaned back inside the Cadillac. In the next moment President Robert Sanders stepped out and a more sustained roar, intermingled with considerable applause, erupted from the crowd across the street.

President Sanders, appearing a bit haggard, smiled in general greeting, briefly shook hands with the dignitaries, and was able to throw only a quick characteristic wave to the crowd—left hand gripping right wrist and right hand held high and widespread—before being hustled into the hotel by his guards. The Chief Executive had been on the sidewalk less than thirty seconds.

A shudder of disappointment shook the frame of the ninety-four-year-old Boardman across the street. He had seen no opportunity whatsoever. Except for just an extremely fleeting glimpse of the President's head over the top of the limousine, there had been no chance. The agents had closed in around him quickly, even while he was shaking hands with the dignitaries, and there had not been an open view of him before he moved inside the hotel. Even if there had been, the distance was much too great to attempt the shot.

The tall old man went over in his mind what had just happened, trying to determine where he may have lost an opportunity, where he might better have placed himself, or how to turn what he had witnessed to his advantage. He shook his head. There simply had been absolutely no opportunity. Even a mad plunge across the street by someone with considerably more vigor and agility than he possessed would have been stopped before midstreet was reached. No, there had been no chance during the President's arrival. Boardman's location had been as good as it possibly could be, since no spectator had been any closer to the President than he, but it still hadn't worked out. He had known that security probably would be tight, but he had not anticipated that it would have been this good.

There was another general breaking up of the crowd taking place now. The great majority already were moving away. But in a moment, Boardman noticed two rather significant things. The police were remaining in place and, perhaps even more important, so were the television crews and reporters. It seemed evident that the President was expected to come out again, probably after his meeting was concluded. Until now, Boardman had taken it for granted that the President would remain overnight here. Disheartened, but not entirely discouraged, Boardman sighed and steeled himself for another wait.

Within half an hour after the President went into the hotel, two things occurred which the old man considered promising. First, there were guests coming and going in the hotel even though the hour was late, and the cordoning of the entire sidewalk on that side of the street was ended. Guests now were being permitted to move at will, under close scrutiny, from the hotel entrance to the middle of one-way Delaware Place, where taxicabs now were being allowed one-at-a-time passage to turn off Michigan onto Delaware to pick up or discharge passengers. Secondly, obviously feeling that they had expressed themselves above and beyond the call of duty, the placard-carrying housewives broke up and drifted off in different directions, thus encouraging a lessening of the sense of strain among the police guards still on duty. Although Boardman had liked the anonymity the crowd had afforded him, even the disappearance of most of that body of onlookers seemed to be working to his advantage. The rope lines along the south curb were taken down and smaller ones were established on the north sidewalk, stretching from the hotel to within four feet of the curb. One of these ran from about thirty feet from the hotel entrance westward to the Michigan Avenue corner. The other, beginning the same distance from the entrance, stretched eastward along the building for forty or fifty yards.

There were perhaps seventy onlookers remaining, and the majority of these generally were drifting toward the more brightly lighted segment of roped area between the entrance and the principal thoroughfare of Michigan Avenue. Perhaps a dozen others, hoping to get as close as possible, headed for the cordoned area to the east of the entrance.

It was toward this latter area that Boardman, too, headed now. It was not a haphazard selection. In his attempt to anticipate what might occur when the President emerged from the hotel—and Boardman now was quite sure that he would, despite the lateness of the hour—the old man remembered something about Robert Sanders; he was only the fourth President of the United States to be left-handed. It seemed reasonable to assume, then, that when the President emerged, he might be closer to the left side of the entry than to the right. If, as he sometimes did when he was not rushed, he stopped to wave at the crowd or come close to it, his left-handedness would more likely incline him to the cordoned area to his left than to his right.

From where Boardman stood now—some four or five people away from the closest point of the roped area to the entry—he still would be about forty feet from Sanders when the President emerged. That was much too great a distance to even attempt hitting Sanders; but if the Chief Executive stopped, Boardman was determined to make an effort to close the gap by quickly ducking under the rope and heading that way, as if to greet him. Then, at the last possible moment and before Sanders could be shielded, he would whip out the revolver and shoot. By then, if all went well, he would be within fifteen or twenty feet—still a long shot for the snub-nosed weapon, but possible.

For two hours more Boardman waited, groaning audibly at times at his own fatigue. Nothing occurred during that interval of an unusual nature except that at one point the same Secret Service agent who had talked with him earlier passed by, saw him standing there, and tossed a nod of greeting his way before disappearing into the hotel. But then, at exactly 2:00 A.M., several men came outside and spoke to the police and Secret Service men still there. At once there was a subdued but definite tightening of security. Again, sharper glances began flicking across the crowd and windows were given suspicious scrutiny. Traffic trying to turn onto Delaware Place was shunted away and even conversation among the spectators became muted.

At 2:15 A.M., agent Ed Grinelski emerged, walked directly to the limousine still at the curb and opened the back door, then returned to the entrance of the hotel. Here he spoke briefly with two other agents, who nodded and moved closer to the cordoned group where Boardman was waiting. Their steely glances studied each face there, including that of the oldest person present. Boardman's sinews tightened, but there was no change in his gently smiling, anticipatory expression.

Five minutes later, with two agents preceding him, with Alex Gordon at his left and another two agents behind, the President emerged, smiling broadly and looking much less haggard than when he had arrived. It seemed evident that he was very well pleased with whatever had occurred during his meeting inside the hotel. Again, as news cameras whirred into action, focusing on him, the President shook hands with two other men who had followed the agents out after him, and then turned to his right and gave his characteristic wave of acknowledgment to the larger crowd on that side, where the onlookers were cheering and waving and inanely crying out,

"Mr. President! Mr. President!"

For a moment Boardman's heart sank. He had been so sure the President would turn to his left, if at all. And then suddenly, now unexpectedly, Robert Sanders turned his back to those to his right and, with Gordon still at his left side and the guards trailing them, walked directly toward Herbert Allen Boardman.

Despite his control, Boardman's jaw dropped and he stared in amazement, but this was evidently construed by the guards as a quite normal reaction. The President passed the first four cordoned people with no more than a cordial nod, but to Boardman he held out his hand as he came to a stop. One of the television cameramen zoomed in his focus for a waist-up tight shot, with Boardman and the President filling his viewfinder.

"I was told," the President said, "that there was a gentleman of quite advanced years who had been standing out here since around ten o'clock, just to see me. I must say, sir, that I am touched and pleased and I consider it a privilege to shake your hand."

Alex Gordon at first had been looking at Boardman sharply, but now his attention went to other spectators crowding around and thrusting out their hands as they called greetings and hoped to touch or be touched by the nation's most important figure. The other guards also were watching these people closely, with some degree of nervousness.

The President's grip was firm and warm, lasting for about five seconds, and Boardman was able only to mutter shakily in response, "Thank you, Mr. President."

Robert Sanders released Boardman's bony hand and then accepted the proffered hand of the man to Boardman's right. At the same moment, Boardman began coughing raggedly and bent over with the spasm, bringing up his left hand to cover his mouth. An instant later he straightened and the revolver was in his right hand.

The President, still with his hand clasped by the other man, heard the coughing and glanced concernedly toward Boardman, and then his eyes widened as he saw the gun. There was no time for more than that. From this point-blank range, Boardman shot and the bullet struck Robert Sanders in the forehead about a half-inch above the right brow. The President's head jerked with the impact and his eyes rolled upward until only the whites showed, but he was still standing. The sound of the shot was terrifying. People nearby were screaming in horror and attempting to scramble away, and those farther away were pressing forward and craning to see better. Agents were already plunging toward the scene.

At the shot, instantly Gordon had leaped in front of the President and already was throwing himself at Boardman and striking at the old man's hand to knock it down, causing the gun to fire again. The second bullet hit the President on the far right side of his chest and slammed him backwards onto the sidewalk, where he lay motionless.

In a daze, Herbert Allen Boardman felt himself being struck, felt himself falling and colliding with the onlooker to his own left as he went down. His arms flailed out and he gripped the man and clung tenaciously to his waist. Someone jumped on him and bore him the rest of the way to the sidewalk. Then there was nothing more than a bedlam of screams and crying and hoarse shouting, the feel of fists hitting him and hands jerking at him, pulling him, punching him, and a forest of legs all around him. For an instant he was able to raise his head slightly, only to have a heavy brown fist thud into his forehead, and then there was silence.

It was exactly 2:22 A.M.

2

Who dares nothing need hope for nothing.

—Friedric H. von Schiller

Men in general judge more from appearance than from reality. All men have eyes, but few have the gift of penetration.

—Machiavelli

I

Oddly enough, the American people were among the last in the world to become aware of the fact that an assassination attempt had been made against the President of the United States. This was not because the news was not almost instantly broadcast in all parts of the nation—even to the point where all three of the major television networks came back on the air with continuous television programming about the incident. The reason was the time of its occurrence.

Since the shooting had taken place in Chicago at 2:22 A.M., it was not until around 2:30 A.M. that the first radio bulletins began being flashed around the nation and the world. CBS was the first nationwide television network to resume operation—at 3:02 A.M. Chicago time—followed by NBC-TV at 3:08 A.M., and ABC-TV at 3:24 A.M. But at such an hour, few people are watching their television screens. By the time all three networks were back in operation, it was after 4:00 A.M. in New York, after 2:00 a.m. in Denver, and after 1:00 A.M. in Los Angeles.

England was the first major country where the news became widely known. By 8:45 A.M. in London, less than half an hour after the shooting in Chicago, the BBC was broadcasting the news on both radio and television. Most of the morning newspapers already were on the streets, but the four largest dailies immediately went into special editions. The London *Daily Express* approached the subject without editorial comment but with a sense of subdued shock and with its usual caution concerning first reports of major news events. The front-page bulletin, accompanied by a Telecom photo of President Sanders with his hand upraised in the familiar wave in front of the hotel prior to the shooting, was brief and to the point.

U.S. PRESIDENT REPORTED SHOT

(May 22—UPI) First reports that President Robert Morton Sanders was the victim of an assassination attempt in the predawn hours today have been confirmed. The President was shot at least twice by a lone assassin at 2:22 A.M. (8:22 A.M. London time) as he emerged from a Chicago hotel following a late-night meeting with financial and industrial leaders.

Reports still unconfirmed state that the bullets, fired at close range, struck the U.S. President in the head and chest, but that the wounds were not fatal. The victim has been taken under heavy guard to a Chicago hospital, but no official report concerning his condition has yet been issued.

A White House spokesman has stated that the First Lady, Grace Vandelever Sanders, left Washington immediately upon learning of the incident and is at this time en route to her husband's side.

Vices-President James Barrington expressed deep shock at the news and presently is standing by in Washington, where intensive security measures are being taken. Mr. Barrington already has temporarily assumed leadership of the nation and is prepared to be sworn in as President should President Sanders succumb to his wounds.

The assassin was apprehended at the scene of the shooting and was taken to the same hospital where the President is being treated. He is under close guard, but officials thus far have withheld identifying him other than with the comment that he is "an older man."

Both the London *Morning Post* and *Times* carried similar stories and expressed "shock and horror" at the reports, promising their readers expanded details in following editions. The London *Daily Mail* described the shooting as "reprehensible and tragic."

On the Continent, West Berlin's *Der Tagesspiegal* lamented the incident and was first to suggest that the shooting was the result of an intricate conspiracy, though without any suggestion regarding who the conspirators might be. On the other side of the Wall in that city, the *Berliner Zeitung* reported the event with subtle innuendo that it was undoubtedly "the first move of the people rising against the imperialistic government's oppression." In Paris, *L'Humanité* expressed grave concern but clearly gave the impression that such an occurrence was not all that surprising, while *Avanti!*, in Rome, voiced outrage and sorrow over the act, which it ascribed to "criminal elements."

Moscow's *Pravda* carried the news in a brief front-page bulletin and, perhaps surprisingly, showed restraint in avoiding any editorial asides of a derogatory nature. Such was not the case with Egypt's *Al Akhbar* in Cairo, which headlined its first report *WAR-MONGERING U.S. PRESIDENT ASSASSINATED* and obliquely suggested in an accompanying editorial that it "already has been discovered through secret sources that the United States President has been slain by a group of Israeli terrorists."

In Kenya, the Nairobi *Daily Nation* reassured its readers that the assassination attempt had occurred some hours after the conclusion of talks between the President and Kenya's own chief of state, Daniel Ngoromu, and that the latter was "greatly grieved" upon learning of the incident, had expressed his concern to both the First Lady and Vice-President James Barrington, and later in the day would be returning to East Africa.

Peking's *Renmin Rabao* carried no mention whatever of the monumental news, and the Japan's *Tokyo Times* had a first report which was practically a carbon copy of that which had appeared in the London *Daily Express*.

It was only after all this had occurred that the majority of the American people became aware of the shooting of President Robert Sanders.

I I

In the modest Oak Park apartment of Paul Neely, Elizabeth Boardman sat with her eyes closed and her feet propped comfortably on the coffee table in front of the sofa. An old Glenn Miller piece, "String of Pearls," was softly playing on the muted FM radio in the stereo console in the hallway leading to the bedroom and bath—the only place there had been room enough to put it—and the faint clinking of the glasses as Paul mixed drinks in the kitchen was a pleasant sound. She was tired, though not especially sleepy, and for perhaps the third or fourth time tonight her thoughts returned to what her father had said about Paul possibly popping the question. She had been flip in her reply then, but it was a question that had been in her own mind. Paul was not an easy man to read, despite their closeness, and she had no real idea when—or even if—Paul would indeed, as Dad had put it, "pop the question" tonight or any night.

Liz Boardman loved Paul in a quiet but very deep way and thought he loved her similarly, yet neither she nor he had ever actually said the words. Hers was not the passionate bloom of first love; Sam Kaiser had effectively stripped her of that forever. When their divorce had become final after all those years together, there had not been, on her part, the slightest twinge of regret in their parting. There was, instead, a strong reticence about ever again becoming so involved with any man that her entire life was affected. Meeting Paul Neely at Oakmont High School did not immediately alter that attitude. It was only after several years of association with him—he as principal and she as school librarian—that they had become closer. A dozen or more different school functions each year, both professional and social, had thrown them together frequently, and so they had known one another remarkably well before he finally had asked her to dinner two years ago, and she had accepted. After that they dated infrequently for a while and then with increasing regularity until now they spent as much time together as possible when away from the school. So far as they knew, no one at Oakmont was aware of their close personal association.

Liz was not entirely sure what her own reaction would be if Paul asked her to marry him. The "if" was the big matter, because even though they'd never discussed it much, she knew that Paul's two previous marriages had gone on the rocks and he probably was disinclined to try it a third time. She was only too aware that the very fact that his two divorces had occurred made him not the best risk in the world as a husband. That the first divorce may have been no fault of his at all was quite possible, just as in her case the reason for her divorce quite patently had been Sam's fault. But the odds against Paul not being at fault to some degree rose astronomically with the second divorce.

"Asleep?"

She opened her eyes and saw Paul standing close by with a misted whiskey sour on the rocks in each hand. She shook her head as she accepted one of them from him.

"Uh-uh. Just contemplating and becoming very relaxed." She tipped her head toward the drink. "Thanks. Looks good."

Paul took a seat beside her and, in the light little ritual they always followed, they touched rims and murmured simultaneously "To you," and then laughed and sipped their drinks.

"Contemplating what?" Paul asked, adjusting his gold-rim eyeglasses as he placed his drink on a coaster on the coffee table. "Me? Our dinner? Your navel?"

She matched his grin. "Definitely not my navel. As a matter of fact I was thinking about you." She arched a brow in an impish expression. "I sometimes do that, you know." She paused, but before he could reply she continued. "The dinner was good, Paul. Better than good, in fact. Excellent. Let's go there again."

He agreed they would and picked up his drink again, twirling it to move the orange slice out of the way so he could sip it. As he so often did, he changed the subject abruptly.

"How's your father, really? You said earlier he was acting sort of preoccupied, but how's his health?"

"Oh, as far as that's concerned, he's fine. Incidentally, he said to give you his best."

Paul grunted. "An incredible man. Just as sharp and active as any man half his age."

"Mentally sharp, yes, but he's been slowing down physically a lot." She took the long-stemmed Maraschino cherry from her drink, put it between her teeth, and pulled the stem away. "Mmmm, good." She set her glass down and looked at him more directly. "I've noticed his slowing down more and more lately, Paul, especially in the mornings. He doesn't really seem to get his feet under him very well these days until he's been up for an hour or so."

Paul bobbed his head without speaking. He was a nice-looking man of near sixty, whose somewhat flaring ears and thin, neat moustache were somewhat reminiscent of Clark Gable, but with gray hair instead of dark. He took another small sip of his drink, then a larger swallow and set it down. Then he half-turned so he was facing her, his arm on the back of the couch and the hand of that arm gently touching her hair, twirling it between two fingers. He leaned toward her and she responded, meeting his lips in a quiet, pleasant way. Other than an occasional kiss of slightly greater intensity, this had been the extent of their physical contact. It was Paul who broke their touch.

"Has he asked?"

She frowned at the change of pace. "Dad? Asked what?"

"About our intentions?"

She looked at him levelly for a long moment and felt her stomach muscles tighten. "Do we have intentions, Paul?" she asked quietly.

"Don't you think we should have by now?"

"Paul," she said, touching his arm, "let's not play games with each other and let's not end each sentence with a question mark. We're neither of us children."

He smiled and put his hand atop hers on his arm. "We aren't children," he echoed, slowly shaking his head, "and you're right, we needn't play games. I'll answer the question myself. I think we should have intentions. I know I have, Liz. For a long time I was pretty sure I'd never say the words again. Liz, I'd like you to marry me."

"All right, I will."

The words seemed to have come without conscious volition and her eyes widened at what she had said. For an instant they were both startled at her response and then she lowered her eyes and her voice was less steady than it had been previously.

"I don't usually reach important decisions so quickly. I won't ask if you're sure. I know you well enough by now to know that you wouldn't have asked at all if you weren't."

"Are you?" He laughed and added, "Another question mark."

"That one's permissible. Paul, I am as far as I can know. I guess no one ever really knows for sure. They can only think they're sure at any particular moment. In that respect, I'm sure. I've loved you for quite a while, Paul."

"It's the first time you've said so."

"You never have."

"I'll rectify that right now. I love you. I think we can be very good for each other."

He drew her to him and they embraced with considerable depth of feeling. This time it was Liz who pulled away, a light laughter in her throat as she did so. Paul looked at her questioningly.

"It's Dad," she said. "I'll swear, he's positively psychic. As I was leaving, he asked if you were going to pop the question tonight, and I told him I had no idea. Evidently he did."

She lay her head in the hollow of his shoulder and reveled in his touch as his hand came up and cupped her cheek, raising her face to him to kiss again. It was a long kiss and, when finished, she snuggled back comfortably on his chest and resumed speaking without looking up, her whispered words barely audible over the soft music.

"He made another comment about us, too."

"What?" Paul's whisper was only slightly louder than hers.

"He asked why I didn't stay with you all night."

Paul Neely was quiet for a moment and then, when she looked up at him, he spoke seriously. "Did you answer him?"

"I told him it was possible. He wasn't surprised." She straightened, looking at Paul intently. "I haven't been to bed with a man since Sam and I were divorced, Paul. Since a good while before we were divorced, in fact. I haven't wanted to. I do now."

He stood, taking her hands and bringing her to her feet after him, kissed her with increased passion and then slipped an arm about her waist, turning her toward the bedroom. She leaned her head against him and they began walking silently. Just as they passed the console in the hall, the music abruptly ended in midpiece. They stopped, looking at one another with puzzlement. Then the voice of an announcer came on.

"Stand by, please, for a special news bulletin."

"On FM?" Paul muttered. "That's odd."

They continued standing there without speaking during the several seconds of silence which followed, and then the same announcement was repeated.

"Lord," breathed Paul, searching her face, "you don't suppose it's war, do you?"

She shuddered. "Don't even think it, Paul."

Still there was silence and then for a third time the same announcement was made, but this time only a few seconds passed before the voice of another announcer came on.

"This is a special bulletin from WBBM-FM news. The President of the United States has been shot in Chicago. Repeating, President Robert Sanders was shot less than a quarter-hour ago while leaving a downtown Chicago hotel. No further information is available at this time. Please stay tuned for further bulletins as they become available."

Liz Boardman's hand had gone to her mouth and the words seemed wrung out of her. "Oh, my God!"

I I I

Herbert Allen Boardman could remember no time in his life prior to now when he had felt so dazed, so dissociated with everything around him, so involved in a maelstrom of events. At first, following the examination and treatment at Northwestern Memorial Hospital's emergency room and then the moving of him to a secluded, soundproof and well-guarded room on the fourth floor, everything seemed to be kaleidoscopic, briefly sharp but then folding in upon itself and mingling confusedly with events preceding and following. A huge dark man was repeatedly asking him questions which he could not seem to comprehend and it was only during the last five or ten minutes that anything had begun to make sense.

The bed felt gloriously comfortable, with crisp white sheets under his naked back. Actually, the first truly clear thought he had was that they had dressed him in one of those ridiculous hospital gowns which covered the front but only flapped in the back; he would much have preferred his own comfortable flannel pajamas.

The large black man, clad in a dark blue suit, temporarily had given up the questioning and had taken a seat on a chrome and plastic chair against the wall. He was writing swiftly in a small spiral notebook with a green cover, and the pad was nearly engulfed in the huge brown hand holding it. He did not look up as Boardman turned his head to see him better, and the old man studied him with rapidly clearing gaze.

To Boardman he looked vaguely familiar, and his brow wrinkled with the effort of concentration as he attempted to determine where and under what conditions he had seen this man before. It came back to him slowly. This was the man who had been only a pace behind the President as Robert Sanders had shaken Boardman's hand outside the hotel. A guard, that's what he was. Some kind of Presidential bodyguard. But even his closeness had not thwarted Boardman.

Abruptly, with exceptional clarity, he remembered it all: the President's approach, the greeting and warm handshake, the incredible frozen moment in time as the gun was drawn, aimed and fired, the momentary astonishment on President Sanders's face, even as the trigger was being squeezed. He could see again the President's loss of consciousness as he was shot in the head, even though he remained momentarily on his feet, long enough for the second, deflected shot to hit his body somewhere. Deflected. That was it. This huge man across the room had lunged at him, struck at his hand and caused the gun to fire again, though Boardman had not planned on firing twice unless he missed the first time. Then the black man had bore him to the pavement under his massive body. And Boardman now remembered that fractional instant as the contorted face of the black hovered near him and as the great brown ball of a fist had struck him.

Boardman closed his eyes again, just as the big man shut his notebook and started to look up. He expected the questions to begin again, but evidently the man had not seen his return to full consciousness. Boardman's head ached violently and he stifled an impulse to raise his hand to feel his forehead where the pain seemed centered. After a moment he heard a light tap on the door and a swift movement to one side as the black man stood. He heard the door open and a respectful male voice spoke.

"Commissioner's here, Mr. Gordon. He's pretty upset."

"Right. He's probably going to be even more upset in a minute. You can stay in here. Watch him. Call me if he comes to.

The door clicked closed, but still Boardman kept his eyes shut.

I V

Alexander Gordon did not at first acknowledge the rather rotund man in the badly pressed royal blue suit who stood in the hallway a dozen feet or so away, waiting with obvious impatience. Instead, he directed his gaze to one of the four men flanking the door of the room he had just left.

"Any word on The Man, Ed?"

Grinelski shook his head. "Nothing. Not since you last heard."

Gordon sighed and looked down the hall at the blue-suited individual. Perhaps forty feet beyond him at least a dozen Chicago police officers in uniform, along with a few plainclothesmen, stood in a loose group, silently watching. Some of them looked resentfully at the black, but Gordon merely looked at Grinelski again.

"The doctor—Evansson—he hasn't come by?"

"No, sir."

"I want to know immediately when he does." Gordon, at Grinelski's answering nod, moved then to stop a few feet in front of the waiting man. He neither smiled nor offered his hand, but then neither did the heavy man who was regarding him sourly.

"I'm Police Commissioner Perello. You're Gordon?"

"I am."

"Then I'd like you to tell me just what in the hell you think you're doing here. What makes you think you can question that man in there," he gestured with his thumb toward the closed room, "without Chicago authorities present?"

"Mr. Perello, I can understand your concern, but I'm afraid it can't be helped. I intend questioning the man further and I don't intend to have anyone else on hand. This is out of your jurisdiction."

"Jurisdiction! *Jurisdiction!*" Blood vessels bulged in Howard Perello's neck and forehead. "Dammit, man, are you nuts? A killer pulls out a gun on a Chicago street and shoots down another man and you're standing there trying to tell me that it's out of the jurisdiction of the Chicago police? What the goddamned hell is wrong with you, anyway?"

Gordon looked at him coldly, not in the least intimidated or ruffled. "It is out of your jurisdiction, Mr. Perello, because the man who was shot is the President of the United States. That makes it a federal matter."

He held up a hand cutting off a retort the commissioner was about to make. "You may recall, sir, that when President John Kennedy was assassinated in 1963, the Dallas police took control in a jurisdictional dispute. You may also recall that in all of the questioning by them of the assassin, Lee Harvey Oswald, not a single word was taped or written down or otherwise preserved. Further, Oswald himself was then murdered while under the jurisdiction of Dallas authorities, and whatever he said to them prior to that time was lost because in their opinion none of it had any importance. As I've already told your officers and your chief of police, sir, this country does not intend to see that sort of thing happen again. These federal agents here —" he indicated the four men at the door and another two at the window where the hallway ended thirty feet behind him "—are members of the United States Secret Service. They are under my command and I have given them orders that no one I have not authorized to do so may come closer to this door than your officers are now. If someone attempts it, he will be told to halt. If he refuses to halt, he will be shot."

Perello blustered. "I resent your comparing the Chicago police force with that cowboy crew down in Dallas. By God, don't you think we fully realize the implications of all this?"

"I sincerely hope you do, sir. I mean to cast no discredit upon the police officers of this city. I'm sure they're good men. But no one—*no one!*—will speak to that man in there except myself until I decide that he may." He paused, regarding the fat police commissioner, and then added in a slightly warmer tone, "Mr. Perello, we do not as yet know anything about this man or what prompted his action against the President. He may have been acting on his own, but equally he may have been acting as an agent of a reactionary group in this country or as an agent of a subversive organization representing some foreign power and bent upon the destruction of the United States. We will not know any of these things until I am able to question him at length. I assure you, we will keep you apprised of anything we uncover which we feel it will be necessary for you to know. But this will be and must be at our discretion."

Perello raised his arm and pointed in Gordon's face, both his finger and his voice trembling with outrage. "I don't know what kind of god you think you are, Gordon, but believe me, your ass is in a sling as of right now! I'll be on the phone to the governor five minutes after I leave here, and then both Illinois senators immediately after that. If you think some fuckin' Fed acting like Dick Tracy's going to come in here and balk me and threaten to murder Chicago policemen, then you're a bigger asshole than I thought! I've got nothing more to say to you."

Gordon's hands had bunched into powerful balls at his side, but he made no reply. His nostrils flared and he took a single step toward Perello. At that the police commissioner spun around and stalked down the hallway, paying no attention to the police officers who parted to let him through. Gradually feeling the anger draining away, Gordon's fists slowly uncurled. He watched until Perello turned a distant corner and then he moved back toward the room where the prisoner was. Grinelski was grinning at him, but neither he nor the other three agents at the door said anything.

The door to the room opened just as Gordon was reaching for the handle and the agent he had left inside, who was emerging, was a trifle startled.

"Oh. Excuse me, Mr. Gordon, I was just coming out to see you." He jerked his head toward the bed where Boardman lay and lowered his voice. "The old man still has his eyes closed, but I'm positive he's conscious."

Gordon made a small approving sound and told the agent to wait outside, then entered the room himself, closing the door behind him, his eyes on the figure of the man in bed. Evidently the old man had overheard the whispered conversation because now his eyes were open and alert, watching Gordon carefully but with no trace of fear. The swelling on his forehead was gradually changing from red to bluish and it was certain he soon would have a distinct bruise there.

Gordon reached into his own coat pocket and removed a cassette tape recorder not a great deal larger than a package of cigarettes. In grim silence he slid the chair over beside the bed, switched on the record button, and set the device on the bedside table with the small microphone aperture positioned ideally to catch any conversation which passed between them. He sat down, then, and spoke quietly to the patient.

"I see you're back with us."

"I am."

"Would you mind telling me your name?"

"Not at all. It's Boardman. Herbert."

"Middle name?"

"Allen. A-l-l-e-n."

Gordon made a gesture toward the table. "Mr. Boardman, as you can see, I am recording our conversation. Are you aware—"

"Later I may object to that thing," Boardman interrupted, "but for now I'll go along with it."

Gordon began again. "Are you aware, sir, of your constitutional right to legal counsel, your right to remain silent if you choose, and—"

"I'm quite aware of my rights under the law, Mr...?"

"Gordon. Alexander Gordon. Chief of security for the President, and whether or not you are aware of them, I am required by law to read you your rights." He withdrew a small card from his pocket and quickly read off the listing of rights, finishing with, "Do you fully understand?"

"Yes, I fully understand. As I told you, I'm well aware of my rights, Mr. Gordon, and for your information I do not care to have counsel present." He gave a short dry chuckle. "As for remaining silent, that depends upon what your question happens to be."

Gordon studied Boardman for a long moment and then asked his age.

"I'm ninety-four."

The black man pursed his lips in a silent whistle and shook his head unbelievingly. "Ninety-four," he echoed. "Why would a man of your age try to kill the President?"

"I'll comment on that briefly, but without much elaboration for the moment, Mr. Gordon. You are wrong in your assumption that I tried to kill the President. Had that been my intention, President Sanders would at this moment be dead. But he is not dead, is he?"

Gordon frowned and shook his head. "I don't know. The doctors are still with him. We've had no report."

Boardman detected the concern in Gordon's voice and his features softened as he smiled faintly. "Don't worry too much. I expect he's not hurt much beyond the extent of a bad headache. Now, as for motivation for my act, I'll explain everything presently, but not to you. You have my name and age already. Do you care to have my address and other basic information?"

This was a situation the like of which Alexander Gordon had never before encountered. He had the sudden suspicion that within that long, frail body there was an iron will and that he probably would be unable to get any other information out of this man than Boardman chose to reveal. That was precisely the case. In the hour of questioning which followed he learned Boardman's Oak Park address and a great deal about his background, but not even the slightest hint of what caused him to commit such an act.

Toward the end of their session they were interrupted by a tapping on the door and Ed Grinelski entered, followed by Dr. Evansson. In somewhat more technical terms, the doctor confirmed what Boardman already had expressed to Gordon concerning the extent of the President's injuries. Relieved, Gordon spent several minutes with the doctor going over with him what he should or should not say to the mob of reporters waiting downstairs for official word. At length Dr. Evansson left the room, followed by Grinelski.

"The President is all right, Mr. Gordon?" Boardman asked.

"Relatively so. Slight concussion and a cracked rib. The doctor wants him to remain here under observation for at least a couple of days in case of complications. Then maybe a day or two of rest beyond that. He should be back at his desk within the week."

"Good. Good." Boardman smiled broadly. So far everything had worked precisely as he had hoped. "It would have distressed me had he been hurt seriously."

Unable to comprehend this old man's logic, Gordon heaved a sigh and once again began the questioning. He was unable to elicit much more than he had gotten in the previous hour. He would have liked it had he been able merely to come to the conclusion that Boardman was insane, but nothing in their conversation thus far had indicated that such was the case. To the contrary, he was incredibly sharp for his age and obviously an erudite individual. Under other circumstances, Gordon was certain he might have liked the man a great deal, but now he was becoming exasperated at getting nowhere and so he tried a ploy he rarely attempted.

"Mr. Boardman, you are not cooperating very well at all, and I must make it clear to you that you are in extremely serious trouble. There are certain methods which can be used to force you to talk. We must—I repeat, *must*—know why you did this and who is behind it. Do you realize that you may very well spend the rest of your life in prison?"

Boardman burst into laughter. "Mr. Gordon," he said at last, still chuckling, "there's no way on God's earth that you can intimidate me. Look at me. I am a very old man. For maybe the last decade I have been living on borrowed time. A very long time ago I began living each day as if it were my last. I'm running down, sir. To me, each day I survive is a real miracle, and each dawn is viewed with amazement because I fully expected that the one I saw the day before would be the last. I live in a frail house, Mr. Gordon, and I suspect that any sort of pressure you might envision to force me to speak would far sooner than that make the last sunrise a reality. As for spending the rest of my life in prison..." he smiled and closed his eyes, "...I fully resigned myself to that when I embarked on this venture. After all," he opened the blue-gray eyes again and they glinted with an amused sparkle, "at my age a sentence of life imprisonment is hardly a fearful prospect."

Gordon's expression was dour, but he admired the man in spite of himself. After a little while he spoke with quiet weariness.

"Eventually we will find out what's behind all this, Mr. Boardman, whether or not you cooperate with us."

"Of course you will," Boardman agreed readily. "I am fully prepared to reveal everything, down to the most minute detail. It's simply a matter of to *whom* I'll make the revelation. It will not, I assure you, be to you. Nor will it be to any other official, federal or otherwise. Equally, it will not be to a lawyer. I have had four lawyers in my lifetime and have outlived them all. I have no desire whatever for another. There is no need. I will fully—and eagerly, I might add—tell everything to but one person, and then only if certain conditions are met."

Gordon's response was sharp. "Who? What are the conditions?"

A triumphant little expression crossed Boardman's face for an instant and, when he spoke, his words seemed to have been rehearsed.

"The conditions first. I must be given leave to speak to this individual in complete privacy. This means you will have to bring him to wherever I am being held and provide us acceptable, private quarters, free from any sort of electronic listening devices. To insure this, I will insist as well that this person be provided with a detector—'bug-seeker,' I believe it's called—with which he and I can thoroughly inspect the provided meeting quarters for any violation of this condition. Finally, we must be uninterrupted during our discussions, except at our own behest, for however long it takes us to complete our business, although it shouldn't take more than a few days—a week at most. After a week, you're no longer obliged to observe the conditions. Agreed?"

"Those are the only conditions?"

"Those are the only conditions."

"What if we should choose to question this person you want to see?"

"Do so if you wish, but I expect it would be to no avail. There are certain conditions which he, too, must agree to which you'll find out about soon enough before I will reveal anything to him."

"I think," Gordon said, after a moment's deliberation, "that we can meet your conditions. Who is the man?"

Boardman hesitated and then gave a faint shrug. "It may surprise you, Mr. Gordon, to learn that I have never met him. I'm looking forward to that. I've admired him for a considerable while. You'll probably recognize his name. He's a writer—John Charles Grant."

V

Even before switching on the ignition, John Grant read the card again. Anne had pressed the envelope into his hand as he was preparing to leave her apartment a short while ago. He had begun to open it at once, but she had taken his hand and kissed it, stopping him, shaking her head and saying he should read it later, when they were not together. He'd nodded and slipped it into his breast pocket. He had kissed her gently then, feeling as always the wonder of her nearness and, at the same time, the deep inner pang of realization that what they shared was so much less than either of them wanted, that this was the way it had to be and he could envision no improvement in their situation.

On the way downstairs from her forty-second-floor apartment he removed the envelope from his pocket and looked at the face of it. He smiled at seeing his own initials in the flourished script of her hand and paid no attention to the instructions on the face of the envelope that it was not to be opened until he was en route to St. Louis.

In a manner of speaking, anyway, he was en route to St. Louis now, so he wasn't stretching the point too much.

The note was short but he reached the lobby before finishing, and stepped out of the elevator automatically, passing through the wrought iron grillwork gate and nodding to the guard who opened it, then locked it after he'd passed through. By then he'd finished the note. At the lobby door he read it a second time while the Marina City parking attendant was bringing his car from the garage.

Now, behind the wheel of his car, the ignition keys still swinging gently, he read it a third time under the dash light, no less moved by its contents than on the previous two readings.

It was a contemporary card an idyllic scene of an attractive girl standing by herself on a beach at deep sunset. On that cover page the printed message began: *It's a lonely world…*and concluded on the inside page with the words:*…when I'm not with you.* Anne's handwritten words followed this, completing that page and continuing on the back flap. She had written:

Like right now. You know where my thoughts are, and where they'll continue to be. You look at me through a picture frame and I can almost hear you telling me how hopeless the situation is. I don't believe it. I can't. I love you, John Grant, too much to accept the ridiculous notion that we'll never have anything more than we have at present. You're just too vital a part of my life. "Hopeless" is the proper word to describe what I feel for you, not for what is a changeable and potentially changing situation. I've spent several minutes trying to express what I'm feeling right now while you're only across the street…

The note had evidently been broken off right at that point and then completed later in the apartment, after he had telephoned her that he would be there soon to spend the night, prior to leaving the city. Her writing had continued with the same thought, but with another pen.

…and also as you read this, when the separation is much greater, although no less effective. Nothing seems appropriate, so I'll assume you're aware of the inward turnings and are going through the same turmoil yourself. I love you more than I could have believed it possible to love anyone. I can't and won't accept the prospect of life without you. It's easy for me to say that. I don't have the horrible complication you do. But what affects you necessarily affects me. I'm sorry about putting both of us through this, but I'm absolutely confident the consequences will be much brighter than the present upset indicates. I love you.
     Anne

Grant slowly replaced the card in its envelope, drumming his fingers mechanically on the steering wheel. He had a momentary picture of himself running full tilt toward the brink of an abyss, realizing he must stop but unable to slow the churning of his legs propelling him toward certain disaster.

As he turned on the ignition and started the car, which the parking attendant had turned off, the radio came to life, its volume low. Someone was talking but he paid no attention for a while, his thoughts vacillating back and forth from Anne to Marie and his present dilemma. How it could be resolved was a weighty matter pressing down on him more unbearably every day and his driving was almost wholly automatic as he gave consideration to the problem. It was not until he was halfway to O'Hare Airport that he realized it was daylight now, and he turned off his headlights. For the first time, then, the muted but excited words of the radio commentator penetrated and he sharpened his attention on it, turning up the volume. By then it was 6:30 A.M.

He listened with stunned fascination as the announcement continued and then, when completed, became a two-way conversation between a pair of commentators who discussed the still sketchy news of the assassination attempt on President Sanders, trying to make sense of it between themselves but without much success. There was a decided aura of mystery behind the whole event which seemed to excite the broadcasters even more than it would have had they been in possession of the whole story. Occasionally they switched to on-the-scene reporters interviewing anyone conceivably connected with the case, digging with futility for anything new to add to the story. They had little success until just as Grant was pulling into the vast, multifloored O'Hare parking garage.

"Stand by," the announcer suddenly said. "We're switching to Peter Dels at Northwestern Memorial Hospital where an announcement is to be made. Peter?"

There was a faint crackling of static and then the sound of numerous voices melding confusedly in the background. The familiar voice of the network correspondent came in a moment later.

"Yes, Wendell? All right we have it. This is Peter Dels in a conference room of the Northwestern Memorial Hospital where we've been waiting for several hours for word on the condition of the President. We've just been informed that Dr. Sven Evansson, head of neurosurgery here, is on his way downstairs to make the first official statement in that respect. Speculation on the extent of the President's injuries has been running rampant here ever since he was brought in unconscious four and a half hours ago, just after two-thirty this morning. It has been pretty well ascertained that at least two shots were fired at close range and both bullets are believed to have struck the President—one in the head and one in the body."

From the studio, Wendell Wright broke in as Dels paused. "Peter, is there a chance that at this moment Sanders is dead and we are presently without a President?"

"There is that possibility, Wendell. There is great fear here, certainly. Fear on the one hand that the President is already dead; fear on the other that even if he is still alive, he will have suffered such brain damage that he will be incapable of functioning any longer as a normal human being, much less as Chief of State. Paralysis is also a possibility. Let me reiterate, though, that no one knows for sure, and what the effect will be on the presidency itself remains at this time pure speculation. However, it seems almost certain that Vice-President Barrington will be taking over the duties of that office."

He paused an instant and, dimly, other reporters could be heard talking behind him. By this time Grant was nosing the car into a parking space on the third floor, but he continued sitting there listening after stopping.

"The First Lady," Dels continued, "arrived here at the Northwestern Memorial Complex about forty-five minutes ago, but she entered the hospital without making any statement and her whereabouts now are not known, although it's assumed she is with—Wait a minute! Dr. Evansson's coming in right now. Stand by."

A sudden rise in the volume of background voices dwindled away almost as quickly as it began and there came an expectant hush. The next voice was somewhat indistinct at first, but then came in more clearly as sound technicians adjusted their equipment levels. The voice was firm and professional, yet with an edge of weariness and strain.

"Thank you for your patience. This has been a trying night for all of us. I'm Dr. Evansson and, though I know you have a great many questions to ask, allow me first to assure you that President Sanders is alive and in no serious danger at the moment."

He ignored the cheers which erupted and went on without pause. "The President has suffered a relatively strong concussion with resultant severe headache and some nausea. He is conscious at this time and his mental acuity seems unimpaired. He also has suffered a cracked rib and a superficial abrasion on the back of his left hand. His condition is listed officially as very good. Now," he added, after a pause, "I'll be glad to answer more specific questions."

"Doctor!" At least a dozen voices were calling out simultaneously, but one continued more loudly than the others and took the floor. "Sir, we've been under the impression that President Sanders was shot twice. In this case and, if true, can you please tell us exactly where the bullets struck him, what actual physical damage they caused, and whether or not these bullets have been removed."

The reply was slow in coming and the words carefully chosen. "Our examination," the doctor said, "indicates that the President was indeed struck twice. The first bullet hit the lower right anterior of the cranium—that is, the forehead—almost exactly a half-inch above the orbit…the eye cavity. Fortunately, the skull is very strong at that point and while it caused the concussion for which the President has been treated, the bullet did not penetrate the skull. As a matter of fact," he went on, "the skin was not broken. X-rays have shown no sign of fracture."

There was something of a hubbub at this, but the surgeon went on speaking doggedly, raising his voice to make himself heard, and the din gradually died away. "The second bullet struck the right side of the President's chest at the juncture of the pectoralis major and serratus anterior musculature, which would be approximately an inch and a half below and slightly to the right of the right nipple. This caused the cracked rib and a contusion of no great consequence. The bullet broke the fibers of the President's suitcoat, but did not break the skin."

"Sir!" It was another reporter. "Can you give us an explanation as to why these bullets failed to penetrate? Isn't that most unusual, especially at such close range?"

"It is. This has been checked rather closely by our staff and our conclusions correlated with those of the investigating authorities who recovered the gun which was used in the shooting. A slight residue of a waxy substance was discovered on the President's forehead, with larger particles of the same substance in his hair above and to the right of the wound. An inspection of his clothing has revealed an even greater abundance of the substance adhering to the suitcoat at the point of impact. A check of the weapon revealed it to be a thirty-eight caliber revolver which was chambered for five bullets. All five chambers had been loaded. Two of these retained only casings of the shells, their charge having been expended. The remaining three were unfired and the slugs, instead of being lead, were bullet-shaped moldings of the same waxy substance found in the area of the President's wounds. That substance tentatively has been identified as paraffin."

There had been a growing murmur as he spoke and it became an uproar as he concluded, taking many seconds to die away. Everyone, it seemed, was trying to speak at once. At last the familiar voice of Peter Dels broke through above the others.

"Doctor, are we to assume from this that the assassin had no intention of killing the President? That President Sanders could not have been badly hurt?"

Again Dr. Evansson spoke methodically, though now with slightly less assurance. "I cannot, of course, know what intentions were involved. I can say only that the wax bullets evidently were especially prepared so as to preclude the possibility of serious injury to whomever they struck. This," he added somewhat hastily, "is not to say the President was in no danger. Had the bullet which struck his forehead been an inch lower, he almost certainly would have lost his right eye. Additionally, there is even the possibility that penetration through the soft tissues of the orbital cavity could have caused extensive hemorrhage, quite possibly resulting in brain damage or even death.

Another flurry of voices followed, but at this moment John Grant looked at his watch, swiftly turned off the radio, locked the car, and sprinted all the way to the terminal. He had been so caught up in what was being said he had forgotten the time. Now he just barely had enough leeway to pick up his prereserved ticket at the Delta counter and race down the concourse to where his flight already was boarding. Five minutes later he was aloft. As soon as the seat belt sign was turned off he got up and went to the lavatory at the rear of the aircraft. Inside, he read the note from Anne a final time, tore it into small pieces and flushed it down the toilet. Back in his seat he became steeped in thought. This time, though, he was not thinking of Anne. He was trying to fathom the intriguing mystery of an assassin who evidently had programmed himself for failure.

V I

The President had insisted upon hearing the chief security agent's entire tape of his questioning of Herbert Boardman, even though Gordon had swiftly briefed him on what had transpired.

Now Alexander Gordon sat quietly in a chair beside the bed and studied the man whose safety had been his responsibility. Time and again he had heard it said that no United States President could ever be fully protected against a determined assassin, because no President of the United States ever had or ever would consent to the stringency of the security precautions which, ideally, the Secret Service wished to impose on him. To do so would be to open himself up to charges of isolating himself from the people, and even the most fumbling politician is aware of the hazards of that. Gordon knew full well that there was simply no way under the existing standards that President Sanders could have been protected from Boardman. The President himself, as soon as Gordon had entered the room, had been quick to absolve his chief of security of any blame. Despite all this, Alexander Gordon still blamed himself, still strove to pinpoint some way in which he might have prevented it. He felt that somehow, some way, he had failed, and he was wretched in his self-incrimination.

After leaving Boardman, Gordon had checked again with Dr. Evansson to see if there had been any change in the President's condition. Evansson's cheerful reply had been "Only for the better," and he went on to tell Gordon that the President had slept deeply for nearly two hours, was awake again, and had asked to see Gordon as soon as possible. There was still some degree of dazedness to the President, but this ought to pass very quickly. The security chief had wasted no time in getting to the President's room. There had, however, been no matter of urgency to the summons. Robert Sanders had merely wished to assure Gordon that he was wholly blameless in the attack and to thank him for acting as swiftly as he had.

"I understand from Grinelski," the President had added with a wry smile, "that the man still had three unfired bullets in the gun. I appreciate your sparing me those."

Gordon had grinned, embarrassed at praise he felt he did not deserve and knowing, too, that this was just one more example of the characteristic thoughtfulness with which Sanders was imbued. The Man seemed incapable of looking on the dark side of things. In this respect he was similar to the way Gordon's own father had been, and he remembered, when he was a very small boy in Cleveland, his mother used to say of his father: "Come the day, Alexander, when the Devil come to carry off your daddy to Hell on his shoulders, you know what your daddy going to say? Well, he ain't going to weep an' wail none at all. No sir! He going to just pat that old Devil on the head and then thank him for not making him walk!"

Now, sitting beside the President's bed, he continued studying the President admiringly. The Chief of State, clad in the same flimsy sort of wraparound gown that Boardman had been wearing, lay comfortably with his feet together and the sheet pulled up neatly to his waist. The head of the bed had been raised to a quarter-upright position, supporting his back. His hands were folded peacefully across his stomach and, with his eyes closed as he listened to the questioning of Boardman, a suddenly sickening vision came to Gordon of Sanders lying peacefully in this same way in a casket, dead and with his feet together, eyes closed, hands neatly folded. He shook his head sharply, disrupting the ugly thought and hoping he never would see it in reality.

Dr. Evansson had warned that while the President was awake and alert now, he would probably soon fall deeply asleep again and when he awakened next time, he might experience a momentary disorientation deeper than he was experiencing now, but that this was normal and would not last. However, if there were important things which had to be discussed with the President, it would be better to do so now, since the next sleep, which should be uninterrupted, might last eight or ten hours.

In point of fact, to Gordon the President looked surprisingly good, considering what he had been through. There was no dressing on his forehead and the swelling, somewhat more violently discolored than Boardman's, was smaller than Gordon had anticipated it would be. It was not much larger than a walnut, but apparently was still spreading a bit, since the upper eyelid was also a little puffy, though not discolored. He knew there were some gauze wrappings around the President's chest, but of these there was no outward indication. Oddly enough, the most superficial injury was the one which looked worst. The back of his left hand had become abraded against the concrete of the sidewalk as Sanders had fallen on it and, while it wasn't bandaged, it had been liberally painted with gaudy methiolate red-orange and had a nasty appearance.

Alexander Gordon sat up straighter in his chair as he heard the tape approaching its close. A few more words of no great consequence had passed between himself and Boardman after the demand to see Grant, and then a final remark by the old man completed the tape. Boardman's voice sounded very calm and normally pitched coming from the cassette's small speaker.

"Mr. Gordon?"

"Yes?"

"Will you be seeing the President before you come back here?"

"I doubt it very much, Mr. Boardman."

There was a pause and then: "If you do...*when* you do...will you please express to him my sincere regret for the pain and shock and inconvenience I've caused him?"

There had been no response from Gordon, only the sound of the machine being turned off.

Now the security chief stood and depressed the Off button of the recorder. Robert Sanders still lay with his eyes closed, the corners of his mouth uptilting in a small smile.

"Interesting, Alex," he said. "Most interesting. I think there is much more to this man than meets the eye." Opening his eyes he turned his head and looked at Gordon, who nodded.

"I'm quite sure of that, Mr. President. In view of the weird aspects of the incident—the man's age, the fact that he was uncannily successful in getting so close to you, or at least getting you to come close to him, the fact that he could easily have killed you, the fact that he deliberately chose not to, but still wanted to appear as if he *meant* to do so—all these things tend to suggest lunacy. Yet, I know that I'm no psychiatrist, but I'd be willing to put down odds that he's no more insane than I am."

The President gave him a peculiar look and then they both broke into laughter. Sanders brought up a hand and gingerly touched his forehead.

"Oh gawd, Alex," he said, still chuckling, "don't make me laugh like that. My head hurts too much."

"Sorry, sir." The agent was grinning.

Sanders's chuckling faded. "This man Boardman," he said thoughtfully. "He took a pretty grave risk."

"He did, indeed, Mr. President. Any would-be Presidential assassin's chances for escaping alive diminish sharply the closer he gets to his target. He was very lucky."

"Maybe. I'm not entirely sure of that. From what we've been able to determine thus far, I've an idea he's a man who doesn't place much reliance in luck. It takes a shrewd man and a desperate one to do what he did. I may be wrong, but ever since hearing that tape, something's been niggling around in the back of my mind, a funny little anecdote with a moral. It was probably kicking around when Lincoln was still splitting rails." He paused, considering, and Gordon said nothing. After a moment more, Sanders continued. "It's that old saw—I'm sure you've heard it—about the farmer getting his mule to follow commands by first whacking him across the head with a two-by-four. The moral being that first you have to get his attention. Alex, maybe that's what this Boardman's doing—getting someone's attention because he wants to be sure he's heard. Could be he wants to say something important to someone."

"But to just an ordinary writer, Mr. President? I'm sorry, sir, but I can't quite buy that."

Sanders shifted into a more comfortable position and closed his eyes again. "Alex," he said, "in the first place, John Charles Grant is not just an ordinary writer. In the second place, more than talking *to* a writer, I suspect our ancient friend may be wanting to talk *through* a writer. I suggest we see to it without delay that Mr. Boardman has his discussions with Mr. Grant." He sighed. "I'm suddenly very weary, Alex. I think I'd like to rest now."

VII

The coffee that Marie Grant had brewed in the predawn hours had smelled good while it was perking, but the cup of it that she had poured for herself still sat untouched on the end table beside her chair and now was barely warm.

For over an hour after completing the deciphering of the last coded entry in the final diary available on the shelf, Marie had sat at John's desk, reading and rereading the numerous passages. A montage of disjointed images and thoughts had been passing through her mind with such rapidity and diversity that she felt dazed and unable to follow any logical train of thought to a conclusion. Within her there was an all-pervading sick feeling. She had eaten nothing since breakfast the previous morning and the emotional strain of yesterday and this night, coupled with lack of food and sleep, had taken a toll. Her eyes were red-rimmed and grainy, yet she knew she could not sleep. Instead, she had risen from the desk chair and replaced everything in the den as it had been—wishing again that John had not taken this year's diary with him—and taking with her only the papers that she had written. These she paper-clipped to the earlier ones which she had hidden in the dresser and then took the entire stack of them downstairs with her.

Always before when she had been upset she was able to find solace by talking with John. Usually he was here, but even if he were not, she could always reach him by telephone. Just the reassuring sound of his voice over the receiver always had been able to impart a steadying effect in her. She yearned to call him now, knowing she could reach him at the Sheraton in St. Louis because he had said that was where Peter Proctor was booked and he had intended staying there also. But even if she did call, what would she say? A fragmentary one-sided dialogue constructed itself in her mind: "Hello, John dear? This is your woman. No, dear, the one on Bobolink Terrace. You remember, don't you—the mother of your children? That's right. Listen, Sweetheart, I've been doing some snooping through your personal things and came across those silly coded entries in your diaries and so I knew you wouldn't mind if I invaded your privacy by just sort of deciphering them a little. No, no real trouble with them, thanks. Just called to say hi and…and…oh, *damn it* John Grant, why aren't you here when I need you?"

The tears came again and she spilled the grounds as she was making the coffee. As if it were the most important thing in the world, she had stood over the percolator for the entire time it popped and plunked and gurgled merrily until a final little wheezing click and rapidly diminishing burbling signified it was finished. She had poured herself a cup and took it into the living room with her. Now it was nearly cold and she still hadn't touched her lips to it.

Periodically as she sat there in the big armchair with her bare feet tucked under her she was wracked by almost uncontrollable shuddering, but she was no longer crying. She felt wholly wrung out and disembodied, lost among a welter of fragmentary thoughts, experiencing a loneliness unlike anything she had ever known before. Unnoticed by her, the night had given way to a muted gray dawn filtering through the heavy cloud layer hanging several thousand feet over the city.

It was at this unlikely hour that the doorbell rang, and Marie jumped as if an electric charge had passed through her. She moved swiftly to the door, for some reason thinking it was Billy coming home early from Jack's house, then received a second start as she opened it and saw two men standing there. Both were in dark business suits and both were fairly tall men. One had receding sandy hair, a small neat moustache, and appeared to be in his early fifties. He was somewhat thin. The other was quite powerfully built, younger, and a Negro. It was he who spoke.

"Mrs. Grant? Sorry to bother you this early in the morning. My name is Alexander Gordon, United States Secret Service." He dipped his head at his companion. "This is Agent Richard Kreps. May we speak to Mr. Grant, please?"

Marie's eyes had widened. "Secret Service?" She seemed unable to comprehend. She accepted the slender leather folder Gordon withdrew from his inner breast pocket and handed open to her. On one side was a United States Treasury Department identification card with his picture, on the other a small, rather flat, but impressively made gold badge. She looked at them mutely.

After a moment or two, when she looked up at the men again, Gordon smiled, took the folder from her hand and returned it to his pocket. "Please, we *would* like to speak with Mr. Grant."

"He…he's not here."

"Can you tell us, please, where we might locate him?"

Marie was regaining control of herself now. In the driveway beyond the men she could see a shiny black sedan parked. It bore no insignia but looked official. She glanced at the men and stepped back inside, holding the door open. "Come in, won't you?"

They entered and stood calmly waiting as she shut the door behind them and then, at her invitation, followed her into the living room. She turned suddenly to face them. "Is there some kind of trouble involving John?"

Gordon shook his head and Kreps said, "We'd like to ask his help, Mrs. Grant, in the matter involving the President."

"The President? You mean the United States President? I'm afraid I don't understand."

"You're not aware," Gordon put in, "of what occurred last night?" At the slow shaking of her head, he continued. "Mrs. Grant, the President was shot in Chicago last night."

"Ohhh!"

"Let me hasten to assure you that he is not seriously hurt. However, we feel sure that Mr. Grant can be of considerable assistance to us in our investigation."

"My God, Mr. Gordon, John *couldn't* be involved in anything like that!" A note of alarm was rising in Marie's voice.

"You misunderstand me, ma'am. I don't mean to imply that he is involved in the shooting. It's just that, for reasons we'd prefer not going into at this time, we're in need of your husband's help. You mentioned that he was not home. Is he in the city now? Can we reach him?"

She shook her head and a strand of the long blond hair fell down over her eyes and she immediately put it back in place. "No. No, he's not in Chicago. He left early last evening to fly to St. Louis. He's meeting there with Peter Proctor, the evangelist, interviewing him for a possible magazine article."

"Do you know where he's staying?"

"Yes. At the Sheraton. That's where Mr. Proctor is staying also. Would you like me to call him?"

"We do want to reach him as soon as possible, Mrs. Grant. If you prefer, and you wouldn't mind my using your phone, I could place a credit card call to him."

"Oh, no, that's all right. I'll be glad to get him for you." She smiled wanly. "Please, forgive my manners. Won't you sit down? I've just made fresh coffee. May I get you some before I call?"

Kreps and Gordon looked at each other and grinned as they sat down together on the sofa. Kreps bobbed his head. "That would be greatly appreciated, Mrs. Grant. It's been a long night."

She carried her own cup into the kitchen, poured the cold contents into the sink and refilled it, along with two others. In a minute she was back with the coffee, a small silver cream pitcher and matching sugar bowl on a serving tray, which she placed on the coffee table before them. As they murmured their thanks, she indicated that they should go ahead. She crossed the room to the telephone stand, picked up the phone book, checked in the front for the area code for St. Louis and dialed direct for the toll-free St. Louis information operator. In a moment she had the number of the St. Louis Sheraton Hotel and was placing a person-to-person call to John there. A clerk listened to the operator's request, asked her to hold on and then was back a moment later.

"I'm sorry, operator, we have no John Grant registered here."

"Ma'am," the operator said, "Mr. Grant is not registered there. Do you care to speak with anyone else?"

Taken aback, Marie hesitated and then asked to be connected with Mr. Peter Proctor's room. While the room phone was ringing she glanced up and saw the two Secret Service agents regarding her curiously. They had not yet touched their coffee. On the third ring the telephone was answered.

"Hello?" The voice was sleepy.

"Mr. Proctor? I'm very sorry to bother you so early in the morning, but it's rather important. This is Marie Grant calling, John Grant's wife. My husband was scheduled to interview you this morning and I wonder if you might happen to know where he's staying?"

"Oh. Oh, yes, Mrs. Grant. Excuse me, I'm not quite firing on all cylinders yet. I just got up. No, as a matter of fact your husband hasn't yet contacted me. He's not registered in this hotel?"

"They said he wasn't."

"Well, maybe he just hasn't arrived yet."

"He left home early last night, Mr. Proctor."

There was a pause. "Hmmm. The hotel here is pretty well filled. He might not have been able to get a room if he didn't have advance reservations. Do you know if he did?"

"No. No, I don't think he did."

"Well," Proctor was reassuring, "that's probably the answer then, Mrs. Grant. He's undoubtedly had to find accommodations in some other hotel. Our meeting's scheduled for nine-thirty this morning, so I'll probably be seeing him before too long. Shall I have him return your call?"

"You're very kind. Thank you, I'd appreciate that."

She hung up the phone, a small frown appearing. It faded as she turned to face the men. Kreps had finished his coffee, but Gordon had not touched his. She smiled and spoke matter-of-factly. "They were crowded. I'm afraid he's had to stay at some other hotel. However, he's to meet with Mr. Proctor in a few hours and Mr. Proctor said he'd have him call home."

The agents got to their feet and Gordon extracted a business card from his wallet and swiftly wrote on it with a slim gold pen. He handed it to her.

"You've been very helpful, Mrs. Grant. This is the number where you can reach me or one of my associates at any time. It's a direct number into a room a at the Northwestern Memorial Complex downtown. The call won't have to be relayed through a switchboard. Would you please give us a call as soon as you hear from your husband? And, also, would you please give that same number to him and ask him to call as soon as possible? We'll accept charges."

"Of course," she said. "I'll be glad to."

She escorted them to the front door and saw them out and then slowly returned to the front room. The two untouched cups of coffee—hers and agent Gordon's—still sat on the tray. She shuddered, suddenly afraid again. So many things were happening at once! She moved to the television set and clicked it on, then picked up her coffee and took it with her to her chair.

A full-screen head of Alban Woodstock, dean of American news commentators, faded in, his mouth moving as he spoke in his familiar measured way, but it was still a moment or so before the sound came up.

"...will come back to Northwestern Memorial Hospital Complex in Chicago in a few minutes for a more updated report on President Sanders's condition. In the meantime, we'll switch now to Mary Breda at Washington National Airport to get a few words from Daniel Ngoromu, President of Kenya, East Africa, who met with President Sanders in the White House last night only hours before the attempted assassination. Mary?"

The studio scene cut to Washington National where Mary Breda, hair in disarray from the brisk wind, stood holding a hand microphone beside the enormous figure of Daniel Ngoromu, his arm linked with that of his tall, attractive wife.

VIII

Ordinarily, Daniel Ngoromu did not consent to on-the-spot interviews, but in view of the gravity of this day and the incident that had transpired so short a time after his meeting with the United States President, he had agreed, stipulating that it would have to be short.

Anita Randall Ngoromu, beside him, was very nearly six feet tall, blond and blue-eyed and with the angular jawline, strong chin and high, pronounced cheekbones often noted on the more statuesque women of Scandinavian heritage. Though now forty-eight years old, Anita Ngoromu retained a figure that was still the envy of many a younger woman. She gave the impression of being smaller than she actually was, but this was a not uncommon illusion because she was most often seen and photographed beside her black husband, whose impressive bulk virtually dwarfed her.

The reporter, Mary Breda, was herself quite a stout woman, yet she seemed rather diminutive as she stood with the couple. What appeared to be a hearing aid in her ear actually was a tiny receiver through which she heard Woodstock's remarks from CBS headquarters in New York. She spoke loudly and clearly in order to be heard well against the wind's rumbling gusts against the hand-held microphone.

"Thank you, Alban. President Ngoromu, you met in the White House for a rather extensive period last night with President Sanders. Would you care to comment on your discussion?"

Ngoromu licked his lips. His voice was deep and rich in tone. "Your President and I had a most pleasant conversation in which a variety of topics were discussed, the majority of which it would not be my place to mention here and now. However, I will say that our thoughts and ideas seem to be in accord in many respects for the forthcoming transition of my country from an agrarian society to an industrial economy, based on the development of petroleum resources."

"When you spoke with him last night, sir," Mary Breda went on, "did the President show any indication whatever of foreknowledge that an assassination attempt might have been in the process of being plotted against him?"

"He did not." Ngoromu shook his head. "But you must realize, Ms. Breda, that all heads of state have many enemies. Simply by the act of assuming the office of President he becomes the target of many foes—radicals, anarchists, whatever. And the longer he remains in office, and the more vigorous and strong a head of state he is, the greater the number of enemies he develops. While the majority of such enemies may try to destroy him through undermining his reputation, misleading a gullible public, attributing to him detrimental policies which may not have been of his instigation, and studiously placing at his feet the blame for all that is wrong and none of the credit for anything that is right, there are equally those in a very small minority who would gladly see him physically destroyed. It is a fact of life which a head of state must accept, however little he likes it."

"Do you, sir, feel that this attempt against the President's life is the action of any sort of organization, foreign or domestic?"

"I would have no opinion about that."

"You have heard, haven't you, that the would-be assassin is a man reported to be ninety-four years old?"

For the first time Ngoromu smiled, his perfect teeth flashing in brilliant contrast against the darkness of his face. "I think perhaps someone may have made a typographical error and transposed the numbers. Forty-nine would certainly be a far more realistic age, wouldn't you think? I suspect a ninety-four-year-old man is far more apt to be found in bed or in a rocking chair than stalking the streets with a gun, intent upon assassinating the President of the United States."

Mary Breda scratched her neck with her free hand, then lifted both eyebrows as she often did when she changed subjects. "Getting back to your meeting with President Sanders, sir, Kenya has been in the news a great deal lately because of the incredibly extensive oil resources recently discovered there. Obviously you discussed these and their development, especially in light of the continuing difficulty America is having with importation of oil from the Middle East. It is no secret that the United States would be wise to provide the funds and technology for the development of your oil resources. Have any agreements been reached between you and President Sanders in this respect?"

Ngoromu lapsed into one of his long pauses, much to Mary Breda's dismay, and when he finally spoke his words were carefully chosen. "If agreements—assuming that some were proposed—were reached between us, it would be, by reason of simple international courtesy, only proper that he, not I, inform the American people of this."

"Is the speculation true, then," Mary Breda persisted, "that President Sanders was planning to journey to Kenya in the near future to continue discussions with you along these lines?"

"I will only say," the Kenyan President responded, "that your President would be a most welcome visitor to my country at any time."

The reporter's eyebrows went up. "What about the other major powers in the world? Are they also bidding for long-range oil resource developments with Kenya?"

The countenance of the big black man became impassive. "I have heard no comment on that. I'm afraid Mrs. Ngoromu and I must leave, Ms. Breda."

He turned and started away with Anita, not acknowledging the reporter's good-bye. Anita looked at him and grinned as they entered the terminal, followed by a small retinue which had been waiting patiently nearby during the interview.

"You fielded those questions very well, dear," she murmured. "As always. I'm proud of you. However," an amused glint came into her eyes and her tone became light, though with a thread of underlying seriousness, "as an interested individual who just happens to be the wife of the President of Kenya as well as a home-grown product of these United States, *are* you going to give my good ol' Uncle Sam the inside track?"

A deep rumbling laughter welled up in him and he faced her. "Well now, 'Neet, do you want me to?"

"Danny, my love," she said, squeezing his arm and smiling back at him, "you know me better than that. I was merely curious. Period." She added, in a broadly bantering way, "I think you know I would never *presume* to bring pressure on you to do anything like that."

"Of course not," he replied seriously.

They looked at one another straight-faced and then suddenly both burst into laughter. Ten minutes later they were boarding for their flight to Kennedy

International and then on to London, Rome and Nairobi.

I X

Although the startling announcement that the President of the United States had been shot in Chicago had delayed the progress of Elizabeth Boardman and Paul Neely toward his bedroom, it hadn't prevented their final arrival there almost an hour and a half later.

Horrified at the news, especially since there was no definite word at the time of the first bulletins about whether the President was dead or not, they had stood in front of the radio tuner as Paul had turned the dial quickly from station to station in an effort to learn more. After a quarter-hour of this, he had shaken his head.

"They ought to have something on television about it." He switched off the radio and started toward the living room.

"On television this late at night?" Liz said, following him.

"For something like this, yes. If they're not on the air yet, they'll be on pretty soon."

He turned on the TV set and as soon as the screen came to life—blank where it was presently channeled—he began slowly moving the selector from channel to channel. At first all were blank and they remained so for another six or seven minutes. Then, coming back to one of the channels he'd checked previously, the blackness changed abruptly to a broad band of black in a horizontal position against a light blue background. In white letters on the black were the words: *SPECIAL BULLETIN*. He stopped it there and in another minute the audio came to life.

"This is the Columbia Broadcasting System resuming from CBS headquarters in New York. The following news programming will be broadcast without commercial interruption. Stand by, please."

A moment later a somewhat disheveled announcer appeared, sitting behind a desk. Neither Liz nor Paul recognized him and the announcer was so excited that he began his report without even identifying himself. It was disappointing because the information he had was no more complete than that they'd already heard on the radio, although he constantly laced his comments with the advisory to keep tuned for late-breaking developments. Unfortunately, the developments just didn't break as quickly as anticipated.

In the first hour about the only solid new developments they were able to glean—intermingled with a dizzying succession of relatively valueless on-the-spot reports—were that immediately after the shooting the unconscious President had been transported with great haste to Northwestern Memorial Hospital, only four blocks distant on East Superior Street at North Fairbanks Court; that the assassin, also unconscious, had been taken to the same hospital, arriving there only a few minutes after the President. Finally, a few new items came to light: the weapon used by the assassin was a .38 caliber revolver and was in the possession of the authorities; that the assassin himself was reportedly an elderly man, perhaps in his late seventies or early eighties, but his identity had not yet been released; that the President was still alive but beyond that nothing was known about the seriousness of his wounds, other than that he had been shot twice—in chest and head; that a widescale roundup had begun, in an area six blocks in radius around the site of the shooting, of all individuals who could not satisfactorily explain their presence downtown at that hour, and that even those whose purposes seemed legitimate were having their identities recorded for more thorough checking.

The initial edge of excitement had begun to fade and Liz, seated beside Paul on the sofa, turned her head and kissed the point of his jaw. "We could," she said softly, "turn off the TV and turn the radio back on. You can hear it pretty well from the bedroom, can't you?"

Paul had nodded and without another word they had done as she suggested. The FM radio was back on with lovely mood music and occasional announcements that interruptions would be made at any further major news developments. These were few and far between and neither Liz nor Paul paid much attention to them. Blissfully lost in the reawakening of a depth of passion which both had assumed forever was gone, their interest in news bulletins understandably was not intense.

It was a good night for them, a night of closeness and soft sounds and incredible touchings, begun with initial traces of shyness but then with increasing boldness and heat, unlocking passions that had lain dormant within each for all too long. It was a night of learning more about one another—mentally as well as physically—than they had learned in their previous two years of association; a night during which they both knew with awed certainty that this was no momentary blending of hearts and minds and bodies, and that a whole new chapter in their lives had begun. They had slept none, but neither felt the need of it. Their happiness was all-pervasive, dispelling ordinary fatigue.

It was not long after the darkness had given way to daylight that they had gotten up, showered together, turned off the hallway radio in passing and then had slice after slice of hot toast and jelly, the closest approximation to breakfast fixings that Paul had in the apartment—and steaming coffee at the tiny table in the breakfast nook of the kitchen. After that they went back to the living room where they sat with more coffee.

They turned on the television just in time to see an airport interview of the East African leader, Daniel Ngoromu, in Washington, D.C. The interview concluded, the scene shifted back at once to Alban Woodstock in New York, who immediately moved into a report of the newest development of the night's sensational news story.

"Authorities in Chicago," he reported, "have just this moment released the identity of the man they are holding in custody for the shooting of President Sanders. That man's age, incidentally, has been confirmed to be an astounding ninety-four years old! He has been identified as a resident of the near western Chicago suburb of Oak Park. His name is Herbert Allen Boardman."

For the first time in her fifty-six years of life, Elizabeth Boardman fainted.

X

Anne Carpenter was totally unaware of the worldwide excitement inspired by the incident which had taken place less than a mile away from her apartment. The aftermath of John Grant's stay with her had begun setting in within minutes of his departure, as she had known it would.

She had watched from the doorway of her apartment his brisk stride down the hallway as he left her; watched until he had vanished around the bend of the curved hall in the direction of the elevators. Immediately she'd closed her door and rushed to the outer glass wall, opened the door and stepped out onto the small balcony. The faintest trace of dawn was just becoming visible then. Forty-two floors below she could see the main entrance, aglow with artificial light. Traffic had not yet begun its morning rush in the city and the paved area between the two corncob towers of Marina City was devoid of life. She wore only a thin, sheer wraparound shortie nightgown and quickly had begun shivering against the dank chill of the early morning, but she made no effort to go back inside to don something more protective.

In a little while he had emerged below, holding something in one hand and beckoning the parking attendant with the other. The two men spoke briefly and then John was alone down there. He was much too far below to see him as anything more than a tiny human figure, but there was no doubt that it was he. She watched as he raised the object he had in his hand and then held it with both hands before him as he studied it and she smiled, knowing it was the contemporary card she had given him. She had known he would read it immediately upon leaving her, despite the instructions on the face of the envelope, but she didn't really mind.

Her eyes misted as she watched and she rubbed the back of her hand across them. Not yet. No impaired vision while he was still in sight. There'd be time for tears soon enough. Once, after he'd finished reading it, she thought he was about to look upward and she raised both arms and waved wildly as the clammy breeze whipped open the pale green garment and caused it to ripple like a flag behind her. But he hadn't looked up after all, and then the attendant had brought his car and he'd gotten into it. Still the car remained there and she knew he was reading the note again, and this pleased her.

At last the car pulled away and was gone. Teeth faintly chattering, she reentered the apartment and shut the door. In the bathroom she gulped down a small orange pill with a swallow of water. She was going to need the mild tranquilizer—she always did—because while it didn't help a great deal, it helped some, and that was a lot better than going through this periodic hell without anything.

The tears had come then, uncontrollably, gushing hotly from her eyes, running down cheeks and neck, hanging pendulously from tip of reddened nose, touching mouth corners with moistly spreading salinity. She simply stood for a long while, trying as she sometimes did to make herself stop, but it was useless, and so she threw herself across the bed and let go in earnest, feeling the whole bed shake with her wracking sobs, repeating his name in an anguished voice again and again.

It happened like this every time he left her, except that every time she was sure it was worse than the time before, and perhaps it was because the anguish was cumulative. Anne Carpenter was absolutely convinced that there was no way on earth, no matter how fervently she might tell him or show him, that John Grant could even begin to realize the depth of her love for him. Life simply seemed to cease existing when he was not with her.

She had no illusions about herself. She knew she was a woman attractive enough to have virtually any man she wanted, and she had always known deep inside that one day a man would come into her life who would affect her in a way that none before ever had, and none afterward ever could. When he did, she would then do practically anything to make that man hers. Whether or not the man in question might already be married was a problem she had considered little. If he were, she would take him away from her. It was as simple as that.

In a vague, almost subliminal way, she hoped that the man she wanted would be unattached when she met him, but the older she herself became, the more she realized how unlikely this was. She didn't like envisioning herself in the role of homewrecker but, should that become necessary, she'd always known she would adopt the role without qualm. Now that the right man had indeed come along and was, in fact, married and she was left with no choice but to lure him away from his wife, she found that it was not quite so easy to be as coldly calculating as she had anticipated.

As soon as she was convinced in her own mind that John Grant was the man she intended having, she made it a point to familiarize herself with his existing situation. For a full day, while Grant was out of town, she followed Marie and the two children, often closely enough to have reached out and touched them. Marie had taken the children to the zoo, enjoying herself to the utmost with them and exuding the aura of an extremely happily married woman and a wonderfully satisfied mother. The three had laughed and run and played together, viewed the animals with interest and amusement together, ate hot dogs together and walked together at times with their arms pleasantly linked. There was, among the three of them, an unaffected closeness that was deeply touching, and at least once during the day, each one remarked, loudly enough for Anne to overhear, the sincere wish that the one missing family member were there to be enjoying the day with them.

It was at that point that Anne very nearly lost her resolve. Only a thoroughly cold and heartless person could set out deliberately to destroy such a family's happiness, and Anne considered herself to be neither heartless nor cold. Then she turned this consideration in her own mind to the rationale that one needed not to be cold and heartless, but rather one who loved with great depth and passion; one who believed with wholly single-minded conviction that what she could offer would bring him more happiness than he already thought he had, and this was a description which indeed fitted her well and was acceptable to her.

The full day of viewing John Grant's family had made her feel a genuine sorrow for them that was unexpected, but she was again unalterably firm in her resolve to have as her own the man who was their father and husband. In the months that had passed since then, she simply could not comprehend why John could not seem to see this as she saw it and why he could not quickly make the decision which she felt was so obvious and so inevitable. When he did not, it saddened her and, to some extent, infuriated her. And when the times came, after he had been with her, that it became necessary for him to leave her and return to them, it hurt her deeply and the tears came with devastating wrenchings she could not control, just as they were afflicting her now. Over the past few months she had shed a great volume of tears.

The odd part of the whole business was that this sort of thing was completely out of character for Anne. Normally she did not go all to pieces. Usually she was not a crier. Since she was about fifteen and until the time when she had fallen in love with John, there had probably not been more than half a dozen times when she had cried, however lightly; and the only time she could remember ever crying like this before John Grant was when Roger had been killed.

Further, other than Roger—and he in a much different way—no one had ever really meant a great deal to her. Not friends, not relatives, not men. That took in a lot of territory, because Anne had known a lot of men in a very few short years. Not even her parents, who were still living their lives separately even though not divorced, evoked a love from her that was not in certain respects sharply limited.

Anne had lived in Chicago and its suburbs all her life except for two years spent in France and England taking a sabbatical at the midpoint of her studies in humanities and sociology at the University of Chicago. She had come to hate injustice and corruption with such intense youthful passion that it practically had become obsessive in her. She was, at that point, positively ripe for meeting someone whom she could adulate, someone whose cause she could make her own, someone whose disciple she could become with such wholeheartedness that nothing else would matter. She was ripe for a burst of fanatical devotion to someone and something…and she found both in the unlikely form of Roger Spotte.

Anne's beauty and innate sexuality were such that she attracted males as moths are attracted to a bright light, and yet, despite this and despite the permissiveness of the era in which she spent her girlhood and young womanhood, she somehow had remained a virgin until near the end of her twenty-first year. That was the year when, having returned to UC, she met Roger Spotte, who was then twenty-four.

She admired Spotte enormously, but hardly for his looks. He was a gawky, loose-jointed young man with long wild hair on his head which was rarely combed, and long wild hair on his face which was rarely trimmed. In his eyes there was a burning intensity which reflected the incipient anarchism in his heart. His one saving grace was that he not only believed in himself, but that he believed unswervingly in his own beliefs—beliefs which included an utter conviction that the world was a rotten place and that, in his own graphic phraseology, "the United States is the asshole of that world." He felt that it was his place, his *destiny*, to change the world to a better one by destroying the government under which he lived and establishing a better one, although he had never really been able to articulate the fundamental precepts of that "better one."

To Anne he was a prince, almost a messiah, and she moved in with him. It was he, at last, who not only filled her mind with burning zeal, but equally filled her vagina with his own thrusting manhood. And to Roger Spotte alone she gave her devotion and her body for the two years which followed. She thought then that she loved him—an opinion she had altered since meeting John—but even if it wasn't real love, it was by far the closest she had ever come to it up until five months ago. Then, five years ago, while leading a particularly violent rock-throwing demonstration against the Chicago police, he left his rotten world with a .38 caliber bullet directly between his eyes.

That brought about a remarkable change in Anne. It was the destruction of one wild seed that had taken root in her soul, but the fertilization of another which was, in its own way, no less extreme. Her own fanaticism, which had run parallel to that of Roger's although milder in temperament and somehow fortuitously remaining off the police blotters, practically vanished overnight. Along with that had gone her attitude toward engaging in sex with anyone but Roger. Over the next two years she had become, both figuratively and literally, what more than one dazed and totally satiated man had called her: "The most gorgeous piece of ass in the whole damn country!" To the delight of most of the men she allowed to pick her up, she was not the one-night-stand type at all. The man who appealed to her, for whatever reason, was in for anywhere from three to ten days of the most incomparable sex he'd ever experienced with the most beautiful woman he'd ever seen that close. A fair portion of those men were never quite the same again afterwards. By her own count—and she kept an accurate record—there were forty-five such men. She took delight in rating them from one to ten, with ten being best, and the highest rating she'd ever given anyone was a six.

Then one day, for no apparent reason, she woke up and took a long hard look at the life she was leading and couldn't believe it. The whole thing, beginning far back beyond Roger even, was suddenly like a life she had only read about, not lived; a strange and unbelievable and entirely repugnant life. That was when the final monumental change had occurred. Anne Carpenter had finally found herself. Within a few days she had found a low-paying but steady job which she really enjoyed in a downtown travel agency. She applied herself as she had never before applied herself to anything—not even to Roger's nebulous cause—and within a year she had learned the business well enough to attempt establishing her own agency. With financial help from her father—all of which she had since paid back with interest—she'd established A-C Tours.

A little at a time, as their lives became more closely enmeshed, she told all this to John Grant, down to the smallest details of those four years when the two wild seeds had sprouted and flourished and then finally died. To no other human being had she ever opened her innermost soul and mind so completely and he had been gentle and understanding, as she had known he would be.

The only person besides John to whom she had been able to speak, at least partially, along these lines was her mother. She still did, to a certain extent, across the distance which now separated them, with telephone calls at least once a week. Susan and George Carpenter had not truly been failures as parents, but neither had they been sterling successes. All through Anne's early years there had been a lot of infighting between them. By the time she was in high school, Anne could barely tolerate either one. They were the impetus, in fact, which sent her out to acquire her own living quarters when she began studying at UC.

With Anne on her own, her parents simply had, by common consent, drifted apart into lives of their own choosing. Legally they were still married, but no divorce could have split them more thoroughly. Anne called her father occasionally at his shop on Chicago's south side, but only occasionally. With her mother it was different. Though she knew she could never again live with Susan Carpenter—even a three-day visit could sometimes have her climbing the walls—Anne got along beautifully with her over the telephone. When either of them needed advice or a friendly word or a shoulder to cry upon, they always had it with one another. But only over the phone.

Anne sat up suddenly. The apartment was bright with daylight and the bedside clock said 8:30. She was shocked that she had fallen asleep. Her mouth felt coppery and she went into the bathroom and gargled, then brushed her teeth. Even while doing so her eyes filled with tears again at the thought of John Grant. The apartment seemed so full when he was here, so incredibly empty when he wasn't. Slipping into panties—she rarely wore bras—she returned to the bed and sat on the edge, then reached for the phone and dialed the number of Susan Carpenter in Elgin, some thirty-five miles west.

"Hi, Mother."

"Well hi, Pussycat!" The nickname from childhood still stuck. "Twice in one week? Next I know you'll be calling every other day."

"No, not really."

Susan detected the off-note in her daughter's voice and her own bubbliness vanished. "What's the matter, honey? Troubles? John?"

"Oh, Mother," the flood was beginning again, "how can you love someone so much that every fiber of your being just *hurts*? How can you love someone so much that nothing else matters, that you just want to crawl off somewhere and die when you're not together?"

"I don't know, honey. I wish I did." She added wistfully, "I guess I've never really loved anyone that much. Did he just leave again?"

"Yes."

"To her?"

"Oh, God, no!"

"Trip?"

"Uh-huh. St. Louis. Couple of days probably, maybe three."

"Couldn't you have shut up shop and gone with him? Couldn't your girl there in the office have handled things? It's not all that long a time."

"No. I've already got Louise snowed under and there's just too much hurry-hurry stuff of my own in the works. In a day or so, maybe, I could have. Not now."

"How's *he* bearing up?"

"Like me—wretched. But in his own way. He keeps tight control, but I can see it. He's still losing weight. Everything's bothering him. Her. The kids. Work. Work most of all, I guess. It scares me, I guess because it's scaring him, too. He hasn't written a creative word in months. Says he can't seem to drum up the enthusiasm anymore. He's been on the verge of a dozen projects like the one he's checking out in St. Louis right now, but he always seems to just shake his head and walk away. He just can't get interested. Mother, John's got to write! He's just *got* to. That's the core of *everything* for him. It's his life!"

Susan Carpenter didn't respond at once, but at last she said softly, "*You're* his life, too, Pussycat."

"Sure I am!" Anne shot back bitterly. "And so is she! And so are Carol Ann and Billy! Without any one of us he'd be tremendously upset for a while, but he'd survive. He'd come back. But without his work..." Her voice trailed off and a moment later she blew her nose.

"Well, dear, then I'd say he has to do one of two things pretty quick: hang onto his work and go to you, or hang onto his work and stay with them. There's just no way he can do both. He'll have to make a choice."

"Only if it's *me!* It can't be any other way. It's got to be *me!*" Anne's voice was becoming shrill.

Susan didn't reply and for almost half a minute there was silence between them. Then it was Anne who spoke again, calmer now.

"I'm going to have to push, Mother."

"Careful! That can just as easily work against you."

"I know. I *know!* He loves me, I have absolutely no doubt of it. But I'm not sure he really *needs* me. Not the way I need him. Not the way he needs his work. If there was only some way besides simply loving him that I could make him realize that he needs me, too!" Another long pause and once again it was Anne who broke the silence. "I...I have to get ready for work now, Mother. Are you all right? Do you need anything?"

"I'm all right. Do me a favor, though; you be all right, too."

"I will, don't worry. Good-bye, Mother."

"'Bye, Pussycat."

Anne hung up, blew her nose again and was just starting to rise when the phone rang.

"Hello?"

An operator's voice came, but not speaking to her. "Here's your party, sir. Please deposit a dollar thirty-five for the first three minutes."

"Okay."

His voice. She heard the bonging of the five quarters in the pay-phone slot, and then the tinnier *ding-ding* of the dime. There was a small crash as the operator triggered the money into the box and then said, "Go ahead, sir."

"Hello?"

"John! Oh, I'm so glad you called. This place becomes an absolute morgue when you leave."

"You don't sound sleepy. Thought maybe I'd awaken you."

"I was up, darling. Thinking of you, in fact, when you called, although that's nothing new. You're in St. Louis?"

"Yep. Just got in. Wanted to give you a quick ring before getting a cab. Has there been anything more about Sanders?"

The abrupt question caught her unawares and confused her. She frowned. "Sanders?"

"Yes. The President? What's the latest word?"

"John, what are you talking about? You've lost me."

"Lord, you mean you haven't heard yet? President Sanders was shot last night. Twice. Over in front of the Continental Plaza."

"Oh, no!" Anne felt as if she'd been punched in the stomach. "When? Who did it? Is he dead?"

"Evidently not, from what I heard on the car radio. They didn't have anything much on who did it. That's why I thought you may have heard by now. There's a hell of an intriguing aspect to the whole thing, too, Anne. The guy who shot him apparently got within just a few feet of him, but then used some kind of wax bullets which wouldn't kill him."

"John, that's crazy."

"Seems like it. Sure raises a lot of questions. Wish I didn't have to hustle off to this meeting with Proctor. I'd like to catch the latest developments, but I won't have time. Fact is, I'd better get moving right now or I'll be late. Tell you what—if I can wrap up this thing with Proctor earlier than anticipated, maybe later on today, I'll catch the first possible return flight. That would give us tonight, all day tomorrow and tomorrow night together."

She caught her breath at the prospect, but hesitated before replying. "I'd like that, love. But, John, please don't give up too quickly on this Proctor thing. It could be just what you've been looking for, something to start all those creative juices flowing again."

"I doubt it," he said shortly, then added with a wry quality which frightened her, "The only creative juices that have flowed from me lately have been when I'm with you, and they're not the kind you put on paper." He chuckled. "Look, honey, I do have to go. Keep tabs on this Sanders thing for me, will you? That intrigues me one whole hell of a lot more than possibly writing about this Holy Joe here. Find out what you can and then you can fill me in on it when I get back. I love you. 'Bye for now."

"I love you, too, darling. So much!"

The line went dead and she slowly replaced the receiver in its cradle. Obviously her mother hadn't heard about the shooting, either, or she'd have mentioned it. Anne considered calling her again, but a glance at the clock changed her mind. She was late already for work. Less than fifteen minutes later she left the apartment.

X I

With briefcase and overnighter in hand, John Grant was knocking on the door to Peter Proctor's suite at exactly 9:30 A.M. The evangelist, in shirt and tie but no suit coat, and with a copy of this morning's *Globe-Democrat* in hand, opened the door and invited him in with warm cordiality. A television newscast was on but Proctor switched it off.

"Nasty business about the President, isn't it?" he said, straightening. "How fortunate he wasn't killed."

As soon as Grant set down his luggage on the floor beside a high-backed and rather uncomfortable-looking sofa and Proctor had dropped his newspaper onto an end table, they shook hands. The evangelist's grip was firm and Grant unexpectedly found himself liking the man already.

Proctor's appearance was not unfamiliar. His picture had been in countless magazines and newspapers and of course his numerous televised mass meetings in stadiums and amphitheaters all over the nation had made his face one of the most recognizable in America. Still, there was a decided difference in seeing him close like this. The man had an enormous personal magnetism which seemed capable of almost instantly putting a stranger at ease. Grant had met only a few people in his life who exuded such ready charm and unaffected affability.

The evangelist was a fairly slight man of medium height, gray eyes and a neatly trimmed but dense shock of dark blond hair. He carried himself well and his long-fingered hands often moved in graceful and completely unostentatious gestures as he spoke. He was about thirty-five years old and unmarried, and Grant had heard it rumored that one of his greatest problems was fending off the multitude of women attracted by his wit and charm, his good looks and his spiritual message, and perhaps even by his money, since he was reputed to be extremely wealthy.

At the invitation, Grant sat down and opened his mouth to speak, but the evangelist's upraised hand stayed him and it was Peter Proctor who spoke instead.

"I suspect, Mr. Grant, that our discussions may have to be put off to another time." He had a strong, well-modulated voice, and an apologetic smile now spread his lips as he added, "Not through my wish, I assure you." He made an offhand gesture toward the newspaper he had been holding. "The whole country seems to be in quite a state over what's happened. Apparently that's why—because of the shooting, I mean—we won't be able to have our talk now. Are you in some way a part of President Sanders's staff, Mr. Grant?"

Growing steadily more bewildered, Grant shook his head, frowning. "No, I'm not. I wonder what would give you that impression?"

Proctor moved across the room to a small escritoire against the wall and picked up a slip of paper, then turned back to face the writer. "There've been two calls for you this morning, Mr. Grant." He chuckled. "One at just about dawn from your wife. I'm afraid I was still a little foggy with sleep and didn't sound especially intelligent to her."

"My wife?" His frown deepened.

"Yes. Evidently she was concerned by an inability to reach you here at the hotel." He looked at Grant steadily. "I explained to her how crowded it was here and that you probably had been forced to take lodgings elsewhere. At any rate, she'd like you to call home immediately. I hope there's no problem."

Grant's lips were set in a grim line and his insides were suddenly churning. Not trusting himself to speak for the moment, he put a hand to the back of his head in a futile effort to smooth down the cowlick and waited for Proctor to continue.

"The second call," the evangelist said, "was not more than ten minutes ago, asking whether or not you had arrived here yet. It was a Mr. Alexander Gordon of the United States Secret Service. He was calling from Chicago and impressed upon me to pass on to you the urgency of your calling this number immediately upon your arrival."

Proctor handed him the note. "So, if you'll excuse me, I think I'll go down to the coffee shop for a short while. Please feel free to use my telephone for your calls. Should it be necessary for you to leave before my return, may I say that it has been a real pleasure meeting you, and I trust we may find another time to talk in the near future."

Grant, the note in his left hand, stood and thanked him and they shook hands again. Proctor airily waved off Grant's apology for the unexpected situation, took his suit coat from the arm of the chair, slipped into it and then was gone.

Grant sat down very suddenly, a welling of alarm flooding him and thankful that Proctor had left him alone here. He had become a little pale and for several minutes he sat motionless, deep in thought. At last he took a seat in the desk chair and placed a collect call to his home. Marie accepted it at the other end and the instant the operator was off the line she was talking.

"John, what's happened? Where *are* you, and where have you been?"

"I'm in Proctor's suite at the Sheraton, Marie. What the devil's going on? Are you and the children all right?"

"Oh, we're all right. It's *you* I'm worried about. John, I've been frantic with worry. I tried to reach you there and couldn't. Then I called Mr. Proctor, did he tell you?" She added hastily, "Of course, he must have, you're calling from there. But where on earth have you been and what's happening?"

Grant had prepared for this before calling. He tried to sound very matter-of-fact about it. "Didn't get here until after eight this morning. Got tied up in a traffic jam on the Kennedy Expressway last night and missed my plane by just a few minutes. There was another St. Louis flight scheduled for midnight and so I hung around. Then that one got canceled because of the fog. The morning flight was the next available one."

"But why didn't you call and let me know? You could've come back from O'Hare and spent the night here and still have caught the morning flight."

"Well, it was pretty late by then to make a call, and I knew if I did call it would just wake you up and worry you needlessly. Anyway, I utilized the time in the terminal going over my notes for the interview this morning. But what's the trouble? Why were you trying to reach me, anyway?"

She hesitated. "You've heard about the President?"

"Yes."

"Two men came to the house early this morning, John. They wanted to talk to you. They were from the Secret Service. Oh, John, I'm scared! Why would they want to talk to *you*?"

"Hell, I don't know, Marie. I don't have the foggiest idea. What did you tell them?"

"I said I'd try to reach you for them, and that's when I called and couldn't locate you and began to get frightened. They want you to call them, John, right away. They left a number for you to call collect."

She read off the number and Grant saw that it was the same number as on the slip of paper that Proctor had given him. He grunted and spoke with a nonchalance he didn't feel.

"Well, I guess there's nothing for me to do but call and see what they want. Quit your worrying now, honey. I'm all right and I have no idea what this is all about, but I'll call right away and then give you a ring back when I find out, okay?"

"All right." She sounded dubious.

Grant said good-bye and hung up, realizing the moment the connection was broken that he should at least have told her that he loved her. He made a mental note to do so when he called back. Picking up the phone again he placed the collect call to the number the agents had left. The man who answered gave his name as he did so, but the name wasn't Gordon. When the operator asked if he'd accept a collect call from a Mr. John Grant in St. Louis, he told her to hold on a moment and put the phone down. In a few seconds it was picked up again and a different voice, much deeper, spoke.

"We'll accept the charges here, operator…Hello, Mr. Grant? This is Alexander Gordon. As you've discovered, we've been trying to reach you. I'm afraid we're going to have to ask you to return here right away."

"Why? What seems to be the matter? And why is the Secret Service interested in me?"

"Mr. Grant, prefer not discussing it over the telephone. Suffice to say we feel it quite urgent that you get here as swiftly as possible. Will you come, please?"

"Well, I suppose so," Grant said reluctantly, "if it's all that urgent. I don't know when the next flight out of here will be, though."

"You don't have to worry about that, sir," Gordon said quickly. "There will be a special plane waiting for you when you reach Lambert Field there. A military officer will be standing at the entrance. Make yourself known to him and he'll take care of the rest. You'll leave immediately?"

"Yes, as soon as I've placed a brief call to my wife."

"Mr. Grant, we'd appreciate it if you didn't. In fact, please don't discuss this with anyone."

Reaction to all this was manifesting itself in Grant in a growing agitation and he answered rather sharply. "Mr. Gordon, I don't know just what's going on, but I do know you scared hell out of my wife this morning. Now I'm willing to cooperate as best I can, but I have no intention of not calling her to ease her fears and let her know what is occurring."

Gordon sighed. "All right, sir, but please say nothing to anyone else and ask your wife to kindly do the same."

"I will," Grant said brusquely. "I should be at the airport in about forty minutes. Good-bye."

Immediately upon breaking the connection he called Marie again, told her what had transpired, said he didn't know what it was all about but that it must be very important if they had a special plane for him, that he loved her, and that he'd call her as soon as possible after his arrival in Chicago. Her fear was not entirely assuaged when he hung up, but at least it was not as strong as it had been earlier.

Grant momentarily considered stopping by the hotel's coffee shop to apologize again to Proctor and possibly set up a future date, but then shook his head. Instead, he took a sheet of hotel stationary from the drawer and swiftly penned a note.

Mr. Proctor,

Again, my apologies for this interruption having occurred. Thanks for your understanding and for the use of your room and phone. I'll be in contact with you or Mr. Farmington again as soon as possible.

Sincerely,

J. C. Grant

The taxi ride to Lambert Field got him there within three minutes of the expected arrival time and the air force captain standing near the entrance snapped to alertness as Grant walked directly to him.

"Mr. Grant?" At his nod, the officer continued. "I'm Captain Builderman. May I see some identification, please?"

Grant showed him his driver's license and a few credit cards and Builderman seemed satisfied. He motioned with his hand toward the street.

"Come with me, please, sir. we have a car waiting."

The car was an official airport security vehicle with a revolvable light mounted on the roof and a cigar-smoking, white-shirted man behind the wheel. As soon as they were seated in the back seat, he started driving without a word. They slowed for a gate which was opened for them by a uniformed guard, but they drove through without stopping. The driver tossed a brief wave at the guard. They continued past a number of hangars and then swung around one of them toward the flight line. They swept to a stop near a huge jet and as they stepped out of the car Grant looked closely at the aircraft and his eyes widened.

"My God," he murmured, "that's Air Force One!"

"Yes, sir," Captain Builderman replied, "it is."

3

We all agree that your theory is mad. The problem which divides us is this: is it sufficiently crazy to be right?

—Dr. Niels Bohr

So-called visionaries are violently attacked or, what is often harder to stomach, laughed at condescendingly by their contemporaries.

—Erich von Daniken

A determined man with integrity has a certain inherent edge over practically any politician or political establishment.

—Robert Morton Sanders

I

Although nearly seven hours of uninterrupted sleep had worked wonders for President Robert Sanders, he was on this awakening a little more disoriented than when he' given Alexander Gordon his instructions earlier in the day. The dazedness was passing quickly, and while his head still hurt, now it was more soreness from the blow it had received than from the headache. He couldn't detect any real pain from his side, but that was probably because it was snugly wrapped and he had not yet tried to move. He had not made any sound on awakening, but merely opened his eyes, and so Grace had not looked up.

The First Lady was seated a comfortable chair a few feet to the right of the bed, an empty cup on a small table beside her and a fairly thick book in her hands. She appeared to be about a quarter of the way into the book and was deeply absorbed in it. Beyond her was another bed which had been moved in for her while her husband was asleep.

He opened his mouth and felt his lips sticking together gummily. His tongue felt thick and coated and he was extremely thirsty. He tried to lick his lips, but it didn't help much and, when he spoke, his first words were a croaky whisper.

"Good morning, Grace."

She started a bit and looked up, great relief in her expression. As she came to her feet she dog-eared the page she was on to mark it—a bad habit from early years which she had never been able to break—and then closed the book, setting it on the table. She placed her hands on his forearm and squeezed, bending to kiss him.

"Bob," she said. "Oh, Bob, how lucky we are!" Her eyes were glinting overbrightly. "How are you feeling? Is there much pain?"

"Thirsty," he whispered, trying to smile but without much success.

She quickly poured a half-glass of water from the heavily misted stainless steel pitcher on his table, put a bent glass straw into it and tried to get him to drink through it.

He shook his head. "Uh-uh. Raise me, will you, and I'll try to drink sitting up." He turned his head, looking around the room puzzledly. "Maybe Alex told me but, if so, I've forgotten. What hospital is this?"

She told him and, still holding the glass, went to the foot of the bed and pushed a button which slowly raised the head of it, accompanied by a faint whirring sound. When it was high enough she came back and held the glass to his lips and he drank eagerly, emptying it.

"That was good. My lips are so sticky."

She poured some more water into the glass and then dipped the corner of a fresh washcloth into it and gently wiped it across his mouth, dissolving the mucus.

"Better?"

"Much."

"Good. More when you need it. How do you feel now?"

"Not bad at all. Surprisingly alert, I'd say. Sore a little, but not much pain."

"Your hand looks bad. It would have to be your left hand, too. Does it hurt?"

He made a negative sound. "Looks worse than it is. I can flex it all right." He looked at her, pleased she was here. "Were you able to get any sleep?"

Grace Sanders nodded, carefully sitting on the bedside facing him, taking his right hand in both of hers. "Three or four hours, I guess. I'm all right, especially now." She squeezed his hand, then gave a light little laugh. "But it's not morning, Mr. President. It's midafternoon."

He raised an eyebrow. "Same day, I hope."

"Same day," she replied. "Are you hungry?"

"Ravenous, but let's wait a while for that. What's been going on? Can you give me a run-down?"

"The whole nation's in an uproar over this and there's been nothing else on the air. A fair portion of the world's press is downstairs drinking coffee by the gallons and wearing holes in the carpeting of the waiting room. Jim Barrington's handling things very well and managing not to make comments that could be misconstrued as anything but genuine concern for you. Early on, some of the reporters tried to pin him down with remarks about this being his moment of immortality—you know, the 'heartbeat away from destiny' line. That was before your condition was known. But he cut them off pretty well in a very dignified way. I must say, Bob, I'm really quite impressed with how he's reacted."

She stopped a moment, thinking of what else to tell him, and then went on. "Let's see now, Mahlora from Hawaii's already preparing a brand new gun legislation bill, though no one really believes he'll be able to ram it through. Telegrams by the hundreds coming here and to the White House. Steve's taking care of the ones here and Hazel's got those in Washington. Steve, incidentally, got here around ten this morning."

"I'll see him in a little while," the President said. Steven Lace was his press secretary and a good man. "What else?"

"Communiques from most of the friendly heads of state and even from some who aren't. Daniel Ngoromu called from New York just after you dropped off. I was here by then and took it. What a baritone he's got! Very much concerned for you. He and Anita were leaving for home in a few minutes and were very relieved that I could give them a little more encouraging word about you than they'd heard. He's a good man, and Anita's awfully nice. I'd like to know them better.

"Oh, incidentally, while speaking of calls, there was one from Mark Shepard over in Ankara. He'd just arrived there from Istanbul and heard the news and was extremely concerned. Offered to come over right away and help if he could be of any use. I told him thanks but that you'd be okay. He was very relieved."

"Did he say anything else?"

"Nothing much, although once he found out you were all right he rambled on a bit." Her eyes were sparkling at the memory. "He gave me the usual line—that I dump you and marry him or, failing that, to at least have an affair with him. That Mark! At sixty-three you'd think he'd stop that sort of talk."

"Not Mark," Sanders chuckled. "Not ever. Okay, anything else?"

She nodded and, in crisp, rapid-fire order went through a raft of matters he needed to be apprised of, including the fact that both of his principal advisers, Oscar McMillan and Albert Jabonsky, were standing by and had much to discuss as soon as he was up to it; that all appointments for the next week had been canceled and those for the week after were now listed as only tentative; that Robbie—their son, Air Force Colonel Robert Sanders, Jr.—had called from Houston, wanting to fly up here immediately, bringing Stephanie along, but in view of the closeness of the Space-Stop VI launching day after tomorrow, Grace had dissuaded him with assurances that his father was in no danger. Finally, the only other thing of immediate importance was that Alex Gordon had located John Grant and that Grant had arrived at the hospital just before noon.

"Has Gordon let him see this man Boardman yet?"

"No. He had the idea you might want to talk to Mr. Grant personally first and, even if not, then you'd probably have some instructions for Alex himself beforehand. You were asleep then, so Alex was going to take a break for some rest, too, before going on with this. Evidently he's still having a lot of trouble with that Perello man— the police commissioner here. Also, some of the papers are already mumbling about government highhandedness, unjustified secrecy, jurisdictional usurpation and that sort of thing. Both the State's Attorney and the federal district attorney are pressing for immediate arraignment of Boardman. Everyone's pretty much up in the air at this point."

"Well," he sighed, "guess I'd better start something rolling. Is Alex available now?"

"He's been sitting outside for the last half-hour or more."

"Send him in, will you please? Oh, and Grace," he added as she started for the door, then continued as she paused, "I'm glad you came so quickly. I know it must have been rough for a while."

"A few gray hairs added," she admitted with a little smile, "but they won't be noticed among the others. I just thank God you've come through it. When I think—" her voice cracked and she batted her eyelashes rapidly and turned away. "I'll get Alex."

I I

"Look here, Gordon," Grant said, leaping to his feet as the Secret Service chief entered the room, "I'm normally a very patient man, but this is getting pretty ridiculous. You've had me cooling my heels in this room for," he shot a glance at the wall clock, "close to six hours now. My requests to see you have been ignored and I'm getting pretty fed up with this whole business. Now either you fill me in on some facts pretty quickly or I'm going to walk right the hell on out of here."

Alex Gordon held up a hand in a placating gesture, a small apologetic smile on his lips. "Look, Mr. Grant, I'm really sorry. I know you've been inconvenienced and I apologize for it but, as you know, we've had something of a situation here. Would you please sit down a moment? I'll try to explain some things to you."

John Grant looked at him for a long moment without replying and then he exhaled heavily and let his face soften into a small smile in return. "All right," he said, taking his seat again. "I guess I did come on a little strong there. But when you asked me to wait in here a few minutes when I first got here, I thought that's what you meant. That was a pretty extended few minutes. I'm glad you didn't say it would be a long wait."

Gordon, still standing, boomed out a deep-chested laugh and then took a seat himself across the low table from Grant. He indicated the tray there with the remains of a light lunch on it. "I see they fed you, at least."

"Sure. Everyone's been very solicitous." He waved a hand with an indication of the room in general. "Lunch, telephone, reading matter, portable television, the works. Cooperation and courtesy up to the hilt, until I start asking question and then everyone suddenly becomes quiet and quickly fades away. Now *you're* here and maybe I'll begin to find out what this is all about."

"That's what I've come for, sir," Gordon said mildly, leaning back and crossing an ankle over a knee. "You said you were going to call your wife. Did you reach her all right?"

Grant grunted an affirmative. "She's still a bit upset, although she understood why I couldn't say much over the phone. Not," he added with irony, "that I could have told her a lot anyway. She's most upset now, I think, because I wasn't able to give her any id ea when I'd be home."

"I have something that I want you to listen to, Mr. Grant," Gordon said, removing a cassette tape recorder from his pocket. "This will take about an hour, and then after—" He broke off abruptly as there was a light rapping on the door, got up swiftly and crossed to it in firm strides. For a big man, Grant noted, he was very light on his feet.

The security chief opened the door a little and looked out, then swung it wide to admit a hospital attendant pushing a cart on which there were two dinner trays abundantly provided with steaming food. Instructing the man to put the trays on the table, Gordon turned to face Grant.

"We'll be in this room for at least an hour," he said, "and then elsewhere for maybe as long, Mr. Grant, so while he's getting set up here perhaps you ought to call Mrs. Grant again and let her know you probably won't be home before..." he paused, "...oh, I'd say nine o'clock, anyway. At the earliest."

Wordlessly, Grant walked over to the desk near the room's only window and picked up the telephone. He wished he could call Anne again, as he'd done earlier on this same phone. In a moment he was speaking with

Marie, reassuring her that he was all right and informing her of his expected arrival time. "I'll have eaten already," he added, "so don't wait or hold anything. You haven't mentioned any of this to the kids, have you?...Good....Right, just make it seem normal and say I finished in St. Louis sooner than expected and will be home tonight, okay?...Fine....Chin up, now. Be there before too long."

The attendant was gone by the time he hung up and returned to his seat. Gordon was waiting, the cassette on the table between them. The agent motioned at Grant's tray in an offhand way.

"Go ahead, sir. There are just a few quick questions I'd like to ask before I turn on this machine. I assume you've been watching the newscasts?"

Buttering a roll, Grant nodded. "All day. They're really not saying very much yet, but what they have said sounds pretty strange."

"It is," Gordon replied. "Have you ever met this man Boardman before?"

"No. Is he really as old as they're saying?"

"He is, but he looks younger. Expect he could pass for eighty or thereabouts. Very tall old man. Have you ever had any contact in any way with him, however remote or tangential? Phone calls? Correspondence?"

"Not to my knowledge."

"Can you come up with any kind of a suggestion as to why he might have tried to make it look like he was trying to kill the President, when in reality he wasn't?" Gordon began buttering his own roll and when Grant, after a momentary pause, shook his head, he reached out toward the cassette. "All right, then, let's listen to this while we eat."

The voices began and as soon as Grant realized it was Gordon's initial interrogation of Herbert Boardman, his interest increased sharply. He really hadn't been too hungry yet, but he chewed and swallowed mechanically while they listened, hardly realizing what he ate and consuming every morsel, along with a couple of cups of coffee, before it had concluded. Sitting back and lighting a cigarette, he raised his brows at Gordon as Boardman began outlining his conditions. He began to suspect why he might be here, but still was stunned at Boardman's specific request for him. A few minutes later the tape ended and Gordon snapped it off and put the machine back into his pocket.

"Well," he said, breaking the silence stretching out between them, "there it is...and there we are. That's the sum total of what we know so far, other than some of his background which we got from his daughter this afternoon. He's a retired electrical engineer. Graduate of the University of Illinois. Totally innocuous life up till now. Never even been arrested for a traffic violation."

"Puzzling," Grant murmured laconically. He looked thoughtful. Stubbing out his cigarette he said, "Are you really going to honor his conditions?"

"Mr. Grant, he may be very old but, as you've just heard, he's not senile. In fact he's very shrewd. He knows there is no possible way we can pressure him and he's totally unmoved by the prospect of prison. He also fully realizes that our number one concern right now is to determine accurately who or what is behind all this, and we can't do that without getting him to open up. And he won't do that unless we cooperate with him. He's deliberately and damned skillfully put us over a barrel and he's the only one who can get us off it. So the answer is yes. I've agreed to the conditions—with the President's concurrence, I should add—and what we need to know now is your reaction.

Are you interested? Are you willing to involve yourself in this and, if so, will you cooperate fully with us?"

Grant didn't reply at once. He put a hand up and unconsciously rubbed the end of his thumb along the line of his chin, his expression unreadable. Inside he was feeling something that he hadn't felt in all too long; the flickering of a little spark that could, with encouragement, become the fire of deep involvement. He cleared his throat.

"I expect," he said slowly, "that it depends considerably upon what you mean by full cooperation, as well as upon what Mr. Boardman has in mind. Remember, he said he'd have conditions which I would have to agree to also. Frankly, you're asking me to bet on a hand that hasn't even been dealt to me yet, and I can't do it. I don't see any way that I could agree to anything at this point, not until I've heard what he has to say, and maybe not even then."

Gordon stood, looking down at Grant, his manner seemingly unchanged. Then he turned and went to the telephone. Inaudibly to Grant, he spoke into the instrument for a few moments and then hung up. He returned to the writer, who had now also come to his feet.

"Mr. Grant, do you mind if I ask if you're carrying a weapon?"

Grant shook his head. "No, of course not. I mean of course I'm not carrying a weapon. Frisk me, if you like," he added in a jocular way, and then was nonplussed when Gordon nodded and did just that, swiftly but very thoroughly. It irked Grant considerably and, as Gordon finished, he spoke coldly. "I assure you, I have no intention of shooting Mr. Boardman."

"I didn't really think you did," Gordon said. "Please follow me."

They walked in silence down a long antiseptic hallway, Grant wondering what Boardman would say to him. They turned a corner and followed another hall several hundred feet to an elevator entrance flanked by two guards. Gordon spoke briefly to them and punched the button. The doors slid apart immediately and he and Grant entered. They emerged on the fourth floor, again under the eyes of watchful guards. Toward the end of the hallway were ten or twelve men who parted respectfully to let them through. Gordon opened a door and stepped aside to let Grant precede him. The writer entered and stopped a few feet inside, looking at the man lying on the bed and hearing Gordon enter behind him and quietly close the door.

"Ah, Mr. Grant. I'm delighted that you've come to see me."

Grant swallowed. "It's an honor, Mr. President."

I I I

"Well, Alex, what do you make of him?"

The door had just closed behind John Grant and now the President and his chief of security were alone in the room. The session had lasted for close to two hours and Sanders was very weary. The writer had been no pushover and even now there was no real guarantee that Grant would come through for him. Even though it might make things more difficult, Sanders liked Grant the better for it.

Gordon shrugged. "I'm not quite sure, sir. I'm just worried that whatever he gets from Boardman is going to be kept locked up inside until, in his own time and way, he's ready to open up. What bothers me is that there's no promise at all that when he does open up, it'll be to us. And if it's not, if he takes off on his own with it, there's no telling what the results might be."

The President agreed, pleased but not surprised that Alex Gordon had put his finger on the very element that was bothering him as well. "We may," he said slowly, "be more concerned about that aspect, however, than need be. He has made certain important concessions to us, so let's analyze what we have and perhaps get a better perspective of what this means in light of the possible eventualities."

He held up a hand and ticked off the counts on his fingers, talking as much to clarify his own thinking as anything else. "He has unequivocally agreed to reveal to us what he learns if, one," he folded down the little finger of his left hand with the index finger of his right, "he uncovers evidence of this being a foreign-backed plot; two," the ring finger went down, "a plot involving a domestic civilian organization; three, a conspiracy among any or all of the United States military services; four, a paid political assassination from within my own political party or any other; five, strictly the work of an individual of deranged mind. Now that gives us a good bit of what we were hoping to get from him." He dropped his hands back down to the bed. "On the other hand, he will not open up to us simply on the basis that it might be personally or politically damaging to me, and he's made it reasonably clear that if he turns up anything in this respect, he'll dig through it with all of his ability until he's gotten down to bedrock. I think, in view of his past performances, there's no reason to doubt his ability in this respect, agreed?"

Alex Gordon nodded. "He's bucked the establishment more than once, Mr. President, and each time emerged on top."

"A determined man with integrity has a certain inherent edge over practically any politician or political establishment. No man," Sanders added, a faint rueful ring in his voice, "who makes politics his career can ever get very far without making certain compromises and deals which, even though they might not be technically illegal, would be damaging to him should they be revealed. The politician's stock in trade is his ability to retain the belief of the people. When he fails in this, when he creates a credibility gap and they lose faith in him, he embarks automatically on a primrose path. Witness, for example, what it did to Lyndon Johnson, and even more to Richard Nixon. Compromises, Alex, are a necessity for political advancement, and the greater the advancement, the more far-reaching the results of such compromises. The skilled politician makes as few of them as possible, the least damaging possible, and camouflages them all as best he can. He may make them with the best and most altruistic of motives, but he *does* make them and he goes through his politically active life desperately hoping that he does nothing stupid enough or serious enough to warrant someone digging too deeply into his past. If someone does start rattling bones in his closets, then the immediate reaction is to make offense a defense and eliminate the threat by coming up with something which allows pressure to be applied to such extent that the threat backs off. More often than not, the higher a politician sits, the more retaliatory pressure he is able to apply because of the investigative resources he has at his command. Sometimes this can backfire badly, as it did with Nixon's use of the FBI, CIA, Internal Revenue and other agencies. But above and beyond that aspect, Alex, the danger at every stage for a politician lies in coming to grips with a threat to which no pressure points can be uncovered to utilize in retaliation."

"The determined man of integrity you mentioned earlier," Gordon said softly.

"Precisely. They're few and far between, but when they come along, they drop bombshells at every step. They force government and industry to do things for the public good which both, for one reason or another other—usually economic—are reluctant to do on their own. Ralph Nader, many years back, was such a man. John Grant, today, is another. A perfect example is his devastating—but completely accurate—series for the *Washington Post* some years back. It turned the Interior and Commerce departments inside out and won him a Pulitzer in the process. The point is, that sort of man refuses to be bought off or frightened off and becomes uncannily skillful in avoiding some pretty powerful efforts to frame him for indiscretions or outright crimes which he never committed."

Sanders paused in his monologue, expecting no comment from Gordon and getting none. He interlaced his fingers and cupped the back of his head in his hands. When he spoke again it was with utter conviction.

"And do you know something, Alex? I say thank God that such men do come along occasionally, because without them the world would be in a pretty bad state. Now, I've strayed from our purpose. We're faced with Grant having an inside seat in the matter at hand and have no idea at this point what he'll learn or, more important, what he'll do with what he learns. But because he happens to be one of these men of integrity, I think we can believe him fully in the concessions he's agreed to. At the same time, we are going to have to live up to our end of the bargain, make whatever adjustments are necessary to it, and then hope for the best."

"No skirting of the conditions Boardman outlined for us?" Gordon asked.

"None. We keep tight control of the situation, of course, but we adhere to our agreement."

Gordon bent his head in acquiescence. "What about Boardman's arraignment?"

Sanders made a face. "They're yammering for that already, of course, but we'll have to try to put it off. We've a few factors on our side in that regard. He's an old man who took a pretty solid head blow when being subdued. Evansson said he came through it remarkably well for his age. Minor concussion without any likelihood of complications. Period. All right, the press doesn't have to know that. They saw him being hit, saw him taken away unconscious, know he's being treated here. Keep it that way. For now, condition listed as 'guarded' or 'undetermined' or whatever sort of nebulous label like that Evansson wants to tack on it. Enough to keep him hospitalized and isolated for at least a week, at which time, under Boardman's own conditions, we get free rein."

"I'll see to it. What about Grant?"

"Full cooperation within reasonable limits. That means no interference whatever with him in his first meeting with Boardman tomorrow morning, or in whatever meetings follow. No bugging, no pressuring. Talk with him if you like after the sessions and get what he'll volunteer, but nothing beyond that. If he asks to see me, consider it as priority."

"I think," Alex Gordon commented, "we're going to have some trouble with the press here. The evening papers are pretty upset with the essential news blackout we've established. They'll be even hotter tomorrow."

"Let them be. I'll field that problem from Washington. Tell Bill Byrd to have Air Force One on standby tomorrow. If I twist Evansson's arm hard enough he might agree to let Victor Aiken take the medical reins sooner than expected or, if not Aiken, then Georgetown University Hospital. If I must stay under observation, I'd rather be there than here."

Sanders closed his eyes and brought his arms down from behind his head, folding his hands across his stomach. He lay quietly for so long that he appeared to have fallen asleep, but then he spoke again, still with his eyes closed.

"Grace is probably back by now and we shouldn't keep her waiting outside too long. I told her she didn't really have to leave when you and Grant were on your way here, but she preferred it. She's been reading Grant's latest book, *Monument to Destiny*, and is more than mildly impressed with it."

"Mr. President,..." Gordon began, but then hesitated.

Sanders opened his eyes and looked steadily at the black man, saying nothing. The agent seemed to be weighing something in his own mind and finally he continued. "Sir, there's one last thing you should know. It's something I was going to tell you earlier, but now it seems to be at cross-purposes to your intentions."

"Spit it out, Alex."

"All right, sir." He continued in a brisker tone. "We've been running a number of checks and interrogations today, including a close look into Mr. Grant's background. Both CIA and FBI have dossiers on him, but he's clean throughout. However, we seem to have turned something up here."

Robert Sanders frowned. "After our discussion earlier," he said heavily, "I take it this isn't just a skeleton rattling?"

"That's why I hesitated bringing it up," Gordon admitted. "It could be just that. But there's an outside chance that it might indicate some prior involvement in this thing."

The President sighed. "I agree, then, Alex. Let's have it."

"When Mr. Grant arrived here about noon today, I interviewed him briefly. As you know, Mrs. Grant had difficulty locating him on the phone in St. Louis this morning. He wasn't staying where she'd anticipated he'd be. I asked him about it in passing and he said he'd gotten tied up in an expressway jam the evening before and had missed his evening flight. He said he'd then stayed at O'Hare with bookings for the midnight flight, which subsequently was canceled because of fog, and finally wound up getting the morning flight which put him in St. Louis at eight-twenty this morning. Dick Kreps ran a check and found that he had arrived in St. Louis on that morning flight. However, on a hunch, he also made inquiries about the canceled midnight flight and learned that while there had indeed been a flight scheduled for St. Louis at that time and that it actually was canceled, there had been no John Grant reservation made for it. Discovering that, Kreps then checked on the earlier flight that Grant said he missed and found there had been no reservation made for him on that one, either."

The Chief Executive raised his eyebrows and pursed his lips. "That," he said at length, "has the earmarks of a vigorously rattling skeleton."

Alex Gordon hunched his shoulder. "True, but it also leaves Mr. Grant with an unaccountable absence from the time he left home early last evening until he arrived at O'Hare early this morning. That's also why I frisked him pretty thoroughly for a weapon before bringing him up here."

Closing his eyes again, the President gave a dry, humorless chuckle. "All right, Alex, you win. Check him out."

I V

It was well after seven in the morning when John left the house for his first meeting with the old man who had shot the President, and Marie Grant watched from the open front door until, with a final wave of his hand, he passed from view. She went back inside the house slowly, deep in thought. The welter of events which occurred yesterday had left her in something of a befuddled state, but there was no doubt in her mind of what she was going to do this morning. There would be no recurrence of the mental battle that had buffeted her so mercilessly yesterday.

At any other time and under virtually any other circumstances, she would have been positively fascinated by John's recounting of yesterday's events. He had talked with her well into the night, beginning with his meeting Proctor and subsequent flight back to Chicago in Air Force One, to his meeting with the President and the essence of his discussion with Robert Sanders and Alexander Gordon. As it was, she had difficulty maintaining an air of interest and was wholly unable to conjure up any degree of enthusiasm matching his.

He had noticed, of course, that she was acting in a peculiar manner and had asked her what was wrong. She attributed it to her full day of upset and fear over what was occurring—which was true enough—and he had accepted that. It was obvious, though, that he'd been a bit miffed at her blase attitude and that was reflected this morning when the conversation had been limited to little more than the essentials. Now he was off to Northwestern Memorial Hospital again, and there was no doubt that he would be gone for quite a considerable while, so Marie was once again heading for the upstairs den.

Despite his weariness, John had stayed up later than she in order to do some writing about the day's events. When, this morning, he'd gone downstairs, she'd stepped briefly into the den and noted with a sort of aching satisfaction that the current year's diary was back in its usual place on the far right of the collection of diaries. Yes, now he was gone and her only real quandary was how to proceed from here. She greatly feared that suspicions would somehow be aroused and that John would suddenly remove the books and put them elsewhere and thus she would be unable to finish deciphering the codes of this final volume, the ones she intuitively knew were to be so important. Logic dictated that she should, as swiftly as possible, merely copy every entry in its present coded form without at first attempting any deciphering. That would take more time but, on the other hand, it would take days, perhaps weeks, to laboriously go through the diary if she was decoding as she went.

Still, it was more than a little difficult to suppress the burning desire of such unrelenting magnitude to *know* what was written there and the very thought of not being able to read every word as quickly as possible was unbearable.

Marie made her decision as she removed the book from the shelf and brought it to the desk. She would decipher as she went along. With her stomach a knot of apprehension within her, she began to work. Individual words became disjointed, almost meaningless, so at intervals she paused, unable to keep from going back over what she had deciphered in order to grasp its meaning better in its flowing context. It was another day of copious tears, of incredible hurt, intermingled with an anger of an intensity she had never before experienced—all of it overlain with an aura of unbelievability. This could not be happening. This was not her John. It *couldn't* be. It simply wasn't possible. Yet, here it was, the horrible, damnable, unspeakably painful self-incrimination in his own strong hand.

The first such entry she decoded was early in the book—January 2—and it was short, enigmatic and devastating.

…Lunched together. Delightful. She is positively stunning. We've made a dinner date for Thursday evening and she seems very pleased about it. Certainly I am. In fact, I feel strangely giddy about the whole thing. This will be my first honest-to-goodness date with any woman other than Marie for the past seventeen years.

A fog of apprehension nearly smothered Marie. John had made a connection, but who was the "she" he referred to? *Who?* Marie went back over the entry swiftly to see if she had missed a line, a phrase, a reference anywhere, but she hadn't. It was just as she'd deciphered it—abruptly, disturbingly full in the information imparted, disappointingly empty in what had been omitted. The Thursday entry was the next appearance of the code and she bent to it quickly.

…Incomparably delightful evening which seemed over before hardly begun. We talked endlessly and without pause, even while dining, as if we knew there would not be time enough to express everything we wanted to say. Lunch again tomorrow; dinner perhaps the middle of next week or the following weekend. I think there can be no doubt that this is the knocking of opportunity I've been waiting for, the beginning of a thoroughly delightful relationship, but I can't be entirely sure yet. I want to plunge ahead rapidly, but I'm just a little bit fearful. I will continue to move carefully.

Still neither name nor place mentioned in that entry, nor in the two which followed—a luncheon and another dinner—which differed little except in the progression of John's interest in this other woman and his growing physical desire for her. The next entry after that—for January 20—was much longer and, with a sense of fatalism, Marie knew even before beginning that this was the one she had been dreading, the one she no longer had any doubt would eventually come. But her pulse quickened as she began because this time there was a degree of identification of the woman at the beginning of the entry. Not much; just a single initial, *A*, but at least now she had something tangible. Did it signify a first name or last? Probably the first and, if so, what might it be? Alice? Arlene? Anita? The speculation wasn't getting her anywhere and she continued the work, praying that somewhere in the entry the full name would appear.

…I picked up A at her apartment and we went to dinner. She wore a delightful, fuzzy, pale blue angora outfit which looked molded to her and which had every man in the place mentally slavering (I don't exclude myself!) and every woman emerald with envy. We returned to her apartment by taxi and, as before, I was prepared merely to say good night at the door, but she invited me in for coffee and talk. Abruptly a new element has been added to what had begun as a stimulating and beautiful relationship. I had kissed her before, but those were platonic compared to this evening's. Before long we were making love—deeply, movingly, beautifully, in a manner more exquisitely breathtaking and consummately fulfilling than I had ever known love-making could be. Throughout the night it went on, with quiet, enjoyable talking in between and no real cessation of loveplay at any time to speak of. Once she drowsed off for fifteen minutes, but I stayed awake and continued to touch and kiss her even while she slept. A happy, satisfying experience which continued until seven in the morning. It was unhurried, accompanied by beautiful music softly playing from another room. It was ideal sex, uncomplicated and thoroughly enjoyable, unsullied by coyness, cuteness, or phony acts or words. No promises were

made. No plans were made. Neither of us said "I love you" or other words that were not true or later to be regretted. We were merely two grown people quite happily enjoying one another to the utmost, with no strings of any kind attached. She is extremely attractive in all respects and highly intelligent. She is sensitive, amusing, gentle, loving. It was a happy time indeed, and the selection of partner wisely made. Probably no more ideal or less complicated selection could have been made. No other sexual experience in my life has been so entirely gratifying. I felt wholly and completely satisfied and more relaxed than I have felt for many years. And, wonder of wonders, the black, smothering mood of depression has vanished. At least for right now. I feel good. No, that is not strong enough. I feel great! I am elated, delighted, happy, at peace within myself, relaxed, fulfilled, gratified, and intensely, incredibly amazed at the power of this encounter.

For a long while after this, Marie could do no more. The more she reread what she had deciphered, the more difficult it was to believe. And one line in particular returned over and again, etching itself deeply in her mind and heart: *No other sexual experience in my life has been so entirely gratifying.* What about the seventeen years of what she had always felt—and thought he had, too—was entirely gratifying sex? They enjoyed it always, didn't they? There'd never been problems of any kind in their sex life together, had there? What could possibly be so different about this than what they had known together so beautifully and for so long? Never before had Marie experienced the strong sense of inadequacy which filled her now. She had no idea how it could be possible, but she was convinced that somehow she had failed; that John had strayed because he had been inspired to do so through some lack on her part, some fundamental failing she could not see and of which she had never been aware.

Marie Grant had a terrifying mental image of her whole world collapsing about her feet; of standing there watching this happen and being powerless to stop it; of being swept along with a tide of events she herself had loosed and could no longer control. Why, she thought, why should I be the one to feel guilty? The guilt is his, not mine! But she could not put aside the self-condemnation.

Unable to write more for the moment and equally unable to sit still in the den with those dreadful words before her, she prowled about the house restlessly, automatically picking up, wiping away a film of dust here, straightening a picture there, hardly realizing what she was doing anywhere. At length her legs carried her back to the den and once again she became grimly immersed in the work, on an entry that combined the activities of a couple of days.

…Arrived at A's about 7:30 where, until it was time to leave, we talked and embraced on the couch. Despite having reservations at the restaurant, we still had to wait and we filled this time until our table was ready by having a couple of drinks at the bar. For dinner we both ordered the special bouillabaisse, which was superb, and shared a bottle of chilled white wine—Pouilly Fuisse. Toward the end of the meal we became extremely conscious of one another sexually, almost as if a switch had been thrown for both of us simultaneously. We hurriedly took a cab back to her apartment and within minutes were in bed together. We remained there, enjoying each other's company to the utmost, for just short of 30 hours—until 5 in the morning on Monday. There was, of course, a good bit of sex, but even more important was the closeness and conversation, which was always most interesting and never shallow. She's a remarkably intelligent and deeply sensitive woman of twenty-eight; a consummate lover, fastidious in her dress, habits and personal hygiene, and

compellingly desirable. She possesses a keen sense of humor, though not coupled with flippancy, and she is never coarse in thought, speech or act. She has well-developed cultural tastes and harbors deep feelings toward opera, drama, poetry, art, symphonic music, and literature. It would be impossible here to discuss at length all the numerous things about which we conversed, but conversation never lagged—except when it was just exactly right to merely enjoy and not speak—and it was a thoroughly satisfying, stimulating, relaxing and happy time. We slept very little, probably no more than a total of two or three hours, and that in bits and snatches. We listened to music, drank coffee, conversed, snacked at times from the refrigerator, and made love—all to complete satisfaction. Since A is well aware of my marital status, there is no desire on her part for more than that which I, too, desire; a comfortable, long-lasting relationship to be continued wherever and whenever convenience, opportunity, and good judgment permit. We have found great delight in one another, both physically and mentally. I have many thoughts in regard to what effect this may have on me in respect to Marie and will comment upon that at length in a future entry, but at this moment I don't have the time to write more. A is truly a delight to the soul.

Entry followed entry along these lines, and though mostly she was inflicted with a swirling torrent of emotional responses, there was a small, steady portion of Marie's consciousness which followed the development of John Grant's peregrination with fascination and analytical calm. The cornerstone of her past life and future with John was progressively being chipped away, but there was no longer any consideration within her of stopping. The recurring blows to her self-esteem and confidence were legion, and instead of diminishing or even reaching a plateau, they increased. Time and again she felt the matter could grow no worse and repeatedly she was proven wrong. The final two entries she was able to decode this day seemed almost deliberately geared to strip away whatever remained within her of hope. That John himself was becoming ever more hopelessly enmeshed was reflected in the redundancies he committed in writing about the affair. Yet, in addition to these repetitions, each entry contained new logs being fed to the flames which were consuming the foundations of their marriage.

…A and I seem to be well matched. She's very passionate and reaches climax quickly and often, and I have been possessed of a virility beyond even my wildest expectations. Something new, however, has developed for us both—a much stronger attraction on a plane far surpassing merely the physical. I think she's fallen in love with me, and I believe I'm equally in love with her. It's crazy, I know, for there's no reasonable future in store for us. What I feel is a peculiarly quiet and deep need for her, manifested in a heavy ache whenever we are apart. I feel that I love her as deeply as I love Marie. Both of them are dear to me beyond expression.

The second of the two entries was one of the lengthiest she had yet encountered…and by far the most devastating.

…Though I love both A and Marie, the sexual satisfaction derived from them differs tremendously. For the first time, sex is not only a beautiful experience, as it has always been with Marie, it is now just plain damned good fun, too. There's little A and I have not done in the matter of sex, with many wholly new and incredibly delightful variations engaged in, but there's no need for me to describe the specifics except to say that this time they culminated for me in a

*momentous revelation. My physical relationship with Marie remains unaffected, but what rather frightens me is that there was and is quite a different mental outlook, for things do not any longer seem the same. For one thing, I realize with great impact the tremendous degree of difference between these two women, most particularly in mentality and imagination. Comparisons are odious, yet they are also unavoidable. But how do I state it? Perhaps the best way is to say that Marie, dear and sweet though she is, plods along in heavy shoes through a dark forest, while A lightly dances through beautiful trees with shimmering leaves. Marie looks, but A **sees**. Marie listens, but A hears and feels. Marie glows, but A glistens! And so, what all this amounts to is that abruptly I am involved in a very dangerous situation which I realize might tragically change a number of lives. I don't want to hurt Marie, despite what I feel for A. I love A in one way and Marie in quite another. Both are very real and very deep loves, yet each has its own specific plateau, its own distinct place in my heart. I cannot help but feel that things have evolved beyond the point where I have any real control left; as if I have become, in one stratum of my mind, simply an observer who can only watch events that are snowballing with gathering speed and cannot be stopped. It is a strange and confusing situation and where I go from here I have no idea. There can be neither joy nor contentment if they be derived through creating unhappiness for others, but no matter what course I follow now, it is bound to result in such unhappiness. Awareness of the potential of such hurt is the first matter, and I am deeply and constantly aware of it. I think I can continue to handle it safely and with enough aplomb and covertness that there never be any reason why Marie should suspect, any more than she has ever suspected the way I have felt and the pressures that have bothered me so long and made me want to be with someone else. Nevertheless, I know it will be difficult.*

The return of Carol Ann and Billy from school in the midst of a heated squabble over something entirely pointless snapped Marie from the trancelike state that had enveloped her since deciphering the long passage.

Drawing on a reserve of strength she hadn't realized she possessed, she swiftly put everything away, resolved the argument between her two children with calm reasoning and efficiency, questioned them with her usual interest about their day's activities, busied herself with delayed household chores, and finally fixed dinner for the three of them, since John had been unsure of when he would return and suspected that it would quite probably not be until rather late. And all the while, an anguished inner voice was crying, "No!...No!...No!..."

V

There is a phenomenon in the world of the press with which every newsman is familiar: the runaway story. A child may be lost in the woods and a search instituted, the story of this carried locally. Suddenly that story sweeps a nation, a continent, a world. An intense concern is felt for the little lost child all out of proportion to the importance of the incident. A thousand children may similarly be lost over a period of time and, except locally, no one pays attention. Why, then, does the one instance leap into worldwide prominence? No one knows for sure, but it happens.

A miner trapped deep in the bowels of the earth shares a similar recognition, as does an insipid guitar-plucking moron from the Alabama hills, the old woman who paints passable watercolors with her feet while using her hands to crochet automatically, the murderer whose fourth appeal for a stay of execution has just been rejected. A hundred or a thousand virtually identical people and incidents attract no notice whatever, yet that single case becomes an extravagant exception.

It happened in the murder trial of Dr. Sam Sheppard in Cleveland. It happened in the death of Floyd Collins in Sand Cave near Cave City, Kentucky. It happened in the streets of New York when scores of apartment dwellers looked down to see a man deliberately killing a young woman named Kitty Genovese, who was screaming for help, and no one did a thing to stop it. Sometimes they are insignificant events which snowball and become famous almost because of the insignificance, as when Douglas Corrigan won everlasting fame by the simple expedient of flying his plane from Brooklyn to Dublin and landing without permit or passport, and then laughingly saying he flew the wrong way, thereby forever becoming Wrong-Way Corrigan. Whatever the cause or importance, a news story suddenly and wholly inexplicably captures the attention of the entire world.

Such a ball had begun rolling now and swiftly was gathering an unparalleled momentum. The elements of the attempted assassination of the United States President sparked the interest of the world press—and its readership— as few things previously had ever done. The incident was replete with all the elements required for such a splash: intrigue, mystery, prominence, speculation. The headlines around the world reflected the upsurge of interest.

WHY DID BOARDMAN DO IT?—London *Evening News*

ATTEMPTED ASSASSIN IS 94!—Athens *Akropolis*

WHEN WILL BOARDMAN BE ARRAIGNED?—*Chicago Tribune*

ASSASSIN'S BULLETS COULD NOT KILL!—Warsaw *Kurier Polska*

NOTED WRITER ASKED TO HELP—Copenhagen *Børsen*

RECOVERED PRESIDENT REFUSES COMMENT—*Washington Post*

ISRAELI PLOT STILL POSSIBLE—Beirut *Al Amal*

HOW COULD ASSASSIN GET SO CLOSE?—Bangkok *Post*

MILITARY CONSPIRACY IN U.S.?—Buenos Aires *Herald*

STILL NO CONDITION REPORT ON BOARDMAN—Toledo *Blade*

IS BOARDMAN A PATSY?—*Dallas News*

Perhaps no headline, however, summed up feelings so well as that which appeared in the New York Times:
QUESTIONS ON ATTEMPTED ASSASSINATION
REMAIN UNANSWERED-WHY?

Television and radio broadcasts were no less embroiled in the mystery. Commentators editorialized and asked questions. Reporters held man-on-the-street interviews. Pollsters conducted their polls. Panel discussions were commonplace. But in all there was little more than speculation—intriguing, mysterious, delicious speculation.

The world was waiting for answers. Impatiently.

V I

John Grant had been listening to Herbert Allen Boardman and asking questions of him for the past eight hours. He was himself growing weary and he wondered how the old man could go on like this hour after hour, showing no visible signs of fatigue. Grant longed for the opportunity to sit in solitude in some dim, quiet bar booth with a tall cool drink in front of him and nothing to do but consider the things Boardman had told him.

Although Grant was not yet convinced—not completely—by Boardman's claims, the instantaneous and total disbelief at the old man's initial outrageous remarks had gone through an evolution. Outright disbelief had become strong skepticism, then that had given way to considerable doubt. The doubt began to ease and admit of a remote possibility, and then of a possibility perhaps not so remote at that. And now the possibility was being strengthened by a strongly interwoven thread of probability.

With each step of this mental evolution he had passed through, Grant's inner fire of interest and enthusiasm had burned brighter. Now it was flaring even more, licking at the story sense that had lain dormant within him for so long. If—and he reminded himself firmly that it was still only an if—if Boardman's relation was indeed true, then nothing he'd ever before encountered held such significance; no news story in history had ever had the impact that this promised. Certainly he had a much better perspective now in regard to Boardman's motivation for the attack on the President. The act had been unbelievably extreme and yet if—that same *if* again!—Boardman's reasoning proved valid, then even such an act as he had committed could be considered justified.

The very fact that his own reasoning had carried him this far was indicative to Grant of how strongly he already felt about the matter and how deeply involved he was becoming. Now, even as he continued to listen to Boardman, a remote part of his mind reviewed the events of this incredible day.

The atmosphere of chill emanating from Marie had started the day on a sour note. He could understand her apprehension of the day before when unable to locate her husband and confronted by Secret Service men looking for him in vague connection with an assassination attempt on the President. That was enough to unnerve anyone. He could see as well how that sensation could have maintained itself at a high level through the bewildering day of not having any clear idea of what was going on. But why should she have been so remote and uninterested last night as he explained in full all that had taken place down at the hospital? She'd even shown little reaction to the fact that part of that day had been spent in close conference with the President of the United States. He had attributed the lack of reaction to a backlash of the day's events, but a night's sleep should have restored her. Obviously, it hadn't.

The dark mood filling him lasted until he reached the Northwestern Memorial Hospital Complex, parked in the multifloored parking garage directly across Superior Street, and walked toward the hospital entrance, the heavy little four-track portable tape recorder held in one hand by its sturdy handle, his double-snapped briefcase in the other. Before reaching the entry he had been besieged by reporters swarming around him with pads and pencils, microphones and cameras, yelling questions at him in a tumult of voices. Why was he here now? What had he done here yesterday? Did he have an inside track to the President? To Boardman? What was the significance of his tape recorder? How was he involved? Was he representing a news agency? How come he was getting preferential treatment?

He'd shaken his head, muttering repeatedly "No comment," waving off the microphones thrust his way, blinking against the photoflash burst of blinding light, and pushing his way through the crowd, which gave way only reluctantly. They followed him inside the building, creating a din which caused floor personnel to come running to restore order.

Alexander Gordon and Steven Lace were inside and, ignoring the newsmen, they whisked Grant to the same room in which he'd waited so long yesterday. Lace was a harried-looking individual with an earnest, clean-cut appearance whose ability to mollify the press without really saying anything was legendary. Though young—no more twenty-eight—he was already nearly bald and his horn-rimmed glasses imparted an owlish expression. He shook Grant's hand with unexpected warmth and briefly commented on having read and been highly impressed with *Monument to Destiny*, considering it well deserving of the high literary acclaim it had received.

Inside the room it was Gordon who took over as the press secretary stood by. He led Grant to the table where a portable device lay and explained that it was the sort of listening device detector that Herbert Boardman had requested as part of his conditions. Gordon showed Grant how to activate it and how to use the pencil-like probe at the end of the wire to check baseboards, windowsills, picture frames and other such areas for "bugs." A needle dial on the face of the small metal box at the other end of the wire would bounce wildly if the probe came within half a foot of any sort of bugging device.

"We've left Boardman in the room he's occupied since being brought here," Gordon said. "We'd thought about moving him to a different room with more spacious quarters which might have been somewhat more comfortable for you both, but were afraid he would feel that we'd been busy bugging that room with nonde-tectable devices. He knows we've done nothing to the room he's in since he was brought there and the likelihood that it was prebugged is faint, even to him. I want to assure you," he told Grant, looking at the writer directly, "that the President has instructed us to abide completely with the conditions Mr. Boardman has stipulated. No tricks, no deceptions. You know how vital we feel the information will be that you'll be getting from him, but we won't pressure you to reveal what he's said. However, we're also confident that you'll live up to your own promise of informing us at once if you uncover evidence indicating Boardman's in cahoots with some organization plotting an overthrow of the government or if you conclude that Boardman's insane."

Grant nodded but made no comment until Lace added that he'd like to be included in the next session after this one with Boardman, if the old man would agree. At that his nodding stopped.

"Even if Mr. Boardman went along with it, which I doubt, considering what he told Mr. Gordon on that first taped interrogation, I won't agree to that. I've stated clearly that I'll relate anything I find which indicates a threat to national security, but I'm in full accord with his desire to make the interviews strictly between himself and me. Incidentally," he added, "how'd the press get wind of my connection so quickly?"

"You were seen here yesterday," Gordon explained. "Some of the Chicago police saw you being brought to President Sanders's room last evening and let it slip. You're not exactly unknown, Mr. Grant. The President hopes, of course, you'll be discreet when they collar you for comment as they just did."

"They won't be put off easily, Mr. Grant, we know," Lace interjected, "so we'll give them enough to partially satisfy them. Beyond that we can only request that you continue with a 'no comment' line."

"That was my intention, at least for now, and if I do decide to make any comment, I'll let you know first."

"Fine, fine!" Lace obviously was relieved. He indicated Grant's tape recorder with a finger. "You're planning to record your conversation with Mr. Boardman?"

"Yes."

"I think that's a good idea. I'd like to suggest that you turn the tapes over to us for safekeeping, with the guarantee that we would not listen to them except with your okay, but I have to admit," he laughed sheepishly, "that I don't really think you'd go along with that."

"You're right. I wouldn't. I'll see to their safekeeping. That is, providing Mr. Boardman agrees to my taping the sessions. He may not want that and, if not, I'd have to agree with him."

Gordon spoke up again. "The old man's daughter, Elizabeth Boardman, has been in the waiting room for over an hour this morning already. She's demanded several times that we let her see her father, and she came down pretty hard on me when I told her that it wouldn't be possible for a while. She's a librarian at a high school and seems like a nice enough woman, but she's pretty upset right now. Chances are good she'll be even more upset when she learns you've been given leave to see her father, maybe for hours, when she's not even given a few minutes with him." He shook his head sympathetically. "I feel for her and understand what she's going through, but right now you're the only person outside of my own men and the doctor who is going to have access to that room."

"Is she all alone?" Grant asked with some concern.

"No. The principal of the school where she works out in Oak Park is with her. His name's Paul Neely. His actions seem to show somewhat more than a very strictly principal-librarian interest in her."

"Would it help any if I talked with her briefly? If I explained that her father requested my presence?"

"I don't really think so," Gordon replied. "I'll be explaining that to her soon enough, anyway. Right now the important thing is to get you up to Boardman's room. Let's go."

The three men stepped back out into the hallway. Lace shook hands with Grant and moved off in a different direction as the writer and Secret Service chief headed for Boardman's room. It was on the same floor as the President's room, but in a different wing. Grant saw that it was guarded just about as carefully as that of the President. Inside the room, Gordon reassured Boardman that the conditions were being observed, gave them an extension number to call if they needed anything, and then exited.

Even though Boardman was very old, he exhibited little of the frailty of age that Grant had expected. His handshake was firm, his gaze direct and sharp, his speech not halting. He also seemed to find a certain amount of humor in the situation. When Grant prepared to give the room a going-over with the detector device, Boardman stayed him with a casual movement of his long-fingered hands.

"No need, Mr. Grant," he said, smiling. "That," he added, pointing at the device Grant was holding, "is simply a little form of insurance. The fact that they've provided it is, in itself, pretty much a guarantee that we'll find nothing with it. We can better utilize that time in discussion. I see that you've brought a tape recorder. That's good. I hope you're planning to record our entire conversation…but I must add here that it will have to be in accordance with some stipulations I'll soon make. You may as well get it set up at once and then we'll get down to business."

The writer nodded, amused at the way Boardman so quickly was taking control. He opened his briefcase to remove a new five-inch reel of tape from its cellophane-sealed box and put it on the machine. The twelve hundred feet of recording tape would permit a run of two hours per track at a speed of one and seven-eighth inches per second. With the capacity of four tracks per tape, this gave him a solid eight hours of recording time. Grant was sure that for this session, one tape would suffice; nevertheless, he had brought along three of the new five-inch tapes.

As he rigged the machine, running the tape across the recording head and onto the empty take-up reel, he listened to the conditions Boardman was outlining. Grant had to promise to hear him out completely before forming any conclusion; that in the initial stages of the comments by Boardman, questions or comments should not be interjected, although he was free to make note of any questions he wanted to ask and ask them later if he cared to; that at least until the end of their second session together he would say nothing of what had passed between them to any other person; that at the conclusion of their third session together he was to call a press conference and make a statement to newsmen in his own words and in whatever way he saw fit about what he had learned, without allowing himself to be muzzled in this respect by federal or local authorities; that he refrain from telling any authorities about what was discussed until after that press conference; that he give his absolute word to abide by all the conditions for a maximum period of one week, at the end of which time he would be free to follow whatever course he chose.

The conditions were hardly more than Grant would have imposed under the circumstances and so he agreed readily enough to them, his curiosity mounting. Now, more than ever, he was anxious to hear what Boardman had to say and, with the machine rigged, he made the final steps to begin recording.

Boardman remained silent as Grant set up the machine on the bedside table, plugged it in and tested and adjusted the recording level, and then carefully positioned the microphone so it would catch with equal facility and clarity both sides of their conversation. Himself taking a seat beside the bed, Grant pressed the red Record button, gave the date, time and subject, and then nodded at Boardman.

"I'll begin," the old man said, "by identifying myself as Herbert Allen Boardman, of 926 Crescent Hill Drive, Oak Park, Illinois. I am ninety-four years old and in full possession of my faculties. I admit fully, openly, and in the absence of any form of duress, that I did shoot the President of the United States, Robert Morton Sanders. I had no intention of killing the President, though I could have. This fact will be evident from the nature of the injuries suffered by the President, indicating that the ammunition used in the gun was specifically designed to be nonlethal.

"I will further state at the outset here that due to my age I realize that at any given moment I could suffer a fatal stroke or coronary attack. Therefore, it is my desire very quickly and as succinctly as possible to go over my reasons for doing what I have done. Once this has been accomplished and the essence of what I wish to express has been recorded, then it will be possible to go back over the entire matter in a more leisurely manner and in much greater detail to explore it fully and to respond to any questions which it may occur to Mr. Grant to ask."

With that preamble out of the way, Boardman began speaking in a strong, steady voice, often closing his eyes for long periods as he spoke, at other times watching with something akin to amusement the reaction of Grant to his words. He never faltered in his speech nor groped for words to express what he meant—and though at times his terminology was very involved and couched in scientific phraseology, it was clearly understandable. For fully two hours he spoke without pause except for the few moments it took Grant to turn the tape over for recording track number two.

At Boardman's first explanatory comments following the preliminary remarks, John Grant had come decidedly close to labeling the old man a thorough crackpot. Had he not made the promise to hear him out in entirety, he was convinced that he would have walked out before the session was more than a half-hour under way.

"The supposed assassination attempt on the life of the President," Boardman began, "was positively not at the instigation of any group, organization, political party, military branch, or any individual other than myself. It was planned and carried out by me without any other person having prior knowledge or even suspicion of what I intended doing. It was accomplished in the manner which took place for a very specific reason which will become clear as I get further into the subject of what motivated me to do as I did.

"I am," Boardman continued, "an alumnus of the University of Illinois, where I took my degree in electrical engineering nearly three-quarters of a century ago. I believe that I am the oldest living alumnus of that university."

He paused and took a sip of water from the glass on his bedside stand. His eyes were bright and, peering at Grant over the rim of the glass as he drank, he gave the impression of enjoying himself. As he replaced the glass, he continued in the same pleasant conversational tone. "However, though I was trained in electrical engineering, I very early developed—and retained—a strong interest in the geophysical history of the earth. I was, of course, properly indoctrinated in my earlier schooling with the then current, and largely still unchanged, theories regarding the formation of the earth and its development through geological eras. Part of this indoctrination, naturally, dealt with the recurring Ice Ages, so called, that the earth has known—those periods of the alleged advance and retreat of great glaciers from the polar regions, advances and retreats which covered so much of our globe and of which so much physical evidence remains.

"The more I delved into the actual physical evidence, Mr. Grant, the more skeptical I became of the existing theories. There were many pieces of physical evidence which, in certain respects, appeared to be at variance with the theories. This troubled me and I investigated further and began finding a great deal of irrefutable evidence that the theories concerning the earth's history were not valid, that they were based on misinformation, misinterpretation of available evidence, and with total disregard of existing evidence which did not coincide with the popular theories."

Boardman stopped and regarded Grant searchingly, momentarily biting his lower lip as he considered something. He continued then in a suddenly more intense tone. "While I am fully aware that I have, in you, something of a captive audience, Mr. Grant, I'm equally aware that if I attempt to continue at this point in a chronological manner, I run the risk of beginning to bore you before I reach my point."

He shook his head, cutting off the mild protest Grant was about to make. "Please, let me go on. With this thought in mind, therefore, let me at this time insert a comment here that may startle you."

The old man had been leaning comfortably against the inclined head of the bed, but now he raised himself to an erect sitting posture and stared unwaveringly into Grant's eyes. When he spoke, his words were more deliberately spaced and clearly enunciated.

"Beyond any shadow of doubt, unless instant remedial steps are taken, all civilization and, in large measure, mankind itself, will soon be destroyed."

For a moment Grant's jaw dropped, but then he caught himself and frowned deeply, a huge disappointment blooming within him. Oh, for Christ Almighty's sake, he thought, the old man's a goddamned Doomsday nut! A sharp wave of disgust and anger swept over him and he opened his mouth to speak, but Boardman, his eyes blazing at the expression on the writer's face, forestalled the remark with a savage chopping motion of his hand.

"Wait!" he said curtly. "Remember the first two conditions you've agreed to; you're to hear me out completely before forming any conclusions, and you're to hold any comments or questions until I have finished." He allowed an uncomfortable silence to develop between them and then abruptly smiled broadly and leaned back.

"However," he murmured, some genuine amusement in his voice, "in reply to your unspoken remark, you are most assuredly not suddenly being confronted by a crank or a madman. It is only human nature to think that at the moment, but I guarantee you that by the time we have concluded this day's talk, I will have provided you with enough proof that you will no longer consider insanity on my part as being a probability. Now, let me go on uninterrupted, if you please.

"I mentioned that I came across actual physical evidence which was at variance to existing theories. There were only two possible courses of consideration at this time: either the physical evidence I was encountering was being misinterpreted by me, or else the most highly respected geological theories in existence then or now were wrong. If the latter, this was tantamount to refuting the theories of Newton or Galileo, Copernicus or Einstein. The ramifications would be shattering.

Boardman puffed out his cheeks in a little wheezing sigh and closed his eyes again, but opened them in a moment and looked sharply at Grant, who still wore a distinct frown.

"I set out, Mr. Grant, not to prove that the long-accepted geological theories were wrong but, rather, that it was *I* who was in error. I was, at the time, only twenty and still a wet-behind-the-ears student of electrical engineering, not geology, at the university. How could I dare to have the unmitigated audacity to challenge some of the world's greatest and most respected theorists? In a wholly extracurricular manner, I steeped myself very thoroughly in a study of geology generally and—more specifically—various distinct aspects of geophysical study—glaciology, oceanography, meteorology, seismology, geodesy, and what have you. Gradually I began taking in as well certain branches of science which were related in a more tangential manner—paleontology, paleobotany, archaeology, anthropology, and so forth. This was not undertaken in a haphazard manner, although I must admit that neither was it done in what might be considered an academically approved manner. I refused to be satisfied with ambiguities, and the more I studied, the more of these I encountered.

"For twenty-five years, Mr. Grant, I made these studies an avocation which virtually dominated my existence. Though my master's was in electrical engineering, I say with all due modesty that I am more qualified for a doctorate in the earth sciences. Try as I might over those years, I could not reconcile the discrepancies I found, the vagaries, the elements of actual irrefutable physical evidence which either threw doubt upon or flatly contradicted existing geophysical theories."

Boardman interlaced his fingers and put his bony knuckles under his chin in a thoughtful mannerism. "Mr. ·Grant," he continued softly, "you have been a political writer and are well schooled in government. You are well aware of the difference between an anarchist and a revolutionary. The former decries the existing form of government and wishes to destroy it, but without any clear-cut idea of what form of, quote, better government, unquote, should take its place. The revolutionary, on the other hand, wishes to overthrow the existing government because he has, ordinarily, a very concrete idea in his own mind, whether rightly or wrongly, of what sort of better government should supplant that which is overthrown. Thus, the revolutionary approach is far more often successful than the anarchistic approach. The analogy is not too far afield in this present case.

"It is not enough to possibly refute a long-established theory. One must be prepared as well to postulate a new theory which takes into consideration all of the requirements of the old theory and yet which equally explains in satisfactory manner the enigmas of physical evidence which first cast doubt on the original theory. After those twenty-five years of thorough study in which I determined to my own satisfaction that the existing theories were incorrect, it then behooved me to postulate a theory which would adequately and justifiably take the place of those which would be demolished. That, sir," he added, a note of triumph and pride entering his voice, "is exactly what I did over the course of the next decade."

Boardman tilted his head to one side and studied Grant, then slapped his own leg and issued a short bark of laughter. "Your expression now, Mr. Grant, is hardly the one of outraged skepticism it was a short time ago, and you still haven't learned what theories have been uprooted or what I propose in their stead. But you will, you will, I promise you! First, though, suppose you call that extension number that our friend Mr. Gordon left and request that someone bring us a large pot of scalding coffee and perhaps even some doughnuts to go with it."

Grant stood up, smiling. "Good idea," he said, "but I warn you, I'm a long way from convinced of anything at this point except that you've definitely earned the right, in my view, of being heard further." He reached out a hand to snap off the machine, but Boardman stopped him.

"No, don't turn it off yet. I'd rather you wind up with a wholly uninterrupted tape so that, should it come down to that, there can be no claim made that the tape was tampered with in any way. Our personal asides won't take up that much time. Now then," he tossed back the sheet and swung his long bony legs over the side of the bed, "if you'll assist a feeble old man into that little bathroom there, I'll attend to a personal matter while you order up the coffee and goodies."

Within five minutes, the interruptions having been seen to and the refreshments on their way, Herbert Boardman cleared his throat and continued.

"I am well aware, Mr. Grant," he said, "that your curiosity must be rather aroused to discover what my findings are that could have led me to make, in all seriousness, so brash a statement as a prediction of the end of civilization." He narrowed his eyes and added, "Note, if you will, that I am not predicting the end of the world. What I predict is an end to civilization as we know it, along with most—but not all—of the human race. What kind of an event could cause this we will get into shortly. More to the moment, however, it is important that you learn what possible connection my refutation of long-existing theories and the postulation of a new one has to do with my supposed assassination attempt on the President of the United States.

"I mentioned," he went on, settling himself comfortably on the bed, "that twenty-five years of study had resulted in the refutation and another ten had gone into the formulation of the new theory. Thirty-five years, sir—half a normal lifetime!" A trace of anger sparked his words now as he went on. "I wrote a voluminous paper on my findings, climaxed by the advancement of the revolutionary new theory and submitted this to the

International Geophysical Symposium being held at that time in New York City."

Boardman grunted in a rueful and indignant way. "I regret to say that I may not have been as respectful as I probably should have been under the circumstances. As a matter of fact, I took some rather roundhouse blows at scientists generally for their proclivity for overspecialization, resulting in head-in-the-sand attitudes among so many. All too frequently our scientists become fantastically qualified experts in one extremely narrow field of study, to such a degree that, for them, virtually nothing outside the spectrum of that specific area of learning exists. They recognize this to a degree, laugh a bit uncomfortably about it, and among themselves call it an intellectual snobbery. Unfortunately, the great majority do little to change this. Thus, on a wider scale, they become educated boobs. For such people, the possibility that there may be very strong and direct interconnection between such fields as, say, archaeology, botany, zoology, geology, anthropology, meteorology, and innumerable others is ridiculous. Even those who are willing to admit the interconnection can really do little about it. There is so much research to be done, so much effort expended on pet projects and so much time and energy consumed in fighting the everlasting battles to get institutions, agencies, foundations or patrons to support their specific programs, that they have neither time nor inclination to branch out and really look closely at their own science in relation to those others with which it intermeshes."

Boardman broke off suddenly, realizing he was becoming agitated, and John Grant nodded in sympathetic accord.

"Undoubtedly that has been something of a problem all through man's history, Mr. Boardman," he said, "particularly in our recent history of extreme specialization. However, we have made enormous technological strides in spite of it. Maybe even because of it."

"Of course we have!" Boardman snapped. "We've become a race of technologically advanced imbeciles living in a world we don't understand and don't have any real desire to know anything more about than what affects us directly and individually. By heaven, I understand that and know I'm probably just as guilty in many respects as the rest. No man can justifiably be expected to acquire in his lifetime much more than a superficial knowledge of all the multitude of fields beyond his own immediate existence of job and family. No man, that is, except that man in whose hands is entrusted the responsibility of learning and interpreting for the rest of us what we need to know about the world in which we live—the scientist. Yet, more often than not, these very people, these scientists, are the ones who become most inextricably bogged down in narrow ruts of specialization."

He stopped, the deep-set eyes flashing and nostrils flaring. Grant, lighting a cigarette, said nothing. As he dropped the butane lighter back into his pocket, Boardman resumed in a much milder tone.

"As you can see," he admitted, "my bile rises on that subject. To shorten a rather lengthy story somewhat, I let that same bile come to the surface far more than was prudent in the paper I wrote and submitted. You don't walk up to a man and smash him in the mouth with your fist and then expect him to smile pleasantly and compliment you on the beauty of your knuckles. In essence, that's what I did. I took the present-day scientists to task in no uncertain terms for their narrow-minded blindnesses, and earlier-generation scientists for having deliberately buried facts which did not support their preconceived ideas. I then added the crowning ignominious touch by thoroughly devastating many well-entrenched theories of some of the world's most respected scientists of the past and present. Finally, I advanced a totally revolutionary theory all my own and demanded acceptance. All this, mind you, from an M.S. in a field of learning entirely apart from that with which the symposium was concerned."

Boardman shrugged and grimaced in memory of his own colossal scientific *faux pas*. "It doesn't take a very great imagination to envision what happened," he said grimly. "It was hardly afforded a thorough reading by the board of examiners and universally sloughed off as the ravings of a lunatic. They sent it back without the membership ever really becoming aware of what it contained. Worse yet, the only thing the membership did become apprised of, through its remarkable grapevine press, was that one Herbert Allen Boardman, insignificant electrical engineer, had had the effrontery to attack and horribly besmirch the entire scientific community, and then had the unmitigated gall to ask for recognition on top of that! Overnight, it seemed, the name Boardman became anathema to every scientist who attended and, in time, to just about all those who didn't. In fact," he issued a raspy ironical laugh, "my initials have now become a standard part of the geological sciences lexicon. When someone does something stupid or brash or gauche, he's put down with the contemptuous comment of 'Don't be such a HAB!'"

"You received no interest whatever from them on your theory, Mr. Boardman?"

"None." He shook his gray head. "Not then, not later. For a long while—years, in fact—I hoped they'd eventually get over it, but that was wishful thinking. Finally, after putting still more years of study into it and even more thoroughly solidifying the findings, I tried another tack that wasn't much better. I decided to write a book about it. I spent five long years writing that book, assuming that publishers would be beating on my door as soon as it was finished to have the honor of publishing it. Suffice to say they didn't.

"Everyone," he added, with a touching little trace of shyness, "thinks he has a bestseller within him. Maybe he does, but only a very few, like yourself, Mr. Grant, have the ability to say it in a way that can make people want to read it. I am now the very first to admit that the book is terribly dry and badly muddled. Even my daughter tried to read it and got no deeper than a few pages into it before tossing it down. The intrinsic importance of the theory simply became lost in a vast disorganized welter of unconnected data. And, despite knowing better by then, I repeated my original crime by making the overriding theme an injudicious and, according to some, entirely groundless criticism of the present scientific fraternity. I pounded the pavement from one publisher to another with that progressively more frayed—"

A tapping on the door made him break off and John Grant got up and walked there in swift strides. It opened just as he reached it and a Secret Service agent poked his head in.

"Coffee and rolls are here, Mr. Grant." He moved aside a bit and pushed a cart halfway through the doorway.

Grant murmured thanks, pulled the cart the rest of the way into the room and shut the door. Wheeling the device toward the bed, he nodded at Boardman to continue and poured the coffee as the old man started speaking again.

"I've always hated garrulous old men," he sighed, "because to me it always smacked of senility. Now it seems that I've become one. Cream and just a little sugar for me," he said, motioning toward the cups. He chuckled and added, "And two of the sugar rolls."

As Grant smiled and prepared Boardman's order, the old man continued. "Every publisher turned it down, most of them without reading more than a few pages. Spent over two years going from publisher to publisher with it and got the same response from all. We appreciate seeing your manuscript Mr. Boardman, but…Well, that's how it went, everywhere. Oh, thanks, that's fine," he said, as Grant placed on the bedside table a small tray holding a steaming cup of coffee and two Danish. He picked up one of the pastries and bit into it with evident relish.

"Love these things." His voice was garbled and muffled. "My daughter says I ought not eat 'em, but I've never been able to resist. Too old a hound to change now, anyway. Actually," he added, a mischievous twinkle in his eyes, "they're the secret of my longevity."

Grant laughed and sipped his coffee as Boardman took another bite, chewed methodically a few times, swallowed, and then went on, picking up his narration exactly where he had left off. "All right, they all turned it down and so that left nothing to do but go to a subsidy publisher. I didn't have a lot of savings and it just about cleaned me out to have a thousand copies published and mailed."

Grant's eyebrows went up questioningly as he munched his own roll. Boardman nodded in response. "Yes, mailed. The subsidy publisher wanted too much for packing and mailing, so I had the books delivered to my home, bought padded envelopes for book mailing, and sent them out myself. Gratis. I sent them to university libraries all over the States and even to some foreign ones. I was hoping some bright, uncluttered and as yet unindoctrinated young mind would come across it, see the value of it and become a champion for me." He took another bite. "That didn't happen."

"What was the title?" Grant asked.

"That was the only good thing about the whole book. I called it *The Eccentric Earth*. I had retained thirty-four copies myself, and so when nothing happened after nearly a year, I sent out all but a few of those copies to book review editors of major American newspapers."

He demolished the remains of his roll in two more large bites and, after another sip of coffee, touched the napkin to his mouth in gentle dabs. Grant finished off his own roll and lit another cigarette, exhaling a plume of smoke. He sipped at his coffee, set it down and asked, "Dead end again?"

"Almost. Only one reviewer paid any attention. Dave Cockrell of the *Enquirer* in Cincinnati. He was science editor then. He sent me a carbon copy of the review he'd written, along with the date it was scheduled to appear. November 23. Not a bad review at all, and very exciting to me, since someone was finally paying some attention. I don't recollect all he said, but in addition to a few remarks like 'ponderous' and 'confusing,' he did bring out the fact that there was quite possibly a highly significant and perhaps even momentous foundation to the book. He urged scientists, in particular, to read it. I think it's pretty likely that he knew of the clobbering I'd gotten from the symposium years before, because several times he referred to my postulation as the HAB Theory."

Grant laughed. "I think I like that. What was the reaction to his review, Mr. Boardman?"

"There was none."

"No reaction at all?" Grant was surprised.

"No review," Boardman murmured bitterly. "I mentioned it was scheduled to run in the paper for November 23. Saturday. As it turned out, John F. Kennedy was assassinated the day before that."

Grant pursed his lips in a silent whistle, but Boardman went on. "Everything else was eclipsed, naturally. The review was scrubbed to make room for a paper full of Kennedy material. Nothing else made any impact. Bigger stories than a review of my book were knocked out or, even if they appeared, who paid any attention? Who remembers, for example, that also on November 23 Aldous Huxley died? For two weeks the papers everywhere had hardly anything that wasn't related to the assassination of President Kennedy. Whatever happened to the review, I have no idea. Cockrell himself died of a coronary a week or so later, and for all I know, they buried it with him."

"What happened then?"

"Nothing. In the years that have passed since then, I've continued working on the theory off and on, sometimes for months or even years on individual aspects, such as how the disaster is going to occur and when and what the results will be." He held up a hand, cutting off Grant as the writer was about to say something. "Just a moment. I have only a little more and then we can get into what the theory itself is all about.

"Mr. Grant, I am an extremely old man. I cannot expect to be around very much longer. I suppose I grew accustomed to having been ignored through all those years and just more or less resigned myself to the idea that my theory wasn't going to create any kind of a stir in my lifetime. But then recently I began to work on a wholly new aspect of it and became very excited again, because I've determined a way in which I believe mankind can avert the tragedy. It is something which would take the combined effort and cooperation of most of the major governments on earth, but it could be done if we acted swiftly enough."

A noticeable excitement was rising in Boardman's voice, and once again, as he had several times earlier in their talk, Grant wondered if the old man was not, after all, mentally unstable. Somehow, he didn't really think so. Maybe, after hearing what the theory was, what the disaster Boardman alluded to was all about, and what kind of a solution he was envisioning which supposedly would save mankind, he'd change his mind again. But right at this moment, John Grant simply could not believe he'd been listening to the rantings of a madman.

Boardman was continuing. "It was at that point that I realized how imperative it was for the world to learn of my findings. I'd already failed twice, quite miserably, in getting at least some degree of consideration for my theory. I did not intend failing again. I had to do *something* which would give me instant importance—or at least notoriety— nationally and internationally; something that would make the press of the world eager to listen to anything I had to say. That, Mr. Grant, is when I conceived the plan of making it appear I was attempting an assassination of President Sanders.

"After all," he added, with what was almost a repeat of that mischievous twinkle in his eyes, "there's a bit of poetic justice in it, don't you think? It was the assassination of a President which thwarted possible recognition of the theory years ago; now another attempted presidential assassination, even though devised to fail, seems destined to force that recognition."

It was a rare occasion when John Grant thought in terms of a cliche , but he did so now. His eyes were crinkling at their corners as he thought, Crazy? Sure…crazy like a fox!

VII

For Alexander Gordon, the thought of not being close at hand to the President was distressing. The years that he had spent as chief of the White House security detail and, more specifically, as personal bodyguard to the President, had caused a significant change in Gordon's life. As a Negro he had been brought up with certain ingrained mistrusts of whites. However much he realized the inherent self-defeating nature of such an attitude, he'd never completely been able to shake it—except where Sanders was concerned.

He had quickly become very much attracted to Robert Sanders and his attachment and devotion had never ceased growing in these three years of their close association. Even though it was his job to do so, he would have given his life unquestioningly at any given moment to protect that of Sanders. It was the role of a Secret Service agent to protect the Presidency, of course, irrespective of who was filling that position, but Gordon's fierce protectiveness of President Sanders went far beyond that standard call of duty.

Not since he was a boy of twelve in Cleveland, Ohio, when his own father died in a grotesque accident in which he was crushed against the concrete block wall of the garage by his own car, had Gordon felt so close to anyone else. His relationship with his mother always had been close, but never quite as dear as that with his father. The fact that it had been his mother who had been behind the wheel of the car, even though the accident had been clearly proven to have been no fault of hers, had made a difference in his attitude toward her that would last for the rest of their lives. He knew this was unfair, but it was there, and no amount of reasoning seemed able to change it.

The devotion Alex felt toward the President was not far in degree from that which he had known for his own father. The fear and anger that had swept him when Sanders had been gunned down had been so intense that Gordon still wondered how he had ever managed to restrain himself from killing Boardman during those first few seconds of encounter. It had probably been a restraint brought about through some subconscious sense that there might be someone behind the old man's action, and if he were dead, chances of discovering who other plotters might be would grow slim. That Sanders had not been killed and that he had recovered and shown far more interest in the man than anger, fear, or the need for retaliation was simply one more aspect of the Sanders character which made the President that much more important to Gordon.

Now Sanders was leaving for Washington, and his departure with Grace at O'Hare was little short of traumatic for Gordon. They stood together at the base of the steps leading up into Air Force One and gripped hands firmly. If Sanders noticed the mist that shimmered Gordon's vision momentarily, he said nothing about it, but his handshake was warm and sincere.

"Alex," he said, "I don't like not having you close at hand any more than you do, but there's no way of getting around the fact that you're needed here badly. Until we learn all we can about Boardman, whether from Grant or from Boardman himself, that matter has to rank as top priority. In the meantime I'll be well seen to, as you know."

"Yes, sir," Gordon said. "Nevertheless, I've ordered that security be tightened considerably around you. I know you don't especially care for that, but under the circumstances I hope you'll let me have my way in the matter for a while at least."

"I don't really have much choice, do I?" He gave Gordon's arm a strong squeeze with one hand and looked at the big black man with a level, affectionate gaze. "Alex, as soon as you return to Washington, I want to have a private talk with you. I know that law enforcement and related work has been your career and you may not want to change that, but I have something in mind which may interest you."

"Mr. President, anything that would allow me to work closer with and for you would take precedence over anything else, as far as I'm concerned."

Touched, Sanders smiled. "Oddly enough, though it would involve working more closely with me, it might at the same time involve being apart from me considerably more than at present. But we'll get into that later on. For now, let me be the one to say 'Be careful' and get back to Washington safely. I've come to depend on you a great deal."

Gordon nodded and stepped back. He said good-bye to the First Lady and then remained rooted in place until the two of them had disappeared into the plane and the hatchway had been closed. When at length he moved back toward the waiting limousine for his return to the hospital, it was with a heaviness inside.

VIII

Although it had been only just over thirty hours since they had parted, Anne Carpenter felt as if she had not seen John in at least that many days. Each time they parted the wrenching was more painful inside and less easy to bear in silence. It used to be that their necessary absences from one another were accepted with at least some degree of inner strength, bolstered by occasional calls from him to her which eased the emptiness until they could be together again.

She knew he was quite equally affected by such separation, but at least when it did become very bad for him, he could somehow get to a phone and call her. She, however, could not call him, no matter how bad it became for her, and sometimes it was just awful—almost more than she could bear. And now it had come to the point where, for Anne, no absences were acceptable or without extreme pain, and the calls he made to her, desperately though she wanted them, twisted the blade of loneliness in her heart. The ache became even worse when anything intervened with plans which were to have brought them together.

John's call from the hospital yesterday had been brief and unsatisfactory. There was a certain pride within her that he was important enough to have been whisked from St. Louis to Chicago aboard the President's plane for some mysterious reason, but she resented the fact strongly that it also had caused a cancellation of the tentative plans they had made for being together a full day and two nights. A suffocating depression had ridden her since his call during the afternoon. She had been unable to concentrate on her work at the office as she should have, and at each ring of the phone she started visibly. Now almost a full day had passed since he'd rung last and a welling of apprehension was taking hold of her.

If only she could be sure of him, all this could be taken in stride. Not sure of him in the respect to his love for her; there was no doubt of that in her mind. What was so nebulous, so frightening, was contemplation of what he meant to do about it. Time and again they had skirted the edges of that subject and always he had recoiled from it, drawn himself away without any form of commitment. On only two occasions had she been able to pin him down to any sort of direct discussion about where they went from here. Both times the conversation had thrown her into black moods which had lasted for days.

Obviously, he was a man tortured by indecision, wracked by a disruptive situation which was untenable for him and yet at the same time insoluble. He loved Marie and his children and could not bear the thought of bringing hurt to them, of leaving them in an act of permanence. Yet, at the same time, his love for her, Anne knew, was just as deep and the pain of not being with her permanently equally abiding. It would all be so easy if only he didn't really care a great deal for Marie. There was no longer a sense of easy acceptance within her that he loved two women simultaneously. She wanted him to love only one—herself—and anything short of that simply was unacceptable.

The call from John had come at midafternoon yesterday and he had promised to call again if he could. Throughout the rest of the day she had waited, and a dozen times at least during the night she had awakened with a certainty that the telephone was about to ring, but it hadn't. Nor had it rung in either the apartment or here in the office today, and her nervousness steadily increased.

There was work she could have been doing, but she couldn't seem to concentrate on it. Travel vouchers, itineraries, correspondence and other items of business were stacked in a pile on one side of her desk and seemed to be staring at her in mute accusation, but she could not work. Instead, on the note paper before her she wrote such things as a string of his names, her own first name and his surname, neatly drawn arrow-pierced hearts with initials enclosed within. The pen in her hand could not seem to move unless its movement were to include him in some way.

A welling of hot tears suddenly and unexpectedly filled her eyes and she dropped the pen, convulsively crumpled the sheet of doodlings in her hand, and clenched it into a tight ball. The tendons of wrist and hand swelled with the pressure of her grip as she blinked rapidly, then eased gradually as she relaxed. When her assistant, Louise Maas, asked her if anything was wrong, she merely shook her head, at the same time dropping the wadded paper into the wastebasket with a small thump. In the next moment she was writing again on a fresh sheet of paper, this time with greater purpose.

Dearest Man,

There is no moment here without you. No breath is drawn or released, and no beat of heart unaccompanied by thought of you. You came and stayed and filled a heart that had considered itself unneedful of anything or anyone. When we parted, you emptied it of all but yourself. Even though now you are not near for me to touch and see and hear, you are yet with me and my mind cries out, "Oh, my Love, my Man!" You emptied my heart, yet left it overfilled with the need of you. Why are you not here, or I there, or we somewhere together? Why must we yearn through the distance which separates us, wanting so badly, so much, yet remaining so alone?

She paused and swiftly read what she had just written and was dismayed at the content. "My God!" she murmured, her words inaudible except to herself, "what kind of juvenile lovesick prattling is that!" She crumpled the page savagely and tossed it into the wastebasket and began anew on a fresh sheet, this time without even a heading.

You think you understand how I feel about you, but there's no way you can. Your love is split between a mate of seventeen years and me. Mine is undivided, all-pervading, unquenchable and desperately, desperately needful. It has blossomed as I had never anticipated it could. Behind me lie the first twenty-one years of childhood, adolescence and young womanhood, followed by four years of ridiculous but hypnotic attachment and excessive sexual experimentation, followed again by three years of inner void which, in retrospect, was worse than anything else. And then suddenly you were there.

Now, at an age when practically all of the friends of my youth have school-age children, I'm just discovering the joy— and the heartache—of being truly in love. I don't envy them their years of youthful parenthood. Those years were, for me, spent in a manner most necessary for me at the time—a sort of drifting semi-solitude. Now, though, I've become weary of sleeping alone, of wandering through an empty apartment, of talking to myself, of doing nothing for any other person and serving only the purposes of self-preservation, of skipping meals because of the loneliness of cooking for one. Do you know it takes less than five minutes to consume a full meal when there is no one to share it?

*I've just now entered a time of life when, later than most people, I feel an urgent need to be wanted, needed and loved. Always before I've shied away when anyone mentioned love. Now I can't hear you say it often enough. The thought of my being in love has always seemed pretty impossible to me. I think a large reason why I associated with so many men during that two-year period which ended three years ago was the novelty of being wanted, even if it was for just a quick romp. I've never really expected people to like me, but I guess all of us, deep inside, have an inherent need to be wanted, and want to be needed. You have become, for me, the solution to that want and need. One of my major complaints with other men was that we shared no interests. All these years, without fully realizing it myself, I've been looking for someone who would conform to **my** expectations. Now, here I am, knocking myself out to conform to yours—and I don't even know for certain what they are! Whatever it is, I suppose, that Marie isn't.*

*No, darling, you don't understand how I feel, and I can't really understand how you can love me as deeply as I know you do and at the same time continue living with someone else. I **do** understand that you still love her. That doesn't stop just because someone new comes along; but John, you can't be a husband to us both, and in my mind you belong with me and I'm trying to be patient until you decide to come home. It has probably become to seem less and less like it, but I **am** trying to be patient and understanding. That's damned difficult when fear and jealousy combine to draw unacceptable pictures of present circumstances and unthinkable glimpses of the void your total absence would leave. I'm so terribly afraid, love! I don't want to die any more than any other normal person, but this daily dread of hearing you deliver the wrong decision is sometimes pretty convincing that it's utterly futile to sit around waiting for the ax to fall. I cannot and will not face the prospect of a life without you, and yet I grow numb with the thought that I may well spend eternity under a stone with the wrong name on it.*

Forgive me, darling, these abysmal thoughts, but I cannot keep them from forming. They do so because…

…I adore you.
Anne

I X

It was as he was leaving Boardman's room in the hospital at nearly 11:00 P.M. that one of the Secret Service agents outside the door handed John Grant the envelope with his name written across the front in the distinctive handwriting he recognized as Anne's. He slipped it into an inside pocket unopened, thanked the agent, and asked him please to tell Alexander Gordon that he planned to resume his talks with Boardman first thing in the morning.

Wishing to avoid the newsmen still impatiently waiting at the entrance, he left through the hospital's emergency room entrance and managed to cross to the parking garage unnoticed by them. Under the dashlight inside the car he read what Anne had written during the afternoon, his heart going out to her in the first part of the letter because of the pain he was bringing her and the love he felt which so nearly matched hers. But then, toward the end, a cold tendril of fear coiled around his heart at the words "…you can't be a husband to us both…" and the fear became a very real apprehension at her final remarks. Though the actual threat of it was not written, the inference to suicide was there. It was more alarming to him in that form than an outright declaration would have been. He groaned, started the car and left the garage quickly.

It was from a public telephone several blocks away that he called her. Though the concern in his voice and words was very real, it was also apparent that there was a great deal on his mind at the moment and he did not wish to talk for very long. He brushed aside her suggestion that he tell her what had happened at the hospital, saying that the telephone was no place for that and he would fill her in better the next time he saw her. The double entendre of that remark broke the sense of strain that had been heavy between them in the conversation up until then. They had concluded on a light note, with promises to be together soon, but the moment he hung up, Grant felt a strong sense of dejection and suspected that Anne was going through the same thing.

Under ordinary conditions, the depression would probably have deepened and remained with him for hours. Yet now his mind was still so filled with the impact of his meeting with Herbert Boardman that the mood inspired by Anne was more or less shunted aside as he considered the great implications of what the old man had told him.

Close to fourteen hours of recorded conversation was on the tapes inside the briefcase resting on the seat beside him. It had been a much longer session than anticipated. The late morning break for coffee and rolls, a similar break for a light lunch in midafternoon, and a somewhat longer period for dinner around eight this evening were the only portions of the recorded tapes that were not filled with steady conversation, and even those areas had a certain amount of dialogue intermingled with the clink and jingle of dishes and silverware.

As he drove north on Michigan Avenue past the Playboy Tower and Drake Hotel and then into the short tunnel which funneled his car up onto the Outer Drive, Grant was steeped in thought. Any possibility that Boardman had acted as he had through insanity was dispelled for him. Whether or not he accepted the old man's theory at face value was something he was not yet entirely sure about. There still were a great many unanswered questions in his own mind—questions he knew would be resolved one way or another in subsequent meetings with Boardman. But the revelations thus far had affected him more deeply than he would have imagined possible and he felt almost dazed by them.

The entire afternoon and evening had been given over to Boardman's relation about his theory—how he had arrived at it, the actual meat of the theory itself, and the incredible connotations imbued in it for the future of man. Assuming, for the sake of argument right now, that Boardman was correct in his assessments and postulations, then mankind as a whole was indeed faced with a disaster of such magnitude that the ramifications were practically incomprehensible.

The theory itself was deceptively simple in expression. It was in the elaboration of it that Boardman had painstakingly undertaken for Grant's benefit that the full impact came crashing through with such force as to leave one reeling under the stunning realization of just what this theory involved.

John Grant already found himself forming a habit of thinking of Herbert Allen Boardman's theory as the HAB Theory, as it had been dubbed so long ago by Dave Cockrell in the Cincinnati *Enquirer* book review that had never been published. And, in essence, the HAB Theory stated that periodically throughout the history of the earth—at intervals ranging from 3,000 to 7,000 years, but averaging about 5,500 years apart—great global cataclysms occur which effectively destroy virtually all of whatever life forms or civilizations have developed on the earth to that point. The cataclysm occurs when the earth is badly thrown off balance due to a massive accumulation of ice at the polar regions. As this polar ice grows and creates an imbalance with its enormous weight, a wobble begins to develop in the rotation of the earth on its axis. Year by year, as the ice caps grow, the eccentricity of rotation increases until finally a critical point is reached. At that point the tilt of the earth reaches a point where it no longer can overcome the centrifugal force of the spinning earth. With devastating suddenness, the polar masses are thrown toward the point of greatest spin, which is the equator. Quite abruptly, the areas which were polar now have become equatorial, and vice versa. The resultant cataclysm is, of course, monumental across the entire face of the earth except at the two points which become pivotal when the capsizing effect occurs. In an effort to paint a better verbal picture for Grant of what occurs, Boardman had made an analogy.

"Picture the earth," he had said, "as a round ball spinning in place on a glass tabletop, its speed of spin very fast and constant. Imagine, then, that on the uppermost point of this spinning ball you drop a tiny glob of molten metal, just slightly off center. The ball immediately begins to wobble. Add more metal, more weight, and that wobble becomes more pronounced. Add still more and the eccentricity becomes so great that the centrifugal force of the spinning ball grips the weight and turns the entire ball so that the heavily weighted portion is thrown to the outermost rim of the spin—the imaginary line encircling the ball where the speed is greatest—which is coincident with the imaginary line on earth known to us as the equator. And that, Mr. Grant, is precisely what happens periodically to the earth. The buildup of ice at the poles reaches such proportions and eccentricity that its weight is thrown some ninety degrees from pole to equator."

A renewal of Grant's initial skepticism had manifested itself at that point. "I'll have to admit I find that difficult to believe, Mr. Boardman. The doubt that strikes me most forcefully at the moment lies in the likelihood of the ice caps growing to such gigantic proportions to begin with. I've always been under the impression that their size remains relatively constant."

Boardman waved a hand as if flicking away a fly and shook his head. That assumption is incorrect. Oddly enough, Mr. Grant, it is the heat of the sun which causes the ice caps to grow." His eyes took on an impish twinkle at the incredulous expression this brought to Grant's face. "You don't believe that now, but you will when I explain. You see, when the sun heats the air, this air rises, at the same time expanding and becoming lighter. Such updrafts are most prevalent in the area where the rays of the sun are hottest—the tropics. With the earth just about a perfect sphere—"

"Excuse me for interrupting, sir," Grant spoke up, "but it's my understanding that the earth is an oblate globe, fatter at the equator than elsewhere."

"I'll answer that, Mr. Grant," Boardman responded somewhat huffily, "but then I'll ask again that you hold your questions until I'm finished. True, the earth is twenty-six miles thicker through the equatorial diameter than through the polar diameter and this bulge is very important in stabilizing the earth. However, that distance, when compared to the entire size of the earth, is very little. A fine ivory billiard ball probably appears to you to be a perfect sphere, but in almost all cases is not. Ivory billiard balls warp from a tendency to absorb moisture, but this warpage is too slight to be detected by even a close inspection. In large measure, this is how the earth is affected. The earth is within one-sixth of one percent of being a perfect sphere, and this makes it a truer sphere than an ivory billiard ball.

"Now, let me go on. With the earth nearly a perfect sphere, the currents of warm air rise in the tropical areas and then, at high altitude, move toward the polar areas. Here they converge from every direction, collide and, becoming colder and heavier, flow downward. Now their direction is reversed as they near the ground and they flow with greater velocity back toward the equator. There is, as a result, a continuous updraft of warm, humid air moving toward the poles and a continuous downdraft of cold, dry air moving at or near ground level toward the equator. When air is warm it absorbs considerable water. When it cools, it can no longer hold that moisture and drops it as precipitation. That precipitation at the poles falls as snow. Most of this snow does not melt because the temperature prevailing there is just too low. Instead, it impacts upon itself and gradually turns into ice—glacial ice. As this process continues without pause as a normal physical course of events, the ice caps continually increase in size.

"This is not merely speculation, Mr. Grant. It has been *proven*. Consider this: a symposium on Antarctica was held in August 1960 in Helsinki, Finland, by the International Union of Geodesy and Geophysics. At that time the renowned polar explorer from Russia, Dr. Pyotr Shoumsky, reported that his then recent studies had proven conclusively that the south polar ice cap was growing at a minimum rate of two hundred ninety-three cubic miles of ice annually. To really grasp what a fantastic amount this is, let me make a comparison for you. Lake Erie contains water totaling a hundred and nine cubic miles. Thus, a blanket of ice forms on top of the existing ice at Antarctica *each year* which is almost three times the volume of water in Lake Erie. Such a volume is equivalent to a layer of ice a mile wide and two miles high from New York to Chicago. And let me reiterate, this is the buildup for one year only! It recurs year after year."

As Grant sat there silently digesting this, Boardman took a small pad and ball-point pen from the drawer in the bedside table and did a series of swift calculations. In a few minutes he murmured in satisfaction and cleared his throat.

"Let me bring the fact home to you even more pertinently," he said, glancing up from the paper. "Each *day*, two billion seven hundred and forty thousand tons of new ice is added to the Antarctic ice cap. This means that in a year's time—every year—close to seven hundred and thirty-three *billion* tons of weight is added that wasn't there before." A triumphant glint was in his eye as he looked at Grant. "Impressed?"

"Considerably!" Grant's mouth was dry.

"Shoumsky's figures, incidentally," Boardman added, "were fully corroborated by a couple of very esteemed men in the field—Franz Loewe of France and Malcolm Mellors of Australia. There's no mistake."

"Well, how large is the ice cap at the South Pole now?" Grant's voice was a trifle croaky as he spoke.

Boardman wrinkled his lips. "The present ice mass resting on the continent of Antarctica is considerably over five and a half million square miles. Again using the United States for a comparison, if the present pole were located here at Chicago, there would be a covering of ice two miles thick from Atlantic to Pacific and from the top of Hudson Bay in the north to Key West, Florida, in the south."

Boardman shifted and sat erect in the middle of the bed and raised a finger, the softening of his voice in no way diminishing the jarring effect of his words. "Even this great mass of ice wouldn't be such a real threat if it were perfectly centered over the earth's axis of spin at the pole, but unfortunately it is not. Part of it, true enough, does cover the pole, but the greater mass of it is considerably to one side of the polar center. And *that's* our villain. The off-axis placement creates the eccentricity—the wobble—in the earth's rotation. Consider this: a very slight earth wobble was discovered by astronomers in 1885. It amounted to only a fraction over an inch. By the mid-thirties, this had increased to just over six feet. Thirty-five years later, in 1970, its radial movement was close to eighty yards. And right now the wobble exceeds a quarter-mile in radius."

Grant appeared a little pale in the glow of flame from his cigarette lighter, the lines of his face more deeply etched. "How much more does the wobble have to increase," he asked, little puffs of smoke coming from his mouth as he spoke, "before reaching the point where the equilibrium can't be recovered?"

Boardman rolled his eyes. "There's no known means of calculating that. It could conceivably happen with another fraction of an inch of added eccentricity. Then again, it might be able to extend itself another half-mile or more. Who knows?" he shrugged. "Eventually, though, it'll reach that critical point of no return and the capsizing effect will occur with essentially no warning. Overcoming the gyroscopic stabilizing effect of the earth's equatorial bulge, and in obedience to the laws of centrifugal force, the weight of the ice will be thrown toward the strongest area of spin, which is the equator. The earth continues spinning on its axis as before, but now with some dramatic differences: the ice caps are riding on the equatorial spin, there's a new axis, and practically all life—man included has been extinguished."

Grant struggled hard not to believe it and felt half-sickened at his inability to do so. "Good God!" he breathed.

"Yes!" Boardman lifted a bony finger. "Precisely! Virtually inconceivable disaster. And this is not just a one-time occurrence, Mr. Grant. It happens over and over again. I've already charted the last nine capsizings of the globe with, I think, a fair degree of accuracy, based on residual evidence. But that barely scratches the surface. There have been thousands of such rollovers, perhaps even millions, during the four-and-a-half-billion-year history of the earth.

"The resultant cataclysm to the earth's surface when such a capsizing occurs," he went on, a far-off expression in his eyes, "must be a stupendous sight to behold. Take the effect on the oceans alone, for example. It's as if you're holding at arm's length in front of you in your hands a basin filled with water and then you suddenly spin ninety degrees to the right! And think of the volcanic eruptions, the rifts—tectonic plates—where the earth splits apart, the mountain chains thrust upward in the areas where the earth surface compresses! Cyclonic winds, mountainous tidal waves, earthquakes, electrical storms of inconceivable intensity, eruptions. The awful grandeur of it all!" The dreamy expression faded, replaced by an apologetic little smile. "Mother Nature on an all-out rampage."

They continued to discuss the HAB Theory at length during the several hours remaining, with Grant now given leave to ask questions. He did so, probing deeply, hoping somehow to find the flaw in reasoning which would negate the postulation, but the angular, gray-haired old electrical engineer fielded all questions without pause and with undeniable conviction. Each time, though, that Grant would broach the subject of the physical proofs Boardman claimed to have amassed to support his theory, he was gently put off.

"I assure you," Boardman told the writer near the close of this first session, "that there are a multitude of such proofs, and I will go over these with you in detail, beginning tomorrow. The only reason I put it off now is that the proofs themselves are matters of lengthy discussion and if we begin now, we'll really not want to quit. We're both too tired for that and we'll be able to think more clearly after a good night's rest. I'd much prefer that you use the intervening hours until we are together again to assimilate what we've covered already, which is quite a great deal. Besides," he gave a short laugh and raised his fingertips to his bruised forehead, his lips turning downward in a faint grimace as he touched it, "for the last couple of hours I've had a growing headache and I'll welcome a bit of rest."

Grant came quickly to his feet, immediately apologetic. "I'm very sorry, Mr. Boardman." He glanced at his watch and was amazed. "I hadn't realized it was quite so late. Nearly eleven. We've more than gone around the clock once already. I really do apologize for so long a session. For me, time stopped existing shortly after I entered this room."

He reached out a hand to switch off the recorder, but then paused with his finger pointed downward at the Off button. He looked over at Boardman, who was watching him curiously.

"One final question I'd like to ask before we quit for the night, sir," Grant said. "You've several times indicated that it's imperative the world learn of your theory quickly. If I remember correctly, at one point this afternoon you said, in that respect, 'before it's too late.'" His brow became furrowed. "Just how much time do you estimate remains before the earth capsizes again?"

Boardman regarded the writer with an expression as sober as any he had worn since Grant entered the room. He tapped a long thin finger on his chin a few times and then folded his hands on his stomach, leaned his head far back, and let his eyes become mere slits.

"Mr. Grant, you may recall my mentioning that the epoch, or interval of time, between such occurrences ranges between three thousand and seven thousand years. The oldest epoch of the past was just about seven thousand years, give or take fifty. The physical evidence indicates that our present epoch is in approximately its seventy-fifth-hundredth year. As this suggests, we've been living on borrowed time for quite a while."

There had been little discussion between them after that. Feeling as if he'd been physically pummeled, Grant had gathered up his equipment. He had taped one full reel—four tracks of two hours each—plus the reel presently on the machine, which was more than three-fourths of the way through its third track. He removed that tape from the machine after recording the time of closing this first session, put it into a tape box, and then put both boxes into an empty compartment of his briefcase.

Boardman's eyes were closed now and he appeared to be asleep. Grant gently lowered the head of the bed and whispered good-bye. This was acknowledged by a movement of the skeletal hand, but without Boardman's either speaking or opening his eyes.

Now, having reached Skokie and nearing his house, Grant was thinking of scores of questions he wished he'd asked Boardman, making mental notes to ask them in the morning. He was also extremely anxious to get into the all-important matter of the proofs. As he turned the nose of the car into Bobolink Lane he suddenly grinned and then began lightly whistling a cheerful little melody.

The literary dormancy that for so long had plagued John Charles Grant had been swept away.

X

The faintest of smiles touched Herbert Boardman's lips as he continued to lie in the position in which John Grant had left him fifteen minutes before. He was pleased with the way the day had gone, pleased with the knowledge that the writer had become so deeply absorbed in their discussion. He also was impressed with the aura of self-confidence and quiet competency that had seemed to emanate from Grant, happy that the man in person had lived up to the expectations formed from readings of what Grant had previously written. If, in this present situation, John Grant could remain as penetrating a writer, as diligent a researcher, and as incorruptible an individual as he'd proven to be in the past, then there was little doubt that the long-ignored theory postulated by Herbert Boardman would reach a worldwide audience.

The smile became a little more pronounced as the old man switched his thoughts to his daughter, Elizabeth.

He really wished Liz could be with him now, not necessarily to talk, but just to sit with him and maybe hold his hand and squeeze it and make him happy in the knowledge of her proximity. The security agent, Gordon, had told him she had been downstairs all day with Paul Neely, waiting patiently despite the Secret Service chief's softly regretful refusal to allow her to visit him as yet. She was deeply concerned for him and Boardman wanted to assure her that everything was going to be fine. Yes, now at last, everything was going his way.

Then, with startling abruptness, Boardman jerked erect in the bed. His eyes were wide and unseeing and his left hand was fiercely gripping the front of the cotton hospital gown. His right arm swept out spastically, came into contact with the stainless steel water pitcher and knocked it to the floor with splashing clatter. Almost instantly the door burst open and a Secret Service guard rushed in, but it was too late.

Herbert Allen Boardman was dead.

4

There have been, and there will be again, many destructions of mankind. When civilization is destroyed by natural calamities, then you have to begin all over again as children.

—High Priest of Egypt to Solon

Perhaps the most valuable result of all education is the ability to make yourself do the thing you have to do, when it ought to be done, whether you like it or not.

—Thomas Henry Huxley

I

In all the fifty-six years of her life, through the tragic death of her mother, a sister, and two babies, and equally through the terrible years of her marriage to Sam Kaiser and the unpleasant divorce that followed, Elizabeth Boardman had never known the depth of sorrow which cloaked her now. A monumentally dear and totally irreplaceable part of her life had been lost in the death of her father.

Throughout the night, after the petrifying bulletin and following the telephone call to Northwestern Memorial Hospital, she had rattled about the big Oak Park house in a trancelike manner, occasionally weeping but more often just moving from room to room in a pointless manner, looking with lackluster eyes at the multitude of objects that reminded her of Herbert Allen Boardman. He was gone; that was the reality of it and she knew it, yet there was something wholly inconceivable about that reality. This was Dad's house and he belonged here—there in the big creaky bed, or in that high-backed wicker rocking chair, or seated drinking coffee at the breakfast nook in the kitchen, or there behind his big desk—but not by any means to be stretched out in a gruesome artificial repose in a satin-lined casket a mile away. A hundred times or more she stood up, sat down, went to the kitchen, the basement, the attic, the garage, the study—all those places where Dad had most frequently been found during his scores of years in this house. A hundred times she was almost positive she would find him there, *somewhere*, and that all this would turn out to be nothing more than a horrible, horrible dream.

Paul Neely was with her constantly, speaking little, comforting with his presence, helping where he could. In his usual methodical way he did the numerous little things that needed to be done but which Liz Boardman simply had no heart to do. Had it not been for Paul, she probably would not even have eaten, but that was one of the few instances in which he insisted. She gave in simply to satisfy him, knowing he would keep after her until she did, but she had no idea of what she ate or drank. She had dozed briefly after daylight came, but at odd times and in different beds, on the davenport, in big comfortable wing chairs. Throughout the night, however, she had roamed the darkened rooms ceaselessly, unable and unwilling to sleep.

Brief word of her father's death had been on the hourly spot newscasts all night, and quite a play had been made of it on the early morning televised news.

A few telephone calls had come to the house during the night and many more this morning. Paul had taken all of them, not bothering her with any but those from the very closest of relatives or dearest of friends. He also monitored the door with all the watchfulness and hostility of a police dog, refusing to speak to the seeming endless string of reporters who knocked, rang bells, banged the doorknocker, or tapped on window panes. Twice he had lost his temper and literally shoved photographers off the wide, wooded front steps, malevolent in his quiet threats about what he would do if they returned.

Still, off and on this morning, there were those who came and could not be turned away—a sister and brother-in-law, and the dear old friends whose hearts were breaking in a way not unlike Elizabeth's, though not in so prolonged or intense a manner. They murmured their soft words to her, placed comforting arms about her ·shoulders, stood quietly and wept with her when she wept. And knowing that it was her wish, they soon left.

Paul Neely alone, of everyone, knew the unbelievable pain she was suffering. For two years he had learned just about all there was to know of Herbert Boardman through Liz; through the soft, proud things she said about him, through the way she saw to his needs, through they way they had talked together, through the loving glances and gentle touches. He knew so well that she had considered him to be the kindest and gentlest of men and the most loving and thoughtful of fathers.

Paul knew equally the utter trauma she had undergone these past two days. They had been so happy, she and Paul, in the full blossoming of their love for one another, and then the initial hours of such a wonderful time were cut so terribly short by the bewildering, unbelievable news that this fine, dear old man had attempted to assassinate the President of the United States. The nightmare had started then and continued all through the day at the hospital; an agony of knowing she was mere hallways and doorways from where he lay, yet unable to see him, speak to him, comfort him.

There were the questions by police and federal agents, the statements given, the hounding by reporters at the hospital, and still the interminable waiting, waiting. Throughout the night and all of the next day, waiting, hoping, praying that somehow, some way, despite the repeated refusals, she would be able to see him. And overriding it all, the incomprehensibility of how a man like her father conceivably could have done what it was said he did.

At length, later yesterday evening, Paul had brought her back to the house in Oak Park. Throughout the first hour of their return the telephone had rung incessantly. In each case the caller was a television or radio or newspaper reporter asking for an interview. Finally they had removed the phone from its cradle and that ended the calls for the evening. It also precluded their getting the news from the hospital officials that came in a far more jarring manner later. It happened, as they sat together before a television program that neither was really interested in, that another bulletin had flashed on the screen, and in this way they had learned, close to midnight, of her father's death. They had called the hospital immediately and been told that it would be pointless for them to come back downtown. An autopsy was to be performed and as soon as the body could be released, they would be informed. Since then, everything had become a montage of mumbles and shadowy figures. Paul Neely was sure it would be a long time before Liz Boardman was a well-functioning woman again.

During one of those blessed respites which sometimes occurred, she and Paul found themselves in midmorning alone and momentarily undisturbed, and he stood with her, holding her close, softly kissing her hair, wordlessly and perfectly comforting her. It was then that the doorbell rang once again.

With a murmured word, Paul left her and went to the front door. The man standing there was tall and well built, with light brown hair and direct eyes of intense blue. Though unsmiling, his features were pleasant and somewhat familiar, although Paul was certain they'd never met.

I'd like to speak with Elizabeth Boardman, please," the man said.

Paul shook his head, his features tightening. "I'm afraid that's impossible. She isn't accepting any visitors. If you'd care to leave your name, I'll be glad to tell her you called."

"I don't think you quite understand. My name is John Grant and it's very important that I see her. Would you please tell her that I'm here?"

The name seemed to ring a bell in Paul's mind, but he still couldn't place where he'd seen or heard of Grant before. He was shaking his head again, even more determinedly, as he heard Liz coming up behind. "I repeat," he said, "she doesn't care to be disturbed."

Neely took a backward step and began closing the door, but Grant moved toward him and placed a hand against the swinging panel, stopping it. Paul scowled and balled a fist, but the touch of Liz's hand on his arm stayed him.

"What's wrong, Paul?"

"This man insists on seeing you. His name is John Grant." He let the door swing open again and immediately Grant stepped back.

"I regret this intrusion," he said, speaking past Neely to the woman. "I would not have come had it not been quite important. As this gentleman said, my name is Grant. I was with your father just prior to his being stricken. May I speak with you, please?"

Elizabeth Boardman did not invite him to step in. She merely looked at him with an unreadable expression. Paul's glance shifted from one to the other and then settled on Grant. The memory of a newscast on television came to him then, an on-the-spot broadcast from in front of the hospital. The pieces finally fell into place for him and he nodded to himself, relaxing somewhat.

"He's not a reporter, Liz, or a policeman." He looked at Grant. "Sorry I was brusque. We've been pestered by newsmen pretty thoroughly the last couple of days. I thought you were another."

"That's understandable." Grant's gaze shifted to Elizabeth and he swiftly explained the connection he had had with her father. "I realize the strain you've been under," he added sympathetically, "first in the matter of the shooting and then as a result of your father's heart attack. If it were not a matter of such unusual importance, I would not think to intrude. Your father and I talked together all day yesterday and were scheduled to talk again today—the rest of this week, in fact. There was great importance in what he was planning to tell me, and now that this can no longer occur, I hope to be able to determine, through your help, what he was going to say. It's imperative that I be permitted to go through your father's papers. May I come in and talk with you about it?"

Liz frowned, now remembering who Grant was and resenting him. Her response was cold. "You may *not* come in, Mr. Grant. You have nothing to say that I care to hear. You're the one who spoke with my father all day yesterday while Paul and I sat waiting and waiting, wanting and needing to see him and not being allowed to. Because of you, I was never able to see him alive again." Her voice became unsteady. "No, I have no intention, Mr. Grant, under any circumstances, of letting you delve through my father's things. The federal authorities have already searched this house enough since the shooting and there was no way I could prevent that. But I can and fully intend to prevent what you're asking. I know you'll consider that unreasonable, but I can't help it. Would you *please* leave now?"

Grant shook his head and spoke swiftly, trying to impress her with the urgency of his request. Her level gaze remained cold and he knew he was getting nowhere with her. Growing angry despite himself at her obstinacy, her unreasonable attitude, his own expression became bleak.

"I regret that I can't seem to get through to you, but I simply can't accept a refusal. I'd much rather have your cooperation, and I'm sure it's what your father would have wanted. But with or without your help, I *have* to study his papers."

"I don't know if that's some kind of veiled threat, Mr. Grant, but if it is, you're making a grave mistake. I warn you, if you try to get to my father's papers without my permission, I'll destroy them before you can see them. Now please, go away!"

She shut the door and turned to find Paul regarding her with a curious expression, but she merely shook her head and walked slowly into her father's study. The tears were welling again. This was the room that affected her most, the room where he had spent more time than anywhere else. This was the desk where she had seen him for the last time, unknowingly kissed him good-bye for the last time. She sat down in the desk chair, avoiding looking at Paul, who had stopped just inside the door and was watching her quietly.

Two of the desk drawers were still partially open and a clutter of papers and letters atop the desk blotter attested to the probing of the government agents who had come here and searched methodically for anything that might shed light on the reasons for his actions. They had taken a few things away with them; a ledger, some notes and letters, the empty casing of the cartridge Boardman had used in his test, the telephone book with the scar and wax debris on the cover, a few other items. The drawers of the desk and file cabinets were still crammed with research notes, papers, clippings, articles—all the very sort of things their recent visitor had expressed such keen interest in seeing, the things that one day she would have to force herself to go through. But not now.

Her natural compulsion for orderliness caused her to close the drawers and gather up the desktop papers into a neat pile which she set to one side. Several paper clips and a rubber band were on the large green blotter and she picked them up automatically and dropped them into the tray in the front of the center drawer. A bit of thread, what appeared to be a piece of the stitching from the corner of the blotter frame, projected from between the leather edging of the frame and the blotter itself, and she plucked at it. It pulled out with a little difficulty, drawing behind it the corner of two folded sheets of paper.

She looked at them uncomprehendingly for a moment. The thread had been firmly affixed to the edge of the papers with a small strip of transparent tape. Dropping the thread, Liz took the edge of the papers between finger and thumb and pulled them the rest of the way out from between the blotter and its holder. It was a letter, addressed to her, the sheets filled with line after line in Herbert Boardman's neat but tiny script. She had been possessed of the strange feeling that somewhere in the big house she would find her father again and now, unexpectedly, she had. In his own way, Herbert Allen Boardman had returned one last time to his daughter.

Liz, darling,

I don't know when or even if you'll find this. There is a good possibility that these may be my final words to you. I don't really think that, but since the possibility is there, then there are certain things I should tell you. By now you'll know what I have done. Undoubtedly this will have caused you much heartache and possibly even some trouble, but I know of no real way to circumvent that; I can only apologize for it. My drastic act of violence is, as you know, completely out of character for me, but it has become necessary as the only means to accomplish an end far more important than any of us individually.

Dear, sweet Liz, I don't think you could ever fully realize how much you've meant to me, the great comfort you've been to me, the unalterable pride you've filled me with by just being your own fine self. No father could love his daughter more than I love you. In a very long and very full lifetime, I've been lucky enough to have remarkably few things to regret. That I must close that lifetime with the greatest regret of all—that of undoubtedly hurting you deeply—is a very bitter pill. Provided I survive my act (and I intend doing all in my power to accomplish that), then it becomes a foregone conclusion that the remainder of my life will be spent in prison. This prospect does not dismay me except in the knowledge of the effect it must have upon you.

You know in a small way, Liz, about the "project"; my theory regarding the earth, its history and future. You've humored me in my years of work on it, I know, but because you never exhibited any real degree of interest in the subject—and believe me, I haven't expected you to—I have never really gone into the matter with you at any length. I wish now that I had. It is far more important than you can imagine at this moment; so important that it prompts me to the drastic action I'll soon undertake. The great need is to make the world aware of this importance. The only way left for me to do that is by becoming so notorious that anything I might say will be newsworthy. If I should survive the act, then it will ultimately bring to me the man I believe could be of the greatest help in following through with what I have begun. I fully intend placing him in such a position that he will be virtually forced to pick up and expand where I leave off, an element of force I could not really hope to achieve by merely contacting the man and asking for his help. This man is John Grant, a writer of great ability and integrity. Even should I not survive my act, Grant will still be drawn into the matter, through your help. Liz, if it turns out that I do not, in fact, survive to speak with him, or that I do survive and am unable to compel the authorities to acquiesce in bringing him to me, then I must rely on you to get in touch with him and place all my papers and other effects at his disposal. With that, I hope, will go your fullest cooperation with him in every respect. I beg you not to fail me in this, honey. I cannot overstate the importance of it.

My dearest daughter, I am running out of both space and time. I therefore utilize the remainder of both to say how much I love you and how very proud of you I am. I also ask that you try to understand what I have done and not judge me too harshly for the way I have finally left you. I hope now, if it is your own will to do so, that you will look to Paul for the comfort and help you will require in this trying time that I have brought upon you. He is, I think, a good and steady man. Whatever you do now, always remember that most of all in this world, I love you, Liz.

I I

A suffocating blanket of depression had settled over John Grant, displacing the anger he had experienced at the unreasonable coldness toward him by Boardman's daughter and by her deliberately thwarting him in respect to her father's papers. Her parting words to him had no foundation whatever. That he could find some way to force her to turn the papers over to him was a stab in the dark and his modified threat to see the papers despite her had been bravado. Possibly he could, with Gordon's help, or even the President's, but her own parting words to him in response had struck a note of dread within him. The very thought that Elizabeth Boardman might actually destroy her father's papers rather than let Grant study them was a blow which sickened him and made him wonder at his own stupidity. He knew that in the past he would never have allowed flash anger to cloud his judgment like that. Now the anger had dissipated and the enveloping depression, a mood only too familiar to him in recent years, had replaced it.

The rapidity with which events were swirling around him was dizzying and disruptive. The exhilaration of his long session with Boardman had lofted him to a plateau of excitement he had rarely attained before, but he had not been permitted the enjoyment of it very long. Marie was still up when he got home, clad in her robe and watching *The Tonight Show* on television, and her reception of him had been cool and distant. Grant had been at a loss to understand why. The ebullience he felt should have infected her and raised her toward sharing it, but it hadn't. Every moment she seemed to be on the verge of a declaration to him, yet such a declaration never came. He had been bursting to tell her about the HAB Theory, but had never gotten that far. His enthusiasm was dying, along with his desire to share the excitement of it all with her. He was still in the process of asking her what was the matter and receiving only averted eyes and a murmured "Nothing" in reply when *The Tonight Show* was interrupted by the bulletin about Boardman's fatal heart attack. Stunned and dismayed, he had tried for over an hour to reach Alexander Gordon on the phone before finally getting through to him.

Gordon explained that he'd been tied up himself in a telephone conversation with the President, discussing how to proceed now in view of the whole new set of circumstances Boardman's death had created. Since the conditions established by Boardman could no longer be considered valid, he wanted to know what Grant's lengthy session with the old man had disclosed. Grant had been cagey, admitting that the session had been quite productive but incomplete and that there was vital information he hoped to get from Boardman's daughter the next morning. He assured Gordon that Boardman had shot the President for reasons of his own and that Grant himself was convinced there was no possibility of a plot or conspiracy involved, and that no other person was concerned in the matter. Beyond that, despite Gordon's impatience and the growing edge of anger he was developing, Grant insisted that he had nothing more to say for now.

There was still the matter of Peter Proctor to resolve. Grant was sure now that he would not be going ahead with that interview, and so this meant getting in touch with George Benedict at *The Covenant* and letting him know his decision, and also either contacting Proctor himself or Lamar Farmington and expressing his regret at not being able to proceed with the development of the proposed in-depth profile.

Then, there was also the all-important matter of his involvement with Anne and what he was going to do about it. The torment he'd been going through these past months in that respect had stretched every nerve to the snapping point and a resolution to the problem seemed no nearer now than at any other time. His gradual loss of weight was continuing and he found himself becoming overly agitated at minor things and short with people around him.

The inability to get deeply interested in anything, to get the creative drive working again, had bothered him tremendously and now, just when it seemed that the fire of enthusiasm had been rekindled, Boardman's death threatened to extinguish it all.

The crowning blow had been Elizabeth Boardman's cold refusal a few minutes ago to let him go through her father's papers and to prevent his doing so even to the point of destroying them if necessary. On leaving there, he hadn't any idea what he was going to do next. Logically, he should contact Gordon and maybe get his help in gaining access to the Boardman papers, but for two reasons he didn't want to do that, at least not yet. Gordon was already putting more pressure on him than he liked to make him reveal what he'd learned. Further, any pressure by Gordon on Elizabeth Boardman just might be the act that would trigger her to follow through in her threat.

He knew that he probably should just go home and make some effort to chart a course of action for himself in respect to the HAB Theory. Doing that, however, would mean facing Marie again and first talking with her in an effort to find out what was bothering her. That prospect did not appeal to him. Marie knew where he had gone and did not expect him home for quite a while, so there was no real need to go back. More than anything else right now, he wanted to shake off the oppressiveness of the mood that was gripping him. There was only one sure way he knew of doing that. It hadn't failed in the past and there was no reason to think it would now.

Having made his decision, he pulled to a stop at a drug store, bought a package of cigarettes, and then called Anne at her office. She sensed his low mood immediately, and when he suggested meeting her at her apartment if she could leave the office, she agreed instantly.

Less than half an hour later he alighted from the elevator on the forty-second floor of Marina City East and followed the curved hallway to her apartment. The rattle caused as he fit the key into the lock made it unnecessary for him to open the door. Anne jerked it open and catapulted herself at him, clinging tightly and kissing him. She took his arm and pulled him inside, kicking the door shut with a bare foot and then leading him to a big chair where she directed him to sit while she fixed him a drink. In less than a minute she was back with it.

"Here you are, Mister," she said brightly.

"You're not having one?" He took the vodka and tonic from her gratefully and, at her negative response, took a sip and then set his glass on coaster she had placed on the table beside his chair. The smile he turned on her was more automatic than genuine and she looked at him with concern. She reached out with both hands, placed her palms gently along his jawlines, and leaned forward and downward, kissing him lingeringly.

"I needed that," he told her, trying to match her lightness but not succeeding.

"Not all you need, John. You're strung out."

Her strong fingers curled, kneading the muscles at the sides of his neck and nape and then onto his shoulders. He closed his eyes, feeling himself relaxing under her ministrations. She stroked his hair, smiling tenderly as the recalcitrant cowlick refused to stay smoothed down. After a moment she kissed him again and took his hand.

"Come."

As if he were a child he let her lead him to the bedroom and stood quietly submissive by the foot of the king-sized bed as she undid his tie and slipped it off, followed by coat and shirt. She undressed him completely, kissing him frequently and lightly here and there as she progressed, kindling his desire and her own in the process. With a swift, sure movement she threw back the spread and coverlet and then the top yellow sheet patterned with huge flowers. She helped him stretch out then on the crisp, cool undersheet. He closed his eyes again as she moved away and when he opened them she had returned with his drink. She stepped out of her own clothes quickly, letting them fall where they would and not bothering to drape them neatly, as she had done his, across the boudoir seat.

He marveled, as always, at the way she moved, at the play of firm muscles beneath smooth flesh, and his hands went out to her as she came onto the bed beside him and let her own hands move gently, lovingly, across chest and stomach and loins. He loved to watch her touching him. In the scores of times that she had done so there had never been the impression that it was done merely to please him, but rather that she derived as much enjoyment from it as he, perhaps even more. On occasion he had watched her more closely in this respect, attempting to see if perhaps this was just an attitude that she wished to portray for his benefit, but he had long ago dismissed that possibility. There could be no doubt that Anne was as much enamored of his body in every respect as she was with his mind and the things he said and did.

"Lots to talk about, sweetheart," he murmured, groaning faintly.

Her head, lying low on his stomach now and facing away, moved slightly in negation. The words were barely audible. "Love now; talk later."

The ice cubes in his barely touched drink had all but melted before he began to talk with her in earnest. Her head was couched in the hollow of his shoulder and her arm lay comfortably across his chest. Her hair, smelling delicately of the lemon shampoo she used, was close to his mouth and tendrils of it moved in little puffs of air from the words he spoke.

He began with the time he had left her last and retraced in summary his visit with Proctor, the return to Chicago, the conversation with Gordon and then with the President, and finally the long session with Boardman. He surprised and pleased himself with the manner in which subconsciously he edited what Boardman had said and rendered the HAB Theory down to its bare essence. By then she was sitting up facing him, her legs crossed Indian fashion in front of her, a look of intense concentration on her face. Her reaction was much the same as his had been to Boardman's words and her conviction of its truth surpassed his own.

"God," she murmured, "think of it! No wonder you were excited by what he said. And to think there was so much more, and yet now he's dead and it's gone with him. Little wonder you were upset and depressed."

"Not the only reason." He went on to tell of his telephone conversation with Gordon last night, and of the agent's swelling irritation in the knowledge that Grant had the information he needed and yet was not prepared to come through with it to him for the moment.

"He knows I have tapes of what Boardman said," Grant went on, "and he's strong on hearing them. Scared to death something's going to happen to me before he has his hands on them, and he'll be left hanging."

"You didn't tell him where you put them?"

"No. I've an idea he'd try to get them if he knew where they were. But I've promised them to him and I'll live up to that promise as soon as I can. I don't intend turning them over until I have duplicate tapes made or a transcript."

"I could do that for you," she said quickly. "Right here in the apartment. My recorder has the foot-stop and all."

He considered that and nodded slowly. "It's a thought," he admitted, "but that would take at least three or four full days of transcribing and I'm pretty sure Gordon's not going to hold still that long."

She obviously had had the same thought. "Then let me make a copy of the tape here from your machine onto mine. One day and we'd have it. Then you could give Gordon what he wants and I'd still be able to make a transcript for you."

He liked that idea and said they'd explore it a little more later, then went on to tell of the unsatisfactory encounter with Elizabeth Boardman just prior to his coming here. She touched his chest softly as he spoke, small lines of sympathetic understanding appearing in her expression.

"My poor darling. No wonder you were so low when you got here. What in the world will you do now?"

"Good question. Wish to hell I had a good answer to go along with it. Right now I don't have any idea. How do I go about gathering proofs for a theory it took him a lifetime to develop and prove? I'll have to move on it quickly and yet now I don't know which way to move. What might seem to be a solid proof to me would likely be knocked flat by any really competent geologist."

They talked more about it but gradually their conversation died away and they lay quietly together, bodies touching in a relaxed and pleasant manner, his hand caressing her back softly, with love, not passion.

The ring of the telephone was a shattering intrusion, jarring them both into alertness. She shook her head at his questioning glance and reached across him to lift the receiver in the midst of the second ring.

"Hello?"

He saw her eyes widen and she paled slightly. A needle of apprehension stabbed him. Her voice was a little shaky as she spoke again.

"*Who* is this, please?...I see...Hold on a moment. She clamped her hand over the mouthpiece and spoke to Grant in a whisper. "Who knows you're here?" His alarm spread and at the shake of his head she continued. "It's a man. He wouldn't give his name. Just said he *knows* you're here and he has to speak with you immediately."

He took the phone from her, hesitated, and then said, "John Grant here."

"Alex Gordon, Grant."

"How in the hell did you know to reach me here?"

Gordon ignored the question. "You saw Elizabeth Boardman today." It was a statement, not a query.

"I did. I told you I was going to. She's upset. Refused to help."

"That may be changed. Now she says it's imperative you get in touch with her immediately. Do it." His tone was peremptory.

Grant saw Anne was still fearful as she watched him and he put his hand on her knee reassuringly, letting her know who the caller was with his next words. "All right, Gordon, I will."

"I want to know what she says to you, Grant. We've had more than enough of being in the dark. We've cooperated with you all the way and now it's your turn. Call back as soon as you finish talking with her, understand?"

Grant's grip on Anne's knee was a little stronger. The fact that Gordon was no longer addressing him as *Mr.* Grant was not lost on him. "I'll call, he said. "I'll let you know what she wants. Beyond that, I'm making no promises."

"Bullshit!" The expletive cracked through the receiver loud enough for Anne to hear it. "Game time's over, man. You've carried the ball enough. You'll cooperate now."

There was no need to ask for an explanation. It seemed to Grant as if a hard knot had formed in his chest. His jaw muscles worked and brows drew together in a frown.

"I don't submit to threats, Gordon. I never have."

"You've never been vulnerable before," Gordon replied flatly.

"That may be, but it still holds. I've said I'll call you. I will."

He broke the connection with a finger on the cradle button and, still holding the phone, spoke to Anne. "Look up the Boardman number, will you?"

She moved nimbly over him, pulled the *Near West Suburbs* phone book from the rack and paged into it swiftly, ran a fingernail down a column of names, and then stopped on one. She read the number off to him and he punched the corresponding buttons on the digital plate as she did so. It was answered by a feminine voice on the third ring.

"John Grant. You wanted me to call?"

"Yes. An apology, first, for the way I acted toward you, Mr. Grant. It was unfair. I'm not normally so unreasonable."

"You were upset. That's understandable."

"Thank you. You're kinder than I deserve." Liz Boardman hesitated and then went on, "I found a letter my father left for me. It…changed my viewpoint. I'll cooperate in any way possible. Can you come back here now?"

Grant's pulse speeded up. "I'll be there in less than an hour."

A moment later he was dressing rapidly, recounting the conversations to Anne as he did so. She began dressing, too, but she was still concerned over how Alexander Gordon had known where Grant was.

John shrugged into his shirt and rapidly knotted his tie. He grimaced. "Surveillance, I suppose. I should've anticipated that. There may be some rough times ahead, Anne."

"We'll meet them," she answered quietly.

He paused with one arm in his suitcoat and smiled. Moving a step closer he kissed her lips and then turned back toward the phone, donning his coat the rest of the way as he did so. He touched seven buttons in succession on the dial plate and then spoke after a moment.

"Grant. She's going to cooperate all the way. I'm on my way out there."

"Good. I want to hear the tapes you made yesterday, Grant."

"You'll hear them. I'm not going all the way out to Skokie for them now, though. I'll bring them in to you first thing in the morning. That's a promise. Don't press me beyond that. It won't work. That's a promise, too."

Gordon allowed himself a little laugh. "You don't bend easily, Mr. Grant."

"I never have. I don't expect to begin now."

"What time will you come in tomorrow?"

Grant glanced at his watch. It was nearly three o'clock. "By eight, I think. No later than eight-thirty."

"I'll be waiting."

Grant looked toward Anne as he hung up. "You still want to help?" At her nod, he continued. "It'll be a hell of a big job. Do you know anyone in the building who has a tape recorder? Besides your own? One you can borrow right now?"

She nodded again. "Kina. She lives a couple of doors down on this floor. She's a Filipino. Sweet girl. Married to an architect. Eric Maxwell. She'll let me use hers, I know. She may not be home now, though. I'll check."

She rang the number and smiled as the phone was answered, quickly said what she needed, thanked the girl, and told her she'd be by to get it in a minute or two. Grant was waiting at the door. He motioned her to come along and she scooped up her keys. He led her swiftly to the bank of elevators and on the way down he explained.

"I'll need my own recorder over at the Boardman place, otherwise you wouldn't have had to borrow that other one. I told Gordon the Boardman tapes were at my house. They're not. They're locked in the trunk."

"You want me to copy them." She bobbed her head, eyes alight. "I'll do it, but I'll have to go out and get a couple of blank reels somewhere. I don't have any."

The elevator stopped and they stepped out in the garage area of the skyscraper. Grant didn't know where his car had been parked so they began walking briskly along the ramps looking and gradually going downward.

"I have some I can give you," he told her. "I loaded up with fresh tapes and a few extra spools before leaving the house this morning. Enough for me to use out there, too. It's going to be a long job for you. If you can get started before four o'clock, you'll be able to finish just in time for me to pick them up in the morning. There won't be much leeway." He raised an arm and pointed. "There's the car."

The ignition keys were in the switch, but the trunk key was not with them. Grant withdrew it from his coat pocket. Inside the trunk was his tape recorder, briefcase, and a shoe box. He opened the shoebox and took out two of the half-dozen new cellophane-wrapped tape boxes inside. A sudden thought struck him as he handed the boxes to Anne.

"I know yours is a four-track recorder, but what about the other girl's—Kina's?"

"I don't know."

"Good think I checked. It may not be. Take a couple more in case it's not."

He gave her the additional boxes, then opened the briefcase and gave her the two boxes containing his tapes of the interview with Boardman. They returned together to the elevators and he pressed both the Up and Down buttons. The Up car got there first. Holding the door open with his back, Grant held her close and kissed her. When they pulled apart, her eyes were glowing.

"For the first time, John, she said, "you really need me."

He kissed her again, lightly, briefly. "Shows you how wrong you can be," he said, smiling. "I've needed you for a long time, Lady."

The door closed between them and a moment later he was dropping to the main floor on the other elevator, where the garage attendant would take his ticket and bring his car down to him.

I I I

The telephone call for John had come about half an hour before and Marie had answered in a spiritless voice.

"I'm sorry," she replied to the request, "but Mr. Grant is not home at present. I'm his wife. May I ask who's calling, please?"

"This is Elizabeth Boardman, Mrs. Grant. Herbert Boardman's daughter. It's imperative that I contact your husband immediately. Is there any place where I could reach him?"

Another wave of the sick feeling flooded Marie. John was supposed to be at the Boardman house right now. That's where he said he was going when he left. Since he wasn't, then it was not unlikely, in view of the diaries, where he was: with A, whoever A might be. The train of logic had taken no more than a second or two. "I don't know for sure, Miss Boardman. I...don't have any number you can call, but let me check and perhaps I can locate him for you. If I do, I'll have him call you at once."

She'd hung up the telephone slowly after saying good-bye. She thought about her initial reaction and shook her head. Perhaps she was overreacting and had leaped to the wrong conclusion. It was a faint hope, but there nonetheless, and so she dialed the number written in ball-point pen on the small white business card still resting on the stand beside the phone. She recognized the voice that answered, even before he identified himself.

"Mr. Gordon, this is Mrs. Grant. I'm sorry to bother you, but would you by any chance happen to know where my husband is?"

There had been a slight pause. "As a matter of fact I do, Mrs. Grant."

"Oh, thank—" She caught herself. "Can you give me a number where I can call him?"

Gordon replied in measured words. "He is momentarily out of touch, Mrs. Grant, but I can get a message to him if it's important. Is there a problem?"

Marie had explained about Elizabeth Boardman's call, thanked Gordon for his assurance that he'd inform John right away, and hung up. Ever since then, she'd been wondering about it. Gordon's remarks had been reassuring, at first, but when she reconsidered them, he really hadn't told her much. The suspicions had returned, but with less strength than at first. There was a doubt now that those suspicions had grounds, and she clung to that doubt as if it were a lifeline.

The raft of papers in her lap was thicker than ever now and she paged back through them to those she had written most recently. The words that John had penned no longer struck her like hammer blows; her mind had rebelled from shock after shock and had thrown up a defensive screen of numbness. The words still penetrated and added to the vast ache within her, but they were expected words now; at this point she had come to expect anything, and so when some of the expectations became reality in his words, they were not great shocks. They merely hurt deeply, very deeply.

...Marie has begun to sense the change in me. I find her studying me when she thinks I am unaware of it. She continues to probe in progressively less subtle ways, attempting to ascertain if any cause for my gloominess exists other than that of my obvious inability to become fired up over any new creative project. I work hard and long, but we both know

*that the work being done, while necessary, is certainly more mechanical than creative. She is so deeply in love with me and since I am, in her often repeated words, the absolute core of her universe, then anything affecting me affects her very deeply as well, even though she may not know the cause. In this present situation there is no real way for me to explain. The thought that I might possible be able to love more than one woman would be alien to her understanding. To admit that although I love her deeply, I love A with an equal depth but in an entirely different way would serve no purpose whatever. It would only crush her and make her feel that I do not love her at all. It's a sad thing, because the last thing I care to do is to hurt Marie in any way, yet I am what I am and feel what I feel and I cannot change that. It is strange to me that I can, on the one hand be so gloriously elevated by what has happened, while on the other be wallowing in a mire of depression on a different plane. I grow increasingly fearful that I may someday hurt Marie very badly, and I don't want to do so. I do love her, but my love is not singularly channelized like hers. One would think that I could not do what I am doing if I really loved her. I don't understand it myself for, as God is my witness, I **do** love her. I also truly love A. All I can do at this stage is to continue to try to keep this latter fact from Marie, which is, in itself, a disagreeable thing to me because I have always loathed deception.*

Marie paused and sniffed, pulled a pale blue tissue from a box at hand and dabbed at her eyes, then blew her nose softly. The rims of her eyes and nostrils were red and she looked as if she were suffering from a cold, though she was not. John Grant knew her well indeed; it *was* incomprehensible to her that he could love another woman at the same time as he claimed to love her. She wadded the tissue into a small blue ball and dropped it into a wastebasket before resuming her reading, this time an entry dated almost a fortnight after the one she had just finished and much longer than any that had preceded it.

…Self-analysis is never a simple matter and it may be entirely impossible, but nevertheless I will embark here on what will be as close as I can get to it. I'm aware that it becomes only too easy to justify in one's own mind those actions which may not honestly be justifiable. To be of any value whatsoever, introspection must be logical, rational, extensive and, above all, thoroughly and unwaveringly honest. With these guidelines in mind at all times, I will begin. It could be argued, I suppose, that what I feel for A is no more than a sudden infatuation founded on a longtime desire for sex with someone different, or some sort of effort to recapture a youthfulness I no longer possess. In all honestly, I would flatly deny such an argument. Of infatuation there is none, if my understanding of the meaning of the word is correct, as I believe it to be. Yet, I would be less than honest if I did not admit that sexual craving for someone different was not what led me into this situation to begin with. I have never been consciously concerned about my age and never was subject to the "growing-old-blues" which afflict many middle-aged men. Still, I am acutely aware of the difference in age between A and myself; with a gap of eighteen years between us, I am, in actuality, old enough to be her father. So, then, what do I feel is the true motivating factor that has placed me where I am at present? The dominant motive is love; of that there is no doubt in my mind. On the one hand my love for Marie dictates that I pursue no course which might ultimately be of anguish to her. On the other hand, my love for A precludes any room for relinquishment. That is my quandary; the two loves are diametrically opposed. Further, above and beyond my love for Marie, there is my duty to her, and I know that in following my present course I am not living up to the requirements of such duty. Some time ago I commented on what

the meaning was of strength of character. Maybe now I perceive its meaning more clearly. Perhaps strength of character lies in having the resolve—no, not resolve, but rather the **capacity**—*in having the capacity to fulfill such obligation as that which I owe to Marie, to the utmost degree. If such be true, then evidently my strength of character is hardly as flawless as I would like to believe, for my well-considered inclination is to say to hell with duty, responsibility, obligation or whatever else one might care to call it. It would be pointless for me to try to justify what I am doing, or try to excuse myself for it. Yet, what do I do about living with* **myself**? *If I bow to the demands of obligation, how do I justify to myself living a life which is a charade, pretending a happiness and contentment outwardly which is absent inside? One might be able to delude others in this respect, but it is not so easy to fool one's self. Thus, perhaps strength of character, if that's what it is, is really more a psychological detriment than asset. How many people, I wonder, are living out their lives wholly unhappy because they are fulfilling an obligation to someone else. Doesn't obligation to* **self** *count somewhere in there? None of this sort of consideration does very much to help me at the moment. In my own present case, I fear, discretion must serve as the better part of strength of character. From the standpoint of logic and honesty, I know that what I am doing is not right. So where does that leave me? Precisely where I expected to be: in a social sense I am morally, sensibly, logically and matrimonially at fault, yet continuing on course with sails billowing full. I am probably a fool, but not a blind one. What I do now I am doing with my eyes open to all the ramifications which might result, and still find myself not only with no desire to change direction, but wholly powerless to do so any longer, if such were my wont.*

IV

If anything, the world press became even more demanding of information regarding the assassination attempt on President Sanders following the death of Herbert Allen Boardman. Here was one of the most explosive stories of the century and yet, as far as dissemination of news to the press was concerned, there had been virtually nothing of substance released. Now, with Boardman's death, allegedly through a heart attack, the newspapers, radio and television were expressing their agitation in blistering editorials.

"Why should it be," queried the *Manchester Guardian* with controlled irritation, *"that the Head of State of one of the most powerful nations on earth can be gunned down and then this notable event be followed by a deadly silence from authorities? Probably no other major news event in the past three decades or more has resulted in so many unanswered questions. Certainly we are aware that this is an internal matter affecting the United States, but as a token of courtesy to concerned people here and in other lands throughout the world, some degree of responsible information is expected from American authorities."*

That was perhaps the least forceful of the multitude of comments which appeared. With the absence of hard facts, dark speculations were rampant. *Le Monde* in Paris broadly hinted that perhaps President Sanders was still alive but no more than a vegetable because of brain damage from the gunshot wound. *"Who, after all,"* the editorial asked, *"has really seen this American President since the attack? It is rumored that he has left Chicago and returned to his nation's capital but is 'resting in seclusion' at Georgetown University Hospital. If the President is indeed well, then he has a moral obligation to his own countrymen to appear before them on television, from his hospital bed if necessary, to assure them of his well-being. If he is not well, as reported, then what forces are responsible for keeping this from the people?"*

In Mecca, Saudi Arabia, *Al Nadwa* was not in the least subtle in its response to the news of Boardman's death. *"What fools do the Americans take the rest of the world to be? Can anyone with a degree of intelligence really believe that Herbert Boardman died of nothing more than an ordinary heart attack? Come now! Tell us, if you dare, who killed him? Who forever sealed the lips of the only man who could clear up so many mysteries?"*

The Hungarian newspaper *Esti Hirlap* in Budapest skirted the same issue but from a different viewpoint. *"The renowned American author, John Charles Grant, apparently was permitted a long period of time alone with the man identified as Herbert Boardman. Is it not well within the realm of possibility that this writer provided the gunman with the wherewithal to destroy himself?"*

The popular James Sylvester editorial on *The CBS Evening News* was no more than a series of very pointed questions asked by Sylvester himself and reflecting the questions being raised by newsmen everywhere in the United States.

"Why is it," the commentator asked in his familiar fatherly tones, "that Presidential Press Secretary Steven Lace has adamantly refused to answer any questions regarding the President and Herbert Boardman? By whose order has he been so thoroughly muzzled? Where is the body of Boardman? Is it being autopsied, or has it already been hastily buried or cremated? What was the connection between author John Grant and a would-be ninety-four-year-old assassin, and why does Grant, who has always exemplified integrity in reporting in America, remain silent and out of touch? Is it not a strange coincidence that a man who allegedly sought to murder the President of the United States and also who allegedly planned to fail in the attempt should himself die of alleged 'natural causes' so quickly after his deed? Why has President Sanders made no statement? Failing that, why has Vice-President Barrington made no statement? Failing that, why has no responsible government authority stepped forward to tell the American people, as it is their right to know, just what is happening in their country these days? Is it not time that these and a multitude of other questions are answered by *someone*? Why is America being kept in the dark?"

V

In his room at Georgetown University Hospital, Robert Morton Sanders was eating a hearty breakfast of hotcakes and sausage. Despite a badly bruised forehead, he sat at a small table and looked quite fit in his own garb of blue silk pajamas and maroon corduroy robe snugly belted at the waist. Comfortable old leather slippers were on his stockinged feet and his hair was neatly combed. Between healthy bites of the breakfast and cautious sips of steaming coffee, he was looking at the envelope of a thick letter he'd just received. The handwriting was precise and distinctive and he recognized it immediately as that of his friend Mark Shepard. It helped to erase the dour expression he had worn ever since putting down this morning's *Washington Post*. He was smiling by the time he had the envelope open and he noticed that it had been dated by Mark on the day before the shooting by Boardman.

Istanbul, May 21

Dear Bob,

Yes, you old duffer, I'm still in the land of the Turks, which may surprise you since in my last letter—a couple of weeks ago, was it?—I told you I'd be heading for the good ol' green hills of Wyoming in a day or two, then back to Columbia to continue molding young minds. The reason I didn't leave as planned is simple; I've turned up some interesting charts here. Three, to be specific. The first (and by far least important) is an old copy of a Mercator—the original done in 1583 using the projections he (Gerhard Kremer, alias Gerhardus Mercator) developed—but the copy, not dated, is poorly rendered. Probably done by some Turkish navigator and valuable only for its age (I estimate around 1450) but important to me because it shows an interesting evolution in Mercator's Projection from his first use of it 15 years earlier. (And, in case you're wondering, it has no real value in respect to the search I've been making for material dealing with my special and important study, which I've detailed to you in previous letters.)

The second and third charts are another matter entirely. Those—hold your hat!—show all the earmarks of being genuine Ptolemys! Let me backtrack a bit to fill you in, in orderly progression.

As you'll recall, my last letter was from Izmir, on the Aegean, where I'd had such high hopes of turning up something significant (something that finally would justify this sabbatical) but was horribly disappointed. The day after I wrote you, I started back toward Istanbul in, of all things, an old Ford (circa 1935) in surprisingly good running condition— a real museum piece that'd be worth plenty on the antique car market back home. Anyway, my driver (Dimitri something-or-other) was originally from Kutanya, a small city we had to pass through, about halfway to Istanbul. (Incidentally, I was heading for Istanbul because I had a little more research to do there before folding my tent and moving on to Ankara for the final wrap-up and then home.) I asked him—Dimitri—if there were any shops in Kutanya that sold old books or maps or whatever, and he lit up and said he'd take me to a very good old shop which (by marvelously convenient coincidence) was very near to where he was raised, and thus, while I looked around, he could visit with some of his relatives there. I figured it was a waste of time and he was putting me on in order to get into his old neighborhood for a visit, but I thought, Well, what the hell, it might be an interesting break in the long drive if nothing else.

To make a long story short, the shop was a real dustbin. Reminded me of the dilapidated so-called antique shops off the beaten path in the U.S.—you know, an incredible mass of pure junk that's been discarded for God knows how long. After about half an hour of poking around, I was convinced there was nothing of any value there and was getting ready to leave when I happened to notice a big old trunk—the chest type, with straps and latches and the upper lid bowed upward. It was off in a corner gathering dust and spiderwebs, full of gouges and scrapes and with the latches broken and the straps falling apart with dry rot, so it looked pretty disreputable. I really can't say for sure what prompted me to take a closer look, but I raised the lid and looked inside. It was empty. The cloth lining of the sides and bottom was downright grubby and ragged, but then I noticed that the cloth covering the underside of the lid was not of the same weave and somewhat cleaner—still very old but newer than the rest.

The shopkeeper was at the door just then, yelling at some old woman (who was screaming back) and so, just on a sudden hunch, I got out my pocketknife and made a tiny slit in the newer cloth, pulled it back a little and nearly shit my pants when I saw about a half-inch of coastline! Had no idea what in the hell it was, but I didn't want to around the shopkeeper's suspicions by looking any further. Called him over and casually asked him how much he wanted for the trunk. He figured he had a live one nibbling and promptly said a thousand lira. I laughed and offered fifty. We haggled for a while and then I gave my "final" offer of 250 ($15) and when he shook his head, as I knew he would, I started walking out. He ran after me, also as I knew he would, and lectured me about taking advantage of a poor shopkeeper who had twenty kids to support (he was only about thirty himself, so they must start early over here) and that I was taking the bread out of their mouths, etc., etc. When I wouldn't budge, he finally agreed to the figure. Although he tried to pretend he'd been rooked, it was obvious that it was probably two or three times more than he ever thought he's make on it, but I let on that I thought I'd made a pretty fantastic deal (which wasn't hard to do under the circumstances). My driver shook his head at my "foolish purchase," but we loaded it into the back seat and got it to Istanbul all right.

*Now for the climax. Behind locked doors and closed drapes in my room, I carefully stripped away all of the cloth inside, and there were the charts, glued—**glued**, by God!—to the underside of the lid. The glue was old and cracked, so it didn't turn out to be quite the trauma I imagined it would be getting them off, though I took my time and completely dismantled the lid in order to do so. Worked all night on it; first on getting the three charts, stuck together, off the lid, and then on separating them from each other. Fortunately, one was smaller and this had been glued in place first, face up, to the trunk lid. At this point I thought there were only two maps. The second, which extended beyond the first about two inches on each side of the width and twice that on each side of the length, was glued only where those overlapping edges met the wood, although there were a few areas where the glue had spread out and stuck the two charts together. I got them off the lid without damage and then separated them from each other with only one little damaged area in the smaller map, and that, happily, was in an ocean area where no writing or charting was involved. But the great surprise was finding, wholly unexpectedly, another chart, still smaller, nestled between the two but not attached to them. I now have temporary backings on them and they're covered with clear acetate while I study them.*

Bob, dammit, I'm so excited I could pop! I really believe at least one's a Ptolemy original, and the other might be even more important a discovery than that. If so, they're priceless, but I couldn't care less about the monetary aspect. Their value to science is inestimable and, even more than that, they're immeasurably important to the "project" you know all about that's kept me researching for so many years.

*I've gone on too long already, but I had to let you know about them, in view of your past interest. Remember how we used to sit and talk about finding "it" for hours? Well, this is **it**! I'll keep you up to date on what I determine from them. I'm all inspired now, and all thought of going home until I absolutely have to has fled. Expect I'll stay most of the summer now, checking them out against existing maps, and only come back when I have to in order to prepare for fall semester. Already I think I've located sites for a couple of "digs" here which might be tremendous.*

Hope you and Grace are in the best of health. Give the First Lady a kiss for me and tell her my bachelorhood remains intact (unlike my virginity), simply because the only girl I ever met that I might have been inclined to marry hooked up with some southpaw joker who became President.

Fondly,
Mark

P.S. Kee-ripes! I never even told you the scope of the charts. On one (the Ptolemy?) it's primarily eastern Mediterranean, Aegean. and Black seas, westward as far as the Gulf of Sirte in Libya, and especially fine in the coastal areas of Greece and Turkey. The other is the strangest chart I've ever seen and if it turns out to be what I think it is, it'll be one of the most important ancient documents ever found. More later. M.S.

President Sanders refolded Mark Shepard's letter and slipped it back into its envelope, a grin still spreading his lips at Mark's closing words. Continuing to think about his lifelong friend, he finished off the breakfast on his plate and poured himself another cup of coffee from the thermal pot on the table. He remembered their early years together and a warm feeling filled him.

Robert Sanders had a handful of very close friends, but Mark had always been closest, ever since they were boyhood pals in elementary and then high school. Even then Mark had been a map nut, hardly able to pass a service station without going inside to see if they had any maps he didn't have yet. And his own ability at drawing them, even at that young age, was pronounced. Sanders still had the truly beautiful map Mark had drawn and given him as a Christmas gift when they were seniors at Lander High School—a finely executed map of Wyoming's Fremont County, itself larger than the State of Massachusetts, with all the places marked where the two of them had had special experiences together: the place where Mark had fallen and broken his leg and Sanders had carried him four miles to Dick Titterington's empty camp and made him comfortable before lighting out to get help; the places where each of them, on trips together, had bagged their first elk or moose or antelope or bighorn; the places where they'd caught, for them, record-sized trout. It was a memento Sanders treasured highly.

When high school had ended for them, they'd gone their separate ways—Sanders to Harvard to study for a life in politics, Mark to Berkeley to major in cartography. A continent apart, they'd lost touch with one another then, except for the usual Christmas cards, each too busy molding his own life to maintain correspondence, though they'd tried at first. It was more Sanders's fault than Mark's that it had lapsed; Mark had always been a more dedicated correspondent. A few years after college—where Sanders met and married Grace Vandelever— came the war in Vietnam and he became a jet fighter pilot. Then came that wonderful, totally unexpected meeting with Mark in Saigon. He was in the air force, too, in the Cartographic Section, engaged in reconnaissance flights over North Vietnam to take aerial photos and draw maps from them. Their friendship brightly rekindled, they'd spent practically every free hour together after that, right up to the night before the mission in which Sanders's jet had been shot down.

In the years which followed, they finally were reunited a second time in Wyoming. Mark was then an associate professor at the University of Colorado. They saw each other occasionally after that and, when that became impossible in the ensuing decades, they kept in touch, faithfully now, by mail—but, again, Mark writing much more often and at greater length than Sanders.

Over the past four or five years, Mark had been following up on a special research project of his own dealing with ancient maps and ancient people. He was now a full professor at Columbia University, but had gone on sabbatical last January to further his research—research which, if it proved conclusive, would set the scientific world agog, according to Mark. Now one of the foremost authorities in the world on ancient maps, Dr. Mark Shepard rarely became excited over anything. For him to wax so enthusiastically over his discovery of the charts indicated they must indeed be quite a momentous find.

A light, tinkling ring came from the white telephone on the table across from the President. In reaching for it, the elbow of his robe came into contact with a small pool of maple syrup on his plate and he grunted with exasperation. Holding the phone to his ear with one hand and dabbing at the sticky stain on the corduroy with a napkin held in the other, he rumbled, "Yes?"

"Mr. President," the brisk feminine voice said, unintimidated at his tone, "I have Mr. Gordon on the line for you." It was his secretary, Mrs. Tierney, who had set up temporary office quarters in the adjoining room, to which special telephone and facsimile lines had been run. All calls were being funneled through her.

"Ah, good. Put him on, Hazel."

"Yes, sir." There was a faint click and she added, "The President is on the line, Mr. Gordon."

"Alex? Good morning. How's it going out there?"

"Good morning, Mr. President. Everything seems to be in hand here, considering what's occurred."

"Fine. I want you to come back here right away. Bring Mr. Grant with you. Bill Byrd's on his way to Chicago now. He'll reach O'Hare by nine your time. How soon can you leave?"

"It's eight o'clock here now, sir. I've been informed that Mr. Grant is presently en route downtown in his car. He should arrive here within a half-hour. Allowing a little preparation time, we should be able to get to the airport and be ready for takeoff by nine-thirty, if that's all right. That would put us on the ground at Andrews around quarter after twelve, your time."

"Excellent. The chopper will be waiting when you land and will bring you to the park area adjacent to the hospital here. Now, what about Grant? Has he opened up any yet?"

"As yet, sir, he hasn't. He doesn't bend very easily to pressure. As I mentioned to you yesterday, he evidently got quite a bit from Boardman before the old man died. He was with him for around fourteen hours and had fully expected to get a great deal more in the succeeding days. I believe he taped the entire session, even during their breaks to eat. Never turned the recorder off except to change tracks on the tape. However, he was very reluctant about disclosing anything yet. Since yesterday afternoon he's been out at the Boardman house in Oak Park. Boardman's daughter has given him full access to her father's papers, and he's evidently worked the entire night on them. He promised he'd be in this morning no later than eight-thirty, at which time he would give me the tapes he recorded in his session with Boardman."

"Any reaction at all on his part to what he's gotten?"

"Nothing specific, Mr. President." Gordon hesitated and then went on. "I talked to him on the phone about ten o'clock last night while he was at the Boardman house and I have to say that I sense a hell of an excitement that he's keeping well under control."

"Now what do you suppose that means?"

"I don't know, sir."

Sanders heaved a deep sigh and was silent for the space of several breaths. "I've got to give the press something, Alex. They're snapping at our heels and there's already hell to pay because of no official statement. Capitol Hill's raising a ruckus, too. The only thing that'll mollify all of them for the moment is if I give them a definite time that I'll make a statement. I don't want to make this a press conference. Not yet. There are still too many question marks." He sighed again, then chuckled. "Well, let's hope Grant has something worthwhile. Come a-running, Alex. We don't operate too well around here without you."

"Yes, sir, Mr. President. Thank you. Good-bye, sir."

The President did not hang up. He jiggled the cradle button and immediately Mrs. Tierney came back on the line. "Sir?

"Hazel, is Steve out there?"

"Yes, sir, he is. Just down the hall at the head nurse's desk."

"Send him in, will you please?"

He hung up without waiting for her reply and bent to finish his coffee. He was just wiping his mouth on the napkin when a light tapping came on the door and the White House press secretary entered.

Steve Lace looked even more harried than customary. He wore, as he invariably did, a vest beneath his suitcoat, and he walked with a springy step, though not quite as jauntily today as normally, and he frequently used his index finger to press his large-lensed horn-rimmed glasses back into place as they kept slipping down on his nose—the usual indication that he was nervous.

Robert Sanders cocked a quizzical eyebrow at him as he came to a stop near the table, recognizing the signs. "Getting to you, are they, Steve?"

"It's getting a little rougher, sir," Lace answered. "Not as hectic here as at the White House, though." He grinned suddenly, a grin that was warm, ingenuous, and made him look even younger than his late twenties. "They're building up a pretty good head of steam that they're going to have to let loose on somebody pretty soon."

"Well," Sanders said, "I guess we've kept you on the hook long enough." He was amused at the relieved expression that came into Lace's face at that. "You can tell them that I'll have a statement for them tomorrow morning at nine." He held up a hand as Lace started to speak. "I know it's a time of day the networks don't like, but it can't be helped. I don't know any way it can be done any sooner, and I certainly don't want to hold off until tomorrow evening. Everyone's mad enough as it is. A simple statement, that's all, and very brief at that. No questions, but you can hint at the possibility of either a follow-up statement of greater length in about a week, or maybe even a press conference. No promises, though."

"Yes, sir. Tomorrow morning at nine. They'll be glad to hear it. *I'm* glad to hear it." He grinned boyishly again and turned to leave.

"Steve."

Lace stopped and turned around. The President had risen and, limping slightly on the prosthetic foot, was walking toward the bed. When he reached it he sat on the edge and began removing his slippers.

"Steve, get some rest this morning if you can. They have a room set aside here if you want to use it. I've an idea we may have a busy night. I want you close at hand."

"Yes, sir. Anything else?"

"Yes. Tell Hazel to ring me at noon sharp. No calls or people until then. Have her order a lunch for three for about one o'clock."

"Yes, sir. Good morning, sir."

By the time Lace quietly closed the door behind him, Robert Morton Sanders had already taken off his robe and was stretching out comfortably on the bed. Within mere minutes he was asleep.

V I

Although his eyes were grainy from lack of sleep and his muscles ached from the long hours of working in Boardman's study, John Grant was highly keyed up. He could remember no time in the past, irrespective of the project on which he may have been working, when he had been so excited over researching. Ordinarily, researching was the most difficult part of his work as a writer. It was often a road strewn with dead ends and difficulties, a long, slow, onerous business requiring enormous patience and self-discipline in the willingness to wade through vast quantities of deadly dull material in the hope of picking up here and there the bright nuggets of information which made his work come to life. Grant felt very strongly about the value of thorough researching and had once had written in his diary:

As I look at it, no other single factor is more important to good writing—non-fiction and fiction alike—than thoroughness in researching. However talented a writer may be, his writing will remain superficial if he has not the determination to research far beyond the needs of any given project before he ever begins placing his thoughts on paper. No writer worth his salt ever utilizes all he knows on his subject in the actual writing; only what he needs to put across well the point he is making. Yet, even though he may not use it all in what he writes, somehow there is conveyed in what he has written, the subtle sense that he knows a great deal more about his subject than he has put down. Conversely, so too it becomes clear to the reader in a similarly subtle manner that the writer knows nothing beyond what he has written when that writer has failed to research well.

Grant had not anticipated remaining at the Boardman house for more than a few hours on this first visit, but after the initial amenities had been concluded—somewhat uncomfortably at first because of the unsatisfactory encounter earlier in the day—he had begun working with Herbert Boardman's papers and quickly became totally immersed.

Now and again Elizabeth Boardman and Paul Neely came into the study with coffee and a bite to eat, talked with him briefly, but soon left him to his own devices, sensing his need to be undisturbed in his work. He'd gotten a call from Gordon about ten and then, close to midnight, had paused in his work to call Marie. Her attitude had been stiff and formal; she was politely glad he'd been able to get into the Boardman papers and, yes, if he was going to continue working even later, why just go ahead because, after all, she wasn't his keeper, was she? He'd hung up slowly, frowning, wondering again what was bothering her lately and knowing that sooner or later it would come to a head and they'd have it out. Within minutes he had become lost again in his studies of the Boardman papers.

He recorded frequently, reading material onto tape that he knew would be essential, but just as frequently he took handwritten notes in his own peculiar form of shorthand developed through years of interviewing and similar researching. Almost before he realized it the dawn had come and the tantalizing aroma of bacon and eggs cooking had wafted to his nostrils from the kitchen. He'd eaten with Elizabeth and Paul and then gathered up his notes and recorder preparatory to leaving. Before doing so, he called Marie, knowing she'd be up getting the children ready for school, and explained he'd have to go downtown to see Alexander Gordon before coming home. Immediately following that he called Anne and, though their conversation was short, it was much more pleasant than the one with Marie had been. Anne sounded weary but nonetheless excited. Only a quarter-hour earlier she'd finished copying the tapes. Throughout the night she had sat up listening to what they contained as the copying progressed, thoroughly fascinated by it all. Now she was preparing to shower.

John told her he'd be leaving Oak Park in a few minutes and would reach downtown in roughly forty minutes. She promised to meet him in front of Marina City with the tapes and he could drop her off at her office on Michigan Avenue on his way to the meeting with Gordon.

Now, moving eastward on the Eisenhower Expressway, which was practically bumper-to-bumper with the normal early morning work traffic, Grant reflected on the night's efforts. While he knew there was still a great deal of work for him to do in collating and then summarizing the badly disorganized Boardman papers, and in other areas as well, he had accumulated enough of the data he needed to become thoroughly convinced of the validity of the HAB Theory. The proofs for that theory, which Herbert Boardman had alluded to in their talk, were indeed impressive. Some of these had been included in Boardman's book, *The Eccentric Earth*, a copy of which Grant had found on a shelf in the study, but those alone had not been as thoroughly conclusive as others that he found in material Boardman had developed long after the book had been published. And of these he had yet barely scratched the surface. Over twenty thousand pages of information, plus maps and sketches and similarly related material, were in the Boardman files. Each of the proofs Grant was discovering opened whole new avenues of research and each was tremendously exciting in its own way. The ramifications became ever-more stupefying the deeper he delved and it had been only with the greatest of regret that he had wound things up for the time being.

His plans were to get this meeting with Gordon, as quickly as possible and then go on home where he would shower and shave, sleep for around six hours, and then, refreshed, return to the Boardman house for another long stint of uninterrupted research. From the extent of Boardman's files, he estimated that he probably could pretty well complete his work there in perhaps half a dozen sessions of the nature of this one just concluded.

The Eisenhower Expressway swept into the downtown area, plunging beneath the massive United States Post Office building, over the south branch of the Chicago Rive and emptying out onto Congress Parkway. At

Dearborn Street, a few blocks later, Grant turned left and drove through the Loop, then across the main body of the Chicago River, on which Marina City fronted. He turned up onto the rampway leading to the entry area and saw Anne standing there waiting.

She was dressed in a crisp white pleated mini-skirt and pastel leaf-green blouse with a collar high in the back and widely flaring in front. Her raven hair fell in lovely swirls over her shoulders to mid-back, with one strand over the front of her right shoulder and curling exquisitely onto the swell of her breast. She was an absolute knockout and looked as fresh and alert as if she had enjoyed a good, full night's rest, though Grant knew she hadn't been to bed at all.

Anne saw him only an instant later and waved before running to meet him, holding her white shoulder-strap purse snugly to her side with one hand, her breasts bouncing freely and excitingly with each step. She was inside the car, shoving his briefcase out of the way and kissing him hungrily almost before he was stopped. When they pulled apart, he grinned.

"You are the most gorgeous thing a man could ever hope to start his day by seeing!"

"Flattery," she said, moving over close beside him as the car began moving toward the down ramp onto State Street, "will get you anywhere at any time. Like right now."

She took his right hand and placed it on her leg above the knee and then slid it smoothly up the inside of her leg as far as it could go. The sheerness of her pantyhose and warmth of her body made him nearly dizzy with the need of her, and he gripped the inner thigh almost savagely.

"Ummm," she murmured, "if it weren't for the fact that they'd probably put us in separate beds in the hospital, I'd almost welcome the wreck we're going to have if you keep driving like this."

He had pulled out onto State Street in a turn to the south that was much too wide. A green Checker Cab was forced to veer sharply to avoid collision and the driver leaned on his horn and shouted some sort of obscenity as he passed. Grant straightened out from the turn just before he would have run into the bridge abutment for the Chicago River separating northbound and southbound traffic. He put both hands on the steering wheel and puffed out his cheeks with a gusty exhalation. His trousers had become uncomfortably tight in the crotch and his eye corners wrinkled with amusement as, with some reluctance, he withdrew his hand from where it was nested and let it come to rest pleasantly but less hungrily on her leg as they crossed over Wacker Drive. When he turned left off State onto Washington Street, she began rummaging in her purse and brought out the two tape boxes.

"These are your originals," she said. "Good thing you gave me four instead of two. Kina's machine was only two-track. Just about filled up all four tapes. I'll put these in your briefcase."

"What'd you do with the copies?"

"They're safe. I put them in that combination-lock-latch suitcase of mine in the closet. God, but it was exciting listening to you and the old man talking together like that. It's really a valid theory, isn't it, John?"

"I think so. Everything I came across last night in his papers locked it in more solidly. I'll tell you more about it later on." He turned left again on Michigan Avenue heading north. "Listen, I've had a thought. I've got an enormous job facing me there at Boardman's. Suppose I take you out with me next time as a research assistant? You know what I'm doing and looking for now, and it would be a hell of a help."

"Really?" She was excited at the prospect. "Of course! Just give me a little warning so I can give Louise some—"

"Louise?"

"Louise Maas," she said. "The woman who helps me. I'll have to give her instructions for keeping matters running smoothly here at the agency."

He pulled to the curb in front of the 333 Michigan Avenue Building and she opened her door, leaned over and kissed him, then slid out with a flash of long, beautifully turned legs. Several businessmen passing on the sidewalk ogled openly, appreciatively, and nearly collided.

"Call me, darling," she said, still leaning in the door.

"I'll always call you darling," he replied, reaching out and squeezing her hand. "Okay. I'll be in touch again as soon as possible. And Anne—thanks."

"I'm the one to say thanks. I'm so excited over this whole thing that I know I won't get a blooming thing accomplished in the office today. Thank God I've got good ol' Louise to lean on." A horn blared loudly behind them and she added hastily, "'Bye now, Sweetheart."

She shut the door and strode briskly into the building as Grant got the car moving again. A few minutes later he was parking in the Superior Street garage across from the hospital. As he got out of the car with the portable recorder and briefcase in his hands, a long black Cadillac pulled up behind with two men in the front seat and one in the back, who was Alexander Gordon.

"You're punctual, Mr. Grant," he said, his dark face projecting from the open window. "Which is a good thing, because we're going places. Bring your recorder and the tapes and let's go."

Grant was surprised at the encounter. "Go where?" he asked. "Aren't we going into the hospital?"

"No, not this one. With that mob of newsmen waiting down there we'd lose a quarter-hour at least. We can't afford the time." He watched as the agent on the passenger side of the front seat got out and opened the back door of the Cadillac for the writer. Grant was ironically sure that more than simple courtesy was involved. He climbed in and settled himself beside Gordon, who continued, "We're leaving for Washington immediately. We'll be seeing the President at Georgetown University Hospital as soon as we get there. I hope you've got some good solid information for him."

"Washington! Cripes, Gordon, I can't go like this. Look at me; I haven't been to bed and I need a change of clothes and a shower and shave. I'm logy. That's a hell of a condition for me to present myself to the President in. Can we swing by my house for just a few minutes, at least, to let me freshen up and tell my wife where we're going?"

Gordon shook his head, took the briefcase from him, and placed it on the floor between his own feet. "No time," he said curtly as Grant put his recorder on the floor between them. "Move it out, Ed."

The big car lurched forward and went down the circular exit ramp with an almost continuous squealing of tires until it reached the bottom and straightened out. Gordon glanced at the briefcase and recorder.

"You said yesterday you couldn't give me the tapes then because they were at your house and you didn't want to go all the way out to Skokie to get them. Yet, you went directly from Marina City to Boardman's and then directly back downtown from there this morning, and here you are with the tapes. Your cooperation with us, Mr. Grant, is leaving something to be desired."

Gordon was obviously no man to underestimate at any time, and the writer was expressionless as he replied with a distinct chill to his voice.

"You've been having me followed, Gordon. I don't like that."

"Did you really expect you wouldn't be?" There was no trace of sympathy in Gordon's tone. "The world is full of things we don't necessarily like, Mr. Grant, but we accept them because we don't have any choice. In this present case, *you* don't have any choice. None at all. You're under a microscope, man, until we can decide just where in the hell you stand."

V I I

"You certainly sound better than last time we talked, Pussycat." Relief was evident in Susan Carpenter's voice.

Anne smiled and switched the receiver to her other ear so she could lie more comfortably as they talked. "I am better, Mother. Much. All of a sudden he needs me—I mean really *needs* me—more than he ever has before."

"That's wonderful, dear. I'm so glad I've finally had a chance to see him."

Anne was bewildered. "See him? How could you have seen him?"

"On television, silly, where else? Haven't you been watching? They showed him going into the hospital there. They tried to get him to talk, but he wouldn't say much. Honey, this whole business is so exciting! What's his connection with it all, anyway?"

"I really can't talk about it, Mother. Only to say that it's a lot more important than anyone realizes right now."

"And you're in on it, too?"

"Well, to a certain extent. Maybe more before long."

"You'll *have* to tell me all about it, Pussycat. Just think, my little Annie caught up in all this intriguing business involving the President! I'd never have believed it."

Anne was silent, knowing her mother's feelings would be hurt if she knew there was no possibility of Anne's telling her all about it. Susan Carpenter had never been noted for her ability to keep things to herself. The pause in their conversation lengthened.

"You're calling from the office, dear?"

"No. I'm in the apartment."

Susan expressed instant concern. "Why? You're not ill, are you?"

"No. Just pooped. I went in for a little while, but had to knock off. I didn't get to bed at all last night and after about an hour in the office this morning I found myself nodding. Nothing to worry about."

"Did you have fun, Pussycat?" A sly note crept in.

"Fun? When? What are you talking about?"

"Last night, with him. John. My God, Anne, he's beautiful! If I'd known what he looked like before you and he got so firmly entrenched, I'd've been there getting my claws into him before you had a chance to." She giggled.

Anne frowned. There was a quality to the words that she didn't appreciate. Susan had spoken in a jocular manner, but Anne knew her mother well enough to realize that there was a strong element of truth in what she said. And Susan was herself a very attractive woman. When Anne said nothing, Susan continued. "Baby, how old is John?"

"Forty-six."

"*Forty-six!* He looks so much younger than that. Do you know that means he's only two years younger than I?"

"I know it, and I also know what you're going to say next—that he's eighteen years older than I." Her voice took on a cold edge. "Hands off, Mother. Don't even consider it! Not for one moment. I'm fighting one battle like that already. I don't intend to engage in another. I mean it."

"My, you *are* defensive, aren't you? I've never liked it when you talk in that tone to me, Anne. You know that."

The brittleness remained. "I know. We usually reserve that for our face-to-face encounters. Which is why we have so few of them. We both know that I'm aware of what you're capable of, Mother, so I'll say this only once." There was measured menace in the words which followed. "He's my man, now and always, and no one is going to get him away. No one!"

An exaggerated sweetness crept into Susan Carpenter's reply. "Someone already has, Pussycat."

"No! He may be living with her now, but not for much longer. He's mine, not hers. He knows it and I know it, and she'll be finding out damned soon."

"You really do need some sleep, Anne." A stiffness was in her mother's voice now. "It should have been self-evident that I was just teasing you about him. I have no interest whatever in your John Grant, except insofar as your interests are concerned. You're altogether too touchy. I'd just as soon you didn't call me when you're in such an ugly mood."

"A mood you inspired, Mother! And maybe you're right. Maybe I shouldn't have called. Maybe I just shouldn't call you again, period!"

She slammed the phone down into its cradle and buried her face in the pillow. Her fists were tightly clenched and there was an anguished, wailing quality to her muffled voice. "He is mine! He is! He is!"

VIII

"It's good to see you again, Mr. President. You're looking better. I hope you're feeling that way now, too."

"Much better, Mr. Grant, thank you. I hope to be discharged from here late today and back in the saddle at the White House again tomorrow, provided I can convince the doctors here that any further coddling is unnecessary." He pointed to the corner of the large room where a three-cushioned tomato-red sofa and three comfortable-looking armchairs of the same vinyl had been positioned in a circle around a low oval table with a slab of thick glass as its top. "Have a seat over there, if you will. You, too, Alex. I'll be with you in a moment."

As the President moved to the smaller table where he had eaten breakfast, his slippered feet made scuffing plops against the tile floor. If one were not sure, it was difficult to determine which of his feet was the one constructed of wood, steel and fiber-glass. With his back to them he picked up the white telephone.

Grant rubbed his eyes and stifled a yawn. He put his briefcase and recorder on the floor by one of the chairs and sat down, hearing the cushion wheeze with escaping air as his weight settled. The graininess was getting worse and he wished now that he'd taken Gordon's advice and tried to get a little nap during the flight. Although he'd washed and shaved in the big jet's well-provided lavatory while en route, he still felt the discomfort of a shirt, socks and underwear worn too long. He also would have given almost anything to be able to kick off his shoes right now.

The time when Grant could have been napping had been spent reviewing the material gathered during the preceding day and night at Boardman's and making as thorough notes as possible. On the way to the plane, Gordon had explained that the President could have no more delays; he must know immediately everything that Grant had learned. This had bothered the writer a great deal. He had expected to be giving a report sometime fairly soon to Gordon, if not to President Sanders, but had anticipated more time to prepare for it. He didn't know how long this present session with the President would last, but he strongly doubted it would be long enough for a convincing presentation, even if he were well prepared. Certainly it precluded any chance of his catching some rest. He had crammed as best he could from his own tapes and notes, making a hasty attempt at some form of organization, and all the while both his nervousness and fatigue had increased. He was also faintly irritated that the rush had been so great that there'd been no way to get calls off to Marie and Anne to let them know where he was going, nor any estimate of how long he would have to remain in the Washington area.

"Hazel," the President was saying into the white phone, "I've decided on a slightly altered situation here. I'll want Oscar and Al in on this, too, along with Steve. They're all available, aren't they?…Where?…Oh, fine, that's all right. Have them come in now, please. And, Hazel, change that lunch order from three to six…Yes, I got the letter from Mark Shepard and I'll dictate a reply after this meeting, okay?…Fine. Oh, I've also signed the letters that go to the families of those killed in that expressway disaster, so you can send them out whenever you're ready…Sure, that'll be fine. Thanks"

He hung up and walked back toward the two men. Gordon, who had taken a seat on the sofa, came to his feet at once. Slower to react, Grant also started to rise, but the President waved him back.

"Sit still. We're casual here. Sit down, Alex. The others will be in momentarily." He sat down himself in the padded armchair chair directly across the glass-topped table from Grant and smiled at the writer. "Alex says we jerked you away rather unexpectedly this morning. I apologize. At this point I didn't have a great deal of choice. I realize you must be rather tired since according to Alex you've had no sleep. Perhaps our talk here will be lively enough to keep you going until we finish."

"Thank you, sir. I'll do my best to keep alert."

"You weren't able to inform your wife of where you were going before you left?"

"No, sir."

"Alex," he swiveled his attention, "would you mind stepping out and asking Hazel to call Mrs. Grant to explain that Mr. Grant is here and probably will be in touch with her later on today?" He looked at Grant for confirmation and the writer smiled his thanks.

"Certainly, Mr. President," said Gordon, rising again and starting away, but then he paused and looked back. "Perhaps, sir, Mr. Grant would also like to have his secretary informed as to his whereabouts." Gordon looked at Grant, the ghost of a smile on his lips.

"By all means, if he wishes it," Sanders agreed.

Grant was startled and hesitated, considering, then nodded with a small, grateful smile. "I'd appreciate that, Mr. Gordon."

As his bodyguard stepped out, the President looked at Grant in a speculative manner. "I don't want to get going on this," he said, "until the others come in, but I do hope you have found some answers to the many puzzles that have been raised by this situation. The press is badgering for answers and I'll have to admit that I'm every bit as curious as they to find out just what happened."

"To a certain extent I'll be able to explain, sir," Grant said. "The whole matter is rather involved and I'm afraid it's going to take a while to give you a fairly complete picture." He stopped. The President had been listening closely and seemed disinclined to speak. Grant mentally braced himself and went on. "Mr. President, what I am going to say here may be the most—"

He broke off at a light rapping on the door, which was then opened. Preceded by Hazel Tierney, four men entered the room in single file. Grant recognized two of them—Gordon and Lace. The President stood, and so Grant rose also.

"Gentlemen," Sanders greeted them, "come in." He glanced at his personal secretary and pointed. "Hazel, the letters are on the table there. Unless it's urgent, no more calls until we're finished in here." His eyes flicked to Grant and then back to her. "Which, I suspect, may turn out to be quite some time."

"Yes, sir."

As she moved to get the letters, the President faced the four men who had entered. "Gentlemen, this is Mr. John Grant. You are all aware of his reason for being here. Mr. Grant, you already know Mr. Gordon, of course, and am I correct in assuming you know Mr. Lace as well?"

"Yes, sir. We met at the hospital in Chicago." He shook hands with Steven Lace and murmured, "Good to see you again."

"These gentlemen," Sanders held out his palm toward the other two, "are two of my principal advisers, Albert Jabonsky and Oscar McMillan."

Jabonsky, taller of the pair as well as elder, was about six feet in height, with dense salt-and-pepper hair, a neat thin moustache and steely eyes behind rimless glasses. About sixty, he was wearing a dark blue pinstripe and well-polished black shoes. He smiled in a perfunctory manner and took Grant's offered hand, though there was no warmth in the grip.

McMillan, on the other hand, dressed in a medium-brown herringbone suit and dark brown patent leather shoes, was almost as opposite as he could be from Jabonsky. Of considerably less than average height and rather heavy-set, only a few scattered strands of brownish hair stretched across the top of his shiny pink scalp. He appeared to be in his early forties and his brown eyes were lively and alert, often squinching together with the amiable smiles he wore so frequently, as now when he shook hands vigorously with Grant.

At the President's gesture as he sat down, the others seated themselves. Sanders and Grant resumed their previous seats and Gordon took the chair between them. The other three sat on the sofa. As soon as all were settled, the President spoke again.

"Mr. Grant was just telling me that what he has discovered during his talk with Mr. Boardman and subsequent to that will take some time to relate. I've ordered some lunch for us, which should be here before long, and if there is no objection, I think we can move along with our discussion as we eat. Mr. Grant," he faced the writer, "you had begun saying something as these gentlemen entered. Would you care to pick it up there?"

"Yes, sir." Grant moistened his lips with the tip of his tongue. He could feel that his palms were wet with perspiration. "I was saying that what I will tell you here today may be the most important subject that has ever been brought to your attention."

Sanders pursed his lips. "Important in what way, Mr. Grant?" he asked quietly.

Grant took the plunge. "For the preservation of mankind, Mr. President."

For a moment there was utter stillness in the room, broken only by the barely audible whine of a far-off jet. Sanders shifted his eyes to Jabonsky and McMillan for a moment and then, with an elbow on the arm of his chair, gripped his chin between thumb and forefinger.

"You don't mince words, do you, Mr. Grant?" There was a faint sense of humor underlying the words. "All right, suppose you tell us about it."

Grant leaned forward with his forearms on the arms of the chair and spoke earnestly. "My talk with Herbert Boardman lasted for just under fourteen hours, and we covered a great deal of ground. I taped the entire conversation, —" he indicated the recorder with an offhand gesture "—and it may be that at some future time you will want to hear what was said in its entirety. I'm sure now, however, that you're more interested in a summary as succinctly as I may be able to give it."

At the President's nod, he continued. "I should perhaps assure you first of my thorough conviction that Mr. Boardman was the agent of no other person or organization. The reasons I say this will become clear as I go along. Mr. Boardman acted solely on his own and, as you're aware, he wished to make it appear his intent was to kill you, when actually it was not."

"If I may interject a comment here, Mr. President," Gordon said, continuing as the President's eyes settled on him. "We have located the man in Chicago who made the special ammunition for Boardman. Run-of-the-mill gun hobbyist named Roy Bujalski. Very frightened. He came forward on his own and told how Boardman had gotten him to make the ammunition, supposedly to shoot a neighbor's dog that had been terrorizing him and his daughter. He said Boardman claimed he didn't want to kill the dog, but just stun it to teach it a lesson. Bujalski checked out reasonably clean, so we're not holding him."

"Thank you, Alex," Sanders said. "Please go on, Mr. Grant."

Grant continued, methodically and thoroughly, boiling down the extensive conversation with Boardman to its prime essence—a task made simpler than he thought it would be because he had more or less done the same thing already with Anne. If anything, his presentation, more organized than Boardman's, was also more convincing.

There was, while he was speaking, a considerably divergent range of reaction from his listeners. Surprisingly, the least amount of reaction came from Alexander Gordon. The Secret Service chief sat with heavy-lidded eyes boring unwaveringly into Grant's, his expression impassive. At the other end of the reactive spectrum, Steven Lace obviously was deeply upset by what he was hearing, frequently glancing at the President and his advisers to see how they were responding. The White House press secretary had actually paled several times as the significance of what Grant was saying was driven home to him, and he seemed to vacillate with mercurial unpredictability between utter disbelief and strong conviction.

Oscar McMillan sat leaning forward with his forearms on his knees for the whole time that Grant was explaining the essence of the HAB Theory, his interest keen and attention unwavering. Once he closed his eyes for the space of a full minute and Grant noticed that the pink of his scalp had become speckled with a fine sheen of perspiration. Albert Jabonsky, on the other hand, was leaning back, one leg crossed over the other more in the manner that a woman crosses her legs than as a man does—with knee almost atop knee and the overhanging leg held nearly straight down rather than with the ankle atop one knee and the legs reasonably wide apart. The tunneled gray eyes grew harder as Grant spoke, and though he smoked cigarette after cigarette, those eyes never left Grant and the cigarettes were extracted from the pack, lighted, smoked and butted out in the heavy brass ashtray in a manner completely automatic.

Of greatest concern to Grant was the reaction of Robert Sanders, and he studied the President closely while speaking. Skilled politician and negotiator that he was, Sanders betrayed through facial expressions little of what he may have been thinking. Occasionally he licked his lips, coughed gently, sighed, rubbed his chin, or changed position slightly, but none of these was really a guideline of any sort to what was passing through his mind.

Only one interruption of any consequence occurred during Grant's initial relation of the essentials of the HAB Theory. This was when a large lunch cart was wheeled into the room and a thoughtful silence enveloped the men as the individual servings were positioned on the low oval table before them. The servers themselves moved with quiet haste, uncomfortable in the knowledge that they were intruding and as anxious to be away as the men in the room were to have them gone. The lunches were light, consisting of delicate finger sandwiches of tuna, boiled ham and roast beef, peach half and cottage cheese on crisp lettuce, and pots of both coffee and tea. As the food was being served, the President invited Grant to break off, if he wished, and eat, but Grant declined, asking ·the others to please go ahead while he continued talking. This seemed to please the President and, following the departure of the servers, the other men listening to Grant followed the President's lead of quietly eating as the writer continued his presentation. Grant's coverage of that initial meeting with Boardman took very close to two hours and he concluded that portion of it with a reemphasis of the three elements that had most intrigued him during the taping session.

"I feel reasonably sure," he said, "that my reaction at the conclusion of meeting with Mr. Boardman was not far afield from what you gentlemen are probably experiencing now. I was smitten by what he said, definitely intrigued, inclined to believe, and yet still filled with a great many doubts. Three things impinged most specifically as a reaction on my part. The first was Mr. Boardman's remarks to my final question in regard to when—assuming, for the sake of argument, the truth of his postulations—such a capsizing of the earth might occur again.

It is extremely significant, I think, to recognize the importance of the fact that all known data indicate that the cataclysm, if an actual threat, is already long overdue. Secondly, in regard to the matter of the doubts that were still heavy in my own mind, there was the strong and calm assurance on Mr. Boardman's part that in our next meeting he would provide proofs which would thoroughly eliminate such doubts.

"Finally," Grant went on after a bit, "there was the comment made by Mr. Boardman which was rather casually given at the time, and its full significance did not really create any great impact on me until after I'd left him. While Mr. Gordon and I were en route here today, Mr. president, I located this particular comment on the tape and positioned it for immediate replay. With your permission, I'd like to have you hear that brief portion now."

"Since you obviously consider it of importance, Mr. Grant," Sanders observed in reply, "then it would probably be well worth our while to listen to it. Please go ahead."

Grant cleared a space on the table and continued talking as he set up the recorder. "At the point where this particular comment was made by Mr. Boardman, we had been continuously in session for about twelve hours and both of us were tired. I remember marveling at Mr. Boardman's ability, at his age, to continue for so prolonged a period. Several times I suggested we wrap it up for the night beginning at about the point where we had been together for seven or eight hours but Mr. Boardman would not have it. At any rate, the comment in question here was brought out by Mr. Boardman to indicate what his motivation had been for the attack upon you, Mr. President, and it was primarily in that light—the aspect of motivation—that I considered it then most pertinent. And since it was part of a chain of events which led up to the attack, it was passed over quickly and we did not get back to any specific discussion of it at the time. Later on, as I realized its significance, I was determined to make it the first matter of priority in the next meeting I had with Mr. Boardman. That, of course, failed to materialize due to Mr. Boardman's death. But this is what he said."

Grant pressed a button on the machine and both reels began slowly revolving in a counterclockwise fashion, with the thin strip of brown tape feeding steadily between the recording heads. Boardman's voice was clear and loud in the room.

"Mr. Grant, I am an extremely old man. I cannot expect to be around very much longer. I suppose I grew accustomed to having been ignored through all those years and just more or less resigned myself to the idea that my theory wasn't going to create any kind of a stir in my lifetime. But then recently I began to work on a wholly new aspect of it and became very excited again, because I've determined a way in which I believe mankind can avert the tragedy. It is something which would take the combined effort and cooperation of most of the major governments on earth, but it could be done if we acted swiftly enough. It was at that point that—"

Grant's punching of a button abruptly cut off Boardman's words. He looked up at the President and was shaking his head regretfully as he continued. "Obviously I should have stopped him at that moment and pursued this matter of what he believed to be a possible way for mankind to save itself. Since I did not, the concern which has been plaguing me most is whether or not anywhere in his papers Mr. Boardman has expressed himself to that end. It was this single item that I was most alert for in my work at the Boardman house throughout late yesterday afternoon and all last night."

"But you have found nothing on it?" The President's words were flat, grim.

"Regrettably, that's correct, sir. However, bear in mind that I've done little more at this point than scratch the surface of Mr. Boardman's files, and I think there is good reason to hope that somewhere in the material I've not yet gone through there may be an explanation of what he was alluding to. Or, if not a full explanation, then at least some clues which would give us a direction in which to concentrate."

"That's assuming that one believes all of this." it was Jabonsky speaking up for the first time, and he was clearly contemptuous and unbelieving. "I find it rather odd, Mr. Grant, that a man of your intelligence and reputation should so easily allow himself to be taken in by the rantings of what was undoubtedly an unhinged mind. Clever, I'll admit, but then many insane people are remarkably clever in achieving their ends. Throughout history every age has had its legion of Doomsday prophets exhorting the population to repent of its sins because the end of the world was at hand. But we're still here, and need I say more? While I'll admit that this Boardman presents his case in a more convincing manner than most, it's all purely speculative and cannot possibly withstand close scientific analysis."

Grant had anticipated some sort of reaction like this and was prepared for it. His response was sympathetic. "That is certainly a normal reaction, Mr. Jabonsky, and one I, too, shared at first. Bear in mind, though, that Mr. Boardman predicts not the end of the world, but the end of civilization as we know it. But even at this, the obvious reaction is to consider such a concept to be the outpouring of a deranged mind. I stated that my prime goal in starting through the Boardman papers was to discover what sort of a survival plan he had worked out. However, I was also maintaining a very sharp eye for anything, regardless of how remote, which could dispute—not prove, sir, but *dispute*—what Mr. Boardman postulates, and I truly hoped to find it. I did not. While I admit that I am not a scientist and as yet I've not delved in any great depth through those papers, nothing I've turned up disputes Mr. Boardman's contentions. To the contrary, I've already turned up a number of proofs which strongly corroborate his contentions, proofs that undoubtedly he would have discussed with me the next day, had he not died."

Grant turned his attention back to Robert Sanders. "Mr. President, I am still not unqualifiedly convinced of the validity of what we're calling the HAB Theory. Competent scientists might well be able to pick apart the alleged proofs gathered by Mr. Boardman. But I do, in all conscience, have to point out that with each and every document I've studied, my skepticism has diminished. I very strongly believe at this point that even though there may be a good expectation of disproving the HAB Theory, just the faintest possibility that it might be true should require that it not be rejected out of hand without benefit of the closest possible scrutiny by well-qualified people."

Robert Morton Sanders stood up and limped away from his chair, his hands clasped behind him and his brow deeply furrowed. He paused in front of the large window overlooking a well-kept courtyard and garden area in which a number of robed patients were strolling and others were being casually pushed along the paved paths by attendants. At this exposure of the President, Alex Gordon became apprehensively alert, but he said nothing. The President remained silent for two or three minutes, his back to the others. When he finally spoke, he did so without turning around.

"Gentlemen, we've listened to what Mr. Grant has had to say to this point without much comment. I'm sure he has more to say before we conclude our meeting. However, before moving on, I'd like to hear from each of you your feelings at this point. No elaboration, please. Just your present gut reaction, so to speak. Al?"

Jabonsky touched his moustache with a fingertip and replied with conviction. "I don't believe one word of it.

Clever, I admit, but totally unacceptable."

"Oscar?"

McMillan was slower in responding. He turned an apologetic little smile on Grant and raised his shoulders in the suggestion of a shrug. "I think I pretty much have to go along with Al's view of the situation. I'm not a scientist, but I can think of a fair number of reasons just off the cuff why this so-called HAB Theory couldn't possibly be valid."

Grant was frowning. He thought that he'd put the explanation over reasonably well to this point, but right now he was obviously batting zero. He was beginning to seriously wonder at his own gullibility.

"How about you, Alex?" Sanders asked, still without turning.

The big agent popped his lips as he opened them. "Before I reply, sir, would you kindly step away from that window?"

The President threw back his head and laughed. "I'm sorry, Alex," he said, laughing as he moved to lean his back against the wall. "I still haven't learned, have I? All right, what's your thought about all this?"

"My primary concern, Mr. President, as is quite obvious, is the issue of security. At this stage I tend to agree with Mr. Grant's conclusion that we're not dealing with any sort of conspiracy, foreign or domestic. Beyond that," his slitted eyes rolled toward Grant, "I really can't buy a word of the old man's theory."

"Steve?"

Lace's eyes were owlish behind the large-lensed glasses and his reply was a high-pitched piping. "I can picture what Orson Welles could have done with this, but I can't buy it either, Mr. President. Not for a minute."

The fatigue Grant was holding it check abruptly washed through him in a wave and his shoulders slumped perceptibly. Zero all the way.

The President dropped his hands to his sides and strode briskly back to his chair, his limp somewhat more pronounced when he walked faster. He stood in front of the chair facing the writer. "I'll refrain from comment for the moment. Mr. Grant, you've given a good summary of your meeting with Mr. Boardman, but nothing yet about your findings since then. I'm sure you'd like to carry this a bit further."

Grant wasn't at all sure that he wanted to carry it any further. It was evident that these down-to-earth men, these realists, were pointing him out to be a fantasist and he was becoming embarrassed and unsure of himself, his earlier convictions haunting him now as having been childish. How could he have let himself become so swayed, so deeply enrapt with what was ever more convincingly looming as the prattlings of a senile old man trying desperately to leave behind him in this world a monument to himself? Deflated to an appreciable degree and feeling a resurgence of the old depression he thought he had whipped, Grant definitely was not very inclined to go on, but he did so anyway, trying his best to mask his disappointment.

"I'll try to recap briefly what I gleaned from Mr. Boardman's papers last night, Mr. President." He reached into his inside breast pocket as the President sat down again and withdrew the soft, leatherbound notebook in which, at Boardman's house and again on the plane to Washington, he had made notes to himself. Opening it, he began by addressing himself to the President with an apology.

"There has been no time, President Sanders, for me to place these data in well-organized form, chronologically or otherwise. I made notations as I encountered them and have tried to establish at least some sort of general order. I'll try not to repeat myself, but there are almost certain to be a few areas here and there where I will have to return to previous data mentioned with other data which is supportive, or at least related, to the earlier material.

"Boardman notes that the geological construction of the earth's surface provides conclusive physical evidence that moisture rising in the tropical and temperate areas of the globe—primarily through evaporation on ocean surfaces, but similarly through the assimilation of moisture rising from tropical rainforest areas—is carried by convection currents over the earth's axis of spin to the polar areas where, being drastically cooled, it falls in the form of snow. This snow is impacted to form glaciers and since there is insufficient heat from the sun's rays to melt the glacial ice, it builds up to form the polar ice caps. These caps, according to Boardman, have appeared randomly at successive areas of the earth's surface. Each time the caps have grown to maturity in one epoch of time, their weight and position of rotation form an eccentricity in the earth's axial spin—the wobble mentioned earlier. Eventually the weight becomes too great, the eccentricity too pronounced, and a capsizing of the globe appears.

Grant flipped a page and went on without looking up. "He goes on to say that his estimates of the duration of our present epoch of time since the last capsizing are derived in part from the lengths of the gorges cut by St. Anthony's Falls on the Mississippi and Niagara Falls. The upstream creepage rates of the falls have been calculated with a fair degree of accuracy by the United States Geological Survey, by the expedient of dividing the gorge length by the creepage rate. The falls were formed at the beginning of our epoch, and utilizing the USGS calculations, simple arithmetic indicates that our present epoch has been in existence for just about seventy-five hundred years."

Turning a page in his notebook, Grant blinked rapidly a few times against the sandiness in his eyes and spoke for a while without looking at the fresh page. "Mr. Boardman told me during our talk that he had charted the duration of nine other epochs previous to our own, and that they lasted between three thousand and seven thousand years each. He was able to determine the age of our present epoch from the falls, but I was interested in seeing how he was able to find out the length of time that other epochs had lasted. I found his calculations for all the epochs he charted, but describing just one of them will suffice for now, I think, since essentially they're all similar."

He glanced down at the notebook again. "The earth material that we know as clay was formed by the grinding up of rocks under enormous glacial weights. Underglacial currents carry this sediment away and deposit it in the beds of valleys or lakes. Just as the years of a tree's life can be determined by counting the annular rings, so too the age of one of these clay deposits is determinable by counting the number of layers it contains. Geologists call these layers varves, and each varve represents one year. Now, in a previous epoch when the North Pole was located at Hudson Bay instead of its present location, these varve beds were forming. They occur over much of the northern portion of North America. Mr. Boardman selected two widely separated varve beds from this glacial period for a test, one of them located at Wrenshall, Minnesota, the other at Hackensack, New Jersey. Core borings at both clearly show the varves, and in both cases they were identical figures of six thousand six hundred. This, Boardman maintains, means that the Hudson Bay Epoch, which he determines as being two epochs previous to ours—or B.P. 2—had a life pan of sixty-six hundred years. Whatever civilization, if any, developed during that span of time, was wiped out with the next rollover of the earth."

Another page was flipped and Grant stood silently a moment, studying what he had written there. He felt completely drained and wished this were all over and he could just go off by himself somewhere and sleep for a week.

"Mr. Grant," the President spoke up softly, "I know you have a good bit more to tell us, and I'm sure that none of us here has any desire not to hear the rest. However, you've had no chance whatever to touch your lunch, and it might be a good time now to take a break and refresh ourselves." He added with a small laugh, "I notice your voice becoming just a bit hoarse, so let's take a fifteen-minute recess."

The group broke up with alacrity, the President disappearing into his room's bathroom, and the other four men moved quickly out through the door they had entered. Grant wryly thought of their exodus as being similar to the rush for the lobby during intermission in a boring play.

Left alone now, the writer expelled a vast exhalation of relief to be stopping for a while, poured some tepid coffee into his cup, and swiftly wolfed down three of the finger sandwiches. His depression still weighted him down. There had been nothing in the demeanor of his small audience to indicate any change of attitude. Rather morosely he began studying his notes further as he ate his salad and polished off another cup of coffee. He was just lighting a cigarette when Robert Sanders emerged from the little room with the sound of gurgling water behind him.

"Feel free to use the facilities here, Mr. Grant," he said, with a wave of his hand toward the bathroom. "I have a brief call I want to make."

"I can just as easily go down the hall if you prefer, Mr. President," the writer said quickly, rising.

"Not necessary at all."

"Thank you, sir."

The President was picking up the white phone as Grant closed the bathroom door behind himself. By the time he relieved himself, washed his face and hands and emerged feeling somewhat refreshed, all the men were back in their places at the table. He resumed his own place and picked up his notebook, but before he could begin speaking again, the President held up a finger like an exclamation point.

"While I very much appreciate your efforts to reduce this material to as brief a presentation as possible, Mr. Grant, I do not wish you to stint in your explanations or feel that you must rush, if you deem a more expanded discourse to be advisable. We are prepared to hear you out fully."

Despite the brief roll of Jabonsky's eyes in evident exasperation at the President's remark, and even though Grant had detected nothing supportive in the reactions of any of the others, the writer felt the tiniest surge of hope at the President's words. He thanked the Chief Executive and continued, a bit more at ease now than before.

"Mr. Boardman," he resumed, "spent a good bit of time in an effort to determine why our present epoch has lasted longer than any others he had yet been able to chart. There are multiple reasons. For one thing, the northern ice cap has been stunted in its growth because it is over the open sea and ocean currents sweeping from the Pacific through the Bering Strait and into the Arctic Ocean form a layer of relative warmth which does not permit the North Pole ice to become very thick—its average thickness being only slightly more than twelve feet. The nearest thing to a true ice cap in the north is located on Greenland, and the nearest edge of Greenland is almost five hundred miles from the pole. The mass of it is much farther away than that.

"Quite a different situation exists at the South Pole, where there is the continent we know as Antarctica. Here an ice cap has formed of proportions which boggle the imagination. It covers the entire continent and is already, according to Mr. Boardman, a third of a million square miles larger than the one which caused the earth to capsize at the end of the epoch preceding ours.

"Incidentally," he added, letting his gaze move across the men who were now apparently listening more intently to every word, "to give you a better picture of how much ice is down there, during the late nineteen-sixties, the United States Coast and Geodetic Survey determined that there was enough ice on Antarctica then to form a layer of ice over the entire face of the earth to the height of a twelve-story building. That was quite some time ago and since then more than three times the volume of Lake Erie in fresh ice has formed every year there."

"That is one hell of a statistic," murmured Lace.

Grant smiled briefly at the press secretary and continued. "Because the northern ice cap is mainly half a thousand miles from the pole and the greater portion of the southern ice cap is not directly over the southern axis of spin, there may be—although I should say, Mr. Boardman certainly adds a big question mark after this—there *may* be something of a stabilizing effect created between the two, except for what he says is a particularly dangerous period occurring once every fourteen months, when their eccentric movements are in a conjunctional alignment with one another.

"More important, however, is the fact that the North Pole ice is directly over open ocean and the currents under the ice are constantly melting it or forcing it to break away into the northern Atlantic in the form of icebergs. The really dangerous situation exists at Antarctica. That ice cap throws off bergs, too, and has been known to be doing so for at least the past three hundred years. That is additional proof that the cap is growing rather than shrinking, as some theorists in the past have postulated. A growing ice cap sheds bergs; a shrinking one doesn't. Shedding icebergs the way it does acts as something of a safety valve in relieving weight accumulation, but not well enough. Far more weight accumulates in one month than is shed away in the form of bergs over a full year."

Grant closed the little notebook, holding his place with his thumb. He smiled tiredly. "Mr. President, gentlemen, I'm now coming into an area of more specific—and, I should add, quite dramatic—physical proofs. There are undoubtedly many more of these developed by Mr. Boardman than I was able to glean in the short time I've had, but even these few that I'm about to describe are very impressive. They also answer some mysteries regarding our planet which science has never been able to penetrate before." He loosened his tie a little.

"One of the points I did *not* ask Mr. Boardman about and which I now regret having neglected is the speed with which the earth rolls over when the capsizing occurs. However, I've gathered from some of his scattered calculations that it occurs at tremendous speed. I've done some figuring based on his calculations and they indicate that the polar region reaches the equator in three to four hours from the moment of passing the critical point of stability and breaking away. This means an average capsizing speed of something in the nature of seventeen hundred and fifty miles an hour. However, that includes both acceleration and deceleration, so the top speed is probably a considerably higher figure, possibly more in the nature of three thousand miles an hour.

"What I'm leading up to," he said, "is that this means that in an extremely short span of time, areas that are tropical have become areas in which the temperature may be fifty to a hundred degrees below zero; and polar areas of bitterly subzero temperatures are suddenly thawing beneath a tropical sun."

Grant opened the notebook again and ran his eyes down the page. "All right, now to some of the specific items of proof. In 1901, one of the mysteries that science has never been able to explain began coming to light. Near the banks of the Beresovka River in Siberia, a prehistoric mammoth was found frozen in the tundra. This, gentlemen, was not a fossil remains but an animal quick-frozen and so well preserved that its meat was still edible— yet mammoths were not known to have existed on earth for eighteen thousand years previous to that!

"That was the first of the mammoths to be discovered in such condition, but far from the last. To date, forty-nine others in similar perfect condition have been found, along with fourteen prehistoric rhinoceroses, throughout northeastern Siberia. While mammoths are known to have inhabited temperate climates, mostly they were subtropical, and the rhinoceroses are known to have inhabited tropical zones only. How, then, could animals living in such climates have suddenly become quick-frozen? Up until now science has been baffled. The HAB Theory, with the abrupt shift of the earth's tropical regions to the pole and vice versa, seems to solve that mystery."

McMillan and Lace exchanged speculative glances at this, but Grant went on without pause. "But the fascinating thing is the condition many of these animals were in when they were frozen. Each of the mammoths as it is found gives concrete physical evidence of the incredible disaster which overtook it. Some of them have been found frozen in upright positions, indicating quick-freeze of such incredible speed as to stagger the imagination. Many of them have been found with full stomachs, and a full stomach in any dead animal can only mean that a relatively healthy animal died with extreme suddenness. Gentlemen, not only have they been found with undigested food in their stomachs, but also with food remaining in their mouths! These were animals killed before they even had an opportunity to spit out or swallow that vegetation they had been eating. And here's another important fact: analyses were made of the food grasses and other plants they had been eating, and these proved to be luxuriant species of trop-ical or subtropical growth never known to science to ever have existed elsewhere except in those climatic conditions.

"Herbert Allen Boardman's theory—the HAB Theory—explains it. These animals obviously were contentedly grazing on the lush vegetation of a warm and pleasant climate at the moment when one of the many capsizings of the earth occurred. Whirled with incredible speed to the polar area, they were subjected to a rapid deep-freeze which kept them in their lifelike condition until now. On our own continent, in Alaska, there must have been fantastic surface disruptions at the time of the capsizing, because while mammoth remains also have been found there in deep-frozen state, these animals invariably have been torn apart or crushed beyond belief.

"Perhaps the most astounding find was the one made by Dr. Ivan Peotyrvich Tomalchoff, Russian biopathologist, in that the animal was experiencing, at the exact time of death, an erection of the genital organ. So far as is known to medical science, erection of the male genitalia can be carried into death—and maintained thereafter—only when that death is the result of suffocation. In fact, suffocation often *produces* such an erection, and the condition in death is inexplicable for any other reason."

John Grant stopped and looked at the men seated near him. None of them uttered a word. Even during the time he took several swallows of water, no one broke the silence. He wiped his mouth with his napkin and then began speaking again, and much of the tiredness seemed to have disappeared from his voice.

"While I've found nothing in Mr. Boardman's papers yet concerning the disappearance of scores of species of dinosaurs from the earth at the end of the Age of Reptiles, it seems to me that the HAB Theory gives a very valid reason for why they vanished all at once as they did—another capsizing of the earth eons before the one which destroyed the mammoths. But," he added hastily, "this is conjecture on my part at this time and I apologize for straying from tangibles.

"Consider this, Mr. President, before I go on with some other proofs: all of this material I'm presenting here is simply material that has been accumulated through one long discussion with Mr. Boardman and one period of looking through his papers in a hurried and fundamentally superficial way. Certainly there are many other items of an even more concrete nature that Mr. Boardman assembled in his many years of gathering data in support of his thesis. Think of what remains for us yet to discover in his papers."

"What you've brought forth so far, Mr. Grant, in the short time you've had for gathering material," the President said, "is impressive. You say you have still other proofs beyond these?"

"Yes sir. Many. But for now I'll only mention a few. In Yellowstone National Park, for example, only a short distance from the Continental Divide, a mountain was split back in the nineteen-sixties by a severe earthquake. Imbedded in the now exposed interior of that mountain are seventeen distinct horizontal layers of trees. These trees are standing upright, as they were in life. Between each layer of trees is a layer of rock which was originally laid down as clay. The HAB Theory contends that each stratum shows trees which existed as a forest during their own epoch of time, and that each was buried by the incredible flooding which occurred when the earth capsized. That split mountain is a graphic record of epoch after epoch of the planet's successive capsizings. Nothing else known to science can explain it.

"There are plenty of other proofs which I touched on in the researching only briefly, as supportive data. For example," he said, letting his eyes go across the men slowly, "one doesn't have to be a paleontologist to know that fossils of fish and marine organisms are found with great regularity high in the Rocky Mountains, the Himalayas, the Andes and elsewhere. They could be present there only if those regions were at some time under the sea— probably comparable to the mid-oceanic ridge of the Atlantic, which is a range of very tall mountains presently at the bottom of the Atlantic for its entire length from north to south. In another capsizing, perhaps those mountains will be exposed and the Rockies will be submerged. But the important thing is the realization that only a capsizing of the earth can cause this to occur.

"Now, then," Grant went on, "while it can't really be considered under the heading of physical proof, Mr. President, consider the following: virtually every tribe and race of man has in its history or mythology or folklore the legend of a great deluge. We have the biblical story of how Noah survived such a flood. The Greek myths tell of their principal god, Zeus, overwhelming the earth with a flood. The Hindus tell of a flood in the ancient past, as do the Chaldean cuneiform writings. And might all this not lend some supportive relevance to the supposed legend of the island empire of Atlantis being lost beneath the sea? Confucius begins his history of China by referring to the receding flood, and an even older Chinese tradition may be particularly significant, because it tells of a time when China itself made a sudden gigantic leap to the Arctic."

"Mr. Grant," the Chief Executive put in as the writer paused, "you mentioned earlier that Mr. Boardman had charted the course and duration of nine of these alleged previous epochs before the present. Do I understand that to mean he has accurately pinpointed the successive areas which he claims to have once been polar regions?"

"Yes, sir, that's correct."

"Just how was he able to do this?"

"Well, as he explained it to me, once he became convinced that he was on the right track, he decided he'd try to locate where the last North Pole had been prior to our present pole. He determined that North and South America together formed the heaviest land belt and theorized that, this being the case, then they were probably riding the equatorial bulge during the last epoch before the present—B.P. 1. He stretched a string around a huge globe of the earth and positioned it so that it passed over the mountain chains formed by the Rockies and the Andes. He then further theorized that if he put another string around the globe at right angles to the first, and then still another string around it at right angles to the first two, that the place where the latter two strings crossed would be the polar locations for that epoch."

"And this worked?"

"Indeed it did, Mr. President. One of the junctions where the latter two strings crossed was in the midst of the Pacific Ocean, but on the opposite side of the globe they crossed at Lake Chad."

"That's significant?"

"Yes, sir. Very. Lake Chad happens to be the near center of Africa's Sudan Basin, and the Sudan Basin forms a vast dent in the earth covering four million square miles, which is about four-fifths the size of present Antarctica. Further, the land around Lake Chad is marked with a multitude of the remains of dried-up, ancient watercourses which have no real connection with one another. These are exactly the sort of watercourses which would form by the runoff of water from a gigantic ice cap suddenly melting under a hot sun. Let me give you a clearer picture." He flicked open the notebook again and paged through a dozen or more sheets before stopping on one. He glanced up at the President.

"Sir, Lake Chad has some remarkable peculiarities. In the first place, over the past half-century it has lost about a third of its area. This means it's a dying lake which is constantly shrinking. It is now down to about ten thousand square miles. Secondly, it is the only large freshwater lake in the world which has no outlet to the sea. Other large freshwater lakes remain fresh because, although they pick up salts from their tributaries, they surrender these same salts to the sea. But Lake Chad never contained any salt at all because, according to Mr. Boardman's postulation, it is all that remains of the Sudan Basin ice cap."

The President was absently tapping the fingers of his left hand in succession on the soft vinyl on the arm of his chair. "Was that the same method he used for determining the other poles?"

"It was. The north polar ice cap for B.P. 2 turned out to be the Hudson Bay Basin. Others he similarly located included Death Valley, the Amazon Basin, the Gobi Desert, Great Slave Lake in Canada, the Matanuska Valley in Alaska, the Black Sea, and the Caspian Sea. But may I go back for a moment, Mr. President, to some other highly pertinent information concerning Lake Chad?"

"Of course. Excuse me for interrupting."

"No problem, sir. Assuming for the sake of argument the validity of the HAB Theory and the pinpointing of Lake Chad as the remains of the ice cap, then we can assume that at the beginning of our own epoch—roughly seventy-five hundred years ago—Africa, or at least its northern third, was at the North Pole. That ice cap, which Mr. Boardman states was four million square miles in area and two miles high, rolled around to the tropics by virtue of one of the recurring capsizings. Adjacent to it was the area we know of now as Egypt, which most archaeologists concur was likely the cradle of our present civilization. Under the heat of the tropical sun, the giant glacier which had been the ice cap melted. It left behind that remarkable four-million-square-mile dent that its enormous weight had caused, and this dent was filled with the water runoff of the melting ice. It became Lake Chad, but at that time a tremendously large, inland, freshwater sea. The earliest Egyptians did not, therefore, live in the dry desert conditions in which we picture them and in which later Egyptians lived. Instead, the earliest Egyptians lived in an invigorating climate because to the west of them was the great Sudan Basin Sea, from which the prevailing westerly winds brought moisture. This certainly helps to account for the incredible architectural accomplishments of that highly developed early civilization. A civilization, incidentally," he added, "which went downhill in direct ratio to the loss of volume of that inland sea through runoff and evaporation. As the Sudan Basin Sea—now called Lake Chad—gradually disappeared, the climate changed, becoming less invigorating, and dried up to a tropical desert. The result was a much less ambitious—in fact, an enervated—Egyptian population and a loss of the skills which had made it so great.

"It's a curious footnote, Mr. President, that there was a race of man contemporary to the Egyptians of 4,000 B.C. to 3000 B.C. who were known as Berbers—an ancient race which still exists today. They lived in the area we now call the Sahara Desert. This ancient race left many well-rendered paintings, including illustrations of swimmers and boaters in a vast body of water. The reason seems evident: that the Berber civilization developed on the shores of the great inland sea where they swam and sailed until it evaporated away to become a lake far distant from their land and known as Lake Chad."

Grant stopped suddenly, as if not knowing what to say any longer. He dropped his notebook on the table with a small harsh smack. A peculiar silence stretched out and then the President leaned forward on one elbow.

"Is that it, Mr. Grant?"

Feeling suddenly as if he had been sapped of all vital fluid, John Grant nodded and then, in hardly more than a whisper, added, "As far as what I was able thus far to gather from Mr. Boardman's papers it is, sir. But if you don't mind, I'd like to make a brief comment of my own."

"Please do."

Grant leaned back in the big chair and laced his fingers together between his thighs. "I don't know what your feeling is, Mr. President, about all this—he swiveled his head—"or yours, gentlemen. What I have given you is not a scientific presentation. I'm not a scientist and it may be that I've muddled things. But I did try to quickly pick out those items which seemed to me to be significant. I haven't tried to convince you of the validity of the HAB Theory, only to present to you what I've uncovered. For myself, while I cannot honestly say that I am one hundred percent convinced of such validity, I do believe there is an excellent likelihood that with further investigation by qualified scientists, it will prove to be true. As a writer and an individual concerned with both the past and future of the human race, I cannot turn my back on this now. Already a great number of questions are rising inside me, questions I feel I have to find satisfactory answers for. If the theory is valid, then isn't it possible that other civilizations of man existed and perished before any that are recorded in our known history? If such civilizations did develop, how great a technology did they achieve before they were wiped out by the cataclysmic disaster of a suddenly capsizing earth? How much time is left in our own epoch? Mr. Boardman thought he had a solution whereby mankind could be saved. If true, we have to find that answer quickly, before our civilization perishes as others may have done."

The men all were looking at him with a sort of curious interest when he finished, but once again no one said anything for a considerable time. Grant had the sinking feeling that all his talk here had been for nothing, that none of these men really grasped the possibilities that the HAB Theory opened. A moment later, when the President called for remarks from them, his suspicions were confirmed.

"It's a fabric sewn together with the flimsiest of thread," Jabonsky said superciliously. "It seems to me, Mr. President, that your press statement should be a very simple one. Herbert Boardman was obviously insane."

"I don't know as I'd go quite that far," McMillan spoke up. "I am much more inclined to think that here was a man more or less thwarted in a lifelong dream of gaining recognition in a field where he had no formal training whatsoever. And, in failing to do it, he most likely reasoned that he would acquire that fame in any way possible to him in the short amount of time he had left to his life. Unfortunately, he picked a rather bad way of achieving his place in history. As for his so-called HAB Theory, it does have its interesting connotations, but there is little likelihood that it could stand up under the examination of truly competent scientists."

"Steve?" queried Sanders.

Lace sighed, adjusted his glasses, and looked at Grant apologetically. "I think I'll have to go along with Oscar's evaluation for the most part. I almost wish the HAB Theory were true, but I just can't swallow it. I'm not altogether sure, though, that we should make a statement declaring the assassination attempt as an act of insanity on Boardman's part."

"Alex?"

The big black man chewed his lower lip and stared at his feet, which were stretched out in front of him and crossed at the ankles. "Mr. President, I really don't know what to say. I frankly think I'd like to hear more before committing myself one way or another."

"Thank you for your comments, gentlemen." The President concentrated on plucking at a little hangnail on one thumb, pursing his lips as he did so. "Mr. Grant," he glanced up at the writer, "my own reaction is that this has been one of the strangest and most unbelievable things I've ever heard."

He paused for quite a long moment, his deepset eyes boring into Grant's. "If," he continued, "we were to announce this sort of story to the press, it is quite possible that we would become worldwide objects of ridicule. To lend credence to this HAB Theory by conducting an inquiry further could also take on the aspect of political suicide.

"Therefore," he went on, a note of briskness coming into his words, "I hope I will not rue what I am about to say." He stood up and walked behind his chair and then faced the group with his hands folded together atop the backrest.

   Mr. Grant, considering the extremely short amount of time you had to prepare and the scope of the subject involved, I can only commend you most highly on your presentation. While you may not have convinced me of the factuality of Herbert Boardman's postulations, you have most thoroughly convinced me that the HAB Theory must no longer be ignored."

5

All I know is just what I read in the newspapers.

—Will Rogers

The legend of the fall of man, possibly, may be all that has survived of such a time before when, for some unknown reason, the whole world was plunged back again under the undisputed sway of nature, to begin once more its upward toilsome journey through the ages.

—Frederick Soddy

I

The address to the nation made by the President of the United States was carried live by all networks, on both television and radio, and was one of the shortest of any thus far made by Robert Morton Sanders during his tenure in the White House. Though momentous in content, it was a very straightforward statement and bore none of the earmarks of the fact that it had been drafted and redrafted, revised and rewritten at least a dozen times during the night.

There was some degree of irritation among network executives, of course, that the President had chosen to request of them "the ungodly time" of nine o'clock in the morning, Washington, D.C., time, to deliver his message. The grumbling was to the effect that Easterners already would be at work and would miss it, that Midwesterners would be getting ready for work and not have time to watch or listen, and that in the Rocky Mountain and Pacific Time zones no one would even be up yet to see it. Still, they acquiesced to relinquishing the air time he asked for and couldn't grouse about it too strenuously since they had been among the most vociferous in demanding some sort of official statement at the first possible moment.

Sanders himself felt remarkably good, despite a nagging thought that it was altogether possible that his reelection as President might be adversely affected by the action he was taking. White House Press Secretary Steven Lace pointed out in what he thought to be an optimistic manner that it might just work the other way around and get the President reelected, but there was an obvious lack of conviction in the remark.

The President showed not the slightest degree of fatigue after working off and on all night with Lace and John Grant in the drafting of the statement. Naturally, it was Lace and Grant who worked right straight through on it while Sanders slept at intervals and roused only long enough, when another draft was completed, to read it and make marginal notations for how it should be revised for the next draft. Grant, too, had been able to get a few hour' sleep while Lace labored over construction of the first draft, but after that they worked together closely.

Late the evening before, Dr. Victor Aiken had come to check on how his illustrious patient was faring. He'd hmmmmd and grunted as he carefully checked the bruised forehead and ribs and followed up by listening to the President's chest sounds with a stethoscope and peering intently into his eyes and ears. At last he had reluctantly acceded to the President's demands that he be allowed to leave Georgetown University Hospital to return to his work at the White House early in the morning. With the decision made, Aiken hurried off to make the necessary arrangements.

With Alex Gordon, John Grant and Steven Lace accompanying him, the President had boarded the big helicopter at seven in the morning. Hardly more than a quarter-hour later he was in the White House conferring with Lace in a small private office close to the Oval Office on some last-minute changes in the statement. Grant had been asked to wait close by.

On occasion, especially if there were a live audience of dignitaries, the President would give his address from the East Room. More often though, as now, such addresses would originate from the Oval Office in the West Wing of the White House. There, at this moment, an organized confusion of preparation was occurring. In the regular network pool, it was the turn of the American Broadcasting Company to cover the speech, with ABC cameras throwing images to their own control rooms and these then fed to NBC and CBS in their respective control centers, resulting in simultaneous network coverage. The two ABC cameras in the Oval Office were linked by snaking cables to a mobile-unit TV control room that had been driven into position outside the White House.

In order to block the interference of daylight streaming in the windows, a large panel had been moved into position between the windows and the executive desk. The panel was coveted with green baize on which, directly behind where Sanders would sit, was the impressive presidential seal. Closely directing all the activities was the pool producer, a thin, sharp-faced man of about fifty named Nelson Vale, who had done this many times before. He paid scant attention to the two White House Secret Service agents in addition to Alex Gordon who were in the room, standing casually but their eyes working constantly.

Having received final approval about an hour before from the President, Steven Lace entered the Oval Office and placed the pages of the speech in a neat stack on the exact center front of the President's desk. During that hour the speech had been flawlessly typed by Hazel Tierney in oversized characters. With the papers ready, Lace himself sat in the President's chair to give the crews of the principal camera and the backup camera the opportunity to focus on his owlish face and lock in. As was customary, there was neither prompter nor television monitor in the room.

Five minutes before nine President Sanders entered, acknowledging with brief, engaging smile the light applause at his return to duty. He took his seat, glanced at the top page of the speech, and then sat waiting patiently. A makeup man with a small kit delicately touched a lock of the President's hair, moving it a crucial millimeter into what he considered a better position, then gently touched Sanders's nose and forehead, cheeks and chin with a powder-puff, whisking it daintily across the skin to eliminate any perspirational shine. He did a reasonably good job of hiding the forehead bruise under makeup, and he was quite certain that his job, aside from the President's, was the most important among this whole assembly.

As the appointed time neared, all activity died away. At exactly nine o'clock, pool producer Nelson Vale held up his hand, a distant expression in his eyes as he listened to his headset. He was the only man in the room who could hear the voice of an announcer speaking the courtesy Tel-Op message over suddenly picture less television screens across the nation:

"Because of the following Presidential address, the program normally scheduled for this time will not be seen today." A pause, and then a different voice: "Now, here from our Washington studio is ABC correspondent Ralston Sheffers." The millions of television screens in the land returned to life as Sheffers appeared in the ABC studio some distance across town from the White House.

"Good morning. This is Ralston Sheffers for ABC. This will be the first television appearance and statement from President Sanders since the assassination attempt which caused him to be hospitalized, first in Chicago's Northwestern Memorial Hospital and more recently at Georgetown University Hospital here in Washington. The President left the hospital this morning to resume his duties. And now, from the Oval Office in the White House, the President of the United States."

In that office red lights blinked to ruby brilliance on the two television cameras. The still-upraised hand of Nelson Vale swung down to a swift point at Robert Sanders, giving him his cue. Under brighter lighting now, which made the forehead bruise still somewhat evident despite the makeup, Sanders permitted himself a small, grave smile and the faintest of nods, and then he began his address.

"Good morning ladies and gentlemen throughout America. It is a pleasure to be addressing you again from this office. The First Lady and I wish to acknowledge with our deepest appreciation the thousands of cards, letters and telegrams which have come expressing concern for my health. I would also like to assure each and every one of you that the injuries which caused me to be hospitalized are rapidly mending and have resulted in no permanent damage of any nature.

"Because of the unique circumstances involved with regard to the incident which took place in the city of Chicago, it unfortunately has been necessary to withhold the dissemination of any specific information until preliminary investigations were completed. Such initial investigations have now been accomplished and a more complex and penetrating study has been initiated at my orders.

"To allay at once the fears and suspicions of a great many people in America and elsewhere, I am happy to state that there is no evidence whatsoever to indicate that the incident of attempted assassination was anything more than the act of one person acting on his own, without the prior knowledge of any other individual, group, or organization. No evidence of conspiracy, internal or external to the United States, has been uncovered, nor is there any longer an expectation that such evidence may be forthcoming.

"The elderly man who enacted the assassination attack—Herbert Allen Boardman—unfortunately himself suffered a fatal heart attack two days later while in the hospital. I say 'unfortunately' in part because certain questions inspired by his deed remain unanswered and, in fact, may never be resolved. Yet, early investigation has answered some of those questions which people everywhere have found to be so baffling. That a man ninety-four years old should even contemplate assassinating a head of state at all is a remarkable matter. That he actually sallied forth alone to carry out his plan is incredible. That he failed in the assassination only because it was an integral part of his plan to fail seems beyond comprehension. It would be only too easy to label this an act of insanity, but initial close investigation has indicated that such was not the case.

"The comments that I will be making to you this morning will meet with a varied reaction in many quarters.

To some they will be alarming, and to others they will be unbelievable at best. I would hasten to say at the outset that it is neither my intention nor wish to cause alarm. Yet, what I have to say is, by its very nature, a matter of grave concern not only for all Americans, but for people everywhere in the world. As for unbelievability, I must preface this statement by saying that my remarks will indeed be based upon incomplete information available through the initial investigation mentioned earlier. As such they are not to be taken to reflect elements that have been proven beyond dispute. Nevertheless, the very fact that I feel so strongly about them as to present them to you today in this address will attest to my own conviction of their importance and the need to ascertain as quickly as possible either their veracity or their lack of it.

"I am convinced that although the man who shot me—Herbert Allen Boardman—acted in a manner suggesting some degree of mental instability, he was neither insane nor even emotionally disturbed. What he did was done in a bold, calmly conceived and executed manner to achieve precisely the purpose he planned. That purpose will become clear as I continue."

The President looked up and then glanced back down as he slid the fourth sheet of the typed speech to one side, cleared his throat gently, and continued in a serious vein.

"Herbert Boardman was a man who, through many decades of scientific study, developed a theory of revolutionary concept and magnitude, a theory deeply affecting all of mankind. Let me, for a moment, ladies and gentlemen, describe the fundamental elements of the Herbert Allen Boardman Theory which, for the sake of expedience, I will hereafter refer to as the HAB Theory.

"It was Herbert Boardman's postulation, based on those years of exhaustive study, that periodically the earth has been subjected to a recurring natural phenomenon of cataclysmic proportions. At intervals of from three thousand to seven thousand years, according to the HAB Theory, the polar ice caps of our globe reach a maturity of growth. At this time their imbalanced weight overcomes the gyroscopically stabilizing influence of the equatorial bulge of the earth. When this occurs, the law of centrifugal force causes a near ninety-degree capsizing of the globe, with resultant cataclysm of incredible consequence.

"Throughout the many years following his original postulation, Herbert Boardman sought to find factors which would *dis*prove its contentions. Instead, he discovered only additional proofs to underline the validity of his concept. In doing so, it is possible that he has opened a great number of doors to man's dim past which heretofore have been locked. There is, for example, as an offshoot of his postulation, the very real likelihood that a succession of civilizations of mankind have developed on the earth at different periods, each only to be wiped out in its turn practically without trace as another cataclysmic capsizing of the earth occurred. If this is true, then the HAB Theory equally opens a vista of frightening potential of what inevitably may be in store for modern man and his civilization.

"The HAB Theory was relegated to obscurity for many years and might never have come to light at all had not Herbert Boardman only recently, in his continuing studies, devised a possible solution, a manner by which mankind might preserve itself from the destruction which such a cataclysm portends. That a solution might be possible prompted Mr. Boardman to make one final great effort to provide mankind with this means of preserving itself. Investigation is now being made into what the solution might have been. It is hoped that this information will be found in his papers, for Mr. Boardman died before he was able to reveal what his proposed solution involved.

"What Herbert Boardman did less than a week ago in Chicago was undertaken to bring upon himself a national and even international notoriety, the consequence of which would be that the HAB Theory subsequently would be afforded serious inquiry—inquiry which had long been denied it through other avenues. I can in no way condone his action, which was unorthodox and extreme and certainly dangerous to himself and others. Yet, while not condoning it, I can, in the light of what has been discovered since his act, understand why he placed the importance of serious inquiry into the HAB Theory as being above any other consideration.

"There is, assuredly, the possibility that under close and serious scientific scrutiny, flaws will be found in both the HAB Theory and the alleged proofs which Herbert Boardman has uncovered which ultimately will show the postulation to be fallacious. I sincerely hope that such will be the case. It is a matter which can be determined only through an open-minded, in-depth study of all of the ramifications of the theory by the finest scientific minds available. Even the slightest possibility that the HAB Theory is valid requires that major consideration be given to its study and to an increased effort to learn what the solution to this grave threat to mankind might be. That possibility seems to be real, and so already I have taken steps to further the inquiry into this matter. Regular reports and releases to the press will be made to keep the nation and the world apprised of the progress of this inquiry.

"Ladies and gentlemen, I thank you, and good morning."

I I

The snowballing of world interest in the situation which had begun with the attempted assassination of President Robert Morton Sanders, then increased with the added elements of mystery and the death of Boardman, grew still more in the week following the President's short address to the nation.

Reaction ran the gamut from profound shock and near panic to utter disbelief and scorn. News stories and editorials approached the subject from every conceivable angle; some with sympathy and approval, others with ridicule and unmasked anger. Numerous radio and television commentators devoted whole programs to analyses of the ramifications of the Presidential address.

Concern for an injured President faded away and newspapers throughout the nation began reasserting themselves along more politically partisan lines, supporting the administration with glowing praise or attacking it with critical virulence, according to their individual, long-established leanings.

The foreign press was no less interested. Wherever the matter was discussed, and whatever the progressing press coverage, a single fact stood out: the HAB Theory had forever left behind the obscurity which had plagued it for so many years. The theory was neither universally believed nor universally disputed, but it was certainly no longer ignored anywhere. The headlines and opening paragraphs of news stories around the world during the week spoke whole volumes.

PRESIDENTIAL STATEMENT A BOMBSHELL

In an early morning coast-to-coast televised address lasting only eight minutes and five seconds, President Robert Sanders today dropped a verbal bombshell into the laps of the American people and, in truth, the people of the entire world...—kansas city star

SANDERS STATEMENT STUNS POPULACE

A brief televised address to his nation this morning by U.S. President Robert Morton Sanders has created a wave of shock and concern throughout London and the remainder of the United Kingdom...—london evening standard

PRESIDENT BACK IN SADDLE AGAIN

Native son Robert Sanders picked up the reins of government again today in Washington with a startling televised statement...—CHEYENNE WYOMING STATE TRIBUNE

"BOARDMAN ACTED ON OWN"—SANDERS

Discounting possible conspiracy, President Robert Sanders told the nation this morning that his would-be assassin, Herbert A. Boardman, acted entirely on his own. In carefully chosen words, the President termed the death of Boardman "unfortunate" and, without actually saying it, justified Boardman's attack upon him in Chicago five days ago. He also launched an inquiry into the so-called HAB Theory...—ATLANTA CONSTITUTION

TILT! HAB THEORY SAYS EARTH TO CAPSIZE

In the grand science-fiction tradition of a Jules Verne, H. G. Wells, or Robert A. Heinlein, President Sanders today foisted upon an unsuspecting American public an incredible postulation he calls the HAB Theory, which predicts that our civilization will soon end in the capsizing of the entire earth...—LOS ANGELES HERALD EXAMINER

SANDERS INITIATES PROBE

Yesterday, in his first public appearance since the assassination attempt six days ago, the Chief Executive launched an inquiry into the so-called HAB Theory...—BALTIMORE SUN

PRESIDENT AGAIN SHOWS AMAZING COURAGE

In speaking as he did in yesterday's televised nationwide statement, Robert Sanders once more has exhibited the courage of conviction for which he has been noted throughout his political career as both United States Senator and President. He clearly has placed his career on the line in an area where most others would have taken the easier road of declaring an aged, would-be assassin insane. Yet, President Sanders is equally noted as a prudent man who rarely, if ever, acts in haste. This factor alone adds weight to his statement and strongly emphasizes the need to consider the HAB Theory with the greatest degree of scientific sobriety and open-mindedness...—NASHVILLE TENNESSEAN

WORLD COMING TO END—HO-HUM

The Silly Season was launched early this year in grand fashion by no less a personage than President Sanders who, during his address yesterday, undoubtedly was abetted by the ghost of the man who tried to kill him…—BIRMINGHAM *NEWS*

BOARDMAN DAUGHTER STILL MUM

Elizabeth Boardman, middle-aged daughter of Herbert Allen Boardman, remains in seclusion in her suburban Oak Park home, continuing her "No-comment" posture at interview attempts by reporters…—CHICAGO SUN TIMES

ISRAELIS NOT INVOLVED

United States President Robert M. Sanders has personally quashed claims made by Arabic news agencies that the assassination attempt last week was the result of a plot by alleged Israeli terrorist groups…—TEL-AVIV *DAVAR*

BOARDMAN AUTOPSY CONFIRMS HEART ATTACK
THOUSANDS FLOCK TO FUNERAL

In a joint statement issued yesterday by officials of the Northwestern Memorial Hospital Complex and the Cook County Coroner's Office, the death of Herbert Allen Boardman has been confirmed as being the result of a massive coronary occlusion. Interest in Boardman soared to unparalleled heights two days ago following the President's address, and Chicago Police Commission Howard Perello cited this as the reason why tens of thousands of curiosity-seekers converged on Rosemont Cemetery today. Graveside services were held at noon and some 400 Chicago policemen had to be called to disburse the mob…—CHICAGO *DAILY NEWS*

NEW LIGHTS TO SHINE ON MAN'S PAST?

The controversial HAB Theory announced by the United States President the day before yesterday holds a promise of unlocking some of the most baffling archaeological mysteries involving pre-Mayan cultures…—MEXICO CITY *NEWS*

J. C. GRANT AVOIDING NEWSMEN

John Charles Grant, Pulitzer Prize-winning author of suburban Skokie, presently closely involved in the investigation of the Sanders assassination attempt, was back in the Chicago area again today after two days in Washington. He reportedly has returned here, following conferences with the President, to continue his study of the Boardman papers. He remains generally successful in avoiding reporters…—CHICAGO *TRIBUNE*

U.S. PRESIDENT TRIES TO FRIGHTEN WORLD
WITH FORECAST OF STUPENDOUS CATACLYSM

United States President Robert Sanders, in an obvious effort to create a state of panic throughout the world, has returned to the duties of his office with a statement predicting a global disaster of cataclysmic proportions. The Russian Presidium of the Supreme Soviet has concluded that this is no more than a bold attempt by the warmongering American government to divert attention from the rapidly expanding oil crisis in the Middle East and threatened embargoes to the West by the Arabian States…—MOSCOW *PRAVDA*

SANDERS ALIVE…(AND WELL?)

The announcement a few days ago by President Sanders that he suffered "no permanent damage" from the assassin's attack last week has met with dispute here. Dr. Percy Utwell, staff member of this city's Seldon Clinic, stated in a televised panel discussion last night that the concussion suffered by the President when struck in the head by a hard wax bullet might well have caused brain damage as yet undetected. Appearing on the popular KDKA program, "Taking Issue with the Issues," Dr. Utwell admitted that he based his comments on what he termed "the Chief Executive's irrational acceptance" of the much-publicized HAB Theory. Dr. Utwell added that he himself considers the theory as being "utterly ridiculous"…—PITTSBURGH *PRESS*

HAB THEORY NAME ORIGINATED HERE

The remarkable HAB Theory, so much in the news since the President's address early this week, received its name many years ago from the Enquirer's former science editor, the late David Cockrell. The letters H-A-B are the initials of the postulator of the theory, Herbert Allen Boardman…—CINCINNATI *ENQUIRER*

AGA RESENTMENT RISES
BOARDMAN LUNACY IS IMPLIED

In the wake of President Sanders's announcement of the HAB Theory five days ago, Clarence Apperly, president of the American Geophysical Union, today issued a prepared statement from his Washington headquarters expressing the association's outrage following a special meeting of the AGA's board of directors.

The statement reads, in part: "We are unanimously agreed that for President Sanders to have made public announcement of the so-called HAB Theory without even the courtesy of permitting qualified professional geophysicists to study the postulation and advise him beforehand as to its reliability is an outrage and insult." Terming the HAB Theory as "absurd," the AGA statement accused the Chief Executive of "a backhanded attack on reputable geophysicists everywhere on the flimsy basis of a preposterous theory advanced by a senile publicity-seeker with no credentials whatever in the science of geophysics." Apperly quoted Shakespeare as he issued the statement to newsmen, saying that the HAB Theory is nothing more than "…a tale told by an idiot, full of sound and fury, signifying nothing." When asked if this should be taken to mean that he considered Herbert Boardman to have been an idiot, Apperly snapped, "Figure it out for yourself!"…—WASHINGTON *POST*

WAS PRE-INCAN EMPIRE FROM ANOTHER EPOCH?

A sharp resurgence of interest in the archaeological remains of Machu Picchu, Sacsahuaman, Ollantaytambo and other Peruvian sites of pre-Incan culture has occurred as a result of the announcement by the United States President nearly a week ago. That these ruins date from another epoch becomes a distinct possibility in light of…—LIMA *LA CHRONICA*

HAS SANDERS COMMITTED POLITICAL SUICIDE?

U.S. Senator Clyde A. Williams of South Carolina last night told members attending the 65th Annual State Banquet of the American Legion that "it is my unqualified belief that one week ago today President Sanders committed political suicide and he will almost surely go down to defeat in his bid for reelection." Williams, chairman of the Senate Select Committee on Standards and Conduct, who has himself been mentioned as a possible contender for presidential nomination, described Sanders's address to the nation as "shocking and irresponsible"…—PHILADELPHIA INQUIRER

WORLD SCIENTISTS SPLIT ON HAB THEORY
POLL SHOWS DISBELIEF HIGH

In an opinion poll of scientists from all over the world concerning the validity of the HAB Theory, the Sunday Mirror has found that while disbelief in the theory is high, the majority prefer to reserve comment until more information becomes known. Correspondents in 17 countries and 38 major cities contacted a total of 488 of the world's most esteemed scientists in 12 distinct branches of scientific study, including geology, archaeology, paleontology, philology, meteorology, glaciology, climatology, anthropology, astronomy, oceanography, physics and geophysics. The following statistics were noted in answer to the single question: Do you believe there is the likelihood that the HAB Theory will be proven valid?

Yes— 4
No—151
Undecided—253
Refused answer—80
—LONDON SUNDAY MIRROR

PRESIDENT APPOINTS SPECIAL HAB COMMISSION

White House Press Secretary Steven Lace announced today in a press interview that due to the continuing possible jeopardy to world civilization as indicated by the HAB Theory, a five-member special commission has been appointed by the President to assemble HAB data concerning this situation. He added, "This commission's purpose will be to gather and organize HAB Theory data and search for clues Herbert Boardman may have left behind relating to his admission of having devised a plan for saving mankind."

Lace said no chairman has yet been chosen for the commission, but that there will be mutual cooperation between the commission and John C. Grant, who is currently studying the HAB Theory papers at the Boardman residence in Oak Park, Illinois…—UNITED PRESS INTERNATIONAL

"HAB THEORY MINE!" FRUIT-PICKER CRIES

Roberto Rodriguez, itinerant fruit-picker in the avocado orchards near Camarillo, California, was arrested yesterday in the office of Los Angeles Mayor Philip Krogan as he stood on the mayor's desk shouting that the HAB Theory was his.

Rodriguez, 32, claimed to have "dreamed up" the theory five years ago while picking pistachio nuts. He said he met Herbert Boardman on a Greyhound bus ride and between Bakersfield and Amarillo, Texas, he told Boardman the whole thing, and that Boardman subsequently claimed the theory as his own.

Pleading guilty at city court to charges of public intoxication and disturbing the peace, Rodriguez was sentenced to 60 days in the workhouse by Judge Graham Yarbrough. In passing sentence, Yarbrough said, "This will give you ample opportunity to dream up another theory, and you won't even have to pick pistachios while doing so"...—ASSOCIATED PRESS WIRE SERVICE

I I I

Bright midafternoon daylight streaming in the windows of the Oval Office gave the place a more cheery air than it had had when Alex Gordon was here a week ago, when the dark green baize backdrop bearing the presidential seal had been set up behind the desk, blocking away the outside light from television cameras.

Now, clad in a medium-gray, nicely cut gabardine suit, Gordon sat quietly at ease, waiting while the President looked through a number of papers tabbed by Hazel Tierney for his immediate attention. As always, for the White House security chief, there was a feeling of awe which came in just sitting here. This was where Franklin D. Roosevelt had been at the helm of the nation for so long, and where Harry S Truman had conducted the country's affairs with fiery directness. This was where the affable Dwight D. Eisenhower had sat; where John F. Kennedy had favored his ailing back in the famous rocker; where Lyndon B. Johnson was sitting when he glumly announced that he would not run for a second term; where Richard M. Nixon had conducted his affairs and fought so doggedly and so long—and so unsuccessfully—as strand after strand of scandal had been spun around him in the wake of Watergate and related matters.

There was the feeling within Gordon that in some peculiar way, each of these men, along with those who preceded them as President and those who followed, was still here, an eerie essence of a greatness that was almost godlike in its omniscience. Some had been good leaders, others had not, but the very power of the office had wrapped each in the cloak of greatness. Oddly, during one of the first few times that he had sat here in the presence of President Sanders, the Chief Executive had, as if reading Gordon's thoughts, commented on sharing a similar feeling, though not quite with the sense of awe that Gordon experienced.

"Alex," the President had told him then, "sometimes I can feel them standing over my shoulder silently criticizing or applauding whatever it is I'm doing. Except," he'd added, with a mischievous raising of one brow, "when it's one of those damnably delicate decisions which promises to alter the course of history; then the office is suddenly very empty. The ghosts never help much at those times.

There was the familiar whirring sound from the desk as the President signed half a dozen of the documents with the familiar left-handed scrawl that was a flourished illegibility distinctly his. Grace once had laughingly told him he should have been a doctor, since his handwriting was about as legible as that which usually appeared on prescription blanks.

Reinserting the pen in its desktop holder, Sanders leaned back and yawned hugely. Hardly any trace remained of the bruise on his forehead. His mouth snapped closed and now he was looking at Gordon.

"It's one of the occupational realities of this office, Alex, that you never get to sleep long enough or often enough. I sometimes wonder just how many different and converging or interlocking tracks of thought the mind can handle. Every time I think there's no room for taking on a single other element and fitting it into its own separate niche, another handful comes along, and somehow they get fitted. I don't quite understand how, but they do."

Gordon said nothing. It was not the first time Sanders had rambled like this to him, expecting no response and getting none. For differing reasons, both he and the President got a great deal out of it. Gordon enjoyed it because it further cemented the closeness he felt to this man, and because he know that, in a paradoxically ambiguous and definitive way, it was of value to Sanders. For one thing, it permitted Sanders the rare luxury of open and unadulterated verbal introspection, and this in itself had to help clear away the staleness of things that might be locked inside too tightly for too long.

"Now, along those lines, Alex," the Chief Executive said briskly, his gaze sharpening, "we talked very briefly in Chicago about the fact that I might have something I'd want you to do, something that might take you out of the line of work you are doing, the line of work that you enjoy doing."

"I enjoy my work most," Gordon said candidly, "when it involves working closely with you, in whatever manner. I find Secret Service work gratifying, but it's not necessarily the star I've hitched my wagon to."

"I'm glad you feel that way. I truly am. A President has to have those men close to him in whom he can place not only enormous reliance, but men he knows intuitively can accept and handle equally enormous responsibilities; men who can sense without having to ask—and sense accurately—what directions to move in, what decisions to make. Much in the way that I've made use of your abilities in the past, which far exceeds the requirements of your office."

He broke off to sneeze three times in succession, yanking a handkerchief from his pocket and managing to cover the final two. He was shaking his head as he wiped his mouth. "Hope I'm not picking up a bug. Don't really feel like it. What I'm getting to now you've probably gathered already—a greater use of you and even more reliance on you."

"Nothing would please me more, sir."

"Even if it meant leaving the Service?"

"Yes, sir."

"You're not married, are you Alex?"

"No, sir.

"Nor engaged?"

"No, sir." He knew the President was aware of these matters, but enlarged. "I go on dates occasionally, when there's time. Usually there isn't time. I guess maybe I'd take the time if someone came along who was right for me, but that hasn't happened."

President Sanders plucked at his chin with index finger and thumb in a characteristic pinching action. He seemed to come to a decision. "I want you to—"

he stopped momentarily as a tiny, muted tone sounded and a light on his phone winked "—resign from the

Service. I want you to work with me much in the manner of Oscar and Al, but even beyond that in certain respects. Excuse me."

He picked up the phone. "Yes?…Already? Didn't realize it was that late…All right, Hazel. I need five minutes more…Thanks." He looked over at Gordon as he hung up and tilted his head toward the outer office. "Another one of those mental tracks I mentioned earlier. On this one I'm faced with the problem of how to convince a Turkish ambassador to convince a Turkish President to convince a Turkish people—whose economy is largely based on raising poppies, because nothing else grows as well or as profitably there—that its opium production is hurting the rest of the world in general and us in particular. We bought them off once for thirty-five million dollars, but it didn't last long and it won't work at all this time." He paused, thinking. "And speaking of Turkey, Alex, I have a friend over there right now named Mark Shepard who's in Ankara and who just might be deeply involved in this whole HAB business without even knowing it. But those are other matters. Let's get back to you. Do you have anything pending that could make it awkward for you to leave the country for a while?"

"Nothing, Mr. President."

"Fine. I want you to go to Kenya, Alex. We've got to get some definite commitments from Ngoromu. I've a pretty good idea of what would appeal to him, but I've also had State prepare a report on him and the whole East African situation and I want you to study it. Today." He picked up a metal-clasped fiber binder and extended it toward the black man, who immediately came to his feet and took it, then sat down again.

"Read that this afternoon, Alex," Sanders went on. "I want you to consider what Ngoromu wants, needs, hopes for, and how we can help him get it for our mutual benefit. We'll talk about it later and come up with some working ideas between us. You should leave here by tomorrow, but there's an opening in the schedule for this evening that'll help. Hoskins, over at Treasury, has been vaguely aware that he might lose you. Regrets it, but he's ready to have Dillard take up your reins here. Good man. I think I'll give Elliott a call, too; might help if we got you on State Department status at a quiet level. Wish we had more time this evening to talk. Let me make a quick check here."

Sanders picked up the phone and spoke almost at once. "What's the schedule after five, Hazel?…Is that right?…Well, good! No, I don't mean good that it's happened, but I can sure use the time. Call with my regrets and in the meantime let me have that time slot for Alex…Right."

Plucking at his chin he sat straighter in his chair. "Cancellation for Wolzmann. Stung by a bee and hospitalized with a serious allergy reaction." Harold Wolzmann was Secretary of Defense. "You'll take his hour, beginning at six-fifteen." It was a dismissal.

"Yes, sir." Gordon came to his feet and started to leave with the binder of African material, but Sanders stopped him.

"Alex?"

"Sir?"

"How's Grant making out?"

"Evidently pretty well. We took off the surveillance as you directed. I talked with him just after noon. He said he's finding more than he expected but less than he wants."

"That's typical. Any friction between him and the Knotts Commission?"

Gordon smiled. "Some. No more than might be expected, I guess. He's handling it well. He said then that he might have something important in a few hours. He'll call me if it pans out."

"Excellent. Keep tabs." He picked up the phone. "Ready, Hazel."

On his way out Gordon nodded to Mrs. Tierney, who was showing in a swarthy, round-faced man to his audience with the President. Gordon recognized him as Ambassador Arimo Kozthousa of Turkey. The ambassador was smiling, the widespread lips framed by a dense, black, downturned moustache. Kozthousa always smiled with his lips, but rarely with his eyes.

As they passed Gordon, Hazel Tierney handed him a slip of paper folded once. He opened it as the door to the President's office closed behind them.

> Alex —
>
> J.C.G. called from Boardman house. Urgent. Call him back at that number soonest. H.

I V

At one and the same time, John Grant was haggard and vibrant. The seeming physical paradox stemmed from the fact that the past week had been one of the most exhausting he had ever experienced. It also had been one of the most exhilarating. Too little sleep, erratic and imbalanced meals, intensive researching until his eyeballs seemed loose in their sockets, difficulties with HAB Commission chairman Kermit Knotts, difficulties with Anne, difficulties with Marie, difficulties with his children; all these had been combining to sap his energy. Yet, he was at the same time feasting mentally, creatively, on the most exciting project of his life. He was replacing physical energy with an electric nervous energy which alternately boosted him along in prolonged spurts of activity and then faded, to leave him feeling as if all the cells of his body were collapsing.

Since that ball had begun rolling at the onset of his meeting with Peter Proctor in St. Louis, pulling him into this incredible set of circumstances, it had only increased in speed and importance. Three hours of sleep in twenty-four was becoming the norm, and even then he begrudged himself the times when pure devastating fatigue forced him to rest. Totally exhausted, he would fall into a deep sleep, only to snap awake with no trace of sleepiness—only weariness—remaining after just a few hours.

His time had been almost equally spent between his own residence and Boardman's house, with occasional brief respites at Marina City East. At Boardman's there was never rest, only a concentrated, grinding period of digging deeply for anything of value that had been written or clipped or saved during a lifetime spanning over nine decades; a period of organizing the badly disorganized material, of collating and summarizing, of taking notes until his fingers became stiff and handwriting all but illegible, of tape-recording until his voice was raspy and deadened with fatigue.

At his own house in Skokie there were the necessities which had become irksome because they consumed time, and time was precious; the eating and sleeping, the bathing, shaving, dressing, the constant backlog of correspondence which cried to be answered, the effort of maintaining regular daily entries in his diary—entries which had become progressively shorter when by rights they should have been longer in order to record the fascinating efforts and accomplishments and discoveries of his days. There were, at those times in his own house, the home things which took longer: the talks with Billy and Carol Ann and the children's fascination with his sudden, greater prominence; Carol Ann's huge disappointment—abetted by Marie's tight-lipped accusatory stares—at his rushing home to stay only as briefly as possible for her birthday dinner a few days ago, then rushing away immediately when it was over; Billy's strident anger at his father's not doing anything with him anymore, and Marie's grim, wordless agreement.

Marie had changed drastically in these past two weeks, of that there was no longer any doubt in his mind. It wasn't a cold or the flu or the irritation engendered by a menstrual period; it was a distinct change. The lightness which had always characterized her was diminished almost to nothingness, the lightness of her walk, her smile, her humor, her attitude. Her eyes had become hooded, often averted, and her lips narrowed and downturned at their corners. He had stopped asking what was wrong, weary of hearing the hollow "Nothing" in response, knowing that whatever was troubling her would continue to simmer within for an interval of time and then finally, like a ripened boil, erupt and purge itself of the unpleasantness and then be better. Usually that occurred within a few days, but this time it hadn't. It would, eventually, he was sure of it; but it hadn't yet.

They had made love only once, he and Marie, since his return from Washington, and it had been unpleasant. That was another change. In their years together, it never had been bad. Sometimes it was better than at other times and, on rare occasions, it was ecstatic, but always no less than good. Never bad. Not until this time. In an ironic twist of the old line, the flesh had been willing but the spirit was weak. They had joined, but it had been cold, not really inspiring any responsiveness in either, and with climax itself unsatisfying. Unpleasant. Marie had wept, long and hard, with deep shuddering sobs wracking her frame, and he had tried with strangely alien awkwardness to console her, but with neither determination nor success. The numbing fatigue, held in abeyance by will power alone, engulfed him and he fell asleep, leaving Marie weeping all the harder that he could sleep at such a time as this. Since then their days had been coldly uncommunicative.

Then there was Anne; her joy at his return, her intense pleasure at helping with the research at Boardman's house, her happiness in being really needed for that help, her delight—as always—in the total mutual gratification of their lovemaking, her pleasure in rubbing him, holding him, playing with him even when the weariness was too great for him to respond, only relax and enjoy; all these things were overshadowed by her sudden strange compulsion to pin him down. She wanted his words—the words beyond the heartfelt "I love you." She wanted the promises to her that he was not yet able to make, the plans that he was not yet able to formulate, the future that he was not yet able to foresee. She asked the questions that he had been asking of himself for much longer than she knew, questions which tormented him ceaselessly and for which he had no answer even for himself, much less for her. Always before he had been able to act decisively, confidently, quickly, and now he had become unable to make a decision, unsure of himself or what he wanted, dragging his feet because anywhere he would direct them in forward movement seemed the wrong way.

Early this morning he had picked up Anne in a swing downtown on the Edens and Kennedy expressways and then together they had gone, as they had for the past three days, west on the Eisenhower Expressway to Harlem Avenue and then north to Oak Park and the Boardman house. This morning, as on past mornings, they had run the gauntlet of reporters still keeping vigil over the house, hopeful—though with daily dimming hope—that fortune would smile on them and they would manage to squeeze an interview out of Grant or perhaps Elizabeth Boardman. Fortunately, now there were just reporters, the photographers off on more promising assignments. John Grant walking down a sidewalk no longer was considered a really newsworthy photo. Even the reporters had been fewer this morning and did not pester for a statement as vigorously as before. Anne, with her armful of notebooks, fistful of pencils and other props, looked to be no more than a secretary in Grant's employ and, except for appreciative glances, was not bothered by reporters.

A sort of camaraderie had developed between John and Anne and Liz and Paul. Though Grant knew there was an element of risk in bringing Anne with him, he did so anyway because he really did need her help in the research and, as an aside, there was a sort of intriguing excitement in running the risk of being caught in their indiscretion. After the initial introductions, the four had spent half an hour discussing Boardman and the HAB Theory, speculating on where the research eventually would lead.

"I never really suspected," Liz Boardman had said regretfully that first morning, "that Dad's research and writing and other work on his project—that's how he always referred to it, you know, as 'my project'—was anything more than a sort of engrossing hobby with him. I was pleased, in a way, when he had his book published, but a little bit angry, too, because he'd paid to have it done and he actually couldn't afford that expense. And then, on top of it all, to *give* away the copies! But," she shrugged, "it was his money and he was a grown man." Her eyes misted briefly and her lower lip trembled. "Besides, I was then still with Sam—my former husband—and not living here.

"Incidentally," she added, "I should say that Sam Kaiser at least had the grace to send a condolence card when he heard the news. I also received a cable from David, my son, who's over in Australia. He and his wife went there shortly after they were married. Anyway, getting back to what I was saying, once I made an effort to read *The Eccentric Earth* but, as you're aware now, Dad was a pretty awful writer. He completely lost me in just the first couple of pages. So, after that I just smiled sort of condescendingly at him as he puttered around with his 'project' and never took any real interest. I wish I had. I wish he could have known how interested I'd become—how interested the whole world's become, in fact."

The first morning had set the pattern and each day that followed they spent upwards of an hour chatting over coffee and toast before Liz and Paul, too, if he were there—set off for Oakmont High School. Then John and Anne would dig in and work hard, pausing only occasionally to exchange a smile, a touch, the whisper of a kiss.

With the formation of the five-member HAB Commission, soon put under the chairmanship of Kermit Knotts, a problem developed. Knotts was a very bright and methodical man of about fifty who was totally devoid of imagination and undistinguished by any outstanding physical characteristic other than a penchant for atrocious bow ties. A political science major who graduated from the Ohio State University, he really wasn't cut out for politics, a deficiency he quickly realized. Nevertheless, he had gravitated to Washington and there earned a reputation as a steady and reliable aide to the senator from Wyoming, Robert Sanders, until he left to establish the firm which he now called Analyses, Incorporated. Still, off and on over the years Sanders had utilized his intelligence and tenacity in a number of ways and had never been disappointed.

In his methodical manner, Knotts always did the job well that he was asked to do, but rarely bringing any more to it than he had been asked to provide. He also was a man who followed orders implicitly and had never in the slightest way betrayed any trust that Sanders had placed in him. Apart from his lack of imagination, his one great fault—if fault it could be called —was an absolute lack of personality. It seemed utterly beyond his capacity to exude even a smattering of human warmth and social interest, but neither did he seem to require any. He went his way, never being known by anyone beyond the bland image he projected and never wanting to know anyone else any better. But he was a man who did his assigned task well, and when Sanders needed the services of someone methodical, statistically inclined and reliable, and had called on him to head the committee to collate the Boardman papers, he had accepted. He also fully intended to do his job.

While he was chairman of the HAB Commission, he was not supervisory to John Grant and had, in fact, been specifically instructed by the President to cooperate with the writer in the fullest measure. If Grant needed any special assistance, Knotts was to provide it immediately. Alone of his commission, Knotts came to Chicago. His initial view was to acquire and study the Boardman papers and then send them off to the other commission members in Washington for their perusal and collation along the lines of his recommendations. He had taken it for granted that the papers would be turned over to him without question. When Elizabeth Boardman had flatly refused to do any such thing, he had calmly stated that he would then obtain a federal court order for them.

It was at this point that Grant had spoken with Knotts alone for several minutes and then, expressionlessly, Knotts had waited while Grant spoke to Liz in a whispered conference on the other side of the room. After discussing a number of things they might do, Liz had agreed to a compromise that Grant suggested: after he had finished with any given paper or set of papers, these would be taken by Anne to a nearby reproduction facility to be copied. In this way, Elizabeth could retain her hold on the originals—which she was determined to do at all costs—and each evening Grant could deliver the copies to Knotts in his room at the Westbury Hotel. Knotts was far from enamored of the idea at first, but finally gave in, and since the hotel was only a few blocks from Marina City, the arrangement posed no great hardship for Grant.

At the same time, Knotts was able to lift a considerable burden from Grant. The commission chairman relayed to the writer his instructions from the President to cooperate with Grant and assist him in any way possible, and Grant was swift to take advantage of it. He not only delivered to Knotts the photoduplicated Boardman papers, but also the series of tape recordings he was making to summarize the whole structure of the HAB Theory and its proofs. Grant requested Knotts to have his corps of stenographers at Analyses, Incorporated, make, as rapidly as possible, a full transcript of the summary he was taping, this transcript then to be turned over to the President immediately upon completion. Again Knotts agreed, and once again with display of neither distaste nor enthusiasm.

It had been just before noon when Grant unexpectedly came across the first reference he'd encountered to Boardman's idea concerning the possibility of man's circumventing the disaster that a capsizing of the earth promised. He had been reading the handwritten page for two or three minutes before the realization dawned on him that this was what he had been looking for, or at least a portion of what he was seeking and a substantial lead to where the rest might be.

"Anne!

There had been no reply and he remembered she'd gone to have another raft of the papers copied. With mounting excitement he read the paper through twice more. There wasn't enough here, not by any means, but now he had a direction, a trail to follow. He glanced at his watch, saw it was just a little past twelve, and picked up the phone. Before leaving Washington he had agreed to call at noon each day and report his progress to Alexander Gordon or, failing to reach him, directly to the President. He reached Gordon without difficulty.

Their conversation had been brief. Grant managed to keep his excitement in check and the nearest he came to revealing it was when he told Gordon that he thought he may have found something quite significant, but that he wasn't sure yet and wanted to check further before saying anything definite. If it turned out to be what he thought, he'd call later today.

He was busily rummaging through the files for anything more dealing with what he'd found, and having no real success, when Anne returned with her papers plus hamburgers and milkshakes.

"Read this," he told her.

He stood watching her as the green eyes followed the lines. As his had done, hers began to widen about two-thirds of the way through. When she finished her mouth was slightly agape and she wet her lips with a delicate flick of her tongue before speaking.

"John this is Mr. Boardman's solution, isn't it?"

"Not entirely, honey, but it's a start. What do you think of it?"

"I'm…well, I don't know exactly what I am. Stunned more than anything else, I guess. I never really considered it from that viewpoint before. But, my God, John, what a drastic solution!"

"Maybe. I guess any solution would have to be. But it beats building an ark and waiting around for the flood. Let's dig in, now that we know what we're looking for, and see what else we can find."

Munching the hamburgers and drinking the milkshakes without really tasting them, they began a systematic search, using broad topics and key words suggested by the single page as clues. There were more than five hundred alphabetized topics on the tabs of bulging manila folders in Boardman's bank of file cabinets. Grant started at the head of the files, Anne at the foot, and they worked toward one another. Each time a file folder was encountered bearing a designation that might even remotely be connected with what they were seeking, it became necessary to pause and page through the contents. Since some of these individual folders themselves contained scores of sheets, it was a time-consuming job.

Anne found it. She was leafing through the *T* section at about three o'clock in the afternoon when she passed it by. Half a dozen file folders beyond she paused, reconsidered, then went back to look at it more closely.

"Eureka!" she breathed.

Grant was squatting, engrossed in a bottom-drawer file. Forgetting about the partially open file drawer above him, he jerked his head up and groaned softly as it struck the heavy drawer with a dull, metallic thud. She ran to him, the file in her hand, kneeled beside him and gently touched the injured spot and then kissed it.

"Poor darling."

"Lady," he said, rubbing the swelling and wincing, "I hope your wild outburst which caused this painful result signifies *something*."

She laughed aloud and it was a bright sound in the dimness of the study. Thrusting the folder toward him she said, "See for yourself, Hon."

He took it from her, turned it around to read the tab and then, frowning slightly, looked inside. Within moments a wide grin spread his lips and it stayed there as he swiftly paged through the contents. She was beside him, her head close to his, looking as he looked. When he finished he brought his hand up her back, under the long dark hair, and gripped her neck, turning her head and pulling her to him. In the midst of the kiss she leaned too far sideways on her knees and, compounded by his weight against her, lost her balance and fell, pulling him along. He stopped his fall with his hands against the floor and looked down at her beneath him, her hair fanned out and framing her head, expression a little shocked. He lowered his head and kissed her again, tenderly, but with growing intensity, at the same time putting a hand to her breast and rolling it gently under his palm.

" Wow!" she murmured as her lips were freed. "If I'd known what the reward was, I'd've found it an hour ago!"

"Your reward," he said, helping her to her feet, "is the best-by—God dinner in the city of Chicago! C'mon, work's over for today. You start straightening up a bit while I call Gordon."

It took two calls. Gordon's office informed him that the agent was not available. Calling the alternate number, he reached Hazel Tierney. After hearing him out, she promised to have Alex Gordon call as soon as his conference with the President was finished, which was supposed to be in no more than a few minutes. She was right.

Grant reached the phone in two strides when it rang five minutes later.

"Grant here."

"Gordon. The note says urgent."

"Damned right! You can tell The Man we've got it!" Grant could suddenly hear a clock ticking in the silence behind Gordon.

"The *solution*?" It was a whisper.

"No doubt about it."

The clock was ticking again. "I'll be seeing the President this evening. He'll want to know what it is."

"You don't want it over the phone!" Grant was shocked.

"Of course not. But he'll want to know. Will you be at home this evening?"

"What time?"

"I'll be seeing him at six-fifteen. I'll probably call shortly thereafter. Or he will."

"Okay, I'll be at home waiting. Oh, and Gordon, thanks for calling off the bloodhounds."

"No point. We know you're on our side now." He added, after a slight pause, "How's the summary coming along?"

"All of it, with the exception of this latest portion on the Boardman solution, is in Kermit Knotts's hands. I'll have this stuff to him today and the final transcript ought to be ready in less than a week."

"Terrific. That's fast work. Take care. Be in touch with you tonight."

The connection was broken and Grant hung up. Anne was watching him, a faint frown etching two vertical lines between her eyebrows. He thought he knew the reason.

"Don't get upset." He squeezed her shoulder. "The reward still stands."

The lines were deeper and her nostrils flared. She shrugged off his hand and spoke accusingly. "You're going to be getting a call this evening from Gordon at your house?" At his nod she went on in a biting tone. "You said at home!"

He was bewildered. "Sure, that's right. At home."

"That's *not* your home. It's your house, your domicile, your legal residence, call it whatever you want except home." Tears were glassing her eyes now. "Damn it, John Grant, your *home* is at Marina City East, apartment forty-two forty-three! When you go to her, you go to your house. When you go *home*, you come to me!"

"Semantics, Anne. Words." He was displeased. "Nothing to get worked up over."

"The hell it's not! It's everything. As long as you think of that other place as home, you're not going to leave it. Or her! And you *are* going to leave it—them—and come home because…because…" the tears dribbled down her cheeks and she blinked rapidly, trying to check them, but couldn't, "…because home is where your heart is, and your heart is with me!"

She broke down completely and leaned against his chest, sobbing heavily. Grant put his arms around her and held her close. Now he was the one who was frowning. When he spoke, his words were conciliatory, but the frown didn't leave.

"Come on now, honey. I'm taking us home. I'll drop you off there and go on to my house. As soon as I get through with Gordon's call, I'll come back and we'll have that good dinner."

There was a thoughtful expression on Grant's face as he drove, and neither of them spoke much on the way downtown.

V

The malaise that had been afflicting Marie Grant for nearly a fortnight had not diminished. If anything, it had intensified to the point where nothing seemed clear or made sense to her. In a dim recess of her mind there was something struggling to free itself, a desperate knowledge that somehow she had to fight back, that she mustn't just let her world crumble at her feet without at least an effort at combating the enemy. But how? And who? And where to start?

Part of the tragedy was that now, after such a long time, John had become deeply absorbed in a project again, devoting great amounts of time and energy to it, becoming lost in it, and a small part of Marie rejoiced that it had occurred. If only she had not opened a door she now realized should have remained shut! She knew her own actions toward John lately had been driving him away from her even more surely than he was being pulled away, and yet she couldn't help the way she was acting. How else does one act when a comfortable, secure world is falling away? But if she hadn't become hooked on the narcotic of code deciphering, it would have made everything so different! What a perfectly marvelous time this could have been for them—the excitement of all that was occurring around them, the launching of John into a project more important than any that had ever touched him before, the fact that he had become a key figure in a situation of world concern, the fact that he already had met twice with the President himself and undoubtedly would again. All these and more were things which they should have shared, should have reveled in together, should have made a part of *their* lives, not just his. What was worst was that she felt the blame for it inside. John had tried to share at first, tried to tell her with boyish excitement of the wonderful and intriguing things that were happening. She had not listened, *couldn't* listen, because the horrible cloak of misery that had been spun around her made anything else unimportant. And now it was too late, because John had shut a door. He no longer was inclined to share. At a time when she should have been most receptive to him in any conceivable way, this was when the hurt within her had made that impossible and she had turned herself away from him.

With a desperation that made her ache inside, Marie wished she could stop decoding the diary entries. She had even considered destroying the volumes bearing those coded entries, or at least ripping out the offensive pages and destroying them, but she couldn't bring herself to do it. Not yet. Later, perhaps, when she finished, when there were no more of the addictive entries left, which wouldn't be too long a time now; maybe then she could sit before the fireplace and feed them one by one into a crackling blaze. But not now, because now she was deciphering another series of the outpourings from the pen of the stranger who was her husband. They were entries for five different dates within a three-week period ending only five weeks ago.

*...I haven't written much in this coded portion of the diary lately, mainly because it takes considerable time to do so and I've had little time to spare recently. Now it becomes necessary to take the time and effort required to do some serious writing about the present situation. Marie has become aware that something is radically wrong and I can sense that she is confused and hurt and, I think, perhaps a little afraid that I don't love her anymore. No assertions of my love for her have seemed effective in assuaging her doubts. She doesn't know what it is that's wrong, only that **something** is troubling me, depressing me, and she has the idea that she is at fault. Whatever fault there is lies within me, not her. I've been uncommunicative and unhappy, knowing all the while that I am increasing her concern and unhappiness in being that way, yet unable to help myself. I really wish I could. A and I have certainly opened a Pandora's Box, and where we go from here is anyone's guess. The suspicions Marie tries not to show, the subtle scrutiny of me that she has been making lately, makes me all the more edgy and irked, tending to make me feel as if I'm on a leash, and that's a very unpleasant sensation. Marie may suspect that I have fallen out of love with her, but in truth I haven't. It's just that I love A very deeply as well and I refuse to deny my love for either of them. God, what a **predicament**!...*

Marie bit her lip, forcing back the tears. Not now! She couldn't cry now. She had to finish. There was still a thread of hope—stretched unbearably taut, it was true, but still there. John still loved her and his love for her *had* to prove stronger in the end than what he felt for this intruder who had entered their lives. She shuddered and continued decoding the entry.

...marie might vaguely suspect that I could be having a fling with another woman, but I don't believe she could conceive that I might actually be in love with another. After all these years, how little she really knows me and, significantly, how little she really understands human nature. She is a good mother to our children and, I suppose, a much better wife than I deserve. There is no way for me to even attempt explaining to her how I feel—which I would rather do than be so damned deceptive like this. The deception becomes more complex and extensive each day.

Where I go from here where A is concerned is unanswerable. The love that I have for her is founded not just in sex but in the wholeness of her, in all those things that make her what she is, and I know with a certain fatalism that sooner or later she and I must come to the point where what little we share now becomes not enough for either of us. This is when undoubtedly we will begin to engage in some very serious discussions about what lies ahead. I don't relish the thought because, from my vantage at present, **no** *view of the future bodes any substantial promise for us, and progressively less happiness. Yet, it is not in my power to forego seeing her any more. "O, what tangled webs we weave...!"*

There was hope there, of a sort—vague, nebulous, perhaps foolishly insubstantial—but Marie grasped at it frantically and mentally clutched it to her breast. John realized there was no promise in what lay ahead, no happiness in such a future. As time progressed, wouldn't he realize this even more? If he ever really considered all that was involved, wouldn't he know that it was pointless to pursue his course any further? It would be difficult for him to break away from the excitement he was experiencing, the adventure, but she had yet within her that strong spark of faith which said he could do it—and would! She bent to the next entry at once.

...It seems as if my life is falling apart. I am reaching a decided crisis point, in my marriage, in my affair, in my life. I am not happy at home anymore. My life over the past couple of years seems somehow to have become dull, rutted, increasingly uninteresting. It's a comfortable life, I have to admit, but like my own writing of late, it has become prosaic. I know that Marie wishes for nothing more than my happiness and it grieves me that her efforts in this respect are not successful. The sense of being stifled grows each day, becomes constantly more oppressive, suffocating, frustrating. I wonder, perhaps, if the basis for all this has its genesis not it Marie, but in my writing. Writing is my life and always has been. I eat it, breathe it, sleep it. It dominates my life. But over the past couple of years, perhaps even more, I've watched the fire of inspiration grow less and less bright. Though I write about as much as ever, it is increasingly uninspired. I am suddenly on the sidelines, watching as an integral part of me is deteriorating—aware of the degeneration and desperately wanting to check it, but unable to do so.

Despite the depressed nature of that entry, it caused the spark of hope in Marie's breast to flare a bit more brightly. This was the first coded entry since he met her that John had not mentioned A, had not given rein to an outpouring of the crippling love, as he called it, that was dominating him. She hoped he would continue thinking in this vein, feeling a wave of sympathy for him flush through her, wanting so terribly to reach out and help, but not knowing how. She sniffed and blew her nose and then returned to the task of deciphering the next entry with considerably more hope than previously.

...My situation is worsening. Whatever I will do about it seems calculated to hurt those I love most dearly and am most responsible to and for. The only real easing of tension and pressure seems to be when I am with A. I feel empty, lost, when we're apart, exultant and having some measure of peace when we're together. Damn it, this tells me something! Increasingly A becomes the focal point of my present existence and I become all the more inclined to do whatever I must in order to share the remainder of my life with her.

It was at the close of this entry that Marie made her decision. It was time for her competition to become real, a flesh-and-blood reality instead of an invulnerable shadow—a menacing, ghostlike, disembodied wraith known to her only as A. If John was going to become lost to her, then it was not going to happen because his wife had merely stood silently in the alcoves watching it happen. Somehow, she knew, she must learn the identity of this creature called A. If the only way to learn this was through directly confronting John and asking, then that was what she would have to do.

There was a grim satisfaction within Marie at having come to this decision. Just the very act of planning to end the passiveness that had been gripping her made her feel infinitely better. It was not a feeling which lasted for very long. The first sentence of John's next coded entry, three days later, filled her with horror.

*...I have never been inclined toward suicidal tendencies, and yet the thought of it comes into mind frequently these days. Why this moroseness enveloping me lifts only when I am with A is inexplicable to me. It doesn't make much sense to me, with this being the case, that I go on trying to live a charade in such an intolerable existence as my life has become of late. Marie means a great deal to me, just as I love Carol Ann and Billy. But the love I harbor for them is a far cry from what I feel for A. The fact remains ever present that life without A is inconceivable for me to contemplate. Yet, I can conceive of no way that life **with** her is possible unless I abdicate all responsibilities here and go there, even in the knowledge that there is almost sure to be no degree of true happiness in that direction. It is a vicious circle and perpetually frustrating. Little wonder, perhaps, that suicidal thoughts have impinged on my consciousness lately...and not unpleasantly. Even that is hardly an answer, though, for wouldn't wife and children be even more deprived by such an irrevocable loss? And what about A? It would end the problem and frustration for me, assuredly, but at what cost to those others whom I love so much? The damnable circling continues unchecked.*

Marie stopped writing and sat with her eyes closed for a long while. Despite John's vehement assertions of his love for this other woman, she could not believe it. His feeling was no more than a runaway infatuation. How could his so-called "love" for her and his experiences of mere weeks possibly be compared to a true love developed through seventeen years of sharing joys and sorrows, triumphs and failures? How could a mere sexual gratification possibly compare with the wonder of creating children together and watching them grow and become a part of the ever-deepening love that she and John shared?

There were no tears in Marie's eyes at the completion of this entry. A sick hollowness and unbearable ache inside, yes, but no tears. The wonder of it all was how John could do this to her and to Billy and Carol Ann. Had he no conscience, no compassion? Was he devoid of moral turpitude? Where was the integrity, the honor, the decency that were characteristics of the man she had married?

She opened her eyes and, sighing deeply, tackled the unusually long coded entry which remained.

*...It seems obvious that my health, both physical and mental, is being considerably affected. I damn the fates that have caused me to be so introspective, so concerned with sense and reason. I have, goddammit!, a real dilemma here and so what do I do? For Christ's sake, **what do I do?** I've been thinking a lot these past days of another aspect of this whole mess. Not of Marie or myself. Not even of A. I've been thinking about the kids. What of carol Ann and Billy in all this? What are the ramifications for them? They need a father to help and guide them, although often enough I doubt my effectiveness in this respect. Anyway, they love me and need me as all children need a father to love and care for them. I fell uncomfortably sure that I've never been any great shakes as a father to them as things stand. I know, too, that whatever course I follow, they will be provided for very well insofar as material needs are concerned. True, they need a father, but I feel as if I have been only a half-father to them, and is a half-father any better than none? Might he not be **worse** than none? They might, in truth, be better off without me entirely than with me as I am now and have been in the past. The thought comes with ever greater frequency that within only a few short years from now, both of them will be gone, living their own lives elsewhere. Do I then give up what possible future peace of mind I might have just on this basis? For that, again, I have no answer. If I stayed and wound up, because of the continuing depression over this situation, blowing my brains out, would this be better for them? And I think that is more of a probability these days than just a remote possibility. If one can't find **some** degree of inner peace and happiness, then life itself becomes pretty pointless. What a dilemma! I'm unable to resolve **anything** and I wonder to myself, am I unique in the way I feel and in the way I am reacting? My God, other men have fallen in love outside their marriages and have left their homes and wives and children behind. Sometimes it has worked out and sometimes it has not, but at least they seem to be able to take the steps. They make their decision and go ahead with it. Don't they experience the inner turmoil that I am encountering? Is it so easy for them? Don't they consider the choices, the feelings of others, the ultimate effects of what they're doing or plan to do? Or, having considered them, do they just go on and do it anyway, and to hell with the consequences? Is it normal for **me** to feel such concern for all parties at my own expense, and at Anne's? Don't my own needs and wants, as well as Anne's, have to be considered somewhere along the way, if I am to live with myself? I don't know. I just don't know.*

Marie stood up slowly, her features devoid of expression. With automaton stiffness she carried the sheaf of papers she had written to the bedroom and carefully put them with the others at the back of the dresser drawer beneath her lingerie. Returning to John's den, she replaced the diary on the shelf where it belonged, checked to see if everything looked right, then snapped off the light and started downstairs to fix dinner. Of all that John had written in these entries, only one word of it kept ringing in her mind with a bitter exultation. At last she had a name instead of an initial. *Anne!*

She knew now that she would no longer hesitate in confronting John with everything. She would at last be doing so in her own way and in her own time, starting just as soon as he came home.

She was halfway down the stairs when the front door opened and John walked in.

V I

Alexander Gordon returned the small spiral notebook to his breast pocket and waited patiently for the President to continue. This past twenty minutes was marking a turning point in his life and, as always when a man reaches one of those crossroads, he wondered if he had made the right decision.

A few hours ago he had been chief of White House security, a man who had spent his entire adult life, after leaving the Los Angeles Rams, in federal law enforcement work, first with the FBI and later with the Treasury Department's Secret Service. Yet here, at a mere suggestion from this man sitting across the Oval Office desk from him, he had put aside that past and was now attached to the Department of State.

Robert Sanders, with practically no trace remaining of his forehead injury, at the moment was steeped in thought, his elbows on the desk, one hand lapped over the other and his chin resting against the hands, looking at Gordon but not really seeing him. It wasn't the first time Gordon had seen the Chief Executive do this, and he took a measure of pride in the knowledge that there were few people in whose presence Sanders allowed himself the luxury of such detachment. Before long, Gordon knew, the President would clear his throat and instantly be ready to move ahead in whatever direction he had been considering.

Their talk had begun twenty minutes ago and in that time Sanders had spoken almost continuously, with Gordon making occasional notes to himself. Now and again the President had asked for Gordon's views, in light of the material he had been studying, and he had seemed pleased at Gordon's response. With characteristic directness, the President had explained the urgent need now existing to establish a solid and exclusive alliance with the government of Kenya which would be stronger and longer-lasting than any in the past. With new Arab oil embargoes on the verge of being used as a blackmail device to force the United States to lessen its ties with Israel—which Sanders positively had no intention of doing, most particularly in the face of such blackmail—the newly discovered Kenyan oil field could well be the key to the continuance of the United States as a world power. A massive embargo by the Middle East countries, which had lasted only a few months during 1973-1974, had proven only too well how the Arab oil nations could quickly, and at only minor inconvenience to themselves, bring powerful nations to their knees. This knowledge was a club with which, ever since, they had threatened to bludgeon the world market if higher prices were not met and certain favors given. Among these "favors" was the gradual elimination of support to Israel by other nations, beginning with the smaller, most oil-import-dependent countries first and gradually working up to the giants.

Up until only a few years ago, America had been able to wield a club of its own in response. As much as the United States economy pivoted on petroleum imports from the Middle East, so too the Arab States had been uncomfortably dependent upon importation of American wheat surpluses. An uneasy stalemate had existed for many years, until a benevolent hand from nature had let the Soviet Union step more pertinently into the picture. For decades in the past, Russia's wheat crop had been an agricultural yo-yo. For a while it would do well, even to the point where it seemed a surplus of Russian wheat would occur; but then a series of growing seasons rife with winds, freezes, rainstorms of great intensity and severity, with resultant flooding of the rich wheat lands of the Steppes, would result in almost total crop failures and grain deficiencies which crippled that largest nation on earth. But in the past five years nature had been more than kind and Russian wheat coffers not only filled but overran. Wheat exportation became more important to the Russian economy than at any other period in its history. What all this amounted to was that with Russian grain available to the Arab States in unlimited quantities, the club of petroleum embargo in Arabic hands now was poised for a crushing blow to the United States. That blow could not be parried in any other way now except by America's finding another oil source. Kenya was the answer.

The object, as Sanders explained it to Gordon, was to offer the Kenyans something in exchange which the other bargaining powers either could not or would not match. That important something was what Gordon had been listening to the President outline until his conclusion a few minutes ago.

Sanders abruptly dropped his hands to the desk top and cleared his throat. "That's pretty much the picture at this time as far as Kenya and President Ngoromu are concerned. It's a gamble, undoubtedly, but one we have no choice but to take. Your role in this, Alex, could provide the turning point in our favor. Now, let's go on to something else. What about Grant? He called back?"

"Yes, sir. He didn't say much, for which I don't blame him, but he did make it clear that he's located Boardman's solution. He sounded pretty excited about it. I told him I'd be seeing you and would get back to him as soon as you let me know what you wanted to do at this point. He also said Kermit Knotts would have the final tapes tonight on the summary, including the solution bit, for transcription."

"Grant's at his home?"

"By now, yes, sir."

Sanders picked up his phone. "Hazel, get John Grant on the line for me, will you please?…Yes, at his home."

He recradled the device and shook his head, dark eyes thoughtful and brow furrowed. "I'm not at all sure where we're going to go with this HAB thing, Alex. I was advised in the strongest possible terms by Al Jabonsky not to make the statement, and Oscar pretty much backed him up. I rejected that advice and went ahead and now there's a good possibility that I may regret it. The press is going out of its mind trying to get more and the opposition's having a ball roasting me. I can only hope that Grant can—" He broke off and snatched up the phone as it signaled.

Good, thanks…Hello, Mr. Grant?…Fine, thank you. Alex Gordon's here in the office. Says you've come up with something…You're sure on that?…No, I agree, the phone's not the place, but I want to see you in the morning reasonably early. Can you be here?…How about ten o'clock?…Excellent. At the same time, be considering some recommendations from your viewpoint about what our logical steps should be now, projected as far as you can. I'm going to have a number of people here to sit in, after you and I have gone over it alone for a while…Go on…That sounds a little forbidding…All right, you undoubtedly know best at the moment…Can you also give me a fairly tight summary of what else you've turned up since you left here?…Fine. Be prepared to spend a few days in Washington. I'll see you at ten tomorrow…Please extend my apologies to Mrs. Grant for pulling you away again on such short notice, and my best regards as well. Good night."

The President stood up at the same time as he replaced the phone and Gordon got to his feet at once. Sanders nodded, coming around the desk.

"Apparently he has it, Alex. From what he's indicated, we may not be all that pleased to hear about the solution."

He gripped Gordon's arm warmly and began walking with him toward the door. "I wish you were going to be here for it."

"I'd have liked that, Mr. President." He stopped when Sanders did at the door to the outer office and accepted the offered hand wordlessly.

"Extend my warm personal regards to President Ngoromu and his wife. Tell him I hope to see him again in the near future." He paused, then added, "Also, that I greatly appreciated his calling the First Lady on the morning of the shooting. Be careful, Alex."

"Yes, sir, Mr. President, I'll do that." The answer covered it all and Gordon started away. "Goodbye, sir."

VII

Marie Grant stood with her back against the bedroom doorjamb, where she'd been ever since following John upstairs, and watched him pack swiftly and silently, his face set in hard lines. Neither of them had said a word to one another for five minutes or more and the atmosphere between them was frigid.

In a way, she was glad the telephone call from the President had come. It was very nearly a "saved-by-the-bell" interference, because their conversation to that point had been strictly downhill. Another few moments, she knew, and the damning words would have been spoken and then there would have been no stopping. It would come to that eventually, this was clear, but now that she'd made the decision, she was in no real hurry to follow through. The fact that they had been heading in that direction anyway was strictly the result of a conversational evolution she hadn't anticipated. The wonder of it all to her now was that it hadn't occurred the moment he stepped inside the house. Certainly she'd been prepared for it.

Inadvertently, Carol Ann and Billy had been the ones to prevent an explosion then. They'd plunged into the house only seconds behind John, Billy's arms tightly wrapped around Carol Ann's waist and she with a headlock on him, both of them grunting and shrieking and gasping as Billy tried to drag her down onto the floor. Both were laughing so hard and were so preoccupied with their activity that they hadn't seen their father stop to toss a greeting to Marie on the stairs. They had run into him and it was enough of an interruption that they were able to break apart and stand poised and panting for a renewal of happy hostilities.

"Mother!" Carol tossed an appeal up the stairway. "Tell him to stop *tickling* me."

"Dad!'! Billy's grin was that of a co-conspirator. "Grab her till I can get her down."

The twelve-year-old plunged at his sister but was brought up short as John Grant caught his passing wrist and spun him back. "Hey, c'mon now, you two. Take it easy." He swatted Billy in a jovial manner on the bottom and then ruffled his already wholly unruly hair. Hi, sweetie," he added, reaching over to put his hand on Carol Ann's shoulder and draw her to him. Her arm slipped around him automatically.

"Hi, Daddy," she said, smiling up at him with a little toss of her head to get her hair out of her eyes. The femininity of the movement delighted him and his grin broadened.

Marie's eyes were suddenly glistening and she continued down the stairs. Her husband disengaged himself from Carol and came to her, tilted her head up slightly with a finger under her chin and kissed her lips lightly. He tasted his own lips then in an exaggerated pantomime not unfamiliar to any of them.

"Licorice!" Billy yelled.

"Banana?" That was Carol, eyes dancing.

"Raspberry?" murmured Marie mechanically, on cue.

A shake of the head as Grant smacked his lips more, supposedly continuing to try to identify the quality of his wife's lipstick.

"Onion soup, that's what!" Billy again.

"Watermelon?" Carol.

"Butter pecan?" Her heart wasn't in it, really, but Marie played out the game. Sometimes it went three or four rounds, but today only two.

Grant shook his head and then raised a triumphant finger. "Aha! You've been to Roosha in my absence. Eet iss wahd-kah!

Marie snorted. "That's a roundabout way of saying you'd like a drink. Vodka and tonic, I assume?"

"A bloomin' seer, that's what you are. Hi, honey."

"Hello. I'll get your drink." She moved off toward the bar.

The kids were off again, Carol with a shriek as she plunged out of sight around the corner to the kitchen and Billy in clattering pursuit. The boy stopped, letting her go for the moment, his body out of sight but his fingers and face from the nose up visible as he peered around the doorway like an anachronistic Kilroy.

"Hey, Dad, speaking of watermelons, what do you get when you cross a collie with a watermelon?"

Grant rolled his eyes. "A red-white-and-green collie with black spots?"

"Nope.

"A barking watermelon?"

"Nope."

"All right, son, you've got me. What do you get when you cross a collie with a watermelon?"

Billy yelped a high-pitched laugh and ducked out of sight, leaving a single word hanging in the air behind him.

"Melancholy!"

The kitchen door banged and then there was silence inside the house except for the sound of ice cubes clinking into a glass. In a moment Marie was back and wordlessly handed him the clear, cool drink with a dark green wedge of lime in it.

He raised one eyebrow. "You're not joining me?"

She shook her head and her smile was forced. Grant shrugged, raised his glass and said "Cheers!" and then sipped, an appreciative murmur escaping as he swallowed.

Marie braced herself. "I want to talk with you, John."

His eyes narrowed at her tone and abruptly all levity was gone. He shook his head and partially lifted the briefcase he still held in one hand. "Can it be a little later, hon? I've got to go up to the den. Some damned important stuff turned up today. I have to go through it thoroughly before five-fifteen. What time." he said casually, turning toward the stairs, "are you planning to have dinner tonight?"

"It'll be a little late. I don't even have the roast in yet. It slipped my mind."

Grant had stopped on the third step and was looking back at her with an unreadable expression. "I'm really not that hungry. For a big dinner, I mean. Since you haven't put it on yet, how 'bout saving it for tomorrow and let's just have something light—soup, maybe, or a grilled cheese sandwich?"

Her reply was listless. "If that's what you want. I'll tell the kids. You'll be a hero." There was a thin vein of bitterness in her words.

Grant continued upstairs without reply and Marie moved into the kitchen. Carol Ann and Billy were still sparring, but in the back yard now. Marie watched them from the window and her eyes misted. What was in store for them, she wondered. So innocent, so unknowing.

Carol Ann's blouse had pulled out of her skirt on one side and she twisted violently to elude Billy's rush. He stumbled and, in falling, his outstretched hand caught the front of that garment. Like dominoes falling in succession, every button of the blouse popped off and she stood there shocked, the garment still half on and half trailing down to Billy's hand on the ground. It was badly ripped. She was wearing no bra and one breast, about the size of a small grapefruit, pink-tipped and firm and quite pretty, became exposed. She yelped and covered herself with her arms in an X in front of her and ran for the house.

"Hey, Sis," Billy chortled after her, "you're really growing up. And *out*!"

Carol Ann stopped just inside the kitchen door at the sight of her mother standing there watching. She dropped her arms despairingly and snatched up the trailing shred of garment that had flapped into the house behind her like the tail of a ruined kite.

"I'm sorry, Mom."

"Don't fret about it, honey. Those things happen. Go on up and change into something else."

Carol Ann vanished and Marie called out the door to Billy that they'd be having soup and sandwiches for dinner tonight, and that he could eat anytime he cared to.

"I'm not hungry now, Mom. Could I go over to Jack's and eat later on when I get back?"

"What time is 'back later'?"

"Seven-thirty or eight?" he asked hesitantly, expecting a refusal.

Marie nodded. "No later than eight," she said, and smiled faintly as he raced out of the yard before she could change her mind. How grown-up they were getting, both of them. She had the sudden feeling that she may have just witnessed one of the last times that the two of them would romp like that together, and again the kitchen swam in her vision.

The roast, which had been on the sink sideboard thawing, she now put into the meat tender in the refrigerator. Just as she thudded the heavy door closed, Carol Ann reentered, wearing a fresh white jersey blouse and, quite obviously, still no bra. Marie was going to say something about it but changed her mind, knowing her daughter immediately would say that none of her friends wore bras any more. She didn't want to get into that hassle again now. She merely nodded her permission when the girl asked to go to Peggy Dinito's house until about eight. And then Carol Ann too, like, Billy, was gone.

Marie moved about downstairs, straightening a cushion here, realigning a picture frame there, sitting down and picking up a magazine and then throwing it down almost at once. She went to the basement, sorted some dirty clothing and tossed a load into the washer and got it going, then came back again to the front room. She was procrastinating and she knew it. Difficult things are always easy to put off.

"Marie!" It was John calling from his den. "Would you please fix me another drink?"

"You can come down and fix your own damned drink!" His voice had been a trigger and she was shocked at the sharpness of her own reply.

Grant came down at once, frowning, and he started to speak while he was still on the stairs. "What's wrong with you, anyway, Marie?"

"That's my question. What's wrong with you?"

"With me? What makes you think anything's wrong with me?"

"I don't think it, I *know* it. And *you* know it, too."

His expression changed subtly and his eyes became masked. He made an effort to keep the ring of puzzlement in his voice. "Honey, I haven't the foggiest notion what you're talking about."

"Ohhh!" It was practically a growl and she moved up to face him, standing tensely only inches away from him on the thick carpeting at the bottom of the stairs, her fists tight and fingernails digging into the palms of her hands. "Damn it, John, don't you waste that injured innocence on me, you hear? I don't buy it!"

"For Christ's sake, Marie! If you've got something on your mind, then spit it out and quite beating around bushes. I've got things to do."

"I'll just bet you've got things to do. I'll just bet you have!" She wanted to plunge ahead, to confront, accuse, berate, but she couldn't make her tongue bring out the words. Not yet.

"I don't know what you're leading up to," he said, his brief flare of anger fading to a level coldness, "but I can't say I care for your attitude."

"My *attitude*?" She changed the emphasis. "*My* attitude? Let me tell you something, Mr. John Charles Grant, the attitude that's at issue here is yours, not mine. And your actions along with it!"

He regarded her for a long moment and was on the verge of a retort when the telephone rang. Marie was closest to the telephone stand and she took a couple of steps snatched it up. "Hello!" Her voice was scarcely less sharp.

"Hello, Mrs. Grant?" It was a woman's voice. "Is Mr. Grant there, please? This is…"

"Who's calling?" The harshness in her voice, now laced with suspicion, was all too clear and cut off that very identification.

There was a brief pause on the other end and then the woman continued, "This is Hazel Tierney, Mrs. Grant. Secretary to the President. President Sanders would like to speak to Mr. Grant. Is he there, please?"

"Yes. Yes, of course." She was instantly contrite. "I'm sorry. Excuse me, please. One moment." She held out the receiver to him. "A friend of yours wants to talk to you. The President." She remained standing there as he put the phone to his ear.

"This is John Grant, Mr. President…Oh, hello Mrs. Tierney…Of course." He waited quietly, his eyes not meeting Marie's stony gaze, and then, "Good evening, Mr. President. I hope you're well?…It's Mr. Boardman's solution, or at least his basic outline for it…Yes, sir. I've been studying it ever since talking with Mr. Gordon. It's much different than anticipated. It's rather drastic, in fact, but he said in his notes that it's the only hope…Well, I don't know that I am, Mr. President, but evidently Mr. Boardman was convinced of it. I don't think you want me to outline it here for you, do you?…Yes, sir, of course. Whenever you want me.. That'll be fine, Mr. President. I've given Mr. Knotts a Xerox copy and I'll bring along Mr. Boardman's file on it, although it's pretty weighty. He wasn't a very accomplished writer. I think, though, that I can give you a pretty fair breakdown of what he's envisioned…" He paused for a longer period, listening carefully. "I think, Mr. President…" he hesitated and then went on, "…Thank you. It's just that it may be better, sir, if you alone heard Mr. Boardman's plan at first…To a degree it is, sir. I just thought you might want to be prepared for a possible reaction from the others…Yes, sir, I was planning on doing that, with your approval…I'll be there, Mr. President…I'll do that, sir. Thank you…Good night, sir."

He hung up the telephone slowly, nibbling at his lower lip, then pressed a button on a phone caddie, which sprang open. He ran his finger down a list of numbers, stopped on one and picked up the phone again. While he was punching out the numbers, he spoke to Marie with out looking up.

"President Sanders sends his regards to you, and his apologies."

"Apologies?"

"For pulling me away at short notice. I have to leave at once. May be in Washington for…Hello? Yes, please. When is the next flight to Washington, D.C.?…Right…That'll be fine. Reservation for one, please. Coach." He gave his name, address and phone number, withdrew his wallet and flipped it open to read his credit card number aloud, received confirmation, and broke the connection. He continued what he was saying to her as he checked another number—the toll-free Sheraton reservation center—and punched out a new set of numbers, "…for four or five days. Maybe longer, depending on what the President needs.…Hello?…Yes, I'd like to make a reservation, please, a single, beginning tonight for at least four days at the Sheraton Park in Washington, D.C…That's right…Yes, guaranteed. Arrival in about three-four hours…Yes. Thank you." Again he provided the necessary information and then hung up.

Oddly, though obviously he was going to be away again, Marie found a grain of comfort in it. This was all so spontaneous there was no way it could be something involving the woman named Anne, and that alone was encouraging. There was still a smoldering anger within her that urged her to pick up the conversation where it had broken off at the President's call, but he seemed to sense she was about to speak and he shook his head savagely.

"No more talk. Not now. I've got to move."

He went upstairs and she stood there alone, not knowing whether to follow or not, feeling if she did she might not be able to refrain from plunging them disastrously into the conversation again. She heard him moving about between his den and their bedroom and finally she was able to convince herself that now was the time to maintain silence. The period he would be gone on this trip would give her an opportunity to formulate in her own mind how the ultimate confrontation should take place. A carefully thought out course of discussion would be better than one like now, when both parties were simply wading in, not knowing where they were going and letting the confrontational chips fall where they would. That could be utterly disastrous. After about five minutes she walked heavily upstairs and came to a stop in the bedroom doorway, leaning there against the jamb, silently watching him pack.

The clicking of the latches on his luggage as he snapped them closed seemed to put a period to the mood prevailing between them. He looked up from the two-suiter and briefcase, his expression pensive, somewhat sorrowful.

Her words were not entirely steady. "You haven't had anything to eat."

As if on unspoken command they came to one another and embraced, tightly, silently, the contact speaking more eloquently than words possibly could have at this time. Marie felt the tears flowing but couldn't stop them, knowing they were coursing down her face to his neck and then down into his collar. He felt them, too, and his arms tightened around her. His whisper into her hair was hoarse.

"I love you, Marie."

"John. Oh, John! Always love me. Please. Always. I couldn't bear it if you didn't."

Their kiss had a tender saltiness, and when they broke from it he reached out and with his middle finger gently touched the corner of her eye, let his finger slide across her closed eyelid and down her nose, pausing on her lips, reaching her chin and uptilting her head again for another brief kiss.

Her arm around his waist, his around her shoulders, they walked slowly downstairs side by side. At the door he kissed her again and said "I'll call," and then he was gone.

VIII

As he drove away from the house on Bobolink Terrace, John Grant's forehead was deeply lined and a muscle in his check just above the heavy jawline alternately swelled and relaxed. A wave of love for Marie filled him and he felt that in all their years of being together he had never loved her more than at this very moment. She was all and everything that a man could hope for in a mate. He wondered at himself—at how he could do what he had done to her, at how he could be so deeply in love with her and at the same time be at least as equally in love with another. He wondered how he could perpetrate the deceit, with its interwoven web of lies, for he always had considered himself an honorable man, with his word being his bond. Where was his honor now, his honesty?

Time and again he had attempted to analyze his own actions, his motivations for them, his persistence in them. Long ago he had come to the conclusion that he was not in any way justified in what he was doing, and so he did not look for such justification. He was honest enough with himself to know what the erosive results of that would be: he would begin to look for fault in Marie, for anything, irrespective of how insignificant, which could be magnified in his own mind until it became an unbearable situation and then that unbearable situation would, in effect, become the justification for all this. No, that was something he would not, *could* not do.

He turned onto Dempster, heading for Edens Expressway, still deeply steeped in thought and driving automatically, wisely keeping his speed low in deference to the distracted state of mind he was experiencing. He thought of the joy that life with Marie and the children had resulted in over the years, and the thought that what he was doing was clearly jeopardizing that happiness caused a constriction of his abdominal muscles. He thought, as well, of the incredible happiness he felt with Anne, and the simultaneity of loving two women struck him again with a stab of fear, because despite his love for Marie and his life with her, he no longer could envision his future life without Anne's being a part of it.

The scene with Marie had shaken him. No clue had been given to what had set her off and he harkened back to recent events to see if there had been any moment of carelessness on his part which would have given rise to suspicion in Marie that he was unfaithful to her. He could think of none and so continued to bear the knot of worry within him of what this was all about. He had no doubt that if Marie ever learned about Anne she would immediately confront him and deliver that fateful ultimatum: her or me. He frowned, realizing that, in a manner of speaking, this was the very ultimatum he had recently received in the note Anne had written to him in which she had said, "…you can't be a husband to us both." But, God, how could he ever make a decision between them? It would be easier to decide which of his two eyes he wished to retain.

Now, with the green and white signs announcing the upcoming Edens Expressway, and with his heart still abundant with the flood of love for Marie, he pulled to a stop by a telephone booth in a shopping center to call Anne, hating himself for his own weakness. He had long since given up trying to figure out how he could do something like this. He knew no answer to that question, only that he was powerless to stop it.

"Ready for your reward, Lovely Lady?" he asked when he got her on the line. "I'm on my way to your place now."

"I've had thoughts about that." Her voice was throaty, low.

"Elucidate."

"You're not going to get out of paying the reward," she said, "but let's save that for another time. I can fix us something here and that way we wouldn't have to take so much time with dinner. I've something else in mind."

"Dear Lady, how shrewd of you to recognize that through his stomach is only one of *two* best ways to a man's heart. Am I to assume that your intention is to combine them?"

"That's a reasonable assumption."

"I accept the change in plans without hesitation. You will receive your reward tomorrow evening instead. Are you booked?"

"Only with you. Can you get away, though?"

"What about your calendar for the next two or three nights after that, as well? And the days, too. Can Louise Maas run A-C Tours for somewhere between three and five days without making the business bankrupt?"

"You're serious?"

"I'm serious. I want you to go to Washington with me tomorrow morning."

She sucked in her breath. "Christ, yes, John. Of course!"

"All right. I'll see you within forty minutes. There is something you can do while I'm coming. It falls under the purview of your chosen profession. Call O'Hare. TWA." He gave her the number of the flight and its time. "Cancel that one and make another for the two of us for very early morning. One that will get us there in time to take our bags to the hotel, get checked in, and give me time to get to the White House without having to rush."

"The White House? You have an appointment there in the morning? What time?"

"Ten o'clock."

"Nine, our time. Hmmm, that's pretty early but okay, there's an Early Bird flight on United a few minutes after five, so no problem. What about the hotel?"

"Call the Shoreham and make reservations for us there beginning tomorrow. I've already made a single reservation at the Sheraton Park, right across the way from the Shoreham. For obvious reasons, let that one stand. It's guaranteed and it'll give me a place to check for phone messages that might come from…my house."

There had been just that slightest pause before he said "my house," because he had nearly said "home." He was sure Anne had noticed it, but she didn't react.

"It's as good as done."

"And I'm as good as there."

"Everything'll be waiting."

"Everything?"

"Everything."

She had not been exaggerating. She met him at the door just over half an hour later wearing a beautiful robe in bittersweet-orange nylon jersey with very simple lines, close fitting, moving silkily across the contours of her body, from widely flared collar to ankles. A belt of the same material was looped at her waist with enough snugness to tauten the material over her breasts and highlight their peak attractions. In a silhouette-halo effect, her long black hair flowed in graceful, softly gleaming curves over her shoulders and back in striking contrast to the orange material. Her feet were bare.

Practically dazzled at the beauty of her, he started to say something, but she stopped him with a long index finger touched gently to his lips. She put her other hand to his face, too, and then let her fingers move with cobweb softness across his cheeks to the back of his head where the fingertips just barely interwove. The clean, fresh scent of her filled his nostrils as she leaned forward very slowly and deliberately, barely touching her lips against his, let the tiniest tip of her tongue flick across the crease between his upper and lower lips. His arms went around her and the warmth of her skin through the smooth material was electric beneath his hands. They pressed more closely together. The kiss became more impassioned, but only briefly. and then she moved her lips to his nose and eye and temple, kissing each lightly in turn. She kissed his ear then, momentarily holding the lobe between her teeth and then releasing it and whispering into his ear so softly that it was a voice heard more mentally than audibly.

"John Grant, with the strength of all I know or am or will ever be, I love you."

The corners of his eyes became wet and his hand came up, buried itself in her hair and pressed the side of her face tightly against his own. He was brimming with the loveliness of the moment and a part of his mind knew at that instant that come what may, should he live only another year or another fifty, the memory of this exquisite moment would forever remain vibrant and fresh inside. His whisper in the room was equally soft and somewhat unsteady.

"Anne Carpenter, I love you. Now. Always."

They moved into the apartment, filled with the wonder of their love for one another. They made love. They ate, but he really didn't know what they ate because he scarcely glanced at his plate. They made love. They talked in soft whispers to one another, but the talk with eyes and hands and bodies was more significant, more memorable, and he hardly knew what his tongue had said or his ears had heard. They made love. They showered together and they lay together quietly. And they made love beautifully, wonderfully, fulfillingly, each glimpsing the greatest mortal paradise that it is given to a human to know.

In the midst of the late night hours, when Anne had drifted asleep close against him, John lay listening to the music of her rhythmic breathing and felt the gentle little puffs of her breath against his skin. In the faint glow from the green-lighted clock dial, a hint of moisture glinted on his outermost eyelashes. He was, at that moment, thinking of Marie.

6

I

"All right, Mr. Grant, let's have you begin things with the supposed solution that Herbert Boardman devised. I'll have to admit I'm a little concerned with the ominous sound you've given it thus far. I think we'd better ascertain very quickly just how drastic—your word—the solution is and whether it can be applied practicably."

The President settled himself comfortably in his leather chair and let his eyes rest on John Grant, seated across from him in the heavy wing chair. The writer, in a medium-beige suit, off-white shirt and subdued dark brown tie with diagonal stripes, nodded and glanced at the top sheet of a collection of eight or ten typewritten sheets stapled together which he held in his lap.

"In order for you to better understand the possible application of Mr. Boardman's plan, Mr. President, I'd like to lay a bit of foundation before getting directly to the plan itself."

"Go ahead."

"Well, sir, from the very beginning, Mr. Boardman had the idea that if there were any solution to be found at all, it would have to be something dealing with Antarctica, because that's where the source of the problem lies. He undertook a pretty thorough study of the continent and its ice cap. Through a series of solidly based indicators, he determined that the ice cap is growing with phenomenal speed."

The President shifted his eyes to the portrait of George Washington on the opposite wall and said in a quiet voice, "What kind of indicators? Is it something we should get into here as we go along?"

Grant considered this briefly and then shook his head. "I think not, at the moment. They're remarkable in themselves and I believe you should know about them, but it may be distracting to get off on them right now. I'd suggest we go ahead for the moment with what he deduced from those indicators and then how he went on to formulate his plan. We can get back to his basic foundations later, if that's all right with you, sir."

"I will want to hear about them, but I suspect you're right; we'd better go through this phase of it as quickly as possible. I've asked some people here this morning whom we'll join a little later. It'll be important for them to hear it, too." The President saw Grant glance at the large platelike ashtray on the chairside table and he pointed a finger toward it. "Smoke, if you like. It won't bother me. I gave them up about eight years ago." He grimaced. "At Grace's suggestion."

"Thank you, sir," Grant said, reaching inside his coat and taking a pack of cigarettes from his shirt pocket. He placed them on the table, along with the slim gold lighter Anne had given him. As he was doing so, the Chief Executive continued.

"Assuming for the moment that Boardman's indicators are factual," he said, and Grant gave an affirming gesture, "then explain what you mean by phenomenal speed."

"The continent of Antarctica is fairly large, Mr. President. About two-thirds larger than the United States. It covers an area of about five and a half million square miles, as compared to just a little over three million square miles for the United States exclusive of Alaska. The evidence that Boardman found indicates that this Antarctic land mass was essentially ice-free at about the time the ancient Egyptian culture started deteriorating—roughly 4500 B.C. , which puts it at about sixty-five hundred years ago."

Instantly Sanders sat up straighter. "Repeat. You say. Boardman found *evidence* that Antarctica was ice-free

"Yes, sir, he did."

"Hold on a moment." The Chief Executive picked up his phone. "Hazel? You may have some trouble finding him, but I want you to put in a call for me right away to Dr. Shepard over in Ankara, Turkey…No, I don't know for sure which hotel…Yes, that's right, Mark Shepard. Call me as soon as you've got him."

He replaced the instrument and returned his attention to Grant. "Continue," he said.

"Yes, sir. The annual snowfall at the pole was far greater then—and, of course, still is—than summer melt-off could eliminate. The weight of snowfall upon snowfall over the centuries caused an impacting which resulted in extensive glacial formation—the beginning of the ice cap. Up until about three thousand years ago the ice cap grew higher and wider but was still far from covering the entire continent, and the greatest height and density of the cap still was not far from the actual pole, the axis of spin. Then glacial movement began. As the ice reached a thickness of between one and two miles, its weight became such that it began an outward creepage in all directions. From that point on the buildup in height slowed down considerably, but the expansion of the ice cap in an outward direction greatly increased. Roughly at about the time Christianity began, a couple thousand years ago, the ice had covered the continent, though the greatest thickness remained closer to the pole."

Grant paused, shook a cigarette from his pack and touched the clean long flame of the gold butane lighter to the tip. He exhaled a cloud of smoke and went on. "Now, as this weight of ice pushed outward, it shoved a lot of debris along in front of it, pretty well scouring the surface of the ground beneath right down to bedrock. But the great weight of the ice, still growing every year, was getting to be even more than the bedrock could withstand. It began to cause an actual underground flow of the rock itself—a process called isostasy—which caused it to extrude toward the outer limits of the pressure the ice cap was creating."

Sanders held up a hand, stopping him. "I think I know what you mean but just so I'm sure, can you clarify that a little?"

"Certainly. Let's compare the Antarctic continent to a flat pan of mud. In the midst of that mud you gradually lower a large flat weight—a block of concrete, for example. The gradual lowering of that weight is comparable to the gradual buildup of the glacial weight. As the pressure increases and the weight sinks lower, it begins causing the mud to squeeze out from under it. As the pressure becomes greater, more of the undermaterial gets extruded and forms a raised rim all around the perimeter of the weight. That, in essence, is what's happening at Antarctica. The weight of the ice cap is squeezing the material of the continent out from under it. The extruded material forms a range of mountains before it, all the way to the coastal areas and even beyond. There's good evidence that in this way not only is the ice cap growing, but the continent itself is expanding."

The President's eyes flicked down to the small gold clock on his desk and then back to the writer. Noticing this, Grant hurried on.

"The danger lies in what happens through the creation of this perimeter of mountains, Mr. President. The new mountain range serves as a barrier which prevents the flow-off of the glacial ice into the sea. In effect, a huge basin has been created, an actual impoundment of sorts. This allows a much increased volume of ice to accumulate inland and add its weight to the ice cap."

"How much and how fast?"

Grant flicked a few pages, studied one a moment, and then looked up. His words hung like icicles in the room. "Just short of eighty-five billion tons every month."

President Sanders shifted in his chair, inhaled deeply, and then said, "Continue."

"This buildup has progressed through the centuries. About three hundred years ago, some of the edges of the ice cap pushed beyond the continental mass. This was probably because of two reasons: first, because the mouths of continental rivers did not allow for as great a barrier of mountains to be thrown up at the perimeter as elsewhere; and then also because the depth of the ocean close to the shore of the continental mass allowed some portions of the pushed-up mountains to literally be shoved off the continent and slide down to the bottom of the sea. It was at that time that the first icebergs began being sloughed off by the ice cap into the water. This tends to act as something of a safety valve, because it gets rid of some of the weight that has accumulated."

"But not enough?" the President interjected.

"Nowhere near enough, sir. As a safety valve, it's very imperfect. I think I may have mentioned before that even today, with a regular flow of icebergs being shed into the sea from the South Polar ice cap, there is still more new ice accumulated in one month than is carried off by icebergs in a year. To go on, pretty much the same thing on a smaller scale is occurring with the ice cap presently on Greenland. Just as with Antarctica, Greenland's land mass has become a depressed rock basin with the weight of the ice cap upthrusting a range of coastal mountains before it. Much of the rock floor of Greenland is now well below sea level, because of this extrusion of rock forming the giant ice basin. The mass of the ice caps at both poles is increasing every day and right now the weight of the Antarctic ice cap is around three tons per square inch."

Most of Grant's cigarette had burned away in the ashtray without being smoked and he stubbed it out, continuing to talk as he did so. "As a sidelight, sir, this sheds a whole new view on why some present areas of the earth are so far below sea level—areas such as the Dead Sea region in the Middle East, the Valdes Peninsula in Argentina, Death Valley in California, and so on. These areas, according to the HAB Theory, were once polar seats and became deeply indented by the weight of the ice caps which grew over them."

Sanders issued an impressed little grunt. "Interesting. Shall we move on to Mr. Boardman's plan now, or is there more preliminary material you want to cover?"

"No, we're right at that point, sir. Mr. Boardman had his plan filed under the letter *T*, for thermonuclear power. The file is extensive but he sums it up fairly well in one particular comment he wrote which I'd like you to hear right now."

The President waited patiently as Grant turned to the last page of the sheaf of papers he was holding and read aloud in a level voice.

"'I am convinced that modern man has it within his power to simultaneously achieve his most spectacular triumph over the forces of nature and equally save himself from extinction or severe retrogression. For the first time in the history of the earth, man possesses the ability to prevent the capsizing of the planet. Through the use of thermonuclear devices strategically placed at intervals along the twelve-thousand-mile coastal rim of the gigantic Antarctic ice basin and then detonated simultaneously or in series, great pressures can be alleviated. The leveling of upthrusted coastal mountains, created by the pressure of the South Pole ice cap, through judicious use of such thermonuclear devices will permit vast amounts of ice to break free to float off as icebergs in the ocean, gradually melting as they are carried northward into warmer waters. In addition, a considerable amount of ice would be melted instantly at the time of the detonations by the intense heat generated in thermonuclear reaction. In substance, either we limit the growth of the Antarctic ice cap, or else we accept a limitation to our civilization's existence. There are no other alternatives.' That's it, sir."

The President's expression had congealed into hard lines. He toyed absently with a small iron whale paperweight, saying nothing for quite some time. At last he let his gaze fasten on Grant again.

"Your initial appraisal that the plan was drastic was not an overstatement. Offhand I can think of a number of arguments against it. Good arguments."

Grant stood and sifted about in his briefcase for a moment before extracting a sheet of blue paper on which there were neat lines of tiny handwriting. "I expect, Mr. President," he remarked, "that Mr. Boardman has covered those and more on this sheet. There are only two arguments against such implementation, however, which he feels are matters in which considerable resistance would be met." He glanced up and Sanders gestured him to continue.

"The first is the radioactive peril. The accumulation of radioactivity and radioactive dust and moisture in the atmosphere from the detonation of a whole series of multi-megaton thermonuclear devices would undoubtedly be high, even with what we term 'clean' devices. The radioactive fallout might so pollute the air and seas that it would be as liable to exterminate man as the capsizing of the globe, though not as rapidly. Mr. Boardman suggests that all-out effort be undertaken to devise thermonuclear devices that are much cleaner than any we have now—up to at least ninety percent clean. With devices such as those, a certain amount of hazard would undoubtedly still exist, but fatalities would be greatly reduced and it would be far less a peril to the whole of mankind than would be the capsizing.

"The second argument is a very complex one, with numerous problems which would have to be carefully studied. If such an action were taken to reduce the ice weight and better stabilize the earth's rotation on its axis, this would necessarily mean the introduction of a fantastic volume of water into the oceans of the world. Mr. Boardman estimates a minimum rise in all ocean levels of at least eighteen feet and perhaps as much as thirty to fifty. The ramifications are grim. All coastal areas and low lying lands throughout the world would be inundated. This would result, for example, in loss to the United States alone, almost the whole state of Florida, most of New York City, Long Island and Cape Cod, and such major cities as Boston, Norfolk, Savannah, Mobile, New Orleans, Galveston, and Los Angeles, to name only a few. Inundation would be just as severe for other coastal areas throughout the world and a great many island societies would simply cease to exist. If, in the face of this, any shipping industry remained, it couldn't reasonably function due to increased navigational hazards from icebergs. Then there are also such considerations as what this would do to the ocean temperatures, the climate of the entire earth, and what the effect of so much fresh water intrusion would do to marine life everywhere. Still, while the solution is certainly drastic in the extreme, Mr. Boardman insists it is the *only* one whereby the greater majority of mankind can avoid being annihilated." He dropped the blue paper back into his briefcase. "That's it, sir."

As Grant sat down, the President rose and immediately Grant started getting up again, but Sanders waved him back. "That's all right, stay seated."

The President walked around the desk and crossed the Oval Office slowly, deep in thought, the limp more pronounced than usual, when he would consciously try to lessen it. He stopped near the door to the outer office, facing it, his hands locked behind him. Twice Grant saw him shake his head, and then the President turned and limped back to a stop in front of him.

"You've found nothing else which might give some indication of how much time we might have remaining to us before this cataclysm occurs?"

"Nothing more than Mr. Boardman himself told me, Mr. President. It could happen tomorrow or in a year or perhaps not for fifty or a hundred years. There's just no way of knowing. Still, from what I've gone through in his papers and in comparing the life span of our present epoch with others that have preceded it, the fact becomes clearer all the while that it has to be very close. No epoch previously known has lasted for within five hundred years of this present one. I'd say that whatever course we take, we'd better act as swiftly as possible, and even then we're apt to lose the race."

"All right then, let's go talk with these other people."

It was as both Grant and the President were leaving the Oval Office that Mrs. Tierney caught the Chief Executive's attention.

"I have Dr. Shepard on the line, sir."

"Good!" He beckoned Steven Lace, who was standing near Mrs. Tierney's desk, and then looked at Grant and then clapped his shoulder warmly. "This may take me five or ten minutes, so you go with Steve here on down to the conference room and I'll be along directly."

II

The two men seated in a comfortable private office in the Kenya capitol building in Nairobi had been measuring each other, each in his own way, ever since their conversation began. Since Nolokoi Igoravich Solavitska did not speak either Swahili or the native Kikuyu tongue and Daniel Ngoromu could not speak Russian, their conversation was taking place in a language in which both men were quite fluent—English.

The Russian was unusually tall, at least six and a half feet, but so thin that he gave the impression of a scarecrow caricature. A prevailing joke in Moscow was that one had better watch carefully what he said, even when in the open expanse of Red Square, because Solavitska very well could be lying down in one of the cracks between the large red paving bricks, hidden and listening.

Actually, Solavitska was neither a spy nor a member of the NKVD, as the apocryphal story suggested. He was a man who handled very special personal contact jobs for the Presidium and he was responsible only to that body. Ordinarily, he was quite gregarious and he would have had great difficulty making himself inconspicuous anywhere. He weighed less than a hundred and fifty pounds fully clad and, because of his skinny height and skeletal features, along with a distinctive sort of disjointed gangling gait, he always was clearly evident in whatever collection of people he joined.

The smart dark gray suit he wore was sharply creased and cut well to his peculiar anatomy and, as was something of a trademark with him, his necktie was the exact same shade of red as that which appeared in the flag of the USSR. His dark hair was liberally peppered with gray and cut in a close crew cut fashion, as he had worn it for most of his fifty-two years. His nose and chin were both long and straight and his eyes were a warm brown and highly expressive; yet those same eyes could, on occasion, become masked or even intensely hard and cold. Mostly they did not.

Solavitska had been sent as a friendly emissary to Kenya to meet with the Kenyan President and to feel him out, to extend the Russian hand of friendship in an even warmer grasp than previously, to learn his weaknesses and then, finally, to accomplish his mission. This was one of the greater talents that Solavitska embodied—the ability to penetrate the facades that individuals usually presented and detect what lay far beneath the surface, then use this knowledge to Soviet advantage. On occasion he had misjudged his man, but far more often his appraisals were so accurate that they seemed more like months-long studies of a personality rather than the result of a seemingly casual meeting or two.

For over an hour he had been having just such a casual discussion with President Ngoromu and he had formed some fairly solid conclusions about the enormous African's character and how he might best be reached for what the Presidium had in mind. These conclusions, involving a large amount of preliminary study before this contact, were quite well drawn. By far the single factor of Ngoromu's character that most interested him was this man's great ambition. Solavitska had correctly determined that the black leader was very hungry to increase his power and to extend it far beyond the borders of Kenya or even those countries bordering this East African nation. Ngoromu, Solavitska felt certain, envisioned himself as very nearly something of a messiah to all Africans and wanted to amalgamate them into one nation under his own strong leadership. Such being the case, the Russian had concluded in his own mind, Ngoromu would surely be most receptive to any sort of proposal which could help him achieve that goal.

"As you are undoubtedly aware, President Ngoromu," he was saying, "the economic fortunes of my own country have taken a dramatic turn for the better over the past five or six years." He crossed his long bony legs comfortably and smiled the well-known broad smile which exposed practically all of his teeth, half a dozen or more of which were made of stainless steel. "In this respect our countries are much alike, for it is the mother earth that has favored us both. We, in Russia, have been favored by her bounty on the vast surface of our land through wheat. Yes! Now no other nation on earth produces as much as we of this vital crop, and our possibilities for expanding the production of the important commodity are virtually limitless. You, here in Kenya, on the other hand, have been favored by a similar bounty, but from far beneath the surface in the form of oil. Yes! Not even the great fields of Saudi Arabia can come near matching what you have been blessed with here, and soon no other nation on earth will produce as much oil as you. Your opportunity for expanding, like ours, is boundless. We are both very lucky, are we not?"

Ngoromu, as usual, took his time in answering. "We are, Mr. Solavitska, but with one difference." He knew the Russian was moving in on the object of his visit here. All the talk before this had been a gradual maneuvering of the conversation to this turn, as if by happenstance the subject should arise. He continued, after another pause, "Yours is a commodity in full production. Ours," there was a wistfulness in the faint rise and fall of one shoulder, "is but a potential."

"All major nations are keenly aware of that," Solavitska observed seriously, "and all are keenly anxious to participate in the development of that potential." He laughed in a high key. "We are certainly no exception. It would be an insult to your intelligence to even suggest we are not."

"Yes," Ngoromu said dryly.

"Yours, of course, Mr. President," the Soviet went on, uncrossing his legs and leaning forward on bony elbows against the arms of the chair, "is not an industrial nation. To be of any use to you, your wonderful resource must be developed and you, therefore, are in need of someone to help you who can provide unlimited aid in such endeavor, is it not so?"

The reply was an uncomfortably long time in coming, but Solavitska was well aware of Ngoromu's irritating habit of being unnecessarily slow in making replies or comments when engaged in discussion with leaders of other nations, or their ambassadors or emissaries, and he waited patiently.

"We have reached a conclusion along those lines, Mr. Solavitska."

"And undoubtedly some governments have already made proposals to you, such as during your recent visit to the United States. Ah," he held up a hand with unusually long, narrow fingers, "don't say a word! I would not think to pry. What you have discussed is no one's business but yours. But others are not unaware of all this, and since you are here in Kenya again and bargainers from the world over still tap at your door and are given entry, then one is led to assume that no agreement has yet been reached."

He stood up suddenly, unfolding himself and rising so high it seemed he suddenly had been elevated on stilts. He raised a long stiff index finger, almost hitting his own eye. "So! May it not be the possible answer, Mr. President, that the bargainers until now have fallen short? Industrial goods, machinery, technology, ah!, these are items that each would bargain with. That is a fait accompli, eh? But what can they offer beyond that? A good ragout may be only merely good until the skilled cook comes who can add that special ingredient that others have not."

Now it was Ngoromu who stood and, though he was not as tall as his guest, the very bulk of him greatly overshadowed Solavitska and added emphasis to the cadaverous aspect of the Russian. There was the faintest of smiles on the black leader's lips and a glint in his eye that the Moscow emissary thought he recognized.

"It might be good for us to have some refreshments as we continue our chat, Mr. Solavitska," he said, following a long pause. "We have some vodka, although I must hasten to say that it is American, not Soviet."

"Ah!" The hand went up again. "The Americans make a reasonable vodka. A trifle weak and somewhat without body, but reasonable. That would be most pleasurable, Mr. President."

Ngoromu touched a thick, dark finger to a button on a panel of his desk and had hardly lifted it away before the door opened and a male secretary entered and stood waiting respectfully just inside the portal. The Kenyan President inclined his head to indicate a small low table with comfortable hide-covered easy chairs on each side of it. The secretary vanished as swiftly and quietly as he had entered. Ngoromu moved around his desk to where Solavitska still stood and held out a hand, palm up, in an invitational manner toward those same chairs.

"Shall we sit where we can comfortably continue our discussion, Mr. Solavitska?"

The tall, lean Russian nodded and the physical contrast between them became even more startlingly apparent. At six and a half feet in height, the Russian had seemed incredibly tall, due to the narrowness of his frame, but it became obvious now that he was not a great deal taller than the black leader. Now with the two standing close together, Ngoromu actually seemed to dwarf him. As they walked to the chairs and sat, Solavitska moved with a peculiar ungainly jointedness, whereas Ngoromu was sure and smooth in his movements, big with the bigness of a large lion, but with the same sense of reserve strength and agility.

Ngoromu was physically an enormous individual. Large-boned, massively built and standing three inches over six feet in height, the President of Kenya weighed exactly three hundred pounds, although by no stretch of the imagination could he have been termed obese. He was simply a very huge man. His skin was extremely dark— darker, in fact, than that of most Kikuyus, the tribe of his ancestry—and under certain conditions of lighting, such as that in his office at this moment, it took on a blue-bronzed character that was oddly striking, appealing. He had dense, closely cropped hair which matted his scalp as if he wore a heavy woolen skullcap. The hair at his temples was graying and imparted a distinguished aspect to his general appearance. His eyes were only slightly protuberant and his nose somewhat lacked the full, broad-nostriled flatness common to his tribe. His lips were full, but not obtrusively so, and they covered a set of teeth which were startlingly white, beautifully proportioned, and had never known a cavity.

Daniel Ngoromu was forty-seven years old, impressive as a man and greatly admired as a dedicated leader of his people. His command of the English language and his overt affection for the United States—of which Solavitska was disgruntledly aware—stemmed from a twofold source. He had been educated in America, majoring in political science and graduating with high honors from Stanford University. That was the prime factor for his feelings toward the North American nation, but the secondary reason was closely related. It was while he was attending Stanford that he met Anita Randall, another political science major, who had taken a special interest in him. A bond had quickly developed between them, at first in an educational vein but rapidly expanding to other interests, for each found in the other a remarkable and unexpected affinity for many things. Physical attraction was there, too, although only much later and as an outgrowth of a mental attraction far more important.

Anita Randall was twenty-one when they met, Daniel Ngoromu only twenty. She was not of the ilk who, because it was the currently chic thing to do, decided to link herself to a black man. As a matter of fact, she abhorred the sense of gross exhibitionism and social flaunting that this sort of arrangement bespoke. What initially attracted her to him was that in the classes they shared, she discovered him to be a young man of great perception and depth, a man of unusual compassion and yet filled with determination and strength and with a burning desire to learn, to try to understand his fellow human beings and what motivated them. The mutual mental attraction eventually dissolved whatever physical restraints may have existed between them. She considered him a man, not a black man; and to Ngoromu, Anita Randall was positively one of the gentlest, most intelligent and stimulating human beings he had ever encountered, man or woman, black or white. Their eventual sexual closeness came as a natural evolution in their association. It was never flaunted, but neither was it hidden. It was extremely gratifying to both, often rapturous, always profound. It was also a relationship seemingly without future beyond that of close friendship. No promises were made and none expected, and there never had been any trace of romanticizing about a possible life together.

There was an augury of destiny about Daniel Ngoromu even then, which Anita Randall was quick to sense. Daniel himself knew it, knew where he was going, what he wanted. He had seen his country evolve from a relatively benevolent colonialism to a fierce but essentially directionless nationalism, and then through a succession of quasi-nationalistic leaderships during which internal political struggle was rife and growth as a nation stagnated. He had seen some of the most gifted and altruistic leaders of East Africa destroyed by emotional power-seekers who, themselves, soon fell by the way as intertribal struggles for political ascendancy continued. Even before leaving Africa for America, Daniel Ngoromu knew one day he would return and become Kenya's leader. He knew as well that merely leading Kenya was not enough; that one day his great vision of unifying all of East Africa under a single strong leadership—his own—was his ultimate goal. It would be a unification with Kenya as the hub and surely including the Somali Republic, Uganda, Rwanda, Burundi, Tanzania, Malawi, and Mozambique. Eventually it might extend to include Zambia and Rhodesia, perhaps even Ethiopia. It would become the greatest nation of Africa, a proud and powerful unified people in a proud and powerful land, with the model for its governmental foundation being not that of the United Kingdom, which some might expect, due to the background of British colonialism, but rather patterned after that most incredible of time-tested political documents, the Constitution of the United States of America.

Eventually he returned to Kenya, alone, and in time he had become, as he had known he would, President of that nation. Over the years his popularity had only increased, but what was most significant was the fact that intertribal friction had practically vanished, gradually being replaced by the strong and unified nationalism that Ngoromu had set out to initiate. That he had staunchly resisted—and defeated—a burgeoning communism was a fact well known to Nolokoi Solavitska, and the Russian took this as an indicator, with considerable justification, of the tremendous personal ambition in Ngoromu, an ambition he planned to utilize to the benefit of the USSR in this current international manipulating to gain firm inside footing in the development of the fabulous Kenyan oil resources.

The fact that Daniel Ngoromu had been able to end, for all intents and purposes, the intertribal frictions that had always existed in Kenya was, to some degree, due to his marriage the year before he became President. The Kikuyu, ever since the leadership of Jomo Kenyatta, had always been Kenya's most politically ambitious tribe. They were not, however, the strongest. The Masai to the south and the Samburu to the north, hereditarily closely allied, remained always a potentially powerful force. The fact that overt friction between the Kikuyu and them did not develop was merely because the two warrior tribes which flanked the Kikuyu were not at all politically inclined. Long before independence and ever since, they had remained aloof, considering themselves the dominant race on earth and simply tolerating the machinations of the politically maneuvering Kikuyus, so long as they did not tread upon Masai or Samburu toes or attempt to bind them with governmental restrictions they had neither desire nor intention of obeying. And, realizing this, the governing Kikuyus had moved only with the utmost prudence, taking care to in no way offend the warrior tribes.

It was Daniel Ngoromu who had changed this. His marriage to the tall and graceful Ngaia Loolmalasin was the key factor, since she not only was a Masai, but also daughter of Lombora Loolmalasin, acknowledged leader of all Masai, and his wife, Loriyua Rumumaik, formerly of the ruling faction of the Samburu. It was not a marriage predicated upon political expediency, which neither Masai nor Samburu would have tolerated. Ngaia and Daniel were simply a good match and, having weathered the expected tribulations of the intertribal marriage, they found that they equally had inaugurated a new understanding and respect between the Kikuyus and the Samburu-Masai coalition, if such it could be called. At any rate, Daniel Ngoromu, on assuming leadership of Kenya, became the first President of that nation to have the unqualified approval and support of all the major tribes. And, shrewd individual that he was, Ngoromu made the most of it. It appeared a foregone conclusion that he would remain President of Kenya for as long as he should live, providing his leadership retained the benevolent strength it had exhibited thus far.

The one great crisis in Daniel Ngoromu's Presidency had occurred six years ago. Three years prior to that, Ngaia died suddenly of the dread disease, *nagama*—sleeping sickness—which she had contracted during an inexplicable plague of tsetse flies. Her death had left Daniel Ngoromu so totally bereft that for months afterward he did not function well at all. Only gradually did he regain his control and, even then, his hands were full with the responsibility of continuing to raise their five children, the eldest of which was then only fourteen.

That was when Anita Randall entered the picture again. Her note of condolence to Ngoromu when she learned of Ngaia's death initiated a correspondence between them which ultimately reinstituted the closeness they had shared so many years before. On his several successive visits to America, Daniel was able to set aside time to be with Anita. After one such visit six years ago, she had returned to Kenya with him and shortly afterward they had announced their marriage. The ramifications within Kenya could have been tragic. Interracial marriage was infrequent at best and rarely involved any high governmental official. It was simply too politically risky. Never before had it involved the President and for some time there were ugly murmurings. It had been Anita, not

Daniel, who inadvertently smoothed the troubled waters. Both her care for and her love of the five children born of Ngaia and Daniel could not have been more genuine had they been her own offspring. As weeks became months and the months became years after their wedding, her love for the children and theirs for her had won the grudging admiration of both Masai and Samburu and, in a simple but significant ceremony, they accepted her as one of themselves. The Kikuyu quickly held a similar ceremony and the rumblings were forever put to rest. Since then, Daniel Ngoromu's stature as a leader had only increased and he was now indisputably one of the most powerful men on the African continent.

His dream of unifying all of East Africa and, eventually all southern, western, central and possibly even northern Africa as well, remained strong in him. It was of this great ambition that his present visitor, Nolokoi Igoravich Solavitska was intensely aware.

Having finished toasting the President, he sipped his drink and then held the glass before his eyes and murmured, "It is not bad vodka, even by my own standards, which are high." He raised the glass again. "Another toast, if I may, to your very lovely wife."

Ngoromu nodded, smiling faintly at the more than mere approval in Solavitska's voice. It was not an unusual occurrence among many of his white male visitors. He raised his own glass and said, "I cannot help but give that toast my complete accord," and then threw back his head and laughed with genuine pleasure.

Solavitska issued a high-pitched tittering sound. "Mrs. Ngoromu is Scandinavian?"

"Danish by ancestry. She is American by birth."

"Ah!" Solavitska acted as if he hadn't known this. "Then of course she would wish to see her own country of America obtain the benefit of aiding yours."

Ngoromu blinked slowly. "She is Kenyan now. She wishes only what is best for Kenya."

"Perhaps what is best for Kenya," Solavitska murmured, "would not be what is best for America."

"Perhaps it may be," Ngoromu said, touching a blunt finger to the side of nose in a thoughtful way, "that America does not cook as tasty a ragout as Japan or France or England.

"Or Russia?"

Ngoromu looked at Solavitska in a droll manner and both men laughed. The Soviet pursed his lips, making his face appear more than ever skull-like. "Yes! It may be, Mr. President, that you would like to know of the special ingredients which make the Russian dish tastier than any other's?"

"Just the special ingredients?" Ngoromu questioned.

"Many cooks can speak well of the basic ingredients," Solavitska replied, speaking more briskly now. "Let us speak in other terms. Basic ingredients which would be of interest to Kenya are all things the Soviet Union can provide in amounts equal to or even exceeding those of other countries. As short a time ago as the nineteen-seventies, the Soviet Union was far from the lead in exportation on the world market, with exports totaling only fifteen and a third billion dollars annually. Now that figure has nearly trebled and we are first of all nations in products exportation. Cattle, hogs, wheat, fish, coal, steel, timber, other exports—we have them all in abundance. And, of course, the technology Kenya needs for production of its latent resources."

"Perhaps, then, bargaining would have to depend on how tasty the special ingredients would be to Kenyans."

Ngoromu, after his lengthy pause, spoke the words slowly, as judiciously as if he were threading bits of bait onto a hook.

For an extended time the Russian contemplated the remaining vodka in his glass. He raised the vessel to his lips but spoke quietly over the rim before drinking, his deep-set brown eyes locked on Ngoromu's. "Or even to a specific Kenyan."

Ngoromu remained impassive and the silence stretched out between them. Through the partially open latticed door leading out to the lush gardens came the trilling of birds and a large yellow butterfly wove its way through the upstretched, clublike arms of a euphorbia tree. Still Ngoromu did not speak.

"Shall I go on, Mr. President?"

"Indeed, Mr. Solavitska."

The lanky Russian hunched forward, thrusting his narrow, pointed nose to within a foot of the huge black leader. His voice was subtly lowered. "In Russia, ambitions must be nurtured with care lest they be misunderstood. For a man to exhibit ambitions for himself rather than for the betterment of the people is a dangerous thing. And so, if a man has personal ambitions—and which of us," he raised his palms outward, "does not have some?—he is wise to associate these with ideals of benefit to his country. In such a way, Russia admires men of ambition and rewards them by allowing, even helping, them to achieve their ambitions. Ambitions of other people we also find intriguing." He paused significantly, but when Ngoromu said nothing he went on. "It is known that you, for example, President Ngoromu, have a worthy ambition. One that I admire and that many others of importance consider favorably because it is for the betterment of the people—yours and those of the countries around you."

A veil of inscrutability had covered Ngoromu's eye, and his words, when they came, were deep and soft in the quiet of the office. "It is good to know that you and others approve. Perhaps there are additional matters which you and others know about?"

A widely slitted smile exposed the unusually small teeth behind the Russian emissary's lips, those that were steel teeth glinting in the office light. "Indeed. Indeed. That you are making some headway in gaining support in Somalia and Tanzania is known. That you have made little headway in Rwanda, Malawi and Burundi is known. That you have met great difficulty in Zambia and Uganda is known. That you are unwelcome and feared in Rhodesia is known."

"Those are not secrets, Mr. Solavitska."

"Ah! That is true. But in knowing those matters, we gain better insight into the methods of…bargaining?…no, let us say negotiation, when put into context with other matters of which we have certain knowledge."

There was a slight flaring to Ngoromu's nostrils. "Among the Masai at Amboseli," he said, "there is an old saying to the effect that 'The zebra needs have no fear when he walks in wide circles around the full lion.'"

The two men looked at one another steadily and the Russian ran four pencil-thin fingers through his stubby hair. "Yes! Directness. It is said that the President of Kenya likes directness. Agreed. It is time. President Ngoromu, you will never gain the support of most of those nations you wish, in time, to unite into a single nation of states without strong convincing pressures being brought to bear on certain individuals in those countries who oppose your aims because those aims will be to their personal detriment. Like yourself, many of these are men of great ambition. But, unlike yours, theirs is a more personal ambition. We know what many of these men want most and in many cases it is in our power to fulfill those desires if we ourselves are properly motivated. We consider your oil resources development such a motivation. We are a vast nation, President Ngoromu. It would take over thirty-eight areas of land the size of Kenya to equal the area we have. We are by far the largest nation on earth, yet we produce only just over eleven percent of the world's oil. We need much more than that. And so, you see, oil can be a great motivation to us to help you.

"Yes!" he went on, "Our help will end many insurmountable obstacles for you, and smooth many others. Your task even then will be a great one, but the ultimate goal made much more possible. Without our help, the goal will always remain but a dream." He held up a finger as Ngoromu seemed about to reply. "Wait! I will finish with this: that help could begin instantly and it is, of course, entirely in addition to the normal bargaining of goods and services that would be involved. Bargaining, I hasten to reiterate, which will match or better any that has been offered by other sources."

Solavitska finished his drink in one gargantuan swallow, set his glass down gently and leaned back, crossing his legs. His smile was anticipatory and did not change as Ngoromu came smoothly to his feet. The East African leader turned and walked with heels faintly thudding against the wide, polished, inlaid wooden squares of which the floor was constructed. In the midst of a zebra-skin rug just beginning to show wear, he turned. He stood there for a long while solemnly regarding the Russian before he spoke.

"Mr. Solavitska, you are correct in your knowledge of my ambition to unite the peoples of East Africa under a single leadership. You are right in believing it would help me to be free of the obstacles certain individuals in some of these nations are erecting to prevent this. You are wrong, however, in your belief that without such help the goal can remain only a dream."

Solavitska sat bolt upright, then came to his feet and took two stilting steps toward Ngoromu, but the black leader held up a hand stopping him.

"You are turning down this offer?" the Russian asked unbelievingly.

This time there was no hesitation whatever in Ngoromu's reply. "Unification, to be permanent, can be achieved only through the will of the people to be united. It is the will of these people, in the knowledge that such unification will bring freedom from any form of oppression or subjugation, which ultimately will make the goal a reality. And leaders who do not recognize and act upon the will of their people will not long be leaders."

Ngoromu gestured toward the door and then walked slowly in that direction, Solavitska a pace behind. The black leader continued, "Their leadership will be overthrown not because of outside force, but because of internal pressures they will not be able to stand against, however strong the iron hand may be with which they rule."

He stopped with his hand on the doorknob and was about to add more to his comment, but instead he pulled the door open and stepped aside to let the Russian emissary pass. Solavitska's face was pinched and the dark eyes had become agate hard and very cold. As he left the office stiffly, the deep low voice of Ngoromu followed him.

"Kenya may be interested in the normal ingredients of the Soviet ragout, Mr. Solavitska, but it has a strong distaste for special ingredients which ruin the dish instead of improving it."

Nolokoi Igoravich Solavitska stopped and turned back, but the door was just closing with a gentle click.

I I I

Their room in the huge Shoreham Hotel was on the south side of the building, overlooking a wide, well-manicured lawn which gave way to a heavy growth of trees flanking the expansive Rock Creek Park. It was a pleasant view from their window, verdant and serene, giving little indication of the bustling existence of the city of Washington beyond.

For a long while they had stood side by side in front of those windows, their arms about each other, their heads touching, saying little. That was one of the things that John Grant truly appreciated about Anne Carpenter; she seemed to know intuitively those moments when he had no desire to talk, nor even think very much. There was at such times a sense of floating, of divorcing oneself from all the normal impingements of outside activities, of just drifting apart in a very relaxed way, not really losing contact with the here and now, but viewing it from a dimensional plane on an entirely different level.

They watched the shadows lengthen, the foliage take on the special lush aspect which occurs only at that time of day when the sun's rays are not so harsh. The bright blue of the sky, for a change relatively clear of the pall of smog which so often overhung the Potomac Rive Valley here, gradually deepened with approaching dusk, and here and there the brilliant twinkling landing lights of aircraft on final approach to Washington National became temporarily visible.

As she seemed to know exactly when there was no need to talk, Anne also had a special knack of knowing when that moment was passing and when they could return to the here and now of their lives. Perhaps it was the somewhat deeper breath that Grant had just taken, or perhaps it was a slightly increased pressure of his arm around her. Whatever the clue, she recognized it and, without looking at him or changing position, she spoke quietly in a voice rich with feeling.

"I feel so close to you at this moment, John, so much a part of you. I don't say it very often, I know, but I don't ever want you to feel in any way that I take you for granted. Sometimes I feel so proud of you, so proud of the talent you have, the ability, to reach out and touch a thousand or a hundred thousand or a million different minds with the words you write. I sometimes feel it isn't possible to be so proud of someone else."

Neither of them moved and though she was silent then for a long while, he didn't speak and at length she continued in the same soft, rich tone. "It's a feeling apart from love. The love is there so strong most of the time that usually I'm thinking of you in terms of how deeply I love you, how we love each other and the mingling of our lives, and then you're just my man, the one who is important to me in every respect. But now and then, like now, it comes as almost a jar to me to realize that you are a famous person, an amazingly skilled writer whose words are important to a vast number of people, and I'm awed by it and feel such a swelling of pride in you that it's indescribable." She turned her head and looked at the clean strong lines of his profile. "I'm so proud of you, John."

The catch in her voice turned his eyes to her and he saw the silent tears sliding down her cheeks. He still said nothing, but pulled her close and held her to him, pressing his lips to her neck, breathing the scent of her hair, loving the touch of her hand curled about his nape, with the gently kneading fingers saying as much as words had said a moment before. Her lips were at his ear and her breath was warm against him.

"I won't dwell on it and no response necessary," her voice came again, "but I have times when I can't contain it anymore and have to say the words. I love you. In all my life I've never wanted anything so much as I want to be your wife."

"The strange thing about being so much in love," he whispered against her neck, "is that there is really no way to express it as deeply as you feel it. All the words seem inadequate and in the end they all boil down to those three simple ones, and yet those three are never enough. Still, it's not possible to keep from saying them. I love you, Anne."

They stood that way for a little while longer and then Grant suggested that they go to Paul Young's, a fine restaurant not far distant on Connecticut Avenue, so he could make good his promise of reward. He called and made reservations without difficulty and they caught a taxi at the hotel entrance, holding hands all the way and still deeply lost in one another.

Their table was cozy, the soft background music pleasant and the decor imbued with elegance. After cocktails they shared a superb Chateaubriand and delicate wine, topped off with a smooth, light chocolate mousse. Throughout, Grant talked quietly, telling her of the events of the day. He was far from finished when they returned to their room in the Shoreham, but broke off for the little ritual they frequently observed and which both so much enjoyed—showering together. As always, they washed each other in turn and both the giving and taking were deeply satisfying. The satin smoothness of her skin under his hands as they slid with soapy slickness across every portion of her excited him, and the touch of her lathered hands on him intensified that excitement.

Later, lying in bed together, he continued his relation. During dinner he had gone over the meeting with the President in detail and the reaction of Sanders to Herbert Boardman's description of the only solution he could envision. What had followed then, after the President had finished his phone call, was a meeting in a room to which the press secretary had led him—a thickly carpeted conference room just large enough to contain a table and surrounding chairs sufficient to seat eighteen. Here they had spent half an hour in preliminary discussion with ten other men and two women. They were scientists, distinguished representatives of a dozen different specialized fields.

All had been contacted early in the week by telephone from the White House and asked if they'd cooperate in what the President had in mind, culminating in this day's meeting. None had refused and each was then, at President Sanders's order, provided with Xeroxed transcripts of the tapes Grant had recorded during his session with Boardman at the hospital in Chicago. Very thick, and neatly bound in red fiber binders, the transcripts had been delivered by hand in sealed envelopes to the scientists before noon the day before, with the reiterated request given initially over the telephone that they be read thoroughly and kept strictly confidential before the meeting with the President.

Anne sat up on the bed and turned, facing him, her body softly outlined by the indirect glow of the light from the bathroom. "I was under the impression," she said, "that the Knotts Commission was to analyze the material you passed on to Mr. Knotts and then make recommendations to the President. Didn't they do this?"

"That wasn't their function," Grant responded. "Their job was simply to collate, along the lines I suggested, and then write up the summary I taped and pass it along to the President. It's not ready yet but when it is, it'll be copied and passed on to the selected Scientific Advisory Committee."

"And that committee was the one you met in the conference room at the White House?"

"Right.

"So they haven't seen the summary yet, but they have read your interview with Boardman. What was their reaction on the whole? Skepticism? Acceptance? What?"

Grant readjusted his position on the pillow and interlaced his fingers behind his head. "Nothing at first. Evidently none was desired at first, according to what Sanders said. He opened the meeting by welcoming them and thanking them for their help thus far and hoped they would continue to assist as an official body. Then he introduced me and followed that by asking each to introduce himself in turn. I have a list of their names and titles in my briefcase. Can't recall them all offhand, but I was impressed. Robinson was there, for example."

"Robinson?"

"Dr. Jason Robinson. Curator of geology at the Smithsonian. Edgar Lossing was there he's chief of the U,S. Naval Observatory just a few blocks west of here and, let's see…oh yes, Dr. Irma Dowde, the archaeologist.

Anne had been softly stroking his chest as he was talking but at his last words she suddenly gripped the flesh hard.

"John, really? Hey, she was my professor for several of the Arky classes I took at UIC. Arky and APE were my minors. She's great! Just about the best there is."

Grant winced and gently opened her fingers. "Ouch. Glad your hand wasn't elsewhere. I take 'Arky' to mean archaeology, but what's 'ape'?"

She giggled. "Sorry, darling. And you're right about Arky-ology, but the APE's not ape as in monkey; APE as in the initials A-P-E. Anthropology Education. Campus jargon. She was really there? Gosh, wish I could have seen her. She was terrific. Always said whatever she was thinking, with no holds barred. We were sorry when she left."

"We got a little taste of that today at the meeting. Anyway, she was there and there were others, just about as prestigious. After the introductions the President talked for a short while. Boiled down, he said he appreciated their taking time from their busy schedules to read the Boardman transcript and consider the HAB Theory as open-mindedly as they could. I think some of them had come prepared to get into a really deep discussion about the whole thing, but Sanders changed their minds in a hurry. Told them he'd eventually want them to do that, but not until after they were supplied with and had studied the full transcript of my summary, which he promised them in about a week. Today he wanted no attempt at all-out discussion, which he felt—and rightly so—would be premature. He merely wanted them to hear what I'd told him about the solution this morning, followed by a résumé of whatever else of pertinence I'd turned up this week. Said he'd leave us alone for that, but that he'd be back about five o'clock and at that time he would ask of them only one question."

Grant paused and smiled at her. "You certainly know how to distract a man, don't you?"

"As softly as that?" Her lower lip projected in an exaggerated pout. "It was meant as a comfort, not a distraction. I'll stop."

"It's both, and don't stop. I'll muddle on through with the distraction, if you don't mind." He reached out a hand to the bedside table and got a cigarette and his lighter. She took them from him immediately.

"My job." She put the cigarette between her lips and flicked the lighter, then brought the flame up. Abruptly she jerked and the lighter snapped out before the cigarette was lit. "Now who's the distraction?" She closed her eyes and made a happy little sound, but then shook her head. "Cease and desist! You might be able to handle the distraction, but I can't, and you're at too crucial a point to stop talking now. Here, smoke your cigarette." She quickly lighted it with shallow little puffs and then removed it from her own lips and placed it between his. "Now, go on. What was the President's question?"

"That's what they wondered. He didn't tell them right then." Grant took the lighter from her and replaced it on the table, exhaling smoke as he did so. "He left the room, so I went on and explained about Boardman's plan. Pretty strong reaction on that from everyone. After that I hit some of the high points of supportive evidence. I'll have to admit, there was a hell of a lot of flak to just about everything. I begin to get an inkling of what Boardman was up against. Those twelve, I honestly feel, were doing everything in their power to be as open-minded as possible but, God!, they're really very tightly locked into their long-established theories. Anyway, President Sanders had left us about quarter after eleven. A light luncheon was brought in for us about an hour later and we took a break to eat, then went back to the discussion. Almost before we realized it, Sanders was back again and it was just about five o'clock. Don't think I ever saw an afternoon go by so fast."

"The question, dammit, get to the question! Jeeze!"

Although he had taken only a few puffs on it, Grant leaned over and squashed out his cigarette, then raised himself on his elbows to kiss her. She responded, but then pushed him back on the pillow.

"No more than that until you finish."

"Ah, 'tis a mean taskmaster ye be, lass. All right, here it is. He told them that considering what they'd read in the hospital transcript and what they'd gotten today from me, he wanted each of them to give a simple yes or no answer to this question: Is it even remotely possible that the HAB Theory is valid?'"

Grant laughed, shaking his head. "I think everyone in the room started talking simultaneously at that. They sure didn't like it. Sanders got the floor again and took some slips of paper from his pocket. He told them he knew they'd object strongly to being put in such a position and certainly he did not want them to commit themselves officially in such a manner. He also said he knew the matter could be argued for months. However, he held up the little packet of slips and told them that on each was typed two words: 'Yes' and 'No'. Their answers were to be anonymous, so that none would feel he had been forced to commit himself to an untenable position. Each was simply, in the light of his own specialized knowledge and equally in light of the material just covered, to circle the 'Yes' if he thought the HAB Theory was even remotely possible, or circle the 'No' if he believed it was absolutely impossible. He handed the papers to me and I passed out one to each of them. It took some of them quite a while to make a circle. The papers were then folded in half and I collected them and returned them to Sanders."

Smiling, Grant stopped and reached out for his cigarettes again, but Anne snatched his arm back. "No siree! Not until you finish. Anyway, you just put one out. Come on now, John, don't tease. What happened?"

"Someone in the group just couldn't bring himself to do it, because one of the slips wasn't circled. But of the others, there were four yeses and seven noes."

She frowned. "That wasn't too good, was it?"

"That's what I thought, too, but not Sanders. He looked at them with that sort of sly grin he gets now and then and calmly told them that if only just *one* of them had indicated 'Yes', he would have been satisfied to go on."

"You know,"she said seriously, "that Sanders is really quite a man. I'm glad I voted for him. What happened then?"

"You should have seen the startled looks when they learned the ratio of the answers. Looked like some of them were ready to begin the battle right there. When the symposium's held, we're apt to see some real fireworks."

"Symposium?"

"Uh-huh. After they'd stopped looking daggers back and forth at each other, Sanders asked for opinions on what to do at this point. Should steps be taken to implement the Boardman survival plan? Could other plans be devised? How should the whole matter be approached, considering it's a worldwide problem and not just ours? They did a lot of talking and suggesting, but didn't seem to be getting anywhere until one of them—guess who!—suggested a world symposium be held in New York as soon as possible, with the top scientists of every field even remotely connected with the problem to be invited to participate, the object being to discuss the HAB Theory in an attempt to determine its validity and then, if the general consensus were affirmative, to consider any possible solutions. The symposium would last for a week or ten days and then, *if* an affirmation were indicated, recommendations to be made and, if at all possible, implemented on an international scale. Pretty big stuff."

Anne was impressed. "I'll say! Goes right to the nub of things, doesn't it? Sounds like something Dr. Dowde would suggest."

"You guessed it. She's a powerhouse, it seems. Built like a Sherman tank and just about as direct. Extremely well known, too. From what I gather, you could ask people just about anywhere in the world to name the three most famous living scientists and if they knew any at all, her name would be on the list. Evidently Sanders knows her reputation for getting anything done that she puts her mind and energy to, so he's appointed her to chair the symposium and directed her to draw up all arrangements for the conference, cutting it down to the barest amount of time possible for getting it started. I guess she's off like a rocket already."

Grant reached again for his cigarettes and this time there was no interference by Anne except in the lighting of one. Anne did not smoke except for once in a while puffing on a cigarette without inhaling the smoke, usually at a cocktail party or some similar gathering. However, she never failed to light Grant's if she were within reach, and Grant had become accustomed to it to the point of missing it when she wasn't around.

He smoked in silence for several minutes, the tip of the cigarette a red-orange glow in the dimness as he pulled on it. Then he continued.

"The President wrapped it up pretty quickly after that. He wants all of them to continue to study the hospital transcript and mull over all that we discussed and to contribute whatever they can to it at a similar meeting we're scheduled to have the day after tomorrow. He's also extremely eager to get the transcript of my summary that the Knotts people are working on now. Irma Dowde suggested that as soon as it was available, the summary be reproduced in volume so she could send copies to influential scientists around the world to get their reactions and to encourage them to attend the symposium. The President halfway agreed, although he said he wanted first to read it thoroughly himself."

"Are you included in that meeting for the day after tomorrow?"

"Yes. At the conclusion of that meeting—Steve Lace'll be sitting in on that one, too, incidentally—Sanders'll get to work on another address to the nation, possibly followed by a televised press conference, but he's not entirely sure about that yet. Nevertheless, he wants both Steve and me to work closely with him in preparation." The glow of his cigarette brightened momentarily as he drew deeply on it, then died in a small shower of sparks as he extinguished it.

Anne looked at him wordlessly for a long moment and then suddenly came to her knees and straddled him, kneeling over him and gradually settling back until she was sitting lightly on his upper legs. She reached down with one hand and caressed him, a faint sound like a crooning deep in her throat, and then she took him in her hands, gently, with love. She showed him the way and then lay on his chest. Her hair was tentlike over his face and her tongue touched his lips, lightly, then firmly, then probingly, and then they were joined there also and everything else ceased to exist for now.

I V

Darkness filled the bedroom as Robert Sanders put out a hand and flicked the switch on the bedside light. Grace moved over against him and his arm went around her naturally, comfortably. Her head lay in the crook of his arm, her hand on his chest.

"Bob?" Her voice was hardly more than a murmur.

"Hmmmm?"

"I've heard some of the things you've said to Steve and others, mainly about the steps you're taking in regard to all this HAB business. They give a pretty good indication of what your reaction is to it. But that's the Chief Executive you. What about the *inside* you? How do *you* really feel about it?"

He didn't answer for a considerable while, but simply stroked her hair with familiar tenderness. After a while she began to think that he was not going to answer at all and that she had inadvertently stepped into one of those never-never lands of his business which she so assiduously tried to avoid, but sometimes blundered into. She felt him move his legs and rub the sole of his good foot over the stub of his leg at the ankle. When still he remained silent, she began mentally forming her apology for probing where she had no business, but before she could speak, he answered her.

"For your ears only, Grace," he said, "I do accept the HAB Theory as valid. All the way. There are a number of reasons why, based on more than just the material I've been getting from Grant and Knotts."

"Such as?"

"Such as information I've been getting lately from Mark Shepard and others. I'll tell you all about that in time. Not right now, though. Enough to say that I believe the theory strongly enough that I'm willing to risk everything on that belief."

"That could be dangerous for you. Politically, I mean."

"Not only could be, but almost certainly will be," he replied. "That's the risk I have to run. At this stage I really don't have any choice. If I didn't go ahead with what I'm planning, in my own mind I'd be at fault for being in a position to do what needs to be done and shirking it because of fear of repercussion. Worse, I'd have a tough time living with myself inside. But I'll agree," he admitted, "it could get rough."

"We've had rough times before," she murmured. "We'll manage."

The quiet of the darkened room enveloped them and after a while her breathing became more regular and Sanders thought she had fallen asleep, but then her voice came again, a warm whisper.

"I'm very proud of you, Bob."

V

A cone of light brightly illuminated the desk top in a room deep in the recesses of the Smithsonian Institution. A clutter of books all but covered the surface of the desk except for the small open space at front center where a silhouetted figure pored over an open volume and occasionally made notes on a lined yellow pad. It was just after three in the morning.

The swivel chair squeaked protestingly at the shift in weight as the figure leaned back and yawned prodigiously. Irma Dowde tossed her pencil onto the pad and rubbed the heels of her hands into her eyes, yawning again quite loudly. She knew she ought to call it quits for the night but, as always when caught up by anything which intrigued her, she hated to give up, even for a rest.

Throughout the evening she had worked diligently, mainly without books in the beginning, sketching out ideas and schedules, establishing times and dates for when the HAB Theory Symposium should be held. She had not eaten anything since the light lunch in the White House at midday and she was ravenous, but still unwilling to stop. It had been close to midnight when she was finished with all she could do on that particular matter for the time being. Instead of leaving, though, she had gone to the racks and taken down book after book, grunting at the weight of some of the armfuls she carried to the desk. Occasionally she paused long enough to get another cup of coffee from the percolator on a sink sideboard and return to the desk with it. The big Mexican onyx ashtray was mounded with cigarette butts, even though she'd emptied it once already this night.

She was a very solidly built woman, five and a half feet tall and considerably overweight for her height yet without giving the impression of being fat. Formless was more the word; her body was chunky and squared, unindented from shoulders to hips, almost like a rectangle and her limbs seemed too small for the massiveness of her trunk. Her weight, which had not varied more than a few pounds over the past twenty years or more, was precisely one hundred eighty-five pounds. From the cumbersome walking shoes she perpetually wore to the unattractive cardigans she favored—usually dull browns, grays or black—her clothing was never chosen with an eye for anything more than the utilitarian.

Actually, the only thing about her that really looked feminine were the large brown eyes, soft, alert, intelligent and far more expressive than any other aspect of her physical makeup. She had never been married and, at age fifty, Irma Dowde was quite certain she never would be. It bothered her not at all. Except for a very brief time during her early college days, she had never really been interested in men very much, therefore she had never taken any pains to be stylish. The stringy brown hair, now becoming liberally sprinkled with gray, never had known a fashionable hairdo and, for convenience in caring for it, was kept relatively short.

The one great passion in Irma Dowde's life was her work. Her whole life revolved about it and practically all her energies were devoted toward it. This had paid dividends because, if not the most skilled and respected archeologist in the world today, certainly she ranked among the very top echelon. Egyptology was her specialty, yet she knew more about the ancient civilizations of the Chaldeans, Sumerians, Babylonians, Mayans and Incas than most who specialized in those studies, and her knowledge of lesser-known, vanished civilizations was almost as extensive.

Her interest in archeology seemed almost an inborn trait. Half a century ago she had been born in Dayton, Ohio, and by the time she was eight she was spending every possible free moment at the Dayton Museum of Natural History—a small but remarkably progressive institution that had pioneered in giving youngsters almost free rein to follow whatever scientific inclination was there, helping them but never domineering. By the time she was thirteen, she had devoured everything available in that museum which was even remotely connected with archeology and was participating in digs being undertaken under the museum's auspices in Ohio, Indiana, Kentucky and Pennsylvania. By age fifteen she was a pronounced authority on the prehistoric Adena culture throughout that region.

Upon entering the University of Pennsylvania, a whole new world was opened to her and she plunged into it with relish. She'd chosen that educational institution because it boasted one of the foremost programs of Egyptology in America. Her strides in the studies were remarkable and she graduated magna cum laude with a doctorate in archeology.

Over the next score of years she had traveled widely, participating in digs not only in Egypt and other countries of the Middle East, but in Asia Minor, Japan, Australia, South America, Central America and the southwestern United States. She lectured widely, wrote eighteen books which were considered among the best for the subject matter covered and, for eight years, had taught archaeology at the University of Chicago, whose subdepartment of Egyptology was rapidly becoming one of the most outstanding centers of that study in the world. She was the only person ever to have been elected to three successive terms as president of the American Society of Archaeologists and was twice president of the World Archeological Union.

Irma Dowde somehow managed to convey to the world in general, through her lecturing and books and numerous television appearances, especially on late-night talk shows, a new sparkle and vibrancy to the science of archaeology which it never had enjoyed in the public eye before. It was said, with some truth, that she was responsible for instilling archaeological interest in almost half the students currently entering that branch of scientific learning. In large measure this was due to her widely known outspokenness—usually droll, often hilarious, frequently biting, always refreshing. In scientific circles people often rolled their eyes when the name of Irma Dowde came up, and yet there was a genuine affection for her among the traditionally jealous ologists which no one else had ever quite achieved.

Two years ago, more as a change of pace for her than any other reason, she had accepted the offer to become curator of archaeology in that branch of the Smithsonian Institution known as the National Museum of Natural

History. It was because of her fame, her ability, and her accessibility here in Washington that her name had topped the list of scientists contacted by the White House to see if she would participate in the meeting that had been held at 1600 Pennsylvania Avenue.

Dr. Irma Dowde had accepted with alacrity, experiencing an inner excitement over the prospect that she rarely had achieved throughout the years. There was good reason for this attitude. A single sentence in the President's address to the nation the week before had struck her with singular force. Almost instantly she had been inclined to reject the entire concept of the HAB Theory as pure poppycock, even as the President had been discussing it. But then had come the sentence: "There is, for example, as an offshoot of his postulation, the very real likelihood that a succession of civilizations of mankind have developed on the earth at different periods, each only to be wiped out in its turn practically without trace as another cataclysmic capsizing of the earth occurred."

This had hit at the very core of a facet of Irma Dowde's character which no one but herself knew existed. Beginning with her first trip to Egypt after earning her doctorate, she had encountered certain facts concerning the ancient Egyptians which baffled her, as they had baffled countless archaeologists before her. There were anachronisms, for example, that were wholly unexplainable. One of the first of these which struck her was that within the pyramids were paintings rendered with great delicacy, the finest of lines and hieroglyphs and the most delightful nuances of color in the humans and animals and other figures rendered. In order for these wall paintings to have been rendered at all, it was axiomatic that there had to be an excellent source of light. The trouble was that, as far as was known, the only lighting source available at that time was from fire, whether from crude flaming torches or from the most sophisticated of oil-burning lamps. Fire, especially of a nature to have provided light enough for such painting, would have had to leave a residue—soot or oils on the ceilings and walls, possibly ashy residue on the floors. Of this there was no trace. The floors, walls and ceilings not only were totally free of any fire residue, there was even an absence of dust. To consider that they might have had electrical lighting of some sort was, of course, ridiculous. Yet, there was no evidence in the slightest of any other form of lighting. At length, as other researchers had done before her, Irma Dowde turned her attention elsewhere. But the problem had never ceased nagging her.

There were numerous other enigmas of this same ilk, and all of them taken together were more than merely disturbing. The whole ancient Egyptian culture, as modern man knew it, was enigmatic because, although scientists usually avoided even considering what it suggested, everything about it inescapably pointed to the conclusion that a fantastically advanced culture had suddenly appeared without prior growth. Egyptians lived there and availed themselves of the facilities and advantages of the culture, but with no idea of how to improve or even perpetuate it. Man's whole knowledge of ancient Egypt was of a culture which began at a peak and steadily degenerated thereafter.

Nor was ancient Egypt the only culture in which this same baffling situation existed. The ancient Mayan civilization in the Yucatán and Guatemala was ancient to the Mayans themselves, a cultural legacy they used but did not originate and had no prehistory for. The culture of the ancient Incas in Peru and Chile was in many respects as advanced and brilliant as that of the Egyptians it paralleled, yet there was every indication that it had been inherited by them, not designed by them. By what stretch of the imagination could the Incas have devised such a complex civilization, showing a technology which, in many respects, modern man was hard put to emulate, and yet these very Incas not even possess a written language? By what stretch of the imagination could the Mayans have developed, in less than three hundred years, calculations equal to the best that modern man can compute and a calendar accurate to within seconds for a year? How could they, centuries before development of the telescope, have accurately computed the Venusian year to 584 days? How could they leave behind inscriptions.and calculations dealing in units which projected four hundred *million* years into the future? The ruins of Stonehenge in England, supposedly ancient Druid in origin, in 1963 had been shown by Professor Gerald F. Hawkins of Boston University to have been an incredible astronomical computer and calendar.

For years Irma Dowde had been plagued by thoughts of the achievements of these great civilizations, achievements that had been used by the ancient races we knew but that those races, from all available evidence, could not possibly have developed. What was so frustrating was the fact that there seemed to be no evidence whatever to prove the existence of tremendously greater civilizations before the Incas, before the Mayas, the Aztecs, the Druids, the Egyptians, the Sumerians, and so many others, and yet, unscientific though it was, repellent as it was to her own scientific sensibilities, Dr. Irma Dowde long ago in her own mind had accepted the fact that it had to be so.

Outspoken and direct as it was her nature to be, she might have expressed herself to this end if just one shred of evidence existed to explain how it might have occurred, but there had never been any. And, maverick though she was in many respects, Irma Dowde had no desire to commit scientific and academic suicide by serious expression of these unproven innermost beliefs.

Now the HAB Theory had burst upon the scene—wild, unreasonable, postulated by a nonscientist in the area encompassed, devastating to a whole pyramid of accepted scientific theories. Impossible? Probably so, and yet...and yet, for the first time here was a postulation which gave promise of shedding light on some of the greatest mysteries in the history of mankind! No, Irma Dowde did not accept the HAB Theory, at least not yet. It was possible, probable even, that she never would. But neither did she dogmatically reject consideration of it. If, indeed, there was the vaguest glimmering of a possibility that it might have validity, then it must, *absolutely must*, be given consideration.

Consciously, the formless female archaeologist could not harbor even the remotest hope that this explosive situation the President had opened would come to anything. Subconsciously, there was an electric excitement, an inexplicable sense of participating in the first faltering steps of mankind's most incredible scientific discovery.

Crushing out her cigarette amid the mound of butts, she immediately reached into her pack to shake out another. It was empty and, with a gravelly muttered "Damn!" she crumpled the package into a wad and pitched it into the wastebasket. She held up her left arm and looked at the watch on her wrist, seeing but ignoring the brown age-spots—euphemistically called liver spots—which had begun forming recently on the backs of her hands. It was nearly four in the morning. Time to end things for tonight.

She came to her feet slowly, stiffly, stretching to get the kinks out. The material on her desk she would leave for the time being. No one would bother it. She buttoned up the ugly brown cardigan over the barrel-like shape of her chest. The only things she picked up,to take home with her were her well-filled note pad and the fiberbound bulkiness of John Grant's interview transcription of Herbert Allen Boardman's remarks. She was weary, but when she snapped off the light and walked down the long marbled hallway toward the exit, there was a spring to her step which had been missing for a considerable while.

V I

In all the years of living in this house on Bobolink Terrace, it had been for Marie Grant a warm and happy place. It was home. It was where John was, and Carol Ann and Billy. It was where they had shared the multiplicity of interconnecting things which make up the existence of a man and a woman who have joined their lives together.

Yet in these past two weeks the house had become alien to her. She looked at the things it contained as if she had never seen them before. From room to room she wandered, engulfed by a loneliness apart from any she'd ever experienced. Always before, even when she was alone here, there was a comforting aura to being in this house. It was a nest they had built together, she and John, and even when he was away, somehow he was still here; sitting there in his chair reading, standing there at his basement workbench tinkering with some project, working there in his den with the comforting sound of the typewriter coming to her at almost any hour of the day or night, lying there in bed beside her, holding her, touching her, making love to her and making her happy. Now that essence of his presence, that aura, was fading. Now she walked these rooms alone and she was miserable in her loneliness and in her fear.

Thank God for the children, for the care they required, for the distraction they provided. If it hadn't been for them, Marie felt she would be clawing her way up the walls. But even they were not enough. It was John who was needed here; he was the mainspring of their existence, the nucleus about which all else in their lives revolved. At times like this, when John was gone and the children were in school and she was left with her own thoughts ricochetting endlessly back and forth in the emptiness these walls now encompassed, she really thought she would go mad.

This was the second full day John was gone on his trip to the nation's capital; two full nights and two full days that had been as endless as an eternity. They had been filled with only one bright spot—his call home yesterday to let her know that he had arrived safely and that all was going well. He had met with the President and in just a few minutes after his call he and the President would be meeting with a group of scientists. She had told him then how she missed him, how lonely she was, how she wanted him home and needed him and loved him, and he had responded kindly, saying that he missed her, too, and that he'd be home before long and that he loved her. But after they'd hung up and she was left with her thoughts again, there was a hollowness to his words which only then dawned on her. Again she had that awful feeling that they had been spoken mechanically, that it was merely a response he had known he should give.

Marie had not been in John's den since he left. She knew she probably would have been had the current diary still been there for her to continue the addictive anguish of letter-by-letter deciphering of the coded words which wrenched her heart so viciously. But since John always took his diary on trips with him, she really hadn't been inclined to go in there. It was no longer a happy place. It had become, in fact, the least happy place in the entire empty household. But now, at noon on this second day of his absence, she did go back upstairs and enter the room, hopeful that here, more than anywhere else, the aura of his presence would remain and she could somehow glean comfort from it.

There was little comfort for her in the room. She stood just inside the doorway, her eyes moving from chair to desk, to files and shelves. Empty. Achingly empty. She moved farther into the room and, though she didn't really want to let it happen, her gaze moved to the diary shelf and she saw volume after volume of a recorded life which once was his happiness and hers, but now was a misery of a different kind for both of them. She looked at the farthest right volume for quite a while, unseeingly, and then abruptly her eyes focused and her breath caught in a little gasp. Quick strides took her to the shelf and she had the volume in her hand. It was the current year's diary! John had not taken it after all. She was sure it must have been because of the rush of gathering up the Boardman papers and leaving the house hurriedly to catch his plane, but here it was! In that moment she was no longer a directionless entity knocking about an empty house. She took the book to the desk and paged rapidly into it, finding the date where she had finished her last deciphering. That entry had been dated only five weeks ago. Now she flipped the pages quickly to see what was left and was astonished to find that she was nearly done with it. There were perhaps eight or ten small entries of no more than a few lines each, and one major coded entry, written two weeks ago while he was in the plane en route to St. Louis to see the evangelist.

The smaller entries proved to be little more than mentions of minor activities with the woman named Anne and the love he expressed for her. There was still no clue as to who she was beyond her first name. It was the final long entry that was so unrelentingly shattering.

*…I am writing this while on the plane while on the way to see Proctor—a meeting I do not look forward to with any real enthusiasm, especially in light of this morning's incredible news about the President. I would rather park in front of a television set and follow the developments of the case. I left Anne at her apartment only an hour ago and my heart is still there with her. It is at times of parting from her that I feel the pain of this situation so unbearably and realize that I cannot long continue to be so tormented and that I must make a decision of some kind, however devastating it might be. I am very close at this moment to telling Marie that I want a divorce. I know now that I love Anne more strongly than I ever loved Marie. I sense that one day soon this will all come out in the open and, to indicate how dangerous my mood is, I almost welcome the occurrence. I **must** get better check on my emotions and actions. How is it possible that I can miss Anne so much already? And, if I miss her this much already, then what will it be like tomorrow? What if I could not see her for a week? A **month!** I begin to question whether Marie really needs me as much as she professes on occasion. I also cannot help feeling that Marie and I can never again recapture what we once had—and I have to admit to the possibility that we never really had it, but only **thought** we did. Certainly I don't recall my love for Marie, blazing though it was at first, to have been as strong at any time as that which I currently feel for Anne. I'm torn apart inside by warring factions of love, anguish, longing, hurt, responsibility, morality. I am miserably unhappy with my life the way it is now being lived. Oh, shit! I might as well admit it—my heart is much more with Anne these days than with Marie, and I might well be doing the most generous thing possible to let Marie be free of the heartache I'm heaping upon her. I'm not really a husband to Marie anymore and the chances are that I can never be again. We're*

preparing to land in St. Louis now, so I'll have to reserve further comment for another time.

From the very beginning of her deciphering through the early mentions of the urgings John had felt, through the determination to finally do something about it, through his meeting A, who had finally become Anne—Marie had cherished the belief deep inside that somehow things would work out, that somehow things would work out, that somehow John would come to his senses and ultimately return to her.

Marie Grant no longer nurtured that hope.

VII

"Your President, Mr. Gordon, has led a very exciting life over the past couple of weeks." Daniel Ngoromu leaned down to sniff the aroma of a beautiful red flower of a variety with which Alexander Gordon was not familiar. "Lovely blossom, but very little scent," he continued, straightening. "It is the way with many of the flowers here in our gardens. As I was saying, President Sanders has been making unusual headlines the world over."

"He has at that, President Ngoromu, though not necessarily of his own choosing."

Ngoromu gave a short sharp laugh. "No, I hardly think so. One would hardly choose to be shot on the street like that. But I was thinking as well of his address since then and the rather incredible statements he made. Have you been involved in that?"

Gordon moved casually along the pathway through the capitol gardens beside the black leader, enjoying the warmth of the bright morning, glad they were talking like this instead of stiffly facing one another in an office. He nodded. "I have been, until very recently."

"Can you give me a little better picture of what it is all about?"

"I'm sorry, Mr. President, but I really don't think I'm at liberty to do that. President Sanders undoubtedly will be making another address quite soon and I'm sure many of the questions in people's minds will be answered at that time."

"I understand." He pointed a thick black finger toward white-enameled, cast iron garden furniture—a table with a pair of ornate curved iron seats opposite each other—shaded by a large arbor growth of a salmon-colored bougainvillea. "Come. Let's sit over here and you can tell me why you've paid me the honor of your visit."

The East African leader led the way and seated himself with an appreciative sigh on one of the seats as Gordon took the other. A cheery little gurgling sound was coming from a rocky pool close at hand where water splashed over several layers of fern-grown and moss-encrusted slabs before reaching the main pool, where it sent continuous ripplings toward the little bank of white water lilies near one edge. Dimly below the surface could be seen vague movements of white and red-orange as large goldfish scavenged lazily along the bottom for food.

The two black men had hardly seated themselves before a servant in immaculate white coat and crisply pressed black knee-length shorts appeared, carrying a round tray. He placed a tall lemonade in front of each man, grinning and bobbing his head ceaselessly. On the same tray was a delicate china service dish on which was a small mound of bread cut into little cubes. This he placed before the Kenyan President and then backed off, still grinning and bobbing, for about ten feet before turning and padding away on bare feet.

"Non-alcoholic, Mr. Gordon." Ngoromu had picked up his glass. "However, we can remedy that if you wish."

"No, sir. This will be just fine. Thank you."

They both sipped their drinks and Daniel Ngoromu picked up one of the bread cubes in his free hand and flicked it into the pool. Immediately there was a convergence of fish to the spot and the cube vanished in a swirl. Gordon watched politely, waiting. The President repeated his action and, still watching the swirling waters, spoke casually.:

"You've come a very long way. I am curious to hear the reason."

"President Ngoromu, I've come to discuss further with you the subject that you and President Sanders were discussing in the White House on the evening prior to the shooting."

Ngoromu tossed another cube of bread, not speaking. From all outward appearance, he might not even have heard. His guard was up now and his customary slowness of response was making its appearance.

"As my President indicated to you at that time," Gordon went on, when Ngoromu still did not speak, "the United States has been maneuvered into an increasingly untenable position over recent months. While we have extensive oil resources of our own, we are also the greatest consumer of petroleum products in the world. Our demand far exceeds our production. Approximately thirty-two per cent of our present consumption comes from crude oil importation—from Venezuela, Columbia, Canada, Mexico, and, most particularly, from the Middle East. The Arab States provide over ninety percent of all the crude which we import. We are dependent upon it, too much so, but the fact remains that we are. Now that vital source is close to being denied us and if the threat becomes reality, we will be facing a very grave economic crisis."

Ngoromu leaned his elbows on the network of closely interwoven iron strips which made up the tabletop and laced his thick fingers together around the lemonade glass. When he spoke at last, his words were heavy with implication.

"I'm led to believe, Mr. Gordon, that denial of Arab oil to the United States will not occur if certain concessions are made."

Gordon's brows drew together and his lips tightened. "The concessions demanded will not be met, sir. Since its foundation in 1948, Israel has maintained very close ties with the United States. Over the years there have been differences between us, but amicable ones which have been amicably settled. The ties between our two nations are quite strong. We will not voluntarily end them, nor will President Sanders permit the Middle East to blackmail us into ending them. Some voices in America are being raised for us to do so, as it would be a simple way out of our dilemma. Those same voices have been raised in this manner for many years. Still, we will not do it, no more from internal pressures than from pressures without."

"Obviously, then, your Middle East oil importations will be cut off. How will you prevent the economic crisis of which you speak?"

"Hopefully, Mr. President, through you: through Kenya. Our feeling is that greatly increased reciprocal trade agreements should be established between us. The United States is prepared to meet to the fullest possible measure any reasonable agreement established between us and Kenya in regard to the development of the Kenyan oil resources.

"Exactly what," Ngoromu said, his response coming more quickly, his gaze narrowing and his voice taking on a sharper tone, "is the United States prepared to offer? Trade goods? Machinery? Equipment? Technology? Your President must be aware that other oil-hungry nations are equally prepared to provide these things. Japan. China. England." He was ticking them off on his fingers. "East Germany. France. Russia. Italy."

He stopped talking and scooped up six or eight of the bread cubes and tossed them all at once into the fish pool, smiling faintly at the thrashing which resulted as the goldfish vied for the tidbits.

Now it was Gordon who was slow in replying. When he spoke his words were chosen with great care and spoken in a very deliberate manner. "President Sanders is quite aware that each of the nations you mentioned, and others, is more than willing to develop your vast resources for you, since you do not have the technology here in Kenya to do it yourselves. That, Mr. President, is *not* what President Sanders has in mind."

Daniel Ngoromu turned his head slowly, a spark of interest in his eyes now as his gaze locked with Gordon's. He motioned the American to continue.

"You have nearly eighteen million people in Kenya, sir. Your educational system is one of the best in Africa, and yet it is still far below that of a great many other nations. President Sanders feels that you must know that education is the single greatest source of any nation's strength. It is the desire of President Sanders to assist Kenya in establishing an educational system which, in time, will be comparable to or even surpass the highest educational standards of any nation on earth. It is his desire that the United States, under your direction, sir, assist you in the construction of schools—elementary, secondary and college-level—of a number and quality that no child in your nation need be denied a first-rate education. Through a reciprocal program, these schools can be staffed by highly qualified teachers from the United States, subject to your complete approval, but such teachers to remain only as long as teachers from among your own people are unavailable in sufficient numbers. It is hoped that great numbers of your young people would come to the United States in an educational program geared to teach them how to teach their own people at all levels of education, and that eventually all classes in all Kenyan schools would be taught by highly qualified Kenyans themselves. Universities of the highest quality would be established in Kenya in sufficient number that no young person with a desire to reach higher planes of education would be unable to do so. That is only the beginning, President Ngoromu. It is also—"

Gordon broke off suddenly as two tall women approached them side by side on the path, one black, one white, one quite young and the other middle-aged, and both of them unusually attractive. Ngoromu swiveled his head to see and his cheeks swelled with a happy smile. He came to his feet smoothly. Gordon already was standing.

"Ah, my dears," Ngoromu beamed, "come join us." He moved a few steps toward them and they separated to put him in the middle. He kissed them both and then turned with his arms around their waists to face his guest.

"Mr. Gordon, may I present my wife, Anita," the white woman smiled at the American, "and my daughter, Narai. Ladies, this is Mr. Alexander Gordon, special emissary of President Sanders."

Gordon took the hand of each in turn, murmuring his pleasure, but his eyes most decidedly turned to the daughter. From a distance Narai Ngoromu had looked attractive; this close she was positively lovely. She was very nearly as tall as the six-foot Gordon himself, too slim to be considered voluptuous, yet by no means to be thought of as lean.

Her figure was quite well proportioned, her limbs long and slender and well turned. Her hair was drawn back in a tight hairdo, held at her nape by a broad sterling silver barrette. She had high cheekbones and a wide forehead over large almond-shaped eyes. Her features were delicately formed, with the lines of chin and nose cleanly delineated. Her lips were wide but relatively thin and her nostrils were not in the least broad. Narai was twenty years old and when she smiled, as now, she exposed a set of teeth as perfect and white as her father's—although except for height and darkness of skin, that was the only aspect of her physical appearance in which she resembled him in the slightest. Mostly she bore the characteristics of the Masai in her carriage and in the aristocratic delicacy of her features.

"Welcome to Kenya, Mr. Gordon," said Anita Ngoromu, sitting down in one of the two comfortable wicker garden chairs which the white-coated servant had brought at a run as the introductions were made. "Is this your first visit to Kenya?"

"Yes, ma'am, it is. First time I've been in Africa, in fact."

"And how do you like it, Mr. Gordon?" Narai's voice was a rich contralto and her diction was superb, with no trace of accent.

Gordon shook his head, chuckling. "I'm afraid all I've seen of it thus far from the ground has been the road between Nairobi Airport and the New Stanley Hotel, and from there to here. I'm hopeful of being able to see somewhat more before leaving."

"You definitely should." Anita crossed her long legs and patted the pleats of her flared white skirt. She looked at her husband as Narai sat in the other wicker chair, and reached out to touch his hand. "Please, sit down Daniel…Mr. Gordon. I didn't really want to interrupt, but Narai and I thought we'd take a little drive up to Naivasha and visit Joyce. Dick was in town today and said she's much improved." She looked at Gordon. "Excuse me, the Barretts, Dick and Joyce, are old friends who have a farm just east of Naivasha, about sixty miles from here. Cotton and coffee, mainly. Joyce was stung on the big toe by a scorpion a couple of weeks ago and she's just now getting back on her feet. Anyway, dear," she was turning back to her husband, "we were wondering if it was at all possible that you might be able to go along. We wouldn't mind waiting for a while."

The President shook his big head regretfully. "I wish I could. Too much on the agenda today. But listen," he put a knuckle against his lips for a moment and then went on, "Mr. Gordon and I will be finished here fairly soon, I think, and since he hasn't had an opportunity to see any of the countryside yet, why not take him along? If you don't have any other plans, that is," he said to Gordon.

"I have none, but I wouldn't care to impose, Mr. President."

"No imposition whatever, Mr. Gordon," Anita broke in. "Please, do join us?"

Narai was looking at him with head slightly cocked, waiting for his reply, and when he nodded, her smile broadened. The two women made motions to leave, but Ngoromu reached out and put his hand on Anita's knee.

"No, you might as well stay. I think you'd probably be interested in hearing this. Anyway, here come some lemonades for you. Mr. Gordon, would you mind going back over what you've just been telling me about what your President has in mind?"

"Oh, Lord, I'd forgotten all about him!" Anita said quickly. "How awful about that shooting. He's all right now?"

"Yes, ma'am, he's fine now."

"Don't ask for any information about Sanders's monumental announcement about the HAB Theory," Ngoromu said. "He's not talking. Mr. Gordon?"

Alexander Gordon repeated what he already had told the Kenyan President in respect to education and then continued where he had broken off when the ladies had arrived.

"The President also feels, sir," he told Ngoromu, "that it would be basically wrong for us to come in as a foreign nation to develop your oil resources for you. He feels that this, just as with the education, should be something completely under the control and operation of Kenyans as quickly as possible. Obviously, you are not at this point able to develop it yourself, but it is his thought that we could provide the necessary equipment and personnel to get it going as soon as possible. Where the personnel are concerned, he would like to see every technician sent over to be supplied with a Kenyan counterpart who could begin training immediately at the technician's side. As soon as the Kenyan had mastered the particular job, the American would pull out. President Sanders feels that in this way the entire oil operation would be in Kenyan hands alone within a year or so."

Anita Ngoromu was exhibiting genuine pleasure as Gordon finished and a dimple appeared just to the left of her mouth as she not-too-successfully tried to suppress a smile. She said nothing, though, and after a moment of watching her with amusement, Ngoromu chuckled aloud.

"Please don't say 'I told you so.' I'll concede you did." He faced Gordon again with an apology of sorts. "Bit of an inside dialogue Mrs. Ngoromu and I have been having. Mr. Gordon, you introduced yourself to me this morning as a man without much experience in diplomacy or negotiation. You very definitely have a flair for both. I'll have to admit that when I learned on your arrival that you were black, I was just a bit miffed. I thought perhaps President Sanders had gone out of his way to make a condescension gesture to me."

"If I may say so, sir, I don't think the thought ever occurred to him."

The black leader bent his huge head. "I agree with that thought now. Your President seems to be a remarkably considerate man."

"From a close personal association with him, President Ngoromu, I can assure you that he certainly is."

Daniel Ngoromu stood and immediately the others did the same. He reached out and shook Gordon's hand. "Enjoy your outing to Naivasha, Mr. Gordon. I hope I'll have a chance to see you again before you leave." He looked at his wife and daughter for a moment and then added, as if an afterthought, "When next you are in contact with President Sanders, Mr. Gordon, you may tell him that I am most receptive to his ideas and see no reason why my ministers cannot begin the nitty-gritty of firming up the details with his people as soon as possible."

Narai Ngoromu impulsively clapped her hands and Anita leaned toward her husband and kissed his cheek. And Alexander Gordon, still looking mainly at Narai, quite suddenly was extremely happy.

VIII

Anne lay propped up in bed with both pillows behind her, watching with a dreamy smile curving her lips as

John completed his dressing preparatory to leaving for the White House. A large cheery patch of sunshine lay across the foot of the bed and spilled onto the rug, reflecting her mood. The night had been a glorious one of love and talk and simple quiet nearness and she knew of no other time in her life when she'd been as happy as she was at this moment.

"How long will you be there today, love? Can you come back soon?"

Standing with his back toward her, knotting his tie, Grant tilted his head to see her reflection in the mirror. She lay nude on the bed with one arm behind her head, the other casually at her side, her legs slightly apart, the dark triangle of pubic hair a focal point to the beauty of her entire body, her breasts full and firm and perfectly formed and breathtaking in their creamy loveliness. He turned and walked to the bed and stood looking down at her.

"What a woman!" he breathed. He sat on the edge of the bed beside her, his hand gentle on her stomach, moving upward to hold her breast as he bent to kiss her. Her lips brushed lightly against his as she repeated her question.

"Can you come back soon?"

"God knows I want to," he said heavily. He lifted his shoulders in a small shrug. "At this point I don't know."

She could feel her breast becoming taut, the nipple erect under his palm, and she made a soft purring sound. "There is something so incredibly, deliciously indescribable about the feel of your hands on me, John. I love your touch. Any time, anywhere." She put her hand atop his and rested it there for a moment, then slid it down between her legs, still with her hand on his, glorying in the soft caressing which began at once.

He caught himself, stopped, reluctantly took his hand away, and kissed her again. "You can be certain that nothing's going to keep me away any longer than necessary. Right now I'd better make a call across the street."

He reached to the bedside table and picked up the telephone, dialed nine for an outside line and then the number of the Sheraton Park. "Yes, good morning. This is John Grant, room four twelve. Have there been any messages for me, please?…Yes, I'll hold." He waited quietly a moment and then reached into his inner breast pocket and removed a pen, then stretched to write on the pad beside the phone cradle. "Uh-huh…That number again?…Right, I have it. Anything else?…Fine, thank you."

He hung up and looked at Anne, his lips pursed in thought. She asked the question without speaking and be answered as he picked up the phone again and dialed eight for the long distance operator.

"Elizabeth Boardman. Called last night about eleven. Wants me to call at any time up until seven forty-five." He glanced at his watch. "Hope she meant Chicago time. It's darned near that now…Hello, operator? Long distance to Oak Park, Illinois, please, area code three-one-two…Yes, charge it to my room. This is John Grant in room five twenty-one." He gave her the Oak Park number and waited again. "Hello, Liz?…John Grant here. Sorry to be calling so close to your deadline. Just got the message…Yes…Uh-huh…Wait a minute, let me get some paper here." He set the receiver on Anne's stomach and moved quickly to the desk, took a spiral pad from his briefcase, and returned, kissing Anne's raised knee as he picked up the telephone again. "All right, I'm ready. Go ahead."

Anne watched as his pen flew across the page making cryptic jottings in his own form of shorthand, interspersed with occasional grunts or other small sounds of affirmation. For nearly fifteen minutes he listened and wrote and then finally flicked the button atop the pen to withdraw the point. He replaced the pen in his pocket.

"By all means, Liz…Sure…Glad you let me know about it…Yes, very important, I think…No, I don't know for sure yet when I'll be back. Tomorrow, possibly, but more likely another day or two beyond that. Maybe even longer now, in view of this…Right. You, too…Sure…'Bye now."

She watched him return the pad to his briefcase, close it and then walk back to the bed with it and stoop down over her. She raised her head to meet his lips and

put one cool slim hand on the back of his neck, applying a little pressure to bring him down to her, but he resisted.

"Running late now, sweetheart," he said, straightening. "Have to go. Liz turned up something damned interesting in her father's papers. I'll tell you about it when I get back."

He paused at the door, looking at her longingly, and shook his head. "God, but you're beautiful."

The door clicked quietly shut after him.

I X

"Kermit Knotts didn't mention anything about that when I spoke with him earlier this morning, Mr. Grant." The President was fingering the whale paperweight, but his eyes were on the writer. "Evidently he's making excellent progress on the job, though, and hopes to have the completed transcript of your taped summary to me within two or three days now. I'll give him a call later today and tell him to get this new information from Elizabeth Boardman so he can incorporate it into the summary. She did tell you she'd give it to him?"

"Yes, sir."

"Good. Knotts tells me that she's finally relented and given him access to the original papers—on her premises only—now that you've completed your phase of it."

Grant grunted. "I recommended to her before I left that she do so, since I wasn't sure how long I'd be gone and I didn't want to stall things, especially if something new turned up, like that stuff this morning. She found the file, incidentally, by accident, while she was cleaning out some dresser drawers in Mr. Boardman's bedroom. He'd probably been working on it up there and then just tossed it into the drawer when he went to bed. Anyway, she and Mr. Knotts didn't hit it off too well when they first met, so I'm glad to hear matters have smoothed out now."

Robert Sanders hefted the heavy little iron whale in one hand, thinking. He set it down with a small thud. "What she's turned up does give us another dimension entirely to this matter, doesn't it? The evidence is substantial?"

"Very much so, Mr. President." Grant glanced at the spiral notebook still open in his hands, closed it, and put it back into the open briefcase on the floor beside his chair. "One of the very few hopeful aspects we've come across so far. I guess the question is, what do we do with it at this point?"

"It would seem—" The President broke off as the flasher light on the telephone twinkled. "Excuse me." He picked up the instrument. "What is it, Hazel?"

"I have Mr. Gordon on the line in Nairobi, Mr. President."

"Fine. Put him on."

The connection was not terribly good. A steady, low-key static made conversation difficult and a few times the voice from Africa nearly faded out entirely.

"Alex? How are you doing over there?"

Grant, catching the President's eye, made a motion asking if the President would like him to leave for the duration of this call, but Sanders shook his head and motioned him to stay.

"Quite well, Mr. President." Even Gordon's normally deep voice sounded tinny on the connection. "I've had a long conversation with President Ngoromu today and followed that up with a motor trip with his wife and daughter to Naivasha, about fifty or sixty miles from here."

"Very good. I hope you found President Ngoromu at least willing to consider what we propose?"

"More than that, sir." Gordon sounded pleased. "As a matter of fact he has indicated a willingness to go along with us in the matter. He's instructing his ministers and they're ready to negotiate the details whenever we are."

Sanders raised his eyebrows and laughed. "You're a wonder, Alex! Can't imagine why I haven't used you in this capacity long before now."

"It was your doing, not mine, Mr. President," Gordon protested. "I only relayed your thoughts."

"You're too modest. It could've gone down the drain without careful handling. Alex..." he paused, then repeated himself. "Alex, I have John Grant here in the office. We've just come up with something new and very important in the Boardman matter. I think it'll necessitate our sending him over there."

Grant had been affecting an air of inattention to the conversation, but at this his head snapped around. His gaze narrowed as he listened more closely to what the President was saying.

"I don't know that he'll need your help, Alex, but if he does, provide it in any way possible, will you?"

"Of course, sir."

"Fine. I'll have him brief you on the specifics when he arrives. It may be, since you've established a good line of communication with President Ngoromu, that it would be wise for you to sit in on the meeting. I'll leave that up to you and Grant. And the President, of course. You say you went on a motor trip with his wife and daughter?"

"Yes, sir. They're both extremely interesting people."

President Sanders caught a different inflection in Gordon's voice and a small smile parted his lips. "A question, Alex."

"Sir?"

"How old is Ngoromu's daughter?"

I believe she's twenty-three, Mr. President."

"Are you going to be seeing more of her?"

There was a pause and then a little laugh. "I've been invited to dinner at their home this evening. The invitation," he added hastily, "came from Mrs. Ngoromu."

"You've accepted?"

"Yes, sir."

"Then enjoy, Alex, enjoy. I'll get our people moving on the other matter at once. A good job, old friend."

"Thank you, Mr. President."

Sanders hung up and looked at Grant with a wry smile. "Sprang that on you rather suddenly, didn't I? I apologize, but it occurred to me as I was talking that it was the only logical thing to do at this stage, considering what we've learned. I'm assuming that since you've completed your work with the Boardman papers and Kermit Knotts has all the necessary tapes, you are available—and willing—to go to Kenya?"

"Yes, sir. Certainly. I believe I'd have to make a quick trip home first for what I need to take along in the way of clothing and other things."

"That's taken for granted. You have a passport? What about inoculations?"

"Everything up to date in those respects, Mr. President."

"Fine. We'll fix you up with some diplomatic immunity to cut the red tape on the other end. Will you be able to leave Chicago by noon tomorrow, do you think?" At Grant's nod he said, "Good," and then stood up and once more picked up and hefted the black iron whale, walking around the desk toward Grant as he did so. He didn't stop and Grant snapped his briefcase closed and joined him near the door. Sanders was inspecting the paperweight closely, appreciatively.

"Beautifully made little thing, isn't it?"

"Very nice, Mr. President."

"It was sent to me by a little girl named Amy from Antigo, Wisconsin, about a year ago when we were trying to come to some kind of international agreement to stop the slaughter of whales. She thought they would become extinct and asked me to prevent that. We've tried, but they're still being slaughtered by other countries and they're still endangered." He shook his head sadly. "Odd, isn't it? Everyone seemed to think they'd become extinct in our lifetime. Now there's a good possibility we'll become extinct in theirs."

He dropped the hand holding the whale to his side and looked at Grant steadily. "I'd expected you would be sitting in on tomorrow morning's meeting with the Scientific Advisory Committee. It would have helped, but I guess we can manage. The only thing you've not given them is that last bit of information." He indicated Grant's briefcase. "I know it'll be in your summary that the Knotts people are transcribing, but we'll need it in the morning, so I'd appreciate it if you could write it up briefly for us. Give it to Hazel and she can have copies made for distribution in the morning. Might be a good idea to make a copy for Ngoromu."

"Be glad to, Mr. President."

"Good. Maybe you can be finished with that by noon. By then I'll be all done with the work I've got scheduled for the remainder of this morning. I'm canceling the rest of my schedule for this afternoon. Come back here at noon and we'll lunch together and by then I'll be able to go over with you in detail everything you'll need to know when you get together with President Ngoromu."

X

All the preparations had gone along remarkably well and now, with his luggage on the front seat of the taxi, he paused with the back door open and took Marie in his arms. Her response was not enthusiastic, but then he hadn't expected it to be. She'd been far from overjoyed when he'd called from Washington to tell her about it and ask her to get some of this things ready.

When Grant had gotten home late last night, the atmosphere was decidedly chilly where Marie was concerned, but he was so bubbly in his own enthusiasm over what lay ahead that he took no special note of it. Hazel Tierney had called Pan American while he was still in Washington and made the reservations just the way he'd asked her to, so all he had to do was show up at the proper time at the O'Hare International Terminal.

There were dozens of hurried, last-minute preparations to make, and so what little talking they had done was carried on in a rather broken way, both last night and this morning. Carol Ann and Billy were all agog about the fact that he really was going to Africa. Carol Ann asked him to please see if somehow he could bring back a cheetah cub for her, and Billy badgered about bringing him a real Masai spear and shield which he could hang on the wall of his room.

"How about you, Marie?" he'd asked. "What would you like me to bring back for you?"

She had smiled wanly and for the first time he realized how peaked she was looking. Touching his arm, her eyes were brimming as she replied. "There are only two things I want you to bring back for me, John. They're all I want."

"Name them."

"The first is you. I want you back, John."

The way she said it, the odd tone in her voice, momentarily caused him to frown and look at her closely, but then he decided he wouldn't press it right now with questions that might result in unwanted answers. Instead, he grinned broadly and bent his head to kiss the hand that was touching him.

"That goes without saying," he told her lightly. "I'll be back, you can count on it. What's the second?"

"Your love."

His forehead furrowed more deeply. "My love?"

"Yes. For me. For the children, too, but especially for me."

Again that peculiar note in her voice. A stronger prickling of apprehension touched him, but he smiled and replied as if it had been a joke. "Well, I'll have to consider that." He paused and put a stiff finger to his brow as if he were pondering, and then he dropped it, laughing, and said, "I've considered it. I guess it can be arranged. It's always been there before, so I suppose it'll be there when I come back."

She had looked at him steadily for a moment and then turned and walked away, letting a final comment hang in the air as she left.

"Things have a way of changing, don't they?"

It had bothered him and again he briefly considered pursuing it, but then decided against it and went upstairs to finish off his packing. His Pan Am flight was scheduled to leave at one o'clock this afternoon, but he'd told Marie it was taking off at noon. Leaving the house as he was at just a few minutes before eleven would give him plenty of time.

Now, with Marie so unresponsive in his embrace at the cab, he looked at her and saw that tears were making wet channels down her cheeks.

"Hey," he said gently, "none of that. Come on now, no worrying. I'll be all right and home again before long.

Don't you have a little smile for me?"

She did. A very little smile. He turned from her and bent to hug and kiss the children, where the response was much more effusive. And then the good-byes were over and he was inside the cab, waving a hand out the window as it pulled away, feeling a sudden welling of emotion himself at seeing the three of them standing there on the sidewalk looking after him.

"Expect you're going to O'Hare?" said the driver, tugging down the flag and turning the corner toward Dempster. Grant faced forward and settled himself. "One other stop first. Downtown, at Marina City."

Anne was waiting at the entry to the twin towers, two large suitcases at her feet, a carry-on bag in her hand and wearing downward-slanting white-framed sunglasses. She looked very handsome in her trim sheath of white linen with diagonal slashings of two broad lines of color, one red and one navy. White patent leather shoes with medium heels and coffee-colored hose, along with a slim but wide patent leather shoulder bag of white, completed her ensemble.

The cab driver, who had looked at Anne approvingly and then at Grant with a suggestion of a knowing leer, stowed her luggage in the trunk and slammed the lid. A moment later they were heading north on Dearborn for the intersection with Ontario, which would lead them out onto the Kennedy Expressway.

"All set, memsahib?"

She shook her head and made a face. "You're off to a great start. You've got the wrong country, b'wana."

He shrugged. "*C'est la vie.*"

They looked at each other straight-faced and then burst out laughing. She came into his arms and he kissed her for a long time. When they pulled apart they were on the expressway and both had eyes bright with excitement.

"Is it going to result in any real problem at A-C Tours, your being gone like this?"

She tilted her head, considering, but then made a small negative sound. "Nothing to speak of. Probably a few disgruntled customers who seem to like my personal touch behind their itineraries, but they'll get over it. And honestly," she added, "Louise is really a whiz. If she ever decides to open up an agency of her own, she's going to be a serious competitor. She's super on making arrangements. I was really lucky to find her. Oh, by the way," she added, "I didn't have to do it, but under the circumstances, since she's been such a good sport in putting up with my absences lately, I've given her a pretty healthy raise. She got all flustered and began to cry when I told her first thing this morning. Anyway, to answer your question, no problem. The office couldn't be in better hands, although I do wish I'd been able to give her a definite date for when I'd be back."

"Maybe never."

The green eyes were deep, searching, as she looked at him. "It would have helped a lot," she said in a whispery voice, "if I'd known that."

They lapsed into silence, content to sit closely together, holding hands. As they entered the O'Hare area and approached the rampway leading up to the various terminals, the driver turned his head to them.

"Which airline, pal?"

"International Terminal. First one on the right. Pan Am."

"You got it."

The cab stopped in front and a skycap came with a cart and loaded their bags. Feeling especially high and happy, Grant gave the taxi driver a five-dollar tip, at which the cabbie again glanced appreciatively at Anne.

"Thanks," he said, then muttered in an undertone, "and good luck, buddy. From what I seen so far, you're gonna need it."

Grant ignored him, took Anne's arm, and together they entered the terminal in the wake of the skycap. It was fairly crowded inside with an overriding polyglot din. People were queued up in front of a series of money exchange counters, turning their American currency into the medium of exchange for wherever they were going, or vice versa. It was with a sense of pride that Grant realized heads were turning to ogle Anne as they passed. When they stopped at the Pan Am counter he impulsively kissed her on the temple. She put her arm about him and he hugged her close for a moment.

"May I help you, sir?"

The couple ahead of them had gotten their tickets and were moving off and the counter agent had directed his question to Grant.

"Yes. Reservations on Flight fifty-eight. John Grant and Anne Carpenter."

The clerk thumbed through the reservation file, plucked out a slip of teletyped paper and said, "Grant, John C.?" and at the nod continued looking until he found Carpenter, Anne L.

"Let's see now," he murmured, studying the sheets, "Nonstop Chicago to London Heathrow. Change to BOAC Flight twenty-two there for Nairobi, Kenya, with one intermediate stop in Rome." He looked at Anne's sheet more closely and then glanced up at her. "I see you have the travel agent status. May I see authentication of that, please?"

Anne dug in her purse and showed the properly official cards which, as an international travel agent, allowed her to travel anywhere in the world at a fee amounting merely to the tax of an ordinary ticket.

"Some people have all the luck," Grant groused in a jovial manner. He handed the agent his own American Express card.

"Some people," Anne retorted, making a little face at him, "have their expenses reimbursed by the government."

With their tickets ready the agent checked the weight of their four suitcases and found them well within the limitation allowed and tagged them. He also put tags on their hand luggage—Anne's small bag and Grant's briefcase—and then handed them their tickets.

"That'll be Gate Number Four on the C Concourse. They'll start boarding in about half an hour. Enjoy your trip, folks."

"Time enough for a quick drink to send us on our way, if you like?" Grant suggested as they moved away from the counter.

"Pretty early in the day but a sterling idea, nonetheless. Lead on."

Anne hooked her arm in his, briefly put her head on his shoulder, and walked to the cocktail lounge. They wordlessly clinked their glasses together as a toast and sipped. Anne shook her head.

"I really can't believe it," she said. "Africa. With you! God, I've been smiling so much my jaw muscles ache.

It's like some crazy wonderful dream come true. John, I feel like we're setting out on our honeymoon. From now on you can refer to me as Anne Grant. Mrs. John Grant, that is."

He looked at her levelly a moment, detected a mischievous twinkle in her eyes and nodded in response. He reached out and put his hand over hers.

"Nice name. Has a certain lilt to it. We'll have to take it under advisement." He took a sip of his drink. "Did you let your mother know you were going?"

"Uh-huh." She sipped her own cocktail and then set it down. "I was half inclined not to at first, because the last time we talked we sort of cut things off with some icicles hanging down between us." She shrugged. "It's happened occasionally, so no real problem. But, anyway, yes I did call her and now I'm glad I did. She's terribly excited about the whole thing and very happy for me—for both of us," she amended quickly.

"What are you supposed to beware of this time? You were advised to watch out for something, weren't you?" He was smiling as he took another swallow of his drink. A long time ago Anne had told him that whenever she was on the verge of going anywhere, the last thing her mother would say to her would be to tell her to be careful and watch out for something. That "something" might be drunk drivers or martians, low-flying pigeons or mean people or men in brown suits, but it was a warning that always came.

Anne laughed brightly and tossed her head to one side. "Yep. Never fails. She told me to be careful and watch out for tigers."

"Tigers? In *Africa*?"

"Hey, who just called me memsahib not long ago? Anyway, your response was exactly what *I* said to her," she laughed lightly, "but Mother said that one can never afford to take chances with such matters, so to be sure to watch out for tigers."

They talked a little more as they finished their drinks and fifteen minutes later arrived at the International Terminal security check station in the long hall just before a stairway leading down to the passenger loading gates. There was time only to go through and board their plane.

A considerable crowd had swelled at this check station as friends and relatives said their good-byes. Only ticketed passengers were permitted beyond this point. Grant and Anne passed through the metal-detecting arch without difficulty and waited briefly as the slow conveyor belt brought their hand luggage and Anne's purse through the X-ray machine. They recovered these belongings and then moved with the general surge of the crowd toward the head of the stairs and then downward.

Just a couple of steps before moving out of sight of the waiting area, Grant looked back. His eye fell on a woman standing in the hallway outside the security check area, her face in her hands, her blond hair dancing with the spasms of her sobs. In that fractional moment that he saw her, she raised her head away from her hands, exposing an expression of the most abject misery he had ever seen. And in that final fleeting view of her, he realized that it was Marie.

X I

The Washington Post

WORLD SYMPOSIUM SET ON HAB THEORY

by Donald Barron

WASHINGTON, D.C., June 6 (AP). White House Press Secretary Steven Lace today announced at a news conference that on a directive from President Robert M. Sanders, a symposium of the world's foremost scientists will meet soon in New York City to discuss the highly controversial HAB Theory.

The 10-day symposium, which begins on Friday, July 1, will be attended by approximately 2,000 to 3,000 scientists in various fields from all over the world. No nation, Lace said, will be excluded from sending representatives if it chooses.

The action taken today, according to Lace, followed three days of closed preliminary talks in the White House between the President and a dozen renowned scientists whom he has appointed as an official Scientific Advisory Committee. The 12 are primarily from the Washington, D.C., area. After having studied documents pertaining to the matter, Lace announced, a third of the Committee agreed that in their opinion the HAB Theory was "within the realm of possibility." As such, according to President Sanders's recent address, it poses a threat to the entire human race.

The purpose of the symposium, which will be centered at Manhattan's Waldorf Astoria, will be to discuss in greater depth whatever evidence may be uncovered prior to commencement of the symposium which either corroborates or refutes the basic hypotheses of the HAB Theory. If, in the view of the participating scientists, the theory is valid, symposium attendees will culminate their 10 days of discussions be establishing recommendations aimed at preserving mankind from extinction brought about by the HAB Theory cataclysm. Lace went on to say that Sanders was hopeful, if such were the case, that a top priority survival program could be established involving a cooperative international effort on a global scale.

The Press Secretary also announced the appointment of Dr. Irma Dowde, curator of archaeology at the National Museum of Natural History, not only as chairwoman of the Scientific Advisory Committee, but also coordinator and chairwoman of the HAB Theory Symposium. In addition to organizing the details of the projected symposium and establishing an elite list of scientists the world over to be especially invited to participate, Dr. Dowde will see that each of the participants receives copies of whatever material is available or becomes available on the HAB Theory prior to the meeting. This will include a detailed summary of the HAB Theory being specially prepared for the President.

According to Lace, investigation of the Herbert Allen Boardman papers is continuing at this time. Boardman, the ninety-four-year-old man who recently attempted an assassination of the President and who subsequently died of a heart attack, is the man who postulated the HAB Theory.

Lace said the investigations into, and correlation of, the Boardman papers has been undertaken by both the HAB Theory Commission under the chairmanship of Kermit Knotts and by the Scientific Advisory Committee, as well as by special presidential aide John Charles Grant, Pulitzer Prize-winning author. Grant has been conferring at fairly regular intervals with the President on his findings, and tomorrow the Knotts Commission is expected to provide the President with a more comprehensive written report on the Boardman papers, as summarized by Grant.

Lace reported that Grant, now acting on behalf of President Sanders as a special emissary to President Daniel Ngoromu of Kenya, East Africa, left the United States for that country today. The Press Secretary refused, however, to divulge the reason behind Grant's mission.

7

The most beautiful thing we can experience is the mysterious. It is the source of all true art and science.

—Albert Einstein

When a scientist states that something is possible, he is almost certainly right. When he states that something is impossible, he is probably wrong.

—Arthur C. Clarke

I

The long black Cadillac limousine bore the flag of Kenya; black, red, and green stripes with crossed spears behind a warrior's shield in the center. It pulled to a smooth approach in front of the Nairobi Hilton at exactly three in the afternoon. The heavy rain just after noon had washed the air thoroughly, leaving in its wake a sweet freshness and the streets of the Kenyan capital filled with puddles of various sizes and depths. One of these, near the curb in front of the hotel, looked like a potential hazard for splashing and so, as the big car pulled up, John Grant took Anne's arm and moved back a few paces. It hadn't been necessary. Seeing the puddle, the driver of the limousine slowed to such extent that the tires hardly made a ripple in the water as the big car came to a stop. Immediately the driver, clad in a gray-green uniform and wearing a bill cap with ostentatious silver embroidery on it, emerged and walked briskly around the front of the car, bobbing his head and smiling at them as he did so.

"Good afternoon," he said in perfect English, showing a wide expanse of teeth as he opened the back door for them. "B'wana and the lady did not have to come out to wait here. I would have called your room from inside."

"*Jambo*," Grant replied in the standard Swahili greeting, and then shook his head. "No matter. We were ready to come down."

Fairly short and heavy, the driver was about fifty and had a round, genial face. He continued holding the door as Grant helped Anne into the car and got in himself, then shut it with a heavy thud after them and reentered the car himself. He spoke to them without turning around as he guided the big car back out into the street, heading toward Jomo Kenyatta Boulevard, a couple blocks ahead.

"It will take only fifteen minutes to reach the Presidential Palace, Mr. Grant. I am David Pemba and am instructed to say that President and Mrs. Ngoromu are grateful that you and the lady were able to accept their invitation."

"Thank you, Mr. Pemba. Miss Carpenter and I are honored."

"Please, call me David."

Grant made no response, but he did nudge Anne and then gesture toward a very old white-haired black man standing in the street near the curb.

"Look. He's still there."

The man was filthy and his dirty khaki clothing was in tatters. The shirt was without buttons and hung open. One leg of the trousers was ripped away above the knee and the other hung in ragged strips from knee to ankle. He was bracing himself with a crooked branch as a staff as he stood on one leg, the opposite bare foot flat against the standing leg just above the knee. His free hand was clenched in a bony fist and held in the air. He was facing the hotel and yelling raucously in a language incomprehensible to the Americans, who could hear him faintly as they passed. They had seen this same man here earlier in the day as they had walked around Nairobi, visiting shops and markets.

"Why does he stand there shouting like that, David?" Anne asked. "We saw him there late yesterday and again this morning."

Again their driver responded without turning, both hands on the wheel and looking straight ahead. "Yes, he is still there. There are not many times when you would not see him. He is known as Kambu. He shouts curses at the hotel because he claims it was built on his land and he was never paid for it. Neither is true. Actually, the land his family owned is where the street is now, not the hotel, and he was paid for it long ago by Mr. Kenyatta's government. Later, the hotel paid him something, too, just to get him away. But he keeps coming back. He has become something of a Nairobi landmark."

"How long has he been doing this?" Grant asked.

Pemba turned briefly and his cheeks swelled with the wide smile. "At least forty years," he said. "I remember him there the same way when I was a young child, back in the late nineteen-sixties when the hotel was being built. At first he was arrested several times, but he always came back and since he really does no harm now he is left alone. He is very old and cannot shout his threats very much longer."

Grant was curious. "What kind of threats does he make?"

David Pemba barked a high-pitched laugh. "He says that his fist will soon shake the air hard enough to make the hotel tumble down."

They were on Jomo Kenyatta Boulevard now, gliding smoothly past the long line of ornamental date palms which lined the median strip. As they moved along, Pemba indicated various points of interest—churches, mosques, governmental buildings, interesting shops, lovely gardens and parks. He turned onto a road which skirted past the iron-fenced governmental capitol and soon afterward they were on the outskirts of town on a highway listed as B-16. A large sign showed the distances to Thika, Fort Hall, Meru and Nanyuki. Numerous Africans in a wide variety of apparel walked along the shoulders of the road. The men were mostly in European clothing, the women in simple native print dresses. Most of the women carried large loads; bundles of cane or firewood, jugs of water, baskets of produce. Often a small child would be riding in a sling on the woman's back and just as often she would be in a far-advanced state of pregnancy. The men carried nothing, usually walking in small groups and talking volubly.

About twelve miles out of Nairobi, just as they approached the little community of Ruiru, Pemba slowed from his speed of eighty down to about thirty, passed through the village and then soon took a left turn down a tree-lined drive and quickly pulled to a halt at a gate bridging the gap of a sturdily-built brick wall about twelve feet high. Soldiers with rifles were posted on both sides of the iron gate.

As they came to a stop, a green-uniformed sergeant emerged from a small gatehouse, nodded in their direction, and signaled one of the soldiers to open the gate. Pemba tossed a friendly wave at the expressionless sergeant as they passed through, but the soldier made no further sign of recognition or greeting. Glancing back, Grant saw that the gate was shut behind them immediately.

The drive was a long one of smooth macadam curving past neat plantings of trees and shrubbery and occasional statuary. There were numerous well-tended flower beds alive with colorful blooms which caused Anne to murmur appreciatively and squeeze Grant's hand.

Grant himself was impressed. "Beautiful grounds. Does the wall go all the way around, David? How much of an area is there?"

"Exactly sixteen acres, b'wana, Pemba replied, "with the wall all the way around. This entire place—the palace and other buildings, the wall and road and plantings—all were done by President Haru Mzembe, who succeeded President Kenyatta. There is the Presidential Palace ahead of us now."

He was pointing toward a large, red brick building which really didn't look much like a palace at all. With white Doric columns in front and a white-railinged balcony extending the length of the building's front, it reminded Grant of one of the antebellum mansions in Natchez, Mississippi, lacking only the large live oaks draped with Spanish moss. In a circular area rimmed by the drive a fountain spurted water upward to fall back on itself and into a pool in front of the mansion. Completing half the circle, Pemba pulled the Cadillac to a stop in front of the brick steps leading up to the huge house. A houseman in white coat and full-length black trousers was waiting for them and immediately opened the back door as the vehicle stopped.

"*Jambo*," he murmured, adding, "Welcome. Please follow me. The others are waiting."

Grant thanked David Pemba, tossed him a wave, and, holding Anne's elbow, followed the houseman up the eight broad steps which led to the brick terrace in front of the building. Anne glanced at her own crisp, close-fitting powder-blue dinner dress and white shoes and made a disapproving sound.

"At the hotel I felt overdressed. Now I'm beginning to feel as if a formal would have been much more appropriate."

"You look fine, honey. Perfect. But isn't this some layout?"

"I'm half expecting to find Rhett Butler and Scarlett O'Hara in the parlor."

Grant laughed softly as they moved across the close-fitted bricks toward the large white double door topped by an arched, multipaned window of leaded glass. As they neared the door it was opened by a houseboy, also in white coat but wearing black shorts. He was no more than twelve years old and had large liquid eyes and a smile more friendly than merely respectful. He bowed gravely as the houseman led them past into the large entry room with twin curved stairways leading to the upper floor on each side and a massive crystal chandelier hanging in the center. They walked across the exquisitely patterned marble tile floor to another double door, one side of which was open, with the sound of laughter coming from inside.

The houseman stopped in the doorway and said, "Miss Anne Carpenter and Mr. John Grant," and then stepped aside for them to pass.

It was a large parlor in which an ebony concert grand piano seemed almost small in the expansiveness. Numerous chairs and settees were positioned about the room, with small tables here and there, each with fresh flowers or statuary in the center. A half-round alcove to one side had a bank of eight latticed windows overlooking a lovely garden. Here a long, curved sofa was positioned, with eight or ten comfortable chairs of dark wood and red velvet arranged in a sort of semicircle facing the sofa over a low, broad coffee table also of very dark wood.

There were eight people seated here and all of them came to their feet as the two Americans entered. Grant recognized Ngoromu from news pictures, but the only person there he'd met before was Alexander Gordon. Both the President and his wife came toward them at once, both smiling and Anita Ngoromu holding out both hands to them as she approached.

"I don't see Scarlett or Rhett anywhere," Grant murmured in an undertone only Anne could hear.

"Welcome Mr. Grant. Miss Carpenter." Anita took their hands briefly, then turned and continued, "We're so glad you've been able to join us. This is my husband, Daniel."

They shook hands and any sense of formal discomfort they may have had quickly fell away at the easy, genuinely friendly greetings. Ngoromu was openly pleased with their presence.

"Mr. Grant," he said, "we've been hearing a great deal about you from Mr. Gordon, and it's a pleasure to welcome so illustrious a writer to our home. However," he turned his glance on Anne and took her hand, "Mr. Gordon might have been a bit more effusive in expressing what a beautiful woman would be accompanying you."

Anne colored and immediately Anita took her arm and Grant's and said, "Come, join us. We'd like you to meet the rest of our family. Mr. Gordon you know, of course, and beside him there at the couch is our eldest daughter, Narai. The remaining three girls in turn are Lomai, who is twelve, Mari, who's seventeen, and Olo, who is nineteen. The young man is our son, Thomas. He's fifteen."

There was a remarkable similarity in the physical appearance of Narai, Lomai and Olo, and some of the same in Thomas—a tall, lean, aquiline appearance with finely cut features and all of them quite attractive. Mari, however, was much shorter, rather more heavily constructed, though certainly not fat, and with a broader flare of lip and nostrils. Gravely but with smiling eyes, each shook hands in turn with Grant and Anne, as did Alexander Gordon.

"Pleased to finally meet you, Miss Carpenter." Gordon said softly, a faint smile playing on his lips. He chuckled then and added in an undertone for her ears only, "Had I seen you before, I certainly would have been more effusive, as Mrs. Ngoromu suggests."

"It's good to meet you, too, Mr. Gordon." Anne was pleased, but her voice was low and level and her eyes met his directly. Grant was looking at them curiously, but their conversation went no further. President Ngoromu held up both hands, halting the talking that had begun among his children.

"All Ngoromus below the age of twenty are at this point excused," he said, smiling. "The adults wish to converse in relative peace."

Except for Olo and Tom, who seemed a bit put out over the edict, the Ngoromu youngsters obviously were glad to be excused and trooped out, still talking and laughing among themselves. Narai resumed her seat on the sofa and, at a gesture from Ngoromu, the rest of them sat down as well, with John and Anne side by side on the sofa a short distance from the eldest Ngoromu daughter and Alexander Gordon.

"Mr. Grant," Ngoromu said, after signaling for drinks and hors d'oeuvres to be brought, "I'll have to admit that my curiosity has become very keen over the rather enigmatic cable about your forthcoming visit which I received from President Sanders." He paused, but at Grant's hesitation, made a motion with his huge hand which took in the other members of the group seated here. "I think I'd like my wife and daughter to sit in on this, if you don't mind. I believe you've also received instructions that Mr. Gordon is to remain with us and, if inclined, to contribute to your remarks."

Grant nodded. "I have no objection, sir. My hesitation was based on the fact that an explanation of my visit is apt to take a considerable while; something, perhaps, that you'd care to save for discussion in your office?"

"To the contrary, Mr. Grant, I'd like to hear it now, and I'm quite sure that both my wife and daughter," he turned his eyes to them and then back to Grant, "would be most interested as well. Mr. Gordon has told us that what you are here to discuss has something to do with the recent attack on your President, and on the remarkable statement he subsequently made to the nation. This is true?"

"Yes, sir, it is."

"I can't imagine why I should be singled out to have a special American emissary sent over just to brief me on it. It makes me assume that I or my country may be more involved than we presently realize."

"Your observation is correct, Mr. President, but President Sanders feels that before I explain to you how you and Kenya are concerned in this, it would be well to fill you in completely on the details from the beginning. Shall I start?"

Daniel Ngoromu pursed his lips. He had not been utilizing his usual ploy of slow replies and showed no inclination to do so.

"Certainly."

"It might be a good thing," Grant began, "to take your questions as they come to mind, so please feel free to stop me and ask anything you care to. That, of course, applies to everyone else here, also. Mr. Gordon already knows a good bit of what is concerned here, and if there's anything he cares to add as I go along, I hope he'll do so. The same is true of my research associate, Miss Carpenter."

For the next couple of hours, with only occasional interruptions from the five who were listening, Grant went step by step over the events which began with the attempted assassination. Even for Gordon and Anne, who knew much of what he was going to say, having the matter expressed clearly, concisely, and in a very well organized manner now gave them both a far better and more convincing picture of the situation than they'd had previously.

Grant did not pause when the cocktails and hors d'oeuvres came, indicating that the others should go ahead but refraining himself except for a sip of his drink. The servants silently served delicate finger sandwiches, marinated mushrooms on toothpicks, Astrakhan caviar on buttered rice crackers, and lightly chilled Bordeaux white wine in fine long-stemmed crystal. They withdrew just as silently as Grant went on with his monologue. Twice the writer rose and walked about some as he spoke, though always staying fairly near the Kenyan President. Once he paused briefly to sip some of the wine. Now and again he lit cigarettes as he talked. He had just reached the point of his discussion where the meeting with the Scientific Advisory Board had begun in the White House when the resonant reverberation of a deep-toned brass gong sounded distantly.

Ngoromu sighed, glancing at his wristwatch. "The time for dinner has crept up on us, Mr. Grant. I'll leave it up to you whether or not you care to continue the discussion at the table. You may wish to enjoy your dinner without having to talk your way through it."

Grant shook his head. "I'll welcome having something to eat, Mr. President, but if it won't interfere with your own dining pleasure," he let his gaze sweep briefly across the group, "and that of the others, I'd just as soon go on with it as best we can."

"Excellent!" White teeth were flashing as Ngoromu slapped his own knee. "I was hoping you'd say that. I think we're all so fascinated at this point that we don't want anything to interfere very much."

They paired off as neatly as if it all had been planned in advance. Ngoromu offered his arm to Anne and led her to the spacious dining room, followed by Grant escorting Anita Ngoromu and Gordon with Narai. More chilled wine already had been poured and, at Anita's direction, they seated themselves at the table for eight, joined there by Olo and Thomas. The President and his son had seats at opposite ends of the table, with Grant and Anita to the President's left and right respectively. To Anita's right were Gordon and Narai, and to Grant's left were Anne and Olo.

Dinner began with a delicious chilled vichyssoise and chunks of firm white Kiwaihu Bay lobster on crisp lettuce, lightly topped with an exquisite lemon-flavored white sauce such as the Americans had not tasted before. The entree, served on beautiful hand-painted china depicting in Oriental delicacy the splendor of 17,000-foot Mount Kenya, was individual wild fowl about the size of a Cornish hen. Anita called the bird redleg, but she added that it was more properly known as the scaly francolin, a game bird of Kenya's eastern forested highlands. The taste was as delectable as any fowl Grant had previously eaten and, even though he continued talking while the meal progressed, he enjoyed it immensely. Dessert was a minted chocolate parfait in frosted glass. Also, two large silver trays of fruit—apples, figs, oranges, grapes, bananas and plums—were placed on the table. While they enjoyed these delicacies along with the rich, dark Aberdare coffee—one of Kenya's principal agricultural exports—Grant came to the purpose of his visit to Africa.

"President Ngoromu, one of the most interesting aspects of the entire situation involving the HAB Theory is the recent discovery which has brought me here. President Sanders is quite pessimistic about the feasibility of Mr. Boardman's projected solution—that of reducing the Antarctic ice cap weight through controlled use of thermonuclear devices. He very clearly sees the need for it and strongly hopes that, if no other solution can be devised, international agreement with all nations can be reached for instituting such a project. However, he strongly doubts it. At the moment he feels that with numerous scientific minds working on the problem, an alternate solution can be arrived at which had not occurred to Herbert Boardman. However, while he hopes this will occur, he is not optimistic about that, either. Approaching the situation from this viewpoint, he realizes the necessity and fully believes you will too, sir—of preserving as many people as possible, as well as a considerable amount of modern man's technology and culture, should the capsizing of the earth occur."

"Yes, I can see the need for that, Mr. Grant," Ngoromu said slowly, but his broad dark brow was faintly wrinkled, "but as yet I fail to see what that has to do with Kenya."

"A very great deal, Mr. President," put in Alexander Gordon. "Mr. Grant briefed me on it in my room late last night at the New Stanley and I must say that it involves your country so much that even the development of your oil resources here pales in importance."

Anita Randall Ngoromu murmured "Indeed!" and Narai's eyes had become wide. Both Thomas and Olo were equally surprised. All at the table knew the incredible importance to Kenya of the oil resources and it was difficult to imagine anything which could take precedence over development of the petroleum potential.

"Your story sense is not strictly confined to your writing skill, Mr. Grant," Ngoromu said. His forehead had smoothed and he was now smiling. "You know as well how to build anticipation in your audience through the spoken word." He chuckled and indicated the assemblage at the table with widespread upturned palms. "You now have us all on the edges of our seats, so please continue."

Grant touched a fine Irish linen napkin to his lips following a sip of his coffee. "Herbert Boardman foresaw the possibility that the cataclysm, for various reasons, would not be averted. This made him curious to know what portion of mankind and his civilization might possibly survive when the cataclysm took place. Carefully studying the reports of hydrogeologists and glaciologists who made extensive studies and mappings during the International Geophysical Year and since then, he found that the greatest mass of the ice caps for both poles lies to the east of the true polar axis. In the case of the North Pole, almost all of the ice cap's weight is confined to Greenland, eastward of the pole. More important, though, is the fact that fully two-thirds of the weight of the incredibly large Antarctic ice cap lies eastward of the actual pole."

"Wouldn't that cause the earth to wobble as it turned, if the weights were so much off center like that?" The question was asked by Ngoromu's son.

"Considering that you weren't in the other room when I discussed the very fact of such a wobbling, Tom," Grant said approvingly, "that's a very astute observation. You're absolutely right. It can and has caused the wobbling of the earth which Mr. Boardman contends will eventually cause the earth to capsize when a point of nonrecovery is reached."

Thomas grinned, delighted that he had contributed something of a worthwhile nature to the conversation, and not missing the pleased little nod that his father sent his way.

May I say something, please?" It was Olo who, up to now, had remained silent. At her father's nod she went on. "Mr. Grant, you said that most of the weight of the two ice caps is east of the poles and this is what causes the wobble. Doesn't this also mean that when the capsizing finally does occur, the direction will be more to the east than to the west?"

"Indeed it would, Olo, and that's the whole point I'm leading up to. The peak of the wobble gave Mr. Boardman the foundation he needed for calculating exactly on what line of latitude the earth would capsize when nonrecovery was reached."

He paused to light a cigarette and consider how to proceed and then reached out and took a large orange from the fruit tray at his end of the table. "It's a bit difficult to picture in the mind's eye what comes next, but maybe using this orange to represent the globe will help clarify it."

He held the orange at eye level in his left hand, with his thumb at the bottom and middle fingertip at the top.

Now he directed his remarks to the President of Kenya again.

There are two points on the earth which will remain essentially undisturbed at the time of such a rolling-over of the planet. Those two points are not the polar areas but rather the pivotal points when the capsizing occurs. Assume that this orange is the earth and I am holding it with my middle finger on the North Pole and my thumb on the South Pole. The weight of the ice caps causes the eccentric wobble like this."

Grant pivoted his wrist back and forth so that his thumb moved up toward his face and then back again toward the tabletop. He continued.

"Note when I do this that the two points wholly unaffected by the move are the pivotal points—the points on or near the midpoint of the orange, comparable to the equator of the earth—which are the points closest to my palm on the left and toward you, Mr. President, on my right. When, in fact, the earth does tilt and not make its recovery, it will move sharply like this."

Again he pivoted his wrist so that the orange turned a full ninety degrees and held it there so that his thumb was toward his own face and the back of his middle finger was toward Anita, across the table from him.

"As you can see by that, every portion of the globe has been relocated except for the two pivotal points on the equator, here and here." He used index finger to touch the median parts of the orange to left and right.

Ngoromu was looking a little bewildered as he massaged his earlobe between finger and thumb. "I can see clearly what you mean right there," he said, "but what about the matter of the rotation of the earth? Those pivotal points are not constant because the earth is always revolving on its own axis. With that in mind, how can any one point—or two specific points, I should say—be accurately determined as the pivotal points?"

"Again, sir, through the weight of the ice caps and by being able to accurately know the peak of the wobble reached by the earth at the present time. The capsizing occurs only when the weight becomes overbalanced and reaches a point of nonrecovery. That point can be reached only at the very apex of the wobble. Through astronomy— taking successive star-movement photos at different locations on the earth—it is seen that the amount of detectable wobble differs at various observation points. Identical wobbles are recorded only at points on the surface of the earth which are diametrically opposite each other. Again, let me use the orange to illustrate."

Grant reached into the inside breast pocket of his navy blue suit coat and withdrew a long, freshly sharpened yellow pencil. He pushed the pencil through the orange so that it protruded on both sides and then again held the fruit as he had been holding it before, with thumb down and finger up, but now with the eraser of the pencil toward his face and the point toward Anita.

"When the capsizing occurs, as I demonstrated before, the earth turns approximately ninety degrees." Once more he turned the orange so his thumb was toward his face, and now the pencil eraser was pointing straight upward. "You see that not only is the least amount of movement at the pivotal points located to left and right on the globe at the equator, but that the greatest movement is also located on the equator at the point where the pencil goes through. The star charts show us these movements very accurately. Therefore, we are able to determine with considerable accuracy just where the pivotal points are located, because the successive star photos show no wobble whatever at those two points. The peak point of the wobble occurs once every fourteen months and, unless something unforeseen occurs, the capsizing will take place as that peak is reached. Assuming that to be the case, then the line of the capsizing is determinable as well as the two pivotal points."

There was a momentary silence as Grant set the orange down on his service plate, pulled out the pencil, wiped it on his napkin and replaced it in his pocket. Anita Ngoromu spoke softly, asking the key question.

"Those two pivotal areas, then, Mr. Grant where are they located?"

"One is in the midst of the Pacific Ocean, Mrs. Ngoromu, a few hundred miles off the Philippines. The other is on the African coast of the Indian Ocean about thirty miles north of the town of Malindi, at Formosa Bay.

Ngoromu jabbed a fingertip down on the tabletop and at the same time looked at Grant sharply. "That's in Kenya."

"Correct, Mr. President."

"What it amounts to, President Ngoromu," Anne put in, green eyes flashing with excitement, "is that when the cataclysm occurs, the safest place in the entire world will be right here in Kenya."

It was then that everyone was talking at once as the magnitude of the declaration came home to them. Olo's voice was high-pitched, strident, as she talked with Thomas, and his cracked frequently. Narai was listening carefully to what Gordon was telling her. Anne, Grant, Anita and Ngoromu were continuing their own discussion.

"You said, Mr. Grant," the Kenyan President remarked, "that the peak of the earth's wobble occurs every fourteen months. Was Mr. Boardman able to calibrate when the next peak will be reached?"

"Yes, sir, he did. The next peak will come somewhere around the middle of July—between four and six weeks from now—but Mr. Boardman, judging from his notes, was optimistic about our surviving that one. He was much less optimistic about the next one after that, which will occur in mid-September of next year. By then another hundred billion tons or more will have been added to the Antarctic ice cap. If we survive that one, then we'll have until mid-November of the year after next."

"Let's hope," Ngoromu said fervently, "that we have at *least* that much time to prepare. You say there will be no effect at all from the cataclysm on the Kenyan coast?"

"No," Grant replied, "that's not entirely true. There's no place on the globe that would be unaffected entirely. It's just that much *less* effect will occur here than anywhere else."

"The tidal waves will have to be gigantic, won't they, John?" Anne asked. "If so, then even the Kenyan coast wouldn't be very safe, would it?"

"That's probably true for the actual coastal areas," Grant admitted, "but the tidal waves probably won't reach too far inland, especially if the elevation of the land increases rapidly. As for volcanoes erupting or earthquakes occurring, there's no way of being really sure where these *won't* happen, but we can be pretty certain where they will."

"The strain on the crust of the earth must be incomprehensible," President Ngoromu said, more to himself than to the others, but Grant responded.

"Absolutely. There are areas where the compressing of the earth's crust will be so severe that vast new mountain ranges will be thrust up to absorb the wrinkling effect. By the same token, other areas of the crust will be stretched so badly that splits will occur and this will result in tremendous gaps forming in the crust. Almost certainly, at some previous capsizing of the earth, Mr. President, this is how Africa's Great Rift Valley came to be formed, as well as our own Grand Canyon. And, on the other side of the situation, this is no doubt how the mountain ranges were formed the Himalayas, Andes, Rockies, Urals, others."

God!" Anita breathed. Her large circular gold earrings glinted as she shook her head. "What a concept!"

Her husband nodded his huge woolly head and now he looked at Grant in a speculative manner. "I now see the reason for President Sanders's sending you to see me, Mr. Grant. Obviously there is a great deal we must discuss. I suggest we move into more comfortable seating in the parlor and continue our talk there."

They did so and within a few minutes a fresh silver urn of coffee was on the parlor coffee table, flanked by two silver trays bearing cups, spoons, cream and sugar on one and a variety of cookies on the other. They helped themselves as the discussion continued.

"No doubt," said Ngoromu, seated in one of the red velvet chairs beside its twin in which Anita sat, "your President has some idea of how to proceed from this point. Otherwise you would not be here. Will you explain what he has in mind?"

Grant made a somewhat helpless gesture. "Actually, what ideas President Sanders has are tentative, although no less urgent because of that. There are still many questions unanswered. To be perfectly frank, the HAB Theory has not yet stood the test of being battered in every conceivable way by the scientists who will be analyzing it next month. Analyzing it with considerable skepticism, I might add. It may be that they will find proofs which will refute the theory."

"But you don't really think so, do you?"

"No, sir, I don't."

"What about President Sanders?"

"At this point, President Ngoromu, it would take a great deal to persuade him that the theory is false."

"How do you feel about it, Mr. Gordon?" Ngoromu rolled his large eyes toward the former Secret Service agent.

Alex Gordon chewed at the corner of his lower lip for a moment, considering. "I haven't been quite as close to this thing as Mr. Grant or our President, sir, but I have to admit that I'm reasonably convinced that the theory is good and the peril genuine. President Sanders seems to feel—and I agree with him entirely—that even if there is a *remote* possibility that the theory is correct, action must be taken at once, since there's no real way of knowing just how long man may have to work on effecting his survival."

"Narai?"

The dark beauty closed her eyes for several heartbeats and then opened them again, looking steadily at her father. "The magnitude of the whole idea is difficult to picture," she said. "I suppose at this point I have a wait-and-see attitude. It would be easy to go off half-cocked on something like this."

"It could be argued that one could just as easily delay too long, dear," the big African leader pointed out, surprising Grant with the comment. "What about you, 'Neet?"

Anita Ngoromu brushed a cookie crumb from the front of her chic mauve dinner dress and set her cup and saucer on the table before her. "I can see Narai's point. It's a great temptation to say let's wait and see what the scientists have to say when they conclude their studies, but there's a danger of losing too much time in doing that, time which may be desperately needed. It's a luxury I don't really think we can afford, considering what we know of the HAB Theory so far and the destructive potential of a shift in the earth. I think if President Sanders is going along with it to this extent, that says a lot. Too, I keep coming back to the thought that Mr. Boardman very deliberately lay his life on the line just to get some serious attention for his theory. I don't think anyone would do something like that very lightly. Going back to how President Sanders feels, I don't see how we can afford to do less at this point."

"But what could we do about it here in Kenya?" asked Thomas at the far end of the sofa. "Especially when Mr. Grant says no one's even *sure* of anything."

"The things we *are* sure of, Tom," Grant said, "have all supported the probability of the HAB Theory's being factual. Under that basis alone it would be wise, President Sanders feels, to get busy without delay with what we should be doing now."

"And *that*, Mr. Grant," Ngoromu spoke up, "is exactly what I want to hear about. Just what are your President's ideas and what does he suggest for implementing them?"

"Bear in mind, please," Grant said, "that these thoughts of my President are offered only as the *first* steps to be taken here toward preventing man's extinction and the destruction of all he's accomplished over the centuries. Other steps can be put into operation as they're decided upon. Naturally, since the known evidence indicates that Kenya probably will be the least affected area in the world in the event of a capsizing earth, then he feels that here is where steps need to be taken first. He—"

"You've twice mentioned steps to be taken here in Kenya, Mr. Grant," Ngoromu interjected with an edge of impatience apparent. "Let's be a little more specific. What sort of steps does President Sanders have in mind?"

Grant puffed out his cheeks with a heavy exhalation. "All right, sir, here it is. First, President Sanders thinks there should be built in Kenya, far enough away from the coastal area to be safe from tidal waves and equally far enough away to be above a rise of perhaps several hundred feet in the level of the oceans, a gigantic complex of interconnected indestructible buildings. These buildings, with walls thick enough to withstand heavy shock from water, storms, tremors or whatever, would become living and working quarters for a wide variety of people highly educated in every known aspect of human endeavor. Equally, there should be a great multitude of storage areas where the accumulated knowledge of mankind could be gathered together, not only on microfilm, recorded tapes and photographs, but, in those instances where the document is especially valuable in its own right, in the original form.

"Further, there should be storage areas for various types of tools which man has developed to improve his lot, storage areas for carefully selected fertile seeds of the best hybridized grains man has developed, and storage areas for the preservation of the best possible examples of his art—paintings, statuary, poetry, music, literature, whatever.

"Structurally," he went on, "these buildings should be built quite low, probably no more than thirty feet in height except where necessity for some reason or another would dictate greater height. Buildings would have to be constructed at many different areas within the complex which would serve as life-support systems, providing the electrical energy, heat, cooling, circulation whatever else might be required to make the complex self-sustaining under the most adverse conditions. A series of hydroponic structures could be built to perpetuate cuttings of the best fruit stock, timber woods, medicinal plants, vegetable hybridizations, and so on."

Grant took a quick sip of his coffee and then continued. "A highly important part of the complex would have to be devoted to education—from the most primary instruction through all levels to the highest studies achieved by man in his institutions of higher learning. An equally extensive medical facility would have to be part of the complex, not only to care for those who would be here, but to perpetuate man's medical knowledge, techniques and devices. Whole sections would be devoted to water purification and sanitation.

"It doesn't end there. A rather extensive section, properly supplied for its food and water needs, would have to be provided which would house a wide variety of animal life especially those animals upon which man has become most dependent for food, leather, fur, protection, plant propagation and fertilization, predatory value, or whatever, such as horses, cattle, sheep, hogs, chickens, other fowl, dogs, cats, beavers, birds of prey, and even such insects beneficial to man as the ladybird beetle, the honeybee, the praying mantis, and others. When these were provided for, other animals of perhaps lesser actual value to man for his survival could be provided for, simply as a matter of esthetics and to prevent their almost certain loss."

"Good Lord," murmured Anne, who was hearing this for the first time, "it's as if you're talking of putting a whole nation under roof."

"Wrong," Grant said quickly, "not a whole nation, but a whole *civilization*. A cross-section of the best of mankind of all races, and the best that any of those races have achieved culturally, scientifically, educationally, medically, agriculturally, technologically, whatever."

There was a long silence when he stopped, each person in the room deep in his own envisioning of what necessarily would have to be the most extensive and complex construction project ever undertaken by man. At length the huge African leader came to his feet and walked slowly across the room, his hands clasped behind him. The silence in the room continued except for the double clicking of Grant's cigarette lighter. As he turned back to face the writer, Ngoromu crossed his arms over his chest.

"Several questions immediately come to mind in contemplating such a project," he said. "Fundamental questions, that is. First, exactly where is it envisioned that such a complex should be built? Second, how much land area would the complex cover? Third, who would build it? Fourth, how would it be funded? Fifth, where would the raw materials come from, and the construction equipment, and the technicians? Sixth, when should it be undertaken? Seventh, who should have control over it?" He paused. "There are other points, but those will do for starters."

Now it was Grant who rose and came to a stop a few paces in front of Ngoromu, the others in the room watching both men with fascination. "Again, Mr. President, the answers are largely dependent upon you at this stage. The complex should be built as close to the pivotal point as possible, yet in an area where the ground elevation is no less than five hundred feet above present sea level. Since the pivotal point is just north of Malindi in the Formosa Bay area of coastal Kenya, then the nearest inland plateau of that elevation would probably be best. A very rough guess would be somewhere between thirty and sixty miles inland.

"As for how much land it should cover, the only answer possible now is that it should be as much as possible. A starting plan might call for a full four or five square miles to be covered with the interconnecting buildings— these buildings to interconnect, incidentally, not only through sealable doorways, but also through a labyrinth of underground passageways, also sealable—but built with the idea in mind that continually more would be built, perhaps eventually covering scores or even hundreds of square miles of land.

"Who's to build it?" Grant shook his head. "That all depends upon who is willing to help. It should, of course, be as fully an international project as possible. Yet, there is always the likelihood that some nations would have nothing to contribute and that others, who might have much to contribute, would refuse to go along with the project. It is conceivable, I suppose, that no other nation could be convinced enough to pour a vast amount of its energy, resources and finances into so nebulous an undertaking. President Sanders, therefore, has authorized me to extend to you the assurance that no matter what other nations might or might not do, the United States will cooperate to the fullest possible extent, even should it come down to no more than a joint operation between Kenya and America only. Other nations will eventually cooperate—President Sanders is positive of that—but there is not time to wait for all this to be argued out by the various governments. It must, start now. Tomorrow, if possible. The United States is willing to bear almost the entire burden of construction cost at first. And that comment applies to your question of how such a project will be funded, though ideally, the World Bank—that is, the International Bank for Reconstruction and Development—will recognize the great need and assist. At the beginning, too, the United States will shoulder the burden of being the source for materials, equipment and technologists."

Grant turned and walked to a small table beside one of the red velvet chairs and there squashed out his cigarette in an ashtray. Remaining there, he turned to face Ngoromu again.

"As for *when* it should be undertaken, the answer can be nothing else except immediately. As I said, tomorrow, if this is possible. There is no way of knowing how much time we have left. The fourteen-month cycles of the wobble's peak are thought to be when the capsizing will occur, but we can't plan on this for certain. We have to make use of every day we have. Each one permitted to go by without the project under way is a day which might prove crucial in the extreme later on. Perhaps everything we do will be too late, there's no way of knowing—but we *must* start.

"Let's see, what else? Oh yes, you asked who would have control over it. This, too, becomes dependent upon who is involved in the project and to what extent. Possibly some sort of international board of governors would have to be established, but President Sanders's feeling is that since the project must take place here in Kenya, then the leader of Kenya should serve as chairman or president of this international board. As you've pointed out, President Ngoromu, there are a multitude of other points to be considered, but the urgency of the matter requires that a start be made at once. Whatever needs or problems arise above and beyond these points are matters which can be attended to as they present themselves."

Another heavy silence enveloped them, stretching out to the point where it was growing uncomfortable. Deep in thought, Ngoromu's expression was impassive, and he was oblivious of the fact that all eyes in the room were on him. He made a peculiar humming sound deep in his throat as he considered all this, and at last he directed his gaze at the writer.

"You've said, Mr. Grant, that the urgency of the matter requires that a start be made. This may be, but I am skeptical over the willingness of other nations to contribute as fully as would be required in an international project of this scope. Regarding belief in the impending cataclysm, I do agree with your President that if the faintest possibility exists, then we must act at once. Yet, I have the gravest of reservations about committing my country to the disruption that would necessarily result from such a construction endeavor here as President Sanders envisions."

The huge black man took a step closer to Grant and his words became a bit more harsh. "His offer to bear the costs at first is generous, but is it not possible that the apparent altruism of your nation in this matter may be no more than a rather devious means by which America would hope to firmly entrench itself on the African continent? Could not the impending oil crisis for America have more to do with this than meets the eye?"

Ngoromu swiveled his head and stared for a long moment at Gordon, but when Gordon licked his lips and seemed about to make a comment, the Kenyan President waved him off and redirected his attention to Grant.

"Americans," he said, "somehow never seem to see themselves as other nations see them. The American illusion is one of a mother country extending herself to the limits of her ability to help underprivileged nations raise their standards of living. In many cases the vision of foreigners is quite different and America takes on the posture of an aggressive, often ruthless meddler in the affairs of other nations, stretching out its so-called helping hand only in an effort to exploit the very people it purports to assist. How many wars, for example, has America fought or supported since the time of its own Civil War? Ten? Twelve? Fourteen? And how many of these wars have been fought on American soil? None, Mr. Grant. I have no intention of seeing Kenya, or any other part of East Africa, become a new theater of war for America in which it can test itself—at *our* detriment, sir!—against some other foreign power, while at the same time enjoying all the comforts of peace within its own borders. That will never occur so long as I lead Kenya or any other part of Africa."

He stopped again, regarding the writer with a dark level stare. After a moment he ran the tip of a pink tongue over his lips and spoke again. "You have said, Mr. Grant, that the urgency of this present matter requires that a start be made. Despite my instinctive wariness, I am forced to agree. You may tell President Sanders that Kenya will cooperate. Beginning tomorrow. The start has been made."

I I

The New York Times

HAB THEORY SYMPOSIUM
STIRRING SCIENTIFIC FUROR

A Special Feature by
Times Science Editor Ralph Zeitler

NEW YORK, June 10—If famed archaeologist Dr. Irma Dowde gives the impression of competence, it is well founded. The curator of archaeology at the Smithsonian Institution is, among world scientists themselves, one of the most highly regarded professionals in any scientific field of study. Probably no other individual President Robert Sanders might have picked to chair the forthcoming world symposium in this city on the HAB Theory three weeks from now could have been better chosen in any respect.

An example of her competence can be seen in her whirlwind approach to the obligations imposed upon her when she was named coordinator and chairwoman of the HAB Symposium by the President four days ago. During that interval she has met daily with the Chief Executive and with all members of the select Scientific Advisory Committee (of which she is also chairwoman) in extensive discussion sessions, weighing and correlating all material thus far gathered in regard to the HAB Theory. Part of this has included author John Grant's summarization of the papers from the files of the postulator of the HAB Theory, the late Herbert Allen Boardman; a summarization made possible, following Grant's taped summary by the production of a transcript of the summary by the HAB Theory Commission under the chairmanship of Kermit Knotts. The Commission submitted the completed summary transcript to the President three days ago and, while no official news release has been made regarding its contents, it is reliably reported to be a highly impressive and convincing presentation.

Drawing on the Grant summary and her own studies to this point, Dr. Dowde has duplicated the 50-page document and sent it under Presidential Impression to heads of state and select scientists in 138 countries throughout the world.

"The Grant summary," Dr. Dowde said last night, "explains as concisely as possible what we know of the HAB Theory to this point and lists some of the more important contentions of proof in its support. To this I have added the request that each government extend highest priority to the selection of its top scientists to represent their nation at the forthcoming symposium. I have also asked that each government make further copies of the summary and place these in the hands of those scientists who will be selected as representatives, for their detailed study prior to the commencement of the conference."

Dr. Dowde went on to say that a listing of the top scientists in a wide variety of fields was compiled and in each report going to the heads of state was the recommendation that the scientists whose names were on the list be chosen, if at all possible, as representatives. Certainly, if this is done, no more prestigious gathering of scientific minds will ever before have been accomplished.

The symposium is to be held for 10 days beginning July 1 in this city's Waldorf Astoria and already many Manhattan area hotels are solidly booked for that period. Dr. Dowde reports that she has been in direct communication by overseas telephone with many of those she hopes will attend the symposium. She stated in last night's interview that the HAB Theory has created a greater furor in the scientific community than anything else in her memory. Opinions, she related, vary from harshly and dogmatically rejective to enthusiastically approving.

"There are almost sure to be some hot debates involved during the symposium," she said. "Each participant is being asked to draw up a listing of whatever data he can find in his own particular field which either supports or refutes the postulation in question. Hopefully, each of these points will be discussed thoroughly during the meetings. The ultimate object of the symposium will be first to make a determination of its acceptibility, and then, if reasonable acceptance is established, to discuss what may be done to preserve mankind from the near extinction projected by the theory.

"Further," she added, "a special request has been made to each scientist contacted—and will be made to any others who will yet be contacted—to draw up, as completely as possible, a listing of scientifically inexplicable discoveries of the past. It is quite possible that these may acquire new relevance in light of the HAB Theory."

Asked to clarify this statement with some specific examples, Dr. Dowde quickly and succinctly rattled off a number of mysteries that have always puzzled scientists and which remain, at this time, unexplained and largely ignored. Included among these were some intriguing anachronisms.

Why, she asked, should it be that a human footprint clad in a shoe with even the marking of the stitching threads visible on the sole, was found embedded in 15-million-year-old sandstone in Nevada?

How were the ancient Peruvians able to smelt platinum, as they did for their ornaments, when the melting point of that metal is over 3,150 degrees Fahrenheit, a temperature which can be reached artificially by man only through relatively modern, sophisticated furnaces.

Why are tropical or temperate mammals such as rhinoceroses and mammoths found quick-frozen whole in the Siberian Arctic?

Why should there be distinct networks of river beds on the floors of our oceans, where no sea currents could possibly have carved them?

Why have modern scientists almost totally ignored the indisputable evidence that races of giant human beings, upwards of 12 feet in height, once inhabited the earth and that some of these had double rows of teeth instead of single rows like modern man has?

How can it be that a mechanical device found in 1900 by sponge divers near the Greek island of Antikythera and accurately dated to 65 B.C., has been identified as nothing less than a marvelously advanced astronomical computer and planetarium?

How is it that in the tomb of Chinese General Chow Chu (A.D. 316), his remains were found clad in an aluminum girdle, when aluminum itself was not isolated until 1825 by the Danish scientist Oersted, and the aluminum electrolytic process was not developed until 1886?

How is it possible that the ancient Egyptians and Babylonians of nearly 3,000 years ago knew about the passes of Venus and about the existence of the moons of Jupiter and Saturn, none of which can be detected without a telescope, and yet the telescope was not invented until 1610 by Galileo?

Declining to elaborate further on these matters, Dr. Dowde said that they and others would quite probably be discussed in greater detail during the symposium. According to the renowned archaeologist, the list of these mysteries in science is extensive and she openly admits that scientists have a well-developed knack for ignoring such matters.

"I would hope," she said with refreshing candor, "that many of these subjects will be brought out of their closets and dusted off in lively and penetrating discussion during the symposium. It is time, I think, that we scientists—and I include myself—stop this ridiculous business of hiding our heads in the sand and pretending that certain things do not exist when, in fact, the physical evidence of them is before us."

Dr. Dowde pointed out that we no longer live in the Dark Ages and that scientists will no longer be burned alive for heresy because of making postulations that are opposed to current beliefs. "You would be amazed," she said, "at the incredible things many respected scientists believe but refuse to admit publicly for fear of academic scorn or scientific ridicule."

It is her hope, Dr. Dowde remarked, that the possibilities opened by the HAB Theory will encourage all scientists to be not only more open minded in their consideration of these mysteries, but more open in their remarks on these heretofore "undiscussable" subjects. She states, however, that there will undoubtedly be many attending the Symposium who "will fight tooth and nail to defend existing theories which the HAB Theory, if valid, will weaken or destroy."

Whatever else might occur, the HAB Theory Symposium is shaping up to be one of the most controversial meetings of scientists in history and the eyes of the world will be on its outcome.

III

"You certainly look a lot better than I expected, considering what you've been through, Dad."

The air force colonel looked across the table at his father and mother, noting that no traces of any bruising remained on his father's forehead. Actually, he looked pretty good. A bit more tired-looking, true, and he'd aged some since Christmas, which was the last time they'd seen one another, but really surprisingly good for all the pressure he was under.

Robert Morton Sanders put down his coffee cup on the saucer with a faint clink and smiled. "It's all that clean living I do, Robbie. All the sleep I get, too—at least five hours every night, except when I'm busy."

Robert Morton Sanders, Jr., erupted in a short dry laugh. "Which is just about always," he said. "I'll swear, Dad, I don't know how you keep up the pace. Although I'm glad to see you're not campaigning very much this time yet. I suppose that'll come later though."

Grace Sanders spoke up. "You father has always contended that an incumbent President can't help but be reelected unless he's a total incompetent, an out-and-out charlatan, an absolutely blind egotist, or a victim of circumstances for which he has to take the blame whether guilty or not. And even then he'd be an odds-on favorite if he campaigned with a certain amount of vigor." She looked at her husband and winked. "I don't have any doubt that he'll be keeping me First Lady for another four and a half years."

"Provided the world doesn't tilt before then," put in Stephanie, and then joined the laughter of the other three. The colonel's wife was a reasonably handsome woman of thirty-three, three years younger than Robbie, but already beginning to show a slight double chin. Her hair, which years before had been a luxuriant brown and very thick, was now streaked with gray, obviously thinner and a bit more coarse. There was something of an unhealthy pallor to her complexion as well, as if she hadn't been out in the sun for a long time, which in itself was odd, since she had always been the outdoorsy type and the Texas sun is not especially kind to the skin.

"We've laughed about it," the President said, "and I suspect that's what people all over are doing—certainly the comedians on television are making the most of it, from what Steve Lace tells me—but there just could be more truth to it than we care to admit."

Until now, as if by unspoken agreement, there had been little talk about the HAB Theory. For one thing, the family got together so infrequently that Grace liked to keep their conversation light and pleasant, if possible, and steer clear of matters of presidential concern. For the most part, Sanders would go along with that. Yet, Robbie and Stephanie had flown up to Washington this time only because his father had specifically requested him to, so obviously there was something definite in the wind. The meal had been a very pleasant get-together in the privacy of the First Family's own quarters in the White House and they'd chatted about a wide variety of things. Now it seemed that the elder Sanders was ready to get down to the point of his having Robbie get up here. They waited for him to continue, but he seemed in no hurry to do so. In the short silence he finished the last swallow of coffee in his cup and then looked over at Grace.

"I wonder," he said slowly, "if you ladies would excuse Robbie and me for a short while? There's a matter I'd like to discuss with him." He glanced at his daughter-in-law. "I don't think I'll keep him away too long, Stephanie."

"However long you need him is fine, Dad," Stephanie said.

"We'll sit here a while longer, dear," Grace put in, touching his hand. "I think I'd like another cup of coffee and Stephanie has some new pictures of the twins that she's promised to show me."

Sanders nodded appreciatively and both he and Robbie rose and left the room, strolling side by side toward the small, cozy study where the President did a great deal of his work. As they walked along the heavily carpeted short hallway, Sanders spoke without looking at his son.

"How goes it down in Houston, Robbie?"

"Not badly. Space-Stop Five's still performing beautifully and now Space-Stop Six has turned out to be just about the most trouble-free launch we've had. That was the day after you got shot."

The elder Sanders closed the door after them as they entered the study. They seated themselves in deep, soft leather, overstuffed chairs placed at angles to each other with a small table between on which there was a tall lamp and a heavy sterling silver ashtray.

"Any people problems?" Sanders asked.

"We were worried some at first that we might have some personality conflicts in the confinement up there with so many aboard, but not a trace of it so far. That's fairly remarkable when you consider that there are twelve astronauts aboard this one and half of them are women. Hell, there were minor conflicts during the Skylab Project back in the seventies and even more serious ones after that aboard Space-Stop One, Two and Three almost from the beginning. Nothing desperately serious and certainly no more than anticipated, but there *were* clashes. I suppose the compatibility in these recent manned efforts is because there's more for them to do now, as well as more diversion and roomier quarters. It's a wonder to me that the three men each in One, Two and Three weren't at each other's throats constantly because of the cramped quarters and overlapping functions they had to perform. Jesus, they were bored stiff half the time! I'm damned glad I wasn't in on those. They answered a lot of questions for us, but they were a lot of headaches, too. We had a lot less trouble nine years ago with Space-Stop Four with six men inside than with the previous two. And, as I say, none at all yet with Five, and it has seven men and three women. We're hoping for the same now with Space-Stop Six, although," he reached out and knocked lightly three times on the table, "it's still pretty early to make any real judgment; they've only been up for less than three weeks now. It may be a different story when they've been up there four months."

The President nodded and then jabbed a button at the base of the lamp and a warm glow sprang to life. The twilight was growing deeper outside the narrow window and soon it would be full dark.

Sitting as they were this way, in a relaxed manner under the soft light, the physical resemblance between father and son was more evident than it had been under the harder light of the dining room. There was that same strong line of chin and jaw, a trace of the same gentle firmness in the set of the mouth, a similar directness in the gaze. Robbie was an inch less in height than his father's six-one and was considerably more solid and chunky than the President, but the resemblance definitely was there. In some instances, even the mannerisms were the same; the small wave of the hand while emphasizing a point, the raising of one eye brow in question, the lifting of one mouth corner in amusement, the pinching of the chin when steeped in thought. But Robbie, even out of uniform like this, had much more of a military bearing about him than his father had ever developed, though understandable so, since eighteen of the younger Sanders's thirty-six years had been spent in the United States Air Force.

"I'd hazard a guess," the President remarked, continuing the conversation, "that the compatibility among the present ten in Space-Stop Five and the twelve in Space-Stop Six is due to the diversions you've dreamed up for them. The microfilm library, for example. It'd take them a year or more to read all that's been made available to them, even if they read full time."

Robbie gave a little shrug as if to minimize his own significance. "It helps," he admitted, "but then so do the exercisers and miniaturized video tapes, and I had nothing to do with them."

"What's our tally now, son, on orbiting craft?"

Robbie shot a glance at his father, but the elder Sanders was leaning back, looking idly toward the ceiling without much expression on his face. It was the first time his father had called him 'son' in conversation for years.

"Total, you mean?" the colonel asked. "Since the initiation of the space program?"

"No, what I'd like to know is how many do we have orbiting right now."

"Manned? Unmanned?"

"Both."

"Total of seventeen, but that includes eight for either communications or weather, plus the two manned craft, Space-Stops Five and Six."

"That leaves seven unmanned. How many of those can we dock with and enter?"

Robbie looked puzzled. "All are dockable. That's a built-in on all. Four, though, are thin-skinned. They can be opened and checked inside, but there's no way to enter. The remaining three can be entered. The Cosma Nine unit up there is tight with equipment and if we had to do any repairs, it'd be rough. The two Phobos units, though, are pretty roomy. Three men inside comfortably, if necessary, with room for work. What do you have in mind?"

The President didn't reply. For a long while he continued contemplating something and then at last he looked back at his son and smiled.

"Sorry," he said. "Momentary cogitation. Are you still smoking?"

The younger man nodded, not terribly surprised at the abrupt change of subject. "And still those vile cigars, as Stephanie calls them. You'd think after fifteen years she'd be accustomed to them, wouldn't you? About the best you can say is that she's tolerating them. Even the twins are badgering me to quit, but I wouldn't be surprised if she put them up to it. I smoke cigarettes more at home now than cigars, but Jesus! I enjoy a good cigar."

"Smoke one now, if you want," Sanders said. "Are you going to give them up as Linda and Laurie want you to? As I recall, you tried to quit a couple of times in the past."

The answering laugh had an affectionate ring, but he was shaking his head. "No, I expect I'll be puffing away when they finally carry me off. The only thing I've given up is giving up. That in itself makes smoking a whole lot more enjoyable."

He stripped away the cellophane from a long dark cigar he'd taken from his breast pocket and lit it, sighing with pleasure at the first puffs. A heavy wreath of smoke drifted away toward the duct near the door. "Old Rudyard Kipling told it right when he said, 'a woman is only a woman, but a good cigar is a smoke.'" They both laughed.

"I know someone who agrees with you completely, Robbie," the elder Sanders said, his eyes twinkling. "You know him, too."

"Only one person that could be, Dad—Uncle Mark. I don't think I've ever seen him when he wasn't chewing on one, as often unlit as lighted."

The President laughed again. "True," he said. "Mark Shepard once told me in all seriousness that he smokes seven cigars per day, and eats four others."

The humor of it struck them both and once more the small room reverberated with their laughter. It was Robbie who spoke next.

"Is Uncle Mark still over in Turkey?"

Sanders nodded. "In and out of Ankara. He's onto something very big, but I'm not yet sure exactly where he's going with it. Anyway, I've just sent him five boxes of the cigars he likes best. The reason I've done so is because I got a letter from him the other day saying the Turkish cigars he's been forced to smoke over there, simply because there aren't any others available, are very fat and very strong. He says they're composed of twenty-five per cent ragweed, twenty-five per cent mattress stuffing, twenty-five percent rope, twenty-five percent crankcase oil, and fifty percent camel dung."

Robbie guffawed. "That," he said, "totals a hundred and fifty percent."

"Exactly—and so Mark went on to say the way they do this is that when they have the cigar finished with the first four ingredients, they weigh it and then they punch a hole in one end and pump in half again that much weight with camel dung."

Again there was a deep-chested laughter from both men and then they fell into a comfortable, reflective silence. Robbie felt good being with his father again. There had been times in the past when they couldn't get far enough away from each other, but in recent years they both thoroughly enjoyed their occasional visits.

"Anything else about the space program I should know, Robbie?"

The fact that his father had returned to the subject made the colonel realize that this was the key reason for his being here and the levity diminished. He leaned forward and gave the characteristic little wave of the hand which was holding the cigar.

"Budget problems, of course, but then when haven't we had those?"

"The appropriations cutbacks hurt?"

"They hurt like hell, but we've lived with them before and we'll manage this time."

"I tried to keep it from happening."

"I know you did. I appreciate that. I keep getting the sly old look that says, 'You're the President's son, so how come you can't get him to make Congress come through with the allocations we need?' Their thoughts, Dad," he added quickly, "not mine."

"You didn't have to say that," Sanders said softly, "but I'm glad you did. It's difficult to push too hard for increased space program appropriations when my son happens to be number two at NASA, because then it begins to smack of favoritism, even though it's not."

"I know—and so does almost everyone else—that you'd never be guilty of that, Dad." He leaned over and tapped the long first ash of the cigar into the shiny metal ashtray.

"Never's a long time, Robbie."

Something in the President's tone caused Robbie's gaze to sharpen. He looked at the older man in silence, a further measure of the easiness between them disappearing. When Sanders unconsciously pinched his chin between thumb and index finger, Robbie knew they were coming to the crux of the discussion.

"When a politician has a relative who is damned good in his line of work and wants to use him in that capacity, he's almost sure to get criticism about favoritism from the opposition and even some of his own party. Nepotism is an ugly word in politics, Robbie."

"As I said, you've never been guilty of that."

"True. But I'm about to be. At least that's what it's going to look like. Maybe it is. I don't think so, because I don't know of anyone more qualified than you to handle what I have in mind. Still, there's probably an element of nepotism to it, even if only subconsciously."

Robbie said nothing and Sanders went on. "I've talked over my idea with Oscar and Al and they've both strongly advised against it, saying it would be bad at any time, but especially so in an election year. I agree with what they say but I'm not taking their advice, which doesn't make either of them very happy. I haven't followed much of their advice at all lately. As I said, I've made up my mind to go ahead anyway, providing you want to take it on."

"I've never known you to talk around the edges of anything, Dad," the younger Sanders said. "I suspect I'm going to turn down whatever it is you're planning to involve me in, but let's hear it anyway."

"All right. I know you're sincere in thinking you're going to turn it down—this matter I'm beating around the bush about but I think I know you well enough to say you won't, once you've heard me out. Let me backtrack a moment, though. What's your feeling on this HAB Theory?"

Robbie shrugged. "Sounds pretty far out, what I've been able to from the papers. I don't think I can buy it. At least not unless there's a whole hell of a lot more of a convincing nature that I don't know about."

"There is, Robbie. Let me fill you in on some of the facts from the preliminary reports of the Scientific Advisory Committee—facts that haven't been released to the press yet."

As the colonel stubbed out his cigar and almost immediately withdrew another from his pocket and unwrapped and lit it, Sanders talked. For fully twenty minutes without interruption he explained the essence of what he knew so far and concluded with the Boardman survival plan involving the use of thermonuclear devices to reduce the Antarctic ice cap. Robbie was holding the cigar gently between his lips and at the same time rolling it back and forth between his fingers, a habit of long standing which he couldn't seem to break. It was a habit, in fact, which had caused one of the more serious arguments in his household. Immediately after he had inadvertently dropped a long gray-white ash on the new carpeting at home, Stephanie had become furious. She'd stood in front of him with arms akimbo as he rolled the cigar in his mouth like that and then told him that his sucking on it was a symptom of repressed homosexuality. The remark had infuriated him and it took a long while to calm things between them. After that he didn't smoke cigars much in the house, but she'd planted a seed of worry in him and he wondered if what she'd said was true. Now, realizing he was twirling the cigar again that way, he removed it from his mouth and set it down on the slot of the ashtray.

"That's one hell of a solution."

"To one hell of a problem, Robbie."

"You'll never get Congress to appropriate for something like that, Dad, much less arrive at some kind of international agreement to do it."

"Not even to save mankind from extinction?"

The air force colonel sniffed and momentarily drummed his fingers on the fat leather arm of the chair, shaking his head. "*If* you could prove that this HAB Theory were valid and *if* you could establish an actual date for when this great cataclysm is supposed to occur, you *might* just possibly get cooperation. But you can't, and they won't. I'm no gambler, but I'd give odds of a thousand to one against it. And, Dad, I don't want any part of it, so you're wrong in thinking I wouldn't turn it down. I wouldn't touch—"

The President held up a hand, cutting him off. "Quit jumping the gun, Robbie. I haven't even approached the point yet. I tend to agree with you that there'd probably be no cooperation, nationally or internationally, on ice cap reduction along those lines, even if we had the proofs you mentioned. But now that you've heard the known facts, how do you view the theory?"

Robbie pursed his lips, considering, then sighed. "All right, I'm more convinced now than I was before you began, but fifty-fifty is about the best percentage I can muster up for believing it. And if you've told me all you have, Dad, then I have to put it on the line and say I think you're on damned thin ice. Jesus! You're apt to lose reelection over something like this."

"I suppose that's possible," Sanders said resignedly, "but I also know at this point there's no other way for me to go. Just before he left for Africa, John Grant finished correlating the Herbert Boardman material and dictated a summary of the whole thing, including some of the more convincing proofs, onto tapes which he passed on to Kermit Knotts. Knotts's people finished the final transcript of that summary and it runs fifty pages. It's pretty convincing stuff. I'll give you a copy of it first thing in the morning. I want you to read it carefully."

"Sure, I'll be glad to, but don't expect it to change my thinking very much."

"It will, Robbie. It will." The elder Sanders glanced at the door. "Well, let me get on with what I want to say before we have a couple of impatient women beating on our portals. Robbie, because I believe, as you do, that there's precious little likelihood of Boardman's survival plan being adopted, it becomes necessary to think of how else—assuming the reality of the theory—that man and his civilization might be preserved. I told you about the pivotal point centered over in Kenya and the word I've just received from Grant about Ngoromu's willingness, reluctant though it might have been, to go along with my idea for a survival complex there. I've already started the ball rolling on that without consulting Congress and it's going to take one devilish lot of push on my part here to get them to go along with it, but as an alternative to the ice cap reduction plan it may not look so bad. Now, there's only one other possible area besides Kenya where man is going to be safe if and when such a capsizing of the globe occurs. If anyone should know where that is, it should be you."

Robbie, in the process of reaching toward the ashtray for the stub of his cigar, abruptly drew his hand back and sat stiffly upright.

"By damn!" he murmured. "Now I see what you're driving at, Dad. Space!"

"Exactly. Space. Anyone orbiting at the time of such a cataclysm will be physically unaffected by it. And any of man's knowledge and artifacts orbiting with him will also be unaffected. I'm hoping that as a result of the symposium we're going to be able to arrive at a cooperative international agreement for a crash program on the production and launching of a whole multitude of orbiting vehicles from different nations, each with payloads contributing toward the whole of the effort—the construction of not just a Skylab or Space-Stop sort of facility, or an even larger space station, but rather a vast orbiting complex, almost a city, similar to but not as extensive as the Kenya complex."

"Jesus H. Christ!" Robbie was stunned. "How many people?"

"Haven't gone that far in the planning yet. Thousands, eventually. First things first. Initially we've got to find out what kind of worldwide reaction we're going to get on the concept. If we can't get international cooperation, we'll have to try to do it on our own on a smaller scale. But whether done nationally or internationally, Robbie, I want you in on the ground floor of it. You've orbited, you've explored more on the moon than anyone else, you've had space in your blood ever since you were old enough to know what space was. It's all you thought about through high school and the Air Force Academy and just about all you've worked on for the last fifteen years in the space program. It's why you're number two man at NASA and why no one's more experienced and qualified in every respect than you to handle it. And, to paraphrase a great patriot back in seventeen sixty-five, if this be nepotism, make the most of it." He reached over and placed his hand atop Robbie's, a rare physical demonstration of his affection for his only offspring. "Well, Robbie, are you still so sure you're going to turn it down?"

"God Almighty, no! How could I? But qualified or not, Dad, this naming me to the post is going to give you some bad headaches. I don't see how you can escape it.

"Son," the President said in a determined voice, ever since Herbert Boardman gave me that initial real headache, I've had headaches at practically every turn. At this point it doesn't make a lot of difference. What matters is that *I* believe in what I'm doing. Even if the HAB Theory should prove to be fallacious, I still won't regret taking these steps now. If I'm bumped from office because of it, well then, so be it. It won't be because I did something I knew was wrong, but because I did something I felt was right."

Robbie's expression was one of deep pride in his father. He doubted that he himself would have had the plain, old-fashioned guts to do as his father was doing. Earlier he'd remembered a line from Kipling's poem about Maggie and cigars, *The Betrothed*, and now another of that writer's poems came to mind. He stood up and put his hand on the older man's shoulder and squeezed gently.

"Dad, I think Kipling must have been prescient when he wrote his poem *If*, because he had to have patterned it after you."

Genuinely pleased at the accolade—he remembered so well helping Robbie to memorize the poem when his son was only twelve—Sanders chuckled appreciatively, but shook his head.

"You're probably thinking of the lines, 'If you can make one heap of all your winnings and risk it on one turn of pitch-and-toss, and lose, and never breathe a word about your loss…' Well, don't count me as down and out yet, Colonel Sanders, because I may not lose." He grunted faintly.

"As a matter of fact, Dad," Robbie put in softly, "I was thinking of the entire poem."

"Now that's probably as great a tribute as I've ever received." He clapped his hand to Robbie's forearm as his son released the shoulder and resumed his seat. "But, Robbie, a lot can happen between now and next November. For that matter, a hellish lot is going to happen in the next month. I'd say there's pretty good reason to believe that whether or not I'm reelected is going to depend on what conclusions are reached in this HAB Theory Symposium. If the scientists support the theory, I'm in. If they don't, I'm out, no matter what candidate the opposition runs against me. It's just that cut and dried. Now, there's one more thing I have to find out from you. How fast, at the fastest, can we have half a hundred rockets ready to put payload into orbit? I mean from the date the contracts are let to the moment of lift-off."

Robbie wrinkled his brow. "Hmmm, that's hard to say, Dad. There's one manned and two unmanned units on the pads and just about ready to go now—two more Phobos units and one of the new Deimos units."

"What are they rigged for?"

"A variety of functions on the Phobos units. Mainly astronomical data relay and telemetry stuff. Deimos is different. Much bigger and it's the first really serious step with hydroponics in actual orbit. It's being rigged with a variety of self-recycling vegetation. High oxygen-producing plants. Only two men, though. Our first space farmers, the newspapers are calling them."

"Be prepared," the President said, linking his fingers over his stomach, "to forgo anything they're geared for right now. There may be another, far more important use."

Robbie opened his mouth to speak, frowning, but his father went on first. "What about the rest? How long for half a hundred rockets from contract date to lift-off?"

"Well," Robbie drummed fingers on his knee, "that's hard to answer. A lot's involved—appropriations, size of payload, whether or not they're to be life-support systems, whether or not reentry recovery's a consideration, other matters."

The President stood, his manner now more brisk. "Appropriations are my concern; you'll get all you need. Size of payload—as great as possible; what, twenty tons? Thirty? Fifty, is possible? Whatever we can do with a guarantee of successful launch and orbiting. Except for maybe ten of the first fifty, life-support systems unnecessary. These are just going to be orbiting boxcars carrying freight—the building materials needed for construction of the space complex. After we get this phase going we can start thinking about what we'll need in the way of rockets capable of transporting large numbers of people, and by that I mean women and children as well as men. Recovery's not a matter of concern. We may even want to dismantle them in space as additional construction materials. So give me an approximation, son. How long?"

"Half a year at the very best."

"Even with top-priority, crash project status?"

Robbie reconsidered. "Well, maybe four and a half or five months."

"Plan on it then, beginning the moment the symposium ends. If it ends supporting the HAB Theory, I may get pretty good cooperation out of Congress. Whether I do or not, we'll forge ahead, if I have to do it on the basis of Presidential dictate by reason of national emergency. I'm apt to be calling on some presidential prerogatives and powers that have never been put to the test before. I may be impeached. But, damn it, Robbie, we are *going* to get that space complex in the works!"

"You know, Dad," the younger Sanders came to his feet beside his father, and respect was a deep undertone in his voice, "I've heard people say you've been wishy-washy as a President, wanting to please everyone and in the process pleasing no one, that you're too hesitant about taking a firm stand on any real issues of moment. All I can say is that they sure as hell won't be saying that much longer."

"I take it, then, that you're in all the way?"

"Solidly."

"Fine!" He clapped his hand to Robbie's shoulder, his arm around his son's back. "Now, let's get back to Grace and Stephanie. I want to see those pictures of Linda and Laurie."

I V

For John Grant, Anne's absence from the hotel room this morning to, in her words, "splurge some of my savings on wearables," gave him the only solitary time he had had since their arrival in Nairobi three days ago, time he had not really wanted because he knew when it came there was something he had to do.

The memory of Marie's tortured expression during that instant before boarding at O'Hare haunted him. It had struck him with the force of a physical blow at the time, and in the recurrent mental images the blow was little softened. How he had managed to mask his own feelings from Anne, he didn't know. For some unfathomable reason he'd felt it would be a mistake to tell her. Instead, he feigned airsickness, which untruthfully he told Anne sometimes rose in him during flights, though not always. It had put a damper on their enjoyment during the trip to Kenya and he had regretted that for Anne's sake, but he was in no mood for any kind of enjoyment.

It was not until after getting settled in Nairobi and having the long talk with Alexander Gordon the evening before the Ngoromu dinner that he was able to regain his equilibrium to some degree. The HAB Theory matter was paramount and so he had concentrated on it almost to the exclusion of all else, and he was gratified to find Ngoromu strictly a man of his word. So swiftly were Ngoromu's ministers and U.S. State Department negotiators moving that it looked promising for an actual physical beginning on the survival complex within a week.

For Grant, these activities for the most part effectively blocked out thoughts of Marie and what he must eventually do, though not so effectively blocking out that damnable image of her at the airport. He knew that no matter how long he lived, he would never lose that mental picture. And no matter what Marie might have said had she confronted him at the time, her words could never have been as eloquent as her expression.

Anne had been gone for the better part of an hour now, and in that interval John had been working on his letter to Marie. He had encountered difficult forms of writing before, but not any so difficult as composing this letter to his wife, mainly because he had no real idea what he wanted to say. Often he paused in the midst of a sentence for long moments. But at last he had completed it and, considering the length of time it had taken him to write, it was surprisingly short. He retracted the point on his ballpoint pen and lay it on the desktop, then picked up the sheets of hotel stationery and reread what he had written.

Nairobi, Kenya
Saturday, June 12

Dear Marie,

Well, now you know. It doesn't make any difference who she is—you'll learn soon enough as it is—or where and how we met. What matters is the knowledge I've lived with for all too long, and which you've just discovered, that our marriage is in serious trouble. I think you've probably sensed this to some degree over the past couple of years and, judging from your actions, more pertinently in recent weeks.

I think what I'd better say first is that, despite the present circumstances, I love you. I know you probably won't believe that now, but it's true. I've never stopped loving you and don't really suppose I ever could. But, Marie, something began to go wrong with our marriage, at least for me, a long time ago. I don't know exactly what caused it to begin turning sour, but it did, and I have become progressively more discontent and unhappy. This was hard enough to bear when there were no outside complications. Now those complications have arisen and I have been undergoing mental turmoil ever since. You see, Marie, notwithstanding the fact that I love you, I find that I also love someone else. How does one reconcile the knowledge that he simultaneously loves two women? This is a problem I've lived with for a number of months now and I am no closer to a solution than at the beginning. The thought of losing either of you fills me with dread, yet now that you've become aware of the situation, it seems obvious that I will be compelled to make a choice. How, in God's name, do I choose?

It may be that in view of what you have learned and what I am writing here, you will want a divorce. The thought makes me sick inside—not only the knowledge that I would be losing you, but Carol Ann and Billy as well, and the life that all of us have shared for so long. Yet, if it is a divorce you want, then I will not oppose it, nor will I argue any over the disposition of our mutual possessions or custody of the children. By no means will you, or they, ever have to worry about financial matters.

It may be, too, that despite the terrible hurt I've given you, you will want to continue our marriage, provided I sever contact with the other woman. There's the rub, because I could not do that. I love her very deeply; every bit as deeply as I love you. I no more want to give her up than I want to give you up.

I know that when we talk in person about this, you will say I should consider you, consider the children, consider our home, our life together, consider this and that and the other. Much of the torment I've been living through for so long, Marie, is directly due to exactly such considerations. I have considered until my mind spins, and still the dilemma persists.

When I return—and as yet I'm not sure when that will be, though probably not for two or three weeks, since the President has asked me to stay on for a while here to help coordinate plans with President Ngoromu—we will talk.

Maybe together, hashing this out as calmly as possible under the circumstances, we can arrive at a decision. What that decision will be, Marie, I simply don't know. I'm not optimistic about anything right now. Nothing. Least of all future happiness for any of us—you, her, me, the kids—irrespective of what the final outcome may be.

I am not consumed with guilt and will not be coming back dripping repentance. I don't regret in the least having met her and having fallen in love with her, any more than I regret having married you, and still being in love with you. My only regret is that I've caused you a very great hurt already, and yet the matter is far from resolved.

John

It was a very unsatisfactory letter and he knew it, but he didn't know how to improve it, so he quickly folded the sheets, put them in an airmail envelope, affixed the proper postage and addressed it. He was halfway across the room en route to the lobby to mail the letter when the door opened. Anne stood there, her arms filled with bags and boxes.

"Hi, Mister," she said cheerily. "Come give your woman a hand. I'm about to collapse."

He casually thrust the letter into his inside coat pocket and then took the packages from her and carried them to the sofa where he put them down. She had followed him, trying unsuccessfully to kiss his neck as he walked, but then came into his arms smoothly the moment the packages were down. The kiss started well but she soon realized the enthusiasm was all on her part and she pulled away, peering at him searchingly.

"What's the matter, sweetheart?" She tossed her head to get her hair out of her eyes.

"Nothing."

"Oh come *on*, I know better than that! I could've gotten a better response from a dead turkey. What's wrong? Something to do with that envelope you put in your pocket? Who's it from?"

"It's not *from*, Anne, it's *to*; I wrote to Marie."

"Oh?"

Amazing, he thought, how much chill could be packed into that little two-letter comment. He shrugged and turned away. Hell, it was coming out into the open now, so she might as well know. He took out his pack of cigarettes but she took it from him. Her smile was forced.

"My job, remember? You're not at your house now. Light me."

She puffed rapidly, shallowly, as he held the flame of his lighter to the cigarette, and all the while her eyes never left his. When he dropped the lighter back into his pocket and took the cigarette from her with a murmured thanks, she took him by the hand and led him to the bed where she sat on the edge and then tugged on his hand until he sat beside her.

"Anne," he said, puffing out a little billow of smoke, "Marie knows about us."

"*What!*"

He nodded glumly. "She saw us together."

"You're serious?" She was stunned. "Where? When? How could she?"

"At O'Hare, when we were just going down the steps to our gate. I caught a momentary glimpse of her, but there's no doubt it was Marie."

"Oh my God!" she whispered, eyes widened and a hand at her throat. She had paled visibly and apparently didn't know what to say after that. After a moment her color returned and she was under control, but the bridge of nose was pinched in a frown.

"You weren't airsick on the way over after all, were you?"

"Sick in a way, but you're right, not airsick."

He was expecting her to be angry, but surprisingly she smiled and squeezed his hand. "I can't really anticipate what this means now—to us. I'd be lying if I said I wasn't scared. I am. Scared silly. I can't comprehend why you didn't tell me before." She stopped, thinking, then gripped his hand in both of hers. "I'm scared, yes, but in a way I guess I'm relieved, too. Maybe it's the best thing that could have happened—for all of us."

His uncomprehending expression spoke more than words. She hurried on.

"Don't you see? You were having such a *terrible* time making a decision and now it's out of your hands. She *knows!* It's all out in the open. We don't have to hide anymore. She'll want a divorce and you can give it to her and then we'll have each other."

"Anne, honey," he said, sadness in his words, "it isn't all that simple. I don't know that she wants a divorce. Hell, I don't know for sure that *I* want a divorce."

"You don't want me?"

"Of course I do. God Almighty, Anne, I want you so badly I'm half out of my mind with it."

"Then what's the problem? I'm all yours, John, for God's sake. All yours! Forgive my French, honey, but now's the time to shit or get off the pot. I told you before that you couldn't be husband to both of us and you damned well can't. And Marie will say the same thing. So that makes it pretty clear, doesn't it? All you've got to do is make your choice. And naturally, it's going to be us. It has *got* to be us, John. She's had you for seventeen years, and it's my turn now."

"And what about Carol Ann and Billy?"

She shook her head and made an irritated little sound. "You'd be divorcing *her*, John, not your children. It's not as if you'd never see them again."

He shook his head. "They need a father."

"They *don't* need a *half-*father," she shot back, "and that's exactly how you've described yourself any number of times. It's not as if they wouldn't be provided for, John, and I'll repeat, it's not as if you'll never see them again."

The misery was heavy in his voice. "Anne, I don't know. I just don't know."

She stood up in front of him and took his cheeks in her palms and kissed his lips tenderly. When she pulled back, she stopped with her face only a couple of inches from his, her hands still cupping his cheeks, her eyes now overbright but locked on his, searching.

"Listen to me," she said. "I love you. More than anything in life. More than life itself. For twenty-eight years I've been nothing, no one, drifting and alone. Then you came along and somehow you made me whole. You brought me to life. You made me important, to myself as well as to someone else. Nothing else matters, John. Nothing. Only you and me—us!" Crystal tears were sliding down her cheeks now, but she paid no attention. "Everything is so meaningless without you. If I can't be a part of you, then life itself is pointless. Oh, God," she was crying harder now, her voice beginning to break, "how do I measure my love to show you how strong it is? How do I tell you?"

"You don't have to," he said, "because I know." He brought up a hand and gently wiped away a tear on her cheek with the ball of his thumb. "Because I feel the same."

She caught his hand in hers and then reached and took the other one, too, clasping them both tightly together between her own. "Then tell her, darling. Please, please tell her. You know—we both know!—that without each other we can't be happy. Do you want to go through the rest of your life with her, unhappy because deep inside you know that you love me more? You know you could never again have the happiness, the *completeness*, that you and I have together. You *know* that, John. Tell me now, as honestly as you can, from your heart: do you really believe you can ever again be as happy with Marie as you once felt you were?"

He didn't answer for a long while, but she waited, still holding his hands, eyes still steady on his, and at last he replied. "In my heart, Anne, I know that I could never recapture what Marie and I once had. And I know if I turned away from you, I would regret it all the rest of my life. But, darling, can't you see that I still feel a love for Marie and for the children? Can't you understand that I have a very deep responsibility to all three?"

She didn't reply at once. She loosened her grasp on his hands slightly but did not let them go. Leaning forward, while at the same time drawing his hands toward her, she kissed the back of one, then the other. He could feel the wetness of her tears on his skin. After a moment she let one of his hands go and reached up and fingered the top button on her lime green blouse in the way she sometimes did when considering a knotty problem. She nodded then, faintly, and sat down beside him again, still holding his hand that was closest to her.

"Yes," she said softly, "I can understand that, John, and God knows I admire you for it despite myself. But are you really ready to make a martyr out of yourself? Are you really willing to live that role? You might be thinking you couldn't be happy with me because you wonder what sort of happiness can be founded on the heartache of others. But you can be. Believe me, John, you can be! And I know in my heart that you *will* be if only you let yourself."

His words were raspy. "I would gladly give my right arm just to *know* that. But I don't. And, Anne, much as you want to believe it, you can't know for sure, either."

"All right, I'll go along with that. I can't know for sure, but I do *feel* it deeply inside, and I think you do, too. You have got to be honest with yourself! Just as you feel deeply inside that with Marie you could never really be happy again, you must feel that we could be. So what more needs to be said? Love, like life, is reaching out and grasping what you feel is right at the time when you feel it. It's never free of risk. It never can be."

He smiled ruefully at her and now it was he who raised her hand and kissed it for a long moment, after which he nodded slowly. "I guess you're right. All along I guess I've been looking for guarantees, and there just aren't any."

A shudder went through her and she closed her eyes for a few seconds. When she opened them again and spoke, her voice was husky. "A few moments ago, while I was standing, I was tempted to take off my clothes. But, John, it wouldn't have been fair to make that kind of influence a factor. I want you to decide to come to me not because you physically want me, but because you love me. I think now you'll do that and I feel better."

"Oddly," he said, "I do too, somewhat. It wouldn't have been right then. It still isn't now. Not yet, anyway."

Her hand came up and cupped the back of his neck and he leaned toward her with the slight pressure of it until their heads were touching . Neither spoke and they simply sat that way for a long while.

V

While the upcoming scientific symposium in Manhattan was never played down as unimportant, its prestige and news value abruptly skyrocketed not only in America but throughout the world as a result of the brief White House bulletin issued by Press Secretary Steven Lace three days after the *New York Times* published its feature involving Dr. Irma Dowde. The bulletin was brief and to the point.

Due to the importance of matters connected with the HAB Theory, President Sanders announces his intention of delivering an opening statement to the participants of the HAB Theory Symposium. His statement will be presented at the general luncheon which begins the symposium in the Grand Ballroom of the Waldorf-Astoria at noon on July 1. Copies of the address will be made available to the press.

Not even the International Geophysical Year—perhaps the most significant and newsworthy internationally cooperative scientific event heretofore—had stirred as much worldwide interest or generated as many news stories.

Suddenly, scientists who had held themselves coldly aloof from comment or who, in various ways, had been openly derogatory in their remarks about both the forthcoming symposium and the HAB Theory altered their stance. Many who had scoffed at the theory in the beginning and who had made it clear that they had no intention of attending the symposium, now were having strong second thoughts about the matter. Scientific history was in the making and, as a direct result, scientific reputations of considerable proportions were apt to be established by those who participated.

At the Smithsonian, Dr. Irma Dowde, found her office deluged with letters, telegrams and cables begging invitation to the event, and the telephone rang so constantly that several assistants had to work full time taking the messages. The problem now, where the symposium was concerned, was becoming one of providing space enough for all those who wished to participate. Yesterday, four days after the initial White House bulletin announcing, an amending bulletin was issued to the press by Steven Lace.

The HAB Theory Symposium is now scheduled to begin at 10 A.M. Eastern Daylight Time on July 1 and the President's opening address, previously scheduled as a luncheon address, has been rescheduled to 10:30 A.M. at the Felt Forum in the Madison Square Garden Center so that adequate seating can be provided. The change has been made because of the great volume of requests for attendance being received by the coordinator of the symposium, Dr. Irma

Dowde, and because of a reluctance to turn away any scientist of any country who wishes to participate in the symposium. It is now estimated that no less than 3,000 scientists from all over the world will attend.

The world press had rarely before experienced a summer season so pregnant with story material. While here and there pieces were still appearing concerning the assassination attempt against the President of the United States, that newsworthy event was being replaced by articles dealing with the three primary—and now more intriguing—areas of interest: the HAB Theory Symposium which would begin in another fortnight; what the President would say in his address there; and, most significantly, the imagination-stirring aspect of the scientific enigmas, as touched upon by Irma Dowde.

Hardly a day passed since announcement of the HAB Theory by President Sanders that newspapers throughout the world did not carry stories in some way related to it. The aura of excitement over the possibilities it opened continued at a high level. As was so often the case, the *New York Times* was the pacesetter for the many follow-up stories elsewhere.

The major news and wire service agencies had been quick to provide their subscribing newspapers with features similar to the Ralph Zeitler interview of Dr. Dowde which had appeared in the *Times* nine days ago. Services such as Associated Press, Tass, Reuters Limited, Jewish World News Agency, United Press International, South African Press Association, Australian Associated Press, Deutsche Presse-Agentur GMBH, London International Press Limited, and others, set the tenor for sidebar stories on a more local level in major cities everywhere.

Just such a sidebar story, first published in the *Arbeiter Zeitung* of Vienna, was subsequently picked up by wire services and republished in many areas.

In view of the current fervor to unearth scientific mysteries which may be discussed soon at the symposium to be held in New York, Austria has a very great mystery of its own which invites close scrutiny. The director of the Salzburg Museum, Dr. Frederic Gottlund, who will be attending that symposium, states that in the museum's collection is one of the most baffling anachronistic artifacts ever discovered.

The object is a cube of iron-nickel alloy tempered to an unusual hardness. It measures 5.08 centimeters by 7.62 centimeters and has a weight of 785 grams. Two sides of this cube are convex, while the other four are perfectly square to extreme precision. An odd geometric groove of consistent precise dimensions traverses the edges of the cube. Obviously, according to Dr. Gottlund, a manufactured device for some unknown purpose, but that is not the foremost mystery. The utterly baffling fact is that this cube was discovered in Lower Austria in 1877, embedded in a block o coal. There is no possibility that it could have been artificially implanted there. The vein of coal in question is estimated to be 300,000 years old.

One would think that such a find, astounding as it is, would be a once-in-history discovery, but not so. Just eight years later, in 1885, at Vöcklabruck, another of the cubes of metal was found, this one smaller, in a block of coal broken in the Isidor Braun foundry. It measured 67 millimeters by 47 millimeters but was otherwise identical, including the two convex surfaces and the incised groove.

Not to be outdone by the *New York Times* report of the human shoe imprint found embedded in sandstone in Nevada, as described by Irma Dowde, the *Chattanooga News-Free Press* came up with a great oddity of its own along the same lines.

Perhaps the scientists converging on New York for the HAB Theory Symposium will give some consideration to Tennessee's famous fossil footprints. Found during the last century near Brayton in Bledsoe County, about 35 miles north of here, these footprints are not in sandstone, such as those recently described by Dr. Irma Dowde, which were only 25 million years old. The series of footprints of bare human feet near Brayton are embedded in solid granite which is probably hundreds of millions of years old. Not only that, the human who made those prints must have been gigantic, for the heel alone measures 13 inches in width.

The newspapers of Peru were having a field day with their stories of unanswered questions regarding the pre-Inca civilizations which built the great structures at Machu Picchu, Cuzco, Ollantaytambo, and Sacsahuaman. Each of the stories asked or implied the same question: were these the remains of a civilization made extinct by a previous capsizing of the earth? The remains were a continuing enigma to archaeologists, and undoubtedly one of the most bizarrely baffling was a spectacular discovery made in 1952 at an altitude of over 13,000 feet in the Andes. An editorial in Lima's *La Chronica* appealed to the scientists everywhere who might attend the symposium.

The august scientists now preparing to assemble in symposium in New York have a grave responsibility. If, in fact, the postulations of the HAB Theory are accepted by them, then by their pronouncement mankind finds itself facing the most horrendous jeopardy imaginable. Could it be, as the United States President has suggested, that previous civilizations of man were destroyed by just such capsizings of the entire planet? Could it be that this was what caused the extinction of the mysterious race which originally built the amazing cities—the ruins of which are extensive in our country—long before the ancient Incas were living their own highly advanced civilization? Perhaps at last we are on the brink of a new age of extensive study into the mysteries of which we Peruvians have become heir. Perhaps now one of the most puzzling of these, the incredible find at Marcahuasi, only 80 kilometers northeast of this city can be solved.

The discovery, made in 1952 by Dr. Daniel Ruzo, is a great amphitheater of rock in which are magnificent sculptures— but sculptures which, according to all we know, are wholly anachronistic. Here, for example, among carvings of familiar South American animals and people, can also be seen unmistakable carvings in white dioritic porphyry stone of camels and cows, lions and elephants, and other animals which have never lived here, along with finely carved heads, in the same material, of Semites, Caucasians, and Negroes, all of whom came to this continent less than 500 years ago. There is even a perfect rendering of the turtle's long-extinct ancestor, the amphicelydia; yet in all recorded history, the amphicelydia is known only from its fossilized remains. It lived during the Upper Triassic Period and became extinct about 180± million years ago. Where, then, could the sculptor have gotten his model? There is also a rendering of a horse, but horses became extinct here 9,000 years ago and did not reappear until brought by the Spanish conquistadors in the 16th century.

Dr. Ruzo's great discovery too long has been ignored. It is now time for science to take a fresh look at the mysteries of the past which titillate and haunt the imaginations of all knowledgable Peruvians.

We applaud the courage of the President of the United States; and for the scientists who will attend the HAB Theory Symposium we wish the open-mindedness and clear vision to see—and perhaps to solve—our ancient mysteries, as well as to preserve our present civilization.

In a somewhat less hostile manner than exhibited in its usual coverage of American events, Peking's *Renmin Rabao* paid homage to two of the fourteen Chinese scientists who already were en route to the United States to attend the symposium.

The hearts of the citizens of the People's Republic of China go today with 14 of her sons who journey to America to represent us in what may be a significant scientific symposium.

The two leaders of this group are Dr. Ting-Wuo Lin, professor of geophysics, and Dr. Ho-Chung Chow, professor of archaeology,1 both of the University of Peking. The two men and their party left for New York this morning to participate in discussions concerning the so-called HAB Theory.

This is no new concept to the Chinese. Our ancient book, The Story of the Ten Stems, *tells of how our country made a sudden flying leap to the Arctic and remained there for over three thousand years and that there was death and destruction, but those who survived managed to adapt to the colder climate. Then, after the three thousand years were over, again our China made another gigantic leap and returned to almost where it was before and where we remain now. And what little child among us does not know that K'ung-fu-tze* [Confucius], *in writing the history of China, tells how our present situation began with the receding of waters that had been raised to the skies? Thus, it is not unexpected to find the Americans now claiming to have discovered what we have known for so many centuries. Undoubtedly now, too, they will be even more surprised to learn some other secrets that the Chinese people have long known about such matters.*

The London *Evening Standard* published a listing of a hundred scientists from a wide range of fields who were preparing to attend the function, but added that probably a few others would join that list before it was complete prior to the beginning of the symposium. Among the most prestigious are astronomer Robert Fitch, archaeologists Philip Graceland, Edmund Crenshaw, Irene Rutman, and Sidney Rotheringill, anthropologists Peter Douglas Hempstead and Alice Anderson, geophysicist Joseph Snell, and philologist Thomas Addison. A sidebar story said that the director of the London Museum of Natural History, paleontologist Percival Heathly III, would be attending, adding:

…hoping, among other matters, to receive comment about a most peculiar anachronism involving a prehistoric human skull in the museum's collection.

"The skull," Dr, Heathly told the Evening Standard *reporter, "was found early in the Twentieth Century in what was then Northern Rhodesia. The cranium has been Carbon-14 Radioactivity Dated as being that of a man who lived some 38,000 years ago. It is now in a case on the ground floor of the museum. The very peculiar thing about it is that the skull shows evidence of death having been caused by a very modern means."*

Dr, Heathly said he would be taking numerous photos of the skull to the symposium so they can be studied by scientists attending and perhaps some conclusions drawn regarding the cause of death.

In the same edition of that paper but on a different page was another story dealing with the symposium. It was a story reasonably representative of a certain number that were appearing elsewhere in newspapers around the world.

HAB THEORY ASININE: OXFORD PROFESSOR

Dr. Owen Holder, professor of geology at Oxford University, today in an interview at his Wyecliff Hills home, said that he considered the HAB Theory to be "the most asinine proposal" he has ever encountered.

"There are always fools coming up with ideas that are pure poppycock, and there are always fools who will believe what they say. To bestow upon it even the dignity of an acknowledgment that it was ever conceived is an outrage."

Dr. Holder said he had received a copy of the Grant summary of the controversial HAB Theory.

"Although I looked it over to some extent," he said, "I simply could not force myself to read such utter balderdash. The fact that some bona fide scientists are taking it seriously is, to me, a sad commentary on the state of our present average scientific mentality."

When asked if he was planning on attending the symposium on the HAB Theory (see SCIENTISTS PREPARE FOR HAB SYMPOSIUM, *page 1), Dr. Holder admitted that he was. When asked why, considering how he felt about it, the geology professor said that was precisely his reason for going.*

"There have to be some there," he said, "who will have the courage to get up and take issue. I intend being one of those, and I'm quite sure there will be many others. This Boardman chap who made the postulation was obviously nothing more than a modern-day Charles Dawson."

When asked to explain what he meant, the Oxford professor simply said, "Attend the symposium and you'll find out." He declined to continue the interview after that.

Finally, also in London, a second opinion poll of scientists from all over the world was published by the *Sunday Mirror.* An effort was made to reach the same 488 scientists in 17 countries who had previously been polled, but two had died—one of natural causes and the other in a vehicular accident—and seven others were not able to be reached. Nine other scientists, not previously polled, were contacted to make up for those missing. A comparison was drawn between the first such poll, taken a fortnight ago when details on the HAB Theory were sketchy and the more recent one where more information was know. The question asked was exactly the same: Do you believe there is a likelihood that the HAB Theory will be proven valid?

	First Poll	*Current Poll*
Yes	4	52
No	151	144
Undecided	253	235
Refused Answer	80	57

V I

The day had been a good one for all four of them. Long and tiring, perhaps, but good to get out into the sunshine and fresh air, to see something different and interesting, to get away from the long involved talks they'd been holding day after day with President Ngoromu and his Ministers.

Now, standing here on the edge of the precipitous escarpment road overlooking the Great Rift Valley, John Grant felt fully relaxed for the first time in many days. Anne was standing beside him and perhaps twenty feet away stood Alex Gordon with Narai Ngoromu. The black couple were looking out over the great natural phenomenon, their hands interlocked and occasionally squeezing a silent message, their attention really more inward than outward and, for the moment, totally oblivious of Grant and Anne. As the latter couple watched, Gordon released his hand and slipped his arm around Narai's slender waist, and almost unconsciously hers moved around him. They leaned their heads together and continued standing silently.

Grant smiled, putting his own arm around Anne's waist and leaning to touch his lips lightly to her cheek. His words in her ear were barely audible.

"Looks like our big friend is smitten."

Anne faced him, green eyes bright. "I'll tell you something, Mister, Alex was smitten before we even got to Africa. He may not have known it at that time, but it was obvious the first night we were all together at the palace. Narai knew it, and so did I. Now he knows it and so do you." She sighed and shook her head in mock despair. "You men are sometimes so obtuse." She kissed him lightly on the lips. "But we love you in spite of it. Maybe even because of it." She kissed him again.

Grant gave a quick glance over at the other couple but they were still lost in themselves. He and Anne then walked to a little wider standing place close to the brink of the cliff and stood looking outward and downward into the Great Rift Valley.

"Well, there it is," he told her.

As good as this outing had been for himself, Grant knew it had been equally good for Alexander Gordon. Both of them had been putting in long sessions with the Kenyan ministers and the two groups of American negotiators. Each of these groups—that involving Gordon and concerned with establishing the groundwork for the cooperative petroleum resources development, and that involving Grant and the initial work on the huge survival complex—had been laboring upwards of twelve to fourteen hours daily and an enormous amount of work already had been accomplished in both endeavors.

Gordon's group involved nine Kenyans, including the ministers of finance, internal development, foreign affairs, and health, each with his principal assistant, except for the minister of internal development, Kibwe Bomba, who was aided by his two chief assistants. President Daniel Ngoromu sat in on the sessions as much as possible, trying to divide his time between the oil negotiations and the survival complex group, yet still allowing time for the handling of other pertinent business in the governing of Kenya. The team of negotiators sent by President Sanders included six highly experienced individuals under the leadership of none other than Donald Elliott, secretary of state, who did practically all of the talking for the United States during the negotiations.

Elliott was wearing two hats here, because he also was key man on the United States side in the discussions about the survival complex, which involved Grant. Eight Americans, in addition to Elliott and Grant, were negotiating on that front, with Kibwe Bomba also sitting in when possible, but with most of the actual negotiation for Kenya being handled by the minister of foreign affairs, Wautura Kelemmo.

In both groups, everyone present was keenly aware that these undoubtedly were the most important negotiations Kenya had ever engaged in and they proceeded with careful haste. Much already had been accomplished, but a very great deal remained yet to be done, not the least of which was making allowance, where the survival complex was concerned, for the inclusion of other nations which might wish to participate. It was difficult to conceive that other nations would not want to participate and it was essential, early in the game, to establish a solid foundation for all that lay ahead.

Site location for the complex had already been decided upon by Ngoromu and initial groundbreaking had occurred over a week ago, though the negotiations were far from over. Thus far there had been no serious problems and the smaller ones had been ironed out quickly. Both sides seemed eager to cooperate with one another to the fullest. The only real bone of contention had come over a relatively minor thing, and it involved some early horn-locking between President Ngoromu and Secretary Elliott.

"President Ngoromu," Elliott had said in one of their initial sessions, "just to simplify things where paperwork and vocal reference are concerned, we really should have a name for the survival complex. Something easy to remember. I've given it some thought and, under the circumstances, think we ought to name it Hab City."

Ngoromu had closed his eyes for several seconds, a faint smile touching his lips, as if he were recalling something pleasant. But he looked at the thickly gray-haired Elliott and slowly shook his head in negation.

"You don't like that name?" Elliott asked, frowning. "After all, it's after the HAB Theory and, of course, the initials of the man who, in a way, is responsible for all this. I really think we should call it Hab City."

Grant had grinned about that time. It was well known, that when Donald Elliott said "I really think…" about anything, it meant his mind was made up and he intended to see it done that way. Ngoromu, expressionless, was still shaking his head.

"I have given it some thought, too, Mr. Elliott. We'll call it Ngaia."

"What?"

"Ngaia. N-G-A-I-A." Ngoromu spelled it out slowly.

Elliott was the one shaking his head now. "No," he said, "that will never do, sir. Americans just are not accustomed to words beginning with two consonants like that together and then followed by three vowels. I really think, sir, for the sake of simplicity, that Hab City is the proper terminology. Mr. Grant," he shot a glance at the writer, "since words are your specialty, would you kindly express to the President here the dissatisfaction Americans would find with such an unfamiliar sort of word? En-guy-yuh. No, it's just not right."

Grant shifted his eyes to Ngoromu and again detected that faintest glimmering of a smile. He looked back at Elliott. "Mr. Secretary," he said, "it may be that there is a very specific reason why President Ngoromu wishes to use the name Ngaia. I don't think it would take Americans very long to get used to it."

Elliott didn't like the answer and he turned his back on Grant without replying. "I really think," he said to

Ngoromu for the third time, "Hab City is the only fitting name."

"The complex, Mr. Secretary, will be named Ngaia."

Elliott's nostrils flared slightly. He was clasping his wrist behind him with one hand and was rapidly rubbing the thumb over the fingertips of the hand that was being held. His voice was flat.

"Is there some particular reason for selecting such a name?"

"There is."

Elliott waited for the black leader to continue, but Ngoromu said nothing.

"Would you care to tell me, sir?" The fingers were still being rubbed.

"I'll be glad to, Mr. Secretary. Ngaia is the name of the mother of my children. My first wife."

A faint tinge of color came to Elliott's normally pallid cheeks and he nodded, but he still didn't give up entirely. "Would you have any objection, then, to calling it Ngaia City, sir?"

"I would have no objection to that."

"Fine! Fine!" He broke into a toothy smile and it was as if he had won a major battle. "We'll hereafter refer to the survival complex, gentlemen, as Ngaia City."

As they had begun their drive from Nairobi this morning, Grant had told Gordon, Narai and Anne about the exchange and Narai had turned briefly to look at him—she was driving the Mercedes-Benz—and smiled broadly, exposing teeth as white and beautifully formed as her father's. She was talking as she looked back at the road.

"That was Mother's doing as well as Father's. Even before Mr. Elliott got here, they were discussing the complex one evening and Mother said it would have to have a name and that she would like to have the privilege of naming it. Father consented, of course, and when Mother said 'Let's call it Ngaia or even Ngaia City,' I really thought for a moment he was going to break down. He loved Mother—my real mother, I mean—a very great deal."

"He loves Anita, too," Grant put in softly.

"Oh, yes! I didn't mean to imply that he doesn't. I think he loves her as much as he loved Ngaia. I think all of us do."

They had fallen silent then for a while, enjoying the passing scenery. Gordon had had a chance to get out and see a little of the African veldt with Narai, both on the trip with her and Anita to the Naivasha area and then later for half a day to Nairobi National Park, about ten miles south on Highway A-109, the Mombasa Road. Grant and Anne, however, had seen none of it and so everything was new and exciting.

Actually, it was a sort of farewell trip, since Gordon would be flying back to the United States in the morning, his preliminary work here in Kenya finished for now and other work for the President awaiting him back in the States. Grant and Anne would be staying on for at least another day, perhaps two, while Grant continued the work with President Ngoromu and the secretary's team in wrapping up the Ngaia City preliminaries. When Narai and Gordon invited Grant and Anne to accompany them on this full day's drive up toward Mount Kenya and the Northern Frontier District, at first they had refused, feeling that Alex and Narai probably would rather have this last day together alone. However, the black couple wouldn't hear of it and insisted, so here were the four of them making a great oval tour of just over three hundred miles.

Grant had watched the clustered modern buildings—offices, businesses, hotels, churches and governmental structures—gradually be replaced by residences as they left the center of Nairobi early in the morning, thinking that it really wasn't a great deal different from many cities in the United States. As they began leaving town on Highway B-16, he broke the conversational lull.

"Narai, what's the population of Nairobi? Of Kenya, for that matter?"

"Well, at our last census four years ago I believe it was in the neighborhood of three hundred and seventy thousand for Nairobi, and just over eleven million for all of Kenya. Kenya, incidentally," she added, briefly throwing him a glance, "is not terribly big when compared to a country like America, for instance. It has an area of roughly twice the size of your state of New Mexico. Anyway, of that eleven million population currently, somewhere around fifty thousand are Asians—primarily from India or Pakistan—and another fifty thousand are white people from Europe, America, and elsewhere. We used to have a lot more of both groups at one time. By 1968 there were over two hundred thousand Asians here, but President Kenyatta felt they were establishing a strangle hold on our economy, so that year he ordered most of them evicted. There were also a great many whites here before that, when we were still a British colony and protectorate, but their number was reduced drastically—and mostly voluntarily—when we gained our independence in 1963. Many of the whites had begun leaving a decade before that, at the start of the Mau Mau uprising."

"I read Robert Ruark's novel about that," Anne spoke up. "It must have been a terrible time."

"It was, but perhaps not quite as bad as pictured in *Something of Value*. Ruark did a somewhat more accurate job of writing in his next book about us, called *Uhuru*, but I understand it didn't sell as well because it wasn't quite as grisly. At any rate, what I was getting ready to say was that we'll be passing the Aberdares on this tour."

"The Aberdares?" Anne wrinkled her brow.

"Yes. Remember how Ruark wrote about them in *Something of Value*? It's a small range of mountains to the north of us—a national park now, but it was the final stronghold of the Mau Mau before the uprising was ended in 1961. Satimma and Mount Kingagop are the two highest peaks there, both of them right around thirteen thousand feet. It's a very pretty area. I'm sure you've probably heard of Treetops—the resort where tourists can dine in comfort in a lodge built in the trees and watch the elephants and other big animals come to the watering holes below? Well, that's at the northeastern edge of the Aberdare Range."

"Excuse me, Narai," Gordon interjected, "but what's that cluster of buildings over there?" He pointed to a grouping of large estate-type houses.

"Those are the homes of many of the diplomats and higher-echelon government officials. See that large white house there slightly to the right? That's where the American ambassador lives, while remodeling is taking place at the American Embassy. The country club's over in that area, too."

John Grant was sitting in the back seat opposite the driver's side of the car and he studied Narai as she drove and continued to point out interesting buildings and landmarks. She was a most attractive girl and he could see why Alex Gordon had been smitten by her. She had a voice rich and full and well modulated, ordinarily soft and cultured, and her diction in English was perfect, with no trace of accent. This intrigued Grant.

"Is English taught in the schools here, Narai?"

"Oh, yes. Actually, I guess you could call it our second language. Governmentally it's almost our first, since all international business is conducted in English. Our country has a very large number of tribal languages and dialects within those languages. Jomo Kenyatta saw this as a handicap in conducting the business of government, and so in 1973 he proclaimed Swahili our national language. It practically was already, for the most part, but his decree made it official. But, yes, English is taught in all the schools." She gave him a quick look and grinned. "You're wondering about my own use of it, I can see. Well, I learned the basics here and then when Mother—Anita—came to us, she taught me much more."

"She's not telling you quite all of it, John," Alex put in, turning so his arm was over the back of the front seat. "She's also a Radcliffe graduate student in government. She's only home for the summer and will be going back in September."

"Like father, like daughter?"

"Don't forget Mother, too," Narai added. "She's also a political science grad. That's where she and Father met, in their classes together at Stanford. So it's 'like father, like mother, like daughter.'"

They all laughed together. Grant squeezed Anne's hand and he was very glad they'd come along on the tour. He settled back, enjoying the ride, the company and the scenery as they gradually climbed higher in elevation. Numerous coffee plantations were now supplanting the lower-level pineapple farms. A pair of huge, graceful crested cranes flew low across the road ahead of them with a sort of ponderous dignity, the great black-tipped wings beating methodically. Numerous Kenyan women were walking along the road edges here, carrying enormous loads of bananas or papyrus or sugar cane. After they had passed one carrying such a huge load of dried grasses atop her head that she looked like an animated hayrick, Anne spoke up indignantly.

"Don't the men ever help the women with their loads here? Did you see that one? That's awful!"

"Few women in Africa, Anne," Narai said, "have been emancipated. Women's Lib is a long way from reality here. One day, maybe."

"One day, definitely!"

Just before the reached Fort Hall, the Aberdare Mountains began looming in the distance to their left, and almost straight ahead at a greater distance stood a solitary mountain with rugged snow-capped crest. It was Mount Kenya, Narai explained, but still close to seventy miles away. An ancient volcanic cone with an altitude of over 17,000 feet, it was the highest peak in Kenya.

As they reached the small town of Karatina, the garb of the Africans was becoming more primitive. Often the women wore elaborate ornamentation on ears and neck and occasionally the men were in flowing, smocklike gowns rather than trousers and shirt. They pulled to a stop in a small market area and listened, fascinated, as Narai squatted before an incredibly wrinkled, toothless old woman sitting on the ground with several stalks of bananas on an outspread blanket before her, and began a rapid exchange with her in Swahili. After a few minutes Narai nodded and handed the woman a shilling—fourteen cents in American money—and accepted, in return, a cluster of about twenty bananas.

To the Americans, it seemed that the old woman, even at such a ridiculously low price, had made the better of the bargain. The bananas were very small, hardly more than five inches long and not a great deal larger in diameter than Grant's thumb. The skin was an ugly, dirty green color, pitted and streaked and mottled with black. As they reentered the car they joked with Narai about them, laughingly telling her that she could hang them in her garden to scare away the crows, or even hang them on her door to keep evil spirits from entering. She took their comments with a secretive little smile and handed each a banana and told them to eat. They didn't really want to do so and wouldn't until she more or less shamed them into it by eating one herself. The banana flesh inside was firm and ivory-colored, with an extremely good aroma. When they finally ate the fruit, it had the most delicious banana taste any of them had ever encountered.

"It might be compared to some of the oranges they grow in Florida," Narai explained. "Delicious taste, but so awful in appearance that people just generally refuse to buy them. These bananas by rights ought to be one of our greatest agricultural export crops, but import produce buyers from other countries—the United States, for example—take one look at them and turn up their noses. As a result, most of them are consumed here in Kenya."

They soon came to an intersection and turned left, with the Aberdare Range now directly in front of them as they headed toward the city of Nyeri. About a hundred miles from Nairobi, Nyeri was a pleasant, quite modern, quiet place with nice homes and shops, the main thoroughfare divided by a nicely landscaped median strip, the street fronted by banks, auto sales showrooms, bookstores and the ordinary businesses of any small city. Outside Nyeri again and heading back toward another junction with the highway they'd left earlier, cultivation was extensive on both sides of the road as far as the eye could see, just as it had been since leaving Nairobi. And what surprised Grant more than anything else was the fact that here they were, driving through Africa and, except for the crested cranes they had seen sailing across the road and a few smaller birds in brilliant iridescent colors, wildlife had been virtually absent. He asked Narai about it.

"We'll soon be coming into an area where we'll see some of the antelope and other animals," she replied, "but you're right, there are very few large animals in the area we've passed through so far."

"Overhunted?" Gordon asked. "Eaten up by the African population?"

She shook her head and the circle-within-circle gold earrings she wore jingled lightly. "No, not really. Most native Kenyans are pretty much vegetarian—the Kikuyus, Samburus, Somalis, Siolos, Masai, Marsabits. Oh, some of them will eat certain game meats, but not really very much. The Masai, for instance, will eat eland, our largest antelope, but practically no other wild meat. Most of these tribes are agriculturists, basically, not hunters as far as taking wildlife for their own use is concerned."

"Then why don't we see lions and giraffe and zebra and other animals like that roaming about?" Grant persisted. "I expected to see them all over."

"Alteration of their habitat. The agriculturization of the landscape has pretty much made it uninhabitable for them. You may think it strange, but I'd guess that not one person out of a thousand in the area we've driven through has ever seen a wild lion or zebra or elephant. Of course, farther out in the more remote areas that's not the case."

Another half-hour of driving brought them to the vast expanse of grasslands of the Laikipia Plateau, with Mount Kenya much closer now, jutting impressively skyward some ten or twelve miles distant to the right. This was their nearest approach to Kenya's most famous peak, but now their attention was diverted from it by the sight of small herds of wild animals moving about through the grasses. The farther they drove, the greater the size of the herds became. Here at last they were seeing the delicate and beautiful impalas, Thompson gazelles, Grant's gazelles, zebras, and Jackson's hartebeests.

"This whole area is a government reserve now," Narai said. "It used to be, in part, the sixty-thousand-acre Solio Ranch—a cattle operation—and when it was eventually put up for sale, the World Wildlife Association became very concerned that the natural habitat would disappear and, with it, all these animals, so they convinced the government to buy it and set it aside as a reserve. Oh, look, right there by the fence, there's a big kongoni— the one you've been calling Jackson's hartebeest, Mr. Grant. You've given the right name, but locally they're called kongoni. And look, there's a whole herd of them standing over there by those wattle trees."

The reddish and rather large antelope some seventy yards away stared curiously but without fear at the car. Their short, oddly turned horns made them look as if each had four ears. One of the animals, much closer to them, rubbed its neck against the trunk of a short, gnarled tree. Narai pointed, but her comment was not about the animal.

"That's a wattle tree, and it's very important in Kenya. The bark is valuable as a hide-tanning ingredient and the twigs and branches are extremely tough. They're used to make the frameworks of buildings and then plastered with the local mud, which sun-bakes to a very hard composition almost like concrete. Once built, the wattle huts are almost indestructible."

Grant was very impressed with Narai's wide range of knowledge about her people and her land, and throughout the day he, Anne, and Alex plied her with a multitude of questions. At the town of Nanyuki, as far north as they would go, they stopped at a little restaurant and ate an East Indian dish called *samosus*, which the Americans found to be quite similar to the Mexican *tacos*, with a crust not quite as hard as a *taco* and more abundantly filled, but essentially the same. It was a very clean and pleasant restaurant having just five tables and its claim to fame lay in the fact that it was perched precisely on the line of the earth's equator.

On leaving Nanyuki they turned directly west on the road which paralleled the equator and, occasionally seeing small herds of reticulated giraffe browsing on heavily-thorned acacia trees, followed the Laikipia Plateau another ninety-six miles to Thompson's Falls. They stopped there briefly to view the small, picturesque waterfall which plunged from a relatively flat, acacia-thorn-dotted meadow—with many hippos in the pools above the falls—into a gorge some eighty or ninety feet deep. A sudden cloudburst had caught them at the falls and their mad, laughing dash back to where the car was parked had not prevented their becoming drenched. They turned south from the equator here and, leaving the Laikipia Plateau behind, drove to the city of Nakuru. There, at the lake with the same name, they viewed with a sense of awe one of the most spectacular ornithological sights in the world— flamingos by literally millions forming a broad band of pink perhaps a quarter-mile wide and completely encircling the shallow forty-mile shoreline of the lake.

Heading back southeastward toward Nairobi, they stopped briefly in Naivasha, where all three of the Americans bought some exquisite African animal woodcarvings at a little roadside stand. At last, just before sundown, they had arrived at the Great Rift Valley and followed the narrow paved road—built by Italian prisoners of war during World War II—up the escarpment and stopped near the top to overlook this great natural cleft in the earth's crust.

Herbert Allen Herbert Allen Boardman had mentioned this phenomenon in the files which Grant and Anne had gone through at his home. It was, Boardman had said, one of many rifts in the face of the earth caused by overstretching of the earth's skin during one of the capsizings; stretched until the crust had split and drawn apart, leaving a cleft of gigantic proportions and a length of one-sixth of the circumference of the earth. The Dead Sea and the Red Sea were water-filled portions of that rift toward its northern end, stretching southward from the Mediterranean area. It separated Saudi Arabia from Africa proper and, at the mouth of the Gulf of Aden, moved through Ethiopia and into Kenya. From there it went deep into Tanzania as far southward as the border of Mozambique, with one branch of it splitting off northwestward from the water-filled portion of the rift known as Lake Nyasa and forming the basin for the nearly one-mile-deep Lake Tanganyika, second deepest lake in the world. It was an awe-inspiring sight and, in light of the HAB Theory, chilling to behold.

"Well, there it is!" Grant told Anne, who was standing beside him.

"My God," breathed Anne, her arm tightening about his waist, "imagine the inconceivable pressures there must have been to cause such a split." She paused a moment and then added in a low voice which Narai and Gordon were too distant to overhear, "I guess it always takes great pressure before any kind of split is made."

She was not talking about the earth now, and Grant knew it. He looked at her with an odd admixture of sadness and irritation. "The pressures are quite strong enough already," he murmured in return. "I wouldn't want to see them become any stronger."

Her eyes met his unflinchingly, green eyes boring into blue, and it was the blue which looked away. Still staring at him, Anne continued. "Evidently pressures must strengthen or the situation remains unchanged; I on the outside looking in, envying the woman who shares your house; she on the inside looking out, envying the woman who shares your love. All three dissatisfied. How long can it stay this way? It can't for much longer, John. It's about reached its limits."

Her voice remained very low, still unheard by the dark couple nearby who were watching the deep shadows lengthen in the Rift Valley and the low sun turning the massive Ol Ongonot volcanic crater into a 9,000-foot-high silhouette; a black monolithic cone with the top lopped off. With but a brief glance at the couple, Anne continued.

"She can't permit it to stay this way, John, any more than I can. Any more than *you* can, whether you realize it or not. The pressure will increase, you can count on it. If not from her in a very short time, then most definitely from me."

Her eyes remained steadily on him for another minute and then, when he didn't reply, she dropped her arm from his waist and walked back to the car and got in the back. Grant followed, his light mood of the day gone, replaced by a rapidly growing depression. Seeing them in the car and evidently ready to leave, Alex and Narai sauntered casually back and also got in.

"It's always been a stirring sight to me to see the Great Rift Valley," Narai said, pointing the Mercedes-Benz southward for the final fifty-mile run into Nairobi. "Now, in light of the HAB Theory, it becomes more than just awe-inspiring. It becomes something of a warning. I've seen it a hundred times or more, I suspect, but today was the first time it filled me with foreboding."

Just over an hour later—this part of the ride practically without conversation—they left the darkness of the open country and entered Nairobi, and a few minutes after that Narai slid the pearl-gray sedan to a smooth stop before the brightly lighted Nairobi Hilton, a cylindrical building which looked surprisingly similar to one of the corncob towers of Marina City in Chicago. John helped Anne out of the car and, after she said her good-byes to Alex and Narai, he leaned back inside to take Gordon's hand in a warm grip.

"Alex, have a safe journey back. I hope to see you there before very long. Narai," he smiled at her, "it has been a memorable day, and Anne and I can't thank you enough. We'll be remembering it with great pleasure years from now."

"Or at least until the time of the next tilt," Narai reminded with a pixie expression, and the three of them laughed. With their farewell in his ears, he closed the door and watched the car pull away in the darkness, red taillights twinkling as they merged with the stream of others passing by. Then he took Anne's arm and they entered the hotel. Waiting at the elevator door, he suddenly thought he'd better check at the desk to see if there were any messages. He excused himself, saying he'd be back in a moment.

At the desk the clerk checked his box and then handed him a plain white envelope with only his name on it and two airmail envelopes from the United States, both with the same return address in Skokie, Illinois. One was in Marie's characteristic backslant, the other in Carol Ann's flowing but still immature hand. He glanced toward the elevators and saw that Anne had picked up a newspaper that had been on a table nearby and was reading the front page. He put the airmail letters in his inside breast pocket and returned to her slowly, opening the flap of the plain envelope as he did so. He was just taking the folded sheet of paper out when he reached her.

"Mail?" she asked, looking up and folding the newspaper and dropping it back to the tabletop.

"Something. Let's see who it's from."

The elevator doors opened as he straightened the paper and he took her arm again as they stepped inside. He glanced down at the signature first, as the doors closed and the elevator began rising swiftly.

"It's from Elliott," he said, then read the note aloud to her. "'Mr. Grant, Would you kindly give me a call when you return to the hotel? I'm in Room 911. Elliott.' Hmmm, wonder what he wants?"

The atmosphere of chill that had been between the couple since leaving the Great Rift Valley had eased some now and Anne squeezed his arm and smiled, then straightened her face and said with mock seriousness, "Maybe he wants to offer you a job as undersecretary."

"Of course, that must be it!" He tried to smile, but the feeling of bleakness was still strong in him and it didn't come off very well. A few moments later, in Room 1236, Anne put her purse on a tabletop and stretched.

"Ohhh, wow," she sighed, "much as I enjoyed the trip, my sitter is sore. Me for a shower, pronto." She began unbuttoning her blouse. "Care to join me, Mister?"

"Nothing I'd like better, Lady. You go ahead. I'll give Elliott a call first and see what he wants. Then I'll join you."

He sat on the edge of the bed and picked up the phone, asked the operator to ring Room 91 and watched admiringly and yet with a peculiar sense of apartness as Anne undressed completely. The telephone in 911 was answered on the sixth ring.

"Hello?"

"John Grant, Mr. Secretary."

"Thought it might be. You caught me just in time. I was leaving the room to go downstairs. Would you care to join me in the bar? I won't keep you long."

Nude, Anne rubbed her fanny with a grimace, motioned with her head toward the bathroom and disappeared in that direction.

"Certainly, sir. Is there anything you want me to bring along?"

"Just yourself, Mr. Grant. Just yourself. I'll see you there in a minute." The telephone clicked dead.

Grant replaced the receiver in its cradle and stood, hearing the shower begin running. There was a rumbling sound punctuated by a small thud as the sliding glass shower door closed. He walked into the bathroom and slid the door open wide enough to admit his head. Hair tucked under a lemon-yellow shower cap, Anne already was busily soaping her upper body.

"Sorry, honey," he apologized, though not really so sorry at that, "but Elliott wants me to meet him downstairs right away. He said it won't take too long. As soon as I get back I'll shower too and then we can dress and have our dinner, okay?"

"I can think of something we might do between your shower and our dinner."

"Ma'am," he said, winking broadly and feeling a genuine stirring of desire for her, "you shore do come up with some powerful good ideas. See you soon."

About two minutes later he was joining Elliott at a small table near the rear of the hotel's bar. A waiter was already there, taking Elliott's order of Scotch on the rocks, and Grant ordered vodka and tonic double, then sat down across from the diplomat.

The secretary of state handed him a large brown envelope, sealed, and spoke in his brisk manner without preamble. "Inside you'll find some instructions regarding the remaining negotiations. Everything's pretty well wrapped up at this point and by tomorrow night you should be able to leave. Unfortunately, I have to go first thing in the morning. Have to be in Tel-Aviv tomorrow afternoon. The other gentlemen know my wishes, so there shouldn't be any problems. Mainly, you'll just be following their lead, all right?"

"Yes, sir."

"Fine. I want to commend you, Mr. Grant, on the excellent job you've done here as emissary for the President. He's already quite pleased, but I'm sure he'll be more so at my report. Ah," he looked up, "here's the man with our drinks."

The solemn-faced, red-coated waiter set the glasses before them, getting them reversed and then apologizing when this was pointed out and correcting the error.

"Your health, Mr. Grant."

"And yours, Mr. Secretary."

"Umm, that's good. Now then, I understand you and Miss Carpenter accompanied Gordon and Miss Ngoromu on quite a tour today. I'd enjoy hearing about it, if you've time to tell me."

Grant told him briefly. They were nearly finished with their drinks when he concluded and lit a cigarette.

"The Ngoromus seem to be quite remarkable people, don't the Mr. Grant?"

"Yes, sir, I think they are. I like them."

"Good. Good. Never hurts to have friendly relations like that on a more personal level. Well," he glanced at his watch, "I'll have to run." He quaffed the remainder of his drink, set his glass down and stood, keeping Grant in his chair with an outstretched hand. "No, sit still. You're not quite finished yet. Good luck to you."

"Thank you, sir." He accepted Elliott's hand.

The secretary of state started away but abruptly stopped and looked back, a wry expression on his face and a bit of a twinkle in his eye. "I *really* think we should have called it Hab City," he said, then broke into a short brittle laugh and left. It was the first time in two weeks of close association with the man that Grant had heard him laugh.

A moment or so later the writer had removed the two letters from his pocket and placed them atop the brown envelope Elliott had given him. He caught the waiter's attention and signalled for another drink for himself—a double—and then heaved a sigh. There was no doubt in his mind which one he would read first. He picked it up and tore a thin sliver off one end and extracted not one but two brief letters.

Dear Daddy,

It's so hard to imagine that you're really halfway around the world from us, in Africa. We miss you so very much and hope you will be coming home to us before long.

*I've got the **greatest** news, Daddy. I met this boy who's just absolutely the greatest! He's just moved in a couple of blocks away from us and will be attending my school, except he's not a sophomore like me. He's a senior. (**Will be**, that is, when we start again in September.) He's a football player, too, and expects he'll get on our team because he was first-string quarterback in the school he left. Anyway, he asked if I could go on a picnic up to Zion State Park with him a week from Sunday and I asked Mom and Mom wasn't sure but since you weren't here to ask she said she thought it would probably be all right (she knows a lot more about him than you do, and anyway, his parents are going along, too) but that if you objected when you came home, **if** you came home before then, then I would have to cancel out, and that would be awful and I'm sure you wouldn't object, would you Daddy? Anyway, Mom said if you weren't home before then, I could go. I'm so excited! Imagine, a **senior!***

Mom hasn't been feeling too well, but don't worry because it's nothing serious, just a cold she says. If you could see her nose and eyes, all red and puffy (the puffy's just for her eyes) you'd see she's not fooling at all. She didn't even cheer up when she got your letter, so you can see how miserable she must be.

*Billy has been so **obnoxious** lately, I wish you would talk to him when you come home and tell him to stay out of my business and quit pestering me to play his stupid kid games.*

*Well, I better close now. Mom says my room is a total disaster and I have to clean it up. It is a **little** messed up, but not as bad as she makes out. but I'll clean it as soon as I get this in an envelope and in the mail to you.*

I love you and miss you, Daddy. We all do. Hurry home to us, please. (But if you're going to say "no" about the picnic, then don't hurry too much and try to stay until at least the Monday after next.)

Love and XXXX's
Carol Ann

P.S. Were you able to find a baby cheetah for me?
*P.P.S. Billy wrote you a note and so I'll put it in here with mine, but he's such a brat! He never appreciates **anything**!*

*P.P.P.S.S.S. Almost forgot! How **could** I? His name is Art McDermott. The senior, I mean. His eyes are blue like yours and he's got sort of reddish curly hair and he's really **big** and very handsome!*

Grant slowly folded that letter and opened the other sheet Carol had enclosed. It was lined yellow paper and on the inside was Billy's letter to him. He shook his head at the appearance of it. Written in pencil, it was short, badly smudged and generally messy. It was also full of misspellings and poor grammar.

hi dad. Having a good time in Africa? I bet! Wish I was there in Nyrowbee with you. Did you get the spear and sheild? Boy, I hope so! Sis is mad at me again Shes always mad. All of a sudden Shes acting all snootie about Something and thinks shes all grown up and too good for me anymore. I sure do miss you. Mom too. She misses you so much she's always crying when she thins we arnt around to see so you better hurry home. Have you seen any elefents and lions yet? Don't let them eat you. ha! ha!

Love, Billy

P.S. Hurry home, daddy. Please?

Grant put the two letters back into their envelope thoughtfully and very mechanically lit another cigarette, not remembering when he had put out the one he'd lighted while talking with Elliott. He finished his drink in a couple of large swallows, caught the waiter's eye again, and ordered a repeat. Then he looked steadily at the other envelope, not knowing what was inside, not even knowing what he hoped was inside. The depression was continuing to grow. He considered and then discarded the notion of destroying the letter from Marie unread. He finished both his drink and his cigarette, ordered yet another of the former and lit another of the latter. The doubles he was drinking might have been water for all the effect they were having on him. When the new drink arrived he took a large swallow of it, then wiped off the swizzle stick—a plastic miniature of a Masai spear—and used it to slit open the envelope from Marie.

John,

If the letter you wrote me required the mental anguish that this one requires on my part, then I know it was terribly difficult for you to write.

All my life, John, I have heard it said that love and hate are two very close emotions and that one can turn into the other very easily. I never believed it because it was beyond my experience, and even beyond my ability to imagine. Yet, now I'm not that sure anymore. At times recently I have come very close to hating you—for what you are doing to me, to the children, to your home. But most of all for what you are doing to yourself.

Where, I ask myself, is my John—the one I married—the upright, honest, happy, thoughtful John, instead of this one who has suddenly become a stranger to me? The present John is not a very likable person. He cheats, he lies. He steals, because it is stealing, John, to give to another the love and time and thought that should be expended on your children and wife. The present John has become a devious man, a man who proclaims his selflessness to himself while at one and the same time acting in a manner most cruelly selfish. Where are your values, your morals, your ethics? All your life these were your admirable, self-evident traits. How do you suddenly turn you back on them?

*You profess in your letter that despite what is occurring, you still love me. I know you are not trying to deceive me in that instance, but I know equally well that you **are** trying to deceive yourself. It isn't possible, no matter how you try to convince yourself of it, John, that you can really and honestly love both her and me. I am sure that you probably love one of us, and that undoubtedly you are also extremely fond of the other, but one of us takes precedence in the matter of love. There is simply no way it can be evenly divided. To try to convince yourself that it can be is self-delusionary.*

You say that our marriage has become sour, and those words are to me no more than an icicle driven deeply into my heat, for in saying them, whether or not you care to admit it, you have also said which of the two of us you truly love, and which you're merely fond of. You also say that the thought of losing me fills you with dread, yet now that it seems evident you must make a choice, you are unable to do so. You've always had courage, John, but those words reflect the thoughts of a coward, the thoughts of one who is too weak and fearful to make his own decision and flounders about in a state of misery, hoping someone will make the decision for him. In this respect I am deeply, very deeply, ashamed of you. Just as it had been beyond my ken to envision love and hatred being able to supplant one another, so too it had been beyond my ken to envision any time when I could ever be ashamed of you. Yet, on both counts I am proven wrong and I begin to wonder what sort of blind imbecile I have been all these years.

*I can write no more now. The children—**our** children, John, not just mine—have needs at the moment which I must see to, needs which I have always been glad to see to when it has been necessary for you to be away. But these children, John, were conceived as the fruit of our love, and they are **our** responsibility, not just mine. Yes, you are so right, we will indeed talk when you return!*

*The crowning ignominy of your letter was the self-serving sanctimonious avowal that you are not consumed with guilt and will not come back dripping repentance. The utter loathesomeness of that comment defies any power of description I possess. The pen **is** mightier than the sword, John, for you could have slashed at me all day with a razor-sharp sword and not cut as deeply and as painfully as you did with those few deft turns of your pen.*

I couldn't believe that love and hate were allied, but I am wrong. I couldn't believe that I would ever be ashamed of you. Again I was wrong. And I was wrong about the final thing: that it would ever be possible for me to say to you what I say to you now.

God damn you, John Grant! You bastard! You are a rotten, lying cheat and I hope you'll roast in Hell for what you've done. Damn you!

   M.

8

The weapon of skepticism is dangerous—in the past many an over-skeptical scientist discredited himself by rash condemnation and lack of imagination.

—Andrew Tomas

A man who is influenced by the polls or is afraid to make decisions which may make him unpopular is not a man to represent the welfare of the country.

—Harry S Truman

I

The logistics behind setting up the complex HAB Theory Symposium had left Dr. Irma Dowde nearing a state of complete exhaustion, but she had done a remarkable job. For the first three weeks she had worked primarily out of her office in the Department of Archaeology at the Smithsonian Institution in Washington, D.C., but during this final week she had moved her operations to New York City. There, with the size of her work staff growing constantly, as need required it to, she set herself up in the Waldorf Astoria, using the Vertes Suite as headquarters for the HAB Symposium. Seven assistants were working with her now, handling clerical work, taking care of incoming and outgoing telephone calls, accumulating and assembling into packets the mass of printed matter that was to be passed out to each registrant.

Although the symposium was still not officially due to begin until the day after tomorrow, registration already was much heavier than anticipated and the Vertes Suite was a continuous scene of crowded confusion. Initially a total of twenty-five hundred scientists had been expected, but already three hundred more than that had registered and tomorrow was still expected to be the heaviest day of registration. It appeared now that final registration would probably come very close to four thousand individuals.

The registration fee of $100 seemed high at first, but not when all that it provided was taken into consideration. Each registrant was immediately provided with an identification pin of tough, rigid plastic molded in the shape of the earth, with the imprint of lines of latitude and longitude and with a space across the middle where a pressure-sensitive tab could be stuck bearing the wearer's name, field of science and institution or home city. Each person was also given one of the quite sizeable packets of printed materials, including the fifty-page Grant summary of the HAB Theory in its entirety, a twenty-five-page listing of the names, titles, affiliations and addresses of the participants, tickets for two informal banquets to be held during the course of the symposium, plus a certificate promising a numbered special Symposium Edition copy of Herbert Allen Boardman's *The Eccentric Earth*, which was to be shipped to the participant's home just as soon as the new, handsomely bound books came off the press. In addition, numerous addenda sheets of recently received material would constantly be handed out, and three-hole binders were provided for holding this material.

Manhattan abruptly had become the focal point of the scientific world and each airliner or chartered aircraft landing at La Guardia or Kennedy International or Newark almost surely carried its own complement of scientists being drawn to the symposium. As with any sort of convention, the symposium was effecting the reunion of many people who had not seen one another for years, and in hotels all over New York little clusters of learned men and women shook hands warmly and chatted pleasantly in lobbies or hotel bars or in individual rooms. Apart from the significance of the symposium theme, which had drawn them here initially, the meetings were extremely valuable simply for the exchange of ideas that was occurring even before the symposium got under way. But, as always, a phenomenon peculiar to such gatherings manifested itself early; physicists sought out specialists in their own field, as did the anthropologists and paleontologists and archaeologists and other scientists of specific branches of learning. It resulted in remarkably little interchange of ideas *between* the groups, each becoming an island in the assembly of similar islands. For Dr. Irma Dowde, this very aspect underlined what she considered to be one of the greatest problems in science today, and she made a mental note to comment on it strongly during the sessions of the symposium to come.

For the stocky, energetic female archaeologist, this had been one of the most grueling months in her entire career and she was very glad that all the preliminary work of coordination at last was drawing to a close. It seemed to her that ever since accepting the job from the President she had not stopped, and she was as exhausted mentally as physically. The work itself demanded every waking moment of her time and, while in Washington, she had practically made her office in the Smithsonian a home. The amount of work had changed little when she came to New York. As much as she had always enjoyed meeting and talking with fellow scientists, now she had begun to begrudge the time which was lost to those individuals—and there were an amazing number of them who buttonholed her for conversation as she attempted to get everything done. Few here did not know her or, failing that, did not want to become acquainted with her simply because of the prestigious position she held in the scientific world.

Irma Dowde had an excellent ear for languages, and in her years of traveling around the world she had picked up an ability in foreign tongues which allowed her to converse with reasonable fluency in French, Italian, Greek, Spanish, German, Arabic and Portuguese, and to a somewhat lesser degree of fluency in Russian, Japanese, Swahili, Swedish, Africaans, Hindustani, Bantu, and modern Hebrew, as well as a smattering of isolated native tongues of Africa, South America and the South Pacific. This facility alone put her much in demand in polyglot groups as an interpreter, but she was equally valued as a catalyst, for conversations seemed least tedious when she was on hand to inject her pithy and penetrating comments.

Even though English very rapidly was becoming the universal language and was taught in most countries— and few scientists could not use it with relative fluency—she knew there was a good possibility that there might be difficulties with interpretation in some of the meetings. It was just one more problem she simply would have to face if and when it occurred.

Now, early in the afternoon of this twenty-ninth day of June, she was just preparing to leave the registration desks when a stentorian voice halted her.

"Dr. Dowde!" The pronunciation given her name by the speaker was "Dow-dy" when, in actuality, as was quite well known, the letter *e* at the end of her name was silent.

She spun around, frowning, and saw that the one who had spoken so authoritatively was a lean, medium-sized man of about sixty-five whose head had the gleaming shine often noted on those who have been bald for many years. His deep set eyes were a very cold gray, a bit too small and too close together for the size of his head, giving him a pinch-faced expression. His mouth, below the sharp and somewhat hooked nose, was a thin wide line framed by narrow and practically colorless lips. Although she had met him a time or two in years past, she had never cared much for him and was always thankful she'd never had to work closely with him. Nevertheless, her frown faded and she smiled cordially.

"Ah, Dr. Holder. I'm happy you were able to make it here."

"Wild stallions could not have kept me away, Dr. Dow-dy."

"It's pronounced 'Dowd,' if you please." A chill had entered her voice.

Owen Holder shrugged in an insolent manner. He looked at her steadily, his narrowed eyes pinching together even more closely with the frown he wore, and he made an exasperated sound.

"I would think," he said, in his offensive, braying voice—so loud and distinctive that conversations clear across the room broke off and people looked their way—"that a professional scientist of your supposed stature would have shied from, rather than accepted, the position of coordinating this…this *travesty!*" He swung out an arm to take in the room.

"I hardly think any of the other scientists here, Dr. Holder, consider this symposium a travesty."

"Ha! That is the type of comment I expected from you! When this scientific charade gets under way, Dr. Dow-dy, you'll quickly see how many *thinking* professionals consider it nothing more than just that. Of course, to one whose reputation has largely been built on theatrics, it is little wonder why there is an appeal to it all. No doubt you'll get a great deal more television exposure now and become even more famous, won't you?"

Irma Dowde slowly set down the armload of books and pamphlets she had been preparing to carry away with her and in two man-sized strides came to a stop before the Oxford geology professor. She was shorter than he and had to look up at him, but somehow she managed to appear the more formidable of the two.

"I don't know you very well, Dr. Holder, but quite well enough to know that how little I do know you is already too much!" Her words were like whip cracks in the room and someone far in the crowd looking on snickered loudly. Holder flushed and started to speak, but Dr. Dowde cut him off. "I don't understand or appreciate your manner of speaking to me. I would hope that many arguments against the HAB Theory will be advanced at this forum, and I would hope that in the end they will prove strong enough to invalidate the postulation. God help us all if we *can't* prove it wrong! But right or wrong, sir, I think it is our responsibility to bring to this symposium the open-mindedness that all of us, as scientists, are supposed to have—even if we don't often show it. Certainly it is no place to engage in personalities."

"It is, by heaven, when the whole scientific fraternity stands in jeopardy of ridicule for even *considering* such a preposterous theorization!" Holder's entire scalp was bright pink and glistening, and his slightly sagging jowls took on a set of bulldog determination. He pointed a finger at her so that it hung in the air only inches from her nose. "It is, madam, when one alleged scientist attempts to enhance her own reputation by making fools of her fellow scientists and by damaging the very foundation of the institution of science!"

A few strobe lights were flashing now as reporters, drawn to the exchange, made the most of the developing situation. Dr. Dowde, however, had no inclination to let the exchange develop any further than it had gone already. She smiled at the Oxford geologist, but her words were level and cold.

"If that finger is still there three seconds from now, I intend to break it."

Instantly Holder dropped his arm and began to sputter, but Irma Dowde, still smiling, simply turned her back retrieved her material from the desktop and strode away in her ugly flat walking shoes. There was a scattering of applause and some laughter behind her and almost immediately a din arose as practically everyone began speaking at once.

Scientific symposiums never had been noted for dramatic appeal, but the consensus already was forming that this particular symposium was going to be considerably different from any of its predecessors, and in many more ways than one.

Within a few hours hardly anyone who had registered had not heard the story of the altercation in at least one form, and usually in two or three differently embellished versions. Oddly, it established a lightness and eagerness among the participants that they rarely had achieved so early—if at all—at any such symposium.

Six hours later, in the evening, the entire city of New York knew about it, as the evening edition of the New York *Post* carried a page one photo story of the incident. The picture, three columns wide and four inches deep, showed Dr. Holder pointing his rigid finger at Dr. Dowde, whose mouth was open as she made a comment, though the impression was strong that she was on the verge of biting it off. The caption was pithy.

ARCHAEOLOGIST THREATENS TO BREAK BONES OF GEOLOGIST.

During a brief verbal altercation at the HAB Theory Symposium registration desks in the Waldorf Astoria, famed archaeologist Dr. Irma Dowde of the Smithsonian Institution threatened to break the finger of noted geology professor Owen Holder of England's Oxford University if he didn't remove it from in front of her face. The argument may set a pattern of things to come in the controversial symposium which begins the day after tomorrow. (The finger was quickly removed—by Dr. Holder.) See related symposium stories on page 1, section 2.

I I

To Anne, the Marina City apartment had never looked smaller or more barren than it did at this moment. Initially she moved back and forth through it as if she were a stranger to the place, looking at the furnishings and their arrangement, yet not really seeing them. She was extremely weary, but knew that even if she lay down, she would not sleep. There was a feeling in the pit of her stomach as if it contained ground glass, a feeling familiar enough to her at intervals since meeting John and falling in love with him, which always came on most strongly at those times when he left her to go to his own house and family. It was a feeling that had been totally absent over these past twenty-four days in Africa. There they had been able to act like normal people—open and happy in their love, unashamed and hiding from no one. But now, with her return to Chicago and her apartment, everything was wrong again. They were hiding and starting in again to live that same horror of frustration and, because of that, the awful feeling had come back with sickening assault.

She did lie down then, sighing deeply. Part of the weariness was, she knew, due to jet lag; a disorientation created by intercontinental travel, by swiftly moving from one time zone to another and one continent to another and then to a third in a very short time, by sitting for interminable hours aboard aircraft, becoming increasingly unable to rest and gaining little relief from the fleeting naps. But she equally knew that it was not the weariness that was causing the intense ground-glass sensation inside. That came from the deep, sickening fear of what lay ahead now, from the realization that though she wanted desperately to do something to help John, there was nothing she could do but sit back and wait and wonder…and worry.

What was happening right now with him and with Marie was undoubtedly shaping Anne's own entire future, yet here she was, unable to participate, unable to know what was occurring, and the apprehension inside escalated another few notches. The thought came to her that this was undoubtedly precisely the feeling Marie Grant had been experiencing during the entire time that Anne and John were in Africa and a twinge of pity for Marie, for what she and John were putting her through, momentarily swept through her.

Anne's luggage still sat on the floor against the wall close to the closet door, where John had put the bags down hours ago. She knew she should unpack and begin getting things in order to resume the normal pattern of life. She knew this, and yet she looked away from the suitcases, unwilling to do what needed to be done, unwilling to make the moves that would reestablish the existence which to her had become unbearably pointless. She wanted only one thing: to be with John, to be sharing with him, helping him through a time which had to be one of the most crucial times of decision in his life, yet unable to do a thing.

Her clothing still lay in a jumbled pile at the foot of the bed, tossed there a half-hour ago when she thought she would take a shower to rid herself of the feeling griminess that comes with long hours of extended travel. The clothes represented a chore to be done and she fleetingly wished John's garments were in the pile with hers. How eagerly then she would have moved to take these items to the laundry or dry cleaner. She yearned to be able to *do* for him.

She was lying unclothed on the bed and, though it was warm in the room and a pleasant, caressing breeze came through the apartment from the open balcony door, now a chill struck her and her flesh tingled and rose in tiny goose-bumps. What she was experiencing now was a return in force of that hideous ground-glass feeling. Pain has a faulty memory and the *absence* of this feeling in Africa hardly occurred to her while there. The problem of having John, yet not having him, which was the genesis for the inner upset, ceased to exist when they were together an ocean apart from his family. In that short a time it had almost seemed as if the life here didn't exist at all. Now it had come crashing down on her again with greater force than ever and she felt sickened by the weight of the problem. Only John could lift that weight from her and, despite the buildup of her confidence while they were in Africa, now she once again was very unsure and very frightened. A shiver of apprehension passed through her at her own helplessness and the grinding in her stomach worsened.

She sighed and crossed her arms in front of her, rubbing both upper arms with her palms. Then, wearily, she got up and went into the bathroom and started the shower. About half an hour later, much refreshed, her hair done up in rollers and her body clad only in a pair of sheer panties of the palest powder green, she stretched out on the bed for a few minutes and then leaned over and picked up the phone and punched in a number.

"Hello?"

"Hi, Mother."

"Pussycat! You're back! Oh, I'm so glad to hear from you. It seems like you've been gone forever. I've missed your calls so much. The cards and letter were nice, but not the same as hearing your voice. How was it, dear? Did you have a good time?"

"It was beautiful, Mother. There's just no way to describe it adequately. No matter what you read or hear or see in pictures or movies about Africa, you're simply not prepared for the actuality of it. There's an intrigue about it that's really amazing."

"I can imagine. I'd love to see it sometime." Susan Carpenter was silent for a space and then she added, "How's John?"

"He's fine."

"And you?"

"I'm fine, too."

"My, but you're effusive. I detect some hidden something-or-other. Problems, Kitten?" That she used the endearment "Kitten" was indicative of her genuine concern. A takeoff from her more familiar "Pussycat," she seldom used it unless she was truly worried about her daughter.

"To some extent. Well, more than that. Yes, problems."

"Do you want to talk about it?"

"I don't know. I…yes, Mother. Yes, I do. Marie knows."

"Oh, my! How?" The words carried a distinct sharpening of interest.

"When we were just leaving for Africa. At the airport. She saw us there."

Susan Carpenter waited a moment and then asked, "A bad scene, honey?"

"No. No scene at all. I didn't even know it. John saw her, but he didn't tell me until a few days after we were over there. He wrote to her then."

"Did you see the letter?" There was a note of worry in the older woman's voice. "What did he say?"

"All I saw was the envelope, not the actual letter. But I know pretty well what was in it by her reply."

"You saw *that?*"

"Yes. The last night we were there. John left the room for a meeting with the secretary of state and he was only supposed to be gone for a few minutes. After an hour passed and he still wasn't back, I got pretty concerned. He didn't come back at all on his own and after a second hour went by, I went out after him. He was at a table in the bar." There was a slight catch in her voice. "Mother, I'd never seen him drunk before. He just doesn't drink like that. He never has, but evidently he'd been drinking one after another just about as fast as he could get them down."

"Was it her letter that set him off?"

"As far as I know, it was. He wasn't very coherent and I had to get one of the bellmen to help me get him up to the room. And then he got sick pretty badly, so I got him and the room cleaned up and got him into bed. The letters were in the breast pocket of his coat."

"Did you—"

"No, Mother," Anne interrupted in an exasperated tone, "I didn't just read them. I was tempted to, but decided against it, and was just putting his coat on a hanger when I looked around and he was sitting up in bed staring at me in the oddest way. He told me to read them."

"He really wanted you to?"

"Yes. He said, 'Those letters in my coat pocket. They're from Marie and the kids. Read them.' Then he just flopped back and was out. So I read them. The letters from the children were just kid letters. Not much to them. They probably affected him a little, but not really a great deal. But the letter from Marie…" Her voice trailed off.

"Vicious?"

"No. Well, a little at the end, but mostly not. I wish it had been!"

"Forgiving, then?"

"No, not that either. Mother, it was…it was…so…so *full* of hurt, Mother. Such deep hurt. My God, she's my greatest enemy in a way, and yet my heart went out to her. I don't think I ever read anything that so thoroughly expressed the depth of a hurt like that. I wanted to comfort her, to tell her I was sorry, to try to do something to ease her pain. Do you know, I even had the craziest, wildest notion to call her—from *there!* To call and apologize and to tell her I couldn't hurt her like that. I felt…I felt I was *destroying* her. I almost wanted to tell her I was giving up, that I couldn't do this to her."

"You didn't, did you? Call her, I mean?"

"No. No, I didn't. But…Oh, Mother, I don't have anything against her. I don't even know her beyond seeing her once when she didn't know it a few months ago. But she has something I want so much that life's not worth anything if I'm the one who has to do without. I love him, Mother. I love him so much it's just a great big gnawing ache inside, and I don't know what to do. I'm so scared!. I've never been so scared in all my life."

Susan's voice was brimming with sympathy and understanding. "Poor baby. Poor, sweet darling. You've never been like this before."

"No one has ever meant so much to me before, Mother." Anne's voice was a little more under control now. "I want to help him. I want to be beside him and help him through this, and I can't be. He has to face it alone and I keep thinking that if her letter affected *me* that way, then how terribly hard it had to affect him. It was no wonder he hadn't come back upstairs. He's mentioned in passing a time or two how difficult the decision is that he has to make, but I never really even began to understand it until then. I suppose I don't understand it even yet, not the way he does, but now I can see better how awful it must be for him; what it's doing to him. What *I'm* doing to him. I'm not much of one for feeling guilty about anything I've done that I thought was right, and yet now suddenly I feel sick with it. With guilt and worry and fear. I'm so *frightened!* What am I going to do?"

"Are you asking me, Kitten? I mean *really* asking? If you're just talking in order to have a sympathetic ear listening, you know you've got that and I wouldn't want to say anything else beyond ordinary commiseration with you. But if you're really *asking*, then I'll try to help."

"I'm asking. What do I do, Mother? *Now*, I mean. What do I do now besides sit here worrying myself sick and waiting for him to call? I want to help him, but I don't know how. I don't know what to do."

"Pussycat, the greatest help you can be to John right now is simply to do nothing except be available to him in his need. Now is most definitely *not* the time to put any more pressure on him. Just be there to answer the phone if he calls. Be there to welcome and comfort him if he comes. Be there to listen to him, to whatever he wants to unload. Be there and be ready to run whenever he might want you come, or wherever he might want you to go. And Anne, " her mother's voice seemed to drop to a lower pitch and become even more serious than before, "for your own peace of mind, never lose sight of the fact—no matter how much it hurts to acknowledge it!—that there is a strong possibility his final decision will not be in your favor."

When, after an extended pause, Anne did not speak, her mother's voice came again. "Are you there, Kitten? Do you understand at all what I'm trying to say?"

"I understand. I really do. But, Mother, I can't picture a future for me without John. Without him there *isn't* any future!"

"Now, honey, don't talk like that." Alarm had come into Susan Carpenter's voice. "No matter how bad things get, life goes on and you have to adjust. Anticipated fears are often a lot worse than the actuality." Again a silence, and once more it was Susan who broke it. "Well, listen honey, I have to go. But I'm here if you need me. Anytime you want to talk, then call me. Will you do that?"

"Yes. Maybe a lot sooner than you think. And thanks, Mother, for listening. It helps."

"I hope so, Darling. I really do. Keep your chin up now, hear? Bye-bye, Kitten."

"Good-bye, Mother."

She replaced the phone and then lay back on the pillow, squirming a bit until she got into a position where the rollers were not pulling her hair or digging into her head. She stared unseeingly at the ceiling and thought about what her mother had said, and about what John was experiencing right now, and once again the fear rose in her. Somehow, in retrospect, her mother's words seemed more like platitudes and she gained little comfort from them. Her mother didn't know how John had been during that last night and day in Africa or on the long flight back to the States; she didn't know how, after being sick, he had alternately dozed off and then thrashed about in his sleep, moaning and muttering and constantly reawakening himself; she didn't know how once he jerked upright in bed, waking himself with his own fearful shriek, then sat there trembling at the aftermath of the nightmare in which he had discovered both Anne and Marie hung by their hands in a dank cellar and disemboweled. She hadn't seen, as Anne saw, the sick-at-heart expression in his eyes, the deep inner pain he was experiencing which, for the first time, Anne had been unable to assuage.

Anne's mother had warned her against putting any more pressure on John, yet this very day she had put on him the greatest pressure she could, knowing that she *had* to do so, that it was her last real chance to do so. Marie Grant had certainly had a tremendous effect upon John with her letter, so how much worse might the effect be when he confronted her face to face, as he was planning to do immediately upon leaving Anne. It was why Anne knew she had to have her own strong confrontation here in the apartment with John before he left to confront Marie.

She thought about that last night in Nairobi and shuddered. It had been a long one and a bad one, for both of them. The next morning had brought little relief. For the first time Anne had been unable to really reach him and her apprehension had climbed. He had been disinclined to talk and the return flight via Rome and London had been mostly one of moody silence. The closer they had come to Chicago, the more determined Anne had become to unload on him to the fullest. When finally they had touched down at O'Hare, cleared customs, and caught a cab back to the apartment, she steeled herself for what lay ahead. His plan had been merely to drop her off, keeping the taxi waiting while he helped her in with her baggage, and then going right on to his own house. Anne wouldn't hear of it and had insisted that he let the cab go, bring his own things up, too, and talk. He did so, but only with considerable reluctance.

They were both tired from the traveling and from the emotional stress they'd been under. It was not at all a good time for a talk and Anne knew it, but she was convinced that talk under any conditions at that moment had to be better than none at all.

The air in the apartment had been stale, unused, and she had bustled about, opening the doors onto the balcony from both living room and bedroom, allowing a steady breeze to waft through. He simply stood there watching her and, though he hadn't objected when she took his hand and led him to the bed, he refused to let her undress him or herself. He'd consented to lying atop the bed, pillows propped behind his back and head, and accepted gratefully the cigarette she lighted for him. She'd kicked off her shoes and taken a position beside him, sitting upright with her legs crossed under her, facing him, one hand lightly resting on his chest.

It was then that she had begun to talk, slowly at first, hesitantly, softly, but with gradually increasing intensity. She told him that she understood only too well how upset he was, and how torn and tormented inside. She offered her help in any way, simply and without pressure, merely as a matter of fact.

He shook his head, the lines in his face deep. "I thank you for the offer, love, but there's really nothing at this point that you can do, except what I asked of you back in Nairobi."

She knew what he was referring to and nodded. "You asked me to coast, and I've been trying to give the impression of doing that, although I don't think that's an appropriate movement, darling. Coasting is for when the trip is downhill; it's for when you've got plenty of speed and the nearest competitor is too far behind to be a threat. That's not my situation and we both know it.

The green eyes were overbright, restraining the flow of tears only with considerable effort. She put her hand on his arm. "John, try to understand. I've coasted long enough already. With a lifetime at stake, this is no time to sit back waiting for whatever happens. Right now you seem to be deep in a 'I'm-throwing-my- children-to-welfare-and-destroying-Marie's-life-and-Annie-and-I-aren't-very-happy- even-together-anymore-so-what's-the-use' frame of mind. You know every bit of that is ridiculous. We *are* happy—incredibly happy—when we can push aside the knowledge that the happiness is temporary. You and I individually, and we together, have gone over the arguments, although I think you've kept many to yourself. We're both aware of the difficulties involved, but no one ever said it would be easy.

"Honey," she continued, touching his cheek lightly with her fingertips, "I can't dispute the initial injury to everyone, me included, but it will only be temporary. In view of that, how can you possibly even consider a lost lifetime? *How?*"

Although he gave a vague little shake of his head, Grant didn't reply and she didn't seem to expect him to, as she went on without pause. "As much as you keep saying you love me, I'm very much afraid you're still leaning the other way, and I swear I don't know how to make you lean back my way, how to *drag* you back if I could, if I only knew how."

She stopped, but as he propped himself with his elbows to sit up, preparing to say something, she put a finger to his lips and silenced him. He closed his eyes, sighing, but settled back into his previous position.

"Let me go on. Please. You sometimes refer to our six months together versus your seventeen years with Marie. Can't you see that the fact we've gone on for six months under the circumstances says an awful lot? You seem to indicate that if we endure this long enough, maybe the time will get more evenly balanced. It's won't. It can't possibly, so long as both she and I are a part of your life. The misery will just increase and, as that becomes stronger, I'm afraid you'll see *that* more plainly than you see the happiness we've had and can still have. That seems to be your present mood, ever since receiving her letter, and no amount of time is going to improve it."

She hesitated, letting her hand move across his chest and then to the back of his neck, gripping it firmly, pulling him up slightly to meet the kiss she was bending to give him. It was a quiet, pleasant touching of their lips without the heat of passion, yet filled with the warmth of love. She pulled back then, looking at him with a faintly quizzical expression, and she sighed.

"John, I know my thinking is often blurred, because I think primarily in terms of you and myself and us and tend to override other considerations. But I think your thoughts are sometimes too greatly swayed by too many thoughts about the effects on others."

He frowned and met her eyes directly. "In what way, Anne? What considerations am I allowing to sway me that I shouldn't?"

Warning bells clanged in her mind and a sense of panic took hold of her that she was going too far, saying too much, pushing too hard, but the need to go on was inexorable. "Some things," she spoke slowly, "are really superficialities, but if you ponder them enough, as you do in some cases, they take on an importance all out of proportion. For example, part of your disinclination to make a decision in our favor is your fear of a postseparation negative reaction; but, darling, such a reaction can't at this point be known to be a certainty by either of us. Of course there's bound to be a reaction, but it doesn't necessarily have to be a negative one. Even if it *is* negative, we can weather it together. You're worried about living with your guilt over disrupting your family's life, but look at it this way for a change: can you live, period, not just exist, in a continuation of a lifestyle you already know is unsatisfactory to you? I know full well that there's no guarantee of what we could have together, but from the glimpses we've had and the good times we've experienced when the Big Gloom is out to lunch, you must feel *some* sort of assurance of a good life together for us.

"Darling, we're fighting a practically vertical uphill battle, and yet so far we've not taken too many falls in favor of the old-and-established. As a matter of fact, we've managed to land a few pretty good blows ourselves. At this point the score, unfortunately, seems pretty even, but just that fact—that six months is running even with seventeen years—is damned encouraging, and I take that as a signal of eventual victory. I don't want to drag you even lower, John," her hand on his chest squeezed briefly, "but it seems impossible to me to just sit back quietly waiting while you make an unassisted decision that could ruin our lives."

She stood up and strode to the window and stared outward, downward, expecting to hear him speak. When the silence merely stretched out she raised her arms helplessly and let them slap down against her sides and returned to sit by him.

"There are moments," she told him, "when I think I can't stand being without you any longer. But the choice isn't mine. I stand it because I have to, but I draw inner strength for doing so with the sure knowledge that when we finally are together, it will have been a reasoned move and you'll be with me because that's where you want to be. I get the strong feeling that's where you want to be right now, but you're still sorting out the complications. I can't imagine what will finally trigger you—though maybe the letter from Marie is just that very factor—but I hope to God that the reaction is favorable to our side.

"She swung up her legs and straightened them toward the foot of the bed, lying on her side close beside him, her head on his chest, her arm across him. She felt him begin softly stroking her hair and then touch his lips to the top of her head. She made a crooning, contented sound and they were both silent for a little while. Then she gave a little laugh deep in her throat.

"What?" he asked.

"I've certainly been dominating *this* conversation, haven't I? I'm sorry, darling, but this is such an important thing to us, such a crucial time. In a short while you'll be on your way to see her, and I'm trying desperately to fire all my biggest guns now, while I have the chance. There's still more I want to say, but I won't continue if you've had enough."

"No," Grant replied, "I think I'd rather you went ahead. I want to know your feelings, your thoughts. Maybe somehow they'll help. I don't really know how, but perhaps just by helping me clarify my own thinking."

She snuggled even more closely against him, reveling in the touch of him, in the fully-clad, foot-to-head, full-length contact with him. "When I'm alone," she murmured, "I think of us like this together. Sometimes clothed, like now, but mostly not. It's a nice sensation. But, John, mental presence—*imagined* presence—can't do much to ease the pain of physical absence. You're a necessary part of my existence. I can't conceive of a time when you won't be." She sat up again, her eyes on his.

"Now," she went on, "here's a comment you can ponder: You talk sometimes of being selfish if you give in to what *you* want to do. Is that really selfishness? I think not. Your so-called selfishness which involves your coming to me is better described, to my way of thinking, as simply living your life. Only you can determine how you will live your life, John. Other people, myself included, exert an influence, but the final decision you make should be made on the basis of what's best for *you*, not them, and once again that includes me. What brings *you* the most happiness is what counts."

He made no comment but he reached for his cigarettes and she took the package from him. Selecting a cigarette, she replaced the pack on the table and lit it with his lighter which had been lying there, too. The outer half-inch of the cigarette became black because she held it too far into the flame and he chuckled and took it from her.

"Beautiful. Thanks."

They both laughed and then she suddenly buried her face on his chest and her words were muffled as she said she loved him. Again they lay quietly as he smoked, while softly stroking her long black hair. Throughout her monologue he had remained essentially expressionless and, though often in the past she could detect what he was thinking or feeling by the expression in his eyes, that ability seemed to have totally deserted her now and she had no idea how he was accepting all this. She abruptly felt the fear rising in her again and became more desperate to somehow put across what was so overwhelming within her. She licked her lips and sat straighter. She closed her eyes for a moment and then opened them and looked intently at him again, striving with the greatest of effort to keep that rising swell of apprehension out of her voice.

"John, if you really love Marie more than you love me, and if you feel a stronger need for her and feel the remaining years of your life will be better with her, then I have never been so completely wrong in my life. I cannot believe you feel that way. You have made me believe that in these past six months I have come to mean at *least* as much to you as she does. That says a great deal, love, and it's there for you to hear if you'll just open your ears to your own heart. Please, John, don't overlook that potential by thinking so strongly of the possible effect on others. I don't mean this to be heartless and unfeeling; it's just my plea to you to live first for yourself. I'm very certain that I can give you just about everything you need, plus a few nonessential but extremely pleasant fringe benefits. Give us a chance. Please, love, give *us* a chance!"

Abruptly the tears had come, not with accompanying sounds but silently, coursing down her face, and the lump of emotion in her throat made it impossible for her to say more. With the balls of his thumbs he rubbed them away and then held her close, both arms around her, feeling the convulsive soundless sobbing shuddering through her and deeply moved by what she had said. He held her like that for a long while, until the spasms and trembling had abated, and then he raised her face and kissed her.

"It's hard for me to remember a time when I didn't love you," he said, "but I've never loved you more than I do at this moment. I only wish it were as simple for me to act as you make it seem to be, as simple to do what my heart seems to want more than anything else. But it isn't and, as much as I want to, I can't. At least not yet." He felt her stiffen and he added hastily, "I'm not saying I'm going to decide against you. Or for you. I just don't know. Not yet, Anne. Not yet." His voice seemed to be coming from a well and the inner misery it reflected practically broke her heart. "I only know that it's not possible to go on this way much longer. Not for any of us. You said you don't know what will eventually trigger me to make the decision I have to make. I don't know the answer to that. Maybe today I'll find out."

They'd talked only a little more after that, but moving away from the issue. He came to his feet and, as she followed him, kissed her fiercely and held her tightly, wordlessly, for a long moment. Then he released her, picked up his luggage and package near the door, and left with the words "I'll be back" hanging in the air behind him.

Anne had no idea how long she had remained rooted in that spot after he left or, when she finally moved again, how long she roamed pointlessly through the apartment that had become so small and so barren at his departure. Finally she had taken her shower and called her mother in Elgin.

Now she realized with a bit of a start that of the multitude of times John had left here, today was the first time she had not gone out on the balcony to get that final glimpse of him far below. She got up from the bed and, still wearing only the sheer pale green panties and not caring if she were seen or by whom, walked out onto the balcony which was bathed in bright sunlight. Heat waves rising from the concrete corridors formed by the streets made distant buildings shimmer and appear unreal. She placed her hands on the iron rail, far apart, and leaned over looking downward, her bare breasts becoming pendulous from the angle of her body. Forty-two floors below people and vehicles moved, but she didn't see them.

Anne Carpenter was wondering with detached curiosity what the effect would be of a body striking the pavement after falling from this height.

I I I

"What it boils down to, Mr. President, is that the party is extremely concerned." Ross Larkin, Democratic National Committee chairman, squinted over the top of his thick glasses at Robert Morton Sanders. "Fortunately, the Republicans find themselves in the sorry situation of having no candidate for nomination who has captured the public's imagination. If it weren't for this HAB business, there'd be no doubt in anyone's mind, of either party, that you'd be a shoo-in."

"But the party doesn't like my stand on the HAB Theory, is that it?" Sanders leaned back in his chair and let his gaze move away from Larkin to the others in the room—his advisors, Albert Jabonsky and Oscar McMillan, his aide Alexander Gordon, DNC vice-chairman Ted Worthington, and Democratic senators Gregory Talbott of Ohio, Edward Bond of Massachusetts, and Richard Arthur of California.

Worthington shot a sidelong glance at Larkin, caught a barely discernable nod, and spoke up. "President Sanders, the Democratic party has pretty much been in the driver's seat ever since the impeachment threat caused President Nixon to resign. We were on the rocks only once, when Jim Warfield got involved in that suicide scandal just before the last presidential election and we had to dump him. You stepped in as a dark horse candidate and took it, and the whole picture has done nothing but improve since then, with the exception of a slight slump in the national economy picture. That is, up to the point where this Boardman assassination attempt took place. Since then, especially in view of your stand on the HAB Theory, things have been going steadily downhill."

The President nodded at the slight behind-the-scenes politician from Binghamton, New York. Worthington, while himself not an office-seeker, was a skilled political manipulator and undoubtedly one of the most influential blacks in America. Larkin might be titular head of the DNC, but everyone knew it was Worthington who charted the course.

"The polls haven't been encouraging, Ted," Sanders admitted, "but they began moving into a valley long before the Boardman thing came up, predicated primarily on that current economic slump in conjunction with the rise in the cost of living."

"They were slumping then, it's true," spoke up Jabonsky, "but the dip's become a great deal steeper and more disturbing since the Boardman affair." There was a mildly accusing tone in his voice. "It's grown worse after each new development or statement you've given in respect to the HAB Theory."

"You wanted me to keep clear of that from the beginning, didn't you, Albert?"

"I did." Cold eyes behind rimless glasses looked at the President unflinchingly. "I thought it was a mistake then. I think so even more now."

Senator Talbott cleared his throat and spoke in a mild voice. "Mr. President, there are a lot of bad vibrations on the Hill and they're growing worse. There seems to be a general feeling that your actions in regard to this HAB thing are disturbingly impulsive and overreactive, a fear that you are stepping beyond the purview of your office in what you've already said and done and even more for what you may be planning."

"You're evidently trying to phrase it nicely," Sanders commented dryly. "What are they really saying up there? Megalomania?"

"Yes, Sir. Some of them."

"An extremely ominous increase of reactionary sentiment in both houses," put in Senator Arthur. "Mr. President, the fact of the matter is that everyone—well, almost everyone—on Capitol Hill feels you're attempting to ride roughshod over Congress. There are even some faint murmurings of impeachment. They feel you're committing this country beyond its ability to produce, either materially or financially, and that you're doing this far beyond the prerogatives of your office. They don't like it."

Sanders gave a little snort and let his gaze roll over to Bond of Massachusetts. "What's your comment, Ed?"

Senator Bond shrugged elaborately. "Pretty much what the others here have been saying. Plus the hope that you'll get off the horse you're presently riding and participate a hell of a lot more actively in the campaigning. You've still got the edge, but it may not continue that way much longer. Although they're not very happy about the way you've done it, the Hill's pretty much willing to go along with what you've already undertaken in respect to the Kenyan oil resources development. God knows we're all damned well aware of Middle Eastern pressure and anything that can be done to thwart that is apt to get approval.

"We're well aware of what Mr. Gordon accomplished there," he motioned approvingly at the President's aide, who acknowledged it with a faint nod, "and feel it is to your credit that you stepped in as decisively as you did. The opposition was caught flat-footed on that move and they're howling, but because it obviously was done in the best interest of the people, they won't get anywhere. But this current proposal to throw enormous amounts of funds, equipment, and manpower, above and beyond the oil matter, to Kenya for development of a gigantic so-called survival complex has put Congress on its ear."

That can't be helped," Sanders replied curtly. "The Ngaia City complex is going to be built, and with whatever help from the United States that it requires. I've asked Mr. Gordon to sit in today because I thought you might want to ask some questions of him along these lines. Feel free, Alex," he added, turning to his aide, "to discuss whatever they might care to ask."

"Yes, sir," Gordon said. "I think Mr. Elliott will have far more definitive remarks when he returns from the Middle East, but I may be able to help in a general way."

"It's not *our* knowledge, here in this room, of what was done and why that's the problem, Mr. President," the Ohio senator interjected. "The problem is that Congress as a whole wants the opportunity to study the entire matter at much greater length. They strongly object to being told that such-and-such is the way it's going to be. About anything. When it involves something as improbable as the HAB matter, they squeal. And, Mr. President, they're squealing loud and clear right now. I don't think you fully appreciate the trouble you're getting into."

"I'll second that," Jabonsky spoke up, an ugly expression on his face. He stood up slowly, his hard gray eyes on the President. "Sir, I'm going to be blunt. The whole HAB business is becoming ridiculous. It is bad enough when you are willing to possibly jeopardize your own career by the rantings of this lunatic who—"

"Lunatic?" Sanders's voice was cold and he was frowning.

"God damn it, sir, yes. I said lunatic and that's what I meant. What else do you call an old fool who not only gives you a Doomsday forecast but then suggests, as you told me the other day he did, that we can save ourselves by the simple little expedient of flooding and destroying every port city in the world? All we'd lose, he says, is a few piddly-ass little things like most of the world's islands, plus all of Florida and Long Island and Cape Cod and Manhattan and other such inconsequentials. Well, I say, sir, that this is all horseshit! Anyone who could believe such crap from someone so obviously insane has to be sick himself. You have a right to destroy yourself if you're bent on it, but you don't have one goddamned bit of right to destroy this country in the process. You've made me an adviser, but to what purpose, Mr. President, if you won't listen?"

Sanders was shaking his head, looking at Jabonsky in an unbelieving way. "I think you're out of line, Al. The HAB Theory must be taken seriously and that's what I'm doing. And as for Boardman's suggested solution, of course it's drastic. Anything that might possibly prevent a global cataclysm would have to be drastic. It's not workable, I agree, simply because there's no way we could ever get all nations to go along with it, but I wish to God we could." His manner did not soften much, despite his words of apology. "No, I'm sorry, Al. I hate to keep turning down your advice, but it's not in line with my thinking."

The Chief Executive let his eyes sweep over the others as Jabonsky sat down again, obviously seething. "Gentlemen, the Kenyan survival project plan is going through. If necessary, I'm prepared to call on the powers of my office to invoke the amended Emergency Appropriations Act, along with the National Security Emergency Act, or whatever else becomes necessary. I'd like Congress to be with me on this, but it will have to be on my terms. There isn't *time* for Congress to study the matter at length, Senator Bond. There never is in a time of real emergency, which is why the President is endowed with discretionary powers to act without the benefit of congressional debate in a time of emergency. And, gentlemen, we are in just such a time."

"Mr. President." Oscar McMillan was speaking up for the first time since the discussion began. "It would be considerably to your benefit if you would simply hold off for a little while. I'm not talking about the months of deliberation it sometimes takes for House and Senate action on a proposal. I'm speaking more in terms of just a matter of days. The HAB Symposium begins tomorrow and it's scheduled to last for only ten days. I'd strongly advise that you at least hold off any further action or commitment until the symposium announces its findings in respect to the HAB Theory. If they support it, then that will pretty well knock out the flak rising from the Hill. They might—in fact, almost surely will—continue to growl, but you'll have gained a tremendous amount of support. It's only," he added placatingly, "a matter of ten days."

"Those days, Oscar," the President said levelly, "could well be crucial."

"I really don't know how you can say that, sir," McMillan protested, his scalp a more distinct pink than usual and a growing edge of exasperation in his tone. "Even assuming that this HAB Theory is deemed valid, there's no real time schedule for it. We don't have as much as a glimmering of when the alleged cataclysm is supposed to occur."

"That's true enough, and I wish to God we did. I'd feel a lot better, for all of us." The President looked away, but then frowned and looked back at McMillan. "Oscar, over a week ago I directed that copies of the Grant summary of the theory be delivered to you and Al. Your continued opposition in light of that puzzles me." He turned his gaze toward Jabonsky. "Did you receive it?"

Jabonsky nodded and McMillan murmured, "Yes, sir."

Without looking away from Jabonsky the President asked softly, "And have either of you read it yet?"

Jabonsky's jaw muscles twitched and, still without speaking, he gave a small negative shake of his head. The Chief Executive turned his head and looked at his other adviser.

"Oscar?"

"No, sir," McMillan said, obviously embarrassed. "I suppose I should have made time to do so, but I didn't. It's been a busy week and too many things intervened. I apologize."

"Then I suggest," Sanders said pointedly, "that both of you do so immediately upon leaving this meeting. It becomes difficult to properly assess the value of advice from those not in possession of all the information pertinent to a particular matter."

"Yes, sir," McMillan murmured again, stung by the President's comments. Jabonsky said nothing.

Still looking at McMillan, Sanders continued. "If you had read the summary, you could perhaps better understand the position I'm assuming in this entire matter. Oscar, the best evidence we have thus far indicates that we're years—*hundreds* of years—overdue. We have got to assume the cataclysm can occur at any time, and under that assumption there is no time to waste. As I say, even a week or ten days could, in the final analysis, be crucial. I don't intend postponing anything."

"Forgive me, Mr. President." Tiny beads of perspiration now had begun showing on McMillan's sparsely haired scalp. "Despite my unfamiliarity with the Grant summary of the theory, I have to say that I think you're being unrealistic and unreasonable. Everyone does, even your own vice president. Why do you think he's keeping himself aloof from all this business? Mr. President, Jim Barrington's no fool. He knows what you're doing to yourself and to the party. He's smart enough to want no part of it. And he can't be blamed for feeling that way, sir. A little while ago, Al was pretty blunt in his remarks to you, and I'm going to have to be the same. It's painfully clear to quite a number of us that you're staking your career and the status of the Democratic party on such a nebulous premise that it smacks of irrationality."

There was a sudden silence in the room. Sanders's eyes narrowed as he continued looking at McMillan, but then the ghost of a smile tilted his lips.

"You've never been afraid to say what you think, Oscar. I value that highly, which is why you're in the position you occupy. I wouldn't find you so valuable if you agreed with all I said. I know you haven't put an ounce of faith in the HAB Theory since you first heard of it, which is your prerogative. However, I become more convinced of it every day. The Scientific Advisory Board has studied every scrap of material from the Boardman files during the past month, and do you know what their feeling is? No, of course you couldn't know, but I'll tell you now. All of you." He turned so that he was addressing the whole group in general again.

"Three weeks ago today,'" he told them, "that group of twelve top scientists met here for the first time and were briefed by John Grant on what the HAB Theory was all about. At that time I forced them into giving an opinion they didn't want to give. The only reason they did so was because I fixed it so they could answer anonymously. I asked for a simple yes or no answer to the question: is it even remotely possible that the HAB Theory is valid? I thought I might get one yes, or possibly two. As it turned out, gentlemen, *four* of them—hard-nosed scientists, mind you—answered yes. My own conviction in the validity of the theory began to crystallize at that point. Every bit of evidence gathered since then has done nothing but support it."

The President leaned forward with his arms on the desk and began slowly sliding the cast iron whale paperweight back and forth from one hand to the other while he continued talking. "Now, consider this. Each of the scientists has, as of this day, put three weeks of intensive study into the Knotts Commission report, the Grant Summary and the Boardman papers. Today I asked them the same question. *The exact same question!* Gentlemen, the response was unanimous—all yes. Dr. Dowde wasn't there, but I think it's fairly obvious her reply would have been an affirmative also."

The President's eyes went to his adviser again. "Oscar, I may be staking my career on this matter, as you suggest, by acting with such haste. I may also, in the same manner be jeopardizing the status of the Democratic party. I regret that, but I see no other way. You call that unreasonable and I suppose in a way it is, but if I can cop one of Al Jolson's phrases from 'way back, 'You ain't heard nothin' yet!'"

He stood, replacing the whale paperweight on the desktop as he did so, and looked over the group of men. "Gentlemen, my actions may be, in your view, unreasonable, but they are not irrational. I know that all of you believe I'm being highhanded, but I'm afraid it's going to get a lot worse before it gets any better. Between us, I am quite prepared at this point, if necessary, to invoke every power I have and become virtually dictatorial if that's what becomes necessary in order to get accomplished what needs to be done."

"You are definitely toying with impeachment, Mr. President." Jabonsky's warning was issued coldly.

"To hell with possible impeachment! I refuse to be intimidated by that kind of a ghost, or any other kind for that matter. Al, can't you see that in the light of what seems likely to happen to the entire earth, the matter of impeachment becomes a little ridiculous?"

"No, sir, Mr. President, I can't see that at all." Jabonsky's voice was tight, his eyes like ball bearings and his face abruptly more deeply lined, making him look years older. "I must ask you now," he added, coming to his feet again, "is that your final word to me on the subject?"

Sanders frowned, sensing something coming he would not like, but he nodded slowly and replied, "Yes, Al, that's my stand and I intend to maintain it."

"Then, sir," his adviser said, his words measured and with no trace of emotion, "I must regretfully submit my resignation, effective immediately."

There was a stunned silence in the room. The President and his adviser stared at one another for a long moment and then Sanders sighed.

"I'm really sorry to hear you say that, Al," he said, "but under the circumstances I have no choice but to accept your resignation. I wish you felt differently." He stepped toward Jabonsky, beginning to extend his hand.

"Good-bye, sir," Jabonsky said quickly and spun around before the President could reach him. "Gentlemen," he added, glancing at the others, and then strode to the door and was gone.

President Sanders dropped his partially extended hand back to his side and stood looking at the door. An oppressive and disquieting mood filled the room. At length it was Ted Worthington who broke it, coughing lightly before he spoke.

"Mr. President, if you won't alter your present stance, will you then at least take a more active role in campaigning for reelection?"

The President regarded the black man with friendly eyes. He had always liked Worthington and thought the man had a good head on his shoulders. "Ted, at this juncture it would be pointless to campaign. Whether or not I'm to be reelected revolves on just one thing, and that is what sort of conclusion is arrived at by the symposium. If it's an endorsement of the theory—and I can't believe it will be anything else—then I'm in without question. If they don't, then nothing I would do in the way of campaigning from that point on would make a bit of difference. I'll be out."

Ross Larkin, eyes hugely magnified behind his thick glasses, spoke up then. "I was talking with Steven Lace a short while before coming in here and asked him what your address to the symposium tomorrow was going to amount to. He wouldn't tell me except to say that if you wanted us to know, you'd probably tell us during this meeting. Are you planning on doing that, sir?"

Sanders looked at the chairman of the Democratic National Committee and shook his head. "No, I am not. Transcripts of the speech will be given out to the press tomorrow morning. No disclosure to anyone prior to then."

He moved toward the door to the outer office and automatically all the men rose. The meeting was over and not one man among them was pleased with the way gone. After they had filed out with murmured good-byes, Sanders shut the door and returned to his desk, his limp suddenly much more pronounced now that he was alone. He sat quietly a moment and from a dim recess of memory the words of his old friend and patron of over a quarter of a century before, Charles Clepperson, came back into focus clearly. "Don't make the mistake of trying to please everyone. You can't. You never will." Clepperson had also said at that time, "Listen to advice after this and cogitate on it but, by damn, let the decisions be yours, not anyone else's…"

Well, he'd certainly pleased no one today and he hadn't followed advice. But old Clepperson had been right. The decision was his and—right or wrong—he had made it. Now he came back to the present and punched the intercom button with unnecessary force.

"Yes, sir?"

"Hazel, I want you to get Mark Shepard on the phone for me. He's still over in Turkey somewhere. Ankara last I heard, but maybe not any longer. Maybe Istanbul if not Ankara. Find him, wherever he is. Drop everything else and get going on that right away. It's damned important. If you have difficulty locating him, call Ambassador Phipps and get him working on it. I want to talk to Mark tonight. Without fail."

I V

When the cab deposited John Grant in front of his house, his nervousness was at a peak. What would Marie say to him? What would he say to Marie? He was completely at a loss to envision how their conversation would go and his imagination had been taking him in many different directions during the ride from Marina City.

He carried his two suitcases, the briefcase and the long, oddly-shaped package—which Anne had laughingly said looked like a gigantic candy sucker on a six-foot stick—to the front door and rang the bell rather than dig for his key. There was no response and so he set the things down and walked over to the driveway. The garage door was open and the car was gone. Feeling a little better at this minor reprieve from an unpleasant time, he returned to the front door and unlocked it.

Though he was, in a way, glad to find that no one was at home, there was a sense of disappointment in one corner of his mind, the disappointment one always experiences upon returning home, expecting to find people there and instead finding no one. A house always has a peculiarly empty feeling at such a time. He set his bags down at the foot of the stairs and walked into the kitchen to glance at the sideboard, which was where notes were always left, but there was nothing there. It wasn't a surprise, because no one here knew he'd be back today, but he wondered where Marie and the children had gone.

A sense of strangeness was in him as he returned to the luggage and parcel and carried them upstairs, a feeling that he was an intruder here, that this wasn't really his home at all but a place with which he was only vaguely familiar from a long time ago. Weary from the long flight and his mind still filled with what Anne had said to him at her apartment, Grant briefly considered calling her, but then decided against it. He didn't really want to talk with her again right now. He didn't want to talk with anyone and he was glad for this time alone to try to get his thoughts in order.

In the bedroom he set the briefcase unopened on the bed and leaned the big sucker-shaped package against the dresser. Then he unpacked the suitcases, setting the cotton laundry bag with his soiled clothing in it to one side and hanging his suits in the closet. The shirts which were still clean and folded he set on the bed, knowing it would be pointless to put them in the drawers when he'd just have to get them out again later today for the trip tomorrow morning to New York. In his last telephone conversation with the President from Nairobi, Sanders had said he definitely wanted Grant to be on hand for the symposium and that Dr. Dowde had made arrangements for him to stay at the Waldorf Astoria. The President also had said he wanted Grant to call him as soon as he got back home and, remembering that, Grant broke off from unpacking and went to the bedside extension and direct-dialed the White House number. He identified himself to the operator who answered and a moment later Hazel Tierney was on the line.

"President Sanders is in conference at the moment, Mr. Grant. He's been expecting your call and told me to tell you that it won't be necessary for you to call anymore until you get to the hotel tomorrow. He has the Presidential Suite there and would like you to call as soon as you get in. He hopes you'll be able to arrive there before nine tomorrow morning."

"I'll. be there before then," Grant promised.

"Fine. The symposium begins at ten, in case you hadn't heard, and the President will give his opening address at ten-thirty. That'll be in the Felt Forum at Madison Square Garden. Are you familiar with it?"

"Yes. I'll get there all right."

"Very good. From a personal standpoint, I hope you enjoyed your stay in Nairobi."

"Yes, a great deal, thank you. I hadn't been there before, but now I definitely want to return. There's a good bit of Africa I'd like to see."

"I'm sure you'll be going back before long, Mr. Grant. Incidentally, the President is highly pleased with the way you handled matters over there. He's received a most favorable report on your accomplishments from Secretary of State Elliott."

"That was very good of him. I'm glad the President is pleased. Also that matters worked out so well in Kenya with President Ngoromu."

"Yes. Well, Mr. Grant, at your convenience you can submit your accounting of expenses directly to me, either in person or by mail, and we'll take care of it. Been nice talking with you. Thank you for calling."

He said good-bye, hung up the phone, and returned to the unpacking. It didn't take long. Two small packages, the gift-wrapping slightly mussed from the traveling in luggage, he placed atop the dresser. As soon as he was finished unpacking he called Trans World Airlines and made reservations on a flight that would put him on the ground at La Guardia at 7:14 A.M. tomorrow so he'd be able to get to the hotel well ahead of the nine o'clock time set by the President.

He took a quick shower and changed his clothes, expecting that the family would arrive home before he finished, but they didn't. He'd been home nearly an hour when he began going to the front windows to look out. He brewed a pot of coffee and took a cup of it to the front room and sat in his chair there. On the table beside the chair was a shoebox in which was assembled the mail that had accumulated during his absence. He flipped through it, looking only at the envelopes at first, setting aside those which might be important. Into that pile went two letters from his agent in New York, one from his publisher, one from *The Covenant* magazine and several others that had the earmarks of being more than ordinary correspondence.

He read them quickly, finding in them only a few matters reasonably noteworthy. *The Covenant's* managing editor George Benedict was regretful that Grant had turned down the profile assignment on evangelist Peter Proctor and had assigned the project to another writer. Also, both Grant's agent and his publisher were excited about his closeness to the HAB Theory matter and were hoping that a book would result from it. The publisher was already talking in six-figure terms, sight unseen, if he would contract for such a book.

Another glance out the window showed nothing and so he refilled his cup and went back to the mail, going through all that which he had not yet opened. Many were fan letters forwarded by his publisher, some were from friends or relatives, and others were business letters dealing primarily with research feelers he'd sent out a long while ago. None was urgent.

Two hours had passed and the wonder of where his family was began turning into worry. He went upstairs to the bedroom again and scooped up the briefcase off the bed, carried it into his den, and set it on the desk. He sat down as he opened it and began going through the contents. The small spiral notebooks filled with his impressions of Africa he placed in a stack to one side. The four cassette tape cartridges he'd filled with the same sort of material, including the one still in the recorder, he placed beside the notebooks. All this material he would transcribe as soon as he could get around to it.

There was a sheaf of papers he'd typed or had Anne type for him while there, pages that were in the nature of daily reports of his activities with officials of the Ngoromu Administration, and these he would submit to the President. He left them in their file folder, but he placed the carbon copies in a clean file jacket and placed them on the desk also, to file later on. The only thing remaining was his diary.

He opened the book and flipped through the last fifteen or twenty pages filled with his handwriting, both in English and in his own code. When he reached yesterday's date the blank pages began and now he took out his pen and began writing swiftly in English on that page.

Combining entries for today and tomorrow. The trip back to Chicago was not as pleasant as the one going—and I wasn't well then. Time seemed to pass very slowly and I was very much more uncomfortable than I recall being on the way over, perhaps because I'm very tired. Did not even get off the plane during the two-hour stop in Rome, just remained in my seat and dozed. Had to get off at London to change from BOAC to TWA, with a three-hour layover there, but didn't leave the Heathrow terminal. No bad weather encountered anywhere, fortunately, and the whole trip back was basically uneventful and tiring. On the whole, I found Africa fascinating and easily could have stayed much longer. I'll look forward to going again. Evidently there's some likelihood of that, according to an offhand remark by Hazel Tierney when I called the White House to check in after arriving home, but I didn't pursue the matter. Will find out soon enough, I'm sure. Did not talk with President Sanders today, but I'm expected at the Waldorf in New York by 9 A.M. tomorrow, so have made the necessary arrangements. Marie won't be pleased about that, I'm sure. She and the kids were not home when I arrived and still have not come back. Have no idea where they are but expect them home before long.

He paused in his writing for some time and when he began putting down words again, this time they were in code.

Anne's well aware of how upset I've been over the letter from Marie. She could hardly keep from being aware of it, since she had to get someone to help me up to the room after I'd gotten too bombed to get there myself. I was pretty sick, too. Should have known better. She took care of things nicely, but we didn't have a whole lot to talk about on the way back. All along I'd been planning for us to have 24-hour layovers in both Rome and London, but just wasn't in the mood for it and I don't think she was, either. Stopped by her apartment for quite a long while on the way from the airport to here. All we did was talk, Anne doing most of the talking. There was a sense of desperation in her. She's very frightened, wondering what's going to happen between Marie and me today. I can't blame her. I wonder, too. Anne said some pretty important things. Strongly pushy, which was no surprise, but damned pertinent. Many were things I've thought about often enough myself, but she put them into clearer perspective for me. Those, along with other matters she brought up, struck home with me deeply. I think she may have the vague, rather terrifying feeling, for her, that now with everything coming down to the wire, I suddenly don't love her as much. Nothing could be farther from the truth. I was deeply moved by all she had to say. I wonder how it is possible for me to be so close to a decision-making moment and yet remain so indecisive. Oddly enough, a minor impression of Africa, received during our first days in Nairobi, returns to mind frequently. It has a certain uncomfortable relationship to my own situation. This man was a very old native named Kambu, who stood before the Nairobi Hilton, shaking his fist with ineffectual anger at the building he claimed was built on his family's land. The justification of his claim is unimportant. What relates to my case is the persistence in the face of ineffectuality. It does no good to shriek and cry and beat one's breast about something he doesn't like. Either he must stop the self-flagellation and accept the reality, or else he must do something definitive, something along positive lines, even if they are wrong lines, to change the situation. That is my condition now. For too long I've been beating my own breast and wailing about the terrible position I am in, the dilemma I have been facing, without doing anything definitive about it. So now I will become definitive and I will take steps I should have taken long ago. There are so many factors to consider where both Anne and Marie are concerned. God help me in what lies ahead!

Grant put his pen back in his pocket and closed the diary with a sharp bang. He took it to the diary shelf and placed it on the far right. Looking at that shelf, he questioned his own wisdom in writing his thoughts about Marie, Anne, and his own state of mind as he had been doing for so long, even though they were in code. He sniffed. The question was academic, since Marie was already aware of his involvement with another woman. Still, he had written numerous things he would not want Marie to read, primarily because of the hurt they would bring her. He turned and went back downstairs, once again looking out the front window.

He glanced at his watch and saw that he'd been home three hours now. He turned away from the window, heading for the kitchen to get another cup of coffee. He was almost there when he paused, his head cocked. He wasn't sure if he'd heard something or if it was just a feeling that stayed him, but he turned and strode back to the living room window.

Marie was pulling the car into the driveway at just that moment, and he could see Carol Ann with her in the front seat and Billy in the back. They disappeared from sight around the edge of the house and he knew that Marie was pulling the car into the garage, which meant that they'd probably be coming to the back door.

He walked into the kitchen and heard the car doors close and the sound of them coming. As usual, Billy was throwing teasing digs at Carol Ann, and she, predictably, was taking offense and complaining to Marie instead of just letting it roll off her back. Through the four-paned glass of the back door leading off the kitchen he could see that Marie and Carol Ann, both in slacks, were carrying large brown bags, evidently grocery sacks. As they came up onto the back steps, he opened the door.

"Hello, Marie."

She tottered and for a moment he was sure she would drop the two bags she was carrying. He stepped out swiftly and took them from her, noting that she had paled considerably.

"Dad! Dad! You're home!" The tow-headed whirlwind named Billy practically dived into him and small arms wrapped around his waist and hugged with such surprising strength that it even hurt a little, but it was a pleasant hurt.

Another thunderbolt took him from the other side, gripping his head and bending it sideways until fifteen-year-old lips could plant a resounding kiss on his cheek. Carol Ann was holding the big grocery bag with one arm and her eyes were dancing, her grin unable to widen any farther.

"Welcome home, Daddy! Oh, I'm so glad you're back."

Marie had regained her composure a little and now she, too, moved closer and pressed cool lips to his cheek. It was mechanical at best, done for the benefit of the children, Grant knew. There was no more warmth in her eyes than had been in her lips and so he looked away from her and forced a fairly genuine smile for the youngsters.

"How can you both," he wondered aloud, "have grown inches since I left?"

"Oh, Daddy," Carol Ann said, snickering, "you're teasing. Neither of us is any taller."

"I am," Billy yelled, racing into the house and calling over his shoulder, "C'mon, Dad!"

Grant looked at his daughter and realized with a start that she was beginning to turn into a woman. He'd noticed it before and yet somehow it hadn't registered with the impact that it did now. He leaned over and kissed her forehead.

"In Billy's case, he really does look taller to me. But in your case, when I said you've grown inches," he looked at the front of her blouse, "I was not referring to height."

"Daddy! You're awful!" The artificial shock in her voice was belied by the delighted expression she wore. She wrinkled her nose at him and stepped past and into the kitchen. She couldn't restrain looking down at her own chest as she did so and partially stumbled as she crossed the threshold.

"C'mon, Dad!" Billy's voice came again from deep inside the house.

"So you're back." The words were flat. Nothing about Marie exuded any warmth at this moment.

"Yes. Did you think I wouldn't be?"

"John, I've about given up attempting to guess what you might do. Or not do." She turned and stepped into the kitchen and he followed her, setting the two bags on the counter.

"When did you get here?" she asked.

He glanced at his watch. "About three and a half hours ago. I was getting a little worried. Where'd you go? Obviously, the grocery store," he indicated the bags, "but that wouldn't take so long."

"No. Billy wanted to see Jack Coblaum for a minute and I got to talking with Jean and didn't get away for half an hour. You must have gotten home just after we left here. Anyway, then I had to stop and get some gas and go to a couple of different stores." She spoke listlessly. "It all takes time. Things are easier when there are two parents around to share the activities and chores."

The last comment was heavy with sarcasm and accusation and he moved closer to her, opening his mouth to speak, but she cut him off.

"The children don't know. Not yet, at least. I don't intend for them to, either, unless it becomes unavoidable."

"Well, as a matter of fact I had intended walking up to them and saying, 'Kids, guess what? I've been unfaithful to your mother.'"

He had meant it as a sardonic retort but it had come out with a rather brutal heaviness and he was immediately sorry. Her chin quivered and a glassiness came to her eyes, but then the full lips tightened.

"In my letter to you, which I'm presuming you received, I wondered what happened to my John, the man I love and admire, the man I married and bore children for. I wondered where he'd gone." She looked at him with infinite sadness. "I still wonder that."

She moved away, heading for the front room, just as Billy came clattering back and nearly collided with her. He veered out of the way just in time, caromed off the door jamb and churned to a halt in front of Grant. He took his father's hand and tugged on it, pulling him toward the living room.

"Wow, is that ever a crazy-lookin' package in your bedroom. Is it what I think it is, Dad?" His eyes glittered in anticipation.

Grant glanced ahead and saw Carol Ann standing in front of the sofa, an expectant look on her face, and he disengaged his hand. "We'll wait down here, son. Why don't you run upstairs and get that package you're talking about, as well as the two on top of the dresser, and bring them down here?"

Billy was at the foot of the stairs and running full tilt by the time he finished. As he thudded up the carpeted steps, Grant murmured to Marie to stay here with him and Carol Ann and all three of them sat down. Marie's eyes were overbright, but otherwise her countenance was blank.

"We've really missed you, Dad," Carol Ann said. She glanced at her mother for corroboration. "Haven't we?"

"He's been away a long time," Marie said, her words more meaningful to Grant and herself than to their daughter.

Billy came back downstairs only slightly more slowly than he ascended, the large suckerlike package in one hand, the two boxes held against his chest with the other. Grant got up and met him, taking the two boxes from him and indicating with a nod that the oddly shaped one was Billy's. The boy whooped and began tearing at the tape holding the brown paper wrapping around it. Grant handed the larger of the two boxes to Carol Ann, who maintained her composure better, but who was no less excited than her brother. She thanked him and began pulling at the wrappings.

"This is yours, Marie," he said. He handed her the final small package and she took it from him slowly, with some degree of reluctance. He glanced back at Carol Ann and smiled. She had managed to get the wrapping off hers while Billy was still struggling with the tough tape on his. She removed the lid of the box and unwrapped the heavy object inside from the tissue around it. Her eyes widened as she saw what it was an exquisite rosewood carving of a sitting cheetah, its head turned to the left and slightly cocked. The musculature was depicted with amazing accuracy and the entire carving was done in precise proportion. It was polished to the gloss of finest furniture.

"Ohh, Daddy!" she breathed. "It's beautiful! I love it." She went over to him and put her arms around his neck and kissed him on the forehead. "You did remember to bring me a cheetah, didn't you? Thank you so much. I do love it!"

"I'm glad it pleases you, sweetheart. Afraid there was no way to get you a live one. It may interest you to know that the native craftsmen over there in Kenya make carvings like that using only a machette-type knife called a parang to rough out the basic shape and then they use pieces of broken glass to do the detail work and polishing."

"Well, whoever did this one must have worked on it for months!"

"He very likely did, honey."

Billy gave out with a whoop just then. "You got it! You really got it for me!"

The long Masai spear was sword-shaped on the business end and a straight metal spike on the other, with both ends attached to a center shaft of wood a bit thicker in diameter than a broom handle. The whole spear was so beautifully balanced that Billy was able to let the midpoint of the wooden center rest on a stiffly held index finger and the metal ends, each about three feet in length, teetered up and down and then gradually slowed until they lay perfectly horizontal.

"The blade end is used in warfare and for killing lions, Billy," Grant explained, "though they don't have many wars anymore and they're supposedly prohibited from killing lions, although they still do. The spiked end is for practice throwing at trees or other targets or for resting on the ground. They never rest it on the spear end."

Billy lay it on the rug and attacked the circular section of the package and soon extracted a shield formed from an animal's hide stretched across a wooden frame and laced there with rawhide. It was painted on the facing side with black at the top, a rusty color on the bottom, and these two separated by a broad diagonal band of chalky white. It was quite an attractive and nicely made piece of equipment. Billy made a fist and tapped the shield with his knuckles and it sounded as if he were knocking on a door.

"Wow, that's really hard!" He shook his hand. "What kind of hide is it, Dad, to be so hard?"

"That one's from Cape buffalo, Billy, but sometimes they'll also use skin from rhinoceros, elephant or hippo. It's laced on the frame while still raw and dries and hardens just like you see it now. Even that heavy Masai spear could only barely penetrate it at close range. On a long throw, it'd just bounce off."

"Terrific!" Billy, still holding the shield in one hand, hugged his father around the neck and then impulsively kissed his cheek. "Thanks, Dad. Thanks a lot. Jiminy, wait'll Jack sees this!"

Marie was still holding her package, a genuine smile on her face at the pleasure the children were getting from their gifts. The smile faded as Grant turned to look at her. He pointed to the box which she held on her lap with one hand.

"Open it."

She did so and found an even smaller box within, a ring box of navy blue leather with a gold coat-of-arms embossed on it and the name *Boliniere*, also in gold, below the crestwork. She kept her head down so her eyes were hidden, but her hands were shaking as she opened it and then gave a gasp. Inside, on maroon velvet, was a superb solitary topaz, finely faceted in the traditional brilliant cut of diamonds, instead of the broad, flat-surfaced cut usually reserved for the topaz. In color it was between lemon yellow and amber and it sparkled as if with an inner life. It was mounted on gold. The topaz was the birthstone for November, Marie's birth month.

"It's...beautiful." She spoke without looking up and as she tried to say something more her voice broke and she couldn't continue. Abruptly her shoulders were heaving with silent sobs and the children looked at their father with curious concern.

"I guess Mother really likes it, Carol Ann said softly, "to react like that. It's gorgeous, Daddy."

"Gee," Billy said, scowling, "I don't know why she'd cry over that. Seems like everything makes her cry."

Grant's expression was set as he stepped to her and placed a hand on her shoulder. When she still didn't look up, he turned to Carol and Billy.

"Look, kids, your mother and I are going for a little drive together. Alone. Will you be all right for a couple hours?"

They understood, without quite knowing what it was they understood, other than that it was necessary for their parents to be alone together right now. They both nodded.

"Except that I'm hungry," Billy added.

"Rustle up a sandwich and some milk, then, or whatever you want. Will you do that? You too, Carol Ann."

Again they both nodded. Grant took the boxes and ring from Marie's loose grip and set them on the coffee table. With gentle pressure from his hand on her elbow, he brought her to her feet and they moved together to the car. They didn't speak as he backed the car out of the driveway and drove to Dempster, nor as he followed Dempster to its eastern terminus at Lake Michigan. He parked in the lot at Lakefront Park and faced her.

Marie was looking out of her side window at nothing and Grant sighed, knowing her well enough to realize that her nature was such that even now if he were to suggest it, she would gladly turn right around and go back home, not have the talk they needed to have, and be willing to put this unpleasantness behind and try to pick up the reins and continue their married life from there. For Grant it was a temptation because, as close as they were to having it out, he still had reached no decision, still didn't know if he *could* reach one. But he knew, too, that such a move would solve nothing.

A wave of sympathy for her flooded him, but he thrust it down. No. If he stayed with Marie it was most certainly not going to be on the basis of pity. Removing the keys from the ignition, he got out and walked around to the other side of the car and opened her door.

"Let's walk, Marie."

She slumped, as if shriveling within herself, but wordless got out. The closing of the car door was like a punctuation mark, a period. He directed her toward the grass and they strolled side by side there through the scattered hardwood trees, generally heading in the direction of the Greenwood Street Beach. From a distance they might have been lovers, rapt in each other to the point of oneness. Here and there were individuals or couples or small groups, but there was not the crowd that one usually found here. No one was very near them.

"It's a bad time for us, Marie."

They walked eight or nine steps in silence and when he was sure she was not going to reply he spoke again, his eyes on a large fox squirrel moving in rapid bounds ahead of them from one oak tree to another. "I know I've hurt you badly."

She glanced his way at that, the skin between her brows pinched, the hazel eyes in no way warmed by the late afternoon sun. Her long blond hair was back in a ponytail, tightening the facial skin, emphasizing the high cheekbones, heightening the severity of her expression, and yet she was still very attractive.

A woman this beautiful, this devoted to me, he thought, and here I am trying to decide whether or not to spurn her. Seventeen years, almost eighteen, through problems and pleasures, doing things together, sharing life, raising children, and I walk along here as if I had no problems at all, when ten minutes from now I may have dumped a lifetime. He shook the thoughts away and met her gaze for a moment, then looked ahead again, waiting for her to say what she seemed on the verge of saying. She didn't speak.

"For Christ's sake, Marie, say something!"

"All right, John, I will." Her voice was completely under control now, but what she said was hardly what he expected. "Why did you buy me that ring?"

"Huh? Well, it was pretty, and your birthstone, and I was bringing the kids something and so I wanted to get something for you, too. I thought you'd like it."

"Under any other circumstances, I'd be overwhelmed. I've never seen a more beautiful topaz. Somehow, though," an accusing flicker entered her eyes, "the joy and appreciation are diminished when it comes as a form of severance pay."

"That's not how it was meant!"

"Wasn't it? Don't try to con me, John, please. Not anymore. You've done it long enough already."

He grunted. "You're right there. Too long. I don't like deception, Marie. I never have."

"Really?" Her short laugh was bitter. "My, one would never suspect, would he? Not when you have such a great flair for it."

The beach was ahead of them and Lake Michigan was mirror calm, deep blue and with only the smallest of wave action lapping the gravelly sand at the water's edge. He bent and picked up a crooked section of branch from the ground, feeling the brittle bark flaking off under his grip. He swatted his own leg with it and more of the bark fell off. He dropped it to the grass. The silence was descending again and he didn't want that to happen.

"We're approaching it the hard way, aren't we? Let's be more direct. I love her, Marie, but that's not really the problem."

Her nostrils flared as she looked at him. "Then what *do* you consider the problem to be, John?"

He knitted his brows and spoke softly. "What I already told you in the letter. I love you, too."

He never even suspected the blow was coming. Her right hand flashed upward and the open palm smacked across his left cheek and temple with a loud cracking sound and hard enough to snap his head to the right. He took an involuntary step backward, mouth agape, wholly speechless.

"Liar! Liar!"

She spun away, running and almost immediately struck a tree glancingly with her shoulder and went into a disjointed, off-balance series of steps, nearly falling with each before regaining her equilibrium and rushing on. A weird moaning sound came from her as she ran. Sitting on the grass some distance away, a young couple watched curiously.

Grant called after her to stop, to wait. When she didn't, he plunged after her in great pumping strides, closing the gap. She reached the beach sand, very dry and soft this far from the water, and it swallowed her feet to the ankles. Immediately she lost both her shoes and nearly fell again, but she continued running, considerably slowed by the deep sand continuing to swallow each foot as it struck and only reluctantly disgorging it. Numerous people were on the more firmly packed sand near the water and she changed direction, angling back toward the grass for firmer footing.

Still on the grass, Grant veered to cut her off and easily closed the distance, catching her a few steps before she reached the turf. His arm swept around her waist, pulling her off her feet, and the opposing momentums so badly threw them off balance that now they did fall, but he retained his hold on her. She had lost the bow of yarn which had tied back her hair and now the blond tresses were in wild disarray. She was very nearly hysterical, the eerie moaning continuing but broken by choking, gasping sobs. They were quite a distance away from the onlookers near the water's edge, all but one of whom were rooted in place. The single exception was a broad-chested, very hairy man coming toward them.

Marie lay very limply where she had fallen and Grant sat up, pulling her to him, supporting her back with his arm and leaning her head onto his chest. His chin was atop her head and he put his other arm around her and held her closer yet.

"What the hell you think you're doin' to this woman, Mac?"

Grant looked up and saw that the man with the broad hirsute torso was standing spraddle-legged just to the right front of him, meaty hands curled into fists at his sides. He wore swimming trunks and the upper part of his body did not seem to go with the lower. On his chest, stomach and shoulders, and down his arms and onto the backs of his hands the hair was dense and black, often forming little matted curls. Below the bathing suit his legs were thin and practically hairless, weak-looking.

"You're not needed, bud. This is my wife."

"In a cat's ass she's your wife, you bastard!"

The fist thudded to Grant's right temple and he went over sideways onto the sand, pulling Marie with him. He struggled to get upright but was so dazed his limbs wouldn't seem to function properly. Marie was more successful. Sobbing still not checked, she came onto her knees and shrieked at her would-be protector.

"Go away! He *is* my husband. *Go away!*"

"You don't really need no help, lady?"

"No! Leave us alone. *Please.* Go away!"

For an instant longer the man stood there and then he glanced down at Grant who had propped himself up on one elbow, his eyes properly in focus again. The hairy bather shook his head reproachfully.

"You sure got one hell of a queer family life, pal."

As the man walked off toward the beach, Grant came to his feet a little unsteadily. He helped Marie up and, with his arm around her, they walked back in the direction from which they had come. At the point where he estimated that she had first run onto the sand he stopped and unsuccessfully cast an eye around for her shoes.

"I guess it's pointless to try to find them," he said. When she didn't object, he began walking her through the grass again toward where the car was parked. Halfway there he steered her toward a park bench and sat her on it, then took a seat beside her. The sobbing was nearly ended now and she was in much better control of herself. He took both of her hands in his and turned so he was facing her. Her chest still rose and fell heavily from the exertion of the run, and the moderate breeze that had come up kept blowing her hair into her face. Her white blouse had a small rip in the right shoulder from her collision with the tree, and it had pulled out of the butter-yellow slacks she wore. Her bare feet were a little bit grass-stained.

Grant was not quite so disheveled, but his hair was mussed. On the left side of his face the upper cheek, temple and front portion of his ear were red from where Marie had struck him, and a large, angry-looking lump was forming high on the cheekbone and temple, where the hairy bather had hit him. He started to shake his head, winced, and then gave a rueful little laugh.

"We're quite a pair, Marie."

"We always were," she said simply. "Until this year. What's happened to us, John?"

The levity left him as abruptly as it had come. "I wish I knew. My fault, whatever it is, but I'm really not sure myself. It seems that things just started happening and once they did, there was no turning back." He glanced down at her hands, still being held by his, then looked into her eyes again. "I told you that I love her, and that I love you, too. It's a fact. It's also a hell of a dilemma, Marie. I don't want to hurt either of you, yet I'm constantly hurting both. I don't want to lose either of you, yet I'm faced with making a choice, and I don't know how."

Marie's eyes were becoming glassy again and she bit her lip. "Considering the situation, I can't offer much sympathy. John, how can you do this thing? How can you even contemplate the possibility of turning your back on your own wife and children and way of life? We've had seventeen wonderful years together, with far more happy times than unhappy. Does all that mean nothing?"

"All that means a very great deal. That's the crux of the problem."

She was quiet a moment. "What can she offer you that I can't, John?" She looked away. "Is the fact that she's so much younger that important?"

He shook his head as she looked back at him. "No, not really."

"But it is a factor, isn't it? Her youth and her beauty? She's extremely beautiful, John. That's part of it, isn't it?"

He hesitated. "Partly, I suppose."

"I've always tried to be attractive for you, John. I haven't gotten fat or sloppy. I keep myself clean and well groomed and neatly dressed. I'm forty-four, but I can still pass for being in my thirties. But it's unfair to make me compete in physical looks with a girl who's very beautiful and only twenty-eight."

Grant nodded. She was right, of course. He had rarely, if ever, encountered any woman who looked so attractive at forty-four as Marie. A thought struck him and he frowned.

"I know you saw her at the airport with me, but how could you know she was twenty-eight? Another thing, it seems to me that one of the first things you'd want to know is who the other woman is her name and background and such, and how we met. Yet, you haven't even mentioned it. Why not?"

"Because the important thing to me, John, is where we stand, you and I, and what lies ahead for us. What is it you want that I can't provide and she can? Is she sexually that much better?"

Grant looked at her steadily and then slowly nodded, choosing his words carefully. "I suppose that's part of it. I've never found you to be an inadequate sex partner, Marie, but I have to say, too, that I've never experienced sex in a more satisfying way than with her."

Marie's eyes began smoldering again. Her nostrils flared and the words were heavy with bitterness. "Most whores perform better in bed than wives do. They've had a lot more practice."

"Don't, Marie. That's not necessary." He squeezed her hands. "You'll just get us both upset."

She jerked her hands away from him. "Not necessary? *I'll* get us both upset? Let me tell you something, John Grant, whatever upset we're experiencing has not been of my doing. And as for your precious fucking Anne, she's nothing more than a scheming, home-wrecking whore!"

"Damn it, Marie, stop! Name-calling isn't going to help. We've got to—" He broke off and stared at her. "You said 'Anne.' How do you know her name?"

"I know a great deal more than you think I know. Do you think I live in a complete vacuum? Of course I know her name is Anne. I know when you met her and I know how long you've been screwing around with her. I know that you go from me to her, and I wonder how you can live with yourself, doing that."

"When did you find out? How?"

"A thousand years ago, that's when! At least that's how long it seems. Why are you doing this to me, John? Why? What have I ever done to make you want to hurt me like this?"

"Marie, I want to know. How did you find out?"

"How? I'll tell you how. I found out because my brilliant, intelligent, thoughtful and considerate husband had the inconceivable gall to put it all down in black and white, that's how!"

He was thunderstruck. "My diaries! Damn it, Marie, you've been reading my diaries!" He came to his feet and took a few steps away, then whirled back to face her angrily. "How could you dare to invade my privacy like that? It was even in code! By what right do you go picking around through the innermost private thoughts a man has?" He felt sick inside at the realization that she had read his personal writings.

Now she stood, feet apart, facing him and no less angry than he. "How *could* I? Jesus Christ Almighty, John, you're actually asking how *could* I? Well, God damn it, I'll tell you how! Because suddenly the man I loved was becoming a stranger to me. Because a man who had always loved his wife and children and his way of life was suddenly moping around in a mucky wallow of self-pity, for God knows what reason. Because a man who is a fine writer was suddenly unable to write. Because he was depressed and unhappy and because his wife was concerned and wanted to help him. Because his wife was sick with what was happening to them and yearned for the happy days they used to have. And because she found that her man—her honest, candid, trustworthy husband of seventeen years—was suddenly writing more in a childish code than he was writing in English. And because in her naive way she thought maybe if she knew what was troubling her husband, depressing him, making him unhappy and unable to work or enjoy life, she could somehow help him. *Help* him, John, not look for some sort of evidence to club him with!"

His voice was strained. "Doesn't it stand to reason, Marie, that since the writing was in code it was private? The fact that the books themselves are diaries should have underlined their privacy. For you not only to open them at all in the first place, but to then figure out the code and decipher the most private thoughts written…" he flung out his arms in a helpless gesture and then let them fall back to his sides.…I just don't understand how you could do that. I never would have believed it."

"No," she said, a bit more calmly. "I wouldn't have believed it either. I was ashamed and sick. I still am. But this shame and sickness was the result of my concern for you. For *you!*. I wanted to help. The only problem was, I started too late. Your sweet little Anne already had her hooks deeply embedded before I began to read what you'd written."

She folded her arms in front of her and then turned her back to him, her shoulders rising and falling as she took a deep breath and went on without facing him. "Do you know, when I first came to the entries where you felt this…this…*pressure* inside you, when you expressed the need for someone different, I could almost understand. I couldn't feel that way myself. You know that you're all that I've ever wanted or needed. But I know that you're a man and men feel pressures of this sort in a different way than women do, and I could understand that, and my heart wept for you."

She turned to face him again. "Do you know what I wished for you as I went from entry to entry and saw the pressures growing, eating at you? I actually found myself wishing you would find that certain someone who would be a difference—a sexual difference. It was a hurt to me, because it made me feel I was inadequate, but I would have been happy to bear that hurt if, in relieving that pressure in you, it could have made you happy. But you couldn't be satisfied with just a sexual fling, could you? *Could* you? You had to fall in *love!*"

"I didn't go out looking for love, Marie. I didn't ask for it. I didn't want it. But suddenly it was there. How do I explain how it happened when you can't possibly understand the reality of it without experiencing it?" He moved closer to her and she turned her back to him. He stopped behind her and raised a hand to touch her, to take her shoulder and turn her around to face him, but then he dropped it without contact.

"The fact of the matter," he went on grimly, "is that I met Anne and abruptly was in love with her. It grew too fast to put it aside. It became as important to me as the love that you and I shared all these years. That's my problem. You think I don't love you anymore, but you're wrong. I do. Do you think—*really believe*—that I'd be going through the worst form of hell I've ever gone through in my life if there was any doubt of that? Don't you think I've wished—damn it, actually *wished!*—that I loved one or the other of you less than the other?"

Now he did reach out and turn her around and he saw that there were tear tracks running down her cheeks. She jerked her head away, and there was an unspeakable sadness in his voice as he continued.

"Marie, you contend that a person can't love two people to the same degree. What about our children? Do you love Carol Ann more than you love Billy? Or vice versa?"

"That's a different kind of love entirely, and you know it!" she flared. "That's not the love of lifetime sharing, the love of a man and a woman for one another. And since you've brought it up, what *about* our children, John? Don't they figure in here somewhere? Aren't they important to you? Don't they represent something very special?"

For the first time she reached out to him, touching his arm. "John, Billy and Carol Ann are *our* children. They need two parents, not just one. It goes far beyond a matter of financial security for them. We know they'll have that, but they need a father and they need a mother. They need the full-time love and training that two full-time parents can give. They need understanding and guidance from both. They need love—mine *and* yours. I don't want to raise them alone. They're *our* children, John, not mine. They're our responsibility and it's a responsibility we have to share equally. You tell me that you love Anne and me the same. I can't really accept that, but let's say for the sake of argument that you do. Don't the children add some weight of consideration on this side? John, you're just not thinking clearly. Consider this: on the one side there is your wife, your two children, your home, your established way of life, your conveniences, your friends, *our* mutual friends, our relatives, our adjustment to one another over nearly eighteen years, our mutual memories of shared happiness and sorrow, a lifetime of being together with still many years to go. On the other hand, there is this slut, this whore with whom you've shared clandestine love and experiences for only half a year. What else does she have to offer beside a good screwing? What else? The promise of future happiness? Hah! That's a laugh and you know it. You're a man of sensitivity, John. You always have been. She's pulled the wool over your eyes, for God's sake, can't you see that? You could never be happy under such circumstances, knowing what you'd done to the children and me in order to be with her. Isn't it in order to question how and where she became so skilled in bed? Doesn't the sort of past that suggests give you some sort of pause? You've written about her great conversational ability. Am I, then, that much of a drag to converse with? Am I so much more stupid than she?"

She turned and started to walk slowly through the grass, her shadow stretching out far behind her in the rays of the rapidly setting sun. Hands in pockets, Grant fell in beside her, thoughtful. She was looking at her own bare feet moving in the grass as she spoke again.

"You say you can't make a decision between us. For the life of me, John, I can't see why not. Virtually everything is weighted in my direction if, as you say, you really love me. We've talked of a lot of things, a lot of factors which must influence your decision. There are a few others. Can you so easily turn your back on your responsibilities? Can you so conveniently overlook your obligations? I asked before, what happened to the man I married? That man had moral uprightness, honesty, a strong sense of ethics, a vast degree of consideration, a revulsion for deceit. Have you abrogated these virtues? Do they mean nothing to you anymore? Can you abdicate your own responsibilities and obligations?" She looked at him, her chin beginning to tremble again. "Maybe *you* can, but the man I married could not."

Their car was not far away now and they moved toward it, not speaking for twenty or thirty steps. Then Grant spoke again and his voice seemed to be coming from a long way off.

"I've argued those very points in my own mind for months, Marie. I've tried to consider everything which should be considered. If it were possible for me to set the calendar back to a time before meeting Anne, I would gladly do so. But I can't. It has happened and I love her.

He took her arm and held it as they approached the car, then continued to hold it as they stopped beside the car on the passenger side.

"I don't really know what more to say at this point, Marie. Obviously, we're going to have to talk more—much more—but at the moment I think we're both pretty well talked out and emotionally drained. I guess we'd better go on home. I have to repack my things. I'm catching a flight to New York in the morning. The HAB Symposium starts tomorrow and before it begins I have to get in touch with the President. I'll be in the Waldorf Astoria."

She was unresisting, almost puppetlike as he helped her into the car, shut the door and went around and climbed in behind the wheel. Although he slid the key into the ignition switch, he didn't turn it on. Instead, he turned to face her and was abruptly appalled at how she looked. The faint lines of her face had become more deeply etched and harsher. What little color had been in her cheeks had drained away, leaving them ashen, and the normally warm eyes had taken on a lackluster coldness that Grant had never seen before. The full lips had thinned into a straight, colorless line and she looked years older. The whole physical aspect of her was so altered that it was suddenly as if he were seated beside a strange woman he had never seen before and he experienced a repellency toward her that was shocking in its strength. She didn't raise her voice when she spoke, but there was a grating harshness in what she said and the words were flat and cold.

"You're going with that whore-bitch, aren't you?"

His jaw muscles clenched and he shook his head. "I'm going alone."

"Lying bastard! Lying, cheating, heartless son of a bitch!"

"Marie!" He was stunned.

"You son of a bitch!" she repeated. "Miserable fucking son of a bitch!"

"Damn it, Marie, stop!" He reached out a hand to grip her arm but jerked it back as her nails dug into the flesh. She raised both hands, the fingers curved into claws, poised to strike.

"Touch me again and I'll dig your eyes out," she hissed.

They stared at one another for a long frozen period and then gradually her hands lowered to her lap and rested there as clenched fists, colorless bony extensions of her arms. She averted her eyes from him and sat stiffly, staring straight ahead, saying nothing.

He exhaled heavily, started the car and pulled out of the parking lot onto Dempster heading west. No further words passed between them on the way to the house. For now, there was nothing left to say. But as startling as the change had been in Marie, so too, on this drive back to Bobolink Terrace, there was a change in John Grant. It was not as outwardly apparent a change as Marie's, but it was no less significant. Something had just gelled for him. Something that had been in the back of his mind ever since listening to a couple of Anne's comments this morning in her apartment.

First she had said, "I can't imagine what will finally trigger you, " and then later on she had inadvertently provided the key to triggering his decision, in the comment she had made just prior to his departure. She had told him, "Only you can determine how you will live your life, John. Other people, myself included, exert an influence, but the final decision you make should be made on the basis of what's best for you, not them, and once again that includes me. What brings you the most happiness is what counts."

It was necessary to slightly alter what she said, but he knew now that his decision would not be predicated on which direction carried the promise of the most happiness for him, because he knew that no matter what decision he made, he was going to be unhappy. It had now become the simpler matter of deciding which choice would result in the unhappiness he could best bear to live with for the rest of his life.

Before they pulled into their driveway, John Grant had made his decision.

V

Alexander Gordon reached his apartment on Park Road in Columbia Heights about twenty minutes before midnight. The lights on the Tivoli Theater marquee a few doors away at the corner of Park and Fourteenth were dark as he passed, although a number of people were just then leaving the place. As happened on rare occasions, there was a parking place just opening up in front of his building, evidently a theater patron pulling away. He continued a half-block to the corner of Holmead Place, made a U-turn there and came back to the spot and parked.

It had taken him only about fifteen minutes to get there from the White House, and he wished he could make such good time in the mornings. Usually it was closer to half an hour. He arched his back as he walked up the steps into the building, a grating weariness riding him. He felt as if he'd been running at top speed ever since the Boardman assassination attempt, and especially so since the change of jobs to work closer with the President. Now, with the HAB Symposium due to begin tomorrow, there certainly wasn't going to be any letup in the pace for a while. First thing in the morning he'd be flying with President Sanders to New York for the opening address to the members of the symposium, and how long they'd stay up there after that was uncertain. The Chief Executive had indicated he might want to remain for the entire first day sessions.

He muttered when he saw that the light for the outer entry room of the apartment building had burned out again, and he had some difficulty finding his mailbox key and getting it into the keyhole of his own box in the vague illumination coming from the inner entry light. He pulled out two or three letters and a couple of occupant mail folders, shut the box, and then used a second key to open the inner door. He walked up the stairs to the second floor, the carpeting muffling his footfalls. A moment later he was unlocking his own apartment door.

It wasn't a very large apartment—living room, bedroom, bath, and combination kitchen-dinette area—but it suited his needs for the most part. There were times, though, when it seemed very cold and unhomelike to him. His was an isolated and somewhat lonely existence, and that was part of the reason he didn't mind all the erratic hours and unusual demands of his job. There was really nothing here at the apartment to make him want to hurry home.

He tossed the mail on the kitchen table and was turning away, beginning to take off his suit coat, when he abruptly stopped and turned back. A foreign-looking stamp had caught his eye and he swiftly separated that envelope from the others and felt a quickening of his pulse. It was an airmail envelope and the stamp was a beautiful thing depicting a fine sable antelope in the foreground with a snow-capped peak hazily in the background. Gordon recognized the peak as Mount Kenya. The handwriting on the envelope was Narai Ngoromu's.

Taking it across the living room to his comfortable old overstuffed chair, he flicked on the floor lamp and sat down, ripping open the envelope as he did so. There were three tissue-thin pale blue pages with Narai's distinctive right-slanting cursive in clean lines.

Nairobi, Kenya, E.A.
June 27th—10 A.M.

Dear Alex,

Less than three hours ago you left for the States and for the first time Nairobi seems a lonely place for me. I'd probably be even lonelier except for what happened in the interval since your departure, which is the principal reason for writing you so quickly.

Shortly after getting home, I had a call from Father at the Capitol, asking me to come there as soon as I could, so I left at once. I was a little concerned that something was wrong but, to the contrary, things could hardly have been more right. I was ushered right into his office and both our ministers of internal development, Kibwe Bomba, and Foreign affairs, Wautura Kelemmo, were there. I'm sure you've met them. There were also a couple of men I didn't know who were from Nairobi University, Dr. David Gulma and Dr. Bura Baodada, the former a physicist and the latter a professor of archaeology.

Father said both the professors would be attending the HAB Theory Symposium in New York, and so would Mr. Kelemmo. He then asked if I would care to go along and more or less observe from a roving standpoint—you know, sticking my head in here and there at the various meetings to just sort of get a general feeling of what the different groups will be discussing. The professors, of course, are going to be rather busy with their own particular groups, and Secretary Kelemmo can be on hand for only two days, as he has some meetings scheduled with your own Secretary of State Ellis and an undersecretary.

At any rate, knowing you were going to be there, too, I gave the matter grave and prolonged consideration—I must have mulled it over in my mind for at least a second or two—and agreed. Thus, dear Alex, I am going to be seeing you again sooner than either of us expected, and I'm delighted.

Now I'm back home, dashing this off in the hope it'll reach you in Washington before you leave there. I'd see you anyway in New York, but I thought you'd be glad to know I was coming. I warn you, however, I'm going to be very demanding in taking up all your free time (provided you have any) and probably hanging around close by when you're not so free. I don't know if you're aware of it or not, but Father thinks quite highly of you. {His daughter—the eldest one—agrees with him.}

I won't take the time to write much more, since this should get on the plane this morning if it's to reach you, but you might be interested in knowing that matters are still moving swiftly here. Some of this following you certainly know, but let me touch upon it briefly anyway. Based on the Boardman opinion that the pivotal point will be on the Kenyan coast at Formosa Bay, about three miles east of the little town of Kalima Simba, Father has already begun gearing our transportation department for the highway work that will have to be done from Mombasa and Nairobi to the site where Ngaia City is being constructed. The present road up the Indian Ocean coast from Mombasa is a good tarmac road for the first 74 miles to Malindi. Plans are to start immediately in making this into something of a superhighway—our first—with a similar two-lane road paralleling it, each road then to have one-way traffic. From Malindi this double highway will then continue northeastward along the secondary road route from Malindi to Kalima Simba. Future plans call for dredging out the close-to-shore shallows there and making a port suitable for medium-sized freighters at least. From Kalima Simba, the new highway with go directly west by northwest for exactly 75 miles to an expansive plateau (elevation approximately 540 feet) which overlooks the valley of the Tiva River. This is about ten miles east of the eastern border of Tsavo National park and about twenty miles east of the village at present, which is Dadia Badada, located inside Tsavo. On the plateau is where the initial groundbreaking took place which you already knew about. The reason I'm telling you all this is that Father asked if I'd drop you a line and let you know. He thought President Sanders might like to know immediately the exact, rather than just the general, whereabouts of the site we've selected, and that you could pass the information on to him more simply than going through normal channels.

Must fly…literally! I may even beat this letter to America, though I doubt it. I'll see you sometime during the day on July 1.

Cheers!
Narai

P.S. We'll be staying in the Plaza Hotel on Central Park South.

Alexander Gordon put the letter down on his lap, leaned his head back, and closed his eyes. He remained that way for perhaps five minutes, thinking. He had been reasonably sure that he would find the HAB Theory Symposium fairly interesting. Now he suddenly had no doubt of it.

He got to his feet and walked to the bathroom, stripping off his tie as he did so. He flicked the wall switch and then looked at his own reflection in the medicine cabinet mirror and shook his head.

"Man, you know what?" he asked himself aloud. "You grin any wider and you're going to lose the top two-thirds of your head!"

But he didn't heed his own warning and the grin became even wider, and then a low, rumbling laughter welled up from deep in his chest.

V I

It was exactly midnight in Washington when Robert Sanders's transatlantic call from the White House got through to President Daniel Ngoromu in Kenya.

"A surprise and pleasure to hear from you, Mr. President," Ngoromu said. "I trust that the First Lady is well?"

"Yes, she is, thank you. And your family?"

"All very well, thanks. Now, how may I help you?" His deep laughter suddenly came through the receiver. "I have to admit I experience a certain trepidation in asking that. You might tell me."

Robert Sanders laughed with genuine amusement. "Is it as bad as that?"

"Worse. You've rather roiled up what heretofore has been a somewhat sleepy little country." He laughed again.

"It's just the start, President Ngoromu." Sanders was more serious now. "Tomorrow…no," he corrected himself, "it's today, now. Today begins the HAB Symposium."

"Yes?"

"A lot of interesting things will be coming up. There's bound to be a lot of argument and discussion along many diverse lines. However, there's one thing I feel certain of."

"Yes?"

"I don't really have any strong doubt that there will ultimately be acceptance of the HAB Theory by the scientists attending."

There was a pause and then Ngoromu spoke slowly. "Considering what your John Grant had to say, I'd be inclined to agree. And, in view of your expressing this belief, I'm even more inclined to think it is likely. Obviously, you know much more than I about the whole matter."

"That's true," Sanders admitted, "though I wanted you to know that I've dispatched a special courier who's bringing you full information on everything I know to this point. Everything, without exception. For your eyes only, of course."

"Of course. Is that what you've called about? To alert me of the courier coming?"

"No, not really. Have you given any thought to what the result is going to be when the full impact of all this hits the public everywhere in the world?"

"It's already begun to hit, President Sanders," Ngoromu said, a touch of irony in his voice. "So, to answer your question, yes, I have given it thought. A great deal of thought."

"You know you're going to be inundated with people who will do anything to be at the safest place in the world when the cataclysm occurs."

"I know it very well. It's begun already. We have problems. I don't have any idea what the answer is. Do you?"

"I don't," Sanders said. "I wish I did. I wish I could help. It's going to be difficult for you. You'll have to be very hard."

"I'll have to be, yes. As you say, it won't be easy. But then, it's difficult for you, too, over there."

"That's politics, not lives. I don't have to turn away millions of people banging on my country's door for entry."

"No," Ngoromu said softly, then added, "No, you don't. But somehow we'll manage. We'll have to.

There's no choice."

"I'm sorry to have put you in this position."

"Don't be. We'll manage. I'm sorry about our limitations, but it's pointless to wish for what is not. Was there anything else?"

"No, I guess not. I just wanted to be sure you were aware of—"

"We're aware," Ngoromu interjected. "Painfully so. You'll continue to be in touch often?"

"Yes. I'll reach you at once with any new development."

"Good. We'll do our best on this end, but we're going to need a lot of help. A great deal more than either of us thought initially."

"I know. I'm taking steps so you'll get it. And not only from us. It's all laid out in the packet you'll be receiving."

"Fine." He hesitated. "Mr. President?"

"What?" said Sanders.

"For what it's worth, I deeply admire you as a leader."

Sanders smiled. "Thank you, President Ngoromu. That means a great deal to me. Good luck to you."

9

By reason of the constant and repeated destructions by water and fire, the later generations did not receive from the former the memory of the order and sequence of events.

—Philo of Alexandria

Man can learn nothing unless he proceeds from the known to the unknown.

—Claude Bernard

I

A subdued hum of voices arose from the nearly thirty-seven hundred scientists assembled in the spacious Felt Forum auditorium of Madison Square Garden at Manhattan's Pennsylvania Plaza. The seats were very comfortable and the atmosphere reasonably relaxed, yet with a peculiar electric excitement evident in all who had gathered for the ten o'clock opening of the HAB Theory Symposium.

Here and there in the audience could be heard occasional muted laughter punctuating the voices, but this gradually ceased as the time drew closer for the opening of the program. Many of those already seated were studying material from the packets of printed matter they had received upon registering.

At the front left were the members of the press—newspaper reporters, television and radio commentators and newscasters, along with a scattering of magazine writers. Earlier, many from this section had been moving about through the audience, pausing here and there to take brief statements from the galaxy of scientists present and occasionally bathing small areas in bright lights as they filmed brief interviews for later newscasts. Even these men and women of the press, however, soon began filtering back to their own seats in anticipation of the opening remarks.

At precisely ten o'clock, the auditorium lights dimmed, although they did not go out completely, only enough to highlight the more brilliantly illuminated stage. On each side of this stage a trio of Secret Service men dressed in business suits stepped out and stood quietly waiting while, at the same time, the chunky figure of Dr. Irma Dowde emerged from the wings and walked briskly toward center stage, followed by half a dozen men and four women. The ten took seats in a line of chairs a short distance behind the podium, but Dr. Dowde walked directly to the lectern and waited, smiling, for the applause that had broken out to run its course and die away.

"I'd say the old girl's really basking in her glory now," dryly commented Dr. Chester Pearson, of the Royal Society of Geologists in London, during the applause.

"Probably so," said his attractive seatmate to his left, Dr. Esther Gill of Smith College's Ancient Studies Department, "but why not? She's the best. I know. I studied under her for two years at the University of Chicago. She's just what archaeology has always needed."

A number of photographers had left their seats in the Press Section and were now in the space between the front row of seats and the stage, strobe lights winking brightly as they took their pictures. The applause ended but the flashings continued and Irma Dowde's smile disappeared. She directed a somewhat stern look at the still-active photographers and most of them took the cue and quietly moved back to their seats. Ignoring the few who remained, she turned her attention to the audience and again allowed herself a smile.

"I welcome all of you here for the opening of what has every promise of being the most important scientific symposium ever held anywhere. For those of you who may not know me, I am Irma Dowde, curator of archaeology for the United States National Museum in Washington, and chairwoman of this symposium.

"As all of you are aware, what, we begin here today must be of far-reaching consequence. We here must accomplish, in the limited span of the ten days allotted to this symposium, what each and every one of us present would prefer having ten months or perhaps even ten years to study thoroughly before arriving at any conclusions. That is not possible, for reasons which are apparent to all who have read the HAB Theory summary. It is my intention to move matters along with the utmost careful speed and, in that respect, lengthy speeches cannot be permitted—and I include myself."

A smattering of laughter and a small applause broke out at this. "That'll be the day!" laughed Wes Templeton, NBC-TV news reporter. "Whenever Fitz has her on *The Tonight Show*, forget about anyone else getting a word in edgewise."

"Amen!" seconded the lanky *Chicago Sun-Times* reporter beside him, Robert Beltz. "I'd have enough for a book if I compiled all the notes I've taken of what she's said during interviews of her I've covered in Chicago."

"Maybe so," interjected the young and pretty woman to Templeton's right. She was an Oriental, clad in modern dress, and she leaned forward to answer Beltz. "But it's damned seldom she's just bumping her gums. By golly, when she talks, it's worth listening to." She was Keiko Uehara of the *Atlanta Constitution*.

"I'll go along with you both," Templeton said, still laughing, "but you have to admit, she's always good copy."

"Amen!" Beltz repeated.

On the stage, the subject of their comments glanced behind her at the ten individuals seated there. "Without further ado," she went on, "I would like to briefly introduce to you the people up here with me who have already had a great deal to do with the matter before us, and who will continue to be of value during the course of the symposium and whatever follows. I'll ask that you refrain from any applause and that these individuals rise and acknowledge their introductions. Beginning from your left, then, Dr. Jason Robinson, curator of geology at the Smithsonian Institution in Washington, D.C., who is vice-chairman of the President's special Scientific Advisory Committee."

Robinson, a pudgy, round-faced man in dark gray suit and conservative maroon tie, came to his feet, smiled and raised a hand, but then sat down again without speaking. Beside him, a totally bald man with shiny dome, and just as conservatively dressed in a navy blue suit, gripped the arms of his chair preparatory to rising. Dr. Dowde turned her glance to him and continued.

"Next is Dr. Frederic Gottlund, director of the National Museum of Austria in Salzberg, who is well known for his important contributions to the field of paleontology. Dr. Gottlund arrived here nearly a week ago and has been of considerable help in the symposium preparations. Dr. Gottlund?"

Seated in the audience, Dr. Pierre Deschault, aquiline-featured professor of paleontology formerly with the University of Paris and now director of the Paris Academy of Sciences, snorted aloud and looked at Madame Yvonne Deschault, herself a paleobotanist.

"Pah!" he growled softly, then spoke to her in their native tongue, "Gottlund is a windbag and a fool. It is *I* who should be up there."

"You're right, cheri," replied Madame Deschault. "You should make inquiry into why he was chosen instead of you."

On stage, the Austrian scientist had risen as the introduction was made but sat down again immediately as the heavy-set American archaeologist went on with her introductions without pause.

"From the Royal Museum in London we have next its curator of anthropology, Dr. Alice Anderson, who has also been of considerable aid to me here with symposium-related matters."

Dr. Anderson, dressed neatly but somewhat severely in a medium brown knit dress, stood and acknowledged the introduction with a wide smile and then sat down again without comment. About thirty-eight, she was a handsome woman with shoulder-length ash-blond hair which she touched briefly upon resuming her seat.

Irma Dowde nodded at her and then turned her attention to the man seated to Dr. Anderson's left. Of average height and weight, he wore a light blue seersucker suit and a large, perfectly atrocious pink bow tie.

"Next comes the chairman of the President's special commission to inquire into the HAB Theory, Mr. Kermit Knotts. He is responsible for amassing and assembling the Herbert Boardman papers for the President's Scientific Advisory Committee and for the transcript of the John Grant summary of the HAB Theory, which each of you received as you registered for this symposium."

Knotts came halfway to his feet before settling back without comment.

"Mr. Knotts," Dr. Dowde continued, "will be putting his staff's special skills to work during the days ahead as well, to correlate each day's sessions of what we cover, and will present a written report in summarization not only to the President but also for Xeroxing and distribution each morning to everyone present."

She turned her attention to the attractive, smartly dressed middle-aged woman to the left of Knotts. "Of great assistance to Mr. Knotts in his past efforts in the HAB matter and presently aiding me here in New York is a specialist in library science who was formerly head of the Microfilm Cataloging Department for the Library of Congress. We are honored to have her with us today, for she is the person who knew Herbert Allen Boardman better than anyone else: his daughter, Elizabeth Boardman, of Oak Park, Illinois."

Liz Boardman came to her feet and moved in a poised manner to stand beside Irma Dowde at the lectern. There was an expectant hush in the audience as she looked across the expanse of faces while strobe lights flashed.

"I am not a scientist," she said, speaking hesitantly at first, "but at present only a high school librarian. I do not know whether the postulations made by my father are valid or not. That is a matter which will be determined here. Irrespective of whether or not they are proven, I can only say that my father, in all the years I knew him, was an honest man, and with all the fiber of his being he believed in what he was doing and in the truth of what he felt he had discovered. I feel peculiar in my own emotions at present; in one way longing for scientific recognition of what he has done and an acceptance of his theory among you, which would serve as a vindication of the extreme actions he took during the last days of his life…" her voice broke slightly at this point, but she quickly recovered and went on, "…while on the other hand hoping, for the sake of humanity, that you here, with your great scientific knowledge, will be able to show his postulations to have been in error. Though he never sought recognition for himself—only for his theory—I wish he could have lived to see this day. All my life I was very proud of him, but never more than at this moment."

She paused as if she meant to say more, but then simply turned and went back to her seat. A loud applause swept through the audience. It lasted for quite a while and then, as it died away, Dr. Dowde introduced the man seated beside her.

Very active in the HAB Theory investigations from the beginning is the esteemed writer, Mr. John Grant, who has compiled the HAB Theory summary and who has been serving as special aide and adviser to President Sanders."

"Good Lord!" whispered Narai Ngoromu, seated toward the rear of the huge room and suddenly sitting more upright, "there's John! I didn't even notice him when they walked in." She laughed lightly. "I'd better be more observant than that if I'm to learn anything from this whole business for Father."

Beside her, the burly Kenyan minister of foreign affairs, Wautura Kelemmo, smiled broadly and whispered in reply, "Might it be, little lady, that you missed noticing Mr. Grant because your eyes were searching for someone else we've not yet seen?"

The half-dozen thin gold circlets about Narai's wrist jangled lightly as she squeezed Kelemmo's arm on the seat's armrest in reply and nodded.

Back on the stage, John Grant, after standing and immediately sitting down again without comment, had turned his attention to the dapper, bespectacled man in his late twenties who was seated beside him, smiling at him even as Irma Dowde began the introduction.

"As presidential press secretary," the chairwoman went on, "Mr. Steven Lace is a man many of you recognize already. Mr. Lace has a few remarks he wishes to make at this time."

Lace, owlish in his spectacles and with some typewritten pages in his hand, came to the rostrum and took a moment to place the papers neatly before him, although then he looked up and to his right toward the Press Section, which was suddenly more alert, and did not again return his attention to the sheets.

"Mostly at this time," he said in his high-pitched voice, "I wish to make a short statement to the press members present. As you know, President Sanders will be giving the opening address here in a few minutes. Taking news film of the President's talk for broadcast later in the day is permitted but, as you've already been advised, no live telecasts are to be made. Copies of the full text of the President's speech have been available for distribution to the press at a desk which has been set up in the lobby. Those who have not yet received a copy can get it after this meeting is concluded. The copies are limited and will be distributed only to bona fide members of the press who present their credentials. All photographers and other persons present are requested to remain in their seats during the President's address. Thank you."

There was no applause as he returned to his seat without the typewritten pages. None of the three remaining individuals to be introduced made any comment. The first was Dr. Irene Rutman of the Royal Academy of Archaeology in the British Museum, a stern-faced woman of about fifty, dressed in a light gray suit with her hair pulled into a tight bun at her nape. Dr. Heljad Thorgeld, famed geologist and director of the Danish Royal Museum in Copenhagen, was nearing sixty, tall and of serious mien, with thick dark hair quite gray at the temples and chiseled Scandinavian features. These two were acting as symposium coordinators under Dr. Dowde. Finally, there was a petite redhead of about twenty-four, with a good figure and pretty features, wearing a salmon-colored outfit belted at the waist with a white braided cord. She was introduced in glowing terms by Dr. Dowde as Kathryn Lever, an invaluable assistant and aide in helping with the multitude of details involved in setting up the symposium, as well as a doctoral candidate in archaeology at the University of Michigan, doing advanced work in this field at the Smithsonian for the summer.

Over a quarter of an hour had been taken up in the opening remarks by Dr. Dowde and her introductions of those on the stage with her. Now, with a quick glance at her wristwatch, she began speaking rapidly, obviously in an effort to touch upon a variety of matters it was important for those on hand to know.

"Because of the large registration figure for this symposium—one of the largest ever assembled—it would be impractical and needlessly time-consuming to attempt to hold general forum-type meetings each day. Instead, schedules and assignments have been drawn up which place from fifty to a hundred individuals into fifty separate groups. Unfortunately, no one hotel has space enough to hold all these groups, so they will gather daily in the meeting rooms of various hotels. The schedules and assignments already are posted in the lobbies of the hotels where the meetings are to be held. These hotels are the Waldorf Astoria—which is where the headquarters suite is located—the Americana, Statler-Hilton, Park Lane, Sherry-Netherland, Taft, Sheraton-East, Dorset, St. Moritz, Regency, Essex House, New York Hilton, Drake, and Plaza. Please check one of these lists as soon as possible after leaving here, since the first sessions are scheduled to begin at three o'clock this afternoon."

There were some mutterings at this, as well as some pleased expressions, but Dr. Dowde paid no attention and went on with what she was saying.

"For each such group, a coordinator has been selected who will act as chairman and moderator. Highly qualified stenographers have been hired to take minutes of each of the meetings, and these notes will be transcribed and summarized at the close of each day. Each evening at eight o'clock, the fifty group coordinators will meet with me in the Barron Suite of the Waldorf, at which time an effort will be made to further summarize the data from all the groups during that day. This material will then be typed and copied during the night by a staff of workers hired for this purpose, so that by seven each morning, copies of what has transpired will be available to each and every one of you at special desks set up in the lobbies of the meeting hotels. Please do not fail to pick up and read your copy each morning, since much of what will be covered each day will be predicated upon the previous day's summarization.

"At the time of registration, each of you was given a packet of material which included the HAB Theory summary, which it is hoped you will have read thoroughly by now. If you have not done so, please read it immediately following this meeting."

In the audience, Dr. Owen Holder of Oxford murmured to the scientist to his right, Dr. Wilfred Upton, geneticist of Duke University, "I've already done so and it's pure balderdash. Balderdash, I say!"

Upton smiled without amusement and made no reply as he continued listening to Dr. Dowde.

"Only with the fullest cooperation from every registrant can this symposium hope to accomplish its aims. It is imperative that you keep abreast of what is occurring in all meetings."

Irma Dowde paused and glowered across the audience. Even though dwarfed in the vast expanse of the auditorium, she was still a strong figure commanding respect. "This is *not*," she said firmly, "a holiday or a reunion. Many of you have come here with ideas along those lines. For the most part, there is going to be little time for anything besides the work which has brought us together. If you're not willing—*eager* in fact—to be involved in this work, then bow out now. There will be neither time nor inclination to fuss with those who are not."

"Good heavens!" Dr. Holder muttered to the woman who sat in the seat to his left. "How can that…that *person* up there dare to talk to us in such a manner? After all, we're not exactly schoolchildren, are we?"

Dr. Agnet Braendstrum of the Physics Department of the University of Copenhagen, gave him a brief, withering look. "Please be quiet," she said. "I'm trying to listen to Dr. Dowde."

Holder sniffed at the rebuff and ungraciously returned his attention to the speaker.

"I'm sure," Dr. Dowde continued without pause, "that many of us here—most, I'd guess—have attended symposia before. We're all aware of the shortcomings as well as the benefits such symposia have incorporated in the past. There is, in my view, one mistake that has constantly been made in such gatherings which I hope to eliminate from this one. It will not be a popular procedure but it will, I think, be one which will allow us a much freer exchange of ideas than we've ever experienced before. Unfortunately we, as scientists, often tend to become cloistered within the very framework of our own specific fields of science. As an archaeologist, for example, I might be accomplished in my field, yet not know beans about related scientific fields, such as geology, astronomy, mathematics, or whatever."

"She's certainly right about that, much as I hate to admit it," said Dr. David Gulma, physicist of Kenya, to his companion in the next seat.

Dr. Bura Baodada, himself an archaeologist, grunted an affirmative. "Glad she's aware of it," he said. "Maybe she's got some ideas along those lines."

"Yet," the speaker was saying, "whenever groups of scientists come together in symposium, like seems to attract like—the archaeologists seek out and converse with other archaeologists, the astronomers gravitate to other astronomers, and so on. Thus, even while an exchange of ideas would be beneficial, we remain narrowly within the confines of our own branches of science. Hopefully this is a failing we can rectify here. We not only should, we *must*, since the postulations of the HAB Theory embrace a wide spectrum of sciences. Only by fully understanding its impact on one field of science can we relate it to another, and possibly, in the very doing of this, we will be able to view what have long been anomalies or mysteries in our own branches of science in a new and revealing light."

There was a murmuring from the audience, a sense of excitement in what she was saying. In the Press Section pencils were flying across papers as notes were made for stories that would be written.

"Christ, it's about time one of these affairs was handled like this," whispered Ralph Zeitler, science editor of the *New York Times*. "Leave it to old feisty Dowde to be the one to do it."

"Who else?" grunted the reporter beside him, Frank Trapman of the *Boston Globe*. "It won't make her popular, but since when has she ever worried about that?"

Trapman's analysis of the feelings of Dr. Dowde's fellow scientists was only fractional correct. Some didn't like the idea, of course, but by far the greater majority wore approving expressions. Not one among them had not experienced the frustration of encountering anachronisms or contradictions in their own sciences, and few among them had not felt the twinge of guilt which came with ignoring these heretofore unanswerables.

"Imagine!" Dr. Dowde continued. "Just imagine the possibilities that can be opened for all of us and for all mankind. It may happen that in the judgment of this symposium the HAB Theory will be deemed invalid, but in the very exchange of open-minded dialogue among us, between us and across scientific boundaries which have always hemmed us in, we may be entering a whole new plane of accomplishment in understanding our world and its past better than it has ever been understood before."

She waited as the murmur picked up again, peaked, then became subdued. Then she continued, speaking in a more level tone. "For that reason, every effort has been made to avoid having an abundance of scientists of any one field of study in any one particular group at this symposium. As completely as it is possible to do so, each group will be comprised of a cross section of scientists from every field represented here."

Once again the chairwoman looked at her watch, saw it was only just over one minute until it was time for the President to speak, and she hurried on.

"I will, after the principal address here, have a few more things to say. I know most of you are wondering what lies ahead, in regard to scheduling your time. I'm sorry to say that how our schedule runs is very nebulous right now. Much depends on what we accomplish. On a very broad basis, this being Friday, we would hope that the majority of smaller group discussions, arguments, remarks and conclusions could be completed by a week from today, on July 8. On that day it is hoped we can have another general meeting of all members, at which time a final conclusion may be drawn. In the assumption—and, mind you, I say this only for the sake of contingency— in the assumption that we find the HAB Theory acceptable, then the remaining two days—Saturday and Sunday—could be spent in general discussion of various plans of action to meet the emergency that the HAB Theory portends." She glanced toward the left wings and nodded, then looked back to the audience. Her voice became loud and ringing. "Now it is time for our principal speaker. Ladies and gentlemen, the President of the United States."

Over the loudspeaker system in the Felt Forum came the thundering notes of *Hail to the Chief*, at which the entire assemblage stood and applauded vigorously and at length. President Robert Morton Sanders, followed by four Secret Service men, came onto the stage and strode toward the rostrum, his limp noticeable but not disturbingly so. The guards already at the wings remained there, eyes on the crowd, while another half-dozen or more moved into sight and spread themselves out along the front of the audience, between seats and stage. Others appeared and stood at the various exits.

Sanders was met a short distance from the rostrum by Dr. Dowde and they shook hands warmly, and then there was a short interval of handshakes with others on the stage before the President finally moved up into place at the lectern. He was jovial-appearing and evidently quite fit. In his characteristic gesture, he gripped his own right wrist with his left hand, holding the right hand high and widespread, and the standing ovation swelled even more. At length it began to abate and there was a general shuffling sound as the audience sat down. Within another few moments the large hall was in silence.

President Sanders glanced down briefly at the pages of his speech, which had been placed on the lectern for him by Steve Lace when the Press Secretary had been introduced. Immediately after looking up again, Sanders began to speak in the strong, direct manner so familiar to the American public and the world.

"Ladies and gentlemen of the scientific world, it is with gratitude and a keen sense of the magnitude of what we must consider here that I welcome you. Never before in man's history has such a wealth of scientific knowledge in so many different fields—and embodied in so many living scientists who are the most learned in those fields—been assembled in one place. More important, never before in man's recorded history has their composite knowledge been so requisite. You here have assembled in symposium to weigh the pros and cons of a single matter which could be more important and pressing than any problem that man has ever before faced. It is an awesome responsibility and a tremendous encumbrance for any group, however large and learned."

The President let his eyes move across the assemblage and then briefly studied the sheets before him again, slid one aside, and continued. "What you will hear and contribute and consider in these days ahead necessarily must be of paramount importance to every human being on earth, since upon your conclusions mankind as a whole may survive or may be all but extinguished.

"In the ten days which begin today," he went on, a heaviness coming into his voice, "your wealth of knowledge, great though it is, will be taxed to its limits. In a period of ten days you here must weigh all the known evidence, consider the proofs which are offered, and balance them against what you have always known or believed in your own experience. Having done that, you will then reach conclusions of necessity based on a combination of solid data and far-flung speculation. That will not be easy, and certainly it will not be fair to you, because it strays from the cautious precepts of scientific process."

He paused and licked his lips. "Science—just as government does to a lesser degree—tends to move ahead slowly and with sureness, but this is a time when neither science nor government can afford the luxury of relaxed and time-consuming deliberation. Time may be our greatest enemy. Yet, despite this, I would be quick to add that although haste is imperative, it must be haste with care—great care.

A few individuals in the audience began to applaud at this and the others picked it up until the huge chamber resounded with the clapping. Sanders waited patiently until it died away before continuing.

"By this time, each of you here has become familiar with the basic elements of what has come to be known as the HAB Theory. Some of you present have openly accepted the postulation, or at least have concluded that it is reasonable enough for you to direct your thoughts toward what must be done in the immediate future to negate or lessen the effects of the HAB Theory eventuality. Others of you—perhaps as many or even more—adamantly reject it as preposterous, tendentious, inconceivable, and wholly invalid, and perhaps with justification—and to such vigorous extent that it is your considered opinion to reject it out of hand and get back to what you feel is serious scientific consideration. Both views, under the circumstances, are understandable, and it is neither my intention nor desire at this time to make any effort to sway you one way or another in your belief. Yet, in all honesty, we cannot, in fairness to the fundamental elements of scientific thinking, allow ourselves to be irrevocably locked into these extreme viewpoints, either pro or con, without benefit of an open exchange of ideas and information, simply because of personal bias or narrow mindedness."

President Sanders leaned toward the audience, his expression serious yet softened with the suggestion of a smile. "Most of you assembled here occupy positions falling between these two extremes—perhaps leaning strongly one way or the other, but with sufficient scientific open-mindedness to consider what will be advanced to you in these days ahead with a viewpoint at least as impartial as possible to any scientist who is deeply imbued with the science to which he has devoted his life and efforts."

Robert Sanders let his direct gaze shift from his left to the far right and settle on the Press Section, where cameras were rolling and reporters were swiftly scribbling notes.

"I am aware," he continued, "that a great curiosity has manifested itself in the press—and among many of the scientists gathered here—concerning what my own personal views and beliefs are in respect to the HAB Theory."

The members of the press became acutely alert at this and throughout the large audience breaths were held for what would come next.

"It would not have been possible," the Chief Executive said, "for me to have become as deeply involved in this matter as I have been without forming some views. Yet, ladies and gentlemen," he turned back to the audience in general, "my own personal views or beliefs at this stage—and I have no intention yet of publicly expressing them—are of no consequence, simply because I do not possess the scientific background to properly evaluate the information that has been imparted to me."

There was a universal sigh, a releasing of the pent-up breaths throughout the audience, a reaction of something approximating disappointment and at the same time approval.

"If I were to express personal views at this time," the President added, "they would almost certainly influence some of you in your ultimate decision. This must not occur."

There was a spontaneous round of applause at this and, while it continued, the President took a sip of water from the glass on the lectern above his papers. In a little while the noise had abated and he resumed speaking.

"Instead, my friends, it is you, the scientists assembled in this hall from all over the world, whose views become of the utmost importance, not only to me but to other heads of state throughout the world in the decisions which governments must make in time to come. It is upon your experience, your knowledge, your well-considered evaluation that we must now rely and, as I mentioned earlier, this is an awesome responsibility for anyone to have. It must in no measure be taken lightly. There is neither time nor room for pettiness, personal conceits or any form of closed-mindedness due to preconceived positions which do not allow for an unbiased approach to the matter at hand. Far too much is at stake. You here have a job to do for humanity—and I know in my heart that you will do it well."

Another burst of applause came at this, genuine and strong, and the President smiled widely and nodded. As the din faded away he glanced back at Dr. Dowde, who was standing beside the end chair in which her assistant, Kathryn Lever, was seated. He returned his attention to the audience.

"Dr. Irma Dowde of our own Smithsonian Institution in Washington, who has been chairing the Scientific Advisory Committee appointed by me a month ago, and who has also coordinated this HAB Theory Symposium with such competence, will continue to keep me advised throughout the duration of the symposium concerning matters under discussion, along with the evaluations being made and conclusions being drawn. When the time comes for ending this symposium and charting a course of action as a result of the conclusions which have been reached by this body, it is my hope to return here and address you again. It is my hope, but it may not be possible. However, whether I do or not, at that time my own position and proposed course of action will be made clear.

"For the moment, then, ladies and gentlemen, and on behalf of not only the American people, but for all the people of the world united in the brotherhood of man, I extend to each and every one of you our heartfelt appreciation and sincere good wishes for the difficult task which now lies ahead. I thank you."

A tremendous standing ovation came at the conclusion of the President's speech and, while it continued, he turned and walked directly to Elizabeth Boardman who, like the others behind him, was standing and applauding. He took both her hands in his.

"My dear," he said gently, "I arrived in time to hear the remarks you made in regard to your father. They were thoughtfully chosen and beautifully expressed. You said you were very proud of him, as you have every right to be. I like to think that somehow, in some way, he too is equally proud of you at this moment."

Liz Boardman flushed but looked at him directly and said, "Thank you, Mr. President. It's a lovely thought."

"I appreciate your coming here at such short notice," he continued, "and it is I who thank you for your great cooperation already and your offer to aid us here at the symposium in whatever way possible. In that respect I will be calling you in a day or two."

Before she could reply, he turned his head and smiled at John Grant and Steven Lace and then turned and walked, his limp more noticeable after standing so long, toward the wings, raising a hand to acknowledge the continuing applause. Quietly and unobtrusively the Secret Service men moved out and exited the way they had come at about the time the President himself passed from view in the wings.

As the applause ended and the audience reseated itself, Dr. Irma Dowde returned to the lectern with a sheet of paper in her hand. She raised the empty hand to silence the continuing murmur of many voices.

"We're not finished yet," she began in her characteristically blunt way, then grinned at the isolated shout from someone in the audience.

"You never are, Irma!" A burst of laughter came at the remark.

"I will be soon," she replied, "but right now we've still a way to go. We're all gratified, I know, that the President came here to address us, and it only underlines what he expressed so well—we've got one hell of a responsibility facing us, and little time to meet it."

She held aloft briefly the paper she had been holding. "I have here," she said, "some figures I know will interest you. By eight this morning we had reached a total registration of 3,668 scientists representing 116 different countries. There are still some late arrivals coming, so almost certainly we'll top the 3,700 mark. In the broad and specific fields of science or fields related to our needs here, there are presently thirty-six separate headings which included, alphabetically,"—she looked down at her paper and began reading them off rapidly—"anthropology, archaeology, astronomy, astrophysics, biology, botany, cartography, chemistry, climatology, cryptology, cybernetics, electrophysics, genetics, geography, geology, geophysics, glaciology, history, ichthyology, mammalogy, mathematics, mechanical engineering, medicine, meteorology, oceanography, paleobotany, paleontology, philology, physics, physiology, prehistory, psychology—we may need that one," she interjected, causing a new burst of laughter, and then went on—"radiology, thermodynamics, and zoology"

The heavy-set archaeologist stopped and blew out a puff of breath and used her index finger to push back a strand of stringy brown hair which had come loose and hung over the right of her brow. She dropped her paper to the lectern top and looked across the audience.

"Well, I think now we're about ready to get on with our task. There will be assistants at symposium headquarters who will help you in any way possible. I personally will be in and out of that office each day, but mostly I plan to keep pretty much in motion while the daily meetings are being held, dropping in here and there to catch the gist of what is occurring in each group.

"Because of the large number of registrants, please be sure to wear your identification badges to all meetings so that others may know who you are and where you're from, and vice versa. No one not wearing his badge will be permitted entry to the meetings. The group chairmen have already been selected and contacted and they represent as widely as possible all the scientific fields involved here, but just because a group chairman may be a zoologist or geologist does not mean that his group will discuss only subjects which fall under that heading. All matters involving the principal subject of the HAB Theory should be discussed from every conceivable approach by each of the groups. Only through this interchange of ideas from different scientific branches can we hope to get anywhere."

Dr. Dowde held up her arm and looked her watch. "You still have considerably more than three hours before the group meetings begin, and so I have only one last thing to say before ending this session. I believe it would be wise for all group chairmen to select from within their groups another individual who is not in the same field of science as the chairman, to act as vice-chairman. The vice-chairmen should attend the regular nightly meetings. There will be a preliminary meeting of all group chairmen at one-thirty this afternoon in the Conrad's Suite of the Waldorf. Please do not fail to be there. Any named chairman who does not attend this meeting," she warned, "will be dropped as a chairman and a replacement named."

She picked up her paper and leaned closer to the microphone. "And with that, ladies and gentlemen," she said, "I thank you for your attention and declare this first meeting closed."

I I

Rising from his seat at the conclusion of Irma Dowde's remarks, John Grant moved swiftly toward the wings of the stage, unwilling to stay and chat with the others who had been up there with him and who now had formed into a loose group. Grant saw that Kermit Knotts had also broken away and was angling in his direction, but he did not pause. Knotts would undoubtedly be at the meeting with the Chief Executive in the Presidential Suite before long and he could see the man there.

"Mr. Grant."

The low call in a woman's voice came as he passed through the wings and headed for the short stairway which would take him outside the huge auditorium into a passageway leading to the main foyer. He paused and looked to his left and saw Hazel Tierney coming his way.

"Mr. Grant," she repeated, coming to a stop before him, "the President asked me to tell you that the meeting he discussed with you earlier will be in his suite at the Waldorf at twelve-thirty, which is…" she looked at her watch, "…an hour and a quarter from now. You'll be there?"

"Yes, of course. If I'm needed before then, I'll be in my room."

"Thank you." She nodded and made a small notation beside his name on a steno pad and then added with a smile, "I don't think you'll be needed before then, however." She looked past him and gave a little wave. "I see Mr. Knotts. Excuse me, please."

As she moved off to intercept Knotts, Grant continued on his way out. There was already a crowd forming in front of the building, but the writer was fortunate enough to flag down a passing taxi before the rush became heavy. Before another quarter-hour passed he was unlocking the door to his ninth floor hotel room.

Stripping off coat and tie, he sat on the edge of the bed and glanced through the notes addressed to him which he'd picked up at the desk on the way upstairs. The first was from Narai Ngoromu, in her crisp, clear hand.

Hi, John. Just a word to let you know I made it and hope to see you this week sometime. Any possibility that you and Anne might join us ("us" being Alex and me) for dinner some evening? Let me know soonest. Am staying at the Plaza. Room 1102. Father sends regards. Mother, too. Narai.

The second was a written reminder from Steve Lace about the meeting with President Sanders at 12:30, and the third was a note from the hotel saying he had received a call from Marie Grant at 11:02 A.M. and asking that he call home at his earliest convenience. He made a grumbling sound and dropped the notes on the nightstand beside the telephone, then lay back atop the spread and rubbed his eyes.

He looked at his watch and saw that it was 11:40 and let his arm fall back along his side. It felt as if he hadn't had a decent period of sleep for weeks and he longed to just roll over and doze until he woke up naturally, but knew he couldn't do so. Even when the opportunity was there, he couldn't seem to sleep very well. Nightmares plagued him constantly, sometimes jerking him half out of bed with the sound of his own hoarse cry still in his ears.

There was, he thought, a sort of irony in the fact that the most important project he'd ever been involved with was occurring at precisely the same time as the most upsetting emotional situation he'd ever encountered and he wished fleetingly that he had the freedom to give one or the other his undivided attention.

Last night at home had been grim. He had stayed awake throughout the night in his den, trying to work on the HAB data but accomplishing little. He had been acutely aware of Marie lying awake in the dark bedroom next door, occasionally hearing her stir in the big bed or clear her throat or cough, and once he was fairly sure he heard her crying. He might have gone to her then, but at the same time he saw that the shelf where his fiber-bound diaries were kept was bare. He remembered earlier in the evening being puzzled over an enigmatic remark by Marie to the effect that she had "the goods on him" and that he'd pay for what he was doing, but he had shut his ears to her and stalked off. Obviously, this was what she had meant; she had taken them, including even the current year's book, and the wave of sympathy that had risen in him when he thought he heard her crying was submerged in the surge of anger which came at the knowledge that his diaries were gone. He'd been tempted to confront her right then and there, but he knew it would result in another argument and he had no heart for it just then.

Several times during the night he was tempted to call Anne, but he did not; not only because Marie was evidently awake in the next room, but because Anne would want to know all that had happened and he just couldn't bring himself to discuss it any further now. What he wanted more than anything else was time to himself, time in which he could chart his course now that he was sure which way he was going.

At the airport in the morning, with dawn barely streaking the sky, he had called Anne when there was only time enough remaining before his flight to tell her that it had not been pleasant and to give her just a rough idea of how it had gone. He hadn't mentioned that Marie had hit him and cursed him and wound up taking all his diaries. It would have served no purpose except to upset Anne. He was on the phone with her for no more than five minutes.

Lack of sleep and emotional strain had planted a deep-seated weariness in him, but even on the flight from Chicago, when he thought he might be able to catch a couple hours' sleep, it hadn't worked out that way. He'd leaned back with his eyes closed and the stewardess hadn't bothered him, but neither had sleep come. At half past eight they'd landed at La Guardia and in less than an hour he'd checked in at the hotel. Steve Lace had answered the phone when he'd called the Presidential Suite and the press secretary said he'd pass on the word to the President of Grant's arrival, but that The Man was busy at the moment and couldn't be disturbed. Grant had then checked with Irma Dowde and found out when she wanted him at the Felt Forum, and he'd arrived on schedule. There had been time for nothing else.

Now he leaned over to pick up the telephone and in a little while heard a couple of distant rings before the number he was calling was answered.

"A-C Tours. May I help you, please?"

"You're answering your own office phone these days?"

Anne Carpenter's voice became huskier. "Oh. Hi, Missed Man. God, I'm glad you called. I've been so worried. We hardly had any time at all to talk this morning. To answer your question, yes. Louise took the day off for a long weekend, so I'm stuck with answering. Glad I did. Where are you, in your room?"

"Uh-huh. Just got back from the symposium opening." He was trying to speak lightly, but didn't know if it was getting across that way. "Old Salty gave a pretty good speech. Dowde said at the beginning that all speeches were going to be cut short, including her own, and then proceeded to talk interminably. I nearly fell asleep in my chair."

"As many people there as was anticipated?"

"More. Quite a mob. Nearly four thousand."

"Really? I've been trying to get some news on it. The *Trib* had a couple of stories on the fact that it was beginning today, but that's all. Radio news has been talking in circles around it, but so far they don't seem to have much."

"They will soon enough." He fell silent.

"John? Where are we? Your call this morning made me feel a little better, but everything was pretty sketchy. I'm still scared. How about a little encouragement?"

"Look, hon, I'd really rather not go into it much right now. I'm pretty foggy and I'd just like some time to sort things out. Would you mind waiting a little longer? I'll fill you in, I promise."

"All right." The way she said it made it sound very much not all right. She caught her breath as if to say more, and Grant was sure she was going to ask again, as she had twice during the early morning call, if he'd made his decision. He didn't want to tell her yet that he had, and so he spoke up quickly.

"Miss me?"

"Like crazy."

"Prove it."

"The way I'd like to prove it would be a little difficult over long distance wire."

"Then how about making it short distance? We're invited to dinner."

"We?"

"Yep, we. You and I. Anne and John."

"By whom? When?"

"Had a note waiting when I got back a few minutes ago. From Narai. She'd like us to join her and Alex for dinner if we can. Our convenience."

"Gee, I'd love to, but I know I can't get away today, and tomorrow's bad. Without Louise I'll have to go in for at least half the day. Suppose I try to make it later on in the day tomorrow? I could probably get there by six or seven. Maybe earlier."

"Sounds good. Let's plan on it. Let me know when you'll arrive."

"Okay. I'm really excited about it. How's everything going?"

"Pretty well, I guess. I have a meeting coming up shortly with the White House gang. Also had a note waiting to call Marie."

The airiness left Anne's voice. "Are you going to?"

" I suppose so."

"Oh, hell, John! What more can you say to each other after yesterday?" Exasperation was high in her voice. "It should have ended completely yesterday and you know it. You won't say whether or not you've come to a decision, so I can only assume you still haven't. You're evidently still leaving things hanging. Why, John? I don't know how much more of this I can take."

He closed his eyes, not wanting another hassle. "It's just not that easy, Anne. I don't think Marie's going to give up without a fight."

"Well, hell no, she isn't!" She sounded flabbergasted. "You didn't really expect she would, did you? But what's that got to do with it? John, how many times have you told me how unhappy you are and how much you'd rather be with me? What does it *take* to get you to make a decision? If you're being bludgeoned by the life you're living, then for God's sake, isn't it only common sense for you to make a change? And much as I want you, I don't mean just a change to come to me. You'd be wrong to change under that basis alone, and I'd be pretty scared for any sort of future for us if you did. You've got to change things because you need to do it for yourself. *Yourself!* Jesus, can't you understand that?" She was getting herself worked up. "Honestly, I feel like I'm walking around in circles with you. We talked this all out at the apartment yesterday and now here we are, just a day later, starting right in at the beginning again."

"Anne, I—"

"No, wait. You're a man, John. A grown man. A strong man, I used to think, but now I'm really beginning to wonder. Damn it, I *know* it's not an easy decision for you to make, and I'm aware of all the considerations that are bothering you. But you have got to make a decision of some kind if you're ever to have any peace of mind at all. Why can't you do it? Why *won't* you do it? I hate to even mention it, but I'm having fears now. Just when it looks like you've really started the ball rolling, it looks like you're suddenly having second thoughts in all areas, including how you feel about me."

"No!" His denial was instantaneous. "There's no way that can happen, Anne. None."

"Well, then, it seems to me that…just a minute."

He heard her speaking to someone and it was half a minute before she got back to him, her voice lower than it had been.

"Customer. I'll have to go pretty quickly."

"Me too. I have that meeting."

"And your call to Marie?"

He hesitated. "Yes, that too."

She sighed. "All right. Guess I've started lecturing again. Didn't really mean to, but I start before I realize it and then once it starts, it's pretty hard to stop. I know it isn't easy for you, none of this, and I'm sorry. No, I'm really not sorry. I don't know what I am, or even too well where I stand. There I go again. See what I mean? Okay, I'm off. I'll call later tonight and let you know for sure when I'm coming. I'm really looking forward to seeing Narai and Alex again. They're nice people. You're nice people, too. I might even like seeing you again."

"Good. Gives a man a feeling of well-being to know he's missed. Take care, honey." He paused and then said, "And, Anne,—" but the click of her phone cut him off. He grimaced and set the phone down slowly. It didn't matter. He was going to tell her not to worry, but he knew she'd worry anyway, so it didn't make any difference."

Within a couple of minutes he had Marie on the line and knew at once from the stiff formality of her tone that it wasn't going to be a good session.

"You wanted me to call?" He lit a cigarette. "There was a message waiting at the desk."

"I did." Utter coldness in the words. "You said before you left that you'd call, but then you've been forgetting a lot of things lately—like your wife and children and home and—"

"All right, Marie," he cut in wearily, "you've made your point."

"Nowhere near as well as I intend making it today!" The receiver crackled with her bitter, mirthless laughter and then she went on. "I never used to swear much," she said, "but I'm finding that sometimes it's very satisfying to do so. Satisfying and damned well appropriate. I almost ended that comment just now with the words 'you bastard.' But then, it's so appropriate I'd have to end nearly every sentence I spoke to you that way, wouldn't I?". Again the brittle laughter.

"Marie," the heaviness in Grant's voice was palpable, "I'm not going to continue a phone call for this sort of thing. As I've said, you've made your point and if that's all you—"

"And as I said," she interrupted, "nowhere near as well as I'm going to right now. You listen to me, damn you, John, and listen well. I am here alone with two children to take care of and a house to take care of and I don't have the foggiest notion in the world of when the man who is supposed to be here helping is coming back. Or even *if* he is coming back. I damned well want to know. Right now!"

"I told you," he said flatly, "when I left for the symposium this morning that it's scheduled to last for ten days. And that I need time alone to think. I told you that I didn't know when I was coming back, or even *if* I was coming back. That still stands."

"No it does not!" The words were spaced like whipcracks. "God damn it, who do you think you are that you can just walk out and dump everything onto me while you allegedly try, as you put it, to 'find' yourself. Marriage doesn't work that way, John."

"There are times," he murmured, the anger beginning to fill him again, "that marriage doesn't work at all."

When she spoke again there was no alteration of her iciness. "You're talking very foolishly and very dangerously, John, and I hope you consider everything   and I mean *everything*—very well before making any decisions that are going to adversely affect your family. I've put up with a lot from you lately and I'm just about at the end of the string. I'm warning you, if you—

"You're *warning* me?"

"You bet your ass I'm warning you! I've got those rotten diaries of yours. They're locked up in a safety deposit box as of this morning. They're evidence, John. Evidence! So you'd better think twice before you do anything foolish."

"Blackmail, Marie?" he asked softly. "With my own diaries?"

"Damned right, if that's what it takes. *Anything* it takes!"

"I thought I knew you pretty well." His voice was low, grating. "I guess I was wrong. I don't understand your reasoning at all. How could you possibly *want* me back if it takes blackmail to do it?"

"How? How!" Her words were shrill. "Listen, if you think for one damned minute you can walk out on me after all these years and I'll just sit back and watch it happen, you're out of your mind. You want to find yourself, you say. Okay, that's just fine. Find yourself, but I'll tell you one thing for sure—you can't do it alone. You need help. You're sick, John. And you're getting progressively sicker. You'd better get some professional help very soon. Normal people don't suddenly start talking about walking out on lives they've spent a couple of decades or more to build. You've had your head turned by a no-good tramp and you're so infatuated that you're right on the brink of wrecking your own life and the lives of a lot of other people for nothing more than a…a piece of ass!"

Grant didn't trust himself to speak and he remained quiet so long that she finally said sharply, "John?"

"I'm here," he said, "and you may be right. Maybe I am sick. Maybe I should seek some professional help. But that's a two-way street, Marie. If I've changed—and I'll concede that I have, quite a bit—then maybe you ought to carry the thought a step or so farther. Maybe there's a good reason, a reason with somewhat more foundation than the one you've just described. Maybe both of us are no longer the people we once were, or thought we were. Things change, Marie. People change. What I'm saying is, maybe I'm not the only one who needs professional help."

"Oh no you don't! You're not going to do an about-face and then try to lay the blame on me. Listen here, John

Grant, *you're* the one who precipitated all this

mess! *You're* the one who's been philandering around, cheating on your wife. *You're* the one who's confused and bothered and guilty, and…and…you're not going to put the blame on me. Not for *anything!*"

Her voice had begun breaking and once again Grant closed his eyes and wished that he were somewhere else or even someone else. Yet, he was reluctant to discard the thought and he carried it a little farther.

"I've wandered, yes," he admitted, "and I suppose I'm feeling guilty to some degree about it, but not really as much as you might want to believe. The point I'm trying to make, Marie—and I say this with concern, not maliciousness—is that the very fact that I've wandered from you suggests that there's got to be a fundamental reason for my having done so. My being with another woman—with Anne—is not the cause of our problem, it's an *effect* of it. I think we both need to seriously consider what the cause has been."

"The…the cause, damn it, John…the cause is *you!* You and that despicable whore. That's the cause and it's the only cause. And I don't even want to talk to you anymore now." Her stridency rose again. "Don't forget, I've got those damned diaries, and I've got the money, too!"

"Money?"

"Yes, money! You didn't think I was going to let you walk out and leave me without anything, did you? How dumb do you think I am?"

"Marie, make sense. What money are you talking about?"

"Savings, that's what," she snapped. "Seventeen years worth of savings. Joint savings. Only they're not joint anymore. They're in my name as of this morning. So start using your head, John. You'd better come home soon. And I mean to stay. Because if you don't, you're going to be the sorriest son of a bitch on earth. That's all. Good-bye!"

He hung up mechanically after she was gone, his stomach churning with a sick anger, and the self-doubts he thought he'd conquered now returning to assail him with renewed vigor. With a groan and a small descriptive oath, he got to his feet and began getting ready for his meeting with the President in a short while.

I I I

Seated at a little table in the lavish and open Palm Court Restaurant off the lobby in the Plaza Hotel, Narai Ngoromu looked across at Alexander Gordon and tilted her head. Brilliant white teeth shone as she smiled widely at him and her dark eyes sparkled.

Gordon had been looking at her appreciatively. She was easily one of the most attractive women he'd ever seen and he felt proud and happy at being with her, not unaware of the approving glances she had received as they left Madison Square Garden and took a cab to the Plaza, glances she was still getting from men and women alike here in the distinctive restaurant. She was wearing a deep maroon skirt and short-sleeved white blouse with a wide collar which had the effect of emphasizing her coiffure. Her hair had been combed into a large, almost perfectly round

Afro set which framed her face and made her appear even more delicately featured than she was. It took a conscious effort to bring him back to the matter at hand and answer the question she had asked about President Sanders.

"Well, yes," he said, "as a matter of fact I've know him for quite a while and have pretty much lost any credence I may have had in the old adage about familiarity breeding contempt. The longer I know him, the more I respect and admire him. He's a hell of a man, much more so than most people even begin to suspect. I mean above and beyond purely political standing. He's an incredible human being."

Narai reached out and put her hand over his on the tabletop, the gold circlets on her wrist jingling pleasantly at the movement. Her hand looked dwarfed in relation to the size of his.

"Where's it all leading, Alex?" she asked. "From a sort of semi-insider viewpoint, I'd say he seems pretty convinced of the reality of this whole HAB Theory concept, but what's coming now? Isn't be sticking his neck out pretty far? These people that have come here aren't starry-eyed kids; they're a bunch of pretty rigidly opinionated scientists and a lot of them can't help but look on the HAB business as a direct threat to them. Suppose their response turns out to be not what Sanders expects? It could wreck him, couldn't it?"

"Almost certainly, and he knows it." Gordon hunched his shoulders. "But a lot of people still don't realize that when Robert Sanders believes in something, he believes in it all the way. You'd be appalled to know the amount of pressure he's been getting from his own people to pull in his horns some and not make any major moves until there's a strong affirmative reaction from the majority of those that've come here." He shook his head. "That's not his way. He believes it and he's willing to gamble his entire future on his beliefs. There aren't too many figures in politics who'll do that. There never have been, but the ones who have had that much self-confidence have usually turned out to be the most important figures in history. It doesn't necessarily hold that they're *right*, but there's no doubt that they believe in themselves. Lincoln, Hitler, Napoleon, Lenin, Nixon, Slater, others. They've all had this same trait. But it's never easy in the face of constant pressures being brought to bear. Sure, Sanders is sticking his neck out and he's at a point of vulnerability right now that's practically beyond our conception. At any moment the ax could fall and he'd be done. No one knows that any better than Sanders himself, but it won't alter what he has in mind. It's not his way." He paused a moment, then added, "I get the feeling that your father's the same kind of man."

Narai nodded slowly. "I think he is," she said simply, "above and apart from the fact that he's my father. But sometimes it scares me to see the way he moves, too. He has a lot of powerful enemies in Kenya, and they're all poised for that opening when they can chop him down."

"All powerful political figures are in that same position, Narai. It's one of the hazards of the game. And it has to be a hell of a way to go through life. There aren't many who can do it."

He finished the last few swallows of his coffee, set the cup down, and then engulfed her small hand in his own. Impulsively he brought it to his lips and kissed the back of it.

"I just want you to know," he said seriously, "that I'm awfully glad you're here. I've not often been bothered too much with loneliness, but I've been pretty lonely ever since leaving Nairobi. I'm not now."

Her eyes were shining. She let her fingertips touch his cheek lingeringly before drawing her hand back. "You might've been reading my mind to say that, Alex. I'm glad I'm here, too. Or wherever it might be that you are."

Their eyes locked for a long meaningful moment and then Alex squeezed her hand, released it, and looked at his watch. "I'll have to leave," he said regretfully, "for the meeting over at the Waldorf. You're still planning on doing some shopping?"

"For an hour, maybe. I'll be moving around a lot, though, here in the Plaza, when the sessions get underway this afternoon. Four of the groups are meeting here and I want to try to sit in on a little of each of the sessions. But they're over about six, I think. You'll pick me up when? Eight?"

"Uh huh. Far as I know right now, anyway. There could be some changes in plans, but if that happens I'll leave word for you." He smiled as he got up. "I'm really glad you're here."

"Me too, Alex. Try not to let anything intervene. I'd like us to have a good evening together."

I V

No single project in Kenya's long history had ever created such a beehive of activity as the beginning of construction of Ngaia City on the Rematta Galla highlands east of Tsavo National Park. Even though still in its most initial stages, the new complex being formed in the semiarid veldt overlooking the Tiva River Valley had begun taking shape.

Viewing it from the most advantageous viewpoint with Anita and a cordon of engineers and ministers, Daniel Ngoromu felt a quickening of his pulse. It had been his dream for so long that Kenya become an important world state that sometimes deep inside he felt a gnawing frustration at the slowness with which things changed. Years had gone by in the past when no real outward result of all his efforts had been apparent and when the faintest niggling of doubt had touched him that he would ever be able to accomplish his dream. Now it seemed that those doubts had forever been put to rest.

As far as the eye could see in all directions, foundation lines were being laid out, stakes being driven, cords being strung, excavations being dug, careful measurements being made. The ground vibrated with the rumbling of operating equipment, and thick reinforced concrete walls already were being poured in one area. Scores of men worked in small groups, sometimes obscured by the haze of dust being raised by the incredible amount of heavy machinery being moved into the area or already at work.

The Kenyan President felt Anita's hand grip his own and he squeezed it in response and looked at her with eyes filled with a glow which said what words couldn't say. It was a glow that was mirrored in Anita's eyes and she reached over with her free hand and placed it on the powerful swell of his bare lower arm.

"I wonder," he said, only loud enough for her to hear, "if what I'm feeling right now might not be very close to what the architect of the Great Pyramid felt when he saw the ground being laid out for his dream. All this," he indicated the activity in general, "may not become as monumentally beautiful, but it has to be at least as important and, God willing, as permanent."

"God willing," Anita echoed, following his gaze. She turned and faced him, her blond hair turned golden in the rays of the setting sun. "Oh, Dan, I'm overwhelmed. What words can possibly express what you feel at a time like this? I'd like to just rent this space and sit in a chair here day after day watching it grow."

"I know. I feel the same way. Well, we'll be seeing it often enough in the months to come."

She nodded. "It's the first thing I want to do when I get back. I keep telling myself I'll be gone for only a little over a week, but I feel as if I'll be missing so much. I really hate to go, but I promised Narai. Anyway, let's plan to come back here the day after I return from the States."

"We will, 'Neet, without fail." He patted her hand on his arm and then released it, saying he wanted to speak with Tom Umba. He turned slightly and beckoned to one of the men standing apart a respectful distance.

Umba was of medium height and well built, about forty years old and with skin as nearly ebony-hued as that of the President. His piercing eyes were framed by steel-rimmed glasses and lines of strong, genial character were at the corners of his eyes. He was chief engineer of the Ngaia City project and a graduate of both Nairobi University and the Massachusetts Institute of Technology. He was also recognized as the foremost construction engineer in all of East Africa.

Clad like Ngoromu, in khaki shorts and matching short-sleeved shirt, Umba saw the beckoning and strode at once to the Kenyan President and stopped beside him. Ngoromu swept out a hand in a movement which took in the expansive activity before them.

"I know it'll be in your reports, Tom, but let me hear some of it offhand. How's it shaping?"

Umba kicked at a clod of dirt. "Better, I suppose, than we have any right to expect this early, but still not in full swing. That'll take a week or two. We'll have somewhere between ten and twenty storage units finished within another four or five days. They're simple because they don't involve any plumbing or electrical problems of any consequence. They're a couple miles over that way," he pointed, "but that's only the start. We have somewhere just under sixteen thousand men either on hand or presently on the way." He gave a short dry laugh. "The temporary tent cities for lodging them are all but finished, but it gets to be something of a logistics problem just supporting them here. It's improving daily. We have seventeen camps set up already here on the site, plus five others between here and Kalima Simba to the east, eight others active on highway work between there and Mombasa, and a dozen others setting up the road layout between here and Nairobi."

"You've already mapped the layout for the road?"

"Pretty well now. There were three alternatives we were considering for linking with Nairobi. Each had advantages and liabilities. Running straight north on the Kitui and Tana River boundary line up to Highway B-3 and then widening that eastward into Thika and Nairobi would've been all right, except for excessive mileage."

"How much?"

"It checked out at two sixty-five. Part of the problem, of course, is Tsavo. If we could shoot straight west through the park, that would be ideal, but you turned thumbs down on that plan."

"Absolutely. The national parks have become sacrosanct. That won't mean much if and when the HAB cataclysm comes, but for the here and now, people won't buy it. If we start carving up Tsavo, we'd not only have our own people down on us, we'd get criticism from all over the world. We're going to have problems enough without that. All right, what was the mileage for the choice you made and where does it go?

"Two hundred twenty-four miles. It angles up, somewhat west of north, thirty-three miles to Tsavo's northeast corner, then straight west another fifty miles to Mutomo. From there we follow B-26 and B-3 again another hundred forty-one miles through Thika into Nairobi. That route's not only shortest, it gets the most advantage from existing roads and will cost least. Survey's under layout now."

"Fine." Ngoromu nodded approvingly. "What about electricity and water?"

"Electric's being run in already. Mombasa's the prime source for now, but we'll be tapping Nairobi soon as an alternate. We've already begun construction on our own generating plant, but it'll be a while before it's operational. Again, according to your instructions, all cables coming in will be running five feet underground. Where water's concerned, we've lucked out pretty well. Six experimental tapholes either in the bed of the Tiva or adjacent to it show abundant water. Pumping stations are being designed already. Until then, we have eight makeshift wells working full time and they're more than keeping pace with the demand. That," he added, "may change with the increase in personnel. Three or four thousand more of our own people coming in within the next two weeks and somewhere around twenty-five hundred others from the United States. That may make it sticky for a while, but the first permanent pumping plant ought to be in operation within a month, so that'll resolve whatever problem excess personnel creates. All in all, we seem to be in pretty good shape."

"How about the city construction itself?"

"Coming along, sir. We're combining the excavations for the connecting tunnels and the conduit pipes for water, sewage and electricity. That work's top priority right now. Incidentally, as of last Monday we've been on the twenty-four-hour schedule you wanted. Three duplicated shifts, eight hours on and sixteen off per man."

"Good. Keep it that way. Any problem with sewage disposal?"

"Gravity's a big help. We'll have to do some initial pumping eastward to the edge of the plateau slope, but from there on it's all downhill. The plant itself will be set up on the Tana River-Kalifi border, about thirty-eight or forty miles southeast of here, just a couple miles south of the road linking us with Kalima Simba. We're planning initially on six steeping basins, but leaving room to double that pretty quickly, and treble it if it becomes necessary."

"Sounds good on the whole, but there've got to be some bugs."

Tom Umba hunched his shoulders and grinned. "Surprisingly few, so far. Biggest one, I guess, is keeping the men working. They were all pretty well keyed up when they arrived, but Kenyans aren't geared to moving fast. Steadily, yes, but not fast. They run out of steam quickly most of the time, but since they're making more on this project than on any work they've done before, they're coming into line pretty well. I set up a rule that helps. Slackers get one warning to get back to work. If they're found idling again within a week of the first warning, they're dismissed on the spot. On the whole, though, the work's going remarkably well. Heavy mechanization helps and," he grinned at Anita Ngoromu, "I'm glad your Uncle Sam came through with the air cargo shipments as quickly as promised. There's more arriving every day by air, and evidently a tremendous shipment already en route in freighters, but they'll take about eight or nine days."

They talked a while longer and then, the sun having set and the air growing chill, the Kenyan President and his wife, dutifully trailed by ministers and aides returned to the pad where three large Sikorsky helicopters awaited to transport them back to Nairobi.

As they circled once over the Ngaia City site, Daniel Ngoromu, at a window seat, let his eyes take in the vast dusky expanse—now becoming dotted with the twinkling of campfires—where the most incredible under-one-roof construction in man's history was to be erected, and in his mind's eye he saw it there already. And beside him, looking straight ahead, Anita Randall Ngoromu pressed her hands to her body and the color left her face as once again, as had been occurring in the recent past, the waves of incredible pain flooded through her.

V

"I don't need to look out the window to know I'm not in Washington, Hazel," Robert Sanders told his secretary in the small private room of the Presidential Suite. "It's not often I find myself with a little free time like this without someone needing urgently to see me. Let's keep it that way. I want to take fullest advantage of it. I've got—What time is it?"

Hazel Tierney consulted her watch. "A few minutes before eleven, sir."

"Good. That means I've got better than an hour and a half before the meeting with the Scientific Advisory Committee. You can bring that lunch order in whenever it gets here, but I don't want any other interruptions unless they're damned urgent."

"I'll see to it, Mr. President."

Sanders didn't even hear her go out. He sat comfortably in the big armchair, with his feet resting on a hassock. In his lap was a copy of the Grant summary and now, for the third time since receiving it, he began going through it page by page, attempting to fix even more completely in his own mind the full sense of the HAB Theory and its ramifications.

As before, the first seven pages of it meant little to him. They laid out the mechanics of the capsizing of the earth in terms of mathematical formulae, and he skimmed past them. Even after that portion he skipped numerous areas with which he was already thoroughly familiar and devoted his attention to areas he had not yet really studied well.

It was on the ninth page that he began reading more carefully.

...Once the gyroscopic stability of the equatorial bulge has been overcome by the ice cap through centrifugal force, the speed of the capsizing ice cap increases with great rapidity during the first 45 degrees of latitude traveled. This is because the centrifugal is at this time pulling (more properly, throwing) the weight of the ice in an essentially sidewise manner. However, this sidewise pull soon becomes and outward pull the closer the ice comes to the equator. By the time 75 to 80 degrees of latitude has been traversed [see section devoted to Equatorial Bulge Displacement] there is little side pull remaining, but a very strong outward stabilizing pull and the ice cap becomes part of the new equatorial bulge.

Ultimately, the capsizing motion stops when the new bulge of earth materials and ice cap join to stabilize the planet on its new Axis of Figure. Because the Antarctic continent was thirteen miles closer to the center of the earth at its polar location than at the equator, it has moved upward a considerable distance, elevating far more land area that was previously exposed, even though covered by ice. Contrarily, equatorial areas suddenly shifted to the polar regions are thirteen miles closer to the center of the earth than they were on the equatorial bulge and therefore are now submerged beneath the sea. Thus, the kinetic energy created by the capsizing becomes absorbed to some degree in the elevation of great land masses in some areas and the lowering of other land masses in other areas.

More pertinent to the present situation, the next capsizing of the earth will result in the Antarctic continent becoming the center of a great land hemisphere and, at the same time, the Arctic area, including Alaska, northern Canada, Greenland, and northern Europe and Asia, will become the center of a water hemisphere and will undoubtedly become the bottom of a great ocean comparable to the Pacific Ocean we know today.

For clarification, it becomes necessary to discuss exactly what land and water hemispheres are, and their formation. The surface of planet earth is geologically divided into what is known as a Land Hemisphere (this hemisphere presently located north of the equator) which is made up of 46.6 percent land and 53.4 percent water, and a Water Hemisphere (south of the present equator) which contains a bare 11.6 percent land area and 88.4 percent water. Thus, more than three-fourths of the land area of the earth at present is located north of the equator. The principal reason for this has been that, insofar as can be determined, the last three capsizings of the earth have been caused by the excessive weight of the north polar ice cap rather than the south polar ice cap. This becomes a very important point of consideration, since the next capsizing will be caused by the southern ice cap. Much greater devastation across of the entire earth can therefore be expected than during the previous three such cataclysms, which occurred where the land hemisphere was already in existence.

Sanders was so absorbed in what he was reading that he hadn't even realized that Hazel Tierney had reentered the room with a small tray on which were two sandwiches, a couple of cookies and a glass of milk. She placed the tray on the table beside his chair.

"Your lunch, sir," she said.

"What? Oh, thanks, Hazel."

He picked up a sandwich half and began munching on it automatically, not knowing what was in it and not hearing his secretary go out again. He leafed through a few more pages before pausing to read closely again.

…The North Pole does not have a true ice cap now, nor will it have unless, through unforeseeable and unlikely circumstances, the Bering Strait should be sealed. The reason, of course, is that there is no continental mass directly over the North Pole area The nearest such masses are Ellesmere Island in northern Canada, and Greenland. Both have substantial ice caps but, because of the limitation of their land masses, nothing of the significance of that at Antarctica. Further, the flow of water beneath the Arctic ice shelf prevents the accumulation of any sort of ice cap. Pacific Ocean currents force a flow of some 41 billion tons of water daily through the Bering Straight into the Arctic Ocean at an average speed of about 4.5 miles per hour. The ice on the ocean surface over the north polar region is floating ice, averaging only twelve feet in thickness and rarely exceeding 16 feet, over water which averages some 4,000 feet in depth. This whole body of ice gradually moves eastward with the ocean flow, breaking off into icebergs as it enters North Atlantic waters. Dramatic proof of this was inadvertently established by Captain Fridjot Nansen aboard the Fram *and the Russian explorer Nicholai Brestov aboard the ship* G. Sedov. *Both vessels, at different times, became locked in the ice on*

the Pacific side of the Arctic Ocean and at the end of three years drifted free on the Atlantic side.

If this current was not in existence, a northern ice cap would certainly have formed centuries ago. With the weight of two great ice caps being acted on by centrifugal force, the capsizing of the earth would have occurred long ago and man would not have progressed sufficiently to begin understanding the cause...

The Chief Executive leaned his head back and closed his eyes, digesting this information. It was not difficult to visualize the conditions as they were portrayed here in the Grant summary. He opened his eyes again and, coming into a more familiar area, he once more moved rapidly along, skimming the lines swiftly until he reached a portion another few pages along, where his attention became more directed.

During the mid-1880s it was discovered that the earth had developed a slight wobble in its rotation—an eccentricity for which many theories were advanced, but nothing conclusive. When first noted, this faint rocking motion amounted to only about an inch, at a speed of less than two feet per hour. That wobble gradually increased over the intervening years and now it is estimated to be in the neighborhood of half a mile. The linear motion is increased with each increase in the size of the ice cap, and this is reflected in a decided increase in centrifugal force and, with it, greater inertia. The pressures involved in such a rocking motion are incalculable and the buildup of kinetic energy is phenomenal.

Some of these pressures and some of the kinetic energy are expended through the occurrence of earthquakes here and there on the globe, but there comes a time when the relief this provides is not enough. The equatorial bulge being moved away from the outermost rim of centrifugal throw by the wobbling action begins to compensate. Misapplication of mathematics has resulted in general acceptance of the theory that any capsizing of the globe is impossible, but this is an error—the outgrowth of a nonanalytical initial study beginning with the false premise that the equatorial bulge is rigid and immovably solid, but recent geological studies show that in fact it is a yielding ring of earth materials which, when forced to do so by tremendous pressures, becomes relatively plastic in constitution. As such, it both can and does rearrange its constituent parts to accommodate itself to the pressures to which it becomes subjected. As was mentioned above, the equatorial bulge begins to compensate for being moved away from the peak of centrifugal force. It begins moving back toward that force, flowing beneath the crust of the earth's surface, its force attempting to overcome the resistance to movement manifested in the hardrock stratifications. In this way the stabilizing gyroscope of the earth differs from a mechanical gyroscope. The parts of the latter are fixed and inflexible and cannot adjust as the earth gyroscope does as various parts give way before the pressures and yield, then readjust.

The actual start of the capsizing is a result of two widely separated movements. The ice cap approaches and then passes the absolute limit of recovery, while at the same time the plastic fluidity of the earth materials below the crust overcomes the resistance the crust represents. When this occurs, the dominant force becomes the centrifugal force moving both the ice cap and the bulge toward one another at increasing speed. The ice cap moves with the greater speed, not having the resistance to overcome that is faced by the equatorial bulge. The bulge appears to move at this time like a vast underground wave, analogous to the movement that can be created by gripping one edge of a carpet, raising and jerking it downwards and thus causing a large bulge to move away beneath it. But the earth bulge movement is, at its fastest, relatively slow as compared to that of the ice cap, and it is one that is extremely disruptive to the earth's surface, resulting in considerable earthquake and tidal wave activity as well as increased plate tectonic movements.

SURFACE DISRUPTION. Wholly incalculable kinetic energy develops from the movement of the poles and the shifting of the earth's equatorial bulge. Virtually the whole of the earth is in a disruptive movement at this time and, in addition to the kinetic energy developed by the ice caps as they migrate from the poles, continental masses themselves are also in movement and developing enormous amounts of kinetic energy of their own. With their great weight and varying velocities, they collide with the newly forming equatorial bulges and with the ice caps themselves. The kinetic energy thus generated is absorbed through a whole series of earth surface transformations—crushing, wrinkling, folding, splitting, elevating, descending, bending, stretching. What results is the formation of extended mountain chains and equally extensive rifts in the earth's surface. The mountain ranges and rifts are probably always at or very near right angles to the forces being expended. An example of such folding or wrinkling into mountains is the great ridge extending from the Arctic to the Antarctic along the western edges of the North and South American continents, forming the Andes and Rockies-Sierra Nevada chains presently existing.

An example of stretching and splitting is the Great Rift Valley of Africa, extending from the Mediterranean all the way southward across the face of Africa nearly to its southern terminus.

Examples of the crushing, elevating, folding and bending are seen everywhere on the globe in the form of uplifted masses of strata and geological rubble areas. Isolated mountains such as Stone Mountain in Georgia, Steamboat Rock at Dinosaur National Monument in Utah, Table Mountain in Africa, the Rock of Gibraltar off southwestern Europe, and Ayres Rock in Australia—all are clear evidence of elevation through vertical geologic fault, with the mass of earth material raised, exposing the laminations of strata that may have been buried as much as three miles or more beneath the earth's surface.

The wrinkling and folding, producing mountain ranges and elevation of individual masses, such as the relatively parallel accordianlike ridges of the Alleghenies, is evidence which helps to refute previous theories that the earth is shrinking in total volume, resulting in a prunelike desiccation of the earth's surface.

The distinct formation of warpage and bending and elevation in some areas, the wrinkling in others, the stretching and splitting in still others—but none of these as a general reaction occurring over the face of the earth—provides corollary evidence in support of the HAB Theory. This is especially true in relation to rifts and wrinkles.

The rifts most likely occur at the beginning of the capsizing movement, for rigid land masses are suddenly pulled with incredible force and stretch as far as their physical properties will allow, and then split to relieve the incredible pressure. The wrinkles, on the other hand, most likely occur toward the cessation of the capsizing movement, for the slowdown and stop are so abrupt that the momentum of continental masses cannot properly adjust to it and an accordianlike pile-up of earth materials occurs, resulting in the altering of many horizontal tiers of strata to vertical or near-vertical position and similarly causing synclines and anticlines of strata.

Robert Sanders stopped reading, rubbed his eyes, and then finished drinking the milk in his glass. He pinched his chin thoughtfully, staring unseeingly into space for a moment, then bent his attention once again to the Grant summary.

EQUATORIAL BULGE DISPLACEMENT. As noted, the capsizing of the planet, instigated by the migration of overweighted ice cap through centrifugal force to the outermost rim of spin, starts slowly but very rapidly accelerates until a point is reached which is 45 degrees from the Axis of Spin, which is the source of the centrifugal force acting on the ice mass.

Immediately upon passing this 45-degree point, an equally rapid deceleration begins and the ice cap comes to a full stop between 10 and 15 degrees of the former line of the equatorial latitude. The reason for this is that the equatorial bulge—moving more slowly, to be sure, to overcome the resistance of earth crustal materials—has been moving to meet the onrushing ice cap.

Thus, the capsizing of the ice cap is not a full 90 degrees, but rather between 75 and 80 degrees. At the same time, the equatorial bulge has moved 10 to 15 degrees toward the ice cap, with which it merges. Immediately the two masses work in unison to establish the new equatorial bulge for stabilization of the globe, still at right angles to the Axis of Spin. The total distance traveled by the center of the ice cap is approximately 5,500 miles, and the distance traveled by the equatorial bulge is about 2,413 miles—the two distances totaling approximately 7,913 miles, which is the mean diameter of the earth. But while this is occurring, the kinetic energies of both ice mass and equatorial bulge have increased billions of times what they were at the beginning of the capsizing.

RESULT AND AFTERMATH. During and following the capsizing of the earth, incredible surface devastation occurs as earth elements strive to adjust to the pressures and absorb the phenomenal kinetic energy which the rollover has generated.

A general chaos manifests itself in many forms—torrential rains, electrical storms unbelievable in their intensity, dust storms, hurricanes, typhoons, massive and extensive earthquakes, a multitude of volcanic eruptions and, most devastating of all, a monstrous deluge as tidal waves (tsunamis) of fantastic size and power sweep all oceans, pounding continents to pieces, inundating whole mountain ranges, rushing to submerge great land masses that have always seemed high and safe, and at the same time exposing masses of land which were heretofore seemingly at too great a depth ever to move above sea level. Existing mountains will be raised or lowered in relation to sea level, old ranges will be flattened and new ones appear.

There will not be the gradual withdrawal of ice as theorized in the prevailing "Ice Age" concept of alternately growing and receding ice caps. The ice cap, now directly on the equator and fully exposed to the blazing heat of the sun, will begin to melt at once and, while it may have taken thousands of years to reach its present enormous size, it may take only brief decades for the total thawing to occur.

As it disappears, the ice cap will leave behind telltale evidence of its former presence. An enormous depression will remain in the surface of the earth where it sat and this will be ringed by a vast circular range of mountains or hills or elevated plateaus, rising gradually from the center of the depression and then falling away sharply on the outside of the rim—the residue of the earth materials squeezed through isostasy from beneath the great weight of the ice cap as it grew. Glacial striations will clearly show on many of these rocks. River beds will form and glacial runoff will carve itself deeply into earth materials as the thaw occurs and vast quantities of water form from the melting ice cap. At the same time, the tropical areas which were suddenly shifted to polar regions undergo a quick-freezing process and soon are below layers of snow gradually turning into glacial ice as new ice caps begin to form on earth even while the old ones are still melting.

As the great ice caps continue to melt, ocean levels will rise, inundating still more areas of land and, as the isolated ice mass is reduced and its weight is distributed as water throughout the oceans, earthquakes of great strength and violence will continue to occur as the equatorial bulge adjusts and readjusts to equalize and stabilize the rearrangement of such a weight.

At last the violent disturbances buffeting the earth will settle down and a new stability to the planet becomes evident. Earthquake and volcanic activity virtually cease for perhaps hundreds of years or longer. Little animal life remains on the land masses of the globe but what is there, including human life, adjusts to the new conditions and survives, evolving perhaps into entirely new life forms as part of their continuing adjustment. Much marine life has been wiped out, but much remains and it, too, must adjust and evolve to survive in the new conditions, for the ocean temperatures have been greatly lowered by the icy volumes of water rushing into the sea from the glacial runoff. Adjustment in marine life will also have to take place to compensate for the greatly reduced salinity of the sea.

When at last the old ice caps have wholly disappeared and the ocean levels are relatively stabilized, the slow but inexorable process begins all over again. Over hundreds and thousands of years, the levels of the oceans will lower as evaporation sucks up the moisture, carrying it via convection currents to the new polar areas where it falls and compacts and builds into new ice caps until finally those ice caps have become so monumental in size that they begin to wobble eccentrically and eventually capsize the earth once again in a continuing cycle visited upon the earth hundreds of thousands or perhaps even millions of times during the four-and-a-half-billion-year history of the planet.

The President drummed his fingertips on the arm of the chair and pursed his lips in a silent whistle, continuing the little hissing of air as he shifted his position, taking his feet from the hassock and now crossing his legs, using his hands to help position his artificial foot over the opposite knee. More comfortably settled, he resumed his reading, in a new area.

PREVIOUS POLES. Using the same process of location used in ascertaining the location of the North Pole ice cap in Epoch Number B.P. 1 (one epoch before the present epoch), the ice cap for B.P. 2 is found to have been where there is an even larger and deeper depression in the earth than the Sudan Basin—present Hudson Bay. Here the depression, averaging 420 feet below sea level, extends outward in the characteristic circular manner of ice cap residue for 1,800 miles from the center, extending southwardly to the moraines of Long Island, northern New Jersey, Pennsylvania, southern Ohio, the Mississippi Valley and Wisconsin, with the well-demarcated Laurentian Shield being the heights of land virtually surrounding Hudson Bay and providing evidence of the isostatic upthrust of earth materials extruded from beneath the main weight of the ice cap that rested there.

Further, close analysis of the layers of clay (varves) taken in both New Jersey and Wisconsin irrefutably give the life span of that ice cap as 6,800 years, or about 60 percent longer than the Sudan basin ice cap. Additional corroboration is suggested in the fact that the age of the Sudan Basin ice cap comes from Carbon-14 dating of samples of wood uncovered at Tomahawk, Wisconsin, from a lower earth stratum—the remains of an ancient forest. These remains are concurrent with the termination of the Wisconsin Ice Age or, in other words, the thawing of the Hudson Bay ice cap. The age of the wood has been established at approximately 11,400 years. Subtracting from that the approximate 7,000-years of our present epoch, we find that from the end of the B.P. 2 Hudson bay ice cap to the beginning of our own epoch there was an interval of 4,400-years—the duration of the B.P. 1 Sudan basin ice cap.

Identification of Hudson Bay as the location of the North Pole in B.P. 2 is ascertained from calculations showing that it is approximately the same distance from Lake Chad in the Sudan Basin as the latter is from the present North

Pole, indicating a separation of about 10 degrees of latitude.

The ice cap for B.P. 3 is ascertained in the same manner and proves to center itself at the Caspian Sea, which is located in a great depression similar to that formerly occupied by the ice caps for the Sudan basin and Hudson Bay. All three of these depressions—containing the Caspian Sea, Lake Chad, and Hudson Bay—are presently the drainage focus for river systems covering very large areas of territory; rivers which flow into the depressed basins formed by the weight of the ice caps which previously rested on those sites.

The Caspian Sea ice cap of B.P. 3 had similarities to the Sudan basin ice cap of B.P. 1, in that available physical evidence indicates it was landlocked and therefore the glaciation could not slough off to be carried away by the sea as bergs. As with the Sudan basin ice cap, the life of the Caspian Sea ice cap was relatively short—evidently in the neighborhood of 5,000 years.

It becomes possible to trace depression after depression on the face of the earth as the location of a former ice cap. Glacial striations were even discovered on Permian rocks two centuries ago in the Amazon Valley within an area of twenty degrees on both sides of the equator. As a matter of fact, such glacial horizons are found in the rocks of the earth at random places all over the globe. So-called Ice Ages can be traced back through their telltale striations on rock faces not only as far back as the Paleozoic Era's Lower Cambrian Epoch of some 600 million years ago, but some are even recorded as pre-Cambrian, though even those records begin to dim over such a period of time with recurring capsizings of the earth and disruption of its surface. Three such pre-cambrian ice ca[ps are located in Africa, three others in Asia and two in Australia. Five glaciated horizons of the Permian Period (280-230 million years ago) are found in South America and an equal number of the most recent Ice Ages are located in North America.

In the present geological epoch, called the Pleistocene (of the Quaternary Period and Cenozoic Era), which, in essence, takes in the last one million years, many hundreds of earth capsizings have occurred, along with their cataclysmic results. Beyond the Pleistocene there have been many more. A partial listing of some of the more important and obvious ice cap sites during the paleozoic, Mesozoic and Cenozoic Eras can include: the Gobi Desert; Lake Victoria; Mar Chiquita in Argentina; the Black Sea; Death Valley, California; the Amazon Valley; Baikal Lake in Russia; Lake Winnipeg; the Nullabor Plain in Australia's southwest; baffin Bay; the Baltic Sea; the Congo Basin; the Mediterranean Sea; Great Bear Lake, Canada; Great Salt Lake, Utah; the Thar Desert in northwestern India; the Aral Sea in Uzbek; the Painted Desert; Lakes Michigan-Huron-Superior; the Angola Basin off the coast of western Africa; the Bighorn Basin, Wyoming; the Tabor vicinity in northeastern Siberia; the Takla Makan Desert north of the Himalayas; the Canary Basin of the northwestern African coast; Great Slave Lake in Canada; the Argentine Basin 930 miles southeast of Buenos Aires; the Wharton Basin, 900 miles south of Djakarta. And to all these can be added the scores of others known and suspected beneath the surface of the world's oceans.

In every location where records written by nature or man can be studied, each of these sites shows radial striae which pinpoint the seat of a former ice cap. In the matter of duration, geologic evidence indicates that an individual ice cap may grow to maturity in as short a span of time as 2,900 years, although the average appears to be more in the vicinity of 5,750 years. Only rarely does an individual epoch reach 6,500 years, and no other epoch within at least the last dozen has lasted as long as this present one.

Moving along again, the President skimmed rapidly through the next seven or eight pages—the extensive section detailing proofs as related to fossil remains and how the cataclysm had caused the fossilization of soft-bodied animals, fruits, vegetation, and even dinosaur tracks and eggs. He read again about the finding of fossil trees—or at least portions of them—from depths of 13,000 feet beneath the earth's surface through core borings; the discovery of 59 horizontal strata of fossilized trees separated by massive strata of marine clay-rock on nonfossiliferous variety at the Sydney Mines of Cape Breton, Nova Scotia; the fact that Carbon-14 dating of the woolly mammoth remains found in Siberia and North America clearly indicated a time frame of 7,500 years ago. All this material very strongly supported the contentions of the HAB Theory, and President Sanders was no less impressed by it now than he had been the first time he read it.

He swiftly re-read the portion explaining how the epoch duration for the present was determined by the creepage rate of waterfalls through their gorges and then he slowed and began reading more thoroughly again as he came to a different section detailing other forms of evidence supporting the HAB Theory:

Further evidence of earth capsizings can be found in massive mineral deposits which man is in the process of tapping. Highly illustrative among these are the numerous salt beds that are found in subterranean strata. There is only one way to rationally account for their presence; that they were at one time the bottoms of land depressions which filled with sea water during capsizings of the earth, then became exposed again in subsequent capsizings as salt lakes. Gradually, as the waters of these lakes evaporated, the salts precipitated to the bottom as residue.

Seven successive beds of these salt deposits have been found in central New York, and a massive one is presently being tapped a thousand feet below the city of Cleveland, Ohio. Over 30 such beds have been discovered in the American Southwest, some deeply buried, some just under the surface. The most significant on the North American continent, however, is the one which is presently being formed in a lake which, while constantly evaporating, still covers an area about the size of the State of Delaware—the Great Salt lake of Utah. This 2,000-square-mile lake is the last trace of the great prehistoric body of water known to geologists as Lake Bonneville, which covered an area of 20,000 square miles and was over 1,000 feet deep. The great Bonneville salt Flats are on the surface now, but following the next capsizing of the earth they will probably become silted over and eventually, following further capsizings of the earth, become yet another of the multitude of subterranean salt beds.

Coal is another mineral deposit clearly corroborating the successive capsizings of the earth. Coal beds are found in subterranean deposits on a worldwide scale, including the Arctic and Antarctica, and even beneath the ocean floors. Numerous submarine coal mines are presently in operation in the pacific off the coast of Chile and in the Atlantic off Nova Scotia and England. Yet, there is only one way that coal can be formed. It is the residue of vegetation grown in warm temperate, subtropical and tropical lands. Through hundreds or thousands of years, great quantities of vegetative debris—leaves, twigs, fruits, branches, roots—sink to the bottoms of swamps, rivers or lakes. The water covering them reasonably protects them from the oxidation that would have occurred had they been exposed to the air.

At the time of the capsizing of the earth, the submerged deposit of vegetable debris is suddenly shifted to a region of subzero temperature and immediately the water above it freezes. During the polar summer there occurs enough of a thaw to allow siltage to accumulate on the bottom over the mucky vegetation. When the next capsizing of the planet occurs and the deposit is shifted back to a tropical or temperate zone, the layer of silt prevents oxidation of the vegetable matters below it from occurring, while at the same time s new collection of vegetable matter is accumulating on top of the silt. Through repeated capsizings and increasing pressures, the layers of vegetation are compressed into coal and the polar siltage layers become slate or shale. Some of the coal mines in Pennsylvania have shown as many as seven horizontal layers of coal with as many layers of shale or slate interleaved between. Recurrent capsizings of the earth can be the only reasonable and logical explanation for such formations.

Another foundation stone in the construction of support for the HAB Theory postulations lies in the discovery in the relatively recent past of magnetic rocks which vary from the direction of magnetic electrical forces present being imbued into rocks of the earth. The ancients knew of the existence of magnetic rocks, of course, and used them as compasses in their navigation, These were simply magnetized to point north and south by the electrical currents of the earth. But now, much older rocks have been discovered which, though magnetic, do not point north and south, but to differing directions. This is powerful indication that they received their magnetization at a time when the function of the poles differed from what it is at present. Some of the rocks of this nature that have been discovered point toward the Sudan and others point toward Hudson bay. Still others point at other areas where physical evidence indicates ice caps have formed in past epochs. Nonconventionally directional magnetic rocks have been discovered in 15 locations on the European and North American continents. They are corollary to, and proof of, the recurrent capsizings of the earth.

It was as he came to the next section of the Grant summary that a drawn-out sound of "Ummmm" escaped the President in the quiet of the room. This was the area coming up which most intrigued him and the area in which the work mark Shepard was doing over in Turkey bore considerable relevance. The most recent talk with mark on the phone had, in fact, been so significant in relation to the postulations of the HAB Theory that he had wound up talking with him for upwards of an hour. That conversation had gelled a plan which until then had been only roughly formative in his mind. Beginning today he would put that plan into operation, and now he bent with great interest to read what was coming.

It is in the matter of proofs where human history is concerned that incredible new vistas of study are suddenly opened. It is an acknowledged fact among ancient historians that authentic and accurate history of man did not begin until between approximately 7,000 and 7,500 years ago. Actual historical records go back only as far as the earliest known civilizations, such as those of Egypt, Peru, Babylonia, India, Central America, Sumeria, and Assyria. Yet, that 7,500-year period of time represents considerably less than one percent of the time that man has been known, through fossil remains, to have existed on earth.

A curious and yet exciting element of man's history exists in the fact that virtually all cultures in earth, from the most primitive to the most civilized, have in the dim reaches of their history the record or legend of a great flood. In the Bible it is the story of Noah. In the Oriental book, The Ten Stems of China, *tells of it. From the 12 clay tablets inscribed in Sumerian cuneiform comes the* Epic of Gilgamesh, *which recounts the journeyings of Enkidu, a sort of counterpart of Noah. In Greek mythology, Deucalion and his wife, Pyrrha, are the only survivors of a great flood visited on the earth by the great god Zeus. The ancient Brahmans, Chaldeans, Hindus, and Babylonians all had their own records or legends about similar great floods from which only a handful of individuals escaped with their lives. Similar legends are found among the Indians of the Americas and among the aboriginal tribes of Australia, Borneo, Sumatra, Africa and Southeast Asia. Generally, we moderns have looked upon these stories as being apocryphal, but perhaps we have been wrong. Perhaps much more truth underlies them than we had previously suspected. And while the support they provide cannot at this time be considered proof, they do provide interesting and sometimes rather awesome corroboration to the theory of a recurrently capsizing earth.*

Apart from consideration of such legends or so-called records, elements of stronger proof of the HAB Theory's validity have become available in man's history through archaeology. In Iraq, for example, near the confluence of the Tigris and Euphrates rivers, is the site of the ancient Chaldean city of Ur. Evidence exposed by archaeologists digging through layer after layer to a depth of 50 feet proved that over 130 dynasties existed there. Then, at just over 50 feet, they encountered a 10-foot-thick layer of clay. Beneath that layer were discovered the remains of another 10 dynasties, but of such difference that the artifacts recovered from these lower layers bore little resemblance to those discovered in the layers above. Pottery below the clay was beautifully and skillfully painted, but that above the clay was not. Copper artifacts were common in the dynasty layers above the clay, but absent in those below. The archaeologists are unanimous about only one aspect—that the layer of clay had to be the residue of a great flood which buried the city under a great blanket of silt. For the silt to accumulate and turn into clay took a great while and, though scientists are still not agreed to the exact amount of time involved, the general consensus is that the upper layers were all deposited within the last 6,000 years and perhaps as much as 1,500 years prior to that. The significance of the clay layer beginning to form about 7,500 years ago in inescapable.

The ancient Greek, Solon, according to Plato, was told by Egyptian priests in 600 B.C. that 9,000 years previously, Egypt had been invaded by great armies from the powerful island empire of Atlantis, and that afterward Atlantis was devoured by the ocean in a great deluge. The existence of such a place as Atlantis has long been held as a myth, but in view of the accumulation of evidence, perhaps there is more veracity to the story than heretofore believed. That, however, is speculation on the writer's part and not the province of this summary.

The President looked up as there came a light tapping at his door and Hazel Tierney halfway entered the room.

"Excuse me, sir," she said, "but you asked me to let you know when only ten minutes remained before the meeting."

"Oh, yes, thank you, Hazel. Have they begun to show up yet?"

"Yes, sir. More than half are here already."

"All right. Tell Steve to let me know when it's time and they're all assembled."

She nodded and shut the door with a faint click as he returned his attention to the small amount of material left to read in the summary. He went over several more pages quickly, including the Boardman proposed solution to the projected cataclysm. The final comments by Grant he read more thoroughly as the summary came to an end.

More specifically, Mr. Boardman outlined his plan for diminishing the Antarctic ice cap size in the following manner. The initial point at which man has to attack the great glacier is along the entire perimeter of the coastline, which extends for 16,000 miles. The average rate of slope, or gradient, from the center of the South Pole ice cap to the sea is presently 7 feet per mile, as compared to a gradient of 28 feet per mile with the North Pole ice cap on Greenland. The gradient of 7 feet per mile at Antarctica is not sufficient to overcome the barrier rim of mountains holding the ice in check. One of the most urgent priorities Mr. Boardman mentioned was the need to accurately ascertain the annual precipitation in snowfall on the existing ice cap and the ratio of this accumulation to the annual evaporation, ablation, and flowoff. In that manner, it could then be determined exactly how much the flowoff would have to be increased to stabilize the globe on its present Axis of Figure, and then this could be undertaken through the utilization of judiciously placed and detonated thermonuclear devices as previously outlined in these pages.

Mr. Boardman's recommendations ended in the comment that we now have before us a wholly new understanding of the limited time during which our civilization has been developing and the deadly precariousness of its continuance. We have before us, he contended, only two alternatives: either we limit the present growth rate of the Antarctic ice cap, or we accept a limitation to the time we have remaining on this planet in civilization as we now know it.

THIS CONCLUDES THE SUMMARIZATION OF THE THEORY OF A RECURRENTLY CAPSIZING EARTH AS POSTULATED BY HERBERT ALLEN BOARDMAN, SUMMARIZING A QUANTITY OF TEXT, MATHEMATICAL FORMULAE, SKETCHES AND PHOTOGRAPHS EQUIVALENT TO APPROXIMATELY 20,000 PAGES. THIS SUMMARY HAS BEEN PREPARED BY ORDER OF THE PRESIDENT OF THE UNITED STATES FOR CONSIDERATION BY THE SPECIAL SCIENTIFIC ADVISORY COMMITTEE APPOINTED BY THE PRESIDENT TO STUDY AND EVALUATE THE AFOREMENTIONED POSTULATION KNOWN AS THE HAB THEORY.

RESPECTFULLY SUBMITTED.

John C. Grant, Special Aide
to the President
Kermit Knotts, Chairman
HAB Theory Commission

V I

"Paul? Glad I caught you in your office. I know you usually go to lunch around eleven-thirty and it's almost half past twelve here. I was afraid I'd miss you."

Paul Neely's voice, businesslike when he first answered the phone, warmed considerably. "Ah, Liz. I had a hunch you might call. I was going to stick around here until noon on the chance you would. How's it going there in New York?"

"Quite nicely, as near as I can tell," Elizabeth Boardman replied, "but I'm constantly aware of a certain gap. You're not here with me, and I so much want you to be. Paul, I know it's difficult, but…" she hesitated, then went on, "…is there any way you could come here, at least for a few days if not for all of next week?"

"Well, I should say no, because it really is tough right now. We've finally got the summer session going full swing and enrollment's larger than we'd anticipated. That staff meeting was set for next Wednesday, as you know, but it turns out that it's not a good day for several of the teachers, plus the fact that you won't be here, so I've sent out a memo changing the meeting date to a week from Wednesday. As a matter of fact, I had an ulterior motive of my own. I was thinking of possibly taking a day or two in conjunction with the weekend and flying there to surprise you."

"Oh, dear," she sounded contrite, "and now I've gone and spoiled it. I'm sorry, Paul."

"Don't be. You've just convinced me to change it to all week. That'll still give me the following Monday and Tuesday to get prepared for the meeting. Frankly, I'm damned interested in what's going on there. You still haven't told me."

"So far," she admitted, "not really a great deal. The actual symposium meetings aren't scheduled to begin until three this afternoon, but the opening meeting at Madison Square Garden this morning was very interesting. I met the President."

"You met the—" Neely blew out a big breath. "And you're saying nothing much happened? What, dear lady, do you consider to be much?"

"Well," she laughed, "I was speaking then in terms of things being accomplished. Actually, it has been very interesting. President Sanders gave an excellent opening address—registration around thirty-seven hundred, by the way and then when he was finished he came directly over to me, held my hands and told me he thought Father would have been very proud of me for what I said."

"You addressed that group, too? My God, Liz, you really do understate things. That's marvelous. And the fact that Sanders himself would come to you with personal praise! That's just terrific. Well, I can't let any more activities like that pass me by. When do you want me to come?"

"As soon as you can get away, whenever that'll be."

"I've already called and made reservations," he told her. "My plane takes off just short of two hours from now. I'll be landing at La Guardia in about four hours. Four-twenty New York time, I think it is. Can you get me a room there where you're staying?"

"Paul, don't be silly. My room is your room. You don't have any choice. For one thing, there's not a room to be had anywhere in New York this week. Hurry, darling. I'll leave word at the desk where you can find me. There are meetings I have to attend this afternoon, so I won't be able to meet you at the airport, but just grab a taxi to town and you'll find me the Waldorf, okay?"

"Right. I'm on my way. Have to hustle to the apartment and throw some things in a bag and then get out to O'Hare. See you soon." He paused, then added, "I love you, Liz."

"I love you, too, Paul. Hurry. I'll be watching for you."

VII

President Robert Morton Sanders was just setting aside the HAB Theory summary in the smaller sitting room adjacent to the room where the meeting was to be held as Steve Lace entered and stopped just inside the door. It was exactly 12:30.

"Everyone's present, Mr. President."

"Fine," the Chief Executive said, rising from his seat, "we may as well get started with it. We've a lot of ground to cover. Are there enough seats for everyone?"

"Yes, sir. We had some extra chairs brought in by the hotel staff. It'll be fairly casual, though. No conference table and just a lot of chairs, plus the two sofas, all of them generally facing the sofa chair where you'll be sitting."

"Good. I think I'll like that atmosphere better than a more formal meeting table. It'll probably put them more at ease, too. No folding chairs, I hope?"

"No, sir. Either sofa chairs like the one you'll be using, or else nicely padded straight chairs."

Sanders nodded. "Nothing worse," he said as he joined Lace, "than to have to sit through a meeting in an uncomfortable seat." He held up a hand, stopping Lace as the press secretary reached for the doorknob. "What about time? Everyone prepared for at least an hour here?"

"I'm afraid that may be difficult, sir. Dr. Dowde has her meeting with the group chairmen in just an hour from now and she'll have to go to that. Both Dr. Lossing and Dr. Robinson are group chairmen, so they'll have to go, also. That meeting will be followed by the group meetings at three, so it looks like we can only count on those three being here with us for about forty-five minutes at best."

"All right. I wish we had longer, but I guess we'll make out. Let's go."

Lace opened the door, looked into the adjoining room and then said loudly, "Ladies and gentlemen, the President." He stood aside to let the Chief Executive pass.

There was a general commotion as those seated in the larger room began coming to their feet, but Sanders already had a hand out, waving them back.

"Please," he told them, "stay seated. We haven't time to be resting on too many formalities today."

He moved immediately to the large leather-finished chair at the front of the room. Seated to the left of that chair in front of a small table on which was a stenotype machine was Hazel Tierney. The President nodded to her as he sat down, and then to Alexander Gordon and John Grant, who were sitting close to the door leading to the remainder of the suite beyond. Steve Lace, quietly closing the door they had entered from the sitting room, took a seat just to the right and slightly behind the President. Kermit Knotts was sitting in a chair similar to the President's, along the wall to the Chief Executive's right. Four watchful Secret Service agents remained standing, two flanking the entry door, two others along the walls to left and right of the President.

The remaining twelve in the room were the members of the President's special Scientific Advisory Committee. Their leader, Irma Dowde, sat in another of the overstuffed chairs toward the front, closest to Sanders, who smiled at her in greeting and noted with inner amusement that her walking shoes, somewhat scuffed this morning at the Madison Square Garden meeting, had a new shine on them now and he wondered where she had found time to get them polished.

To Dr. Dowde's left and a little behind her, side by side in plush-seated straight-backed chairs were the committee's vice-chairman, Dr. Jason Robinson, the Smithsonian geologist, his short, pudgy, round-faced aspect almost cherubic, and the dapper astronomer, Dr. Edgar Lossing, chief of the U.S. Naval Observatory. The other ten committee members were either in chairs scattered out behind them or on the two small sofas.

"Ladies and gentlemen," Sanders continued, as soon as he was comfortably seated, "once again I want to thank you for the time and effort you've put in on your close evaluation of the HAB Theory and for being here today. I know that you, Dr. Dowde, as well as Dr. Lossing and Dr. Robinson, have limited time available right now, so I'll ask that we move right along. I'm also aware," he added, as she seemed about to say something, "that because of your efforts in coordinating this symposium, you haven't really been able to participate as much in the committee's work as you may have wished. Therefore, be at ease if there are gaps in your knowledge of what has transpired within the committee during this period. I would like this to be a fully open meeting at which any one of you who has anything at all to say can feel free to say it. We're not standing on ceremony here. I'd like this to be a group discussion, not a monologue."

He cleared his throat softly and continued. "I think I should tell you at this juncture that whatever conclusions are drawn from this meeting today will play a very major role in decisions I must make, some of which may be put into implementation today. I think I know fairly well by now, through interim reports from both Dr. Dowde and Dr. Robinson, what your feelings are in regard to the HAB Theory, but just so there's no mistake about it, let me start by asking if there is any member of this Scientific Advisory Committee who is *not* at this time reasonably certain of the validity of the HAB Theory?"

The two women and ten men making up the committee either looked quietly at the President or else glanced at their neighbors, but no individual among them spoke, and after a few moments the President nodded.

"I'm not surprised. Now, what I'd like immediately for press release purposes, as I mentioned to you earlier Dr. Dowde, is a concise and essentially-nonscientific description of the HAB Theory, an explanation of it that the average American will be able to understand. Mrs. Tierney, incidentally, will be recording what transpires here and the press release will be drawn up from her notes. When we're finished with that brief explanation, perhaps then there may be time to move into the less firm ground of what your own predictions may be in regard to when, assuming the acceptability of the theory, that the cataclysm may occur and what recommendations you may have to offer as to how we can best circumvent or meet the event. Dr. Dowde?"

There was a bit of shuffling and coughing and readjusting of positions as Irma Dowde momentarily glanced at her notes. During this interval Grant, Knotts and a few of the scientists lit cigarettes. Dr. Dowde peered through the heavy horn-rimmed spectacles at her papers a moment longer and then let the glasses fall from her face to hang on her chest from the silver chain which encircled her neck and attached to the stems. Having just this week given up smoking, she looked enviously at the long cigarette Kermit Knotts was holding and sighed aloud.

"Mr. President," she began, "I think first of all that on behalf of the committee I should say that our work on this project could never have been accomplished had it not been for the admirable competence exhibited in the combined talents and work of Mr. Grant in summarizing the Boardman papers for us and by Mr. Knotts and his commission in providing an excellent and very swiftly completed transcription. Had we not had the benefit of their assistance, what we have done could not have been possible in the framework of time that was allotted to us. Mr. Grant, Mr. Knotts," she said, facing them in turn, "we sincerely thank you and commend you for a superlative job."

Grant smiled in response to the praise and Knotts, dressed today in a light gray suit and bright green bow tie, acknowledged the accolade with the nearest approximation of a smile that most of them had ever seen on his normally expressionless face.

"To go on, Mr. President," the archaeologist continued, centering her attention on Robert Sanders again, "in order to establish the initial foundation for this discussion, I should point out that we of this committee are, in fact, unanimously convinced of the HAB Theory's validity; to such degree that, while there may be one or two among us who do not totally ascribe to all the findings, we can advance no basis for *not* accepting it in the light of our present knowledge. All of the evidence studied supports with considerable conclusiveness the thesis that throughout its history of some four and a half billion years, the earth has repeatedly and at reasonably regular intervals of time capsized and taken up a new axis of rotation. This rollover has not affected its moving in orbit about the sun, but it has caused regular and almost completely annihilative destruction upon the surface of the earth insofar as animal life on the land masses has been concerned. Nothing in our respective branches of science among committee members can adequately refute this fundamental conclusion. We find the HAB Theory to be entirely consistent with the laws of nature, which are deemed immutable."

Irma Dowde leaned over to pick up a thick packet of loosely bound papers which had been lying on the floor beside her chair. "This," she said, holding it up, "represents the points considered by us in reaching our conclusion. There are numerous points which we incorporated which might be considered as proofs, but proofs only insofar as they fall within the realm of immutable natural law. Many of them require further study and prolonged testing before they can really be called proofs, but certainly they form a basis of evidence which supports the postulations of the HAB Theory virtually in toto. There are equally numerous other items which cannot at this time be called proofs, but which tend to corroborate the tentative proofs assembled.

"These," she dropped the packet back to the thick carpet with a dull thud, "are much too numerous and diverse to make any attempt to go into detail here, but they are substantive and, assuming you have no objection, Mr. President, they will be copied and presented to the members of this symposium at once."

"I think it is probably wise," Sanders agreed, nodding, "that this be done. Your committee has had a month's head start. Providing the scientists newly assembled here for the symposium with your findings will undoubtedly prevent a considerable amount of repetition."

"Thank you, sir. To go on, there are many individual facets of information which serve as evidence to corroborate the conclusions of the HAB Theory. Some are quite pertinent, others only tangential. None, by itself, automatically proves the HAB Theory. Yet, because so many of these facets interlock with one another, viewed on the whole they provide an impressive and undeniable body of substantive material. The more all of these bits of information are fitted together, like the pieces of a puzzle interlocking, the better becomes our picture of the entire scheme of things. Thus far, all pieces have fitted together well within the precepts of the HAB Theory and whole new and exciting vistas of study are being opened in a variety of scientific branches. I think—and I feel certain that I speak for all of us on this committee, Mr. President—that even more than pointing out to us the peril that may be facing the earth's civilizations, the HAB Theory is opening a great new era of scientific discovery."

There were some affirmative nods from the scientists in the room and Dr. Carole Keaton, director of the

Division of Biological Sciences at Cornell University, verbalized the feeling for all of them in a single word when she said, "Amen!"

"However great and exciting the potentials being opened up to science, however," Dr. Dowde went on, "the imperative matter we must consider is that of the threatening cataclysm. Whatever we as scientists may discover through further penetration into the areas opened up to us via the HAB Theory, these will be meaningless if they are lost because of that very cataclysm which the HAB Theory forecasts."

Sanders gave a wry chuckle. "At that remark I'd tend to echo the comment made by Dr. Keaton a moment ago. I'm quite aware of the vistas of new study the HAB Theory opens to various branches of science, and I'm completely sympathetic with scientific eagerness to get moving along those lines. Nevertheless, our great concern now must be to learn all we can about the threatening cataclysm itself—what it does, when it may come, whether or not it could be circumvented or modified or, if not, then how to preserve at least a fair portion of mankind and a vast accumulation of the knowledge he has acquired. If past civilizations did exist and then vanish during such cataclysms—and there now seems to be every reason to assume that such has been the case—whatever knowledge they were able to amass during their tenure on earth was lost. Had they been aware of the potential of such cataclysm, they may have been able to at least preserve their knowledge for those who might survive. By and large, they did not. We seem to have that ability now, if we make use of it in whatever time remains to us. We here may not survive, but if we can preserve what we have learned, then perhaps during the next era of man he will be able to be much more prepared to survive or even circumvent the disaster. That is the goal we must specifically work toward. Now it seems to me that in order to do this, the most important point is to make the people totally aware of the situation. If it can be presented to them in layman's terms so that they fully grasp the significance, the task ahead will be greatly simplified. I'd like to see the HAB Theory become as commonplace a subject of discussion as the weather or the weekend's football scores."

The President paused and when he did not speak again right away, Steve Lace caught his attention and was given a nod.

"Sir," the press secretary began, "I can see a number of problems involved in making the imminence of the peril widely known. There's almost certain to be some degree of panic among the people. It's a pretty fearful prospect to digest, that at any moment in the future they could be wiped out."

"I'm sure there would be some fear," Sanders responded slowly, "but I seriously doubt the prospect of a mass panic. Man's a pretty adaptive creature. He may not like having to contemplate something this fearful, but if he's left with no choice, then contemplate it he will, and he'll use his energies to make the best of the situation that he can, for his own survival."

Lace grunted, not convinced. "Possibly so, Mr. President, but there are other effects as well which could turn out to be highly disruptive. What effect, for example, would it have on the world economy? Might not the stock market collapse? What about international relationships? They're bound to be deeply affected. These are matters which—"

"Those are matters," Sanders interrupted, "which, under the circumstances, Steve, are not of paramount importance. Political and economic considerations fade in importance in view of the basic threat to all mankind. To meet that threat, man has to be made aware of it. This doesn't mean just the scientific community, but man as a species—man as an organism concerned with his own survival, concerned with the survival of the species.

The President turned his attention back to the committee chairwoman. "Dr. Dowde, I think it is important that we go ahead without any further delay. We know that it has taken a great deal of explanation among ourselves to come to the realization of what is involved. That's why I asked you earlier if there was the possibility of boiling this all down to a simple form for publication in the world press."

"Yes, sir, Mr. President," Irma Dowde replied, "to a degree we've done that among ourselves already." She was thoughtful a moment and then swiftly, with commendable conciseness and clarity. she outlined the whole basic precept of the HAB Theory in less than a thousand words.

There was a long period of silence as Dr. Dowde finished talking. Grant, sitting near the door toward the rear, noted the silence with a bit of irony. As often as he himself had made similar explanation of the cause and effect of the cataclysm to others, there was always this brief period of stunned silence as the full impact of what had been said came crashing down on the listener. It was a concept so staggering, so far beyond the powers of reactive words to describe, that the silence always said more than any words could at the time.

Alexander Gordon, sitting nearby, was stony-faced and grim. Knotts, as usual, was expressionless, and the group of scientists were, on the whole, thoughtful. The President was almost imperceptibly shaking his head in continuing awe at the implications of the concept, and Steven Lace was frowning. Hazel Tierney, whose fingers had stopped their slow dance over the keys of the stenotype machine, had lost some of her color. The voices of two or three Secret Service men in the main room of the Presidential Suite could be heard as a vague rumble, the words they were speaking indistinguishable.

"Dr. Dowde," President Sanders broke the silence, "before time creeps up on us and you and your colleagues have to leave for your meeting, I'd like something of an evaluation if you can provide it. In your estimation, is the reaction of this committee apt to reflect the reflect the reaction of the large number of scientists who have gathered here for the symposium? Is it likely that their conclusion will differ drastically from your own? To the extent, perhaps, that they might be expected to conclude that the HAB Theory postulations are invalid?"

Irma Dowde was picking up her papers from the floor and assembling them in her lap, shaking her head all the while as she did so. She looked at the President directly and replied without hesitation.

"Not too likely," she said, "although it may differ in respect to the branch of science involved. The greatest adversary force, I would judge, will be the geologists. However, Mr. President, your Scientific Advisory Committee here in this room is, in actuality, something of a microcosm—including geologists—of the much larger body of scientists gathered in symposium out there." She inclined her head toward the doorway. "They are nearly four thousand people representing a dozen major fields of science which are further broken down into over thirty specialized classifications of study. We twelve of the committee, in this room, also represent those major branches of science and we are quite probably no more or less gullible or skeptical than they. This committee has had an advantage in being able to study the HAB Theory for about a month, and in a fairly cohesive context, thanks to the work of Mr. Grant and Mr. Knotts, and so we are somewhat more aware than they out there of the tremendous importance of the subject at hand. Because of it we have been able, in large measure, to put aside personal bias and beliefs in favor of the more important impartiality you recommended to them this morning, which consideration of the

HAB Theory requires. They will come to this point, too, before the symposium has ended, but they are not there yet. Nevertheless, I feel—and think my colleagues here will agree—that while there may be some individuals among the entire complement of scientists gathered here who simply will not accept the precepts of the HAB Theory, the majority of them, as they delve ever more deeply into the subject, will reach the same general conclusion reached by this committee: that the HAB Theory is indeed valid."

The President came to his feet, at the same time holding out a restraining hand to the others to keep them in place. "It's all right," he said, "please remain seated." He moved to the front wall of the room, glancing down through the curtains at the activity occurring below on Park Avenue, then turning back to face them and speaking thoughtfully.

"There is something that I'd like all of you here to do. By all of you I mean not only this advisory committee, but equally the others here—Mrs. Tierney, Kermit Knotts, John Grant, Alex Gordon. I would like each of you, in your own way, and asking the advice or suggestions of anyone you care to ask, to draw up a listing of what you feel to be the most essential works of man that are presently in writing."

A number of the scientists looked at each other with questioning glances at this, but the President went on without pause.

"By that," he said,"I mean that I want you to draw up a list of the books, pamphlets, maps, or other documents which you feel would be, in event of the HAB Theory cataclysm, the most important books to be saved in order to aid whoever survives the cataclysm to pick up the pieces and resume a civilization as nearly on the level of the present civilization as possible."

Limping slightly, the President moved to the front right of the room and leaned a shoulder against the wall, still talking as he did so. "All of you here are specialists in your own particular fields and so most of you would know very well what written works are the best, most complete and, as far as can be determined, the most accurate of texts where your own field of specialization is concerned. List those books or whatever, but do not feel that you must be limited only to those which deal with your own fields. *Any* book, in any field, which has struck you as being particularly significant in what it portrays of our civilization—technologically, scientifically, whatever. List them. I will be asking others in the fields of art, literature, education, religion, and so forth to do the same. I place no limitation whatever on the number of books to be listed. Priority, I think, should be given to those books which you feel would help the survivors perpetuate civilization, to reestablish themselves, but this should not exclude significant works of any cultural endeavor.

"We have here at this symposium," he went on, "the cream of the world's experts in numerous fields, and it would be a very good idea for each of you to contact the top people in all those fields and ask them, too, to draw up such listings. Are there any questions?"

"Yes, sir," John Grant spoke up at once. "Am I correct in assuming that these books, maps, papers and other documents would then be microfilmed and steps taken to insure that they survived the cataclysm?"

"Quite correct, Mr. Grant. Probably a great many which will appear on the lists have already been put on microfilm by the Library of Congress. Steps can be taken at once to microfilm those which have not. I would think that we should consider having at least six microfilm copies of each book. Perhaps as many as ten or twelve.

Incidentally, because of her experience in such matters, I am going to be asking Elizabeth Boardman to assist in a major way in this respect."

The Navy captain who was chief meteorologist of the U.S. Weather Service Command stood. He was a square-jawed, rather rugged-appearing individual of about forty, impeccable in his uniform.

"Captain Pugh?" Sanders said.

"Sir," Roland Pugh commented, "obviously you would intend placing these microfilms in six or more different locations. May we ask where such locations would be?" He to touched the knot of his tie, adding, "That is, of course, if you've come to any sort of conclusion in that respect."

"Yes, I have, at least partially," the President replied. "As a start, I would envision repositories being established at four locations on the earth and two in orbiting spacecraft. Or, perhaps, only one in an orbiting spacecraft and the other in a craft soft-landed on the lunar surface."

"Those four locations on the earth, Mr. President," spoke up the associate dean of geophysical sciences at Philadelphia's Drexel Institute as Pugh sat down, "where would they be located?"

"I have only vague ideas about three of them, Dr. Kaplan," Sanders replied briskly, returning to his chair and sitting down, "and would rather leave recommendation for that up to this committee. The only one I would suggest for sure at this time is at the Ngaia City complex being built in Kenya. I'd like the committee to very carefully consider what other locations might best provide likelihood of survival for such materials."

"*How* would they be likely to survive, sir?" Rodney Kaplan went on. "I mean, are these to be placed in some sort of time capsule or other such device, or what?"

The President shrugged. "Again, this is something the committee ought to consider. At Ngaia City it would probably be only a matter of establishing a strong, safe location within the confines of the structure. Elsewhere it would be a different matter. Perhaps a very sturdy concrete bunker-type structure which would be able to withstand the cataclysm. On the other hand, perhaps some kind of repository which, instead of withstanding, would tend to roll with the punch, so to speak—a repository built to rest easily on the earth's surface but which, if pressures of water or wind or whatever were brought against it, would be free to roll or float free and finally come to rest relatively undamaged wherever the forces of nature would leave it. I don't really know, but it is something which you here should give serious consideration to at once." He paused and looked out over the group, his head tilted. "Any other questions?"

"Yes, Mr. President," Grant spoke up again. "When we've drawn up our lists of what we consider important materials, what should we do with them?"

"Good question. I think probably the best thing would be to turn them over to Mr. Knotts and his commission for correlation. These could be combined alphabetically, perhaps under specific subject headings, and then turned over to Mrs. Tierney. In the meantime I'll be in touch with the director of the Library of Congress and have him clear the decks of the photoduplication service for the upcoming job. Anything else?"

No one replied and the President now turned his attention to the cherubic geologist from the Smithsonian Institution and continued.

"Dr. Robinson, since the HAB Theory most pertinently concerns itself with the geological past, present and future of this planet and probably will have a greater reevaluation effect upon the science of geology than upon any other specific field it involves, I'd appreciate your specific reaction. Dr. Dowde has already signified that the strongest opposition will probably come from the geologists. In addition to that, since you are vice-chairman of this committee, I'd like your own feelings in regard to what Dr. Dowde has said."

Jason Robinson smiled and blinked rapidly. "I believe that all of us on the committee are in full accord with Dr. Dowde's remarks, Mr. President. Certainly you are correct in your own analysis of the effect that acceptance of the theory will have on the science of geology. It brings me great concern personally, and I know it will similarly affect other geologists. A great deal of our thinking will have to be revised and many scientists—not only in geology—will be deeply dismayed to learn that projects upon which they have spent years of effort will now be rendered useless. That's a bitter pill to swallow. It is, however, one of the hazards of our profession. We all realize that there is the possibility of startling new theories being postulated which will undermine long-established beliefs, but we tend to close our eyes to it and hope it won't happen. When it does, we equally tend to resist it with all our power and to attack the new concept with every weapon available—often quite viciously. We're quite apt to run into some of that at this Symposiums, I'm afraid."

Dr. Carole Keaton was nodding vigorously as the Smithsonian curator of geology finished. "Dr. Robinson is quite correct in that regard, Mr. President," she said, "but all of us know equally that there comes a point at which even the scientist who is most dogmatically locked into his cherished beliefs must give way under the sheer weight of available evidence. That, too, we believe, will occur here very quickly. When such a thing does happen, it's usually quite an embarrassment to each of the branches of science involved, because in light of the new evidence it's only too easy for an outsider to say, 'Well, that's so obvious! How could they possibly have gone so long under that previous fallacious belief?' Such a criticism is really not justified, but that makes it no less embarrassing."

"Actually, Mr. President," spoke up the venerable Smithsonian paleontologist, Dr. Harvey Trautman, ignoring the audible sigh from Irma Dowde, "it's seldom a simple matter to correlate data between different branches of science." Trautman was a doddering but usually mentally acute octogenarian, and he spoke ponderously. "Scientists, by their very nature, tend to be isolationists—isolationists, that is, within the confines of their own specific areas of study. In a word, they have become specialists. It isn't surprising at all. In this age, where science is taking giant strides in practically every field, it becomes axiomatic that the individual scientist must specialize.

"I must say," he added in his agonizingly slow manner of speech, "that one of the greatest blessings of this present HAB Theory situation may turn out to be that it will conclusively prove to us the grave danger of such scientific isolationism. How many heretofore unexplainables might be more understandable if taken into consideration in composite scientific study rather than only by the single branch of science to which it seems most appropriate? I...uh...hmmmm." He stopped and scratched his chin, having evidently lost his train of thought, then looked in momentary mute appeal at the erudite Kaplan seated beside him.

Kaplan nodded and carried on for him. "Most of us as scientists, Mr. President, encounter many riddles within our own fields, riddles for which there are no explanations, however simple or complex. Such riddles bother us enormously, though we seldom allow this to show. Deep inside, though, we wish we had the time to really devote ourselves to exploring the mysteries."

He held out his hands in a helpless gesture. "The simple fact of practicality usually precludes it. Other things have priority. As scientists, we're simply terrifically overburdened with the day-to-day research and studies involved with projects already at hand, and these are almost always limited to a very narrow slot in the field of science to which we've individually committed ourselves. There's practically no opportunity to reach out and embrace tangential studies and problems. And, I also have to admit, little real desire to do so, since our own pet projects are naturally very dear to our hearts.

"Thus," he went on, "we wind up specializing, and the more we specialize, the more we shut out the interference of considering what other branches of science are doing. Example: a geophysicist like myself, who might be deeply involved in the production of a cybernetic apparatus involving complex computer systems for the prediction of earthquakes, has little time or inclination to concern himself with the fact that somewhere on the other side of the earth another scientist, perhaps an archaeologist such as Dr. Dowde, has uncovered remains from a dig which turns out to be pretty conclusive evidence that an ancient civilization may have produced computers of their own just about as sophisticated as the one upon which he himself is at work. He *should* be concerned about it, true, and often if it is brought to his attention he does get concerned about it. But, as a point of fact, it's very rarely brought to his attention because other things more closely allied to what he's working on take precedence. Thus, the archeologist winds up with another of those frustrating riddles which shouldn't go unresolved, but does."

"Doesn't it seem, in view of all this," put in Grant, stubbing out his cigarette in a large brass ashtray, "that many scientists have lost a valuable ability to assess and evaluate productively when something unusual comes along? Isn't the scientist therefore failing himself and his profession through such intensive specialization?"

"Unfortunately, Mr. Grant, to a certain extent you are entirely correct." It was Dr. William Gossett who spoke up now, from near the rear of the room. A renowned specialist in Incan and pre-Incan studies, Gossett was a professor at Georgetown University. He stood and put one hand in his pocket, softly jingling some keys. "But, equally unfortunately, it's too often easy to recognize a failing and extremely difficult to cure it. As Dr. Trautman has pointed out, it's almost impossible in our present age for a scientist not to specialize. In doing so he gains a great knowledge in his own area of specialization, but knows comparatively little about the progress of even relatively closely related scientific branches, and virtually nothing about those sciences not very directly connected with his own." He pulled his hand from his pocket and gripped the lapel of his suitcoat. "We don't like to admit to this limited specialization, but it's there. And when we do have to admit to it, we laughingly call it 'professional cretinism.' Most of us have vaguely hoped that somehow we could change this, but we've never really pinpointed how to go about doing so. Perhaps, as Dr. Trautman suggests, the HAB Theory will help show us the way."

"I couldn't agree with Dr. Gossett more completely," said Barry Eshelman, the husky, outgoing oceanographer who was director of resource ecology at Harvard University. "Certainly in view of that gathering out there of so many scientists from different fields of learning, it appears we may be on the way." His face was somewhat flushed now and there was a distinct ring of defensiveness in his voice as he continued, addressing himself to the Chief Executive.

"We might, Mr. President, be criticized for what we ourselves term professional cretinism, but one has to take into consideration that scientists on the whole, for all their pedantry, are nonetheless human beings, not computers, and there is only so much assimilation of extraneous detail that can be accommodated. One could easily spend his entire lifetime assimilating the knowledge of a variety of scientific fields and be a veritable font of information, yet not contribute one worthwhile thing to the progression of science."

"It's a point well taken, Dr. Eshelman," Robert Sanders replied, smiling, "but so, too, is the point of overspecializing to the extent of becoming unaware in respect to broader concepts. The HAB Theory, obviously, is an example. Acceptance and understanding require the interlocking of knowledge from a wide spectrum."

He stopped for a moment, tapping his chin thoughtfully with a forefinger, and then turned his gaze to the committee's vice-chairman.

"Is it not possible, Dr. Robinson," he continued, "that the establishment of a scientific correlation center, for use by all branches of science, could accomplish much in eliminating this problem?"

"Undoubtedly," Robinson admitted promptly. "Undoubtedly, it could, providing enough funds were appropriated for doing so."

"Of necessity, President Sanders," interjected Dr. Richard Mahon of NASA, "it would have to be a computerized project of enormous scope and incredible complexity." The gray-haired Mahon was associate administrator of advanced research and technology in mathematics for the National Aeronautics and Space Administration in Washington, D.C. "Just the cataloging of the bits of research and information being acquired every day, to say nothing of the correlation of all man's past scientific endeavors and findings, would alone be a monumental task requiring a staff of thousands, perhaps even tens of thousands. Then, making this data readily available to the scientists who would need it would be equally difficult. I don't say it couldn't be done—or shouldn't be—but..." he raised his hands and let them fall back to his sides.

"Assuming even that funds for it could be appropriated," interposed anthropologist Norman Bigham, a rotund deputy commissioner of the Interior Department's Bureau of Indian Affairs, "such a project would require many years to put into operation. Maybe even decades. In view of what the HAB Theory portends...He, too, let his sentence die unfinished.

Philip Greenbriar finished it for him. "In view of what it portends, there may not even be time enough to finish this symposium.' Dr. Greenbriar was one of the nation's foremost zoologists and had recently been named to the directorship of the prestigious Philadelphia Academy of Sciences. In his own way, he was also very nearly as unprepossessing and outspoken as Dr. Dowde was in hers. "I think, Mr. President," he added with emphasis, "that a scientific correlation center has to be one of the goddamnedest most progressive ideas that any administration has come up with since the days of Teddy Roosevelt. But I won't believe it until I see it.

"I also think," he was grinning widely now, "that we've strayed pretty far from the comments you initially wanted from us. We do, as a committee, accept the HAB Theory. But I, for one, am very hesitant at this time to offer any concrete prediction as to when it may occur or what steps should be taken to circumvent it or, failing that, to survive the effects of it."

"I tend to agree with Dr. Greenbriar," said Irma Dowde, breaking her lengthy silence. "I think such matters can better be considered and any conclusions or recommendations more definitively drawn after evaluation by the entire body of scientists at this symposium. I truly believe, President Sanders, that any recommendation for action by the committee alone at this time would be premature. And," she looked at her watch, "I'm very sorry to say that it's past time for the meeting to begin with the group chairmen."

The President nodded and came to his feet. Everyone else rose, too, but the beginning of a general movement toward the door was effectively halted as the President spoke again.

"A final word, please, ladies and gentlemen. Undoubtedly the press is by now aware of this meeting we've been holding and you will probably be interviewed by reporters. For the time being, I would appreciate that you not disclose anything that we have discussed in this room. Primarily because of the effect it might have upon your scientific colleagues in shaping their own views, I ask especially that no word be spoken of this advisory committee's acceptance of the HAB Theory until tomorrow. We owe it to those assembled here to let them begin to argue the points among themselves and establish their own feelings early without being influenced by your decision. I should mention, too, that a matter which may be of extreme significance in your further considerations, and theirs, is at this moment being investigated in Turkey and I hope, before next Friday, to have something of a definite nature for you in this respect. I think that's all for now. Thank you."

As Sanders, holding Dr. Dowde's elbow, moved with her toward the door—she clenching her materials under her arm in a determined manner—the President gestured toward Alexander Gordon and John Grant, who were now standing beside one another at the door, and murmured, "I'd like to see both of you after this."

The pair acknowledged the order and stood aside to let the others pass. Followed by the entire committee, the President and Dr. Dowde left the room and walked through the much larger sitting room which adjoined it, paying no attention to the two Secret Service men who moved quickly to the main door to the corridor or the other two who fell in casually on either side.

"Dr. Dowde," the President was saying to the portly archaeologist, "we've already established that you'll be calling me daily at the White House to report on what's happening here. However, I *would* appreciate a call from you tonight, irrespective of the hour, to fill me in on the first day's meetings and the general tenor of the symposium. Just use that special telephone number I gave you and you'll get through all right."

The President stopped at the doorway to let them pass, shaking hands with each in turn and expressing his thanks. The last to go out was Kermit Knotts, with his odd, puppetlike walk. In a moment they were gone and the Chief Executive returned to the room where the four who remained—Lace, Gordon, Grant and Mrs. Tierney—stood conversing quietly beside the chair where Sanders had been sitting. They became silent as he entered and shut the door behind him.

"Well," he said cheerily, "interesting session, don't you think? Sit down, please, all of you. There are only a few things I want to go over with you. Steve, we'll start with you."

The press secretary nodded, adjusted his glasses, and extracted a small note pad from his pocket. He sat with pen poised. The president pursed his lips and tapped his chin with a fingertip for a moment.

"Steve," he said finally, "just as soon as it's ready, get a transcript of today's session from Hazel and start working on a press release, especially incorporating the simple explanation of the HAB Theory and its aftereffects that Dr. Dowde gave. She stated it pretty succinctly, but if there are any heavy places as you go over it which you think might be simplified, work on it. Be sure to put some emphasis at both beginning and end on the fact that the Scientific Advisory Committee, representing twelve major branches of science, has declared the HAB Theory to be valid, following a full month's study. I want that ready for distribution to the press tomorrow morning, but absolutely not before then. Okay?"

"Yes, sir."

"Good. You and Hazel can get to work on that right away."

The two recognized the dismissal and began leaving the room at once. As they neared the door, Sanders spoke up again.

"Oh, and Hazel, before anything else, place that call for me that I mentioned earlier, will you please?"

He had already turned his attention to Grant and Gordon as his personal secretary nodded and shut the door after her. He blew out a little puff of air and seemed more relaxed now as he headed for the smaller sitting room, indicating that they should follow him.

VIII

John Grant followed Gordon into the room after the President and closed the door, then stood waiting. Sanders continued to the big chair and dropped into it with a sigh. On the table beside the chair, Grant saw, was a copy of his summary. The President was motioning them to be seated, so he took a chair beside Gordon, facing the Chief Executive, who was shaking his head and chuckling ruefully.

"There's just never enough time for the things which need to be done," he said. "We really should have had two or three hours with that group in there."

Alex Gordon nodded, more than familiar with the consistent tightness of the President's schedule. Grant, lighting a cigarette, blew out a column of smoke and dropped the gold lighter back into his pocket. He said nothing, but he was watching the Chief Executive closely.

"Alex," the President went on, "you didn't say much in there," he tilted his head toward the room they had just left.

"Nothing worthwhile to contribute, I guess, sir," Gordon said. "I tend to get a little awed in the presence of so much intellect."

Sanders looked at his black friend with amused affection. "You never need let that occur," he said. He regarded the two men without speaking for an extended time and then he took a deep breath.

"Gentlemen," he said, "I'm about to throw a couple of curves in your direction. First, though, I want you to know that I'm pretty damned pleased with the way both of you came through with what needed to be done. I don't know if Hazel told you or not, but Elliott's been bragging about both of you as if you were top echelon, under secretaries. That's unusual where he's concerned. He's not one who ladles out compliments very often."

Neither Gordon nor Grant said anything, but both were pleased with the praise and slightly discomfited with it. Gordon was smiling faintly, but there was the barest trace of a frown turning down Grant's mouth corners. He was thinking of the President's remark that had preceded the compliment and wondered what sort of curves The

Man had in mind. Sanders noticed it and laughed with genuine amusement.

"You'll learn in a moment, John," he said. It was the first time he'd ever used Grant's given name in addressing him and now it was the writer who smiled. "The work that both of you did over in Kenya," Sanders went on with his line of thought, "is important to a great degree. Alex, I don't know exactly how you won over President Ngoromu, but having been involved in negotiations in other ways several times in the past, I know he's sometimes difficult to deal with. Good job."

Gordon didn't reply, but his eyes seemed a little brighter than usual and his smile had spread. By now the President had turned his gaze to Grant.

"The same holds true for you, John. A fine job, and not only with Ngoromu. I've just gone through the summary for a third time," he tapped a stiff forefinger on the binder beside the telephone on the little table next to his chair, "and I have to tell you that it's really an excellent presentation. Amazing, considering how limited your time was to get it done."

"Thank you very much, Mr. President," Grant said, adding, "A great deal of credit has to go to Kermit Knotts for the transcription of my tapes. I know that wasn't easy."

Sanders gave a brief nod, but his thoughts were elsewhere already. He looked steadily at Grant for several seconds more before speaking softly.

"I'm going to ask a question of you, John, which it's possible you may resent. It's a personal question and don't feel you're required to answer if you don't care to. However, it's a matter I feel I have to clarify to my own satisfaction before going on. You must know that during the first days after Mr. Boardman made his move against me, a great deal of investigation was done. As soon as your name was brought into it, you were one of those investigated."

"I knew I was being followed," Grant said cautiously, glancing at Gordon, "and assumed, under the circumstances, that I was being investigated pretty closely."

Sanders nodded. "At my orders. You'd been investigated quite a few times over the years, John. Much of what you've written in the past has not been of a nature to make you the most popular person in Washington, as you're well aware. Until now, though, there was never anything discovered about you which might be used as a pressure point. Now you've let yourself become vulnerable."

He held up a hand and shook his head as Grant opened his mouth to reply. "No, let me go on.

"Your marriage is evidently in trouble and has been for some time. How the matter is resolved is your own personal business. Under more normal circumstances your present vulnerability could possibly cause embarrassment for this office. In light of present circumstances, I don't consider that a matter of any great moment. I have only two real concerns in this regard. First is my concern for you as an individual and, I hope, a friend, and my desire to see nothing ill befall you. Secondly, I must be concerned in how your problem may affect your capability to work with and for me in what lies ahead of us now. I'd like to lean heavily on you in the days and weeks ahead. What I have in mind for you to do," he shot a glance at Gordon, "both of you, is going to require a good deal of personal judgment and minds free of distractions. What I need to know from you, John—and the answer," he added gently, "has to be as honestly given as you can—is this: are the problems you're having of such pressing and disruptive nature that they're going to interfere with your ability to perform a difficult and delicate task for me?

One that will require an immediate trip overseas and a lot of concentrated effort on your part?"

Grant didn't respond at once. He leaned forward and extinguished his cigarette in the cut-glass ashtray on the small table between his chair and Gordon's, then leaned back and laced his fingers together over his waist.

"Mr. President," he said levelly, "I don't really know if I can give you any kind of a satisfactory answer. I think in all honesty I can say I'm reasonably sure that, whatever occurs of a personal nature with me, I would *prevent* it from interfering with what I'm expected to do. Reasonably sure," he reiterated, "but by no means positive. I'll have to admit that there's also the possibility I'm wrong. I don't think so, but I won't deny that possibility. I should say, though, that this same personal problem has been with me for a considerable while and I've not let it interfere with the jobs I've already done for you—the HAB summary and the conferences with President Ngoromu. Beyond that, there's not much more I can say."

For many long seconds after Grant finished, the three of them sat without speaking—Gordon quietly watching the President; The Man himself thoughtfully tapping an index finger against his chin; Grant lighting another cigarette, his nervousness, if there at all, betrayed only in the fact that it took three clicks of the lighter to get a flame.

"Well," the President spoke at last, "I don't know how I expected you to answer. I suppose I was hoping you'd say definitely that the problem wouldn't affect you in what I have in mind. On the other hand, I guess I'm glad you didn't, because I probably wouldn't have believed it anyway." He frowned and looked at Grant from beneath pinched brows. "I'm not unaware that the same problem was with you in Africa while you were engaged in some difficult work and the fact that you came through with what was needed certainly weighs in your favor. The question that creeps in is how long can a person function in his work as he should when beset with deep and possibly growing emotional pressures? And I suppose there isn't any way you can really answer that, either. I do appreciate your honesty, but not the fact that it leaves me just about where I was before. All right, it evolves then to a matter of judgment and there's no point in putting it off. I want you in, John, because, quite frankly, I don't know who could do a better job for what I have in mind, so I suppose I'll have to take the chance and trust that the problems won't interfere; trust," he amended, narrowing his eyes, "that you won't *let* them interfere."

The President smiled with almost startling abruptness. "Enough of that. Matter settled." He reached out to the small table and pulled free some loose sheets that were under the Grant summary, then turned his gaze to Gordon. "These," he said, holding the sheets up and then dropping them atop the bound summary, "are what concern you, Alex. The job you'll be doing is going to require skillful handling, diplomacy and speed. On those sheets are breakdowns on—"

The ringing of the telephone beside his hand cut him off and he scooped it up before it could ring a second time.

Yes, Hazel?...Good, put him on." He put his hand over the mouthpiece. "Stay seated," he murmured, "this won't take long. Hello, Robbie?...Sure, fine, thanks. How about yourself?...Good. Laurie and Linda?...Excellent. Stephanie okay?...Is that right? Well, I'm disturbed to hear that. You know, that night you and she were here for dinner, she really didn't look too well. Her coloring seemed to be off...Hmmm...Well, keep us posted and let's hope the tests show it's definitely not hepatitis...Uh-huh...I see...Well, just tell her Grace and I will be thinking about her. Your mother'll probably give her a call when she hears...Matter of fact, yes, it is important. Robbie, no holds barred now. Project Noah is on. We're going all the way...Uh-huh...You did read the summary, then?…Good, good…*Ninety* percent? Fine! Better than I anticipated, in fact. I thought it might take you up to about eighty or eighty-five. You always were something of a skeptic…" He chuckled, then nodded, caught himself and stopped. "Yes…Of course, I realize that…Uh-huh…Yes, I know that, but it doesn't make any difference now. I'm out either way if this flops, but it isn't going to, Robbie. I'm positive of it now…No, it really doesn't make that much difference what they come up with here at the symposium, although I'm pretty sure of that, too. The Scientific Advisory Committee, incidentally, buys it unanimously…Yes, me too…The point is, we've passed the last turnaround and from now on it's all the way, as directly and expeditiously as possible…Exactly. You have .everything pretty much in readiness there?…Good…Yes, go ahead with it. All of it…You remember mentioning the night we had dinner about those craft that were nearly ready to go? The two Phobos and the Deimos?…Right. What's the status now?…Uh-huh. I know the Phobos are strictly orbital, but what about Deimos?…Yes, I know you have it set up for orbit, but is it adaptable for a lunar soft-landing?…Good. How long?…No, unmanned will suffice…Ouch! That's a lot longer than I thought…Yes, I'm aware of the problems involved, but I want you to go ahead with the adaptation anyway, okay?…That'd be a great Christmas present…All right, here's what you can plan on now. I'll alert Henry Dexter at the Library of Congress and get him ready for a big job of selecting, packing and transporting to you immediately a large shipment containing pertinent volumes on microfilm. No, by air. Within two days, three at most. Right…I want you to gear all three of them for it. The two Phobos will carry duplicates of whatever's in Deimos. I want those Phobos up and orbiting with payload inside within two weeks, if possible, a month at the outside…Excellent…No, don't concern yourself with that at all. I don't want you getting bogged down in red tape. The funds'll be appropriated, so don't worry. I'll be talking with Andy McKernan over in Defense Appropriations this afternoon on it…Yes, he'll do it. He won't like it, but he'll do it…Yes. There's no time, so get it moving and we'll worry about the administrative difficulties later. Move on all fronts. Phobos and Deimos most pertinently right now, but start the wheels turning immediately for every available priority on the others…Absolutely! I want those first fifty ready in half the time it normally takes…Yes…All right. Hazel has the number in Florida if you leave Houston?…Good, keep me informed about everything. If any snags come up, I want to know immediately…Fine…Good man. Good-bye, Robbie."

The President hung up the phone and returned his attention to Alex Gordon. "All right, let's go on. These," he said, placing his hand on the papers he'd been referring to earlier and picking up the conversational thread exactly where he'd left off, "are breakdowns on heads of state of all the major nations and a substantial number of minor ones. Not all nations because it won't be necessary with some—they'll side with the blocs no matter what happens. But these," he patted the pages, "won't. They'll have to be convinced, and it won't be easy."

He leaned back, uncrossing his legs and then recrossing them in the other direction. "To fill you in briefly," he said, "I now buy the HAB Theory totally. No reservations. That call I just finished with my son was part of a project I'll fill you both in on later today.

"Alex, you, along with Elliott and a number of his best, are going on circuit. Probably tomorrow morning for you, but later for them. Elliott got back from the Middle East this morning. We three will be going to Washington within an hour and we'll be meeting there with Elliott and some of his key personnel at once. He'll want you to brief them thoroughly.

"What it amounts to," he continued, his pace picking up, "is that I want you to talk personally, as my envoy, Alex, to the African heads of state. All of them. Elliott and his men will be in other areas doing the same." He rolled his eyes toward Grant. "I have a different mission for you, John, which we'll get to directly, but let me finish with this first." He looked back to Gordon. "What I want you to tell them, Alex, is not for relay through delegates or ambassadors. I want you to talk only with the heads of state. You're going to have to tell them that I am entirely convinced that the whole of mankind is in jeopardy. From what I'll tell you later, you'll have to explain to them what my plan of action is with this in mind, to prevent the destruction of all that man has accomplished. You are going to have to convince them that their cooperation in the development of Ngaia City and in Project Noah is not only desperately needed, but that it is the only way that they can perpetuate their own culture, their own particular civilization. It is the only way they are going to be able to preserve at least a portion of what their society has spent its entire history building toward. I've pretty well laid out in black and white just exactly what is to be expected of each, and this is what I'll brief you on while we're en route to Washington. It won't be easy, any of it. There'll be a lot of backs up about it, both here and abroad, and a lot of arguments, but they have got to be convinced to help. That's what you and Elliott and his men are going to be doing.

"And John," he turned toward the writer, "while the secretary's men are tops in diplomacy, they're going to need some briefing from you to get prepared for what's necessary. They all have your summary, but a verbal briefing from you will help speed things up. You can show them what areas they'll need to concentrate on most pertinently. You two ought to be able to precede them on your own separate missions by at least a couple of days. Questions?"

Grant and Gordon both began speaking as the President paused and both stopped simultaneously. Grant motioned for Gordon to go ahead, and the black man nodded and continued.

"Mr. President, is it also your idea for me to convince the heads of state I'm to see that the HAB Theory is valid, so they'll more readily provide whatever support it is that you'll ask of them?"

"That's only part of it, Alex. To be blunt, I'm going to lean on these people with all the weight of this office and all the pressure that America, as a major power in the world can bring to bear. They should be able to see easily enough that it is going to be to their own benefit to help. But if they can't be convinced of it through simple logic and reason, then it may have to boil down to threats. Boycotts, embargoes, sanctions, economic pressures, whatever. We're going to force them to help themselves and the only way they can do that now is through full cooperation in what I've laid out. A lot won't believe in the theory's validity yet because they don't have all the facts, but they'll believe it sooner or later. What matters most right now is that you are able to impress upon them the importance of their immediate and fullest cooperation. It's all we need at the moment. Get in and out fast with the agreement to that. The ambassadors in the respective countries have been paving the way for several days. There's not a head of state of any importance who's not aware at this moment that he's going to be paid a visit—an imperative visit— by a special envoy from me personally within the next few days, or however long it takes. They'll be primed. They'll even have a certain amount of background that's been fed to them through diplomatic channels, so you won't be going in entirely cold. That's enough for now, Alex. More on your aspects of it later on."

The President uncrossed his legs and leaned forward toward John Grant, his elbows on his knees. "John, your mission is damned important, too, but this time you're not going to be involved in convincing anyone of anything, although I do want you to take a copy of the summary along to give to a specific individual. Take your tape recorder and extra tapes. You're going to need them. Also a good portable typewriter, which we can provide for you.

"You—both of you, in fact—will be traveling under diplomatic immunity, so you'll have no problems with customs anywhere. In your case, John, that's especially important, because you're going to be bringing something back which you'll be given over there. Over there meaning Turkey.

"I want you to leave tomorrow morning on a direct flight to Ankara. Hazel's already made arrangements for you. The flight leaves just after eleven, I think. On our way to Washington I'll explain what you have to do when you get there. In sum, I'd hope the job wouldn't take you more than four or five days. At any rate, I want you to aim, if conceivably possible, to be back in Washington by next Thursday afternoon. Should this be impossible— and I hope to God it's not!—then you *must* be back here no later than the following Saturday morning. That's all you need to know at the moment. We've got to get moving."

The President stood, and so too did Grant and Gordon. "I'm assuming," he said, "that you're both willing to take on these respective missions. I didn't even think to ask. Are you?"

As both assured him they were, the President smiled. "Excellent. I was sure of it. As I've said, there is still much to go over, but we'll get to the fine points later today. I have a couple calls to make now, but I'll see you both in about half an hour. Be ready to leave."

As the two aides were going out of the room, Sanders spoke Grant's name and the writer stopped in the doorway and looked back. Gordon had already gone out into the other room.

"John," the Chief Executive said, "I don't want you to tell anyone where you're going or what you'll be doing. However, if it would be of any help to you in your own present situation, I can have Hazel call Mrs. Grant and explain to her that you are going to be engaged in a confidential mission for me that will keep you away and out of touch for a while."

"Thank you, sir," Grant said, "but I guess not. Mrs. Grant is already aware that my intentions are to be away and out of touch."

1 0

The stumbling way in which even the ablest of scientists in every generation have had to fight through thickets of erroneous observations, misleading generalizations, inadequate formulations and unconscious prejudice is rarely appreciated by those who obtain their scientific knowledge from textbooks.

—James Bryant Conant

On ancient so-called fables: *Can we not read into them some justification for the belief that some former forgotten race of men attained not only to the knowledge that we have so recently one, but also to the power that is not yet ours?*

—Dr. Frederick Soddy

I

The second call from Grant—the one at three o'clock on this Friday afternoon—had upset Anne far more than she'd let on at the time. She had been fully prepared for his absence in New York for the ten-day duration of the HAB Symposium, but her loneliness had been mitigated to some extent when he'd called at 10:45 this morning with the invitation to dinner in New York with Narai and Alex. She'd made flight arrangements and was scheduled to land at La Guardia at six tomorrow evening. Then had come the second call, in midafternoon, and he was calling from Washington instead of New York. His news then dismayed her—that he'd be leaving Washington tomorrow morning on a mission for the President overseas, but that he couldn't tell her where or for how long or anything else about it. The call was very brief because he was about to enter a conference with the President, the secretary of state and others. He was sorry their own plans were disrupted, but it couldn't be helped. And that was it. Period. He was gone before she'd hardly had a chance to say anything.

As soon as they hung up, she knew she couldn't work anymore today and so she'd closed shop. Now, nervously turning her car off Sheridan onto Dempster and heading west, she was beginning to have second thoughts about what she was doing about what had seemed like such a logical and reasonable thing to do while she was still in the office, immediately after John's call.

She made an exasperated sound, disturbed at her own nervousness and fighting it down, her lips set in a grim line. A taxi in front of her stopped without warning to disgorge a passenger and she had to veer sharply left to avoid colliding with its rear end. Fortunately, no traffic was in the other lane.

"Damned fool!" she shouted out the open window as she swept past and, in the rearview mirror, saw the cab driver stick his arm out the window, his hand upraised and the middle finger stuck stiffly upward in obscene response.

She broke into genuine laughter. The buildup of tension was abruptly gone and the conviction that she was doing the right thing was back again as strongly as it had been in the office.

She was on her way to see Marie Grant. Though she had seen Marie at reasonably close hand once before, they had never spoken to one another. To Anne, it was somehow important that this should occur, although it wasn't the dominant reason for this undertaking. No, most of all she hoped that in some way, calmly and quietly, she could put across to Marie her sorrow for her and what was happening to her; that she felt no animosity toward Marie and sympathized with her being in such a difficult position; that maybe somehow matters could be worked out on a friendly basis, eliminating perhaps much of the pain of a situation which necessarily had to be extremely painful. She would explain, again as unemotionally and reasonably as possible, how deep her love was for John, and his for her, and how for his own peace of mind both women should now stand back and let him carry out in his own way what had to be done, and that he should have this opportunity without either woman making any further effort to influence him. After all, he was a grown man and certainly fully aware of all the ramifications involved, and it really wasn't fair at this point for either of them to exert any more pressure on him. Anne would accept—and she hoped Marie would accept—with grace whatever John did now.

Again, as she had when leaving the office, she wondered if she should have called her mother and talked it over with her first, telling her what she had in mind. There was still time if she wanted to do so. She made a negative sound. No, her mother might try to dissuade her or get all involved in waxing philosophical about it or, even worse, approve and start rattling off a series of suggestions that would only serve to get Anne confused. No, the time to call her would be when this was all over and when she might very much need to have someone to talk with.

Even knowing that it was most unlikely that he could do so, she had been afire with hope, once John told her about the impending trip, that he would ask her to go along with him as on the African trip. He hadn't even suggested it and, though she knew it was unreasonable of her, she felt left out and a little irked. She'd been so eager and excited this morning about the idea of being with him over the weekend and of seeing Narai and Alex for dinner. Now even that had been canceled. She sighed. John's world was certainly not one of routine, and anyone who entered the framework of that world had better be prepared. In a way it was terribly exciting, but it also would be nice to be able to make plans and then be reasonably sure of having them occur on schedule.

So steeped in her thoughts was she that she very nearly missed the intersection of Keeler and had to brake sharply and make a very sloppy turn to the left.

She held her breath, wondering if a Skokie patrol car were lurking nearby, but then relaxed as there was no indication she had been observed. It was only the second time she'd ever driven down this street—the first time being that day early last spring when she had parked early in the morning near the Grant house and then followed Marie and the children all day on their outing to the zoo. Now, three months later, she was back again, but not simply to park and watch and follow this time. She had been sure of her love for John then and of her intention to have him, and nothing meanwhile had changed her mind. If anything, her resolve had strengthened. At that time the question mark had been John himself, how he really felt and what he really wanted to do. Now, as far as Anne could see, he had answered those questions through his confrontation with Marie.

The question of whether this justified her own decision to confront Marie was another matter. Deep inside there was a fear that John would be furious with her for taking the initiative, but for Anne it was important that it be done. She had to admit to herself that quite likely nothing of any real value would be accomplished by this meeting, at least not in any tangible sense, but if nothing else there would be a sense of relief in having everything out in the open, in putting behind the furtiveness and vague sense of shabbiness that had so long plagued both her and John. Even while thinking this, at the same time there was a small hope inside that Marie would not even be home.

She had been driving very slowly since turning onto Keeler, yet had already passed Lee Street and was approaching Bobolink Terrace. At the corner she turned right and in just a few hundred yards was pulling to a stop in front of the fine, old, refinished brick residence where the Grants lived.

Two boys were wrestling on the front lawn, giggling and grunting and rolling over and over down the slight slope toward the sidewalk. She recognized Billy at once and, as she got out of the car, paused to watch, feeling an odd tugging inside to be this close to the son of the man she loved. As she started up the front walk the two boys broke apart and sat up, still giggling, and then Billy got to his feet.

"Hi," he said, looking at her curiously.

He had a cowlick at the crown of his head, just like John had and Anne felt the tugging inside her intensify. She smiled at him.

"Hello," she replied. "Who's winning?"

Billy grinned. "Jack thinks he is," he indicated the boy on his knees on the grass behind him, "but it's easy enough to see who's standing and who isn't."

The boy named Jack gave vent to mock outrage and immediately tackled Billy around the backs of the legs and brought him down. They rolled over twice and then Billy managed to pin Jack down, his knees on the boy's shoulders and striving to maintain his position as Jack bucked ineffectually beneath him.

"Is your mother at home?" Anne asked as the more boisterous efforts momentarily faded away.

"Uh-huh. Inside." He was panting heavily. "Just go on up and ring the bell."

The dread came pulsing back at the boy's words and Anne was no longer smiling as Jack gave an especially hard and unexpected lunge, throwing Billy off, and once again they were grappling and rolling. The nervousness was increasing rapidly as her finger pressed the doorbell and chimes sounded from inside.

Marie Grant answered the door clad in a pair of faded blue jeans, an old shirt and frayed white tennis shoes, and in her rubber-gloved hand she was holding a heavy scrub brush. Her long blond hair was held back in a ponytail, but a lock of it had come free and hung over the corner of one eye. She brushed it away with her forearm, but it immediately fell back over her eye. Beyond Marie, Anne could see that the interior of the house was spotless.

Marie started to smile but then stopped abruptly and her eyes widened. Her lips parted and she paled considerably. She gripped the edge of the door tightly with her free hand and steadied herself. Anne nodded, trying to smile but failing.

"Yes," she said simply, "I'm Anne Carpenter."

"How do you *dare* to come to this house?" Marie's voice was no more than a raspy whisper, her brows pinched down and nostrils flaring.

"I think we need to talk, you and I," Anne said. "May I come—"

There was no time for any more than that. Marie's hand flashed upward and struck Anne a severe blow at the corner of the eyebrow with the brush she was holding. For an instant Anne staggered and then slowly raised her hand and touched her fingertips to the spot and then looked at the blood on them, for the first time realizing that already blood coursing down her cheek from the split brow had begun to drip from her jawline, and part was running down her neck. She seemed unable to comprehend what had happened.

Marie was raising the brush again, more deliberately now, an expression of utter hatred on her face, her lips contorted and the cords of her neck taut. Anne took a step backward, out of range of another blow but not beyond the verbal barrage.

"You stinking whore!" Marie hissed. "Stinking, homewrecking whore!" The words began rising in volume. Get away from here! *Get away!*

At another level of consciousness Anne was aware that the noise of the two boys behind her had stopped, and without looking she knew they were watching, but even as she fumbled in her shoulder bag and took out a small handkerchief and held it to her brow, her attention remained centered on Marie. Anne suddenly jerked her head to one side and felt the slight wind of the scrub brush as it whirled past her ear and into the front yard beyond. A throbbing pain was beginning in her forehead now and she started turning away, not knowing what to say.

Marie stayed where she was in the doorway, unaware that the boys were watching the tableau in frightened fascination, unaware of anything except the younger woman—the great enemy—moving away carefully.

"I'm warning you," she said, her voice low and harsh again. "You stay away from my husband!"

Anne was about ten feet away now, but she stopped at that and looked over her shoulder at Marie. She shook her head and refused to let herself wince at the pain this caused. She regarded Marie for a long moment and then spoke levelly.

"You have no husband."

I I

If a single word could describe Irma Dowde, that word was indefatigable. Though she had not spent a busier day in her life and had not even had time to gulp more than a hasty sandwich and glass of milk after the conclusion of her meeting with the group chairmen, she felt buoyant, almost electrically charged with the excitement of what was occurring here at the HAB Theory Symposium.

She had hoped to be able to sit in for at least a short while on no fewer than one of the group discussions in each of the fourteen hotels where they were being held, but as it was turning out this first day of the conference, it was unlikely she would even leave the Waldorf, as her work here was far from finished.

She felt herself to be on a treadmill, followed and ably aided wherever she went by her young archaeological assistant, Kathryn Lever, and her every move dogged by a mob of reporters and cameramen, shooting their film footage or stills and firing questions at her continuously.

Following the briefing of the discussion group chairmen, she'd snatched that bite to eat and then held a short meeting with Kermit Knotts and his corps of steno-typists, carefully explaining what was expected of them, the dangers of becoming bogged down in petty details when a strong overall view was far more essential to their purposes, and advising on what sort of notes should be taken and how they should be correlated. For the most part, as near as she could determine from the initial reports already received, the meetings had begun well, with pertinent and serious discussion being carried on by each of the eight groups of up to one hundred meeting here in the headquarters hotel. However, it wasn't until nearly half an hour after the group discussions had started that she was able to begin making the rounds of these individual meetings.

Outside the closed double door to the first meeting room, the Duke of Windsor Suite, she paused with her hand on the knob and held up the other stubby-fingered hand to silence the hubbub of continuing questions from newsmen.

"Ladies, gentlemen," she said firmly, "there is a meeting in progress in this room at the moment and I have no intention of allowing it to become disrupted by a swarm of people entering in midsession. Each of the group discussions is already well covered by members of the press inside. I do not intend being here more than ten or fifteen minutes, and if you care to wait in the hall until I come out I have no objection, but I cannot permit you to enter. While I appreciate your need to get your stories, I am much more aware of the necessity to accomplish, without interruption, the work which needs to be done here by symposium members. I ask your cooperation in this matter. And," she added darkly, "for those of you who will not cooperate, each of the groups has been instructed to appoint door marshals who will refuse entry, forcibly if necessary, to anyone not authorized to attend. Come along, Kathryn."

She opened the door and stepped inside, followed by the young redhead, who quietly closed the door behind them. All of the seats in the room were filled and, though a few heads turned their way with smiles and nods as they entered, attention was riveted closely to the front of the room. Bending her head in silent greeting to the two door marshals, Irma Dowde took a standing position along the wall with her assistant.

At the moment the chairman of the group was speaking and the archaeologist recognized him immediately as a man with whom she had worked on two occasions in the past and whom she considered as being one of the best in his field. He was a tall, well-built and ruggedly good-looking Greek with slightly curly sandy hair, graying at the temples—Dr. Michael Balourdos, chairman of the Department of Archaeology at the University of Athens. He was speaking in English in a strong, rolling baritone with only a small trace of accent.

"...so many peculiar references," he was saying, "made at various times by the ancients now have considerably more meaning in light of what we have all read in the HAB Theory Summary. Whether or not at this moment we here are inclined to accept the theory, certainly many aspects of it are providing us with insights into puzzling matters that have always mystified us.

"Ah," he said, directing his attention toward the back of the room, "I see that Dr. Dowde has joined us and I welcome her." Heads swiveled throughout the audience to see the chairwoman. "We've been discussing some peculiar archeological findings that become more relevant in light of this theory, Dr. Dowde," he went on. "Perhaps you may contribute to the discussion. Specifically, we're trying to establish ancient references to times when capsizings of the earth, as outlined in the HAB Theory, might have occurred. With your wide knowledge of ancient Egypt in particular, perhaps you may recall something that would provide food for thought?"

Irma Dowde pursed her lips in thought, nodding slowly. "I've encountered quite a few such matters since becoming involved in this business. One of the most curious factors of Egyptian history," she went on, "is that insofar as we've been able to determine, it presents itself as a culture that has never known a youth, a foundation. It was an old and highly mature civilization at the very dawn of recorded history. We trace that history back through thirty-one dynasties, the latest of which ended in 332 B.C., and the oldest of which began in 3188 B.C. I use the term 'oldest' with some reservation," she added hastily, "since obviously there had to be much history of Egypt prior to 3188 B.C., but beyond that date we come up against a blank. We find Egypt at this dawn of history as we know it— a powerful, highly cultured civilization but, oddly, one without any record of previous heroic ages and without even any trace of mythology. It is just suddenly there in all its grandeur, a nation that had never been young."

She caught herself and looked at Balourdos. "I'm sorry," she said, "this is your meeting and I didn't mean to come in and usurp it."

"No, please continue," Balourdos protested, "We're most interested in whatever you have to say."

"All right, then, as briefly as possible let me make just a few more points. We also find, when we discover Egypt in what we call the First Dynasty, under King Menes, that it is at its absolute zenith of culture in painting, sculpture, architecture. From this peak period, the Egyptian culture steadily declines." She paused, then added almost as an afterthought, "It is very much as if the Egyptians abruptly found themselves the inheritors of a great ready-made culture of which they could take advantage, which they could utilize and even to some degree emulate, but which they themselves did not create and had not enough ability to improve upon or even, for that matter, perpetuate for very long."

"Dr. Dowde." The call for attention came from a man who was perhaps in his late twenties, studious-looking behind large horn-rimmed glasses, who came to his feet near the left front of the group. As she paused and looked his way, he continued.

"I'm Robert Quaife, associate curator of Egyptology at the American Museum of Natural History. I'm very curious to learn how you could possibly relate Egypt's lack of preliminary history to the HAB Theory." He paused and then added, almost apologetically, "I really don't see any basis for equating the two."

"As yet I make no such direct relationship," Dr. Dowde replied, ignoring the flash of a strobe light as a newspaper photographer took her picture, "but I do think there are grounds for some serious speculation. As you must know, Dr. Quaife, ancient Egypt first appears to us on the historical record at a higher order of culture than it is able to maintain at any subsequent stage of its history. This very strongly suggests that it drew its greatness from a source higher than itself, a source which very suddenly and inexplicably disappeared. It's at least worth considering that, if the HAB Theory does reflect actuality, then at such a capsizing of the earth, a fundamental ability among this civilization for creative progression ceased to exist and the process of dying out began."

Quaife, still standing, scratched the back of his head and then continued hesitantly. "But what you're saying doesn't seem to coincide with what the HAB Theory portends, which is a massive destruction to the face of the earth which virtually wipes out any construction by man and, for that matter, man himself."

The chunky archaeologist shook her head. "Not necessarily so, Dr. Quaife. There are, as you recall from reading the

Grant summary, pivotal areas at the times of the capsizings of the earth which remain relatively unaffected. Assume, for the moment, that the Egypt we do not know—the one predating the First Dynasty—stood at or near such a pivotal point. Or probably even more likely, fairly close to one of the poles. The effects of the earth's capsizing might thereupon be felt most strongly by the people but with little seriously destructive effect on structures or artifacts."

"One moment, please," broke in Dr. John Fleming, slowly unfolding his long, gangly frame from a seat in front. He was chairman of the Physics Department at Queensland University, Canberra, Australia, and also vice-chairman of this particular discussion group. He continued, "While admittedly I have no great liking for all the wrenches the late Herbert Boardman has thrown into the science of physics, I must also admit that I'm intrigued by the theory and intend giving it a great deal more study. But you've just said something, Dr. Dowde, that I have no recollection of having been covered in the Grant summary. I don't recall reading anything to the effect that an area close to the poles would remain relatively unaffected by a so-called capsizing of the earth."

"I apologize for springing that bit of information on you so unexpectedly, Dr. Fleming," Irma Dowde responded. "You will be receiving—everyone here will—supplementary sheets of HAB Theory data not contained in, or at least not enlarged upon, in the summary—data which is still being assembled and found to have especial bearing to our studies here. One of these is a supplement you'll probably be receiving later on today or first thing tomorrow. In the summary, close attention was paid to what Mr. Boardman termed pivotal areas, as being the safest places on earth for survival in event of the capsizing he postulates. However, two other areas on earth also will be relatively unaffected at the time of the capsizing, and these are the two areas of the poles themselves. The summary did not elaborate on this point simply because at first it was assumed that little human life would be involved in such areas. Later, however, too late for full inclusion in the summary, it was discovered that Mr. Boardman considered these areas highly important to the survival of man."

"How so, Dr. Dowde?" Fleming obviously was interested, yet the ring of skepticism was clear in his voice.

Irma Dowde stood a little straighter. "Having traced to his satisfaction that the Sudan Basin was the site of the North Pole in Epoch Number B.P. 1, Mr. Boardman states his conviction that the Egyptian culture was at that time a flourishing civilization at the edge of a glacial continent, directly on or near the Arctic Circle."

"Oh, come now," Fleming put in quickly and a bit superciliously, "a highly advanced civilization at the edge of the Arctic Circle?"

There was a smattering of laughter at this, but at once another scientist in the midst of the group, the heavily blond-bearded Dr. Hjalmar Mathiessen, geographer at the University of Iceland, sprang to his feet, bridling.

"There is nothing particularly amusing about that," he declared, shaking his shaggy head, "or farfetched either. I might remind Dr. Fleming that the capital of my country, Reykjavik, is quite a highly advanced civilization, with over a hundred thousand people living in the city at present. There are other far-northern cities similarly situated close to the Arctic Circle. Fairbanks, Alaska, with a population of over eighty thousand. Nome, Alaska, for another."

"Do not forget Murmansk!" shouted a voice from the back, heavy with Russian accent, and laughter swept the group.

Immediately Michael Balourdos raised both his hands high to quell the disturbance. "Please," he said firmly, "to a certain extent interruptions can be handled, but we cannot afford to have the meeting degenerate into comments being hurled back and forth without identification. I will reiterate what I asked of you before this meeting began. If you have something germane to contribute, please be patient enough to wait for a break in the discussion and then rise, identify yourself, and make your statement. Thank you. Dr. Dowde?"

"As a matter of fact, Dr. Fleming," Irma Dowde continued, "Dr. Mathiessen is quite correct. There are present major centers of civilization at the fringe of the Arctic Circle, so this is certainly not an inconceivable possibility. In his papers, Mr. Boardman suggests that the Egyptian culture, at the time the North Pole was located in the Sudan Basin, was situated at almost exactly the same distance from the pole of that epoch as Fairbanks, Alaska, is today situated from the present North Pole. According to Mr. Boardman, one of the two pivotal points was located in the area we now know as Sumatra and the Malay Peninsula. The other was located in the border area of Ecuador and Peru. Do we have a botanist here?"

Half a dozen or more hands went up at once and Dr. Dowde pointed to a thin, sharp-faced woman of about 50 sitting at the midpoint of the group, a couple of seats from the center aisle. She stood immediately.

"I am Dr. Emilia Parodi of Buenos Aires."

"Dr. Parodi, do you have any background in the historical origin of fruits and vegetables?"

"Yes," she replied with a small shrug. "It is one of the courses I teach at the University of the Argentine."

"Excellent. Can you tell us, please, as briefly as possible, what the origin is of some of our more important fruits and vegetables?"

"It will probably be of some interest," Dr. Parodi said, her voice high and clear, "that the seats of origin of most of the world's important staple vegetables and fruits are the areas you've just mentioned as being previous pivotal points—the Sumatra-Malaysia area, and the Ecuador-Peru area. Most of our fruits have originated, as best as can be determined, from a large radius of southern Asia, of which the Malay Archipelago appears to be the hub, fruits such as cherries, pears, apples, plums, olives, figs, grapes. Others, too, perhaps—apricots and peaches, citrus fruits, bananas and coconuts and mangos. On the other hand, the basic vegetables seem to have originated primarily in the upper Andes—Ecuador and Peru, as mentioned, but also Bolivia and upper Chile. They would include both white potatoes and sweet potatoes, yams, maize, numerous beans including lima and navy beans, pumpkins, squash, peppers, and many others."

The botanist seemed to have finished, but just as Dr. Dowde was about to comment, she went on with a certain degree of hesitancy. "It has never been clearly explained before, but perhaps now it may be; there were cobs and kernels of popcorn found in ancient Peruvian burial grounds which were thought to be unique to the world until, some years later, identical species of popcorn were found in ancient urns buried in the Naga Hills in the border country of Burma and Assam. Heretofore, this has been a very uncomfortable coincidence."

"Thank you, Dr. Parodi," said Irma Dowde, smiling. "I think the ramifications of what you've just said are quite clear. One further question, though. Is there any botanical evidence existing which links such fruits and vegetables to Egypt?"

The Argentine botanist shrugged elaborately. "I have heard of none, Dr. Dowde. The fruits and vegetables that are found there now came to that land as they came to Europe and North America—through gradually being transported there by migrating peoples."

As Dr. Parodi reseated herself, the archaeologist nodded and spoke to the group in general. "Is it not possible, then," she said, "that an Egypt originally having had a cold climate might account for the very notable lack of early Egypt, as we know it, having virtually no such fruits and vegetables? And, as another point to bring forth incidental to this, is it not strange that in one of the pivotal areas, South America, we find another ancient civilization, the Incas, which, precisely like the Egyptian civilization, seems to have drawn its early cultural and technological level from a source it could never quite emulate, and which it was unable to maintain? Both the cultures of Egypt and Peru seem to parallel one another in being the slowly dying remnants of much greater civilizations of which we have no knowledge whatever."

"Assuming, then, Dr. Dowde," came a woman's voice from the left rear of the room, "that the HAB Theory has validity, then wouldn't it—"

"Excuse, please," broke in Michael Balourdos from the front. So the steno-typist can properly attribute your comments, will you stand and identify yourself before continuing?"

"Oh, yes, I'm sorry." The woman, an attractive blond of about thirty in a gray pants suit, stood at once, somewhat flustered. "I'm Rosemary Cantrell from UCLA. Anthropology. What I started to say, Dr. Dowde, was wouldn't it then be reasonable to assume that the Eskimos of today were living in a tropical climate before this present epoch, and that when the earth rolled over they managed to survive and adapt to their new conditions?"

"Possibly," Irma Dowde conceded.

"And that when the pending capsizing does occur again—*if* it does," she added with a nervous little laugh, "—that these same Eskimos might become as prominent then as the Egyptians were at the beginning of their history, as we know it?"

"According to the Boardman postulations," the archaeologist replied, "when the next capsizing occurs the new poles will be located in the Pacific in the vicinity of the Philippines and in eastern Brazil. As an anthropologist, Dr. Cantrell, your deductions along these lines would undoubtedly be more pertinent than mine. The Eskimos are, of course, relatively primitive in their present society, but there is probably some justification for assuming that a portion of their culture will remain and that perhaps even the more developed culture of Fairbanks, Nome and other northern cities may persist to some degree. All that is purely speculative at this point, but along those lines I might ask here for the view of a paleontologist."

A florid-faced man of middle age sitting only a few seats away from where Dr. Dowde was standing immediately came to his feet.

"I'm Hubert Sizer," he said crisply. "Colorado State University."

"Thank you, Dr. Sizer. Allow me to ask, you have read the HAB Theory summary, have you not?"

"I have."

"In particular, have you read those portions dealing with the woolly mammoth remains found in Siberia and Alaska?"

"Yes. I was familiar with the discovery of them before reading the summary, however, and with the inexplicable nature of such occurrences."

"You've also read the portion in the Summary regarding the rising and falling of continental masses, to form land hemispheres and water hemispheres, depending upon how the capsizing of the globe is triggered?"

"Yes."

"Could you mention other areas in the vicinity of Siberia and Alaska where mammoth remains of similar nature have been found?"

"Well, yes, I suppose so. They've been found on Melville Island in the Canadian Arctic, in Alaska and Siberia on both sides of the Bering Strait, on the New Siberian Islands and on Wrangel Island."

"Heretofore has there been any way of stating how these mammals of identical species could have been found on land areas separated by frigid seas?"

"Well," Dr. Sizer said, clearing his throat, "a land bridge across the Bering Strait has always been a matter of conjecture. However, there's no real proof for it. Nor is there any explanation as to how mammoths might have gotten to Wrangel or the New Siberian Islands. Swimming in such seas would have been, for them, totally out of the question, and it is doubted that a Bering Strait land bridge would have connected those islands to the mainland of Siberia."

"Doesn't it now seem likely, Dr. Sizer," Irma Dowde pressed on, "if we assume the validity of the HAB Theory and take into consideration the Boardman postulations of rising and falling land and water hemispheres, that Asia and North America were almost assuredly part of an unbroken land mass during B.P. 1, including the islands you've mentioned, and that the mammoths and probably the Eskimos or their forebears once roamed freely throughout this region in a tropical or subtropical climate?"

Again Dr. Sizer cleared his throat. "Well now," he said, hedging his words, "I wouldn't want to be committed to this as a definite pronouncement without considerable further study, but I suppose it is a reasonable possibility if one does in fact accept the HAB Theory."

"And that the race of man in that region was able to adapt to the change in climate and survive, but such mammals as the mammoths and rhinoceroses could not adapt and thus became extinct?"

"Well, again, yes," Sizer said, even more discomfited now, "but still only on the basis of the HAB Theory's being valid, and I'm not at all sure I'm in accord with deeming it such."

"Excuse me, Dr. Sizer. I had no intention of putting you on the spot. I only wished for all of us to get a better general picture of the interlocking nature of all these bits of information data which, if taken in an overall view, provide fascinating possibilities, but which, if closeted in one particular field, seem to have no relationship to anything reasonably explainable within that field."

She looked about her a bit sheepishly and chuckled. "I came in here to learn how the discussion was going and find myself dominating it. I apologize, Dr. Balourdos, and thank you for allowing me such liberty. I must leave now."

"Dr. Dowde, please, a final question before you go?" From near the right front, a portly man wearing a tweed jacket and striped bow tie stood. He had only a narrow fringe of gray hair from temple to temple across the back of his head. "I am David ben Ribal, historian at Beirut University in Lebanon. You mentioned earlier that the culture of the Egyptians appeared full-blown, without any history antedating the First Dynasty. Yet, if memory serves me correctly, it was about the year 450 B.C. when the Greek historian Herodotus journeyed to both Memphis and

Thebes on the Nile and talked at length with the priests there about their country and its history. At that time, again if memory serves me correctly," he added, though Irma Dowde was sure his memory was functioning quite well, "Herodotus was told by the priests of Memphis that their records went back eleven thousand years, and the priests of Thebes said their records covered the past seventeen thousand years. That seems very much to be in opposition to the idea of a capsizing of the globe on the average of every six thousand years. Even if they had survived such a cataclysm, wouldn't accounts of it have played important roles in what records we find of them, and in what the priests themselves told to Herodotus?"

He sat down immediately, but before Irma Dowde could reply, Balourdos spoke from the front of the room.

"I would like," he said, "if Dr. Dowde has no objection, to comment in that respect."

"None whatever, Dr. Balourdos," she responded, "but as soon as you finish I will have to be leaving."

"Dr. ban Ribal," said the Greek archaeologist, "you pose a most interesting question. Perhaps not so surprisingly, the identical question came to my own mind as I first read the summary in Athens. We have, of course," he added with some degree of pride, "a great library at the University of Athens dealing with the lives and activities of ancient Greeks. I delved into the matter to some degree and discovered some rather startling facts.

"You are," he said, leaning his hip against the head table, "quite correct in your recollection of the priests of Thebes and Memphis relating to Herodotus that their historical records extended back, respectively, seventeen thousand and eleven thousand years. Unfortunately, those records were on papyrus and skin scrolls, housed in one of the greatest libraries of antiquity, the Alexandria Library. Much of that library, along with a large portion of its collection of seven hundred thousand scrolls—the equivalent of ten thousand textbooks of today—was lost to fire during the reign of Caesar. Nevertheless, the Alexandria Library was rebuilt and continued to be a great font of knowledge and repository of ancient records until A.D. 390. In that year the Bishop of Alexandria, evidently insane and a religious fanatic, led a mob through the streets of the city and pillaged the library of half a million of its scrolls, all of which were burned in a street bonfire at the order of the bishop. Not too long after that, the remainder of the collection was destroyed by the invading army of Caliph Omer. So much," he added sorrowfully, "for the written record of Egypt's past.

"Fortunately, though, during his visits to Memphis and Thebes, Herodotus noted some other very peculiar information passed on to him by the priests. Information," he added meaningfully, "which heretofore was greatly puzzling and largely discounted as imaginings. Now, in light of this present HAB Theory, the histories written by Herodotus take on a great and rather frightening significance.

"Assuming," Balourdos continued, "that an observer in one of the so-called 'safe' areas of earth at the time of a capsizing were looking at the heavens, he would note a drastic change in the course of the moon, stars and sun. They would suddenly no longer be rising and setting in the directions they had followed before. The sun might strangely rise in the south instead of the east, and set in the north instead of the west, because of the shift of the planet's surface in regard to its rotation. Or it might even shift a full one hundred and eighty degrees, so that the sun would appear to rise in the west instead of the east.

"For the sake of example here," he went on, "imagine that at the moment of the last capsizing of the earth it was nine in the morning in Memphis. The earth began suddenly moving sideways even while continuing the normal rotation from west to east. To an Egyptian looking upward at such a time, it would appear that the sun had stopped in its path, then moved about erratically for a while and finally set very close to where it had risen.

"An impossible supposition?" Michael Balourdos asked of no one in particular, and then answered himself. "So it has always seemed. Consider, though, what else it was the priests of Memphis related to Herodotus. They told him with great assurance that in the history of their country, spanning eleven thousand years—or, as they put it, three hundred and forty-one generations—Egypt had had three hundred forty-one kings and a similar number of high priests, and that twice during this span of time the sun had risen where it set, without any great change in the productivity of their country. In a framework of reference based on the HAB Theory, this heretofore inexplicable statement begins having considerable relevance. Mr. Boardman suggests in his postulations that the tendency is for the earth to capsize back and forth in somewhat the same pattern time after time, unless there is a change from a water hemisphere to a land hemisphere. The possibility becomes clear, then, that Egypt was fortunately situated where it could survive with little damage two distinct land hemisphere capsizings of the earth.

"In other words," the big Greek archaeologist concluded, "in B.P. 2 the earth was located approximately in the position it is now, but with the North Pole at Hudson Bay instead of at its present site. When the capsizing occurred, the planet rolled over, and the area now known to us as the Sudan Basin became the site for the North Pole. The Egyptians then lived in a climate not unlike that of Fairbanks or Reykjavik. Another—"

"Or Murmansk!" came the voice from the rear again, causing a brief outburst of laughter. Balourdos ignored it and went on.

"Another rollover occurred and once again the sun seemed to stand still and then set where it had risen, and what had been the North Pole became the Sudan Basin of today. The reference by Herodotus to the sun rising and setting twice in the same direction in ancient Egypt fits into the precepts of Mr. Boardman's theory very nicely."

"I'd like to add one small point to the one you've just made, Dr. Balourdos," Irma Dowde said, standing with her assistant next to the door now and obviously ready to leave. "When the tomb of Senmut, the great Egyptian architect of the Eighteenth Dynasty, was opened, there was discovered on the ceiling an astronomical panel which depicts the constellations of Sirius and Orion moving in a direction directly opposite to the direction in which they move at present. That could well be one more item of confirmation to the veracity of what the priests told Herodotus, and what he wrote." She looked around the room. "And now, ladies and gentlemen, if you'll excuse me, I really must leave. Thank you, and please continue your discussion. I think we're beginning very well indeed."

She nodded to Kathryn Lever and, with a light applause rising, began to leave. Before the door closed behind her, Dr. Balourdos was already continuing the discussion.

"The records of Herodotus aren't the only records of ancient shifts of the earth," he was saying. "As we've read in the summary, China has its tradition of a leap to the Arctic and back. Other cultures have legends or records of the sun standing still in the heavens or rising where it should have set, or incredibly long or short days or nights. Consider, for example, the Biblical story of Joshua fighting the Battle of Jericho, and how the sun stood still in the skies and the walls—"

The clicking of the door behind them cut off the continuing words of Michael Balourdos and the young redheaded archaeologist opened her eyes widely in exaggerated wonderment.

"Wow," she said, "fascinating stuff. I hate to leave."

"Me, too," Irma Dowde admitted brusquely, "but we stayed longer than I'd intended as it is. Let's move along to the Louis the Sixteenth Suite and see how it's going there."

As they stepped away from the door, the newsmen once again converged on them.

I I I

For Narai Ngoromu the day had been both exciting and disappointing. During most of the afternoon she had moved from one symposium meeting to another among the discussion groups assembled in the Plaza Hotel. When she and Alex Gordon had parted, following their luncheon together immediately after arriving at the Plaza from Madison Square Garden, she had gone up to her room to freshen up a bit. She had found herself humming as she moved about in the beautifully furnished suite on the eleventh floor overlooking Central Park. Once, in the midst of unpacking some of her things to put them in a dresser drawer, she stopped and laughed aloud.

"Narai," she told herself, "you are acting like a schoolgirl. Where is your dignity, your decorum?" She laughed again and answered herself. "Out the window, that's where!"

The luncheon with Alex had been all too brief, but the knowledge that they would be spending a delightful evening together alone in this fabulous city would more than make up for it. She'd never met any man, apart from her own father, who was at one and the same time so strong and so gentle. In many respects, she realized, the similarities between Daniel Ngoromu and Alexander Gordon were quite remarkable. Both were highly intelligent, competent men, exuding an aura of self-confidence which was immediately apparent. Both spoke softly yet meaningfully, wasting no time in exaggerations or long-windedness. Neither became excited quickly or, by the same token, seemed much affected by matters that did not work out to their expectations. Both her father and Alex were physically large men, yet both moved with masculine grace and sureness. Alex was, admittedly, a more handsome man than her father, yet both seemed to project a distinct animal magnetism which set them apart from others. Each had a strong but quiet sense of humor and the ability to meet success or the lack of it with equal poise.

As she stood studying the garments hung in her closet, trying to decide what she would wear for this special evening with Alex, her smooth brow wrinkled in a faint little frown, not over the clothing decision but over a thought that had touched her a number of times in the past few weeks. She had never felt herself drawn to any man as she was drawn to Alex Gordon, yet he didn't fit the picture she had always envisioned of her future. She'd always imagined herself someday falling in love with a man who was a year or so older than herself, just as her own mother, Ngaia Loolmalasin, had with Daniel Ngoromu. The imaginings culminated in her eventually marrying that someone and settling down to a beautiful life of sharing everything. One of her stronger fantasies had been that one day she and the man who won her would wind up on a fine big ranch in Kenya, maybe north of Nairobi up around the Laikipia Plateau or even more northerly than that, in the Northern Frontier District. They could raise cattle and a variety of crops and have a huge rambling house well staffed with servants. Somehow, though, that vision just didn't seem to fit the sort of life Alex Gordon would really care a lot for. More immediately bothersome, Alex was forty-one years old, only six years younger than her own father, and close to twice her own age.

The telephone had interrupted her thoughts. It turned out to be Kenya's minister of foreign affairs, Wautura Kelemmo, whose room was on the same floor of the hotel but some distance from her own. He told her that since he had to be in Washington, D.C., tomorrow morning to meet with President Sanders and Secretary of State Elliott, he wanted to take in as much of the symposium today as possible, and would she care to accompany him on a round of the various meetings? She agreed at once and they met in the lobby just before three o'clock and went up to the second floor together to the first of the four meeting rooms where discussion groups were just now going into session in this hotel.

Their plan was to stop by briefly at each of the meetings to give Kelemmo the opportunity to take in as many as possible in order to form a general picture of what was being discussed. This first meeting, of about sixty individuals, was being held in the large gold and green Savoy Room. It was being chaired by Dr. Agnet Braendstrum, professor of physiology at the University of Copenhagen and member of the Danish Royal Academy of Sciences. Her vice-chairman was the distinguished astronomer, Dr. Robert Fitch, director of the Royal Astronomical and Meteorological Society of London as well as curator of astronomy at the British Museum of Natural History. However, the matter under discussion when Narai and Kelemmo entered and took seats was not directly connected with the specialties of either of these two.

The group was involved in a rather animated discussion regarding the pros and cons of Herbert Boardman's recommendation for combatting the threat posed by the South Polar ice cap—that of using thermonuclear devices to set free vast portions of ice presently bound to the Antarctic continent by the upthrust of coastal mountains. The man who had just then been recognized by Dr. Braendstrum was a portly, neatly dressed, gray-haired man who stepped to the front of the table at the head of the room, thanked the Danish scientist, and then turned to face those who were seated.

"For those of you who do not know me," he began in a strong voice, "I am Clarence Apperly, a geophysicist and presently director of the AGA, that is, the American Geophysical Association, in Washington, D.C. Our organization numbers over seven thousand members who are primarily geologists and geophysicists. By the very nature of what this HAB Theory postulates, we represent the branches of science most immediately and most deeply affected. I must admit that when this HAB Theory was thrust upon us so entirely unexpectedly, we were dismayed. A great many of us still are.

"We have," he continued, "as I assume to be the case with all of you here, spent long hours reading, studying, and discussing among ourselves the Grant summary. There are a great many interesting and possibly valid aspects to it and there are some of our membership who have, in essence, indicated that they are inclined, with certain reservations, to accept the findings. Except for just one thing, perhaps many more of us would accept it. That one matter prevents me, and many others, from doing so. Unless it can be resolved for us beyond any dispute, we will never accept it. I should add that while this is my own very strong personal feeling, I also say this as the official voice of the AGA.

"I have spent many hours on the matter I have just alluded to, and now I wish to present it here for the record. The HAB Theory contends that when a capsizing of the earth occurs, the ice caps are suddenly relocated to the equator and areas which were previously equatorial become sites for the new poles. This goes wholly against long-established geological estimates which, for example, place the age of the South Polar ice cap at approximately thirteen million years. All right, if we say for the sake of argument that our geological time estimate is wrong, then this brings up some very disconcerting contradictions. Consider: after the alleged capsizing, the ice now on the equator begins to thaw, but it is a process which takes scores of years to complete. By the same process, the tropical areas now at the pole freeze, very quickly on the surface but much more slowly to any great depth. Largely, this is due not only to the great amount of heat stored within the earth strata, and the insulating factor involved in such stratification, but equally to the warmth of surrounding oceans. True, with the thawing of the ice caps, the temperature of the oceans gradually lowers but it takes a great while. We estimate that while snows would very quickly blanket the ground surface of the continent that was now at the pole, it would take about three hundred years before a true polar ice cap would even begin to form. In the case of the continent of Antarctica, which has an area of some five million square miles and a mean diameter of twenty-eight hundred miles, the ice cap would have begun forming first at the location of the true pole itself which, in Antarctica, is slightly off from being centrally located. For the glacier to grow first upward and then gradually outward enough to completely cover the continent, so that no actual land of the continent was visible, would take from as little as forty-five hundred years to as much as six thousand years."

Apperly paused to turn his head and clear his throat and then went on. "Now, the HAB Theory sets the last capsizing of the earth at about seventy-five hundred years ago. That would take it, on our present Gregorian calendar, back roughly to the year 5500 B.C. This would mean that until at least the year 1000 B.C., and possibly until as late as 500 A.D., the continent of Antarctica would have been visible in its actual form.

"Now, the high civilizations of Egypt, Babylon, Sumer, Chaldea, whatever, were in existence at least five thousand years ago. The question then becomes, why, if Antarctica was visible as a continent for anywhere from two thousand to thirty-five hundred years while man was progressing and plying the oceans of the world in his ships, there is no mention of Antarctica as a land mass? Why is there no map which has ever shown it as anything except what it is today—a fantastically huge glacier two miles high and far overlapping the continent it covers?

"Of the greatest importance to the AGA, however, is that there *must* be some conclusive evidence given, through a geologically sound dating method, showing that a warm climate existed on the Antarctic continent only six or seven thousand years ago. Quite frankly, I do not believe that this can be done. And I reiterate that until and unless this major matter can be resolved beyond dispute, geologists everywhere will be hard put to accept the HAB Theory."

Finished, he returned to his seat amidst a sustained applause. While this was in progress, Wautura Kellemo touched Narai's arm.

"Shall we move on?" he whispered.

She nodded and they rose to leave. Hardly anyone took notice of them, as now another member of the group had risen, identified himself as Dr. John Stanton, thermodynamicist of McGill University in Montreal, and continued the discussion.

"I would like to return," he began, "to the matter we were initially discussing, about the effect Mr. Boardman's proposed solution would have on the earth. The coastal destruction this so-called solution would cause on a worldwide scale is incredible and certainly totally unacceptable. Beyond the actual flooding of coastal area and inundation of island and peninsular societies, as we discussed earlier, the side effects would themselves almost certainly generate an ecological disaster of monumental proportions. Atmospheric radiation increases and the subsequent lowering of ocean temperatures would—"

His voice was cut off as Kelemmo shut the door behind Narai and himself. He shook his head as they began moving away and said, "The ramifications of this entire situation are beyond comprehension."

"Aren't they, though?" Narai agreed. "I really hate to leave this meeting." She was facing him as they walked down the thickly carpeted hallway, her eyes bright with excitement. "And to think that there are forty-nine other discussions just like this one taking place all over the city right now. Wouldn't it be fascinating to have tape recordings of each one?"

"It'd take a year just to *listen* to all of them, much less analyze what was said," Kelemmo grunted. "I don't envy Dr. Dowde's task of trying to make any real sense of it all."

"She has plenty of help," Narai said, "but, even so, it has to be a formidable job. Okay, Mr. Minister, where to now?"

"The Crystal Room, just ahead of us here."

Arm-in-arm, they passed beneath a fine crystal chandelier overhanging a junction of their hallway with another and were just approaching the Crystal Room when a voice behind them spoke hesitantly.

"Excuse me. Miss Ngoromu?"

They turned and saw a bellman carrying a small silver tray on which was an envelope. Narai nodded and, puzzled, accepted the envelope as the bellman extended the tray toward her. She hesitated and Kelemmo immediately removed a bill from his money clip and placed it on the still-extended tray. The bellman bobbed his head and smiled, thanking them both, and then moved away.

Narai's name was on the envelope and she broke open the lightly sealed flap and removed a piece of paper. The handwriting was none that she recognized, but then it became clear that it was the hand of whoever had taken the telephone message. A wave of disappointment washed over her as she read it.

Narai. Greatly sorry. No dinner together tonight. Am returning to Washington this afternoon under orders. With Grant. Will miss rest of symposium. I'll call you sometime this evening, late. Probably after 11 P.M. Again, sorry. Alex

"Bad news, little lady?" asked Kelemmo gently.

She nodded, trying to mask the disappointment with a smile. "A little. Nothing monumental. I was going to dinner tonight with Alexander Gordon. He can't make it."

"Oh, I'm truly sorry to hear that. If you would care to join Mr. Bomba and me, we were planning to dine together at—"

"No," she said quickly. "Thank you, but I think not." She touched his arm and now her smile was more genuine…"I appreciate the offer."

The remainder of the afternoon had been no less interesting, but for Narai the enjoyment of everything had been diminished. Instead of abating, as she had thought it would, the disappointment of not being with Alex tonight had increased as the day progressed. Still in the company of Kelemmo she dropped in on the remaining three group discussions being held in the Baroque Room, the Terrace Room, and the White and Gold Room of the Plaza, and then one meeting each in the nearby Sherry-Netherland, Essex House, and New York Hilton hotels. The discussions taking place were lively, sometimes heated, and always interesting. Yet, while she listened carefully and made notes of what was being said, the element of thorough enjoyment laced with keen anticipation had gone. One part of her mind continued methodically to catalogue what was being said, in order to relay the information to her father, but at least half a hundred times while the meetings were in progress she glanced at her watch, mentally willing the hands to move faster toward eleven o'clock.

It was during this period that Narai Ngoromu realized with something of a shock that she was very much in love with Alexander Gordon.

I V

As she left the Vanderbilt Suite in the long, T-shaped corridor on the third floor of the Waldorf Astoria when the group meeting she was attending broke up at six o'clock, Elizabeth Boardman moved with the crowd into the main hall. She was thinking about what the group had discussed today and wishing, as she had wished a dozen times or more during this day, that her father had lived to attend it. A time or two she was stopped by scientists wishing to meet her personally and talk, but she excused herself quickly, saying that she should report to Dr. Dowde at the symposium headquarters suite as soon as possible.

She had just reached the bank of elevators and turned left into another corridor on her way to the Vertes Suite when someone tapped her on the shoulder. She stifled a sigh and put an automatic smile on her lips as she turned, but immediately it became genuine.

"Paul! You got here! Oh, I'm so glad to see you."

Paul Neely was grinning broadly, no less delighted than she. "Hi, Liz," he said. He leaned forward and kissed her lightly and then tilted his head as he looked at her. She was wearing a becoming aqua dress with white belt, shoes and handbag. "You look terrific. I'd better watch out or one of these erudite academicians will be stealing you away from me."

She shook her head, laughing derisively but clearly pleased at his comment. "No chance. I'm spoken for. When did you arrive? Here at the hotel, I mean."

He shrugged. "Oh, around forty minutes ago, I suppose. I found your note at the desk—where I left my bag, incidentally—and came right up here. Tried to crash the meeting but the gendarmes turned me back. So I just stepped aside and waited. Then, when it was over, you got mixed up with the crowd and it took me a while to get to you."

"I'm sorry, Paul," she said, touching his cheek. "I should've thought of that. I was pretty sure you wouldn't get here until after the meeting broke up. I'll make sure you're not kept out in the hall again. Come on. I ought to see Dr. Dowde briefly—she's chairing this whole thing—and I want you to meet her. Amazing woman."

She took his hand and led him farther down the hallway toward the green-decorated Vertes Suite. The doorway to the symposium headquarters was clogged with a milling mass of people, mostly reporters. The couple was seen and Elizabeth Boardman immediately recognized. A sizable segment of the news people broke away from the rest and converged on the pair, firing a barrage of questions.

At first Liz tried to answer but the hubbub became so great that she finally began shaking her head and saying "No comment." The reporters were not discouraged and, beyond those encircling her, Liz could see that the outer foyer of the Vertes Suite was crammed with others trying to interview Irma Dowde. Over the confusion of voices she could hear Dr. Dowde's name being called aloud and once or twice a phrase or two as she replied. It was equally obvious that for the moment there would be no way for Liz and Paul to get close to her, or even to talk if they did so. Liz shook her head and leaned close to Paul, speaking into his ear.

"Come on, we'll see her later and get an official ID badge for you then. Right now we're going to the room. I can't cope with such confusion."

They gradually eased their way through the welter of bodies thrusting cameras and microphones at them and squeezed into a crowded elevator going to the lobby, so Paul could get his bag. Five minutes later they arrived at Room 3711, where Paul took the key from Liz and unlocked the door. He stepped aside and let her precede him, but stepped in immediately behind and caught her wrist. He kicked the door closed, dropped his bag and pulled her to him.

"That kiss downstairs was only a polite 'Hello, how are you' sort of thing. This one's for real."

"I would say," she murmured as they finally pulled apart, "that all the signs indicate you might have missed me a little."

"Enormously. More than I thought, and I'd thought it would be a lot. Gosh, but it's good being here with you." He gave her a speculative glance and then added, "Are you tired?"

"Whipped," she admitted. "It *has* been quite an eventful day."

"I gathered as much, from what you said over the phone and the way those reporters were acting downstairs. Therefore, a suggestion."

"Suggest away."

"First, a nice hot shower. Second, a little nap for maybe half an hour. Third, I take you downstairs to Peacock Alley off the main lobby for dinner."

"Sounds good. Are you planning on joining me for the first two as well as the third?"

"I'd been toying with the idea."

"I rather suspected that you might have been." She cocked a brow at him. "Which might somewhat alter step number two."

"It might," he conceded.

"I didn't really want to sleep, anyway." She kissed his lips gently and there was a tender expression in her eyes as she pulled away. "Paul, I feel so good. So wanted and needed. I hope it'll always be that way."

She turned her back to him and said, "Unzip me, please," but then turned to face him again before he had a chance to do so. She reached out and touched his arm. "Oh, a thought. Maybe you'd better call down and make reservations. They're awfully crowded here. It might be too late already to get a table."

"No problem," he said. "I made eight o'clock reservations for us as soon as I arrived." He turned her around and unzipped her dress, saying as he did so, "Now suppose you start telling me what's happened here so far?"

She nodded and began as they prepared to shower.

V

Irma Dowde undressed slowly in her room, grunting softly over the effort it took to bend over and untie her heavy, blunt-toed walking shoes and kick them off. She wriggled her toes in the delicious sense of freedom which came immediately after release from the imprisonment they had suffered since very early this morning. Except for brief intervals she had been on her feet constantly, and for someone built as heavily as she, it was very hard on the feet. She sat on the edge of the bed, still wriggling the toes and alternately rubbing one foot over the other as she reached behind her and began unbuttoning her blouse.

In her usual methodical manner, she carefully hung her skirt and jacket in the closet, grumbling over the ridiculous coat hangers which disconnected from the hook portion in the closet. Her soiled clothing she put into the plastic drawstring bag and then put the bag on the floor in the closet. She stood naked in the middle of the room, luxuriously letting her stubby fingers scratch the multitude of places which itched from being so long confined. Whole series of red marks began appearing on the flabby, puckered flesh of belly, thighs, and buttocks, and on the sides of the heavy, pendulous breasts which hung in a flattened manner nearly to her waist.

She groaned with delight at the sensations brought by the scratching and then caught a glimpse of herself in the room's big mirror and shook her head.

"You are indeed," she murmured to her reflection, "a true vision of feminine loveliness."

She snorted at her own remark and then glanced at her watch, nearly blanketed by a fold of flesh at her wrist. Ten after eleven already and quite late to be calling the White House, but the President had insisted that she call him with a report of the day's activities regardless of what time she finished. She arched her back as she removed the watch and set it atop the dresser, then changed her mind and took it over to the nightstand. As long as it was this late already, being a little later wouldn't hurt, and what she wanted more than anything else right now was a good hot shower.

Twenty minutes later, much more relaxed and comfortable and clad in a formless, ankle-length nightgown of faded yellow, she carefully laid out her clothes for tomorrow. Then she padded to the bed and propped up the two pillows to support her back while she talked. On the nightstand she placed two spiral-bound steno pads—one blank, the other well used—and a ball-point pen, then turned out all the lights except the one in the bathroom and the one beside the bed. In another moment she was lying on the bed, resting back comfortably on the pillows, her knees up and the pads in handy reach.

She put in a quick call to the hotel operator and left word to be awakened at six in the morning. Then she dialed eight for the long distance operator and gave her the number she had been instructed to call.

"This is the White House," came a soft masculine voice. "The switchboard is closed to incoming calls. Normal switchboard hours are from eight to five daily. Please call tomorrow."

"I have a long distance collect call," the operator said, "from Dr. Irma Dowde in New York City for President Robert Sanders."

There was a slight pause at the other end. Then, "Does she have a code class to her call, Operator?"

Irma Dowde spoke up. "Yes, I have. P-E-0 number one."

"We will accept, Operator." There was a businesslike briskness to the male voice now. "Please put her through and remove yourself from the line."

"Yes, sir. Go ahead, please," she said.

"Dr. Dowde?"

"Yes."

"We were instructed to expect your call." There was a click as the operator disconnected herself. "Operator?" There was no response and the male voice went on. "Hold on, Dr. Dowde. I'll ring the President. He's retired for the night, so it may be a short while."

The wait was about a minute and a half and then came another clicking sound and the President's voice, somewhat thick with sleep. "Dr. Dowde? I'm glad you called. How'd it go today?"

"Exceptionally well, sir," she replied. "I had some reservations about how the evening meeting with the group chairmen would turn out, expecting it to be rather confused, but it went surprisingly well. We concluded about an hour and a half ago. Mr. Knotts had about ten of his staff there on stenotype machines to take down the summarizations of the chairmen. On the master chart we had groups alphabetically listed by the hotel in which the discussions were held, so that's the order in which they were called upon to speak."

"Were the Knotts people who attended the individual group meetings this afternoon of value?"

"Indeed yes, Mr. President. I'm quite sure that without them there would have been no adequate way for the group chairmen to have presented their reports so concisely and well."

"There had to be some difficulties."

"Only one major problem insofar as the actual functioning of the individual discussion groups was concerned. I more or less anticipated that it might happen." The archaeologist paused, but then went on when Sanders made no reply. "It's in the matter of linguistics. By far the greater majority speak and comprehend English well, but there's a small percentage who don't and these individuals had difficulty both in following what was being said in their groups and in contributing to the discussions. Here and there during the day I was able to help a little in this respect, as were some others, but not really as well as was needed. Part of what we did tonight was to endeavor to place any who could not understand English beside someone who could interpret for them during the talks tomorrow, but it's still going to be a problem. I don't really know what we can do about it at this juncture."

The President made a little sound and said, "Wait a moment till I get some paper here. All right, where are we having the most difficulty? Slowly, so I can take them down."

Dr. Dowde turned a pages of her own pad before replying. "Four languages in particular," she said. "Africaans, Hindustani, Chinese, Japanese. Then there are three others which aren't quite as much a problem, but where it wouldn't hurt to have some help. Arabic, Portuguese, Turkish."

"Got it. We'll get our United Nations Interpretation Section on it right away. They'll be in touch with you in the morning. Be prepared to tell them how many of each you need and what specific dialects, if any."

"Yes, sir. Thank you." She sounded relieved. "There will be need for specific dialect help for China, I'm sure, and possibly the Arab states."

"Okay. Any other problems?"

"We do have," she spoke reluctantly, "a small core of individuals who have obviously closed their minds to any possible acceptance of the HAB Theory. I mean," she amended quickly, "above and beyond the expected argumentative nature of those not yet convinced. Naturally, we anticipated a good bit of friction to arise because there are a great many who won't give in easily to a theory which undermines so much of what was previously accepted. This is good, I think, because in most cases the arguments which ensue generally seem to be establishing the theory more thoroughly than ever, rather than undermining it.

"But what I mean by a problem," she went on, "is that there are perhaps three or four people being unreasonably disruptive in their comments—batting down every pro-HAB argument under discussion with diatribes that are far more emotional than scientific. The problem is not so much that they disagree with the HAB Theory as it is that they become so vehement in their arguments and get so far off the track in their comments and interruptions that the meetings they're involved with tend to get stalled or become chaotic. There's been," she admitted, "even a certain amount of temper involved—insults, name-calling and, in one case a very minor physical altercation. I think it could worsen."

"Any specific motivation?" the President asked.

"I suppose there must be, but there's no way to know for sure."

"Have you made notes concerning those causing the most trouble?"

"Well, not really, Mr. President, but I know who they are."

"Let me have their names and we'll initiate some quiet checks on them."

Irma Dowde became even more reluctant. "I really wouldn't want to contribute to the injury of their careers, Mr. President. They're being dogmatic, true, but I don't really feel that should be cause for possibly ruining them. I wouldn't want to take part in anything like that."

The President's response was sympathetic but firm. "It's not a matter of an intent to deliberately ruin careers or cause injury, Dr. Dowde, but both of us know full well the extreme importance, to all humanity, of the matter involved here, and if these individuals are creating stumbling blocks simply for the sake of impeding progress in the discussions—that *is* what you've indicated they're doing, isn't it?"

"Yes, sir, to large extent."

"Then," Sanders continued, "we can't allow possible injury to individual feelings or careers to be an influencing factor. Good, strong, well-founded argument we welcome; deliberate harassment, on the other hand, has to be eliminated, if at all possible. In that respect, I'd like you to provide me with the names of those individuals who seem to fit into the latter category."

The heavy-set archeologist sighed. "All right, Mr. President. You're correct, of course. There are two men in particular who evidently are doing their best to undermine the purpose of the symposium, plus a third who's more or less borderline in this regard." She shook her head, obviously still hesitant to provide the names, but then went on. "Unfortunately, all three are either chairing or vice-chairing individual group discussions—one chairman and two vice-chairmen, to be specific—and they've been disrupting not only their own group meetings, but the evening summation as well. I'm sure we'd have finished tonight's session much earlier had it not been for them. The one who is a group chairman is Dr. Owen Holder. His group is meeting here at the Waldorf."

"Who is he?" the President inquired. "His credentials, I mean."

"Dr. Holder," she replied, "is professor of geology at Oxford. England. He's highly respected in his field."

"All right. And the other two?"

"Dr. Percy Utwell is vice-chairman of one of the three discussion groups meeting at the Taft Hotel. He's an M.D. on the staff of the Seldon Clinic and Medical Research Laboratory in Pittsburgh."

"Who's chairing his group?"

"Dr. Omi Damshad. He's a cryptologist and a good man. I know him well. Presently curator of the National Museum of Antiquities in Tehran."

"Uh-huh. That's good. Now, who's the final one?"

Once again Dr. Dowde hesitated and then began slowly. "I'll reiterate, Mr. President, that this individual's borderline in respect to out-and-out harassment, but he's being argumentative irrespective of whether or not the matter under discussion is in his own field or not. He was the one, incidentally, involved in the minor altercation. He shoved Dr. Gottlund of Austria deliberately and they had to be separated before anything more serious occurred."

"His name?"

"He's Dr. Pierre Deschault, director of the Paris Academy of Sciences. He's a paleontologist, and a good one, too, just as Gottlund is, but he's also known to be pretty thin-skinned and hotheaded. His wife, Yvonne, incidentally, is herself chairing a group here in the Waldorf and doing exceptionally well. She's a paleobotanist and associate curator at the National Museum of Natural History in Paris. She's also connected with the Paris Institute."

"What hotel is Deschault's group meeting in, and who's chairing it?"

"He's in one of the four groups at the Americana. The chairman is—just a moment..." she flipped a few pages in her assignments book, found what she was looking for and nodded as her finger stopped at the appropriate place, "here it is—he's an Australian. Dr. Colin Hastings. Director of the Australasian Society of Engineers in Sydney. Mechanical engineering."

"All right, I have it. Now, we can't very well eject them from participation in the symposium, but I'd suggest, if the problem persists, that you remove them from their leadership positions and perhaps in that way they can be tempered somewhat."

"If that's what you wish, Mr. President," she said, but she was pretty sure she wouldn't follow through. "In respect to Dr. Deschault, I think I can solve the problem fairly easily. Tomorrow I plan to exchange his vice-chair-manship with the vice-chairmanship of his wife's group. She may be able to exert a sort of leavening factor on him."

"Excellent idea. Any other problems?"

"Nothing worth mentioning, sir."

"Good. Now, what's been accomplished today and what's the general feeling so far?"

"It's still too early to be certain about anything," she replied, "but indications are that increasingly more are becoming convinced of the solid foundation to Mr. Boardman's postulations. I don't want to become too optimistic at this stage, but I'd say the chances are good for a pretty general acceptance of the HAB Theory by the time the symposium's finished."

She gave a short laugh and added, "I've been trying to keep uppermost in my mind the gravity of this whole business and what it portends but, in all honesty, sir, I'm most excited about all the new prospects of study that are opening. So *many* things becoming more understandable now than ever before!" Her tone of voice had become electric. "So *many* things that've been hidden in museum basements and so many topics that've been more or less ignored or even made to appear not to exist because we had no answers for them—and now it's as if a dam has burst and everyone's suddenly eager to talk about them, to dust them off and bring them out into the daylight for serious consideration. I've never encountered anything like it before. I don't think the *world* ever has! I truly believe, Mr. President, that we are at this moment crossing a threshold into a great renaissance of science."

There was a tinge of amusement in Sanders's voice at her enthusiasm. "One that's long been needed, would you say?"

"Without hesitation," she replied, "and I think a great many others here—far more than I first anticipated—are feeling that way also, or at least beginning to. Mr. President, you and I both sense the validity of the theory—you, I think, even more than I—but even if it should prove to be invalid, what it's done already has been to take science by the coattails and give it a good shaking. One that it's needed for decades—centuries even! I don't see how, at this point, the theory can be disproved, but I most sincerely wish it could be, simply because of the avenues of new study and research that have been opened. It's a springboard into the future and now there may be no future. It's like a man who has been blind since early childhood and then, on the very day that the doctors restore his sight, they also tell him that he has a hopelessly terminal illness. He has so much to see, and so little time in which to see it. In our case, as scientists, we now have so much to do, and yet so little time in which to do it."

"That's what I've felt from the beginning," Sanders agreed thoughtfully. Then he added with a degree of briskness, "Now, suppose you give me a breakdown on what went on during the discussions today."

"Yes, sir." She opened the nearly filled steno pad to its first page and began. "I should mention first that in all fifty groups, in accordance with instructions I previously gave to group chairmen, the discussions began with the request for anyone to rise and speak who felt he had found proofs which would indicate faulty premise to Mr. Boardman's postulations. In most cases such discussions occupied about the first hour of the three-hour initial discussions. Sometimes the entire three hours were filled with such argument, but just as often it branched out within mere minutes to discussions of the new light that the postulations were shedding on scientific enigmas which have baffled us all for so long. Among the—"

"Just a moment, Dr. Dowde," the President interrupted. "Before going on, *were* there any indisputable proofs offered against the HAB Theory?"

"No, sir, none. Not indisputable. Occasionally some fairly heated rhubarbs occurred but—and here's the excitement of this whole business—*because* the arguments were not confined to simply one scientific field, or even a small number of fields of closely interrelated study, the interlocking factors of many fields brought up by other specialists showed instead that the alleged proofs against the HAB Theory were themselves based on faulty premise." She hesitated. "That's a terrible sentence I just gave you to digest, but I hope you caught the gist of it. In no case were the Boardman postulations *proven* wrong. In some cases," she admitted, "there's considerable doubt remaining, but so far no *proof* of invalidity.

"One of the most important presentations made thus far *against* acceptance of the theory," she went on, "was given by Dr. Clarence Apperly, who's director of the American Geophysical Association in Washington. It's a pretty powerful organization in scientific circles. He contends that no hard evidence has been presented to show that the Antarctic ice cap is any younger than the thirteen million years geologically established as its age, and that it can't be shown positively that the continent of Antarctica had a warm climate about the time when the HAB Theory states the last capsizing of the earth occurred. Unless such proofs can be shown, Apperly said, then geologists in general and the AGA in particular simply won't endorse the HAB Theory. His point was well made and if it's not shown to be in error, acceptance by the majority, whether geologists or not, is unlikely. I have people already doing a lot of digging in this respect. Whether or not we'll find something to satisfy Apperly and his people, I just don't know."

Irma Dowde evidently expected some indication of distress on the President's part, but instead he surprised her.

"Hmmm," he murmured, "very interesting. Go on."

"Well," she continued, "that's the only *really* glum note that's come up. In by far the greater majority of cases, contributions by specialists in a wide spectrum of studies are interlocking in unexpected and exciting ways and they tend more to confirm than dispute the HAB postulations."

"What about the matter of Mr. Boardman's proposed solution?"

"Quite a bit of discussion about that, Mr. President. That matter alone was discussed to some extent in seventeen of the fifty sessions. No satisfactory conclusions reached yet, but the consensus seems to be that the proposed solution is much too drastic and its immediate results—to say nothing of the long-term effects would be so devastating that it's wholly out of the question. I'm quite sure, though, that there'll be more discussion about it."

"Anything—beyond merely generally supportive—which adds basis to the HAB Theory?"

"Quite a lot of individual little pieces which are falling into place now in many fields, sir, but only one so far which might be considered a substantial proof. As a matter of fact, it's one of the most astounding things I've ever heard or encountered. Everyone here's been talking about it. On the surface, at least, it appears to fully corroborate recurrent capsizings of the earth."

"Ah!" The single sound from the President carried with it a strong quickening of interest. "Let's hear about it."

The Smithsonian scientist became hesitant again. "I don't know that we should get into it right now, Mr. President. It came about during the afternoon meeting here in the Louis the Sixteenth Suite and it's quite involved. It may take much longer to explain than you'd care to put on it right now. I'd planned to drop in on the meeting for only a few minutes and wound up staying for over an hour. Practically all of it will be in Mr. Knotts's summary in the morning and you might want to wait until we can send one down to you by special courier first thing in the morning."

"It's that important?"

"We believe so, sir, yes."

"Then by all means I want to hear about it now, however long it takes." When still she seemed dubious about continuing, he added. "Go ahead, I'm listening."

The scientist, wishing fervently that she hadn't disposed of all her cigarettes, took a deep breath and scrunched down a bit more comfortably on her pillow, changed ears with the telephone, and then began.

"The meeting in the Louis the Sixteenth Suite had been in progress just over half an hour when I got there with my assistant, Kathryn Lever. I gathered that they'd begun the session according to directions, but then had gone off quickly on the tangent of trying to answer the question of why, if previous civilizations had in fact existed on the earth, some sort of permanent and definite records have not been found. Definite," she added, "as opposed to the questionable nature of some of the so-called records as deciphered from the Egyptian hieroglyphics.

"It was at this point, Mr. President, that the group chairman, Dr. Ho-Chung Chow of Peking, took the floor. He was still talking when I left over an hour later, and he had the entire group in the palm of his hand."

"Dr. Chow is—? Sanders left the sentence hanging.

"Excuse me, sir. He's an archeologist—head of the archeology department at the University of Peking. I'd never met him before but his reputation precedes him and I've known *about* him for years. He began by saying — incidentally, he speaks English fluently—by saying that such definite records were indeed in existence and had been found many years before. In China. He then went on to describe the discovery and subsequent study of a large number of peculiar stone disks that had been found in some underground repositories in the Himalayas near the border of Tibet. I'd heard and read rather tantalizing bits and pieces about these disks over the years and so I was immediately very interested. He said that these—"

"Pardon me a moment please, Dr. Dowde," the Chief Executive broke in. His hand evidently covered the mouthpiece of the phone but Irma Dowde could still hear his muffled voice as he said, "No. No, it's nothing to worry about at all, Grace. Sorry you were disturbed. Go on back to bed. I'll be a while yet."

His voice came back clearly again. "I'm sorry for the interruption," he said with a little laugh. "The First Lady gets concerned if I'm called from bed at night to the telephone. Her first thought always seems to be that we've been attacked somewhere and I'm declaring war." He laughed again. "Go on, please."

"Yes, sir. Dr. Chow said that the discovery of the stone disks was made in 1938 by Professor Chi Pu Tei, an archaeologist who was leading a body of his students on an expedition into the Bayan Kara Ula Mountains in the then-disputed frontier territory of Tibet and China. The precise location was not given by Dr. Chow, but he said it was in the general area of where Chang Thang Province of Tibet and Tsinghai Province of China abutted.

"That area, sir," she added as an aside, "has been what is termed 'Positively Forbidden Territory' for the Western world since the year 1938, which now, in light of what Dr. Chow had to say, was probably not at all coincidental. At any rate, Professor Chi Pu Tei and his students discovered what was first described as a series of caves or caverns, but later admitted to be a complex system of artificial tunnels and underground storerooms. These tunnels are perfectly squared and the walls, ceilings, and floors are highly glazed, as if somehow the passages and rooms were carved by a device emitting heat of such intensity that it simply melted its way into the mountains."

"As might occur," the President put in, "if you pushed a red hot nail into a block of wax?"

"A good comparison, Mr. President. Yes, probably very similar to that, at least in appearance. All right, to go on, the archaeological group followed some of these passages and encountered larger chambers in which numerous undescribed implements were discovered. The implements evidently differed from one chamber to another, but one item was found in common in each of the chambers—the stone disks I mentioned earlier. Apparently in each of the chambers they were found in the same position—on a smooth cube of rock, glazed just as the tunnels were, with anywhere from five to twenty of the disks neatly stacked on top."

"I take it," Sanders said as the scientist paused, "that there is something especially significant about these disks?"

"Very much so, President Sanders. Each of them was twenty-two point seven centimeters in diameter by two centimeters in thickness, which is about three-quarters of an inch thick by nine inches in diameter. Each disk also had a perfectly circular two-centimeter hole in the exact center. The edges of the disks were regularly indented all the way around, almost like a cogwheel, though neither sharply defined nor amorphous. Somewhere in between the two, most like the flutings on a pie crust. However, we've yet to come to the most peculiar characteristic of the disks. Each had a twin groove which began at the center hole and gradually moved in an expanding spiral in counterclockwise manner to the outer rim. The individual disks bore a certain similarity to the phonograph records of today. There were evidently slight differences from disk to disk in the actual groovings, but the basic similarity was standard."

What about the other items—the implements?"

"Dr. Chow did not comment to any length on what the other items were that were stored in the chambers or what has happened to them, but he did say that all of the stone disks were removed and taken for study to the Peking Academy of Prehistory."

"How many were there?"

"A total of seven hundred sixteen."

"Go on."

"Nothing was heard about this discovery," Irma Dowde said, after changing ears again, "by Western world scientists for the next twenty-seven years. During that period, Dr. Chow says, the disks were being studied intensively in a project headed by Professor Tsum Um Nui, at the Peking Academy."

"Question," the President said. "Before we get too far away from the area where these disks were originally discovered, did Dr. Chow say anything about that particular region—who inhabits it? What it's like?"

"As a matter of fact he did, Mr. President, in passing. But it does bring out another curious element which has a distinct tie-in later on. The Bayan Kara Ula Mountains area is one of the most isolated and least known areas on earth today. The nearest city of any consequence is Lhasa, Tibet, about four hundred miles to the south through virtually impassable terrain. It is an area presently inhabited by two tribes of very unusual people."

"Unusual in what respect?"

She sighed. "They simply do not fit into any racial category established by anthropologists for the races of the world. For one thing, they are both of pygmy stature. The tallest and shortest adults have measured at four feet seven inches and three feet six inches respectively, but the average height is four feet two inches. They are yellow-skinned. Their heads are disproportionately large and sparsely haired, and their eyes are large but not Oriental in aspect, with pale bluish irises. Their features are very nicely formed, most nearly approximating Caucasian, and their bodies are extremely thin and delicate. Adult weight is estimated by Dr. Chow to average, in our system of weights, about thirty-eight to fifty-two pounds. The tribes call themselves Dropa and Han. Now, if I may go on?"

"Unusual. Very unusual," Sanders muttered. "Yes, please continue."

"The disks, as I was saying, underwent extensive study by Professor Tsum Um Nui, interrupted at times by war. It took him and his coworkers only a short time to discover that the spiral grooves were not sound tracks but, rather, an incredibly ancient writing inscribed in some unknown way and very nearly microscopic in size. The disks were determined to be no less than three or four thousand years old at the youngest, and more likely anywhere from eight to twelve thousand years old. This would make them the oldest known form of writing in the world. Deciphering was incredibly difficult. It was twenty-four years—in 1962—before Professor Nui and a young colleague found the key and began laboriously deciphering. That young colleague happened to be our present group chairman, Dr. Ho-Chung Chow. The deciphered spiral text of the stones, even though only a small amount was completed, was so startling in its content that the Chinese government prohibited any publication of the papers of Nui and Chow. Then, in 1965, in a manner which Chow describes with a peculiar smile as 'very mysterious,' an article written by the Russian philologist Vyacheslav Saizev appeared in *Das Vegetarische Universum*, a German magazine, and in the Russian-English magazine, *Sputnik*, telling about the disks, their qualities and composition, and a little about what had been deciphered from them. It's rather startling."

Irma Dowde paused, sneezed twice explosively, excused herself and blamed the room's air conditioner and then went on. "Dr. Chow accidentally bumped one of the disks against a metal table, and though it didn't damage the disk, through his hand he could feel a strange vibration. He then suspended one of the disks with a strong line and tapped it with a metal rod. For nearly half a minute the disk rang with a clear, perfect tone, much in the manner of a tuning fork. Subjected to close analysis, the disk was found to have a very high cobalt content, which in itself is incredible in stones of such age. Further, there was a high metallic content to them. All indications are that these disks were at some time part of some sort of advanced and sophisticated electrical system. The articles in both *Sputnik* and *Das Vegetarische Universum* presented very little of the deciphered text, but what was there was significant in light of the HAB Theory. Dr. Chow read the passage aloud to the group and I took it down verbatim. At least I think I did. I have a strange sort of home-grown shorthand I use, and if you won't mind my stumbling a bit, I'll read it through."

"By all means, Dr. Dowde, please do." There was not the faintest trace of sleepiness or impatience.

Irma Dowde had been referring to her notes at intervals as she made her relation to the President, but now she held the pad closer to her eyes and, after a wide, stifled yawn, read slowly aloud.

"'This is our story as the Dropa have given us this means of preserving our words forever on one of their many ecal.' I don't know that word 'ecal' at all," she said, "but it evidently refers to these peculiar disks. Continuing, 'The Dropa stopped their great sky ship in the air above us and terrified all our people. At first our men and women and children hid themselves in caves, but then wonder overcame fear and they emerged. Ten times during the night the fear rose again as ten times smaller ships came out of the larger ship and floated to the ground among us, and ten times we fled into the caves before sunlight. But then the Dropa entered our heads with calming sounds and they made signs of friendship, and they told us inside our heads that we should not fear them, for their intentions were of a peaceful nature. As they worked with their great machines and cut into the mountains they told us of the great disruption and flood that was to come again, as it had come so many times before, and that there was little time remaining to preserve mankind, but we did not understand. In all our history there had been only one flood and that was the great flood which was ending as our lives here were beginning. But they told us to fear not because this was a safe place. Then, all but fifty of the Dropa, their work finished, returned to the big ship and disappeared into it and then the big ship moved quickly from our sight to return to the other safe place.'

"That," Irma Dowde said, "is all, up until that time, that had been deciphered from one disk. It represents, according to Dr. Chow, only about one-twentieth of one percent of the grooving on that particular disk. Since then, Dr. Chow told us, the efforts at deciphering have gone on. The entire first disk has been translated into a volume of nearly two thousand pages, but he said he could not—which might well mean *would* not—tell us what else was said there. The other seven hundred

fifteen disks have similar but more extensive double grooving, however it's more difficult to decipher. In fact, according to Dr. Chow, no real progress was made on them over the years that have passed since then until a significant key was discovered just ten years ago.

"There is still great difficulty, as he tells it," she continued, shifting her weight a little to get more comfortable on the bed, "but little by little the deciphering is being accomplished. Five complete disks and a portion of another four have been deciphered. He declined to comment at all in respect to what they revealed except that he did say one of the disks began by the Dropa people commenting on their regret that their larger sky ship had been severely damaged in the turning of the earth—his exact phraseology," she added quickly, "and they had failed in efforts to construct another. The most modern mineral-dating techniques have now shown the oldest of the disks to be approximately eleven thousand five hundred years old and the others spaced in between that to the latest, which is approximately seventy-five hundred years old. The oldest disk is the one which comments on the damage to the ship by the turning of the earth. The newest is the one, evidently recorded by the progenitors of the Han tribe, telling of the visit by the Dropas and their warning of destruction.

"The corollaries to be drawn here, Mr. President, are momentous. "*If,*" she added with emphasis, "the ancient writings are to be believed. And *if* the entire discovery and deciphering is to be believed. Taken in reference to Mr. Boardman's postulations, they fit much too well to be mere coincidence. According to Boardman, our present epoch is somewhere around seventy-five hundred years old, which ties in perfectly with the capsizing of the earth which he claims to have occurred about that time, and which the Dropa were obviously aware was approaching.

Again, according to Boardman, the epoch before our present epoch—that is, B.P. 1—lasted only about four thousand years, which again ties neatly to the eleven-thousand-five-hundred-year dating of the oldest disk and the capsizing of the earth to end Epoch B.P. 2 and begin Epoch B.P. 1—further linked by the Dropas' referring to the damage their large sky ship had suffered in the turning of the earth."

There was an extended silence on both ends of the line as Irma Dowde finished, and then at last the President spoke, a sense of wonder tinged with disbelief in his voice.

"You chose your word well when you said it was startling, Dr. Dowde. It's an awful lot to chew. It also opens one hell of a keg of worms. My immediate reaction is to be extremely skeptical of any ancient race on earth having had the ability to fly."

"I think we've all felt that way, sir, but we're coming up with an enormous number of references to the ancients having had the power of flight. This is especially true, sir, with the Chinese. There are numerous accounts of the Chinese having built flying machines, only to have each in turn—and sometimes the man who built it as well—destroyed by the emperor then in power because of the dangerous potential they had for war." She started to say something, stopped, then went on anyway with a sense of reluctance. "I think, Mr. President, that maybe it's time we began treating such stories with our minds more open."

"*Touche*," he said. "My own words coming back to haunt me. You're correct, of course. All right, assuming they possessed flight ability, is there any indication where the so-called big ship of the Dropas came from and where it went?"

"Nothing concrete insofar as where the ship came from, but it certainly lends itself to speculation in any number of directions. As for where it went—the translation says 'to the other safe place,' signifying that for the coming flood and destruction the Dropa were predicting, there were only two safe places. That, again, ties in with Boardman's theory regarding the pivotal points as being safe at the time the earth was capsizing."

"Yes," Sanders murmured, "I caught that. Anything else?"

"Yes, a couple of items which seem closely related and are very important in respect to both the Chinese discovery and the HAB Theory. I know it's getting very late, though, sir, and if you prefer I can have all this material in your hands fairly early tomorrow."

"No. If you don't mind and aren't too tired yourself, I'd just as soon hear all you have on it right now."

"I don't mind at all, Mr. President, and I won't take too much longer with it. One of the items is strongly corroborative of the genuineness of the Chinese discovery. The same Russian philologist who wrote the pieces which appeared in the two magazines, Dr. Vyacheslav Saizev, made an extremely important discovery subsequently on his own. He'd heard rumors of unusual rock paintings and cave paintings having been found by some villagers in the far southeastern USSR, fairly close to the border of Sinkiang, China. Just north of the border of the state of Kirgiz, SSR, lies a little village called Fergana. On a straight line from where the stone disks were found, it's just over a thousand miles distant. With considerable difficulty, Dr. Saizov got to Fergana, and after months of fruitless searching, he finally found what he sought: a small area of caves in which there were some of the most incredible prehistoric rock paintings ever discovered."

She turned another page in the pad and now only a few pages remained. She sneezed abruptly and violently and nearly lost her pad. "Excuse me," she apologized, "no warning on that one. Now then, the painting of particular interest that he found depicts an individual, somewhat stylized but more in the manner of a Picasso stylization than the usual stick-figure types commonly observed in ancient cave paintings. Saizev estimates, probably with considerable accuracy, an age of about nine thousand years to the painting. The individual pictured is dressed in what can only be some form of spacesuit. A large clear globe encircles his head and appears held to the collar by a row of rivet heads or lock nuts of some kind. Positioned in front of his mouth, which is open in speech, is an excellent representation of a microphone, from which wires come out the bottom and attach to some sort of power pack. There are numerous dials and gauges on the suit, without exception connected to thick wires draped in layers over his right shoulder and coming from his back. The seams of his suit are clearly visible and he is wearing heavy gloves. His head, incidentally, is large for his body. There are flames erupting from the right side of the clear globe over his head and the right side of his face appears to be burning. His expression is somewhat agonized and he seems to be calling for help into his microphone. But—and this is what is so significant, sir," she added, becoming more excited, "in his gloved hand, the right hand, he holds at chest level an exact duplicate of the Chinese stone disks, complete to hole in the center, groovings and the peculiar cog-flutings on the outer rim. So accurate is the painting that the groovings can be seen emanating in counterclockwise manner from the center hole to the outer rim, identically to those found in the tunnels in the Bayan Kara Ula Mountains. That's all I have on it."

The President was silent except for a faint, wondering "Hmmmm," just barely audible to the archaeologist. After a moment Dr. Dowde spoke again.

"Shall I go on with the final item, sir?"

"Yes, of course. Forgive my lack of comment." He gave a short laugh. "It's just that I'm overwhelmed."

"All of us are, Mr. President. Even the most skeptical. I'll finish now as quickly as possible. This last matter is an item of my own deduction since leaving that meeting this afternoon. As you may recall from John Grant's summary of the HAB Theory, Mr. Boardman postulates a shifting of the earth on its axis of approximately eighty degrees at the time of the capsizing action. What I wanted to determine was this: under the assumption that the deciphered message was accurate and the so-called big sky ship left the Chinese safe area for the 'other safe place,' then where was that other place? Fortunately, the manager of the Waldorf has a very nice world globe in his office and allowed me to use it shortly after I left the meeting. The alleged 'safe area' in China where the stone disk s were found lies at approximately ninety degrees east longitude. Thus, the other safe place should be located a hundred seventy degrees from there, which allows for the earth shift of eighty degrees instead of a full ninety. That would take it to eighty degrees west, on the opposite side of the earth. That line of longitude, Mr. President," she added softly, "passes through Peru and Ecuador."

"The Incas!" Sanders said immediately.

"Not directly, sir," she replied. "Rather, pre-Incan. But this is not the principal point I'm making. Back in 1965 an Argentine citizen, Juan Moricz, who is an amateur archaeologist, was poking about in the Ecuadorian Andes about a hundred fifty miles south of Quito, in the Province of Santiago. He stumbled across another of the most significant archaeological finds of the past century—of *any* century, for that matter," she amended. "He found a cave held in superstitious awe by the Indian tribes of the area. After finally gaining their confidence, he was allowed to enter the cave to explore. What he found is just about as amazing as the Chinese discovery and closely allied to it.

"The initial, naturally formed cave gave way to a smooth shaft, obviously artificially made, which went straight down in three distinct drops, each of two hundred and fifty feet. At the level of two hundred fifty feet below the surface was a platform leading into a vault of considerable dimension; radiating outward from this vault was a whole series of artificial tunnels. The same situation was found at the five-hundred-foot level and at the bottom, seven hundred fifty feet below ground level. The important aspect is that these tunnels evidently were made in exactly the same manner as the tunnels in the Bayan Kara Ula Mountains in China. Perfectly squared and highly glazed, as if formed by means of intense heat. There are, Mr. President, thousands—perhaps even tens of thousands—of miles of these tunnels beneath Ecuador and Peru. Mostly they're still unexplored because the radiation in them is very high and compasses refuse to operate down there. Only a few hundred miles of them have been explored and those mostly in a cursory manner. There are a great many chambers filled with artifacts and statuary but, most important, there is one chamber in particular of immense consequence."

The scientist licked her lips. Her throat felt dry and she wished she had brought a glass of water in from the bathroom and put it on the nightstand before she began this call. She swallowed and went on.

"That chamber, with the unusual, highly glazed walls, ceiling and floors, measures four hundred fifty-nine feet by four hundred ninety-two feet. In the center of this room is a huge table around which are seven chairs. They are fashioned of an unknown material, as heavy as stone but not of stone. Nor are they metallic or wooden. The closest approximation seems to be some sort of extremely dense plastic material, but far heavier than any plastic known. Forming a perimeter around the table and chairs is a ring of sculptured animals. Well, no," she corrected herself, "that's not quite right. They're made of the same material and appear to have been molded."

"What kind of animals, Dr. Dowde?"

"Some which represent animals indigenous to the area, others which definitely are not and never have been. There are jaguars and cougars, but also there are lions, elephants, wolves and bison. There are monkeys, gorillas, and bears, as well as small invertebrates such as crustaceans and gastropods. All this—the furnishings and statuary—are intriguing, but they fade in significance to what else is in this room, some fifty feet from the table. You are undoubtedly aware, sir, that archaeologists were for many years agreed in the belief that the Incan and pre-Incan civilizations existed without any form of writing except a peculiar sort of record-keeping through the tying of knots in lengths of cord. Yet, fifty feet from that center grouping is an incredible library permanently preserved in metal leaves. Each sheet of metal is one point six millimeters thick—about a sixteenth of an inch— but thirty-eight inches long by nineteen inches wide. Yet, they're so sturdy that standing on the narrow edge and extending upward over three feet, they remain perfectly rigid, with no sign of bending. The metal most closely resembles zinc, but it definitely is not zinc. Neither is it tin nor any other known metal or alloy.

"These metal pages stand side by side, held in place by great blocklike pieces of material of the same substance the furniture is fashioned from. And, Mr. President, each of these thousands of leaves has stamped on it in regular order, just as if stamped by a powerful press, line after line of a peculiar boxed form of writing. The characters are wholly unfamiliar and seemingly of a sophisticated hieroglyphic nature, but whatever culture produced this amazing library also left with it the key to its deciphering. In a special niche, obviously made precisely for the purpose it is serving in one of the huge block bookends, is what appears to be an alphabet of fifty-six characters stamped in a gridwork of squares on metal of the same type as the leaves, but much thicker. A sort of stele."

Stifling another yawn, Dr. Dowde turned to the final page of her notes and read the figures there aloud. "The metal stele is an inch and a half thick, five and a half inches wide and twenty and a half inches long. From top to bottom there are fourteen rows of hieroglyphic characters, with four characters per row, confined within boxes which are exactly three and a half centimeters square—that's roughly an inch and three-eighths. None of the characters are the same, but these very characters are used in different combinations in the rows of characters on the metal leaves."

"Comparable, then," the President put in, to someone today placing at the front of a large book a listing of the alphabet?"

"Precisely."

"Dr. Dowde, let me ask a question here. I take it that this particular matter was not a subject under discussion today at the symposium. How have you come by so much information on it?"

"Years ago, Mr. President, when I first learned about Moricz and his amazing find, I was intensely interested and did quite a bit of research on it. I've talked with Moricz himself about it on a number of occasions. It's a project I think I could have devoted the rest of my scientific life to studying, except for the fact that there's no possibility of studying it anymore at present, for a reason I'll be explaining to you shortly. First, I'd like you to know what the writing on the leaves amounts to."

"Yes, by all means, I want to hear that."

"Unfortunately, it'll mostly be a disappointment."

"How so? Haven't they been deciphered?"

Irma Dowde issued a sour grunt. "Other than Juan Moricz's early—and successful—efforts in this respect, no attempt has ever been made to decipher them, although for a trained cryptologist it would probably be a relatively simple matter. The metal stele of boxed characters is far more important to the deciphering of those hieroglyphics than was the Rosetta Stone in the deciphering of Egyptian hieroglyphics."

"Then why," Sanders demanded, bewildered, "has no attempt been made other than the early ones you mentioned?"

"Only the Ecuadorian government, in its infinite wisdom, knows the answer to that," she replied sardonically. "For the first four years after his discovery, Juan Moricz maintained secrecy about it, but he gradually realized the fantastic significance of his find and knew it should be placed in the care of reputable scientific teams for close study. One of the big stumbling blocks was that he was not an Ecuadorian. Nevertheless, in June of 1965 he petitioned the government of Ecuador to give him legal title to the entire system of tunnels and their contents, with the stipulation, in accordance with Article Six Hundred Sixty-six of the Ecuadorian Civil Code, that though the treasures discovered became his personal property, they also remained subject to state control. In his petition, Moricz expressed his full knowledge of the immense cultural value of his find and promised to give full and unfettered access to reputable scientific teams and individuals for study.

"At one time," she added wistfully, "I hoped to head just such a team as he was talking about. But, getting back to Moricz and his petition, initially the governmental red tape regarding discovered treasures, archaeological deposits or significant historical finds prevented anything from being done. At last Moricz was granted the legal deed for which he had petitioned and everything seemed fine. Then, somehow, word got out that a great many of the archaeological treasures in the upper level passages were of solid gold or platinum. Those precious metals were undoubtedly Moricz's undoing. In just over a decade from the time he first petitioned for ownership, a governmental seal was placed on the entrance and has remained there ever since. It is now perpetually guarded with, supposedly, entry permitted to no one. What purpose this accomplishes is anyone's guess. Moricz has told me that he's convinced that at intervals certain high government figures are entering the tunnels and gradually disposing of great quantities of the gold and platinum. He constantly repetitions the government for removal of the decree, but just as constantly meets a blank wall. Outside institutions and agencies have at times tried to help, but with no better results."

"You mentioned earlier," President Sanders said, "that Moricz made early and successful attempts at deciphering the language. Is anything available on what he deciphered?"

"Oh, I meant to bring that up and then became sidetracked. It's important. During the four years' interval from when he first discovered the metal library until the time he petitioned the government, Moricz spent a great deal of time first learning how to decipher the hieroglyphics and then gradually translating the printed metal leaves. He admits that he did not decipher them in sequence, but rather a leaf here and there taken at random from the entire collection. He says he did this in order to try to get a quick, overall view of what was written. However, he has positively refused to relate to anyone what be has learned."

"Why, for heaven's sake?"

"He reasons that he will continue trying to win his case with the government for another ten years. If by then he has not succeeded, he says he will write a book faithfully detailing all he discovered and in that way, at least, when he dies, his heirs will be left comfortable through the proceeds from the book. There is, however, in the original petition to the government in 1965, of which he gave me a copy, an exceptionally good clue given by him to what he discovered in those metal pages."

"Yes?"

"I called my secretary in the Smithsonian this evening and had her dig out my copy of that petition and dictate the relevant passages to me. I wanted you to hear his exact words here. Under the heading of what his discoveries encompassed, he wrote as follows:

'The objects I found are of the following kinds:

1. Stone and metal objects of different sizes and colors.

2. Metal plaques engraved with signs and writing. These form a veritable metal library which might contain a synopsis of the history of humanity, as well as an account of the origin of mankind on earth and information about a vanished civilization.'

"So you see, although he tempered it with the word 'might,' he's quite definitive regarding the message this library has to convey."

"And there's no chance he could be persuaded to reveal what he's learned?"

"Not so long as he's convinced he's eventually going to be given back the rights to his discovery, and he's unalterably sure that that's just what will happen eventually. Pardon my terminology, sir, but it's pretty damned frustrating."

Again they were both silent and then it was Sanders who spoke. "That's it, then? I mean insofar as the day's symposium business is concerned?"

"Oh, a great many other interesting things, but all this will be in the summarization you'll receive in the morning from Knotts's people."

"Fine. There's one thing I'd like you to see to personally there, Dr. Dowde. I want two copies of each day's summation to come to Washington—one to me and the other to be placed into the hands of Henry Dexter, administrative director of the Library of Congress. He knows what to do with it and it should be delivered to him personally, to no one else."

"Yes, sir." Irma Dowde jotted a few lines on her pad. "Is there anything else?"

"No, I don't think so. I've kept you up long enough after what had to be an exhausting day. Oh, I did want to apologize for taking John Grant away from you so unexpectedly. I know you were counting on his assistance there. I'm afraid I need him more at the moment. I'm sending him out of the country tomorrow morning and anticipating his return next Thursday afternoon. He may not make it, but I'm assuming he will. He'll be returning with data that I think may be of extreme importance in substantiation of the HAB Theory. In this respect I want you to hold off that general vote of the scientists on whether or not they accept the HAB Theory. Don't give out the ballots until Friday noon, but all the votes should be in by Saturday morning early enough so they can be tallied by noon."

Irma Dowde was frowning as she jotted on her pad again, but she only murmured that she would see to it.

"I also," the President continued, "want you on Thursday to forego the usual meeting of the group chairmen to discuss the day's meetings. Instead, set up a meeting with them for, say, nine o'clock that evening. You can also include anyone else in that session, geological and archaeological specialists in particular whose convincing is especially important to us. Be prepared for a two-hour session at least."

He went on swiftly, explaining what would take place then, while Irma Dowde made notes. When finished, he paused a few moments and then added, "I must say that Grant did extremely well in his briefing of Secretary Elliott's team late this afternoon. We were finished by six o'clock. Alex Gordon did well, too." He paused again and then gave a little snort. "I'm rambling, so I guess it's really time to quit. Many thanks for the call and don't hesitate to ring me at any time of day or night if something comes up you feel I should know about right away."

"Certainly, Mr. President. I'll be sure to do that. Good night, sir."

"Good night. Oh," he added hastily, "are you still there?"

"Yes, sir, I'm here."

"I just wanted to let you know, Dr. Dowde, that I think you're doing one hell of a fine job. Good night."

There was a click and the connection was severed before she could respond. She slowly hung up the phone, smiling, deeply pleased at the compliment. A glance at her watch on the nightstand shocked her; she hadn't realized they'd talked for over an hour. Raising herself slightly, she dropped the steno pads to the floor along with her pen, punched the pillow into a more comfortable shape and depressed the button at the base of the nightstand lamp.

Irma Dowde sighed deeply as she settled down on her side, then smiled again in the semidarkness as she abruptly realized that she was very probably as happy as she had ever been in her life.

V I

Anne Carpenter could not remember a time—not even after Roger Spotte was killed during the street demonstration—when she felt lower than she felt tonight. Everything seemed to be wrong. Only the early morning hours had been bearable—not good, because somehow things were never really good when John was not with her, but at least bearable. Then had come his call in the morning with the invitation to join him in New York, but even the joy at that prospect was tempered by the knowledge that as soon as he hung up from talking with her, he was going to be calling Marie.

From that point on, until the call from John at three, she thought off and on about Marie, and such thoughts were hardly conducive to improving her day. How could the woman be so blind? Couldn't she see that he no longer loved her, hadn't loved her, in fact, for a very long time? Anne knew that if John suddenly stopped loving her, she would sense it immediately, so how could it be that Marie didn't, even though John hadn't really told her so? Then again, maybe she did know. Maybe she was just hanging in there for no other reason than the security a continuing marriage, however sour, provided. But that was selfish! She wasn't thinking of John at all if that was the case, but only herself, and of nothing more than preserving the marital status quo under any circumstances. Couldn't she see what this was doing to John? She probably never even let herself think about it. But what if she *had* to think about it? Wasn't it possible then that she might see the hopelessness of a future with John which, if continued, could only wind up destroying him? If she felt anything at all for *him*, wouldn't she rather, for *his* peace of mind, give him up than see him gradually suffocating in a way of life he had outgrown?

It had been at about this point in her reasoning that the second call from John had come, from Washington this time, and everything had fallen in. And it had triggered her to act on the reasoning concerning Marie that John's call had interrupted. So she'd driven up to the house in Skokie and received the crowning blow literally as well as figuratively.

She hardly remembered the drive back to Marina City after that, nor parking her car and going up to her apartment—her lonely, damned and double-damned lonely apartment. Her mouth had tasted coppery and she'd gone to the bathroom to brush her teeth and gargle, still in a somewhat disjointed state. Then she saw her own image in the mirror and was jerked back to reality, appalled by her own appearance.

The blood which had flowed so freely from the split brow had coagulated into a horrible cinnamon-colored stain down her face and chin, and dried blood drippings were all over the white collar of her blouse and even more extensively on the front of her navy blue linen jacket. A few splatterings were even on the matching skirt and she knew she would never wear that outfit again, whether or not the stains were removable.

Worst of all was the condition of her eye. The brow was thickly scabbed and swollen, and the swelling had moved down to her eyelid until now vision through that eye was limited to a narrow slit. The skin of the upper eyelid, where not coated with caked blood, was already becoming purplish-blue and it was clear she was going to have a black eye—the first in her life.

The anger came then, at last, and she tore at her own clothing, kicking off her shoes in her fury, popping buttons and splitting seams as she ripped the garments from her and then threw them on the floor.

"Bitch!" she snarled, stamping on the wadded clothes. "Miserable, no good, rotten bitch!"

She kicked savagely at the pile to scatter it, but the momentum of the movement carried her stockinged foot into the porcelain base of the toilet and she let out a little cry and sat down on the toilet seat, squeezing her toes with the pain.

Then the tears came, washing away the anger—silent, shoulder-heaving sobs and tears which were crystal bright sliding down one cheek, but turning pinkish as they slid down the other, softening the dried blood in their progress. And, after a while, even the tears were gone and she simply sat there holding her toes but no longer massaging them, aching inside with a deep and desperate loneliness for her man.

In time she stood up and turned on the shower, removed her lingerie and stockings, tossing them into the same pile to be discarded. She wanted to keep nothing she had worn this day, not even the midnight blue patent leather pumps she'd only worn twice before. Nothing.

She stepped into the shower, briefly adjusted the faucets to make the spray a little warmer, and then simply stood there for a long while with the high-pressure water needling pleasantly at her shoulders and nape and back. She shampooed and rinsed twice, wincing occasionally as she inadvertently pulled the flesh of temple and brow. She daubed carefully and for a long time at the split brow, biting her lower lip at the sting but gradually cleansing away all the scabrous material on the spot. She had expected the wound would begin bleeding again, but it didn't.

Outside the shower she toweled herself mechanically. Rarely, no matter how bad she felt, did a shower not have the capacity of bettering her spirits. This evening it didn't. She paused in the middle of drying and frowned, realizing with a bit of a start how really grim she was feeling. Not only hadn't the shower helped give her a lift, this was the first time in months that she hadn't carried the bedroom extension phone into the bathroom and set it on the floor in case John called while she was showering. And the realization that John had *not* called caused her to sink even lower.

With the towel in a turban-wrap on her head, she shrugged into a bulky white terrycloth robe and belted it snugly about her waist. At the bed she slipped into a pair of old, comfortable, tapestry-cloth slippers, and a minute later, apartment keys in her robe pocket, she was walking down the long curving hallway with all the clothing she had worn today bundled in her arms. Without even a lingering glance at the garments, she thrust them into the incinerator chute, dropping one of the shoes on the floor as she did so.

Grumbling, she scooped it up and threw it into the chute, then slammed the lid with unnecessary force. She spun around and very nearly collided with Kina Maxwell, who had a brown paper grocery sack filled with trash to feed into the same opening.

"Oh, sorry Kina," Anne said, jerking to a stop and then, too late, averting her face. "Didn't see you there." She took a step to move past her, but the Filipino girl gripped her upper arm.

"Anne, what's wrong? What happened to you?"

"Nothing. Nothing's wrong, Kina. I...I'm all right. Thanks." She was already moving on, pulling out of the younger woman's grip and leaving her staring after her with concern. She didn't look back. The last thing she wanted was to be questioned right now, however helpful the intentions.

Back in the apartment she considered fixing herself something to eat, but she had no appetite. She moved to the sofa and sat down listlessly. She knew she should set her hair, but she just had no desire to do anything at all. Across the room the blank screen of the television stared at her and she resolved to turn it on in a little while. Some special filmed coverage of the HAB Theory Symposium was scheduled and there was the possibility that she might see John somewhere in the footage.

Suddenly she felt tears running from her eyes again and she sniffled. Where was John now? What was he doing this minute? Was it possible he was thinking of her, as lonely for her as she was for him? No, not likely, not if he was tied up in meetings with the President and secretary of state and whoever else was involved. And he must be tied up with them yet, or he would have called by now.

"Oh, dammit, John Grant," she said aloud, "call me! Please, *please* call me. I need to hear your voice and to talk to you. *Please!*"

The telephone remained silent and after a while the tears stopped flowing and she simply sat there in the growing darkness, lost within herself. When the door buzzer rang twice in succession she jerked involuntarily, startled, then realized it had to be Kina Maxwell. She always rang twice like that and she wasn't the type to let Anne's behavior in the hall pass without further checking.

Anne walked to the door, flicking on a light switch in passing, using fingertips to smooth away any lingering tears on her cheeks, and mentally framing both an apology for her rudeness and an explanation for her eye. Then she snapped the bolt and swung the door open.

"Hi, Lady," said John Grant, his teeth gleaming in a wide grin. "I couldn't leave without saying I love you. In person."

11

In the highest ranges of thought in theology, philosophy and science, we find differences of view on the part of the most distinguished experts—theologians, philosophers and scientists.

—Charles Evans Hughes

Science is the search for truth—it is not a game in which one tries to best his opponent, to do harm to others. We need to have the spirit of science in international affairs, to make the conduct of international affairs the effort to find the right solution, the just solution of international problems, not the effort of each nation to get the better of other nations, to do harm to them when it is possible.

—Linus Carl Pauling

I

The world press was in its glory.

Momentous stories of wars, famous murders, revolutions, scandals, impeachments, scientific and technological breakthroughs, and other such items all had their moments of glory in the newspapers—the time of initial, flashing impact when most of the world was aware of them. They were like meteorites streaking across the heavens, suddenly and excitingly brilliant, but rapidly expending themselves until soon all that remained was the memory of the explosive and unexpected bursting upon the scene. In this respect, the HAB Theory was unique, for instead of a short-lived meteoric spectacle, it was a continually expanding supernova, with its successive bursts of fiery interest encompassing every nation and every individual in some way.

The biggest story of all right now—and there was hardly a newspaper on earth which didn't carry it verbatim—was the White House press release given out by Steven Lace on Saturday, the second morning of the symposium. In addition to commenting on other matters, it contained an almost word-for-word transcript of the essence of the HAB Theory as it had been presented to the Chief Executive by Irma Dowde during the meeting in the Waldorf's Presidential Suite the day before. Publication of the press release was like the bursting of a dam. Now the whole world knew just what the HAB Theory meant.

There were so many facets of the HAB Theory subject to be covered and, unlike news stories of the past which were of extreme importance to major portions of the world but never to the entire world as a whole, the theory and the symposium it had inspired created news of vital, immediate, and lasting concern to every nation on earth, without exception. There had not yet come the time, as always before had occurred with major news events, when eventually the story had exhausted itself and become something of a huge bore to the reading public.

The major world newspapers—as well as governmental and network broadcasting systems of radio and television—tended to take the broad, overall view, with full coverage to some extent of all that was occurring. On the other hand, the more local press in isolated areas of the world or in less important areas within major countries were more interested in stories with a local or regional tie-in to their individual circulation areas, and there seemed to be an inexhaustible and constantly renewing supply of just such items. The news stories, articles, features, editorials, polls and reports became a geographical chronology of HAB events on a worldwide scale.

Stockholm *Expressen*

U.S. PRESIDENT OPENS INTERNATIONAL SYMPOSIUM

President Robert M. Sanders opened the HAB Theory Symposium in New York today with an eight-minute address to an audience of nearly 4,000 scientists from 114 nations. The speech, beginning at 10:30 A.M. (4:30 P.M. Stockholm Time), was delivered with a strong sense of solemnity. The President pointed out that the matter they were on hand to discuss and consider could be a matter "more pressing and important than any problem man has ever before faced." He also told them that from the conclusions they reached, "mankind as a whole may survive, or may be all but extinguished."

President Sanders stressed that time may be the greatest enemy and he asked them to proceed with haste, but also with care. He pleaded for openmindedness, asking that the scientists not be locked into preconceived views. While he hinted that he had already formed his own opinion, he refused to divulge what that opinion is. However, in view of recent developments, it is generally assumed that he at least admits to the possibility of the HAB Theory's being valid...

London *Sunday Express*
Feature Magazine

FRAGILE FOSSILS
SUPPORT HAB HYPOTHESIS

Heated words have passed between a French scientist of Paris and our own Dr. Percival Heathly III, director of the London Paleontological Society and curator of paleontology at the British Museum of Natural History. The verbal fracas occurred at the HAB Theory Symposium in New York City.

In a group discussion, of which he was chairman, meeting in the St. Moritz Hotel, Dr. Heathly was in the process of stating that he was especially impressed with a certain paleontological proof offered in support of the theory by its postulator, Herbert Allen Boardman, the proof being cited that occasionally such delicate and fleeting impressions as raindrops in mud have become fossilized. The Boardman postulation is that this could not occur unless, in mere moments after the raindrops struck, the mud was subjected to intense cold and quick-frozen.

It was then that the French paleontologist Dr. Pierre Deschault, of the Paris Academy of Sciences, interrupted and accused Dr. Heathly of being "a gullible old fool." Deschault went on to say that fossilized raindrops were common and easily found today in many places in the very process of being fossilized. To underline his contention, Deschault offered as evidence the writings of over a century ago by an individual whom he termed as being "a good English scientist," Sir

Charles Lyell, the renowned geologist who died in 1895.

Deschault pointed out that Sir Charles had visited the Bay of Fundy in Nova Scotia and found, deposited by spring tides, extensive stretches of sandy mud. For 10 days during the neap tides, this red mud bakes under a hot sun and solidifies to an impervious degree for up to eight centimeters. In this hardened mud Sir Charles found not only the perfect impressions of footprints where birds and small mammals had walked while the mud was still soft, but also a multitude of small pockmarks caused by raindrops whose impressions had been baked into the mud along with the tracks.

Deschault, in what many scientists on hand described as "a highly deprecating manner," went on to say that this "good" scientist, Sir Charles, took some slabs of the mud and carefully split them and, as he reduced their thickness, he found similar tracks and raindrop impressions made during previous neap tides on the underlayers, each set impressed at different times.

"Thus," Deschault concluded, "no one worthy of having the title of paleontologist could possibly swallow the Boardman postulations."

In reply, Heathly, with the sure calm befitting his nature, admitted that certainly raindrops were forming pockmark fossils in this manner, but that the impressions were just that— ordinary little pits whose sides were smooth, evened by the slight settling of the mud within a few minutes after the initial impact of the drop.

*"However," he added, "neither that explanation nor any other I've ever heard until now explains how the **immediate** impression of the raindrop in the mud is preserved, when an extremely delicate shell-like crater is formed with beautifully fluted edges from the initial splash. Nothing could cause such a transient impression to fossilize except the process outlined by Mr. Boardman. Unless, of course, the eminent Dr. Deschault knows of some other such process?"*

Amid the laughter of those assembled, Deschault's only reply was a bilabial fricative...

Hong Kong *Tiger Standard*

ANACHRONISTIC BURIAL
STILL PUZZLING SCIENTISTS

The opening of the HAB Theory Symposium in New York has reignited the fires of interest in an anthropological enigma first discovered near Peking many years ago.

The apparent anachronism stems from an excavation made at Chou-Kou-Tien in 1933 by the esteemed German anatomist and anthropologist Dr. Franz Weidenreich. In the process of excavating, Weidenreich uncovered a grave in which there were the skeletal remains, quite well preserved, of four people from widely separated areas of the earth.

Carbon-14 radioactivity dated to the year 28,000 B.C., one skull belonged to an old caucasian man; a second to a young woman of Melanesian extraction; the third from an Eskimo; the fourth, Arabic. The question of how, so long ago, they got into a common grave is a mystery the HAB Theory Symposium scientists might well consider...

Nashville Banner

PRESIDENT'S POPULARITY SAGS

JABONSKY RESIGNATION LINKED?

Recent polls by the independent firms of Gallup, Tren-duv, Roper, and Baedly have all indicated a distinct dip in the popularity of President Robert Sanders. The slump first became evident several months ago with the extreme rise in the cost of living index but has become more pronounced in recent days as an apparent result of the President's personal involvement with what has been termed "arbitrary handling" of fiscally extensive programs (i.e., foreign aid, especially to Kenya) and his equally personal involvement in matters concerning the so-called HAB Theory.

Interviewed this morning on ABC's Good Morning America, *former chief presidential adviser Albert Jabonsky was reluctant to divulge specifics in regard to his recent sudden resignation, except for one brief moment when his customary iron control seemed to slip and he stated that "President Sanders is becoming distinctly megalomanic."*

Reno *Gazette*

CAVE FIND BAFFLES PROFESSOR

Professor Luther S. Cressman of the University of Oregon, who discovered a previously unexplored cave in eastern Nevada, which has now been named Lamos Cave, has made a new discovery there which he claims to "baffle me as nothing ever has before."

In a remote chamber of the extensive cavern, Cressman discovered, neatly stacked, 200 pairs of woven, modernistic-looking sandals. Carbon-14 dating, Cressman says, shows them to have been made in 7,030 B.C....

Santiago *Clarin*

PERUVIAN MYSTERY INTRODUCED
AT HAB THEORY SYMPOSIUM

Dr. Eva Tobazo, professor of prehistory at the University of Santiago, has brought up for consideration by Hab Theory Symposium scientists in New York a Peruvian mystery of many years ago.

Dr. Tobazo pointed out that a number of vases were found in the Nazca District not far from Pisco, Peru, in the 1920s by Dr. Julio Tello. The enigma lies in the fact that paintings on the vases depict llamas with five toes.

"The llama of our present age," she told a discussion group in the Regency Hotel, "has only two toes, but in an earlier evolutionary period the animal went through tens of thousands of years ago, they had five toes..."

New York *Post*

A TREE GROWS...UNDER MANHATTAN

Construction workers today excavating at the corner of madison Avenue and 48th Street for erection of the new E.

I. du pont de Nemour Building, uncovered at a depth of 60 feet the well preserved remains of a tree tentatively identified by a HAB Symposium botanist as "closely related to the red cedar."

The scientist, Dr. Gaylord Wheaton, curator of botany at the Field Museum of Natural History in Chicago, stated that the discovery "neatly dovetails with the HAB Theory postulations"…

Rangoon *Burman*

TIBETAN FOLKLORE LINKED TO HAB THEORY

Dr. Alon Kelawa, professor of philology at the University of Burma, was one of those present at the HAB Symposium discussion in New York when Dr. Ho-Chung Chow of Peking made his startling revelation regarding ancient spiral writing found on stone disks in the Sino-Tibetan frontier district (see "Chinese Discovery,' page 1.)

Dr. Kelawa, who studied for many years in Tibet, spoke later in that meeting after Dr. Chow had concluded his remarks. He told of encountering Tibetan folklore of "sky people no larger than an 8-year-old child, but with large heads, who landed from the heavens in a sky ship near one of the villages." According to the ancient story, the little sky people approached the village and made efforts to communicate, but the villagers considered them harbingers of evil, killed several of the "Heaven Devils," and chased the others into the hills, but they escaped into "smooth tunnels" which the villagers feared to enter, but which they thereupon sealed with rocks…

New York *Daily News*

CHOW REVEALS SECOND CHINESE DISCOVERY

Dr. Ho-Chung Chow, University of Peking archaeologist, who Friday stunned members of the HAB Symposium with his relation of an intensely important archaeological discovery unknown to the Western world for a quarter of a century, today added another note of excitement to the discussions.

Chow related that a colleague in his department at the university, Dr. Chi Pen Lao, was exploring caves in July 1961 in Hupeh Province west of Oyang. In the Hohan Mountains at the south shore of Tung Ting Hu (a large lake) he entered a cave and followed it inward and downward. At 32 meters (105 feet) beneath the surface he encountered a large domed room with glazed walls, from which numerous squared tunnels moved off deeper into the mountains in a confusing, inter- connecting network. As in the main chamber, the tunnels had a glazed surface as if they had once been melted.

Chow described some of the unusual items found by Dr. lao, but stressed that no spiral disks had been located here. However, an intricately rendered painting on one wall depicted a wide variety of animals all being driven in one direction by men above them riding on what he called "a shieldlike flying platform" and clad in very modern-looking trousers and jackets. The men held what appeared to be long pipes to their lips, which they were pointing toward the animals…

Dayton *Journal Herald*

SPECIAL ENVOYS SENT ABROAD

In a press conference called at the White House early today, Presidential press secretary Stephen Lace announced that "a team of envoys" had been dispatched late yesterday under orders of President Sanders to conduct individual "confidential missions" to heads of state throughout the world.

Declining to answer any questions, Lace told reporters that most of the envoys were select members of the State Department, including Secretary Elliott, but also that one of them was special Presidential aide John C. Grant...

Atlanta *Constitution*

PREHISTORIC DEATHS
SAID CAUSED BY BULLETS

Two prehistoric skulls discussed today at the Hab Theory Symposium in New York have lent credence to the HAB postulation that highly advanced human civilizations may have existed in previous epochs of time and were wiped out by the sort of worldwide cataclysm the HAB Theory forecasts.

One of these skulls, presently in the Moscow Museum, is that of a large animal called an auroch, which is a type of bison of the Neolithic Age—4,700 to 10,000 years ago. The skull provides an anachronistic enigma, because in the very center of its brow is a neat circular hole of a nature which could have been caused by only one means known to man—a bullet. Scientists have heretofore withheld speculation about what might have caused the hole, which is about the size of a modern .44 caliber bullet. Now it is being openly and very seriously discussed as having a bearing to the HAB Theory.

Equally startling is a human skull with the same sort of injury, but dated back to approximately 38,000 years ago. This skull is now in the collection of the British Museum of Natural History in London. The director of that institution, paleontologist Percival Heathly III, discussed it with his group of HAB scientists in the St. Moritz Hotel today.

Heathly said that the skull, that of an adult male, was originally discovered in a cave near the Zambezi River of Rhodesia. The left side of the cranium shows a perfectly round hole 1.15 centimeters in diameter, which approximately the same size as that in the skull of the auroch. The right side of the human skull, however, has been shattered.

"Had the injury been caused by a cold weapon," Heathly said, "such as a spear or arrow or even a round-bladed knife, there would have had to be radial cracks emanating from the circular hole. Further, it is most unlikely that, had it been caused by such a cold weapon, the right side of the cranium would have been so thoroughly shattered."

All the evidence, according to Heathly, points to a bullet which entered from the left side and then, flattened in the process of penetrating the bone, continued its course and blew out the right side of the cranium. Close study of the bone edges on the right side indicates it was blown outward from a force inside the skull.

One member of the discussion group was Dr. Sven Evansson, who was the first to treat President Sanders in Chicago following the shooting of last may 22. Evansson, who is chief of surgery at Northwestern Memorial Hospital, closely examined a large number of photographs, including extremely closeups, of the skull and its injuries on both sides of the cranium. Also involved in the close study was Dr. Kenneth Walker, neurosurgeon of South Africa, who is chief of staff of University Hospital in Johannesburg. Both specialists concurred in the conclusion that the injury could only have been caused by a bullet.

Evansson, who was with the U.S. Medical Corps in a MASH unit during the war in Vietnam, told the assembled scientists, "The injury is unequivocally identical to the hundreds of injuries I witnessed in postmortem examination of soldiers shot through the head by rifle bullets."

I I

I *still* don't see why you didn't let me know right away when you got in yesterday," Narai Ngoromu said, watching the waiter as he placed their cocktails before them and left.

"Well," Anita replied, "I did check to see if you were in, but you were busy in a meeting, so I didn't want to bother you. The desk clerk in the Plaza said you were attending one of the HAB group discussions."

"That wouldn't have mattered at all!" There was still a lingering petulance in her tone. "We're going to have little enough time together as it is. You should have let me know."

"Dear, bear in mind that I had a few things to do, too—some calls to make and people to see, so I got tied up. But," she added lightly, "I knew I'd be seeing you today, and here we are."

"Yes. And it's just great. I'm so glad you're here."

"How about the symposium? Are the discussions going well?"

"They're terribly fascinating, Mother," Narai said, reaching across the table to touch Anita's hand in a loving gesture, "but honestly, after three days of them, my head is *spinning!*"

A delicate, melodious laughter rolled from her lips and evoked a smiling response from Anita Ngoromu. At a table next to theirs here in the Four Seasons Restaurant on East Fifty-second Street, a nicely dressed middle-aged couple looked at them briefly but with curiosity, undoubtedly wondering why an unusually attractive middle-aged blond woman of obvious Scandinavian extraction should be addressed as 'Mother' by a young and beautiful and very dark Negro woman.

"You're planning to remain until the end of the symposium, Narai?" Anita patted the girl's hand and then took a sip of her frozen daiquiri. "Mmmm, that's delicious."

Narai was nodding. "Uh-huh. Maybe even a few days afterward, although I'm not sure of that yet. Depends."

The older woman cocked a quizzical eyebrow. "On what?"

Narai's residue of smile became a little sheepish. "On what I hear from Alex, I guess."

Now it was Anita's turn to laugh aloud. "Ah-ha! Do I detect that someone has been touched by the lightning?"

"I guess so, Mother. Alex is so…he's so…" she fumbled for the proper words.

"Wonderful?" Anita suggested. "Manly and handsome and athletic and bright and engaging?"

Narai nodded, but her expression became melancholy. "All those things. I…didn't realize how much I was anticipating being with him until all of a sudden it wasn't possible anymore, and then I just felt crushed. I still do."

"Will he be back before the symposium ends?"

"It's not likely, but I am expecting to hear from him and I don't want to leave until I do. I don't know where he's gone, but I'm hoping to find out. If I do, then I'd sort of like to detour to wherever he's going to be, then go on home from there."

"That would be nice, dear, if you're sure it wouldn't interfere with his business. From what you've said, he's evidently on an extremely important mission."

Narai shrugged. "That's what I gathered from what he said when he called that night, but he couldn't tell me what it was all about or where he was going. But, no, to answer your question, I'm sure we could arrange things so my visit wouldn't interfere." She picked up her whiskey sour and made a toasting gesture toward Anita. "To your health," she said. She sipped lightly, appreciatively, but over the rim of her glass she saw a fleeting, vaguely disturbing expression pass across her stepmother's features. She set her glass down slowly and was about to speak when the waiter stopped at their table.

"Another drink, ladies, or perhaps you'd care to order now?"

They had already glanced through the dinner menu and halfway decided what they'd have, but when Anita murmured that they might as well order, both picked up their menus with the distinctive cover decoration of four stylized trees, depicting the seasonal changes for which the restaurant was named. Narai gave her order and then, while Anita made her selections, she looked around the restaurant, which was now filled. Large rubber plants stood at each corner of a square pool of water lighted from beneath, its placid surface turning with mild currents. Tall, narrow windows only a few feet wide but easily twenty-five feet high, rose from almost floor to ceiling in two of the walls. They were coveted by an unusual form of drapery like bellied slattings of reed which undulated with increasing pulsations from ceiling to floor, until the result was akin to a series of waterfalls, with delightful soothing effect. Flowering plants and frilly-leaved ferns in hanging baskets were suspended by thin, almost invisible wires to the thirty-foot-high ceiling, around the perimeter of the room. It was a beautiful place to dine.

"I so much enjoy coming here," Anita said abruptly. The waiter was gone. "Your father and I ate here perhaps four or five times and were never disappointed.

He—"

"How is father?" Narai interrupted.

"Why, he's just fine." She frowned faintly. "That was a sort of out-of-the-blue interjection. Not like you, dear."

"What about you?"

Anita was confused. "What do you mean, what about me?"

Narai was looking at her steadily, unsmiling. "Just that, Mother. What about you? A moment ago I toasted your health and I saw something in your expression that bothered me. How are *you* feeling?"

The older woman was suddenly very busy buttering a roll and replied without looking up. "All right. Same as always, I guess. You remember the old saying, you can't—" She broke off and looked up as Narai's long fingers curled with strong grip about her wrist.

"Mother...don't. You're holding something back. I know it."

"Honey," Anita protested, putting down the knife and roll, "I just don't know what you're talking about. I'm as fit as...I'm...I'm..." She broke off and turned her face downward, hiding from Narai's concerned gaze. The wrist Narai was still gripping began trembling and Narai was shocked to see a single tear drop onto the edge of the bread-and-butter plate with a tiny splatter. In a moment the trembling stopped and, still without looking up, Anita spoke more calmly. "I'm all right now, dear."

As Narai released her wrist, Anita took up her napkin and briefly touched her face with it and then cleared her throat and looked up at the black girl, a poorly formed smile crooked on her lips.

"I'm sorry, Narai. I didn't realize it was showing. I'll have to learn better control, and pretty quickly at that. I don't want Dan to see through me the way you just did." She shook her head with firmness and repeated, "I don't want that."

"Don't want father to know what? For God's sake, Mother, what's wrong? Are you ill?"

The momentary closing of Anita's 'eyes was the same as a nod but she confirmed it with her next words. "Ill, yes, in a way. Narai, I'm dying."

"Oh my God!" Narai covered her mouth with the tips of her fingers of both hands and took a deep, pained breath, as if she'd been struck. "How?" The word was muffled, almost inaudible. "You've been to a doctor?"

Now Anita did nod. "Yesterday. And in May when I was here. Several doctors. While your father and I were in Washington. When he thought I was out shopping, I'd taken a hop up to Baltimore and was in Johns Hopkins having tests run. We left before I could get the results. They've been writing me every week to please come in or else go to my own doctor in Nairobi. I didn't." She shrugged. "Afraid, I guess. Wanting to put it off and finding it easy enough to do, because I knew I'd be coming back here now. The letters weren't specific, but they sounded grim. Now I know why."

Outwardly Narai had gotten control of herself, but her stomach was still churning and her voice was whispery. "What is it, Mother? Is it cancer?"

"Not as you're probably thinking of it, no. It's leukemia, honey."

"Oh, Mother." The anguish was evident, and Anita patted the back of her hand.

"Don't ask the questions, Narai. Is there any hope? Can it be cured? Might they be wrong? The answers are all in the negative. It's called chronic lymphistic leukemia. There's treatment, but there's no cure. And no way of knowing for sure when the end will come. Conceivably, a year…maybe more. Realistically, almost surely no more than six months. Possibly three, and maybe even less. Treatment isn't going to help much. Unfortunately, I had it for quite a long time before I knew it. Couple of years, possibly. They might have slowed down the process if they'd caught it in time. Might have, but not for sure. They've made me an outpatient—transferable to Nairobi Hospital—and they've put me on chemotherapy, but even they admit there's not much it'll do at this point. It's an oral medication—the newest treatment—but the best it could possibly do is slow it a bit. Probably not even that."

She smiled wanly, feeling more Narai's pain right now than her own. She continued in a gentle voice, trying to make it easier for her dark stepdaughter. "There's a fairly good chance I won't linger, either, which will be a blessing—as people will undoubtedly say when it's all over." She gave a short, mirthless laugh. "Most likely there'll come what the doctor calls a blastic crisis, at which point the leukemia abruptly changes from the chronic to the acute form. Most likely," her voice shook a little, "only a matter of hours from that point."

"Is it…" Narai had trouble getting the word out, "…painful?"

"At times. More so lately, but only at intervals. Mostly just tired all the time." Her smile became rueful. "A little weight loss, so far, but more to come. Now and then some fairly strong attacks of depression, but I've hidden them pretty well, I think. I intend," she added with more firmness, "to keep it that way. Narai, I don't want your father to know about this. Not a whisper. Not a hint."

"But, Mother, he *should* know. He has a *right* to know. He loves you and—"

"He absolutely *must not know!*" The last three words were low and well spaced and very intense. "Narai, I want your promise that you won't tell him."

"I don't understand why not, Mother. Father wouldn't want you to put on some kind of a brave act, you know that. It's not fair to him or to you."

"Stop it, Narai! Think! You're old enough to remember. When your mother died, your father wasn't himself for months. He could hardly function. I don't want him *anticipating* my death and going into the same sort of tailspin. He mustn't learn of it. Narai, *promise!*"

Narai's lips were set in a tight line and Anita gripped her hand. "Honey, listen to me. Your father is right now, this minute, doing something that may result in the survival of mankind. It's taking every instant of his every waking hour, and even that may not be enough. He *can't* be diverted not in any way, not by any thing, not by any body! You're here at the symposium. You know the importance. I don't have to explain it. Narai, please...*please!* Give me your word."

Narai Ngoromu promised.

III

Although it was the Fourth of July and a holiday, the scientists at the HAB Theory Symposium were attending their group meetings as usual. As a result, most of them missed the holiday's pyrotechnical displays—but not those who attended the group meeting in the Conrad's Suite of the Waldorf, presided over by Dr. Owen Holder. The fireworks witnessed there were verbal rather than visual, but they quickly became the talk of the entire symposium.

Twenty minutes before the 9:00 A.M. start of the session the scientists began assembling and taking their seats. The suite was a beautiful room with a predominantly orange motif and a series of long mirrors fitted to the walls and nearly reaching the high ceiling. The plush seats were very comfortable and arranged to face the outward-curving head table. Nearly all of the one hundred chairs were occupied when the eminent Oxford geologist entered at one minute before the hour and moved to his chair at the head table. Seated to his right was the vice-chairman, Dr. Ian Johnson, professor of biology at the University of Rhodesia in Salisbury, and to his left was Dr. Charles Dovering, ichthyologist with the University of Madagascar in Tannarive.

Holder glanced at his large gold watch, extracted from a vest pocket, saw it was exactly on the hour, snapped it closed with a loud click and called the morning's session to order in his most professorial tone. Silence settled over the group and he was just about to begin speaking when the door opened and Irma Dowde strode into the room. With poorly concealed impatience, Holder waited while she quietly found a seat.

"I see," he said, when she was settled, "that we are honored today with the presence of Dr. Dow-dy. It has been called to my attention that she has tended to dominate the discussions of those group meetings she has visited, and I would appreciate not having that happen here."

His rude remark occasioned an awkward silence, but when the archaeologist made no reply, Holder turned his attention to one of the scientists seated before him, Vincent Bartell, cyberneticist and vice-chairman of the Department of Physics at Harvard University.

"Dr. Bartell," he said, "yesterday you were remarking about what you stated was evidence that past civilizations had knowledge of cybernetics. I must say, I find that hard to believe and I'm sure others do as well. However, we'll hear you out. Are you prepared to conclude your remarks this morning?"

"I am," Bartell said, rising. He was a neatly dressed medium-sized man with crew-cut hair and unusually thick lips. He seemed to have taken no offense at Holder's aside and quickly took a position in front of the curved table. Facing his listeners, he picked up from where he'd left off in the last session. In clipped, precise words he said that many ancient writings discussed strange machines with unusual powers.

"Quite a number of ancient Greeks and Egyptians," he told them, "are reputed to have had ambulatory automatons which were powered by something referred to as 'lightning-in-a-jar.' These were allegedly perfectly functioning robots which could talk and walk and do simple household tasks. All of them, unfortunately, were reluctantly destroyed by their owners because of public outcry—a growing fear among those who didn't own one of the handy servants, that the gods would object to man's making and using such a creation."

Bartell concluded with a discussion of the device which had come to be known as the Antikythera Computer, a device discovered in the ancient wreckage of a ship on the bottom of the Aegean Sea near the Greek island of Antikythera. Found in 1900 by a sponge diver, the device was an odd conglomeration of strange dials and gears, wheels and rods, and spheres of brass and bronze. Although badly corroded, it was possible to reconstruct what it had been, although this had not occurred for many years. The archaeologists who initially studied it were totally baffled as to its purpose. They were able to date the wreckage of the ship to around 55 B.C., but the amphorae—wine and oil vases—recovered from the wreck with it were more accurately dated to 65 B.C.

"There is the strong likelihood," Bartell added, "that the mechanical device was very ancient then. At any rate, probably because it presented an embarrassing enigma, the device wound up in a storage room of the National Archaeological Museum of Greece in Athens. There it remained for nearly sixty years, out of sight and out of mind."

He shook his head. "It wasn't until half a century later that the mechanism came under the close scrutiny of Dr. Derek Price of England, who was then with the American Institute for Advanced Study at Princeton. He made a meticulous reconstruction and wound up with a device about the size of a large portable typewriter case, which he positively identified as a complex and highly sophisticated computer and planetarium. It was designed for and capable of advanced astronomical calculations. Dr. Price wrote of his findings in *Scientific American*—the June issue of 1959—and later stated that the device was certainly neither the first nor the last of its kind. He is not a man who makes rash statements and yet he said at the time that finding a thing like this is like finding a jet airplane in the tomb of King Tutankhamen. That, Mr. Chairman," he said, turning briefly to Holder, "is all I have."

Holder watched the Harvard scientist walk back to his seat and then sniffed in a derogatory manner. "Such a device as that, coming from such a remote time," he said flatly, "is obviously preposterous and impossible.

Undoubtedly the work of a charlatan."

"Under the circumstances, Dr. Holder," Bartell replied, unruffled, "any form of charlatanism was not possible."

"Are you calling me a liar, sir?" Holder thundered.

"No, I am not." Bartell was frowning now. "I am merely stating that from what is know about this matter, there can be no possibility of trickery of any kind."

"Ridiculous! Of course there was trickery."

Irma Dowde came to her feet. "Dr. Holder," she said clearly, "may I ask what your own reaction is to the studies in 1963 by Dr. Gerald Hawkins of Boston University? You may recall that, as an astronomer of considerable renown, Dr. Hawkins proved that the ruins in England known as Stonehenge were actually a highly accurate astronomical computer and observatory, designed for observation of the moon and sun and for calculation of forthcoming eclipses."

"That's another thing just as ridiculous!" Holder declared. "And you needn't explain his findings to me as if I were a student. I'm quite aware of what Hawkins wrote. That doesn't mean I accept it as gospel. I will remind *you*, Dr. Dow-dy, that as was pointed out three years later by Richard Atkinson, the work by Hawkins was tendentious, arrogant, slipshod and unconvincing." He brought up his arm and pointed across the room at the symposium chairwoman, adding, "There are always so-called scientists who will do anything for publicity."

Irma Dowde maintained her calm and pointed out that any scientist who advanced revolutionary postulations became the target of critics, and that the work of Hawkins subsequently had been fully accepted, despite the attacks upon him.

The discussion went on in a strained atmosphere. Dr. Siegfried Gozan, electrophysicist of the University of Budapest, brought up the enigma of electrical batteries having been in use more than two thousand years before in the ancient city of Babylon. A timid little man, Gozan was hesitant in his delivery and, when finished, cringed visibly as Holder snorted again in his irritating way.

"I'm really surprised at the attitude of the people at this symposium," the chairman said loudly. "You people are scientists, or so I'm led to believe, but evidently our concept of science differs considerably. Can't you see that such so-called archaeological 'discoveries' of this nature are hoaxes, again by the publicity-seeking pseudo-scientists?"

"Dr. Holder!" Irma Dowde's voice had a sharp quality to it now and she was on her feet again. "As chair of this entire symposium, I would like to point out that you have a responsibility, as group chairman, to maintain an open mind during these discussions, especially in view of physical evidence which cannot be denied. Dr. Gozan is not making up what he reported, nor is he the dupe of a hoaxster. I am familiar with the matter he has brought up and to that I'd like to add that in 1938 this whole matter came to light through the efforts of the German archaeologist, Wilhelm König. He was a highly respected scientist who discovered in the site of ancient Babylon, not far from present Baghdad, a large number of pottery jars designed to be electrical storage batteries. Eight years after that his speculations along these lines were proven when a General Electric Company scientist, Willard Gray, studied his find and then duplicated the jars and metal rods and other paraphernalia and wound up with a workable battery."

Holder sprang to his feet, once again pointing at her. "You be quiet, Dr. Dow-dy, and not interrupt again unless you're recognized. *I* am chairman of this group and I don't intend seeing it disrupted." As Irma Dowde, grim-faced, resumed her seat, he continued. "I will suggest to all present here," his gaze swept over the group, "that the possibility exists, if one does not wish to romanticize, that Dr. König, for all his fame and alleged respectability, himself constructed the battery jars and planted them on the Babylonian site and then later conveniently 'discovered' them."

At this there was a horrified hush and in the protracted silence a small, soft-spoken man of saffron coloring and easy smile came to his feet seeking recognition. This was Denzil Ramasamy, professor of prehistory at the University of New Delhi, and he had already contributed much of value to the symposium in regard to ancient India. As Holder nodded toward him, he removed a folded paper from his inner pocket and began talking quietly.

"Artifacts might possibly be planted on archaeological sites," he conceded, "but there is no possible way for anyone to plant a modern writing as an ancient document, since the age of the materials used in the writing is clearly determinable and cannot be duplicated in undetectable manner. Because we are now on a subject in which I have an interest and upon which I was prepared to speak, I would like to offer this for consideration." He held up his paper and then unfolded it. "What I have here is a copy I made of a passage in one of India's oldest known documents, the *Agalstya Samhita*, which is proven to be of great antiquity. This is a literal translation and it should be noted that while it may sound very modern, no modern terminology has been used. This is exactly how it is written." He cleared his throat and read from the paper.

"'Place a well-cleaned copper plate in an earthenware vessel. Cover it first by copper sulfate and then by moist sawdust. After that, put a mercury-amalgamated zinc sheet on top of the sawdust to avoid polarization. The contact will produce an energy known by the twin name of *Mitra-Varuna*. Water will be split by this current into *Pranavayu* and *Udanavayu*. A chain of one hundred jars is said to give a very active and effective force.'"

There was open amazement on the faces of many of the scientists as he finished and refolded the paper. "I am not," he concluded, with a small shrug, "a physicist, but it seems evident to me, as it must to others here, that the ancient terms *Pranavayu* and *Udanavayu* signify hydrogen and oxygen, and that *Mitra-Varuna* could be nothing but what we describe as cathode-anode—the negative and positive poles of a battery."

As Ramasamy sat down, a burst of discussion filled the room, which Owen Holder strove to silence and succeeded only by rapping the head table loudly with the bottom of an empty water glass. Holder's face was pinched and ashen and as the din began fading he came to his feet and jabbed his finger in the air toward Ramasamy.

"You, sir," he brayed, "are a liar! For the sake of sensationalism, you wrote that material yourself!" There were gasps from the assembled scientists but without pause Holder shifted his pointing finger to the Harvard cyberneticist and continued. "And you, sir, are an idiot, guilty of criminal gullibility! You blindly believe the so-called discovery by Wilhelm König, who undoubtedly planted the alleged batteries in Babylon."

"Dr. Holder, you must stop this!" It was Irma Dowde, once again on her feet and now in the middle of the center aisle, her eyes blazing. "I cannot allow you to conduct a meeting in—"

"Shut up!" Holder shouted at her. "You're the worst of the lot!" He swung both arms out to take in the entire assemblage. "You call yourselves scientists. Pah! You are all *fools*, willing to be led like sheep by monstrous hoaxsters. I warn you, this...this...*woman*," he was pointing at Dr. Dowde again, "is no more than a modern

Charles Dawson. He only made laughingstocks of the archaeologists and anthropologists. Dr. Dow-dy is going to make laughingstocks of scientists in all branches of science—of all who are taken in by the deceits and monstrous hoaxes of this incredible Boardman garbage!"

The diatribe shocked everyone present, stunning them into aghast looks at their neighbors. In mentioning Charles Dawson, Holder had touched a sore spot for all conscientious scientists. Dawson was the unscrupulous amateur archaeologist who subjected the academic world to its most infamous embarrassment by "discovering" in 1908 what was hailed as "the missing link" which proved Charles Darwin's theory of evolution—the Piltdown Man. Dawson was greatly honored and highly acclaimed for his discovery of the famous bones near Piltdown in Sussex, England, and he was still basking in that glory at the time of his death in 1916. But then, years after the discovery, a few skeptics at the British Museum of Natural History subjected the bones to a dating process—the carbon-14 radioactivity test—and a tremendous shock washed across the world. The bones had turned out to be nothing more than those of an ape—with teeth and jawbone skillfully altered—which had died eight years prior to Dawson's great find.

Now, in the hum of voices that began rising, Irma Dowde marched to the front of the room and stood facing the audience. She held up a hand for quiet and silence fell at once.

"I regret," she told the participants, "that an occurrence such as this could have happened. As head of this symposium, I am officially removing Dr. Owen Holder from his chairmanship of this discussion group and appointing vice-chairman Dr. Ian Johnson to assume the duties of chairman."

Holder began sputtering angrily, but the archeologist silenced him with an upraised hand and continued. "Dr. Holder is welcome to remain in this meeting if he wishes, but I now instruct the door marshals to eject him—by force, if necessary!—should he create any further disruption here."

"He won't, by heaven!" Holder shouted. "I will no longer be party to this meeting…to this entire charade called a symposium. I refuse to submit to the dictates of a tyrannical female charlatan!"

Staring straight ahead and his back as stiff as a broomstick, the Oxford geologist stalked from the front of the room. At the door he paused, his hand on the knob. "I'll have nothing further to do with this travesty," he said. "I'm checking out immediately and returning to England." Then he was gone.

Still in front of the room, Irma Dowde expelled a huge breath and then apologized again to the scientists in attendance for what had happened.

"I feel," she continued, "no anger toward Dr. Holder, only a sincere sympathy. In part, he was right. We must be wary of those who might, for personal aggrandizement or profit, perpetrate hoaxes under the guise of science. But, at the same time, we must not shut out new concepts or new interpretations of old discoveries simply because they do not conform to past precepts. Many of us still live and study and teach in the shadow of the Dark Ages. We remember times when a visionary like Giordana Bruno was dragged into the Piazza del Fiore in Rome in 1600 and burned alive because he wrote that there are an infinite number of suns and that planets revolve about these suns, and that the possibility exists that some of these other worlds are populated."

She shook her head vigorously. "We no longer physically destroy our visionaries, but even today it is often academic or scientific suicide to postulate too boldly, or even to treat with seriousness the mysteries of the past which have been unexplainable in terms of science as we know it. We, here and now, at this symposium, have the opportunity of dispelling those strictures forever. It's time we did so. I only hope we will. From what I can see, we are off to a good start in this direction, with but few exceptions, and it is high time."

There was a rousing burst of applause which became a standing ovation as Irma Dowde left the Conrad's Suite. She strode down the hall, feeling drained and sorry, one hand in the pocket of her ugly gray cardigan, the fingers touching the folded piece of paper on which she had written down the information she had received in a personal call from President Sanders this morning. Among several interesting notations, it included the information that for the past ten years Owen Holder, professor of geology at Oxford, had been developing a new theory of his own dealing with the formation and development of the earth. The theory was totally apart from the postulations of the HAB Theory, and if the symposium scientists accepted Boardman's theory as valid. it would result in all of Holder's years of effort having been in vain.

I V

Anne Carpenter, standing with her back to the expansive front-room windows of her Marina City apartment, looked slowly back and forth over the incredible mass of newspaper clippings on every available flat surface of the living room and dining room and gave voice to a groan.

"Gawd," she murmured, "do you think we'll ever get any semblance of order out of this chaos?"

Kina Maxwell, on her hands and knees about at the dividing line of the two rooms, simply snorted and then, for perhaps the fifth time, repositioned the pins holding her waist-length deep black hair in a partially twisted pile atop her head. The pins kept working loose as she was moving about among the individual clipping piles.

Standing at one end of the dining room table, just beginning to open yet another of the thick bundles, Susan Carpenter glanced over at her daughter and smiled. "Oh, we'll get there, Pussycat, never fear. We may run the risk of smothering in newsprint in the process, but we'll get them arranged somehow. I have an idea we're going to need more than that box of a hundred large envelopes you bought."

There was quite a striking resemblance between mother and daughter, though certainly no doubt which was which. They were of approximately the same height and carriage and with a very similar general bone structure. Anne's hair was much longer and not shot with gray, as was her mother's, but their movements, their manner of speech and their gesticulations left little doubt as to their relationship. Though certainly well groomed and attractive, Susan would not have been mistaken by anyone for much less than her actual age of forty-eight.

"Gosh, I hope not," Anne replied. "Surely we won't wind up with more than a hundred specific categories, will we?"

Kina snorted again and then came erect on her knees, holding the small of her back. "Hah! I'll bet we're already past that point. Look at this mess!"

Little open islands of carpeting were visible for stepping areas but, except for that, practically every inch of floor space was covered with the clippings, along with every level surface on the chairs, couch, coffee tables and elsewhere. The table where Susan was working was about half-covered with piles of clippings and the other half with bundles of the same which had not yet been opened, their thick rubber bands stretched to the breaking point. In addition, over near the front door on a chair was a stack of complete, unclipped Chicago newspapers for the past five or six days. The stack was nearly two feet high.

"Lord, when I volunteered to get clippings for John of what was going on in his absence, I never anticipated anything even remotely like this. And still four more days to go before the symposium's over."

"Don't count on the clippings coming to a sudden stop just because the symposium ends," Susan said dryly. "I've a hunch we've only begun."

Anne shrugged and rolled her eyes. "Well, all I can say is that I hope he gets back soon. He'll probably go into an apoplectic fit when he sees all of this. He wanted material for his projected book on HAB; God knows, he's going to be getting it."

"It'll take him a year just to go through all these," Kina said, once again starting to put individual clippings from the wad of them in her hand onto their appropriate stacks.

"Uh-uh, not John. He'll go through this stuff like lightning and I'll be willing to bet that in three or four days he'll have it all assimilated. He has a fantastic ability for doing that. You should have seen him zipping through more than twenty thousand pages of the most disorganized files you ever saw, over at the Boardman house."

"He'll *have* to be good to get through all this," Kina muttered, bending to her work. The other two joined her and for a little while there was no more talk.

Thus far most of the piles had only two or three clippings each. Occasionally there were those with only one, but just as often some of the piles had a couple dozen or more. There was a lot of juxtaposing going on as new categories were formed or as it became evident that already established categories should be further divided.

"Hey, here's an interesting one," Kina said suddenly. "From the Miami *Herald* with Monday's dateline. The headline says, 'Divers Find Remains of Civilization in Bahamas Waters—230 Feet Down.' Listen to this." She read the brief article aloud to them:

"'A team of Scuba divers from Miami today reported an archaeological find which is certainly of great significance in regard to the HAB Theory. The discovery was made in a "blue hole" about two miles from Cat Cay in the Bahamas.

"'The team, led by Ken Littlejohn of Coral Gables, explored some of the holes which were first entered during the late 1960s by divers from aboard the famous Jacques Cousteau research boat *Calypso*. Littlejohn's party, however, reported finding a network of tunnels previously overlooked, which had been hidden by coral and marine growths.

"'Inside the caves at a minimum depth of 230 feet they discovered a circular domed room in which there is an only slightly smaller circular domed construction with several arched entryways. The outside of the construction is highly glazed and liberally decorated in bas-relief with a wide variety of animals, some recognizable but many entirely unfamiliar.

"'According to Littlejohn, the construction is a part of the floor of the room, and there is good reason, he says, to believe that both the room and its structure were sculpted in some unknown way from the solid rock material in which the tunnels and room are located."'

Kina's eyes were large and round when she finished reading. "Gosh," she breathed, "isn't that amazing? Now, where do I file it?"

"Start a new pile, I guess," Anne said, "or else put if for now with those other clippings about Atlantis or the underwater tunnels leading inland along Ecuador's coast."

She returned to her own filing, but then straightened, holding a single clipping. "Now it's my turn," she said. "Lend an ear. This one'll set you back on your heels. The headline says, 'Ancient Medical Arts Support HAB Claims.' It's from the *Pittsburgh Press*.

"'A discussion group of the HAB Symposium,'" she read, "'today devoted itself to the topic of ancient medicine in respect to the HAB postulation of high orders of civilization in previous epochs.

"'The meeting, in a suite of the Sheraton-East Hotel, was chaired by Dr. Lya Pompara, who is chief of the Philippines National Health Service and—"

"Bravo!" cried Kina. "I wondered when a Filipino was going to get into the act. I've heard of Pompara since I was just a kid in Manila. She's supposed to be terrific."

"'—and,'" Anne continued reading, "'professor of internal medicine at the University of the Philippines in Manila. Pompara opened the meeting by reading an item which is quoted here in its entirety: "Take on the tip of a knife the contents of the pox inflammation and inject it into the arm of a well man, mixing it with his blood. A fever will follow, but the malady will pass very easily and will create no complications. Thereafter, the second man will forever be rendered invulnerable to the same disease." When she completed reading it, Pompara revealed that this was a passage outlining an immunization process against smallpox and that it was written in the ancient Brahmin book of India known as the *Sactya Grantham*, which was compiled 3,500 years ago. She added that Edward Jenner (1749-1823) is credited with discovery of smallpox vaccination in 1796.

"'Pompara, before relinquishing the floor, also noted that ancient records from Thebes show that the use of penicillin was widespread in Egypt 4,000 years ago, although Alexander Fleming received modern credit for the discovery of penicillin in 1929. Both the use of penicillin for the treatment of infection and the process of vaccination for smallpox were obviously not newly discovered at the ancient dates noted, she added, but rather they represent medical arts which were dying at the time and which vanished soon thereafter.

"'Other discussions during the meeting covered the use of anesthetics in Peru and Egypt some 4,500 years ago, the successful technique of brain surgery in hundreds of cases in Peru about the same time and, catching many of the conferees by surprise, the use in China of an X-ray machine in 206 B.C., and the use of a machine which may have combined both X-ray and fluoroscope in India in 500 B.C. In the latter example, a physician named Jivaka wrote that he made great and good use of the machine in diagnosing the maladies of patients, adding that "placed before a patient, it illuminated his body as a lamp illuminates the objects inside a house; it revealed the nature of maladies."' Well, how's that for an eye-opener?"

"Amazing," Kina repeated.

Susan nodded. "I've always contended," she said, "that there's just nothing new under the sun."

"Yes there is," Anne put in. She swept out an arm to take in the whole of the cluttered rooms. "Filing all this stuff is what's new. If we're ever going to finish, we'd better keep at it." She began bending over to place a clipping on a pile, but then straightened and added, "I'm really grateful for the help you two are giving me. It was especially good of you, Mother, to come all the way in from Elgin."

Both Susan and Kina sloughed off the words of appreciation and continued their filing, and Anne joined them. They didn't talk for quite a long while after that. The majority of these clippings, taking in the first six days of the symposium, were Xeroxed copies provided in packets by a downtown Chicago international clipping service, but quite a few were items Anne herself had clipped from the numerous newspapers of Chicago and its suburbs. With many, the headlines alone told the stories. In others it sometimes took a paragraph or two to appreciate their value:

GOLDEN ICONS MAY BE AIRCRAFT

Three solid gold models of what appear to be nothing less than delta-winged aircraft, found in archaeological digs in Ecuador, Columbia and Peru, were wind-tunnel tested at the New York Aeronautical Institute yesterday and found to be aerodynamically sound. —Quito El Commercio

WERE THERE REALLY GIANTS IN THE LAND?

Many thousands of reports of giant human remains found throughout the world during the past two hundred years are presently being given new study as a result of the HAB Theory Symposium. Not only the bones of races of giants have been discovered but also, in many cases, the artifacts these races used—such as gigantic stone chairs, a huge skillet weighing over 200 pounds, a metal ax head with a weight of 38 pounds, a large...—London Observer

MASSIVE FOREIGN AID INCREASE TO
KENYA FOR SURVIVAL CITY STIRS CONTROVERSY

—*Milwaukee* Journal

IMPEACHMENT BILL INTRODUCED BY WINTHROP

A Bill of Impeachment against President Robert Sanders was introduced to Congress today by Senator Harold Winthrop (Rep., R.I.) on grounds of presidential malfeasance, irresponsibility, and...

—*New York* Times

BAGHDAD PROFESSOR AT HAB SYMPOSIUM
CITES OLD RECORDS

Dr. Tobas Darab, director of the Asia Minor Antiquarian Society of Baghdad, has strongly recommended to fellow scientists attending the HAB Theory Symposium in New York that "a new, penetrating and unprejudicial look be taken at all ancient writings having to do with floods, mysterious lost powers, flying machines, medical devices, alchemical skills, and other such enigmatical matters."

Among the ancient works Darab cited for inclusion in such study were the 225-volume Tibetan commentary on the Kantyua, called the Tantyua, the famed Varahamara Tables of India, the Yoynich Manuscript discovered in Italy but not of Italian origin, the Zoroastrian books with an alleged but unconfirmed age of 11,600 years, The Epic of Gilgamesh…

—*Baghdad* News

HAB CULTS FORMING

Authorities here report a new series of cultist groups meeting in at least six separate locations of the city. According to alleged "reliable inside sources," the cultists are basing their mystic rites on recent HAB Theory revelations…

—*Los Angeles* Herald Examiner

ROME PUNDIT DESCRIBES ETERNAL LIGHTS AND ETERNAL LADY

Dr. Anna Viale, cryptologist and chief of the Roman Institute of Antiquities, today at the HAB Symposium in New York teamed up with Dr. Hussei al-Ahrid, prehistorian of the University of Damascus in Syrian, in a group discussion presentation at the Sherry-Netherland Hotel.

The topic of the two scientists was a description of numerous tombs found in Italy, Greece, Syria, and Egypt which, when opened after thousands of years of being sealed, contained glowing lights. In most cases the lights were described as "glowing globes on pedestals" which emanated a light without the generation of heat and from no observable power source.

Dr. Viale said one such tomb, found along the Via Appia outside Rome, was opened in 1485 and was found to contain not only glowing lights, but the body of a young woman coated with a strange salve. There was no doubt that the tomb had been sealed for at least a thousand years. When the protective salve was removed from the body of the woman, who was described as being about twenty years old and of very comely features, the flesh was found to be as firm and whole as if she had passed from life only moments before. The body was placed on display in Rome for a week or two and was seen by thousands of visitors, but then decomposition set in and it was reburied…

—*Rome* Avanti!

ELLESMERE ISLAND MYSTERY DISCUSSED

As a result of a HAB Symposium discussion yesterday in the New York Hilton hotel, plans are underway here for a new investigation into the mysterious object far beneath Ellesmere Island.

Dr. Rolf Dadier of the Canadian Observatory in Ottawa will be heading up the expedition. The object, as described to HAB Symposium scientists, was discovered in 1968 beneath the weather station called Alert, located at Ellesmere Island's northernmost edge, 475 miles from the North Pole. The object, though never seen, has been seismologically measured and is described as a near cylindrical mass 65 miles in length by 64 miles in thickness. The edge closest to ground surface begins at a depth of 15 miles.

The unknown object, scientists reported, emits a magnetic distortion of incredible power and…

Toronto Star

MAYAN CALENDAR "IMPOSSIBLE"—BUT TRUE

Dr. Carlos Sanchera, professor of mathematics from this city, today told a HAB discussion group in New York's Drake hotel that the Maya culture, in the short span of its existence—only 256 years—could not possibly have developed the mathematical ability to produce its incredibly accurate calendar.

In what he termed "a far more reasonable approach," Dr. Sanchera admits to a belief in the HAB postulation that a former culture, extinguished by a capsizing earth, was responsible for its development...

Guatemala City La Hora

SECOND VISIT OF U.S. ENVOY ENDS

Alexander Gordon, special envoy to President Ngoromu from the President of the United States, ended his visit here yesterday, following a tour of the Ngaia City construction site. No clue has been given as to the reason for Gordon's one-day visit...

—Nairobi Baraza

ARE GEOLOGICAL TABLES WRONG?

HAB Symposium geologists are openly expressing bafflement over a series of archaeological "proofs" which indicate man existed during geological ages as far back as the beginning of the Upper Jurassic Period, about 250 million years ago.

In a group discussion meeting at the Statler-Hilton hotel, Esther Gill, president of the California Archaeological Academy at Berkeley, and Kathryn Lever, doctoral candidate at the University of Michigan and a Smithsonian Institute archaeological associate, presented data which irrefutably shows that ancient man had contact with and close knowledge of animal species which, according to the Geological Tables, were extinct upwards of 230 million years before man was previously thought to have appeared on earth. Among the many examples presented by the two archaeologists were:

1) An ancient rock carving discovered in 1924 in the Hava Supai Canyon of northern Arizona by the Doheny Scientific Expedition, which depicts a Tyrannosaurus rex (extinct carnivorous lizard of the Upper Cretaceous—beginning 110 million years ago) standing on its hind legs and preparing to attack an unsuspecting human being.

2) A rock carving of amazing accuracy and great antiquity on a cliffside overlooking the Big sandy River of Oregon, which depicts a stegosaurus of the Upper Jurassic—beginning 150 million years ago.

3) Ancient Panamanian ceramic pottery on which are finely executed paintings of pterodactyls, extinct flying lizards from the Lower Jurassic, beginning 180 million years ag.

4) Sculptured heads of toxidons, extinct mammals of the Lower to Upper Tertiary—13 to 63 million years ago—carved in the stone calendar of Tiahuanaco in Peru.

Geologists and anthropologists, as well as archaeologists, have long contended that man did not appear on earth longer ago than 1.7 million years...

New York Daily News

POPE DECLARES HAB INVESTIGATIONS
"IMMORAL...SACRILEGIOUS"

Scientists presently attending the HAB Theory Symposium in New York are making light of the Holy Beliefs of Catholicism and other religious denominations, according to Pope Benedict XVII at Vatican City today...

—*Associated Press*

WIFE, DAUGHTER OF KENYAN PRESIDENT
ATTEND HAB SESSIONS

—*New York* Times

HAB-INSPIRED TV SERIES SLATED

A new half-hour weekly television series, to be entitled The Archaeologists, *is in production now and...*

—*Variety*

MILD 'QUAKE HERE TERRIFIES RESIDENTS

—*San Francisco* Chronicle

DOWDE CITES SCHLIEMANN
AS "GOOD EXAMPLE"

HAB Symposium Chairwoman Irma Dowde, in last evenings meeting of the group discussions chairmen, hailed the German archaeologist Heinrich Schliemann as "a good example of the sort of outlook that we, as scientists, must have."
The Smithsonian archaeologist said that Schliemann, at a time when Homer's Iliad *was looked upon as sheer fantasy by other scientists, was convinced that it contained history as well as legend. Painstakingly following clues in the Iliad, he deduced where ancient Troy might have been, excavated at that location and found it, in one of the most thrilling archaeological discoveries of all time...*

Toledo Blade

EVANGELIST ACCEPTS HAB REALITY

Peter Proctor, famed Chicago evangelist, stated yesterday to a crowd of 6,000 at Red Rocks Amphitheater here that he is "in full accord with the reality of the HAB Theory," and that he feels the teachings of Christianity are "wholly compatible with that reality."
In an interview at his hotel last night, Proctor revealed that he will soon be embarking on a major evangelistic tour of the nation, during which he will be presenting a program entitled The Promise of the Cataclysm. *He will begin this tour with an appearance at...*

—*Denver* Rocky Mountain News

The silence in Anne Carpenter's apartment, which had been unbroken for the better part of an hour except for the rustling of papers, suddenly was shattered by a burst of laughter from Susan. Surprised, Anne and Kina looked up and saw the older woman almost convulsed with amusement. Even though not knowing the reason, the two younger women were themselves grinning widely by the time Susan caught her breath well enough to speak.

"Oh, this is just absolutely priceless!" she gasped, then burst into laughter again. After a few moments, once more in control of herself, Susan continued. "I don't know," she said, "maybe it's not really all that funny; maybe its just a relief in the midst of a tiresome job, but anyway, take a look at this, will you?" She was starting to crack up again as the two younger women came over to her and looked at the clipping she was holding.

It was an advertisement from the amusements page of the Philadelphia *Bulletin*:

*NEW! * NEW! * NEW! * NEW!*
GIRLS! GIRLS! GIRLS! GIRLS!
Troc Theater
presents
!!! The HAB Girls !!!
starring
The Roll-Over Queen
EARTHA TILT
*…with her **incredible** globes…*
and
The Pivotal Princesses
KATTA KLISM and ANN GWISH
!!!…PLUS…!!!
…for a Tidal-Wave of Laughs, that Zany
End-of-the-World Comic
"CAP" SIGHS

All three of the women were laughing heartily now, but it was Anne who recovered first. "You're right, Mother, that's priceless I've half a mind to have it framed and give it to John as a present when he comes home."

She stretched prodigiously. "Well, since we're interrupted now anyway, I'd say it's time we took a real break. All in favor of vodka martinis say aye."

The vote was unanimous and in a few minutes the three were sitting around the small table in the kitchen sipping their drinks, still amused over the burlesque show ad.

The discoloration of Anne's eye was beginning to fade away and, with the judicious use of makeup, she was able to conceal the injury pretty well. The small split in her brow probably would leave a hairline scar, but it wouldn't be too noticeable after it was healed.

Kina glanced at her wristwatch and frowned. "Oh-oh, look at the time. Nearly five already. And this is Wednesday, which means Eric'll be home in about half an hour. I'll have to scoot." She smiled at Anne. "Hate to leave you with all this mess, but Eric's a bear if his scotch and soda's not in his hand within thirty seconds after he walks in the door, and if his dinner doesn't follow within half an hour. Tell you what, though, Eric has a meeting with a client tonight at seven and probably won't be back until after ten, so I'll be here later to help you finish, okay?"

"That's sweet of you, Kina," Anne replied, "but I feel as if I'm taking advantage of you. Seriously, I appreciate all the help you've been already, but please don't feel you *have* to come back tonight. Mother and I can wrap it up pretty well, I'm sure."

Kina was finishing her drink in hasty gulps and she shook her head as she set the glass down. "Oh, I don't. I *want* to. It may be a mess, but it's kind of fun, too. And who knows, maybe we'll find something else about Eartha Tilt. I'm dying to know more about those *incredible* globes!"

They all laughed and in a moment Kina was gone. Susan shook her head. "She's such a nice girl. Kind of kooky, but a doll." She looked at Anne with a more serious expression. "Have you told her how you got the shiner?"

"No. Not the real way it happened. She's curious about it, I know, and so I just said I'd stumbled in the office and fell against one of those big upright filing cabinets. I don't think she believes it, but she's not one to probe."

"How about John? Did you tell him?"

She grimaced. "I didn't know whether I should or not. He was awfully concerned on Friday night when he saw it, and you know how he is; he wanted to know everything. And so," she sighed deeply, "I wound up telling him. He got pretty angry."

"At you?"

"At *me*? No, of course not. At *her*. Oh, he was a little upset at first that I went out there to begin with. And he got even more ticked off when he found out that Billy—his son—saw the whole thing. But mostly he was furious about what she'd done. That's when he told me something he said he guessed now he should've told me before. On the day that he and Marie went to the park for their talk, she clobbered him, too. Totally unexpected, just like with me, but she didn't have anything in her hand at the time. Then some man hit him, too."

"Some *man*? Who? Why?"

Anne laughed briefly. "A stranger. Sort of a knight-in-shining-armor type, I guess. John said after she smacked him, she started running away and he ran after her and finally caught her. Some man in the park evidently thought he was molesting her and came charging over and belted John a good one. But they finally convinced him it was a personal thing between them and he left. Anyway, John was about as angry as I've ever seen him when he learned what happened to me. That's when he called her and—"

"From here?"

"Uh-huh. First time ever. He didn't give her much of a chance to talk. Just read her out pretty well and then wound up telling her that he'd finally sorted out this whole situation in his own mind and that at last he knew what had to be done, but that he couldn't do it right now because he was on his way overseas and was going to be gone for ten days at least."

"Just that? He didn't tell her why?"

"Mother, for heaven's sake, he wasn't even able to tell *me* why. It's a secret mission for the President. All he was able to tell me was the same thing, that he was going abroad—he wouldn't say where—and that he didn't know for sure when he'd be back. He was evidently stretching things just to get here to see me before he left. The plane out of O'Hare got him back to Washington with only just enough time to do whatever he had to do there and then catch his overseas flight. So the answer is no, he didn't tell Marie anything about it. Only that the next time he saw her, matters would be settled for once and all."

"So now what, Pussycat?" Susan asked softly. "What happens when he comes back? Does he come here or does he go there?"

Anne's expression changed and she frowned. "I don't know for sure, Mother. Here, I think, but I really don't know that for sure. He talked about how glad he was going to be to have this time alone, apart from both of us, so he could reflect on the decision he's made." Abruptly a tear rolled down her cheek and she brushed it away in an exasperated manner. "*Reflect* on it, he said, and then plan his next moves. Naturally, he'll *have* to see her again to finally settle things, as he told her, but I'm hoping he'll come here first."

"Well, dear, I don't know. You've got to realize he's got a lot to bear in—"

"I *know* it! But I'm so afraid something'll happen that will make him have second thoughts if he seers her first, and he'll reverse his decision. I want him to come to come home to *me*, not her. He's *got* to come back to me now."

Susan looked at her daughter more sharply. "Got to? Annie, honey, is there more to that than you're saying? You're not pregnant, are you?"

Anne shook her head. "No. Sometimes I wish I were. I've thought about it. But I don't want him coming back because of a sense of obligation for something like that. He's got to come to me first of all because he loves me, and then because he realizes that his life with her is over and there's no way to ever take it back to what it was. No," she shook her head again, "I'm not pregnant. But if I thought for a minute that he wouldn't come back to me, I'd make sure I got pregnant. It'd be a way of having a part of him, at least. Not to make him come back. Just so that I'd have *something*."

She picked up her drink and gulped the last swallow. "I don't think I have to worry now, though. He's made the decision and that's what's most important." As she set the glass back down, her mother's hand covered hers.

"You really love him deeply, don't you, Kitten?"

"Yes, I really love him deeply, Mother."

They were silent then for a few minutes. When Anne spoke again it was in a lighter tone of voice. "Well, we still have a lot to do in there. Tell you what. It does feel good to sit down for a while, so why don't we stay put for now? We'll get back to the clipping service packets in a little bit. Right now I'll get that stack of Chicago papers and we can split them up and go them here at the table and cut out whatever we find about HAB, okay?"

"Sounds good. My legs feel ready to fall off."

Anne got up and brought in the pile of newspapers for the last six days and put them on the floor between them, then found two pairs of shears in a kitchen drawer and they started. There were plenty to clip, but they'd hardly begun with the latest editions on top of the pile when the telephone rang. Reaching far over, Anne picked up the kitchen extension from the wall.

"Hello?"

"Miss Anne Carpenter, please."

"Speaking."

"This is the overseas operator. We have a call for you from Turkey. Hold on, please."

Anne covered the mouthpiece and spoke to her mother excitedly. "It's *him*, Mother. John! Calling from—"

"Here is you party, sir," came the operator's voice. "Go ahead, please."

Susan started to get up to leave the room but Anne caught her arm. "No, stay. It's all right. He's in—"

"Anne?"

"Yes, darling, yes! I'm here. Oh, John, thank God you called!"

"What's the matter? Is something wrong?"

"No, no, everything's fine, perfect. I'm just so glad you called. You can't know how much I've missed you."

"Yes I can, because I've missed you the same."

"I love you, John. So much! Are you okay? I've been going out of my gourd wondering how you are and where you are. Where *are* you now?"

"Yes, I'm okay. I'm in Ankara." He paused but didn't seem inclined to elaborate. "How are you doing? Is everything all right? Are you okay?"

"Me? Fine. I'm fine."

"How's the eye?"

"Pretty good now. Swelling's all but gone and the discoloration's leaving, too. By the time I finish with makeup, it's almost invisible. You should've seen it over the weekend, though. Sunday it looked like I was peering out from behind a piece of rancid meat."

He was quiet a moment and she knew he was remembering Friday night and his call to Marie. It wasn't something she wanted him to dwell upon. "I miss you, honey," she reiterated softly. "Much more than it's possible for me to say."

"I know," he said. He was back with her. "I'm glad we had Friday night, but I can't say I cared very much for Saturday morning, getting dragged out of a comfy bed while it was still dark to go traipsing out to the airport."

"I'm glad for Friday night, too, Mister. If you'd ever picked a time when it was really necessary for my peace of mind to have you here, you couldn't have been more on target than you were then. It was a beautiful thing for you to do, John. I hope you have some small idea of how much I appreciated it."

"Actions speak louder than words," he said, laughing, "and yours were speaking clearly and loudly. It was important to me, too. Now tell me, what have you been doing since I left?"

"I'm up to my earlobes in newsprint for one thing, Mr. Grant, and it's all your fault! Good grief, you ought to see this apartment. There must be five thousand-clippings piled all over the place. Kina Maxwell—you remember her, from down the hall? The one who let me borrow her tape recorder?"

"Uh-huh."

"Well, she's helping me put them into categories and file them in large envelopes. So's Mother. She's right here now, in fact. Mother is, I mean." She glanced up at Susan and saw her mouth some words and nodded. "She says to tell you 'Hi."

"Say hello back. Glad to hear you're getting the clippings. What's going on with the symposium? I've sort of been out of touch with that end."

"Evidently it's really something. All kinds of fascinating stuff coming out of it. Some friction, too. Irma Dowde lowered the boom on one of the group discussion chairmen who was out of line and he left in a huff. Some guy from Oxford. Lot of other things happening, too. Exciting."

"Like what?"

"For starts, they've reported a significant underwater archaeological find in a cave two hundred feet or more deep in the Bahamas—which seems to prove that the cave in question was on dry land instead of under the sea. Then there was a small earthquake in San Francisco that got everyone shaken up, mentally as well as physically."

"I shouldn't wonder," Grant said, chuckling. "So what's the general attitude of the scientists at the symposium now?"

"Hard to say for sure. A lot of little proofs have been showing up which, individually, don't seem to mean a lot, but when taken in total concept become very important. What seems to be hitting home with a lot of them is the way everything seems to interlock. It's like a jigsaw puzzle coming together. The piece that is the blue of the sky doesn't seem to have any relationship at all to the one that is green for water or red for a barn, but when they get put into place, they each begin to contribute to the whole picture. There are some gaps yet, but they're filling in. Don't go getting all fired up about that, though; on the opposite side of the fence there are some large segments of the scientists—most especially the geologists—who are still pretty far from accepting the theory yet. Pollsters from both Roper and Tren-duv have been buttonholing symposium members each day and reporting the results daily, but they're pretty inconclusive. All in all, there seem to be a lot more pluses than minuses. Most of the scientists won't commit themselves on the record, but off the record, except for the geology factions, it looks pretty good."

"Glad to hear it. Are they still planning to have the official vote on Friday morning? The one Dowde was setting up?"

"There's some kind of change in that, according to the papers. Ballots were all made out and they were supposed to have been passed out to everyone, through the group discussion chairmen, tomorrow. Now I see in the paper where they won't be passed out until noon on Friday. Each of the hotels has a box at its desk where the ballots are supposed to be dropped by eight in the morning on Saturday. Then I guess Dr. Dowde's people will tally them and announce the results. Around noon on Saturday, I think."

She paused, considering, then added, "Oh yes, there was a bill of impeachment introduced in Congress against the President, and the President himself is scheduled to make a major address next Sunday evening. He wants it to be relayed to all the major nations by satellite simultaneously, so maybe you'll get a chance to see it over there wherever you'll be. Where will you be then, do you know? Or can't you tell me?"

"Yes, I can tell you, I guess. As far as I know right now I'll be either in New York or Washington. I'm leaving here in the morning. Going directly to Washington and then on to New York. I think I'm expected to finish out the Symposium, but I should be in Chicago next Monday at the latest."

"John, really? Here? On Monday?"

"That's how it looks, unless I can get away from the symposium sooner. However it turns out, prepare to meet a limp rag at O'Hare. That's probably how I'll be feeling when I get home."

There was no response and after an interval he said, "Anne?"

"Yes, yes, I'm here! How can you expect me to answer, you big dope, when I'm bawling my eyes out?" She sniffled and took the paper napkin Susan was extending toward her, then wiped her eyes and blew her nose.

"You'll meet me, then? I'll call from New York or Washington to let you know the exact time."

"Ye gods, you have to ask? Of *course* I'll meet you! I'll have a big brass band there. No," she amended quickly, "everyone does that. I'll hire the Chicago Philharmonic. I'll have—"

"Just have yourself there, Lady. That's all I want."

"I'll be there. Count on it."

He hesitated and when he spoke again he was more serious. "There'll be some difficult times coming, Anne. Very difficult. And unpleasant."

"We'll make it all right, John. Together we'll make it all right. No one ever said it would be easy, but we'll make it."

He spoke slowly. "I guess one of the first things I'll have to do is file for divorce. Incompatibility, isn't that what they call it?" There was a fine edge of bitterness in his voice. "Well, that's something to think about then. I may be in Chicago for only a couple days. Then I'll probably have to go back to Washington. I'm hoping you'll be able to arrange your schedule so you can go with me. Think so?"

"Shouldn't be any problem," she said. Now it was she who became serious. "John, I've wanted this, you know that. But I want it to be what *you* want to do. It has to be done because deep inside you know that for *yourself* it's the best thing to do."

"That's the only way it can be, Anne. It just took me a while to determine what was best for me." He became cheerier. "All right, can't have you and Susan becoming slackers. Get back to work on those clippings. And I'm going to hit the sack. It may be only quarter after five in the evening on Wednesday there, but it's fifteen minutes after one in the morning on Thursday here, and I'm whipped. Take care, love. Say good-bye to your mother for me."

"John?"

"What?"

"I love you."

"I love you, too. 'Bye."

Anne hung up the telephone slowly and then turned to her mother, who was once again clipping. She picked up her own shears.

"He said to tell you good-bye."

Susan was smiling as she looked up. "Felt like an eavesdropper, sitting here like this while you were talking," she said, "but I'll have to admit I'm glad I was. Now you won't have to go through the process of calling me to tell me the latest. Honey," she reached out and gripped Anne's hand, "I'm happy for you. I guess you both know it'll be a pretty tough way to go for a while but, as you said, you'll make it. I'm sure of it."

"I am too, Mother." She put down the shears and placed her other hand atop Susan's and squeezed it. "And I'm glad you were here to eavesdrop, too." She laughed at the expression on Susan's face and then her mother joined in.

"Oh," Anne said suddenly, disengaging her hands, "he said something you didn't hear that I should tell you."

"What's that?"

Her daughter's eyes were dancing. "He said he couldn't have you and me becoming slackers and told us to get back to work."

"Good heavens!" Susan exclaimed in mock fright, her eyes open wide. "Then let us be at it!"

They bent to their work again, turning the newspaper pages slowly and scanning the headlines, pausing frequently to clip out an article and mark it with the date and source, speaking little to one another. They worked for perhaps another ten or fifteen minutes when there was a sharp gasp from Susan and Anne looked up quickly. The older woman wore a peculiar, unreadable expression.

"What is it, Mother?" Anne was alarmed. "Are you ill?"

Susan shook her head and murmured, "No. Just a minute, Kitten." She fastened her eyes to a small article near the bottom of a second-section page of the latest edition of the *Daily News*. She was still shaking her head as she wordlessly clipped the article out and marked it as she had the others, then handed it to her daughter.

Anne frowned, still trying to read her mother's expression. Then she read the article.

DIVORCE SOUGHT BY WRITER'S WIFE

A divorce petition was filed today in the Cook County Circuit Court by attorneys for Marie Fischer Grant of Skokie, wife of the prominent Chicago-area author, John Charles Grant. The petition was filed under the grounds of infidelity.

Mrs. Grant refused to answer questions by reporters at her home late this morning. Grant himself was not available for comment. Very active in the HAB Theory matter, he has recently become a special aide to President Sanders and is currently out of the country on a confidential mission by direction of the President.

John Grant is well known for his best-selling novels and nonfiction books, the latest of which is Monument to Destiny. *Eight years ago he was awarded a Pulitzer Prize for his* Interior Motive *series published in the* Washington Post.

V

Breakfast in the dining room of the American Embassy had been a delightful affair and John Grant acknowledged to himself that there was something to be said for being the recipient of such VIP treatment as he had received since arriving here in the Turkish capital. All through breakfast the four of them—the ambassador and his wife, Mark Shepard and himself—had engaged in stimulating discussion about Turkey and its rich historical heritage.

The Ambassador, former governor Charles Phipps of Delaware, was a gifted conversationalist and skilled raconteur with an amazing store of knowledge in a wide variety of fields. A very distinguished-looking individual, he was tall and graying, with warm, intelligent eyes. His wife, Diane, was dark and attractive and equally endowed with intellect. She was a very soft-spoken woman with a lilting laugh so delightful that simply to hear it evoked a warm feeling. Both had read most of Grant's past writings and were aware, in a limited way, that his visit here with Mark Shepard dealt in some manner with the HAB Theory and was a matter of top priority directly from the

President, yet there had been no trace of even the most subtle probing for enlightenment as to his mission. The closest thing to it was the ambassador's comment just now as a second serving of coffee was being poured.

"I hope, Mr. Grant, that you've been thoroughly successful in accomplishing the task which has brought you here. We only wish you could remain with us longer."

"Most definitely successful, Mr. Ambassador, thank you," Grant replied, putting a teaspoonful of sugar in his coffee. "As for staying longer, I'd very much like to do so. Especially now, since Dr. Shepard's put me on the track of an unusually interesting story possibility above and beyond what brought me here."

"Excellent. Is it something you'd care to tell us a little bit about at this time?"

Grant smiled. "I have no objection, but perhaps Dr. Shepard should be the one to tell you, since he knows the subject so well."

Mark Shepard, in the process of lighting his second cigar of the day, grunted in a rumbling sort of way and shook his head. He was a lean man, with a strong, deeply lined face and somewhat protuberant eyes. A thick dark moustache made his face appear fuller.

"No," he said immediately, "I think you should tell them, John. I've discovered from long experience that there's no better way to ruin a good cigar than to light it and then not smoke it because you're too busy talking. You go ahead and if you get stuck, I'll kibitz. Bear in mind though," he added, pointing the cigar toward Grant, "that Air Force One will be picking you up, according to what Ambassador Phipps said, in about an hour and a half. That means we should leave here in an hour or less, if you're going to be dropping me off at the hotel en route."

"All right," Grant said. "That's more than time enough. And I'll definitely be depending upon you to kibitz when—not if—I get stuck." He chuckled and turned his gaze to the ambassador and his wife.

"I'll have to preface this," he began, "by saying that I'm not very knowledgeable in Turkish history, but Dr. Shepard is, and he's put me on the track of an individual whose life was so fascinating that it practically cries to be biographized. You may have heard of him. His name was Piri Re'is."

Diane Phipps's brow furrowed as she tried to dredge up the name from memory and the ambassador was already shaking his head.

"No," he said, "not that I recall. Have you, dear?"

"I think," his wife said slowly, "if I'm not mistaken, that he was an admiral in the Turkish Navy."

"Very good!" Grant congratulated her. "Exactly right. I have to admit that I'd never heard of him before. I'm glad I have now. I suspect I'll be coming back here sometime to get into some further research about him, but here's a sort of abbreviated version of what his life was like."

He looked at Shepard, who was leaning back comfortably in his chair, the bulging eyes nearly closed and the perpetual cigar projecting from his lips.

Grant made an apologetic little gesture and grinned. "Can you get me started, Dr. Shepard, by giving me his name again? His real one, I mean?"

Shepard snorted and removed the cigar from his mouth, tapping the first gray-white ash into the fine crystal ashtray to his right. He cocked an eye in a sardonic manner. "Now that's what I call an incisive beginning," he said caustically.

They all laughed, but he went on without pause. "It's a toss-up in regard to what his real name was; the histories give a number of them. It was most likely one of three in particular—Piri Ahmet Muhiddin, Hakiri—or sometimes Haji —Memmed, or Muhyi l'Din. Later in life, after he'd taken the name you mentioned, he sometimes wrote his own name as Piri l'Din Re'is, shortened to Piri Re'is. Okay? Now I hope you'll let me enjoy this cigar in peace for a while."

"I'll try," Grant replied dryly. "His exact date of birth isn't known, but it was probably in the Turkish year of 874, which coincides with our year A.D. 1470. He was born close to Karaman, which is near Konya. That's pretty far from the sea, but very early he became fascinated by the type of life being lived by his uncle, Kemal Re'is, who was a pirate. Evidently when he was only thirteen he ran away from home and joined Kemal, staying with him for many years. Kemal Re'is was an extraordinary seaman and he taught Piri all he knew. By the time he was twenty, Piri was himself an exceptional mariner, and at twenty-five he was said to possess an unrivaled knowledge of the entire Mediterranean Sea and all its islands and coastlines. Around A.D. 1500 the Turks and Spaniards began fighting and Kemal and Piri gave up the renegade life and joined the Imperial Ottoman Navy during the reign of—" He looked at the scientist for help.

Shepard sighed and spoke around his cigar. "Beyazit the Second."

"Thank you," Grant said. "Beyazit the Second, and both were appointed captains. Not long after that Kemal was killed in a storm, but Piri stayed on in the Navy, excelling in sea battles and becoming something of a legend in his own time for the awesome exploits he performed. He remained with the fleet for over fifty years, all through the reign of Yavuz—" Again he hesitated.

"Selim," Shepard contributed.

"…the reign of Yavuz Selim, and most of the reign of Suleiman the Magnificent." He glanced at Shepard and the older man winked. "For a good number of years he was chief aide to the Great Admiral of the Imperial Fleet, Khair al-Din Barbarossa, and…"

"Also known as Barbaros Hayrettin Pasha."

Grant smiled. "Told you you're the one who should have been telling this," he commented to Shepard, then went on. "Piri Re'is had a great passion for old maps and in each port where they put in he would search through the bazaars for ancient charts and maps. There was an especially important engagement with Spanish ships in 1501—important in that something so significant happened it'll have a tremendous effect on our history—but that's—"

"*American* history?" Ambassador Phipps questioned.

"Yes, sir," Grant replied, "but I'll forego any detailing of that particular matter, if you don't mind."

"What a great story teller," Diane Phipps put in. "Gets to the best part and then decides to skip it."

"True," Grant went on, after the laughter had subsided, "but only because I'm not sure I can or should speak of it right now. Anyway, my skipping it will give you greater incentive for reading the book, if I ever get around to writing it. I'll tell you this much of it: that engagement with the Spaniards resulted in something very important concerning a map that came into the possession of Piri Re'is as a result of the battle. To continue, Re'is began preparing an atlas he called *Kitabi Bahriye*, which can be interpreted as either *Book of the Sea* or *The Navy's Book*.

He began it in September of 1520 during the last weeks of the reign of Selim, but in the preface to it he says he started it in the following December. That's because he wanted its dedication to Suleiman the Magnificent to be more impressive, since Suleiman was just coming into power.

"However," he continued, "it wasn't until 1523 that he finished the book—containing two hundred ten beautifully executed maps which he had drawn from his own knowledge or copied from other maps in his collection—and at that time he presented it to Suleiman. He won the emperor's favor and continued advancing in rank. In 1547 he captured Aden. He was then about seventy-seven and four years later, in 1551, he was promoted to *kapudan* of Egypt—which means Admiral of the Fleet then attached to Egypt, which was at that time a dependency of the Ottoman Empire. He held his fleet in the area of Suez and, even though he was now an octogenarian, led expeditions into the Persian Gulf and Arabian Sea.

"With thirty-one ships in command, he took quite a few slaves along the coast of Arabia and captured the port city, of Maskat, losing a few of his ships in the process. He then laid siege to Hormuz on the islands inside the Persian Gulf. The islanders offered him great treasures to leave them in peace and so he accepted and withdrew to Basra in Iran, at the confluence of the Tigris and Euphrates rivers. But then word came that a powerful Portuguese fleet was beginning to block their escape route through the entrance to the Persian Gulf. Rather than risk all his men and ships, Re'is had all the treasures loaded aboard three and attempted to run the blockade under cover of darkness. They were almost through when discovered. One of his ships was sunk but, because of his knowledge of the waters, he was able to escape with the other two around Arabia, through Suez, into the Mediterranean and bring a vast treasure for the coffers of the Ottoman Empire to Cairo. However, the governor of Basra, the Kobad Pasha, then in Egypt as its governor, sent a misrepresentative report to the Emperor in Istanbul—"

"Constantinople, then," Shepard put in.

Grant rolled his eyes. "—in Constantinople and told him that Re'is had begun his expedition with thirty-one ships and was returning with only two. No mention that about twenty-four were still secure at Basra, and no mention of the great treasure Re'is had brought back. It's worth speculation that the Kobad Pasha may have wanted the treasure, or a portion of it, for himself. His report got to Suleiman the Magnificent and the emperor was furious. He sent word back immediately that Re'is should be executed for his failure. And so, at the age of eighty-four, Piri Re'is was beheaded."

"Ugh!" said the ambassador's wife. "How awful. There's real gratitude for you."

Phipps was chewing his lip reflectively. "It ought to make a great story, Mr. Grant," he said. "Are you thinking of it in terms of nonfiction or a novel?"

At this point I really don't know, sir. I'm inclined to make it strictly biographical, but there are a great many gaps right now; too many to make it cohesive if full authenticity is to be preserved. I'll probably be coming back here sometime in the not too distant future to do some digging and if I can't turn up much more than I have now, then I'll probably wind up building a novel based on his life."

Momentarily Grant thought of the doldrums he had been experiencing in his writing just so recently and now two very big writing projects—HAB and the Re'is story—were filling him and he felt almost giddy with the excitement of it. His thought was interrupted by a touch on his arm and he turned to see that it was Mark Shepard who had tapped him and who was now looking at him with an admiring gaze.

"For all my interrupting with pointed comments, John," he rumbled, "I'll now have to back off a bit and admit I'm pretty damned impressed with what you've retained. Hell, I just rattled that stuff off to you in bits and pieces over the past few days. And not in much of a chronological order, either. Your recall—to say nothing of your organizational ability—is phenomenal."

Grant was pleased, but waved off the compliment. "So is my tape recorder's," he said. "Most of that stuff was on tape and I spent a good bit of time last evening going over everything we've covered."

"Impressive anyway. I think Bob knew just exactly what he was doing—as he always seems to—when he chose you to come over."

Shepard glanced down at his wristwatch and then came to his feet. "Well, I hate to say it, but time's our enemy and your chariot awaiteth at the airport. We'd better get moving."

Grant agreed and a few minutes later, after he had thanked all three for their hospitality and assistance, he and Shepard and Ambassador Phipps were in the embassy limousine, weaving through narrow streets choked with traffic and lined by both startlingly modern and obviously ancient buildings. Within a mile they stopped to drop off Shepard at his hotel. With a fresh cigar in his mouth, as yet unlighted, the scientist reached back inside the open window and shook Grant's hand a final time.

"Good luck. By George, I've half a mind to go with you, just to see how you're going to set them on their ears at the symposium. Would, if I weren't so tied up right now with the project. Give Bob my best when you get to the White House and tell him I'll be in touch. Thanks, too, for the copy of your HAB Theory summary. It's been damned nice meeting you. Take care." He tossed a casual wave to Phipps, sitting on the other side of Grant. "Mr. Ambassador."

They pulled away and in less than half an hour had reached Esenboga International Airport. They paused briefly at the flight line gates—a word from Phipps was all that was needed—and then were waved through. The long black car moved slowly past parked airliners and headed toward the far end of the expansive concrete apron where the familiar sleek form of Air Force One was standing, its powerful turbines quietly whining. An Air Force staff sergeant in dress uniform opened the limousine's back door as they came to a stop in front of the steps leading up into the aircraft. He saluted smartly as they emerged.

"Good morning, Mr. Ambassador. Mr. Grant. Everything's ready for departure. May I help you with your bags, Mr. Grant?"

"Yes, thank you," Grant replied. "There's a suitcase in the trunk and you can take these for me." He handed the airman his portable tape recorder and the White House portable typewriter Hazel Tierney had provided. His briefcase and a cylindrical package wrapped in brown paper and about three feet long he retained.

As he was bidding farewell to Ambassador Phipps and once more thanking him, an officer descended the steps carrying a large envelope. Grant recognized him as Colonel Bill Byrd and introduced him to the Ambassador. The colonel handed the envelope to Phipps.

"Directly from the President, sir," he said. Turning to Grant, he added, "I don't mean to rush you, Mr. Grant, but we're on a tight schedule."

"Of course," Grant replied. "I'm ready."

The airman was already disappearing into the plane with his luggage and so now, with a final brief nod to Phipps, he moved briskly up the steps, followed by Byrd.

Right in there, sir," the Colonel said, indicating the door leading into the cabin.

Grant opened it and walked in. Two men in business suits stepped aside to let him pass and as he walked by them Grant was wondering who they were. Then he heard a familiar voice.

"Hello, John. Join me here."

It was President Sanders.

V I

"Hello, Dan."

"Anita? It's you?" Daniel Ngoromu's deep bass tones rolled from the receiver with such clarity he might have been in the next room, and Anita closed her eyes and fought back the tears. The masculine voice continued. "I'm glad you called. I miss you. When are you coming home?"

"Tomorrow. I'm leaving here tomorrow, Dan. Your voice sounds so good to me! New York's just not right without you here with me. I…I wish I hadn't come. I want to be home." Her voice was beginning to break.

"Well, that's fine. But I thought you were going to stay until the symposium was over." There was an edging of concern in his voice. "Are you all right? Nothing's wrong, is it?"

"No," she said, sniffling, "nothing's wrong. I'm…I'm…dammit, I'm blubbering because it's just so good to hear your voice and because we're so far apart and I don't really want to be. I was thinking of staying until this was all over here, but now I don't want to. I want to be with you—underfoot and in the way and asking all kinds of silly questions and…and just feeling *close* to you."

His voice softened. "Then, 'Neet, come on home. I don't perform quite as well in any respect when you're not near. Never. Is Narai coming with you?"

"No. She definitely wants to stay till it's finished. Even then she may not be coming directly home. Narai's in love, Dan."

"In love! In just the few days she's been gone? With whom?"

"Alexander Gordon."

"Gordon! She can't be in love with him. He was just here!"

"What has that to do with it?" Anita said, smiling, her feeling of upset fading. "We weren't sure where he was, but Narai will be glad to know he's there. Anyway, he was here, too, but she didn't get to see much of him. Just enough, I guess, to know it's for real and to be horribly lonely because he's not here. She wants to be with him wherever he is. If he's not back by the time the symposium ends, then she'll leave here for wherever he happens to be."

Ngoromu sounded dazed. "But how could it all happen so fast?"

"Not all that fast, dear. Remember, they spent a lot of time together in Nairobi in June. How long does it take to know it when you finally find someone you love? And forget about their difference in age. It makes no difference whatever to Narai, and she's old enough to know her own mind. You're not concerned about her choice, are you? Alex is a very nice man."

"I know that. I'm not putting him down. He's a damned good man. I'm just surprised, that's all. Listen, it's not just a quick romance sort of thing, is it?"

"No. She loves him and that's that."

"He never even mentioned it to me." The Kenyan President sounded peeved. "Has he asked her to marry him yet?"

"Danny," Anita said gently, "*she* hasn't even told *him* yet that she loves him. Nor has he told her. But she does, and she thinks he does. So do I." She paused as a small needle of pain stabbed her, then went on. "How's it going there? With Ngaia City, I mean?"

"You wouldn't believe it," he said, a rumbling laugh swelling through the receiver. "From the coast all the way to the site it looks like we've been invaded. Construction, highway work, heavy equipment, power lines being buried, people scurrying around like termites from a mound that's been knocked over. But it's coming along well. Faster than I thought. Much faster. A lot more problems than I thought, too, but we're taking them in stride. Tom Umba's incredible. He knows every detail of every single thing that's going on at any given moment. I don't know how he does it. We've got the thick outer support walls in over an area of three acres now, and the honeycomb structure for the individual rooms is working out better than we thought. Provides amazing strength, and we can build on in any direction at any time. We're not greatly concerned with being pretty. We want strong chambers and we want them fast, so that's what we're aiming for. Eighteen chambers under roof so far and more coming. Ten of those chambers, incidentally, already filled with microfilm. We're still on that twenty-four-hour-a-day work schedule Tom established at the beginning. We're going to stay on it until it's finished. We've got one runway operable at the field, capable of handling the biggest thing in the air now. Others being worked on. Both highways—the one coming up here to Nairobi as well as the one going to the coast and then on down to Mombasa—are coming along pretty well. One damned big problem's come up, though."

"What?"

"People. Ever since Sanders issued that press release of his last weekend, we've had big trouble. You wouldn't believe the number of people trying to pour into Kenya. We've temporarily stopped issuing visas and are turning people back. It hasn't stopped them. Now they're entering illegally by boat, plane, by foot across the borders and it's a real headache. We've set up border patrols on the whole perimeter, but they're still flocking in. Tanzania and Somali are having the same problem. And this is just the start. It's going to get a lot rougher."

"What can you do about it beyond that?"

"Hell, 'Neet, I wish I knew! We'll cope somehow, I guess." He snorted. "Tom suggested something in that respect which we've tried out and it's working pretty well. Anyone found without proper papers is arrested. If he's not a Kenyan, he's given a choice; he can be deported instantly or he can join the labor crews at Ngaia City and be put to work—hard work—for which, in return, he gets no pay but he gets his meals and a tent, and the right to stay in Kenya as long as he continues working hard. So far about half are electing to stay—they're calling them 'stickers'—and it's helping."

"How many people, total, do we have working now?"

Ngoromu blew out a huge puff of air. "Altogether? Hard saying for sure. Let's see about four thousand stickers so far, plus our own hired people, about a hundred and thirty thousand of them, including the border patrols, plus over three thousand from the United States so far and another seven thousand expected. I guess somewhere around a hundred fifty thousand by the end of this week. And that'll probably double in the next month or less. Biggest problems are food, water and sanitation, naturally. We've had to put damned near shoulder-to-shoulder guards all around the perimeter of Tsavo National Park, too, to keep them from killing the animals for meat."

"Oh, Dan, you can't let them do that!"

"No, I know it. I told you we've set up the guards, but hell, 'Neet, it's a big problem anyway. You can't guard every inch of the border constantly. The patrols there and at the Kenyan borders have been yelling for permission to shoot to kill, but I don't want anything like that except as a last resort."

"How long before the first rooms are ready? I mean how long before you can at least start storing some important things?"

"You missed what I told you. We're already doing it. As I said, ten of those eighteen chambers are already filled with microfilm containers. Mostly stuff Sanders has sent over by air from the Library of Congress. Crate after crate. It's beginning to look like a huge warehouse. I've been on the phone three times with Sanders since Sunday and I have to admit, he's going all out to help in every possible way without being pushy. He's only made one personal request, and even that was something we needed and so I was happy to agree."

"What was it?"

"Well, you know the daughter of that Boardman man who started this whole business?"

"Elizabeth Boardman? Why, Dan, I've met her. She seems like a nice woman. I rather liked her."

"Glad you did. You may be seeing a lot of her. Sanders asked that I appoint her chief librarian at Ngaia City. It is going to be a tremendous job to catalogue all this material that's coming in and I really hadn't given it much thought. She has excellent experience—used to head the microfilm cataloguing department in the United States Library of Congress, in fact. So I agreed. That wasn't all of it, though."

"What do you mean?"

"She's getting married in a couple weeks. Man by the name of Paul Neely. He's a high school principal at the school where the Boardman woman works now. She thought he could be of value, too, not only in setting up the collections here, but also in helping to establish educational systems when the time comes for it. That's pretty far ahead, so it's something else I hadn't thought about yet, but it's safe to assume we'll have to think along those lines sometime. Besides, it came as a stipulation when Sanders asked her: if Neely wasn't to be included, she wouldn't accept the post. So I consented to both. Administratively, we really haven't given much thought to Ngaia City's future. This Neely may be of some help in that respect, too. At any rate, they'll be coming here."

"Well, I think that's fine, Dan. I'm glad you've agreed to it. Listen, I'd better go now. I want to do a little bit of shopping and then Narai and I are having dinner together just before I catch my plane. Oh, I forgot to tell you. We ate the other night in the Four Seasons. I remembered our times together there and I was sad that you weren't there with us."

"We'll be there again, 'Neet. You'll see. Tell Narai I send my love. Tell her, too, that if she wants to know where Gordon is when the symposium's over to give me a call. I'll keep tabs on where he is and can let her know. Tell her I'm happy for her and as long as she's sure that's what she wants, then she has my blessings."

"She'll be happy. So am I, Dan, just talking with you. That always makes me happy. I love you, dear, and I'm not going anywhere else without you. I'll arrive there at five o'clock Saturday evening. See you then."

VII

John Grant studied the face of the President, who had his eyes closed. There was a faint beading of perspiration on the man's brow as well. The Chief Executive sat across a small, firm table from Grant, his head leaning back against the cushion of the wide, comfortable seat, his hands gripping the armrests with more than ordinary pressure.

Grant frowned. Obviously the President was afraid. The writer had seen this same reaction many times before on people who were taking their first flight in a big jet, but it was something of a shock to see it reflected in the President. After all, The Man had been a jet pilot himself years ago. It was the first sign of weakness in him that Grant had encountered and it was disturbing to witness.

While they continued climbing steeply, Grant mentally reviewed the telephone conversation he had had with Sanders just prior to calling Anne last night. The President had been very pleased to learn that he had finished the essential work with Mark Shepard and was prepared to catch the scheduled PanAm flight just before noon the next day. With only one stop scheduled en route, in Rome, it would put him in Washington some ten hours later, but still at only about six-thirty in the evening, Washington time. It was the best connection he could make, but the President wasn't pleased with it. That was when he had directed Grant to cancel the PanAm reservation and be prepared to leave Ankara fairly early in the morning, that he would be sending Air Force One over to pick him up at the Esenboga Airport. The hours that would be saved, Sanders told him, would more than justify that expenditure of the taxpayers' money, and then he'd added with a laugh, "but I'd just as soon the taxpayers didn't learn of it." However, he'd said nothing about himself being on board the flight, too, and so it had been a shock when Grant entered the cabin and saw him.

Only moments after Grant came aboard the aircraft and got himself settled and buckled in across from the President, Air Force One had begun to taxi out to get into position for takeoff.

"I'd hoped," the President had told him as they were rolling across the apron, "that Mark would accompany you out to the airport. We refueled as soon as we stopped here, but no provision of any kind was made for my arrival and the Turkish government would have been upset—to put it mildly—if they'd known I was on the ground at their airport, so I couldn't get out. But if Mark had been with you, I'd have had him brought aboard for a little while anyway."

John had asked then if he should begin his relation of what he'd learned from Shepard, but the President told him not yet. "There'll be time enough after we take off," he'd said, "but I do want to hear everything. Naturally, that was the purpose of my coming. What work I needed to do in Washington could just as well be done here on the plane on the way to Ankara, and then our discussion on the way back would save a lot of time this afternoon and evening, and time's what we need. I'll tell you quite frankly, I'm much more concerned about that symposium vote coming up than I am over what the vote tally will be next November in the general election. As soon as we get aloft, you can start spelling it out to me."

By that time they had reached the end of the flight line and were in position. The voice of the "Byrd Colonel" had come over the intercom then, announcing that they'd been given clearance for takeoff, and that was when the President had lost a little of his color and leaned back with his eyes closed, gripping the armrests.

Now, as they completed the first sharp climb and leveled off somewhat, the harsh but muted whirring of the turbines eased and could hardly be heard this far forward. They'd continue gaining altitude for the next twenty or thirty minutes, but at a gradual incline. The President still hadn't moved and the writer saw that he looked much more haggard than when Grant had seen him just prior to his own departure for Turkey. Whether it was a reflection of the pressure on him because of all that was happening, or just the fatigue of long hours of flying—hours which were only half over at this point for him Grant couldn't surmise. Maybe a combination of both.

Grant looked out the window and, through a patch of scattered alto-cumulus clouds he could see quite clearly below the Ankara River weaving through the outskirts of the ancient city. Within moments all trace of the metropolis was lost behind them and they were flying due west. In another five minutes the long, sprawling Sakarya reservoir became visible, terminating in the huge power-generating dam, from the bottom of which flowed the clear green waters of the Sakarya River, heading toward its mouth on the southwestern coast of the Black Sea.

"All right, John" came the President's voice, "suppose we begin."

Grant turned back to face him and was once more mildly surprised. The color had come back into the President's cheeks and he appeared much less nervous than before. He made no apology or explanation for his behavior and Grant asked for none.

Sanders pressed the button beside his seat and immediately a voice responded from the intercom.

"Sir?"

Mac," the President said, "I think we'd appreciate some hot coffee and Danish now."

"Yes, sir. Right away."

"As soon as we get that in here," Sanders told Grant, "I'll make sure we're uninterrupted unless some sort of emergency develops, God forbid. By the way, to fill you in just a little before we begin, you may be interested in knowing that construction's moving along at a spectacular pace on Ngaia City. Much better than I'd even dared to hope. We have almost three and a quarter million books in microfilm storage there already. That includes almost everything to date that the scientists of the advisory board recommended. In addition, we're also sending very selective books in their original hardback form for storage, over eighty thousand of them so far."

"Are they set up well enough already in Kenya to handle them?" Grant was surprised.

"So far they are, but not much more than that. They're using a honeycomb structural form which I hadn't considered, but which I concur with as a very wise decision. Phenomenal strength, greater sealability chamber-to-chamber, and they can continue adding on indefinitely in any direction, including upward, though there's no plans for that now. They're planning for the time being on keeping it to two levels, with a roof height of thirty-two feet. Strong, functional design. Not much for looks, Ngoromu says, but who cares? The important thing is it'll hold up well under almost any sort of strain. Elizabeth—"

He broke off as Staff Sergeant Stanley McAllister—the same airman, Grant noticed, who had carried his luggage aboard—appeared with a tray and set it down on the table before them, quickly placed napkins, cups, silver and small plates before them and a wicker basket holding a selection of Danish pastries to one side, along with a container of butter patties and highly polished stainless steel sugar and cream containers. He filled their cups with steaming coffee from a matching stainless thermal pot. Then he stood back.

"Anything else right now, Mr. President?"

"No, that's all, Mac. Thank you."

"Yes, sir." He pivoted smartly and closed the door behind him as he disappeared into the aft portion of the aircraft.

Sanders pushed the white button beside his seat.

"Yes, sir?" It was Colonel Byrd.

"Disconnect all intercom for in here, Bill. I don't want to be interrupted now unless it's urgent. Pass the word to the others in the back. I'll signal you when we're finished."

"Yes, sir. Right away." The intercom went dead.

Sanders turned his attention back to Grant and indicated he should go ahead with his own coffee and pastry. As Grant spooned sugar into his coffee, the President picked up where he had left off.

"Elizabeth Boardman is taking the chief librarian's position at Ngaia City, at my request. Ngoromu liked the idea. Her fiance', Paul Neely, is going also—he and Elizabeth Boardman are getting married in Chicago on the twenty-second, by the way, just prior to their leaving for Kenya. Neely's going as a sort of administrative overseer at the moment, but eventually he'll be helping to establish whatever sort of educational system they'll be setting up there.

"Robbie—my son—has one of the Phobos orbitals packed with a microfilm payload of about eight hundred thousand volumes. Again, these are mostly the books recommended by the Scientific Advisory Committee. Launching is scheduled for noon on Sunday. The second Phobos will be pay-loaded by next Wednesday, and he's scheduled that launch for a week from today. The big Deimos won't be readied for a soft lunar landing until December at the earliest, but it'll be carrying a lot more—upwards of four million volumes on microfilm. We're also moving on setting up repository structures containing floating, corrosion proof cylinders, also filled with microfilm, at Little America, Point Barrow, and on the Philippines.

"The symposium's still an eye-opener every day. Continually more supportive evidence for HAB is surfacing. Seems as if once they overcame that damnable reticence for speculation, which scientists abhor so much, everyone's been jumping on the bandwagon with his or her own contribution. Even without what you've gotten from Mark, I think we have the vote for HAB acceptance in the bag. But what you have will be the clincher. I was pretty sure it would be important, but this week's events have made it crucial, especially for some of the more vociferous unconvinced geologists. All right, I've talked enough. Let's get to what you have."

As the President broke a cheese Danish in half and began lightly buttering one side, Grant set down his coffee cup, removed from his briefcase a sheaf of typewritten pages stapled together and placed it on the table to his left.

"I have everything on tape, Mr. President," he began, "but in that form it's not organized and rather difficult to follow. I spent a good part of the evening going over all that I recorded, putting it in order and making a rough outline. Not only to give some continuity to this, but to make sure I'm accurate on names, figures and dates. As a bit of a preface, I want to tell you about an ancient Turk named Piri Re'is."

With a little more detail than he had given Ambassador Phipps and his wife earlier this morning, Grant retold the Re'is story. Then, referring at intervals to his typewritten notes, he began covering his sessions with Mark Shepard and the results of those meetings.

"Dr. Shepard told me that you've been aware for quite a long while now of his special project," Grant said, pouring refills of coffee for both the President and himself, "but he also said your knowledge of it is more or less sketchy and that I'd better present this to you in its entirety so you'll be sure to have the complete picture."

Sanders held up a finger, chewed a few more times and swallowed, dabbed at his mouth briefly with his napkin and then said, "I only know a little from getting his letters and talking with him on the phone, so just explain it to me as if I knew nothing at all."

"Yes, sir." He took a quick sip of his coffee while he momentarily consulted his notes. Then he began.

"You're aware that Mark Shepard became convinced in his own mind many years ago that the ancients had access to scientific knowledge wholly anachronistic to their time as we know it. Knowledge which gradually vanished. He found this to be very definitely the case in the matter of cartography, which of course isn't surprising since that's his field of specialization. So, taking it from the beginning, somewhat over a decade ago Dr. Shepard came across a long-buried cartographic mystery that had first cropped up in 1929 and then again in the early 1970s before being reburied.

"It was in October of 1929 that a scholar named..." he looked at his notes, "...Khalil Edham-Bey was poking about in the long-stored collection of ancient documents in the Seray Library of the Palace of Topkapi in the Stamboul sector of Constantinople, when he found—"

"When was it," Sanders interrupted, "that Constantinople became Istanbul?"

"The following year, Mr. President—1930—but the Turkish capital was moved from Constantinople to Ankara in 1923."

"Go on."

"He found an ancient map which was drawn and signed by Piri Ibn Haji Memmed, also known as Piri Re'is, and dated in the month of Muharrem in the Moslem year 919, which coincides with A.D. 1513. It was executed on high-quality parchment and was rendered in varying shades of brown sepia, beige, a reddish cinnamon-brown, dark brown. However, the map was torn and what Edham-Bey found was only a fragment of the whole. Why it was torn, who did it and when remains a mystery. But the fragment found in 1929 measures thirty-three point forty-nine inches by twenty-three point sixty-four inches. The whole width of the map is clearly the first measurement and the smaller measurement is what remains of the length. With the lines of projection on the map, Dr. Shepard was able to determine where the center of the map would have been. It was on the portion that is lost. After a great deal of careful calculation, he figured—"

"Mark has seen the original fragment?"

"Yes, sir. He's studied it very closely. It's presently part of the collection of the National Museum of Turkey." Grant's eyes went to his notes again and he spoke for a while without looking up. "He figured out that the fragment represents only a hair over one-third of the length of the original map. His figure is thirty-three point four eight two percent, leaving sixty-six point five eighteen as the portion lost. In other words, he has determined that the missing fragment was another forty-six point nine six five inches, and so the total length of the original map was seventy point six inches. In round figures, the whole map was therefore very nearly three feet by six feet."

"Those figures are important?"

Grant looked up. "Dr. Shepard considers them extremely important. They show exactly what the missing portion of the map contained."

"Which was?"

"Essentially, a map which extended eastward far into the Pacific, but I'll come back to the missing portion in a moment. The existing fragment is primarily a map of the Atlantic Ocean, including the Northern Hemisphere as far up as central France, about in the region of Bordeaux, and then southward to the Antarctic. On the western side it takes in virtually all of the Caribbean area, from the Yucatan Peninsula southward down the entire length of Central and South America, showing the coastlines and estuarial systems in fine detail. On the eastern side, along the torn edge of the map, it runs southward from approximately the location of Santander on the north coast of Spain down through Gibraltar and takes in the northwestern bulge of Africa directly below that, then continues southward to the Antarctic.

"Piri Re'is presented this map in the Moslem year of 924, which is A.D. 1517, to Sultan Yavuz Selim, and no doubt this is why it was preserved in the Imperial Library at Topkapi Palace. It hardly seems likely that he would have presented a fragment, so most probably the map was torn in two by someone there.

"We now come to the matter of the exceptional importance of this map. It not only very clearly depicts parts of North America and all of the Atlantic coast of South America, but it also accurately shows the interior river systems of South America and includes even the eastern slopes of the Andes."

"Wait just a minute," the President interjected. "You say the map was done in 1513. Since America was discovered in 1492, isn't it possible that those areas could have been charted by then by some of the early explorers? Magellan? Cortez? Maybe even Columbus himself?"

"No, sir. Dr. Shepard rules out any possibility of that. Columbus, it's true, made his three voyages from 1492 to 1498, but we know that he touched only the Bahamas, Puerto Rico and Haiti. Magellan was later; he didn't get to the South American coast until 1519, which was six years after the map was drawn. Cortez hit Mexico in 1520 and Pizarro in Peru was much later, in 1531. No, the only real possibility might have been Amerigo Vespucci. He sailed down the Brazilian coast in 1501, from Recife to the Rio de la Plata, which is about where Montevideo is located now, but then he turned eastward into the Atlantic. Besides, neither Vespucci nor Magellan made any inland explorations, and no rivers were explored beyond their own deltas."

Grant held up the thermal jug and offered to refill Sanders's cup. At a negative reply, he refilled his own and stirred in a spoonful of sugar. After a cautious sip, he set the cup down and continued.

"So the question on that particular aspect of the map is, how could the map show not only the complete coastline from the Yucatán to Antarctica with extreme accuracy, but also very accurately chart the courses of such rivers as the Uruguay, the Amazon, the Parana, the Orinoco and others when they'd never been explored? How also could it show that some of these rivers had their headwaters on the eastern slope of the Andes? All right, that was one big question, but by no means the biggest."

"The Antarctic?"

"Right. You know some of the details from Dr. Shepard, but I'll hit the high points anyway. The Piri Re'is map shows the northern shore of the Antarctic continent *without ice!* Explicitly rendered details of the shoreline—and, to some degree, inland areas—are shown, including river systems and mountains. Mr. President, think of it: we didn't know of the *existence* of Antarctica until 1818! It wasn't explored much until late in that century and early in the next, and we knew *nothing* of the continent under the ice cap, much less its coastal configuration, until completion of the scientific research done during the International Geophysical Year in 1957."

"Yes, Mark had told me about that a few years ago. That's part of the reason why I began taking Boardman seriously from the very beginning."

"I see," Grant said, nodding slowly. "That helps clarify a few questions of my own in regard to your immediate keen interest." He looked at his notes for an instant, then looked at the President again, his eyes glinting with excitement. "But, sir, consider: the best geological theories of today contend that the Antarctic ice cap has been in existence for millions of years, as far back perhaps as the Miocene, which ended thirteen million years ago. And at the same time, the anthropologists, archaeologists and paleontologists contend that man, the very earliest forms of man, that is, did not appear on earth until as recently as one point seven million years ago, and that was probably more beast than man. The point is, those scientific viewpoints can't be right under the circumstances. The evidence is in hand that *someone* knew of the existence of Antarctica before it had an ice cap."

Grant broke off and took a sip of his coffee, eyeing the President over his cup. The Chief Executive was steeped in thought. After a moment or two Grant cleared his throat and the President's gaze focused on him.

"Sir," Grant said, setting down his cup, "did Dr. Shepard mention to you anything about another Piri Re'is map, drawn by Re'is in 1528?"

"No, he didn't."

"Then I'd better touch on that before going further into this. It's important, too. The 1528 map done by Re'is, which is also in the National Museum of Turkey, is not as good a rendering as the 1513 map, even though prepared when Re'is had fifteen more years of cartographic experience under his belt. For many years it was treated as something of a curio and not much academic attention paid to it, but it has some extremely important aspects about it which coincide with the 1513 map. It's presented with the same sort of projections and an overlay of the coastal outlines of the 1513 map blend perfectly into those of the 1528 map. But the latter is a map of the more northerly planes of the globe, including the Arctic. This map shows the North Atlantic, along with Greenland, Labrador, Newfoundland, much of Canada and Alaska, and down the eastern coast of North America to Florida. And, sir, this map not only shows Greenland without its ice cap, but it shows the land mass as *two distinct islands!*"

"Sir," he continued, "I'm going to jump ahead of my own chronology here for a moment because of the importance of one thing in this context. During the polar expeditions made by the French in 1947 to 1949, seismic probes were made through the Greenland ice cap by Dr. Paul-Emile Victor and it was then—for the first time, so they believed—that he discovered that Greenland was two separate islands over which a single ice cap had formed."

"And the age of the Greenland ice cap," Sanders asked softly, "according to today's geologists is what?"

"About the same as Antarctica, Mr. President."

Sanders's lips pursed in a silent whistle and he absently squeezed his chin between thumb and forefinger.

"There's more in that respect, sir," Grant went on. "The map showed numerous mountain ranges in Alaska and northern Canada, but some of these did not appear on the charts of the U.S. Army Map Service. Reconnaissance flights were made to check it out and the ranges were found to exist as the Re'is map showed them. They were thereupon added to the present Army maps."

The writer paused, took a small bite from the piece of Danish still on his plate, finished his coffee, and then lit a cigarette. He settled back a bit more comfortably, momentarily wreathed in smoke.

"I'd like to get back now to the chronology I was attempting to follow," he said. "Naturally, as soon as word got out of the finding of the Piri Re'is map in 1929, there was a great to-do about it in the press and a flurry of speculation which was pretty wild. Nothing much came of it. The scientists, on the whole, put it down as lunacy or simply ignored it because it didn't fit with their own preconceptions. It even attracted some very high-echelon attention in the United States Government. Henry Stimson, who was then secretary of state, became interested in the matter and in July of 1932 he directed our ambassador to Turkey, General Charles Sherrill, to request of the Turkish government that an intensive investigation be undertaken to determine if there were other such maps and, if so, their source. The investigation was made and then abandoned in February of 1933 as troubles began looming on that side of the Atlantic in the form of the Third Reich.

"That seemed pretty much to end it," he said, "as far as the government, the press and the scientists were concerned, with but one important exception. That exception was Dr. Adolf Erik Nordenskjöld of Stockholm, a geologist and explorer, who was particularly intrigued by the mystery and, unlike the others, refused to sweep it under the rug. To him the great enigma was not so much the depiction of Antarctica without the ice cap, but the phenomenal accuracy of the maps in regard to the coastlines of the continents and the exact distances between Africa, Europe, North America and South America.

"The projection of the maps, Mr. President, showed a highly advanced ability in the use of both latitude and longitude. Bear in mind, however, the fact that at the time Nordenskjöld began his work on the maps, man had only a hundred years before discovered how to plot longitudes, yet these maps were four hundred years old then and evidence was beginning to show up that even they were simply copies Re'is had made of maps which were much older.

"The problem as Nordenskjöld saw it," he went on, was to determine what sort of geographical projection had been used. He was, in addition to being a geologist and explorer, an exceptionally good cartographer with a wide knowledge of ancient maps. He had, in fact, in previous years, made a very close study of the ancient Dulcert Portolano—which was one of a large number of charts generically called portolanos, which were produced in the fourteenth and fifteenth centuries for navigational use, especially in the Mediterranean.

"He saw at once that the Piri Re'is map fragment had many of the overtones of a portolano. For seventeen years more he studied the maps—the Re'is maps as well as the portolanos—and concluded that they were altogether too accurate to have been drawn by any fourteenth century mariners. He also pointed out the very curious fact that the maps had appeared very suddenly without any explanation as to their origin. He also proved conclusively that the portolanos were extensively copied, but that no succeeding maps for the next two or three centuries showed any trace whatever of progression or development of the mapmaking skills. In fact, maps of the later fifteenth and sixteenth and early seventeenth centuries were much inferior to the earlier ones. Still, he was unable, after all those years of study, to solve the riddle of their projection."

"Did he ever do so?"

"No, sir, he did not. He was still attempting to do so when he died. But he had made a few more conclusions that are important. He believed that the maps used a form of measurement which originated no later than the time when Phoenicia and Carthage were the great powers on Mediterranean waters—in the third and second centuries B.C.—and very possibly even earlier."

Grant noted the long ash on his cigarette and flicked it into the ashtray, then saw that the tobacco had burned all the way down to the filter and then gone out while he was holding it. He couldn't even remember having puffed on it.

"Didn't get much out of that one, did I?" he murmured, smiling. He tossed it into the ashtray and immediately lighted another while the President waited patiently without speaking for him to go on.

"For a long while, Nordenskjöld was of a mind that Claudius Ptolemy had created the maps, since he was the most famous geographer of the ancient world, as well as a highly skilled astronomer and mathematician. Ptolemy, of course, was Egyptian, and a disciple of the great geographer Marinus of Tyre. For many years Ptolemy worked at the Library of Alexandria, one of the greatest libraries in the history of the world. That library contained the aggregate scientific knowledge of the world to that point, on something over a million scrolls dating back to the farthest reaches of antiquity even then. But, just like Marinus of Tyre, Ptolemy was not a good marine navigator, even though he was a great academic geographer. Nothing he ever did indicated that he had the skill to combine those cartographic talents as they were combined in the Piri Re'is maps and the earliest portolanos. The most logical conclusion was, and still is, that within the Library of Alexandria were maps rendered by someone at some former time which exhibited skills even Ptolemy and Marinus did not possess, not the least of which was a very highly developed understanding and ability in the use of spheroid trigonometry. Such skills were not possessed by the Egyptians or Carthaginians or Phoenicians, nor by the Greeks or Turks, nor by the Babylonians or Sumerians or any other ancient or medieval people whose history is even partially known to us. Nordenskjöld took to the grave with him the strong conviction that the Piri Re'is maps and the Ptolemy maps were simply copies of maps of a culture whose level of technology was infinitely higher, and about which we know nothing."

He puffed on his cigarette a few times and then stubbed it out. The President was once again squeezing his chin and there was a faint up-tilting of his mouth corners.

"Begins to home in a little on HAB now, doesn't it?" he remarked.

"It does, sir, yes."

"From the looks of your notes, John, you've still got a lot to cover, so why don't we take a little break here for a moment? I'll order us some fresh coffee and check with Bill Byrd to see if anything's been radioed in that I should know about."

Glad for the rest, John nodded and got up, stretched and then made his way to the lavatory. When he returned and sat down, there was a new pot of coffee on the table. President Sanders was jotting something on a small pad and when he finished he popped open his seat belt and limped to the lavatory also. Fresh cups were on the table and some slices of coffee cake had been added to the basket.

Grant filled his cup and leisurely ate a piece of the cake while he sipped the coffee. He was finished and had poured a cup for Sanders and was drinking another cupful from this pot when the President returned.

"Ah, thank you, John," he said, indicating the coffee as he sat down with a sigh and buckled in again. He cocked an eye as the writer snapped a flame into life with his lighter and lit another cigarette.

"You're smoking those things more often than you have in the past," the President observed.

Grant grimaced. "I know. I try to cut down a little and instead find myself smoking more. I'll be frank and say it's probably due in some degree to a certain nervousness about my own personal problems, but also hasten to add that I don't believe it's affected my work any."

"No, I don't think so either, John, but it may affect your health if you don't ease up."

"I appreciate your concern, Mr. President. You're very probably right, and I'll take it under advisement."

"Meaning," said Sanders with a laugh, "that I should mind my own business. Okay, let's pick up on the map business again, shall we?"

"Yes, sir. One of the most intriguing things to come out of the map study was a translation of all the different Turkish notations Piri Re'is had made on the map fragment. I have a transcript of the entire translation," he added. "You may want to see it later, but there are a few things in particular I should bring up now. On one area of the depicted Antarctic continent, Re'is had written that this land was a very hot place inhabited by large snakes."

Sanders's eyes widened. "You're kidding!"

"Not at all, and the ramifications are staggering, Mr. President. Since mammoths and rhinos moved from their warm temperate or tropical habitat to the pole were immediately quick-frozen, then it stands to reason that once the capsizing occurs, the continent would not be called a very hot place, and it couldn't conceivably support a population of snakes. Mark Shepard deduces from this, sir, that the original map copied by Piri Re'is was evidently drawn *prior* to the last capsizing, at a time when the Antarctic continent was still located on or near the equator."

The Chief Executive nodded wonderingly. "Quite a concept," he muttered. "Mark wouldn't come to a conclusion that momentous without a lot of study."

"He didn't. But he's convinced of it now—convinced that the original maps actually predate the last capsizing."

The President pursed his lips in a silent whistle and thought about that for a while longer and then made a small noise and said, "What about the other notations you were going to mention, John, that Re'is made on the map?"

"Well, at another place he said that in the preparation of the map he'd used eight charts which the Arabs called *Jaferiye* and which had been prepared at the time of Alexander the Great in the fourth century B.C.—*plus* the use of twenty other charts of much greater antiquity."

"Very interesting. Anything else?"

"Something," Grant smiled, "that may upset American historians a bit. From what Re'is says, it begins to appear that Christopher Columbus was not quite the visionary that our textbooks have him being, and he most definitely was not looking for a route to the East Indies. Piri Re'is says Columbus had a map which took him directly to the Caribbean."

As before, the President's eyes widened and this time his mouth fell open as he repeated himself. "You're kidding!"

"No, sir. It's all there. Re'is and his uncle, Kemal, shortly after becoming captains in the Imperial Ottoman fleet, got into an engagement with some Spanish ships and defeated them. That was in 1501. One of the captured Spanish seamen was a navigator and, under questioning, he told Re'is that he had acted as navigator on the pilot ship during all three of the voyages Columbus had made, and that Columbus had accurate maps which led him directly to the Bahamas. When Re'is promised the seaman a berth as navigator in exchange for cooperation, the seaman produced the actual map that had been used by Columbus and presented it to Re'is. Re'is then used that map in the preparation of the map he drew in 1513, and he explains all this on the margin of the map."

"That's incredible," Sanders breathed. "How come this didn't become public knowledge?"

"It did, sir, but then it was quickly buried again, because to admit that Columbus had ancient maps which accurately led him to the New World would mean also admitting the fact of an Antarctic continent that was not only ice-free, but also tropical. The scientists just couldn't hold still for that, and so it was ignored by them. Buried. In fact, after Nordenskjöld died, the whole matter of the maps—the portolanos as well as the Re'is charts—went into hibernation. It didn't surface significantly again until 1956, and that surfacing took place in America."

"Really? That's interesting. How did that come about?"

"An officer of the Turkish navy stopped by the U.S. Hydrographic Office in Washington with a copy of the Re'is map of 1513 as a gift. It created a little flurry of excitement for a while, but then appeared on the verge of dying out again. Probably would've, except that one of the cartographers there—fellow named Walters—had a friend who was an expert on ancient maps. A lot like Mark Shepard, I guess. Anyway, he took this map to his friend, Arlington Mallery, and Mallery was instantly fascinated. He was disconcerted by what appeared to be a discrepancy...no, that's not the right word," Grant shook his head, "more of a distortion...by what appeared to be a distortion to the maps along the western periphery. But then he made a grid and transferred the map to a globe and discovered that it was perfectly accurate, indicating an advanced knowledge of spheroid trigonometry and the ability to calculate longitude. After studying it very closely, he suggested publicly that the land mass at the bottom of the map was the coastline of Queen Maud Land of Antarctica without its ice cap. No one took him seriously because the suggestion seemed so obviously absurd. Some of the criticism levied was pretty tough."

"How so, John? Who was it that was doing the criticizing?

Grant shrugged. "Just about everyone, I guess, according to what Mark Shepard said. Just one example of the type of closemindedness that something out of the ordinary like this can provoke in otherwise highly intelligent scientists. Dr. Shepard told me that a prime example of it could be seen in the comment made at the time by a very highly esteemed Arabian geographer, Prince Youssouf Kamel. He said…just a minute…"

Grant turned a couple of his note pages and then put his finger on an entry bracketed by quotation marks. "Here it is," he murmured. "Prince Kamel said, 'Our incurable ignorance as to the origin of the portolanos, or navigation charts known to us by this name, will lead us only from twilight to darkness. Everything that has been written on the history or origin of these charts, and everything that will be said or written hereafter, can be nothing but suppositions, arguments, and hallucinations.'"

Grant let the notebook pages fall back to their previous position. "Despite critical remarks like that, Mr. President, Mallery didn't give up. He contacted a couple of other knowledgeable men he knew—oddly enough, both of them Jesuits and both astronomers—and showed the map to them. He told them that—"

"Who were those two men, John?" the President queried. "Do you know?"

"Oh, yes, sir. Excuse me. One was the Reverend Francis Heyden, who was then director of the Georgetown University Observatory. The other was the Reverend Daniel Linehan, director of Weston Observatory. That's in Boston. Linehan, incidentally, had been to the Antarctic."

"Did they go along with Mallery's theory?"

"Well, they were intrigued by it, but were wary about committing themselves too much beyond that, except that Linehan confirmed the complete accuracy of the map, even in regard to places still scarcely explored today, much less mapped. The combined interest of the three men resulted in their appearance on a Georgetown University's radio panel discussion. That broadcast was heard by Professor Charles Hapgood, who was with Keene State College of the University of New Hampshire. Hapgood immediately contacted Mallery, discussed the matter, and then himself instituted a comprehensive investigation of the maps at Keene State.

"Hapgood," Grant continued, "is a devoted student of the history of science, and he went to work on the maps with a vengeance. Bits and pieces of research done by others as well as himself began to fall into place, but some of the findings were so astounding that it was inviting academic ridicule even to suggest them."

"Do you know what the findings were, John?" The President was frowning. "Can you give me a breakdown on them?"

"I'm prepared to, Mr. President." He turned another page of the notes and began running his finger down a numbered list, commenting as he did so. "As I mentioned earlier, Antarctica was not discovered until 1818 and there's a long way to go even now before we get it properly mapped. Yet, Hapgood has shown that in every case where mountains are indicated in Antarctica on the Piri Re'is map, echo-locating seismic probes through as much as two miles of ice covering them have proven them to be accurate. And even those were not known for sure by us to be there until 1957, during the International Geophysical Year. Because of the characteristics of the maps, Hapgood became convinced that they were the result of high-altitude aerial photography."

Grant looked up at the President. "There's a point here that I wanted to bring up which is, again, out of chronology but pertinent. Dr. Shepard has a wide collection of satellite photographs of the earth which he's collected—"

"I know about those, John," Sanders interjected. "Matter of fact, I provided him with quite a few of them."

"But you don't know about this, Mr. President: Dr. Shepard detected a similarity between one of the satellite photos and the Re'is 1513 map. He had a photocopy of the map reduced until it was proportional to the satellite photo image. Sir, when he placed the Re'is map on the satellite shot, it was an absolutely perfect match in every respect—continents, coastlines, mountains, rivers, the works. It proves absolutely that whoever made the maps originally did so from a basis of aerial photographs taken from an altitude of over a hundred miles. This was one of the conclusions Hapgood came up with, too. It also explains, according to both Hapgood and Dr. Shepard, the seeming distortion of the continental lines of North, Central and South America on the maps. You see, sir, at an altitude above the earth from which a camera can show everything correctly in a radius of five thousand miles, distortion begins to appear beyond that radius. That was exactly the case in the Piri Re'is maps, as a result of the spherical shape of the earth. There tends to be the sense of lengthening of the continental edges on that curved periphery, and when this is transferred to a flat-planed map, it seems wrong. This point, in fact, is what led many of the earlier investigators of the map to suspect that the maps were badly drawn."

About ready to turn another page, Grant stopped and looked back at a small notation near the bottom of the page he was on and nodded to himself. He tapped the entry with a forefinger.

"Here's an interesting aside, sir, that's related in a tangential sense to the above. In the Nile River not too far from Cairo there's a large island which was named Elephant Island by the ancients, though no one really knew why, since elephants have never been known to live there. Only when aviation came into its own and allowed man to fly very high above the area did it become clear that the shape of that island is practically identical to the outline shape of an elephant—but this is a characteristic that cannot be detected from ground level. So that gives us another question: how did the ancient Egyptians know its shape well enough to name it as they did? Interesting corollary, don't you think, sir?"

"Definitely," the President agreed, but as Grant appeared ready to go on, the Chief Executive held up a finger, stopping him, then leaned his elbows on the table and rested his chin on his hands. "As you're aware, John," he said, "our biggest opposition to the HAB Theory at the moment is coming from the geologists. I can just hear their comments at all this information. They'll say the findings are interesting and intriguing, but all it proves is that maybe somebody's time chart is off—namely, the calculations of the archaeologists and anthropologists. The geologists will possibly agree that maybe there was an early civilization of which we're unaware, which had high technical skills that were lost for some reason, but they'll still point to their own estimates of the age of the Antarctic ice cap, for instance, and continue to contend that a periodic capsizing of the earth every x-thousand years is impossible. We need something to convince them that it is *their* figures which are in error."

Grant downed the remainder of his cup of coffee while the President was talking, and nodded as Sanders finished.

"I agree with you, Mr. President, and I believe that—in addition to the Piri Re'is maps that show Antarctica as a tropical continent—we now have some very convincing arguments in that regard. The fact that stratification and varves from all over the earth show successive changes of climate and fossil remains is a strongly convincing argument. From what I gather, the important thing seems to be not so much to convince them that the periodic roll-overs of the earth do occur, but that they occur in a much shorter time frame than the current geological time estimates allow."

Sanders's brow wrinkled. "Same thing, isn't it?"

"Not quite. They're very tied to figures covering long time spans. They're much more inclined to speak in terms of tens, scores, or hundreds of *millions* of years. To them, a time span of six or eight thousand years is but a second or so in the life of the earth, geologically speaking. And locked into this time-span conviction as they are, they either reject or ignore anything which doesn't conform.

"All right," he continued after a pause, "we come up with something like the Piri Re'is map, which shows conclusively that Antarctica was mapped *before* the ice cap formed. The idea appalls them, because either it means man was around as a highly intelligent creature for a hell of a lot longer than they've given him credit for, or else all the theories for how long it took for the formation of the ice caps, stratification, and the like are in error. Or, worse yet, that *both* are true. What we have to do, as I see it, is to provide the necessary evidence which makes them finally admit that they have been wrong in their time estimates. And I think with what we have now, we're well on the way to that. And Dr. Shepard thinks the geologists themselves have provided the key for it."

"He does?" There was a decided sharpening of the President's interest. "How so?"

"Antarctica is, he feels, the key to the whole thing. If we can show them—*prove* to them—the existence of Antarctica as a warm temperate or perhaps even tropical continent only six or eight thousand years ago, then they'd have to believe. In Mr. Boardman's calculations, he gives the age of our present epoch as around seventy-five hundred years. Prior to the capsizing which occurred then, the Antarctic continent had to be warm. Thus, the development of the major ice cap at the South Pole had to occur in just a few thousand years instead of the thirteen million that the geologists claim."

"If," the President put in thoughtfully, "the ice cap actually grows to maturity in just a few thousand years then it means that the urgency to prepare for the next capsizing is far greater than anyone really suspects."

"That's exactly right," Grant agreed.

"Somewhere we've gotten off the track here, John. What's the proof? You said Mark felt the geologists themselves had provided the key."

"They have, Mr. President. Consider this." He flipped another page in his notes and studied it for a moment or so, murmuring at the same time, "This is a copy of a geological research report which Dr. Shepard gave me. When taken into consideration with Mr. Boardman's theory and the maps we've been discussing, it gains tremendous importance, although up to now it's been basically overlooked.

"Back in 1949," he went on, still looking at the paper, "a geologist from the University of Illinois, Dr. Jack Hough, accompanied one of the expeditions made by Admiral Byrd to the Antarctic. He took a number of core samples from the bed of the Ross Sea and other areas and brought them back to the Carnegie Institution in Washington, D.C., for analysis. The object was an effort to determine what the past history of the Antarctic's climate had been. At Carnegie, the cores were subjected to the then brand-new dating process called the Ionium Method. That process has proven itself to be the most accurate form of dating yet discovered."

"I've heard of it," Sanders said, "but I don't know how it works."

"Let me explain briefly, then. It was developed by a Carnegie nuclear physicist." Grant turned back to a page in his notes which he'd already passed and located a paragraph with his finger. "His name was W. D. Urry. He discovered that there are three radioactive elements in sea water which are always found in a definite ratio to one another. These elements are uranium, ionium, and radium. Dr. Urry discovered that while they're always found in the same ratio in the water, they begin to decay when that water becomes locked up in bottom sediment. However, the *rate* at which they decay differs, and this difference is measurable. Once all water circulation stops, the quantities of the elements diminish, and so it becomes possible to pinpoint the age of the sediments by the amount of change that has occurred in the ratio between the three elements. The sediments are deposited in varves and themselves show the passage of years, much in the manner of the annual rings of a tree trunk."

Grant now went back to the page he had been looking at a little earlier. "When Dr. Hough brought his core samples of the Antarctic sea bed to the Carnegie Institution, Dr. Urry was still there and he was the one who used the Ionium Method to date them. He found that there have been a succession of periods during which the Antarctic area was completely free of ice and that the continent itself, during those periods, enjoyed a temperate or tropical climate. He determined this through sediments which had to have been deposited from rivers flowing off the continent into the sea—the Ross Sea in particular."

"That's all well and good," the President said slowly, "but the important thing is, was he able to determine *how long ago* Antarctica had a warm climate?"

"Absolutely. And with great accuracy. He showed beyond doubt, from every one of the core samples taken, that the last warm period for Antarctica ended almost exactly six thousand years before."

Grant grinned broadly at the expression which this remark brought to the President's face, but when Sanders said nothing, he went on. "Assuming that Mr. Boardman was right and the last capsizing did occur some seventy-five hundred years ago, then this gives us the first really scientific finding of the speed at which the ice cap develops. The sedimentation on the bottom of the sea would not change until the rivers of Antarctica stopped flowing, and those rivers would flow until the ice cap grew out over them."

Sanders made a clucking sound with his tongue, nodding. "What it means, then," he said, "is that after the capsizing occurred, even though the ice cap undoubtedly started forming immediately at the polar center of the continent, it took about fifteen hundred years for it to completely blanket the continent."

"Exactly. And once that occurred, then the sediments became glacial sediments, which are clearly and undeniably determinable."

"Then that *proves*," Sanders said, excitement now strong in his voice, "that it didn't take millions of years for the ice cap to reach its present size, as the geologists contend."

"That's right, Mr. President. It also provides us with a factual framework of dating from which to work, and all at once everything begins to mesh. If we take the HAB Theory's approximate date of the last capsizing as reasonably accurate, then seventy-five hundred years ago means the capsizing occurred in approximately the year 5495 B.C. It was fifteen hundred years before the newly forming ice cap grew large enough to blanket the continent and stop the rivers from flowing. That's the figure of six thousand years ago that Dr. Urry has proven. So that means that until about the year 3995 B.C., the Antarctic coastline was visible and mappable. Further, that date of the capsizing—5495 B.C.—coincides pretty accurately with the best estimates of theologists, mythologists and philologists as to when the flood occurred which involved Noah, Enkidu, Deucalion and others."

Grant picked up the gold lighter from the table and clicked it twice to bring the pencil of flame to the tip of his cigarette. The impact that all this was making on the President was obvious, and Grant was pleased. Blowing out a plume of smoke, he replaced the lighter on the table and continued.

"There are a lot of geologists, Mr. President, who have cautiously admitted to a warm climate having prevailed in Antarctica long, long ago, but for the most part they've explained it as being attributable to the gradual restructuring of the earth's surface through what they call 'continental drift.' They say that, yes, Antarctica did at one time have a warm climate, but over a period of millions of years, continental drift carried it to the polar region where it is now. You'd be amazed at how many buy that theory, but it just doesn't hold water. It doesn't conform to the hard evidence of the core samples, nor to the evidence of the maps, nor to the sudden mass extinction and quick-freezing of animals contentedly grazing in a warm climate, nor to the freezing of raindrop impressions, nor to a great number of other heretofore inexplicable matters for which there is visible proof of occurrence but, until now, no reasonable answer as to how they occurred."

Grant fell silent then, smoking as he studied the President. Sanders did not speak for a long while, lost in his own thoughts. At last he straightened a little.

"You know, John," he said, "not long ago Dr. Dowde and I were talking and I could detect a deep sense of excitement in her. She said then that she felt we were crossing the threshold of a renaissance of science—that a whole new world of scientific investigation in a fresh new light was opening up to us. I agreed, but I see now that I really didn't *feel* it with the depth that she felt it. I am feeling it that way now. It *is* exciting. Tremendously exciting. And I can better sympathize with the frustration she also felt. Now that we're finally seeing the light and moving into this renaissance, it's altogether possible that another capsizing of the earth will end everything before we've even had a good start." He was quiet for another long moment and then he leaned to the side and pressed the communicator button.

"Yes, Mr. President?" It was Colonel Byrd's voice.

"Bill, connect me to the back, will you please?"

"Yes, sir."

There was a click and then the voice of Staff Sergeant MacAllister came on.

"Sir?"

"Mac, how about making up a light lunch for us? Maybe some soup and a light sandwich of some kind?" He looked at Grant. "Will that be all right with you?"

"Fine."

"All right then, Mac, that's all. Bring it in whenever it's ready. Some milk, too, please." He glanced at the writer again. "What would you like to drink? More coffee? Tea? Or, we've got the mixings if you'd like a drink."

"No thank you, sir. I'll go along with milk."

"Right. Milk for both of us, Mac. Thanks."

As the intercom went dead, the President returned to the subject of their discussion. "I'm aware that you haven't talked at all yet about what Mark's come up with just recently, so I presume we have a way to go. Before getting into that, however, I want to interject here, John, how pleased and very impressed I am with what you have assembled in so short a time. I don't see quite how you were able to do so. Don't you ever sleep?"

Grant was both gratified and somewhat embarrassed with the praise and he felt his neck and face warming with a flush. He laughed and shook his head. "Not a lot, sir. Not when something like this comes along—something so exciting and engrossing. I guess somehow sleeping's not so necessary to me at such times and I think I begin running on coffee, cigarettes and pure energy."

"You must." The President smiled, shaking his head faintly. After a moment he straightened a bit. "All right, let's continue."

"Yes, sir. Getting back to what Dr. Shepard told me of Professor Hapgood, he also listed the following conclusions that Hapgood had come to." Grant ticked them off on his fingers as he covered the points briefly. "One. Beyond any reasonable doubt, the original source maps—those copied to draw the maps of Re'is, Ptolemy, Mercator, the portolanos, and others—had to have been drawn before Antarctica was ice-covered and, in some cases, while the continent was still located at the equator. Two. That whoever drew the original maps had an accurate knowledge of all the continents drawn. Three. That the original source maps were compiled through utilization of a stereographic or gnomonic system of projection involving higher calculus and spherical trigonometry and perhaps other forms of advanced mathematics. Four. That while the projective trigonometry used suggests the work of Ptolemy, the adjustment of that trigonometry to the curvature of the earth and the high degree of skill involved in its establishment very definitely eliminates the Alexandrians as the source and, instead, indicates a highly advanced culture unknown to us—a culture in possession of instruments for finding longitude which the ancient cultures we *do* know simply did not possess. Five. That the conclusions are valid, proven beyond reasonable doubt, and that they raise questions of the highest significance involving world history, geology, archaeology, physics, and virtually every other scientific field, questions which demand early and thorough investigation."

Grant grunted derisively. "Do you know what happened when Professor Hapgood published his findings?" He didn't wait for an answer. "Nothing! Absolutely nothing! The scientific fraternity simply ignored it all, swept it under the rug because it didn't conform. And that's where it's been all these decades since then. It took a lot of musty digging for Mark Shepard to piece together the whole story. But think of it, sir, if serious action had been taken back then in the seventies, we'd have had an enormous head start on what we're facing now."

The President was looking at Grant steadily. "It will never be swept under the rug again, John, I promise you. Now, let me ask you something. Just how does Mark feel about all this? If not the world's foremost cartographer and expert on ancient maps, he's certainly *one* of the top men in those fields now. What does he say? Does he go along with the findings of men such as Nordenskjöld, Mallery and Hapgood?"

"Completely," Grant declared. "Only he feels they did not go far enough and that despite the radical nature of their conclusions, they did not fully say what they really believed for fear of ostracism by the academic community.

"In his own studies of the Piri Re'is map of 1513," the writer added, "Dr. Shepard has worked out a projection which places the exact center of the map at the location of Alexandria. I told you earlier that he had, in finding this, been able to compute accurately what the geographical scope was of that portion of the map that is lost. On the existing fragment, we've seen that the western boundary of the map took it to the Yucatán Peninsula in southern Mexico. Well, the eastern portion that is lost continued eastward from Gibraltar through Asia Minor and Asia and far into the Pacific, taking in all of Japan and the Philippines and going as far eastward in the Pacific as

Bougainville in the Solomon Islands. Dr. Shepard wants to believe that the lost section of the map still exists somewhere and says he'll probably be spending the rest of his life searching for it. And that brings us, finally, to the maps he *has* found recently and their relationship to what he's involved in so deeply right now.

"As you know, sir, he found the three old maps last May. One was more a curio than anything else, but the other two he has definitely traced back to Alexandria—one of them having been drawn by Claudius Ptolemy. *Drawn* by him, but not *originating* with him, but I'll get back to those maps in a moment. His project, as you also know, began a long time before he found the maps. For decades he's studied with microscopic closeness the most ancient maps known to man, and he can glance at an old map and almost instantly tell you if it's a Ptolemy or Mercator, a Re'is or Zeno, a Finaeus or De Canistris or Beh Zara or whatever. The old maps have told him a great deal. They've underlined the findings of Hapgood and Mallery and others, but they've shown more than that, too. He's studied them all in the light of these newest developments and has found facts they've included which have heretofore been ignored for the most part.

"The Oronteus Finaeus Map of 1531, for example, not only also shows the Antarctic continent just as the Re'is map of 1513 does, but it has a subtle and important difference. No rivers are shown far in the interior of the continent; they're all pretty much rivers flowing from the coastal ranges, not ice-covered, into the sea. To Dr. Shepard, this is clear indication that the *original* map from which the Oronteus Finaeus map was copied was not quite as old as the original from which Re'is copied."

"How so?" Sanders asked.

"Simply because the absence of interior topography in the Oronteus Finaeus map strongly indicates that it was prepared when the interior of Antarctica had already grown its ice cap, but that the growth had not yet reached the coastal areas. Thus, there's a near certainly that the Re'is map was based on an original map drawn prior to 5495 B.C., while Antarctica was still located in the tropics, while the Oronteus Finaeus map was based on an original drawn probably a hundred years or so prior to 3995 B.C., after the capsizing of the earth and the initial growth of the new ice cap, but before that ice cap covered the coastlines.

"Then there's the map of another Turk, Hadji Ahmed, that's important. The name and style are similar to Re'is, but the map is dated 967, which is A.D. 1559, and that's five years after Re'is was beheaded. The importance of this one is in the rendering of Alaska and Siberia. There's always been speculation of a land bridge once having existed, connecting Asia and North America. The Ahmed Map shows much more than merely a land bridge. It clearly shows the two continents with a land *mass*, not a bridge, connecting them, a mass over a thousand miles wide! That map *had* to have been copied from a map originally drawn prior to the last capsizing of the earth.

"Dr. Shepard points out that the Zeno Map also shows Greenland as two islands, and that point of fact was proven by the French in the late 1940s. There's the Ibn Ben Zara Map, also drawn at Alexandria, which is one of the finest and most incredibly accurate in coastal detail, and which may have been the model for all the portolanos which followed, but which was never improved upon.

"A big and important difference," Grant went on, "according to Dr. Shepard, crops up in the Stone Map of China. This one was superbly engraved in stone in A.D. 1137, but obviously the original map existed long before that. Its importance lies not in the coastal delineations of China, but in the phenomenal topographical detail of *inner* China—with all river systems depicted with every bit as much accuracy as we can achieve today using the most advanced geological surveying techniques, including extensive aerial photography.

"There are others, sir, which Dr. Shepard remarks on, which have equal importance in whole or in part—the 1502 Portuguese map by De Canerio; the Benincasa Chart of 1508; the Reinel Chart of 1510, which is also Portuguese, and which depicts Australia; the 1484 Venetian Map from Italy. They're all of the same ilk. They show a mapping ability far advanced of the abilities of the people who possessed them and who copied them. All right, with that we get to the crux of this whole thing, the maps Dr. Shepard—"

He broke off as Staff Sergeant MacAllister entered with another tray. The soup was a rich chicken noodle exuding a delicious aroma in curls of vapor from the surface. With it were four triangular sandwich sections on crustless rye bread—ham and Swiss cheese with lettuce.

"Thank you, Mac," Sanders said as the airman was leaving. "It looks very good." He looked at Grant. "John, I suggest we postpone the remainder of our discussion until after we've eaten and relaxed a little. I will say at this point, though, that what we have already should go a long way in convincing those not yet sold on the HAB Theory. Are you going to be up to giving pretty much this same whole presentation again this evening to the symposium group chairmen?"

"No problem, Mr. President."

"Good. I've told Dr. Dowde to hold off handing out the ballots for the general vote on HAB Theory acceptance until tomorrow morning. That'll give you the time tonight to brief the chairmen on all this. Those group chairmen can take close notes on what you say and then spend the morning sessions tomorrow relaying your information in their own way to their individual groups. I think everyone attending ought to have the opportunity to hear all about this before coming to a final decision about the HAB Theory."

The two men spoke little as they ate, each glad for the break in the long conversation, and each considering the implications in his own way. The President finished a little ahead of Grant and came to his feet, stretching.

"Uhhhh. Good to unlimber a little. I'll be back shortly." He disappeared through the aft door, leaving Grant alone. The writer finished eating and lit another cigarette, hefting the heavy gold lighter in his palm afterward and reading the inscription in tiny engraved script close to the bottom: *I love you, Mister.*

The faintest suggestion of a smile touched his lips and he felt a stronger swell of the loneliness he'd been experiencing for Anne, along with a welling of his love for her. At the same time there was a deep pain. Leaving Marie would be traumatic, he knew, for both of them, and the matter of trying to explain to Carol Ann and Billy why it was happening was a continuous gnawing inside. No matter how he explained it, there was no way, really, that they could understand. How do you explain, even to yourself, he wondered, that what was there once is there no longer, that the love has gone and is replaced by toleration and ennui which daily becomes harder to bear? For such a long time—since long before meeting Anne—he'd been ridden by such an enormous guilt, inwardly cursing himself, blaming himself for whatever it was that had begun to drive the wedge between Marie and himself, for whatever it was that had made him restless to begin with.

Now the guilt feelings had lessened and were more bearable. Not gone, by any means, but eased and altered. No longer the mental self-flagellation for being to blame. Blame was not a one-way street. The roots of his unease had sprung from soil fertilized by Marie's voluntary loss of identity and his own strong need for the same; from Marie's becoming no more than an extension of him, a satellite revolving on a tighter and tighter orbit about him until it became smothering beyond the point of being borne. Love, he told himself, is a wonderful and beautiful thing, but not when it becomes the zenith of one's existence, not when it becomes the sole reason for living and excludes everything—*everything*—else. Marie had no hobbies, no interests, no life at all, except insofar as it became an extension of him. But how does one tell his children that he must leave their mother because she loves him *too* much?

"That's a pretty grim expression you're wearing, John."

Grant started. He hadn't even noticed the President's return and now he apologized. "Sorry. Guess I was somewhere else."

Sanders nodded slowly. "It always creates a helpless feeling to see someone you think highly of weighted down with a deep problem which you know there's nothing you can do to help resolve. And advice is ordinarily not wanted, appreciated, or followed. Yet, I'm going to risk the possibility of being considered a meddler, John, and say just one thing to you. Whatever the problem, and whatever course you've determined on to resolve it, bear in mind that you have to live with yourself and with the result of your resolution. Important decisions, especially those involving others for whom you're concerned, are never easy, yet sometimes we come to the place when there remains nothing else to do but make them. So, in the end, the *real* decision becomes finding your own inner peace. If you know where that lies, then all the rest, however painful it might be, ultimately falls into place."

Grant considered this. "You're right, of course, Mr. President. The difficulty encountered sometimes is in determining where the inner peace really lies. I didn't know that for a long time. I do now...and, sir, thank you for your concern." He snubbed out his cigarette, then added more briskly, "Shall we continue now?"

"Yes, we'd better. You were bringing up the crux of this map business that Mark's been involved in."

"Correct. The one map, as I mentioned, is valuable for its age and as a curio, but it's just a poor copy of a portolano and of no real significance in itself. The one that Dr. Shepard has now positively identified as having been drawn by Ptolemy is extremely valuable in a number of respects, but two in particular. It provides, for example, an exceptional view of the entire Middle East in about the year 235 B.C., giving exact locations of villages and cities whose existence up until now has been either unknown or only vaguely suspected. It shows travel routes, both land and water, which are largely unknown. These are all placements made by Ptolemy through his own knowledge, but it is evident that the basic outline of the map was

copied by him from a much older chart."

"Evident how?" Sanders interjected. "How does Mark come to such a conclusion as that?"

"I was coming to that, sir. In this case there was no necessity for coming to the conclusion through the logical deductive process. On two margins of the map and partially on the third, Claudius Ptolemy has, in his own hand, written an account of the origin of the map he copied, insofar as he knew its origin. He states that the map—the original one—was on a material he called *utgiz*, which was of almost indestructible nature, but upon which words could not be written or lines drawn by anyone except *Qandhi*. That name," Grant said, looking up from his notes, "is wholly unfamiliar, according to Dr. Shepard. Whether it refers to an individual or a people he has no way yet of knowing." He looked back at his notes. "Ptolemy goes on to say that as a reward—he doesn't say for what—the *Qandhi*—chart was handed down for many generations by the ancestors of the family of Topthopi, who was a priest of Memphis during the reign of Teti. That places it finally in the Seventh Dynasty which, in our calendar, began in 2294 B.C. and lasted until 2132 B.C. Apparently it was ancient at that time. It was Topthopi who took it out of the family heritage and placed it in the Library of the Temple of Ptah. It remained there until just before the destruction of that temple and its library collection in 300 B.C., when it was removed with many other *Qandhi* charts to the Library of Alexandria."

"And that was where Ptolemy saw it?"

"Yes, sir. Claudius Ptolemy copied it as the final chart in a series of copies he had made from the *Qandhi* charts. In his words, he 'brought it forward' to modern use, evidently referring to his addition of the cities, villages, paths, and other markings added by himself. Among many other items spoken of in his marginal writing, Ptolemy said the *Qandhi* chart material would withstand immersion in water and exposure to sunlight or flying sand, and that it could be rolled but not folded or torn or cut, but that it was especially greedy for fire and that when touched with a hot coal would consume itself instantly."

"Some interesting characteristics," the President murmured. "Does Mark have any idea what the substance might have been?"

"More than just an idea, Mr. President. Far more. This is what has Dr. Shepard in quite a state of excitement. He's fairly certain that the second important chart he has is an original *Qandhi* map!"

Sanders's head snapped up at that and he leaned forward. The deep thrumming of the big jet's engines seemed suddenly louder. "Of what?"

"That's part of what has him so bothered. He hasn't yet been able to figure out the projection. He says it definitely uses spheroid trigonometry and highly sophisticated forms of longitude and latitude, but more than that it has a peculiar use of what appears to be a trigonometric parallax. That's a broad generalization and Dr. Shepard says that's not to be taken as a definition of what it is, but rather the closest he can come to describing something he's totally at a loss to explain otherwise."

"But there is a land mass of some kind depicted?"

"Of some kind, yes, sir. It's a body of land, but because he can't really accurately identify any sort of reference point yet, there's no way of even determining its scale. His first reaction was that it was a map of Antarctica on a fairly small scale, but now he's not so sure of that anymore. He does have one idea that's really startling, which he said I should tell you about but which should not be mentioned to anyone else, because he's not in any degree sure yet. It's what he's terming—and these are his exact words—'an immediate gut reaction.' A hunch, nothing more nor less. And he wants to underline that that's all it is until he can figure out a better perspective to the whole thing."

"All right, we'll stick with that. What's his hunch on it?"

"He thinks there's the possibility that it might be Atlantis."

"*Atlantis!*"

"Yes, sir. Possibly. With no other land mass of recognizable form to provide even a clue as to the scale of the map, and without any real certainty as to what form of projection is used, he simply can't say anything definite about it yet."

"Apart from the lines he doesn't understand and the land mass itself, what else does it show?"

"Well, better than telling you about it, Mr. President, suppose we take a look at it. I've brought the maps, as you arranged with Dr. Shepard for me to do."

Grant reached down on the floor beside his seat and brought up the rolled cylinder wrapped in brown paper and held with rubber bands. He was talking as he unwrapped it.

"One of the first things you'll notice about the *Qandhi* map—and Dr. Shepard said I should keep repeating *if* that's what it is—is that although it can be rolled as you roll a thin sheet of plastic, when released it immediately resumes a flat position without any curling."

Using great care, Grant took the paper away and revealed a firm cardboard tube with a diameter of about six inches. "All three of the maps are in here, but I'll leave the other two inside for the time being, sir."

He reached inside the tube with thumb and forefinger and cautiously withdrew what at first glance appeared to be a long cylinder of translucent, faintly blue-green plastic. It, too, was held with rubber bands, and the texture of the material was smooth and not quite shiny.

"Dr. Shepard said that one of the horrors of working over this map," Grant remarked, smiling, "was that he didn't dare smoke his cigars because of the flammability Ptolemy attributed to the *Qandhi* maps. He said to tell you that he ate one whole box of those cigars you sent him just while studying this map."

"Poor man!" Sanders muttered, shaking his head with exaggerated sympathy. "What a horrible deprivation to undergo. One of the great sacrifices in the name of science."

The *Qandhi* chart seemed almost to fly out of Grant's hand once the rubber bands were removed and he released his grip. It dropped flat to the table, virtually molding itself to the smooth Formica top. An incredible series of intersecting lines, both straight and curved, of extreme thinness and uniformity gave the immediate impression of the web of a disorganized spider. Around the edges of the map were a large number of peculiar symbols, similar in some respect to hieroglyphics and yet with more of a letter-character than figure-character configuration. Grant pointed at them without touching the surface of the map.

"There are thirty-one basic character forms that Dr. Shepard has made out, but often two or three are combined to make a single complex character. He's worked long hours on trying to decipher it but, says that so far it's like nothing he's ever encountered before. It's definitely not related to writing by the Egyptians, Sumerians, Chinese, Greeks or any others of the ancient forms we know.

"Oh, by the way," Grant added, "knowing he was going to be turning this original to you, Dr. Shepherd meticulously made an exact copy so he could continue working on it and, if need be, refer to it in any discussions you and he might have in regard to it."

Sanders nodded. "I'm glad he's got a copy," he said, "but not surprised he made one. I doubt, however, that we'll be discussing anything like this other than face to face. Anything else in particular about it that he wanted you to point out to me?"

Grant muttered an affirmative. "This land mass," he pointed to it, "as you can see, is roughly circular, but with what appears to be a peninsular projection. That was what initially gave Dr. Shepard the notion that it might be the Antarctic, but closer examination showed that not to be the case. However, take a closer look at all these markings on the land mass."

They bent to study it, murmuring over the lines forming tiny rectangles and triangular convergences in a pattern obviously of considerable meaning, but not to them. For almost an hour they studied it, now and then leaving it as they talked, but always coming back to look again. Every line was so crisp and sharp that the whole chart might well have been the work of a master draftsman or architect of the present age.

At last they straightened, the Chief Executive, grunting and holding the small of his back with one hand as Grant carefully rolled the map and put it back into the container. In turn, the other two maps were unrolled and studied, though not at such length, and then returned to the tube. As Grant wrapped the cylinder again in the brown paper, the President stood leaning with his back against the door to the aft cabin, his arms folded across his chest.

"The first priority when we get to the White House," he said, "will be to get these over to Dexter at the Library of Congress and get them photocopied and microfilmed. The originals will stay in the vault there for now. We'll use the photocopies for study, and you'll take some up to New York tonight. I'll also get one of the copies back to Mark right away, so he'll have an extra."

"In addition to having made a copy himself, Mr. President, Dr. Shepard also made about a dozen different overlays utilizing various lines of the map itself. He told me to tell you, in case you suggested it, that he really wouldn't need anything else."

"All right, that settles that. However, I want Dr. Dowde to have a copy at once and microfilm copies to be specially dispatched by special courier just as soon as they're ready down to Robbie in Florida so they'll be in the Phobos rockets scheduled for launching on Sunday and Wednesday. Also microfilm copies to all the different storage sites being established. And I'll have Dexter send half a dozen of the copies to Ngaia City. He should be able to get them off tomorrow."

Sanders straightened and continued. "We have a couple of comfortable beds in the next compartment, John, so while we still have the time to do it, I suggest we settle down, relax, and maybe catch an hour's nap. We've both got a busy time ahead of us before this day is finished."

1 2

The debt we owe to the play of imagination is incalculable.

—Carl Gustav Jung

In the fluctuations of scientific knowledge down through the ages, a curious fact becomes evident—the possession of information which could not have been obtained without instrumentation.

—Andrew Tomas

Something deeply hidden had to be behind things.

—Albert Einstein

I

New York Times
Special Edition

HAB THEORY VALID!
SCIENTISTS AGREE CATACLYSM MAY BE IMMINENT

New York—July 9—In a noon press conference at the Waldorf Astoria hotel, Chairwoman Irma Dowde of the HAB Theory Symposium announced that the registered scientists here have, by a large majority, accepted the postulations of the HAB Theory as valid.

In a vote taken by ballot of the 3,716 attending scientists from all over the world, 2,992 votes were cast for acceptance. Only 161 negative votes were cast and 543 abstentions were recorded.

Final tally of the vote was recorded at 11:15 A.M. today and the results were immediately relayed by Dr. Dowd to President Sanders in the White House. Press Secretary Stephen Lace shortly afterward issued a very brief statement to the press which stated that the President was "not surprised at the result, but deeply saddened that members of the symposium had not been able to find proof to disclaim the HAB Theory postulations." The statement also quoted the President as saying that the entire world "owes a tremendous debt to the assembled scientists for the difficult work they have done this past week on a matter of great complexity and urgency."

Dr. Dowde said that during the remainder of today and all of Sunday until 6 P.M., when the symposium officially ends, full attention will be given to the immediate and most pressing problems of the survival of mankind and his civilization, as well as discussions intro the possibility of retarding the capsizing of the earth and its resultant cataclysm, which is now accepted by the majority of the scientists as an ultimate eventuality.

In commenting about the vote, Dr. Dowde said she was convinced even at the beginning of the symposium that the membership would vote acceptance of the HAB Theory by "a slight majority," but admitted that not until the Thursday night address by John C. Grant to the discussion group chairmen was she convinced it would be "a substantial majority."

Grant, who returned to the United States from Turkey on Thursday afternoon and arrived at the Waldorf only half an hour before his scheduled 9 P.M. address, stunned the assembled scientists with a full revelation of some startling recent discoveries by renowned cartographer and geographer Dr. Mark Shepard of Columbia University.

Shepard is presently in Turkey engaged in extensive cartographic research, which led to his discoveries. His recent find of three ancient maps has thrown the scientific world into a state of excitement. One of the maps in particular…

Washington Post

PRESIDENT TO ADDRESS NATION
AND WORLD TOMORROW

President Robert Morton Sanders has scheduled "a major address" on television tomorrow evening at 8 o'clock New York time.

White House Press Secretary Steven Lace confirmed today that the planned major address by the President will still be he'd as previously announced. The address, Lace said, will be confined to matters concerning the HAB Theory and will be of "great urgency and importance." All major networks, Lace added, will air the address and it will also be carried via communications satellites to foreign nations…

Chicago Sun-Times

BOARDMAN DAUGHTER "HAPPY"

Elizabeth Mellon Boardman, daughter of the late Herbert Allen Boardman, whose theory of a recurrently capsizing earth has just been accepted as valid, said this morning during an interview at the Waldorf Astoria hotel in New York City that she is "extremely happy at this vindication" of her father's lifetime work, which previously had been ignored by scientists.

"It now becomes important," she said, "for us to look to the future and to make every effort to preserve mankind. I'm sure my father would have been gratified to know that acceptance of his theory has come about while there is still time to…

Atlanta Constitution

IS MAP 'VANISHED' ATLANTIS?

A new but unofficial controversy is sweeping the scientists attending the HAB Theory Symposium in New York. The question of whether or not the ancient map found by Dr. Mark Shepard in Turkey and known as the Qandhi *Chart might depict the vanished island empire of Atlantis was first brought up at a symposium meeting by Dr. Isaac Soble, prehistorian and professor of ancient studies at Hebrew University in Jerusalem.*

Dr. Soble, author of several books concerning the legendary Atlantis, said that the Qandhi *Chart leads him to believe that...*

Boston Globe

AGA ACCEPTS HAB THEORY...
...WITH RESERVATIONS

In a statement issued this morning on behalf of the American Geophysical Association, Dr. Clarence Apperly, director, said that the proofs cited in validating the HAB Theory are "quite overwhelming," but that acceptance of the theory must now result in what he says "may amount to a complete overhaul of the science of geology."

Apperly also cautioned against taking the results of the vote at the HAB Theory Symposium on Friday as reflecting the viewpoint of all scientists everywhere. "Many are still not convinced of the validity of the HAB Theory," he said, "and there remains the possibility that evidence could turn up which would show the symposium's decision to have been too hastily made and in error." He admitted, however, that he didn't really think that too likely at this point.

The AGA director added that his most immediate curiosity now lies in what President Sanders will say in his address scheduled for...

Rome Avanti!

TURKS 'OUTRAGED AND INSULTED"
HINT INTERNATIONAL INCIDENT

A highly placed Turkish government spokesman this morning expressed anger over the fact that what he termed "an invaluable national treasure of Turkey" had been illegally spirited out of the country "under the guise of diplomatic immunity."

Afsera Gelicusuf, Turkish minister of state, said his government not only was "shocked" by the theft of precious documents, but equally "outraged and insulted." Gelicusuf stated that if it can be shown positively, as suspected, that United States Government officials were involved, "this could very well become a most dangerous international incident..."

United Press International

"TOP LEADERSHIP WILL BE NEEDED"—PRESCOTT

Sen. Richard Abel Prescott (R., Calif.), considered the top contender among Republicans for nomination as the party's presidential choice next month, today said that "now, more than ever before, the American people must exercise great care" in next November's general election.

"They must be very careful," he said, "to vote for the candidate, irrespective of party lines, who will best be able to handle the unique situation now developing."

Prescott, in an interview at the Senate Office Building yesterday, said that "top leadership will be needed for the difficult times which are…"

San Francisco Chronicle

ANTARCTIC ICE CAP NOT OLD
JUST A YOUNGSTER BUT GROWING FAST

In line with their acceptance of the HAB Theory, geologists have now revised their estimates of the age of the South Polar ice cap drastically.

Previous estimates he'd that the Antarctic ice cap was in the vicinity of 13 million years old. Now, however, as a result of evidence presented at the HAB Theory Symposium in New York City, it is believed that the ice cap did not begin to form until only 7,000 years ago, about the year 5495 B.C. This means that the ice cap, presently two miles thick, is growing with much greater speed than previously suspected and thus the danger of a capsizing earth from overbalance becomes a matter of greater urgency. In addition,…

Manchester Guardian

"NO COMMENT"—HOLDER

Professor Owen Holder, geologist of Oxford University, refused to talk this afternoon when telephoned and asked to comment about the symposium scientists' acceptance of the HAB Theory.

Earlier in the week, Holder walked out of the symposium and returned to England, refusing to participate any longer in what he termed "this charade…"

St. Louis Post-Dispatch

QANDHI MAP MAY BE FORM OF CELLULOID

A delegation of 15 scientists from the HAB Symposium in New York has agreed that the material upon which the Qandhi Chart is drawn has many of the characteristics of a material called celluloid.

The delegation announced its conclusion following a flight to Washington this morning to inspect the original Qandhi Chart in the vault at the Library of Congress.

The material called celluloid was widely used during the first forty years of the twentieth century for the manufacture of movie film, photographic negatives, toothbrushes, tool handles, and a wide variety of similar uses. It was essentially phased out of use just prior to World War II because of its high degree of combustibility, its demise hastened by the development of newer, less flammable plastic materials…

New York Herald Tribune

GRANT URGES PUBLIC NOT MISS
PRESIDENTIAL ADDRESS

John C. Grant, author and presidential aide, who has been prominent in the HAB Theory investigation from its inception, has urged that the American public be sure to listen to tune in to the President's major address to the nation, to be televised tomorrow evening at 8 P.M. (EDT).

Grant, interviewed yesterday at Dulles Airport en route to Chicago, said that President Sanders's speech will be of unparalleled importance to every American and, in fact, to all people everywhere.

The Pulitzer Prize-winning author admitted that he was "considering the possibility," when asked if he was planning to write a book concerning the HAB Theory, but he declined to elaborate in that regard.

Grant told reporters his plans were to remain in Chicago only briefly and then return to the nation's capital early tomorrow. He refused comment, however, when asked the purpose of his swift return to Washington.

When asked for a statement regarding his wife's petition for divorce on grounds of infidelity, filed earlier this week in Chicago, the writer said he was aware that such suit had been filed and that he had been served with legal papers on his arrival in New York on Thursday evening. Further questions in that vein, however, were met with terse replies of "No comment..."

I I

The first Sunday morning United Airlines flight out of Chicago's O'Hare International Airport had been off the ground less than ten minutes when the stewardess in the forward cabin served coffee to the couple sitting in the third row.

"Here's your eye-opener," she told them cheerily. "Breakfast in about ten minutes. Would you care to have champagne this morning?"

John Grant looked at Anne Carpenter questioningly and then they both burst into laughter. Grant looked back at the stewardess.

"Why not?" he said.

Anne, sitting in the window seat, hugged his arm as the stewardess left and then leaned over and kissed him lightly on the cheek. "There are times, Mr. Grant," she whispered, her lips still barely touching his cheek, "that I get an overwhelming urge to leap up, throw myself upon you, wrestle you to the ground and then let you rape me. This is one of those times."

"I don't believe," Grant said slowly, "that I've ever heard of rape being committed in such a manner but, hell, go ahead, I'm game to try anything." He grinned and leaned toward her, his hand cupping her breast through the fabric of the smooth lilac-colored silk dress she was wearing. "However," he added, "I do have a tiny suspicion the stewardess might object."

"Piffle! Obviously that would be nothing more than a manifestation of jealousy. Let her find her own man."

Grant's grin became a tender smile and now he kissed her softly on the lips. Her braless breast was warm and firm beneath his hand and he could feel the nipple beginning to protrude against his palm.

"Despite all the unhappiness there's been," he told her, "and more yet to come, I really can't remember when I've been as happy and relaxed as I am right now. And on that—"

She stopped his words with a kiss and then murmured, "Me, too."

"And on that subject," he went on, "there's something I should tell you. Something that I owe you an apology for."

She pulled away a little, searching his face and seeing that he was serious. Her voice was small. "What?"

"You remember when you told me that my final decision should be based on what's best for me and not for others, and that what would bring *me* the most happiness would be what counted?

She nodded without speaking and he went on. "I thought a lot about that and I altered it to fit my idea of the situation. At that time I could see no possibility of happiness anywhere, so I decided that what I eventually would do should be based not on what brought me the most happiness, as you suggested, but on what would bring me the unhappiness I could best stand to live with."

Anne's grip on his arm tightened, but still she said nothing.

"I was wrong in that, Anne. You were right. There is happiness for me, and it's with you. I'm sorry I ever thought otherwise. I know the reason I thought that way—at least I do now. I didn't then. It was a wrong reason. You see, I kept trying to convince you—and, even worse, kept trying to convince myself—that I loved *both* you and Marie."

There was a sound of deep inner ache in his words and he knew she detected it; he knew as well that a reflection of that same indescribable ache was in her. He knew there were no words she could speak right now that would be appropriate, and so did not expect her to reply, but the gentle pressure as she squeezed his hand wrung his heart and he continued softly.

"Love is a funny thing, Anne. It comes on in a rush, but when it leaves it takes a long time to go...so long that you really don't know when it started leaving or even when it's all gone. You become so accustomed to thinking in terms of loving someone that even when it's gone, consciously you can't really recognize that fact for a long while. You reason that things aren't quite what they once were, but somehow you always end with the thought that the love is still there. Things get worse, but the same conviction remains. Things become impossible, and yet there's still that block, that inability to stop insisting to one's self that the love is still there."

He closed his eyes and expelled a deep breath, his expression somber, then looked at her again and continued.

"Only little by little, if you're not destroyed in the process, does the actual realization come that the love that once was there is really not there any longer; that in fact it's been gone for a long time; that in fact it was the silent, unnoticed slipping away of that love which caused things first to be not quite as they once were, and then to get worse, and then to become impossible."

His eyes were sad as he went on. "I don't know what it is inside that makes one incapable of realizing this loss of love when he should. Maybe because of the pain it involves. I don't know. Maybe because it's an admission of failure over a matter in which no one truly believes he can fail, until it happens. But when at last the conscious mind can see and understand what the subconscious mind has known and understood for so long, then suddenly there's a great change. A devastating weight is lifted away. It doesn't end the pain, the sorrow, the regrets. Only time can do that, and maybe not even time. But it places them in their proper perspective. It puts them in their special niches in one's heart and mind, and maybe that's exactly where they should be—not shoved out of sight, hidden and ignored, but stored and remembered and now and then referred to in the process of trying to build a better life. They amount to experience, and experience is what we learn from best. Or should."

Grant stopped talking then, lost in himself, and Anne did not intrude. He could look back now at what had happened last night and yesterday and the night before, and in the months and years before that, with a detachment which let him put the respective joys and sorrows, triumphs and disasters, into the proper niches he spoke of in heart and mind for future reference. And he wished, fervently, sincerely, that in time to come Marie might be able to do the same.

In his mind's eye he could see again the bitterness in her, the love-turned-to-hate that was filling her, engulfing her. He could hear again the denunciations of the last two evenings, the vicious words, the vindictive promises. And mentally seeing and hearing again, he experienced no echoing surge of bitterness and hatred, no desire to rage and threaten or warn of retribution for vindictiveness; only a sorrowful understanding and a hope for whatever would help her.

He could feel again the pain of sitting with the children, with Carol Ann and Billy, trying to explain that he was leaving and not returning; see again the shattered expressions, the incomprehension; hear again the only words of consolation that could be said—that he loved them and that he would write to them and see them as often as possible, and that all was not ending between them—and knowing at the same time that neither of them, Billy in particular, could fully understand yet, but one day they might. But with all of this, when it was over and when the door had clicked behind him, there was a sureness in him that had long been absent, a deep inner knowledge that a chapter of his life was closing, and a new chapter beginning, and that it was right for him. If ever there was to be the inner peace that the President had spoken of, or the inner happiness that Anne had spoken of, then there was no other way than this.

He felt a gentle touch and came back to present awareness as Anne murmured softly, "The breakfast is coming, John, and your coffee's getting cold."

They ate then, enjoying their food and the tingle to the palate of early morning champagne, and they talked lightly and happily about what lay ahead in the forthcoming days.

"I've said it before, but I'll say it again," Anne told him. "Being associated with you, one had better learn to expect the unexpected. History does repeat itself. A month ago, more or less, I suddenly was yanked out of a Michigan Avenue office building to the heart of Africa on not much more than a moment's notice, and now here we go again."

"But not for as long this time," he reminded. "Four or five days there, possibly, or maybe a week. Not three weeks as before. Are you complaining?"

"Lord, no! But it's sure an exciting way to live. Were you surprised when the President asked you to go there again so soon? Especially since you'd been back in Washington for only an hour or so when he sprang it on you?"

"To a certain extent," he admitted. "You know I hadn't expected to get to Chicago at all until the symposium was over, and then only for a day or two. But Sanders is right, the maps and documents must go to Ngaia City without delay. Sure, they *could* have been taken by someone else besides me, but it isn't just a messenger job. The President asked me to give a full explanation of Dr. Shepard's findings to President Ngoromu, and I agreed—not only because of Sanders's reasons, but because I'm damned eager to spend a few days there at Ngaia City to see what's happening. One day I *will* be writing about all this, Anne, and Ngaia City's an integral part of it."

"I know, and I'm glad we're going to see it now. We're going to be a couple of zombies by the time we get there, though. I can doze on long flights, but I sure don't get any real rest." A little laugh rippled from her throat. "I'm so accustomed to setting up itineraries for others, and now here I am taking one that you've set up for me. I'm glad we're going by way of Rio this time. What's our schedule?"

Grant pulled from his inner pocket the itinerary that Hazel Tierney had given him and studied it. After a moment he gave a grunt. "We *are* going to be zombies. Twenty and a half hours from the time we leave Washington National until we arrive in Nairobi."

"Ouch!" She grimaced. "Okay, let's hear it."

"Let's see, this flight puts us in Washington at nine-fifteen this morning their time. Steve Lace will be meeting us there with the package, and from that moment on we don't let it out of our sight. We guard that parcel with our lives. We'll leave D.C. for Kennedy on National Airlines at nine-fifty and arrive there at ten thirty-eight. That gives us nearly an hour and a half to check through the international gates, and we'll then leave New York on Pan Am at noon sharp. The flight to Rio de Janeiro's seven hours, so we'll get in at seven this evening—that's nine o'clock Rio Time—and have an hour to make our connection there on Varig Airlines to Nairobi. That'll be the long flight. Ten hours. Let's see, we'll leave Rio at ten o'clock at night and..."

"Oh, darn!" Anne broke in, frowning. "That'll be eight in Washington—just the time when President Sanders will begin his address. I really wanted to hear that, too."

"No problem," Grant said airily, studying his fingernails in exaggerated nonchalance. "I knew we were going to miss it, so while I was working with Lace on Thursday afternoon, helping him to block out the speech, I asked if he'd bring a final copy of it when he met us at the airport this morning. He checked with The Man and got a go-ahead, so, as it turns out, we'll know what he's going to say almost before anyone else does. We *do*," he added more seriously, "have to make sure no one else sees it before the broadcast, though. And then our copy is to be put into the archives at Ngaia City."

"John Grant, you are a livin' doll! All right, I apologize for interrupting. Go on and finish."

"Well, that's just about it. We fly out of Rio on Varig at ten o'clock and ten hours later we land at Nairobi, where it'll be one in the afternoon when we arrive.

"And," she tacked on to his words, "too pooped for anything."

"*Any*thing?"

"Ah-hah! A sly one you are, Mister. I'll amend that. *Almost* anything."

They looked at each other, grinning, and then touched their glasses together with a tiny clinking sound to toast the exception.

III

Never before in her life had Narai Ngoromu felt such a need for haste. Normally meticulous in her habits, she now raced back and forth in her room at the Plaza, jerking neatly folded lingerie and blouses from the dresser drawers and dumping them in wads in one of the open suitcases on the bed, then pulling clothes off hangers in the closet and similarly throwing them in. Shoes, toilet articles, hosiery, cosmetics, notebooks, everything. When she was finished she had to spread the rumpled contents at least evenly and then finally tug the suitcase onto the floor and climb upon the lid in order to snap the latches closed. By then there was a knock on the door and she ran to it and threw it open, knowing it would be the bellman she had requested.

"Please," she said, handing him a five-dollar bill, "take them down and get me a cab. I have to get to Kennedy International without any delay."

She took one last quick look around the room for anything she may have missed and then moved out quickly and strode down the hall to the elevators. A moment later at the desk, having explained her urgency to the man at the head of the line of those checking out and gratefully accepting his invitation to go ahead of him, she was paying her bill, practically dancing in place at her need to get it taken care of and be out of there. In less than five minutes she was in the cab, which lurched away from the curb to the angry blaring of a horn from behind.

"Kennedy!" she said. Glancing at her watch, she groaned. "Please hurry. My plane leaves in fifty-five minutes. It's doubtful we'll make it, but if you get me there in time for my flight, there's an extra twenty dollars for you over the fare."

"Lady," said the cabby dubiously, "I'll try…but what if we don't make it?"

"Then you'll still get ten dollars extra for the effort. But, please, *try!*"

"You pay the fine if I get nailed?"

"Yes, just get moving!"

"Okay. Hold on. We're gonna fly low."

He took a corner sharply, throwing her against the inside of the door. She snatched at the hand grip and he'd tightly. Breathing heavily, she leaned back and closed her eyes. After a moment a little smile began spreading her lips.

The call from Alex at 7:30 this morning had been the cause for all this. She was up and dressed and just about ready to go downstairs for breakfast when the phone had rung. At first when the operator had told her to please stand by for an overseas call coming in from Africa, she was sure it would be Anita calling from home to let her know of a safe arrival in Nairobi last evening. But then the operator came back and said the call was originating from Addis Ababa in Ethiopia, and that's when her heart had begun to pound. His voice had come on a moment later.

"Hello? Narai? Hello?"

"I'm here! I'm here, Alex. What a marvelous surprise!"

"Narai, listen to me. I have only a few minutes, but I had to call."

"Alex, what's wrong?"

"I want to know something right now. Do you love me?"

"Do I…Do I *love* you?" She put a slim dark hand to her throat and felt a pulse throbbing.

"Yes, that's what I said!" He was almost shouting. "Because I love you! Because I've been missing you so much I'm in a daze. Because I want us to be together. Answer me, do you love me?"

"I…I…*Yes!* Oh Alex, you crazy wonderful silly idiot. Yes, I *do* love you, and I've felt the same way."

"Are you free to leave there whenever you want?"

"Yes. Sure. Of course."

"Then come home. Now. Right away. To Nairobi. I'm heading there this evening. Can you come? Right away?"

"The very next flight out. I'll be on it no matter which route it's taking, so long as it ends up in Nairobi."

"Great. I'll be waiting. I love you. Why the hell didn't we say that to each other before? I love you."

He was gone and for a moment she continued holding the receiver stupidly. Then she dropped it back onto the cradle, snatched up the phone book and swiftly flipped through it until she found the airline listings. She called TWA. Yes, they had a flight with connections to Nairobi, leaving at 8:30 A.M., connecting to BOAC in London and, after one stop in Khartoum, arriving in Nairobi at 6:30 A.M. tomorrow, Kenya time. Yes, first class had space open. Yes, she was confirmed for the flight. Please arrive at least thirty minutes before takeoff time. Thank you. Have a nice flight. Good-bye.

She'd hung up and looked at her watch, then rolled her eyes: 7:43. That left only forty-seven minutes to pack, get downstairs, check out, get a cab, to JFK—normally about an hour's drive—check in and get the tickets at the TWA counter, and then get out to the gate and board. She wouldn't get there thirty minutes before flight time but, if she was lucky, she might make it before takeoff.

Another call then, to the desk downstairs, asking that her bill be made up at once and that a bellman be sent up. Hurry, please. Her own movements felt as if they were in slow motion while, simultaneously, time galloped.

The cabby was a skilled driver and the Sunday morning traffic was blessedly light, with no police in evidence. They screeched to a stop in front of the terminal doors for TWA twenty-three minutes later. She was paying him his fare, plus the bonus, as they halted.

"By God, lady," the driver wheezed, "that's a record for me! By God, that's really a record for me! I need a drink!"

Already she was out of the cab, handing two dollars to a skycap and telling him to bring her bags in to the counter. Fortunately there was an agent who was free and he took care of her at once.

"You'll have to hurry, miss," he told her, handing her the tickets. "Your flight's already boarding. I've checked the baggage right through to Nairobi. Have a pleasant flight."

The concourse leading to her gate seemed endless, but she arrived in time, out of breath and with the calves of her legs aching and a stitch in her side from half-running, half-walking fast all the way. The rampway door had been kept open for her, as the counter agent had called the gate and alerted them of the late-arriving passenger. Then she was on the plane, in her seat and buckled in. Less than a minute later, the plane began to taxi toward the flight line.

Still breathing heavily, she leaned back in her seat and half-closed her eyes. *Alexander Gordon*, she thought, *you've damned nearly given me a heart attack…but I love you! but I love you!*

I V

At exactly 8:00 P.M. the President of the United States appeared on an estimated 145 million television sets in America and other countries. He was seated behind his desk in the Oval Office of the White House and an instant after he appeared he began to speak.

"My fellow Americans…my fellow citizens of the entire world…I speak to you tonight on a matter of the utmost concern to every human being on earth. What I will say may cause fear among many, but there is no way to blunt that fear, for the very existence of man on earth is in jeopardy. But that very fear, controlled and directed, may be the inspiration we will need to prepare for and face the greatest threat to our survival in recorded history.

"Just two hours ago, the HAB Theory Symposium concluded its final meetings in New York City. Slightly over thirty-two hours ago, that body of distinguished scientists accepted the postulations of what has come to be known as the HAB Theory. I need not take the time here to describe what that theory involves. Few people on earth now cannot be aware of the devastating cataclysm it predicts. We have learned a great deal about the mechanics involved when this cataclysm occurs, but we do not yet know *when* it will happen—only that it is long overdue. Perhaps, if there is time, science may be able to determine when it will happen, but we cannot count on that; we cannot sit and wait.

"During this last day and a half of the symposium the assembled scientists have striven to find some feasible method by which we can avert the threat. Their conclusion is not heartening: there is no such means which would not, in its very unleashing, possibly do as much or even more damage to this planet than the cataclysm itself.

Seated in a deep, comfortable chair in his beautiful brick home in nearby Falls Church, Virginia, Senator Richard Abel Prescott casually scratched one knee and then turned to face his wife, Peggy, seated nearby on the sofa. He tilted his head toward the television with a pleased expression and then faced the set again.

"Sanders, ol' buddy," he said aloud, "you just keep right on talking like that and you're going to talk yourself right out of that Oval Office—and me right into it."

"With no means of averting the disaster," the President was saying, "we then are left with no other choice than to make every effort to preserve what we can of our civilization. It is in this direction that hope lies. Already certain steps have been taken along those lines, but they are only beginnings and thus far have involved only two governments. Much more must be done, and it must involve all governments in a cooperative effort unlike any other in history. I appeal now to the heads of state of all nations on earth to join hands in unstinting cooperation for the preservation of mankind.

"Part of this program of preservation, not only of mankind but of man's knowledge and skills, his technology and his culture, has begun. I speak, in this respect, of the joint effort already in progress between the governments of the United States and Kenya.

Although it was 3 A.M. in Nairobi, the lights of the Presidential Palace were aglow. Inside, the entire Ngoromu family, with the exception of the eldest daughters, sat watching the flickering screen, its image momentarily fading at times. The three girls, Lomai, Mari, and Olo, were sprawled on the rug. Their brother, Thomas, was in a chair to one side. Daniel and Anita sat together on the leather sofa. At the American President's words just spoken, the youngest daughter, twelve-year-old Lomai, sat suddenly erect.

"Daddy," she cried, "he's going to talk about us now!"

"Yes, love, he is," Ngoromu replied softly. "Hush now, so we can hear."

"According to the HAB Theory, the safest land area on earth when the cataclysm occurs will be Kenya, East Africa, especially in the vicinity of the coast, which will be a pivotal area during the capsizing of the earth and therefore little affected. On behalf of the United States, I have entered into an agreement with President Daniel Ngoromu of Kenya to construct a vast survival installation in that country. This construction is presently in progress, with a small portion already completed. The entire construction—which is called Ngaia City—will be a honeycomb-chambered building which will have outer walls and roof of great thickness and strength. Eventually, if time permits, this single construction will cover hundreds of square miles. Built to survive the cataclysm, it will provide a refuge for man and a repository for man's most valuable contributions to his civilization.

"Already, I have committed the United States to provide fifty billion dollars for this endeavor. I consider that to be only the beginning. But Ngaia City should not and *must not* be at the expense of—and for the benefit of—only two nations. Again I address myself to all governments of the world and appeal in the strongest possible terms for their cooperation. The knowledge, the technology, the literature, the art, the culture of the individual societies must not be allowed to perish. It will be to the benefit of all governments to participate in this program.

"There is no way that all mankind can be saved in this vast complex, but Ngaia City eventually will be able to house upwards of twenty million people, and these individuals should represent a cross section of all peoples on earth. The cost to feed and house them, to provide for their health and subsistence and education will be enormous. Each nation must contribute proportionately to meet this expense, and each nation which does so will reap proportionately of the benefits. No nation will be excluded from participation, but neither will any nation—not even Kenya—be exempted from sharing the cost and effort.

"Among the more important aspects of Ngaia City will be its capacity to store the knowledge of man. In this respect I have directed the Library of Congress to microfilm every document and every text in its collection which is important to survival and the continuance of civilizations, these microfilms to be sent to Ngaia City for safe storage and cataloguing for the benefit of all mankind. Three and a quarter million volumes which were already on microfilm at the time this project was begun have already been transported by air to Ngaia City and are safely in storage there now. Others are en route and many more will follow.

"In this respect," he added, looking up from his papers, "I should state that in agreement between President Ngoromu and myself, Elizabeth Boardman, daughter of the late Herbert Allen Boardman, has been named to the post of chief librarian of the Ngaia City complex. Her extensive background in microfilm cataloguing and storage with the Library of Congress recommends her highly for this important task.

In their room at the Waldorf, Liz Boardman and Paul Neely, still dressed but with their shoes kicked off, lay propped up against the headboard of the bed, watching television.

"I'm so excited about it, Paul," she said. "I can hardly wait to get all our details wrapped up in Oak park, get the house closed and get over there."

She reached out and touched his chin, turning his head toward her. They kissed lightly, tenderly.

"It's a new life for us, Liz," he murmured.

"I urge all other heads of state," the President was saying, "to likewise direct their own governmental library personnel, in order that the composite knowledge of mankind may be preserved, even should man himself all but disappear. The importance of this I will speak of in a moment. Those nations which have microfilming facilities of their own are urged to assist those nations which do not. Nor does microfilming alone represent the only type of material to be preserved. Actual volumes of great value or antiquity can and should be preserved as well; around eighty thousand of such actual volumes from the United States are now stored at Ngaia City and assuredly others will follow. Eventually, too, the great aesthetic works of man—his paintings and statuary, his art and cultural heritage in a multitude of categories—all should be preserved.

"I have sent personal envoys to the heads of state of all governments, apprising them of the Ngaia City effort, as well as other programs presently developing, and to ask of them their total cooperation in the efforts to come. I now underline the message that these envoys have carried and state that there is no longer any room or time to continue past international jealousies or hostilities. We no longer can afford to be a world of nations; it now has become our responsibility to become a world of human beings, joining our hearts and our minds and all our efforts in order to provide a legacy of the best that man was and is, for those who will survive.

A few miles away from the Kenyan Presidential Palace, in his room at the Nairobi Hilton, Alexander Gordon was stretched out on his bed, propped up with two pillows. He clasped both hands together suddenly and he'd them up to one side of his head, shaking them in a triumphant gesture.

"Right on target, Chief," he said aloud. "You just damned well may be the greatest leader this old world's ever known."

And almost 1,500 miles to the north of Nairobi, the huge BOAC airliner carrying Narai Ngoromu toward home had just taken off from Civil Airport in Khartoum in the Sudan.

She had awakened when the plane landed almost an hour ago, but had snuggled down and fallen asleep again. Now, as they took off, she roused only enough to see a few lights of the city outside her window before lying down on the seat again.

She glanced at her watch before closing her eyes. Just after three o'clock. She sighed. As she got herself comfortable again, she thought of Alex and smiled. In less than four hours they'd be together.

"In addition to the Ngaia City survival complex in Kenya," Sanders went on, "I also have ordered the construction of microfilm storage buildings of a small scale at three other locations. One is at Little America in the Antarctic, the second is on a mountain in the Philippine Islands, and the third is at Point Barrow, Alaska.

These structures could survive the cataclysm, but it is possible they may not. If they are destroyed, there is still an excellent likelihood of the preservation of the microfilms, since they are loaded in special, strong, noncorrosive containers which will float and which eventually may be found by survivors of the cataclysm.

"Far more important than this, however, for the benefit of all mankind, I also have initiated a survival program to begin in this country, but which soon will involve all nations on earth. As my envoys have explained to the heads of state throughout the world, it is a program which we have named Project Noah. This involves the construction, in space, of a gigantic artificial satellite permanently orbiting the earth. This satellite is to be built in stages and eventually will have the capacity for sustaining hundreds of thousands of people. Its purpose will be identical to that of Ngaia City. The initial construction will be even more enormously expensive than the Ngaia City complex, but also its value will be inestimable. In dealing with the HAB Theory cataclysm, we are dealing with a largely incomprehensible force. Our *best* predictions indicate Kenya to be the safest place on earth during the next cataclysm, but should these predictions be wrong, then we cannot afford to let all our efforts be in vain. Irrespective of what occurs on earth, the Noah Station *will* survive.

In the Senior Officers' Lounge at Cape Kennedy, Colonel Robert Sanders sat watching television with a dozen or more of his staff members. Several had glanced at him since the President had begun speaking of the space effort, and now he twirled the half-smoked cigar in his mouth and then removed it and spoke.

"Gentlemen," he said, "you see, seated here among you, a son who is immeasurably proud of his father."

There was an immediate, wholehearted applause at this, but he he'd up a hand, silencing them.

"And if you listen very carefully during the next few minutes, you'll probably hear the shrieks of outrage and the cries of nepotism when he tells them who's in command of Project Noah."

"I therefore now ask all nations who have space-orbital capabilities," the Chief Executive went on, "to cooperate in every way possible with the United States. I have established the Noah Project without the knowledge or approval of the Congress of the United States, not as an act of flagrant abuse of presidential power, but because there is not the time affordable to us for the luxury of debate over whether or not such a project should be approved. I have established Project Noah through presidential dictate by reason of national emergency, under the provisions of the amended Emergency Appropriations Act. In this case I feel it fully justified to argue the matter in Congress after the fact rather than before.

In his Bethesda home, Albert Jabonsky sprang to his feet at this and smacked a fist into his palm with stinging force.

"Now, you megalomanic bastard, they are going to impeach your ass and hand you your goddamned thick head in a basket!"

"As commander of Project Noah, I have appointed one of the most skilled men in space aeronautics in this country's history since the beginning of the American space program. That man has been, for the past eight-years, second in command of the National Aeronautics and Space Administration—NASA—and has proven his abilities time and again. He is Colonel Robert M. Sanders, Jr.

"Well, there it is," groaned Steven Lace to Hazel Tierney in the outer office. "The shit has just hit the fan."

"I make no excuses," President Sanders added, his eyes leveled at the camera and unflinching, "for appointing my son to this position. No one in the United States has better experience or qualifications for the job and so I have—over his objections—appointed him to the post."

In another room of the White house, Grace Vandelever Sanders sat watching the television and her eyes filled with tears at the love and pride she felt for this man who was her husband.

"The present Noah Project is moving forward at top speed. It is our aim at this time to have ready for launching at the end of six months, a total of fifty of our largest payload rockets. These are to be launched simultaneously, or as nearly so as possible. They are to be followed by manned craft filled with space construction crews who will set to work immediately in moving the orbiting payloads to a central docking point where construction of the Noah Station can begin. All other nations with space programs are strongly urged to join with the United States in working toward the culmination of this project; they are asked to coordinate their own launch programs with this one, or as soon afterward as possible, and to send aloft into recoverable orbit additional materials and manpower for the construction of the station. Nations which do not yet have space capability are urged to contribute to the effort by providing personnel and materials to nations which do have that potential.

"As an adjunct to the Noah Station, Project Noah also is preparing to establish at least two orbiting repositories for microfilmed material and another such repository on the lunar surface. At noon today, the first of the orbiting vehicles, carrying a payload of three hundred fifty thousand microfilmed books and documents, was launched successfully and is now established in its orbit, averaging an altitude of one hundred eighty-six miles above the earth's surface. This is a Phobos unit and a second such unit is scheduled for launch with a similar payload at ten o'clock next Wednesday morning. A larger unit, the Deimos, presently is being adapted for a soft landing on the lunar surface, with a payload approximately four times greater than the Phobos. Launch for this craft is tentatively scheduled for December tenth of this year."

The President paused to take a swallow from a glass of water on the desk nearby. Tiny reflections of the portable lights brought in by the television crews to properly illuminate him glinted from the sheen of perspiration now on his brow.

"The Phobos rocket which was launched today," he continued, "in addition to carrying over a third of a million microfilmed volumes, also is carrying a full-sized copy each of the Ptolemy map and the *Qandhi* Chart, whose presentation at the HAB Symposium by Mr. John Grant last Thursday evening was in large measure responsible for finally convincing many of the scientists who were still wavering in their views over the validity of the HAB Theory.

In the Varig Airlines jet presently 37,000 feet above the South Atlantic and already nearly half an hour out of Rio de Janeiro, John Grant picked up Anne Carpenter's hand from the armrest and kissed the back of it. Between his feet and extending under the seat in front of him was the heavily wrapped and sealed package that had been handed to him by Steven Lace in Washington earlier in the day.

"I wonder," he mused, as he lowered her hand, "how the President's making out." He glanced at his watch. He's been talking…let's see…a bit over twenty minutes by now."

"Having read what he was going to say," Anne murmured in response, putting her head against the back of her seat and closing her eyes as she leaned against his shoulder, "I suspect he's in the midst of what will turn out to be the most startling and controversial presidential address ever."

Grant picked up his vodka and tonic from the service tray and held it to eye level. "A toast," he said. "To a truly great American President."

Anne opened her eyes and straightened as she picked up her own glass. "If ever there was anything I'd drink to, I'll drink to that."

"With respect to those maps," the United States President continued, "I now vary somewhat from the purpose of this address to speak directly to the people and government of Turkey. The maps, which were discovered accidentally last May by Dr. Mark Shepard, were taken from Turkey without the approval of the Turkish government. This was done on direct orders from me and I am solely responsible. Because I was made aware by Dr. Shepard of the incalculable historical value of these maps to mankind as a whole, and because I knew there would be no time whatever to go through the diplomatic process of temporarily borrowing these maps in time for them to be copied both for their vital use in the HAB Theory Symposium and for inclusion in the Phobos orbiting space vehicle launched at noon today, I personally engaged in the matter of having these documents brought out of Turkey under the mantel of diplomatic immunity by Mr. John Grant, who placed them in my hands.

"I apologize to the Turkish government for this breach of international ethics. I fully recognize, as does the Turkish government, that there is a tremendous monetary value to those maps, but I would hope that in light of subsequent events, the Turkish government would recognize, as I do, that the greatest value of these maps is not to just an individual or to one people or to any specific government. The great value is to humanity, for the message on the *Qandhi* Chart in particular, if it can be deciphered, may point the way to the salvation of mankind.

"I am not at this time returning the maps to the Turkish government. Those maps, as a matter of fact, are at this moment en route to Ngaia City in the hands of John Grant. They will be put in safe storage and remain there unless their return is demanded by Turkey. In this regard I should add that the most precious and irreplaceable documents belonging to the United States—the originals of both the Declaration of Independence and the Constitution of the United States—are, at the same time and in the same package with the Turkish maps, being carried to Kenya by Mr. Grant. These documents may not have the potential value to mankind inherent in the *Qandhi* Chart, but to every American they symbolize the most priceless treasure this country possesses. I urge that other nations also protect and preserve their most precious national papers by sending them to Ngaia city."

In Ankara, the power suddenly went off in the American Embassy just as the President had begun his apology and explanation to the Turkish government. Cursing their misfortune that this had to happen at such an inopportune time, Ambassador and Mrs. Charles Phipps and their guest, Dr. Mark Shepard, noting that lights were still aglow in other buildings nearby, quickly decided to go out in search of another television set, possibly in the British Embassy a short distance away. As they left the front door of the embassy and began walking toward the gate, a stuttering of machinegun fire split the night in a furious and prolonged blast. Even after all three had fallen, the firing continued for a considerable while.

"Returning now to this pressing matter at hand," President Sanders continued, "recent developments have shown only too clearly that this government of the United States—and all other governments, as well—must keep in closer touch with science in all its various forms. To a very limited degree in the past this has been done through the Interior Department and the Department of Health, Education and Welfare. Obviously it has not been enough. Government has not fully recognized the needs of science, and science has not fully enough kept government informed. Therefore, I take this opportunity to inform the American people that as of this moment, I am establishing a new administrative post of Cabinet level. It will be called Secretary of the Sciences, and I am appointing to this position Dr. Irma Dowde, renowned American scientist, who is presently curator of archaeology at the Smithsonian Institution.

In the Vertes Suite, headquarters of the HAB Theory Symposium in the Waldorf Astoria hotel, Dr. Irma Dowde and perhaps a score of other scientists had paused in their final pickup of symposium materials to listen to the President's address. As the announcement was made of Irma Dowde's appointment to a Cabinet post, there was a rousing cheer.

For the first time in the memory of anyone who ever knew her, Irma Dowde blushed.

"In addition to this appointment," the President added, "I am at this time also establishing a new government institution, under direction of the Department of the Sciences. It is to be called the National Scientific Correlation Center. This government installation will fill a great need for scientists everywhere, both here and abroad, in that it will be a clearing house of correlated scientific data in all fields. Through the revelations that have turned up as a result of the HAB Theory, it has become clearly apparent that, generally speaking, where science is concerned the right hand does not know what the left hand is doing. All sciences are in some way interconnectable, and when they draw farther and farther into themselves in the natural progression of specialization, less and less intercourse between the sciences occurs."

"Lord bless you, you really did it!" In his home in the Philadelphia suburb of Upper Derby, Dr. Philip Greenbrier, director of the Philadelphia Academy of Sciences, was almost beside himself. "By God, you showed an interest in doing it at that meeting, but I never thought I'd see the day. Bravo, Mr. President!"

"The danger of this," the President went on without pause, "has been only too well demonstrated during the HAB Symposium. Facets of information from different branches of science may, if kept isolated, remain fallow, neglected, and misunderstood. But put together they can and do provide a much clearer picture and may possibly resolve many of the enigmas that have haunted science all through the years. This, too, will be quite an expensive operation, but one which this government cannot afford to be without. It can and will be done."

He paused and took another sip of his water and as he did so there was a momentary flickering of the lights. He paid no attention and, setting the glass down, continued.

"As director of the National Scientific Correlation Center I am appointing, with the full concurrence of and recommendation by Dr. Dowde, the curator of geology at the Smithsonian Institution, Dr. Jason Robinson, who was also vice-chairman of the Scientific Advisory Committee to the President, and vice-chairman of the HAB Theory Symposium.

In Georgetown, Dr. Robinson was taken wholly by surprise and nearly dropped the cup of tea he was sipping.

"Son of a gun!" he said wonderingly. "Can you imagine that? Me...as director! Son of a gun!"

His wife, Emma, seated beside him on the sofa, had suddenly glistening eyes. She leaned over and kissed him and said, "Congratulations, dear."

Robinson looked at her and replied, "Son of a gun!"

"Addressing myself again to all who may hear my voice," President Sanders went on, "it has become self evident, through the HAB Theory Symposium, that repeatedly through the centuries discoveries have been made which indicated the existence in some ancient time of amazingly advanced civilizations. Yet, because these discoveries did not conform to the prevailing beliefs and theories as to the generation of man and his tenure upon the earth, the discoveries have been shunted aside, ignored, proclaimed to be hoax or imagination, ridiculed, or even purposely hidden simply because they didn't conform, even though proof of their existence was in hand.

"We tend to move along with the dreadfully complacent belief in our own invulnerability and in the indestructibility of what we have learned. We say to ourselves, when a telephone is invented, can it then be unin-vented? Then we laugh at such a foolish notion. Yet, the evidence is all around us that civilizations existed which had skills of which we today still only dream.

"The *Qandhi* Chart and the portolano charts are only a few examples among many thousands that in some ancient time, a time increasingly likely to have been prior to the last capsizing of the earth, another—or perhaps many another—civilization existed but was lost when the earth capsized and left only the barest handful of humans alive. Humans who then, bereft of the tools and conveniences and knowledge of their lost civilizations, fought an everyday battle for survival; humans who, in a few short generations, turned their history into myth, their cities into legend, their leaders into gods.

"When another cataclysm occurs, will the only legacy we leave behind for the future be a scattered surviving handful of humans who once more will have to begin the long climb upward?

"No," President Sanders said, shaking his head and then repeating himself. "No, we *must not* permit this to be the final result of all our works. Perhaps, by leaving behind what knowledge we possess, those who survive us will be able to avoid degeneration and, instead, pick up the threads of civilization that we have left behind. And then, in knowing the enemy, be able in the thousands of years which will pass before the next capsizing occurs, to avert it, or at least survive it better than we, and better than those who came before us.

"I therefore call on all governments and all people to throw their full energies behind the efforts now begun and yet to be initiated to—"

He stopped abruptly as the lights in the Oval Office dimmed and then went out. During the ten seconds they were off, there was a babble of muffled voices as technicians sought to correct the problem. Then the lights came back on again.

President Sanders was a bit disconcerted and now took another drink of water. He cleared his throat lightly and looked back down at the papers on the desk and continued.

"I therefore call on all governments and all people—"

And then *all* the power went off...

        ...all over the world.

Printed in the United Kingdom
by Lightning Source UK Ltd.
115317UKS00001B/3